DEDICATION

For the past four years, I have labored on this project on most weekends and evenings putting every ounce of my being into this work. In doing so, there is one, who sacrificed our time together, shared, and believed in the dream with me, my wife Rhonda-Lee. It couldn't have been made possible without her love, understanding, prayers, and desire for the manuscript success. For you my love, this book is dedicated.

Acknowledgments

It takes great effort and research when one takes on the task of undertaking a work of historical fiction. Thank you to Kirk and Maria Callison, Wayne and Debbie Loudermilk, and Shirley Owens for the valuable information that they shared with me on that particular era of history. A special thank you to Ellen Martin for all her encouragement while I was writing this book.

PROLOGUE

It was a bright, warm, and sunny afternoon in October of 1959. The trees along the Blue Ridge Mountains were a beautiful gold and red as autumn had fallen upon the Shenandoah Valley. On this day, many visitors had traveled to the little town of Harpers Ferry, West Virginia to celebrate the 100th anniversary of John Brown's raid. The town had drifted back in history with shops decorated as they had been in the late 1850's and Civil War re-enactors dressed in various period clothing mingled along the streets.

Danny Rollins and Jason Thomas were walking along Fillmore Avenue, talking about the events that were taking place and about the Civil War, that the town was famous. The lads soon arrived at the Store College campus where thousands had arrived to witness the re-enactment of the Brown raid. The crowd stood behind a freshly constructed white fence, but the boys, who were small, were able to maneuver their way toward the front for an unobstructed view. Jason stood silently looking across the field at the replica of the old fort. His mind was on what life must have been like for the residents of the town during that period in history. Jason could only dream and imagine what took place, not really being able to comprehend the horror that happen in this little hamlet a century ago. Suddenly, he heard the sound of marching feet and the cadence of drums, and his mind retuned to reality with the passing of the Marine detachment from Washington, D.C. The troops were in perfect step and formation in their blue and gray uniforms. Their eyes were sternly fixed upon their commanding officer as they moved forward to challenge the raiders. The many visitors that attended this re-enactment competed for their attention with shouts and waving gestures, but the Marines' focus could not be compromised. At the front of the command that numbered 90, was an officer on a beautiful black stallion, shouting commands to the officers and enlisted men that were on foot behind him.

Soon, the Marines were taking their place for the re-enactment, about 50 yards in front of the fort. A young officer walked to the entrance of the fort and spoke to the old man with the long grayish-brown beard that opened the door. Danny recognized this man to be none other than John Brown and the young officer as Jeb Stuart. Within minutes, the meeting between the two ended and the young Stuart waved his hat as a signal for the assault to begin. The young lads noticed an officer sitting patiently upon a gray horse behind the first column of Marines; this they assumed must be Colonel Robert E. Lee, the commander of the force. Finally, he gave the order to an officer standing near the firing line and the action commenced. The Marines shouted and responding to a command, they simultaneously fired a volley of musketry. The blaze of fire from the muzzles of their rifles, and the blinding white smoke and noise sent screams and shouts among the spectators. Danny and Jason were bubbling with excitement at the action that was taking place. Some of the Marines were ordered to charge the fort and attempt to gain entrance by using sledgehammers against the doors. When this failed, they picked up a ladder and use it as a battering ram; with this attempt, the Marines succeeded and entered the fort, capturing Brown and his raiders. The re-enactment ended.

Jason suggested to Danny that they should pay a visit to Miss Ann, whom he knew and loved. Danny agreed and said he was anxious to meet her.

Ann Barker was over 100 years old at the time of the town's historic celebration. As the thundering sound of the re-enactment filled the air, she began to tremble, and was reminded of the war which she had lived and experienced. As the sound of battle faded, she looked out the window of her little gingerbread cottage on Washington Street across from the park. She began to wipe the tears from her compassionate hazel eyes as she watched many of the spectators having their lunch. As she focused her attention on the children that were playing, she laughed, because it reminded her of the happier days of her youth at Shenandoah, her home, which was only three miles from her present location. She watched as several men inspected the old cannon that was tarnished from the many years of neglect. For Ann, it was a symbol of pride and tragedy. It was a very jovial time for the community as the High School Band dressed in their blue and gold uniforms performed many patriotic songs of that era, though for Ann, it was reliving history.

Sorrow and despair ruled Ann's heart this day. Her thoughts were upon members of her family that had lost their lives during the war. Often, she was haunted by the tragedy of conflict, and the bitter taste of destruction that she had witnessed as a child. Still, there was the joy of survival and finality of the bitter conflict, and the era of change with the reconstruction period that followed the war.

Suddenly, the silence of her thoughts was broken by a soft knock at the front door. Pausing briefly, she moved her ailing body slowly toward the door. She stopped long enough to inspect her appearance in the mirror that was hanging on the wall. With pride, she arranged her long gray hair and examined the brown and white wrinkled dress that was made from the material that her Mother had given her. It clothed her small frame perfectly. As she open the door, there stood, waiting patiently and smiling, the two boys whom she greeted affectionately with a hug and kiss. Jason introduced his new friend, explaining that Danny shared his interests in history, and Ann was glad to make a new acquaintance.

Ann was always glad to receive visitors. She did not have family that lived near her and life had its lonely times, especially in the stillness of the night. Often, she heard her Mother's voice calling out for her as she laid quietly upon her pillow, and she would cry out passionately for her in return. Many times as she sat during the stillness of the afternoon gazing out the window, her mind would return to the days of her youth and the glorious days of living at Shenandoah.

Once Jason and Danny entered Ann's home, her eyes sparkled with an expression of joy and she asked, "How do you boys feel about the festivities that are taking place?"

Danny answered her question with remarkable swiftness and excitement, "The town has been changed to a different time and era! It has been recreated just like I've read about, only it is more real to life with all of the re-enactors." The lad continued his conversation and enthusiasm, "The Brown raid re-enactment that we just witnessed was as real to life as if we had returned in time."

There was a smile upon her face as she replied to Danny, "I can remember when I was around your age, life was so different. What you will see this weekend, I lived, I experienced, and oh how glorious of a cause it was." Ann continued as she offered the lads some lemonade and cookies, "I can remember going on picnics with my parents and playing games along the Shenandoah. There was a sense of pride seeing the old Jefferson Guard drilling and marching in their colorful uniforms. My Father would always say that they were the best drill unit in Jefferson County."

Jason was looking for an opportunity to get into the conversation and said to the two of them, "I was told by my dad that on his side of the family there were eight in the Thomas family that fought for the Union, and on my Mother's side there were only two that fought for the Confederacy."

Ann began to look at the family portrait that hung on the wall. Her voice trembled in sorrow as she spoke slowly to the boys, "All of my family and their friends fought for the Confederacy. There were some who returned and some who did not. It was a painful time, I hope that you two lads never have to experience what its like."

Jason noticed the sadness and anguish in Ann's voice with her last statement. He was grateful to his friend for the opportunity of getting to meet someone who had lived through this period in history. Having always been instructed that there were many reasons for the conflict, now maybe, he could understand more clearly with a real eyewitness account, and so he asked another question of Ann, "What really caused the Civil War? I have heard so many different explanations that it can become confusing."

Ann paused for a short period of time to reflect on the answer and to choose the appropriate words to satisfy the lad's hunger for knowledge. She had been a teacher of history and still, she had a great desire to share her personal experiences, "The conflict that took place in the little engine house in October of 1859 had only sought to divide the nation over the issue of slavery in a greater way. There was talk of war and the possibility of secession from the Union. Tensions were high. The nation had never experienced such turmoil since the beginning of its youthful history. There were those in the North, who believed that the institution of slavery had to be abolished and brought to an end, and that the Union must be preserved at all cost. The North as a whole believed that secession was not an option, and that the constitution did not grant it. On the other hand, there were those who lived in the South who believed that it did, and that each state was sovereign and could determine its own destiny, even separation from the Union. With these differences and unable to negotiate a compromise, conflict ravaged the land for four long years."

As everyone sat quietly after Ann's explanation, Danny, who was sitting and looking curiously at the pictures hanging on the wall, broke the silence. He asked Ann, "Who is the young man dressed in the Confederate uniform smiling in front of the mansion?"

Ann, rocking in an old chair that her Mother had given her, hesitated and was silent. Her facial expression changed from happiness to sorrow. Suddenly, with tears in her eyes, moving her left hand against her cheek, she looked in the direction of the old Confederate battle flag that covered her wall and again at the picture of the young man hanging on the opposite wall. Staring, as though she was lost in time, Ann began to speak about another time that she had experience.

CHAPTER ONE

It had been an oppressive-humid night in August of 1860. Along the banks of the Shenandoah River, there was the first glimmer of light beaming revealing the shadows of the mountains. It was just before sunrise, and the only sound was the crackling of the fire that burned brightly. After rising very early from a restless night, James Barker, called Pete by his family, welcomed the warm water that occasionally covered his bare feet. On this morning, the young man stood quietly along the riverbank fishing, as he always did when he needed time of solitude. His thoughts returned to years past when his Father, who passed away at forty-five, would often share this area of the Estate with him when he was a child. Memories of those times would always be hidden deep within his heart and cherished. Sometimes he would weep as he remembered his Father's generous smile and recalled his words of comfort and strength. Often, he attempted to draw upon the values that he had been taught, even though his brother looked upon those same values as a weakness. Even though his brother did not agree with his Father's teachings on life and did not share a close relationship with him; it was different for Pete, he always was attracted by his wisdom. The boldness and honesty that he possessed came through the strong and bonded relationship that he had shared with his Father. Now that he was deceased, there was a void in his heart that could not be filled.

Grasping his pole, his warm brown eyes observed the stillness and peacefulness of the water. His attention was turned momentarily to the majesty of nature as a herd of deer on the opposite side of the river relieved their thirst as they gazed about their surroundings without fear. Off in the distance, he recognized the faint sound of a hawk. Turning his attention skyward, he noticed the creature gliding above the low-lying ridge. All of the wonders of nature were magnificent to him, but it wasn't enough to escape his sorrow. For the past hour, he had been deep in thought, reflecting back on the events that had taken place yesterday at Shenandoah, the Barker Estate. He struggled with the anger that he felt toward his Mother, Elizabeth and older brother, Charles. His unhappiness was due to his family's desire to deceive Mr. Robinson, the owner of a small farm called Highland, out of his property. One of the greatest attributes that the young man possessed was his willingness to show compassion for those who were less fortunate. In his life he had learned to be patient, tolerate, and calm in adversity, except when it came to family issues. For Pete it had been an on going problem throughout life competing with his brother and living up to family expectations. On more then one occasion he was known to exert his stubbornness with a flare of temper in an attempt to resist his brother's conceit. On many matters concerning the Estate, Pete did not always agree, and it led to arguments and division between Charles and him. Though in the end, he always attempted to compromise with his brother in hope of a peaceful solution.

The silence, with all of its tranquility vanished when off in the distance the muffled sound of an approaching rider was heard. Slowly laying down his pole, he ran his hands through his long wavy hair as he glanced towards the ridge. Walking over to his prize mare, Victory, he retrieved his revolver, a gift his Father had given him on his 15th birthday. Off in the distance, he observed quietly and calmly a rider upon a pale colored mare. His focus was steady as he cocked the hammer on the pistol and waited for the rider. He recognized the figure on the horse as Hayward Cooper, a tall black man. Haywood had become an employee of the Barker family when Robert Cooper of Philadelphia, a friend of his Father purchased his freedom in 1855, but because of existing Virginia law, he acknowledged Pete as his master.

As Pete lowered the pistol down to his side, he released the hammer and walked over to where his best friend had just dismounted and asked, "Hayward what are you doing out here this early in the morning?"

With the broad smile he was noted for, Hayward spoke in a deep gravel voice that resonated, "Wat are yose doin' out here dis early in de mornin'?" He continued speaking as he turned from Pete grabbing a fishing pole and some night crawlers, "Ta answ'r ya question, I was waken early by sum noise from de barn and after checkin' on de hors's, I jist couldn't git back to sleep, so I grab my fishin' pole and wanted ta com' here ta do som' fishin'."

As Pete walked back over to the fire, he gestured to Hayward to do likewise. The two sat silently fishing, each deep in thought. Hayward began to laugh, breaking the silence. A catfish had taken the bait that he had placed upon his line and was now trying to break free of the hook that held it captive. Hayward was relentless in his efforts and shortly, his determination paid off with the fish as his trophy. After his catch, he cast forth his line back into the water saying as he turned and looked at Pete, "I knows when ya come here at night dat ya is always trouble 'bout sumthin' that has taken place 'tween yose and ya family."

There was only silence; Pete's thoughts were consumed by his family's actions. The expression upon his face changed to despair. He sighed, as if to release his burden and slowly replied, "All of my life my Mother, Charles and myself have had our differences. My family and I have never seen eye to eye on much of anything that I can remember." Pete did not waste any time in getting to the point of his troubles, "I guess you know my Mother wants to buy the Robinson's property."

Hayward answered slowly as he glanced at the water, "Ya Momma for a long time has bin tryin' ta purchase it."

With a flare of anger in his voice Pete cried, "She is taking advantage of that old man. She gets what she wants and will destroy anyone who gets in her way. That's her way of doing business and my brother is following in her footsteps. He is just like her. My sister Rebecca just doesn't care, that's why she is in Richmond attending school. I have tried all of my life to understand my Mother and brother, but I can't."

Pete laid down his fishing pole and walked over to the fire to rekindle it, suddenly he turned toward Hayward with his arms raised in the air, and shouted, "She says that I'm just like my Father. Weak! Well maybe he was, but at least he was honest."

Hayward began to laugh loudly and uncontrollably. Pete believed that his good friend was not taking his feelings seriously, expressing his own indignation, "I'm pouring out my heart to you and your just going to laugh at me, blasted you, why don't you just get on your horse and leave?"

Hayward stopped and wiped his eyes, he paused and then with a serious tone, he spoke to the young man, "Do's yose think at 21 yose knows everythin'."

Hayward paused to give Pete time to respond, but he remained silent, staring at his friend. Hayward continued to speak in a fever pitch, "No. I's didn' think so. Youn'un gonna listen ta me, yose gonna have ta grow up som' day and I feel dat de time is quickly comin'. I'm twice ya age boy, but I's had ta learn at da young age ta do for myself. Do yose think dat be'n de son of a slave man was an easy life? Do's you'd think dat it was easy see'n my papa be'n whipped and sumtimes me be'n smacked across my head with de hand of som' angry overseer." There was a brief silence, and then he continued in a calmer tone of voice, "Yose had everything in life, but yose lack one thing."

"What's that?"

"Long ago, my papa taught me de one thing dats always stay with me in dis life. And dat is, dat yose must always listin' ta and follow ya heart and if'n ya do, things gonna work out."

Pete looked at Hayward wordlessly. Then he turned to look at the river ignoring what his friend said, but still, his heart and mind were troubled.

It appeared that it would be another hot day. There was not even a breeze as a bluish haze clouded the mountains. Hayward suggested that they return to the Estate and attempt to get some of the chores accomplished before the day became too unbearable with heat. Pete agreed, and quickly they made sure that the fire was out before mounting their horses for the short trip back to the house.

With their horses at a trot, Pete and Hayward crossed some low-lying hills not far from the stables. Pete was surprised as he took particular notice of the work that was taking place at this early hour. It was not the routine for the slaves to begin their chores until after breakfast. Daniel Johnson, the Estate's overseer was walking among the laborers with his hand on his pistol shouting orders. As Pete rode over to where Daniel stood, he began to inquire the reason for the break in routine and who authorized it. Hayward's approach was much slower, because he knew Daniel despised him and the rest of the Negro race.

Pete began to speak boldly and with authority as he approached the party of workers, "Why do you have these bucks out so early before they have had time to eat."

Since Daniel's arrival at the Estate five years ago, he had felt resentment for Pete because of his opposition to slavery. He constantly displayed his dissatisfaction with Pete by resisting any authority that the younger Barker tried to exercise. Daniel laughed and causally chose his words with a taste of sarcasm,

"I was told by your older brother, that this here fence has to be mended before Mr. Pierce comes today. And them there bucks are the ones that I chose to do it. Now if ya don't like it, then you need to hash it out with Mr. Charles."

Pete knew that Daniel was unpredictable. Though a warrior with the army from the conflict with Mexico in the 1840's, he wasn't intimated by his words. In a defiant tone, "Maybe I'll just do that."

The cocky overseer replied hastily, "Yea, ya should. Maybe, its best that ya keep ya nose in ya own business."

Pete wanted to continue to challenge him, but instead rode quietly over to Hayward and without a word headed toward the house. As for Daniel, he walked back to where the work was taking place. With a grin on his face, he turned and watched the two of them ride away, knowing that he had scored a victory. Turning his attention to the work at hand, he took his anger out on the slaves with shouting and cursing.

CHAPTER TWO

Caroline Barker had awakened early and was in a pleasant mood. She was looking forward to the reception that was to be held that evening for William Pierce of Richmond. As always, it gave her satisfaction to have the opportunity to entertain and socialize with friends of the family. Before beginning the day's preparations for this event, she decided to take a ride with Ann, her daughter, on their horses to Smallwood's Ridge to view the sunrise. As she was preparing for their time together, she slowly and carefully placed her long blonde hair neatly into a braid. As always, her pale blue eyes would shine at the thought of sharing time with her daughter. On this day, she meticulously dressed in a favored green habit, that fitted her tall frame with perfection, and carefully placed a light gray riding hat with a dark green plume upon her head. After inspecting her appearance in the mirror in the corner of the room, she quietly departed. As she walked out onto the porch toward the stables, she shouted for Ann, who was late, to hurry along. Although, Caroline and Charles had wanted more children, now ten years later, they had only been blessed with a daughter.

As they were riding toward the heights, Ann was excited at spending some time alone with her Mother; she was very close to her, and it was times such as this that she cherished. Her love and devotion for her Mother was unquestionable, and throughout her life she would continue to maintain a strong bond with her.

When they reached their destination, Caroline glanced over at Ann and briefly watched her young cheerful and innocent expression as they both listened to the birds singing aloft on the tree limbs. In the field they laughed and cheered on an old black and white hound barking as it attempted to chase a rabbit. The view on this beautiful morning of Solomon's Gap, where the Potomac and Shenandoah rivers met was worth a thousand words. It was quiet, serene, and precious, and it was times like this that Caroline desired. Time had passed with not a word spoken, only a smile and expression of contentment shine upon her face when suddenly, Ann broke the silence, "Mother, you look so happy, what are your thoughts, if I may ask?"

Caroline softly replied to Ann, "I have always found peace and comfort in coming here. I'm able to escape for a short time from the problems that we adults face." Caroline's expression began to change to one of somberness as she reminisced in a soft and broken voice, "Your father and I would ride here when we first began our courting." Caroline paused to regain her composure and looking at Ann with the glimmer of a smile, she continued, "You are to young to know about these matters and lets just keep it that way for now."

Ann reluctantly replied as she stroked the mane of her horse, "Ok, but only if we can race back to the house."

All of a sudden, Ann, with her mother following, took off at a full gallop down the backside of the heights, pass the Allstadt farm and across the ridge to Shenandoah, the Barker plantation.

Meanwhile back at the Estate, Charles Barker, Ann's father was in the bedroom trimming his black mustache as he whistled his favorite song Camptown Races. His mind was consumed with the overwhelming business of the Estate. Renegotiations on the new government contract for horses were scheduled to begin next month and he had been working diligently on a proposal that he believed would be difficult for the office of the Secretary of War to refuse. After receiving an education in law, Caroline and he had returned to Shenandoah where he could advise his Mother on business affairs, and act as legal counsel for the Estate as necessary. In a short period of time, Charles had become one of the most successful businessmen in the lower Shenandoah Valley, and felt a sense of pride over his accomplishments. With his advice and shrewd business tactics, he had increased his Mother's wealth considerably. Though business wasn't his first love, he was totally committed to the family's success and prestige. His greatest ambition was to run for political office in Virginia, and somewhere in the future, he planned to fulfill his dreams. Charles possessed firm and strong political beliefs and could be blunt with exercising his opinion. He believed that his political and business views should not be scrutinized, even though there were those in the area who would challenge him at various time. For the individuals who dare to, he would forsake their company and demonize their views and insight concerning his conversations.

On this early morning, Charles' mood was positive. He felt confidant that the family would be able to purchase the Robinson farm. It possessed some of the richest grazing pastures along the river. It had been the family's intentions for some time to acquire the small farm to expand their cattle herd, and it would be by any means necessary for its acquisition to become a reality.

Suddenly Charles' concentration was broken by the sound of horses galloping at a rapid pace. Looking out his bedroom window, he watched as the two riders rode swiftly over the backside of the ridge. Recognizing their identity, he dressed in his dark colored waistcoat and buttoned it. Slowly, he walked down the steps onto the back porch to greet them. The wind began to blow gently as he placed his brown hat upon his head to protect his fair complexion. Patiently, he watched as Ann rode slowly over to where he stood. His large blue eyes lit up at her arrival. An innocent smile was on her face as she dismounted her horse and greeted her Father with a hug and kiss.

With Ann by his side, Charles gazed at his wife with admiration as she approached him. Caroline and Ann, along with the Estate, was his whole world. Even though his business affairs had caused him to be negligent of his family in the past, his love for them was still unquestionable. As he helped his loving wife to dismount from her mare, she embraced his tall-medium frame and greeted him with a hug and kiss.

He responded to her touch with a glowing smile that filled his face with joy as he greeted her, "You awaken early this morning."

Caroline's eyes were full of admiration as she calmly replied, "I have been wanting to take Ann over to the ridge and watch the sunrise, something that you and I would do on occasions. Remember?"

For the last several months, Charles knew that he had been guilty of neglecting his wife and daughter and that it had been placing a strain on their marriage. The couple and their daughter were unable to spend as much time together as a family as they were accustomed to, and so he apologetically answered, "I have been aware of your feelings for sometime and I admit that I have been negligent of you, but I have been very busy with affairs that concern the business of the Estate." Caroline continued to exhibit a sorrowful expression as Charles attempted to justify his reasons, "Mother has been pressuring Pete and myself about purchasing more land. It's all due to the fears that she has about Mr. Watson. He is going to challenge us for the government contract."

Charles paused briefly for a response that did not come, reverently he said, "I know that whatever I say, you will not understand, but you must try, it's important."

Hoping for more of a commitment from her husband, Caroline looked at him with sadness in her eyes. She slowly broke his embrace and turned and walked toward the house. As she stopped and turned about to face him, she angrily declared, "Charles, don't you understand? I'm 27 and I'm getting older. I want more of a life then what I have. Is your Mother and Shenandoah more important in life then your daughter and me!"

Suddenly, there was a concern expression upon his face as he looked at Caroline. His disappointment was evident as he attempted painfully to try and persuade his wife to see differently, "It's our life, you do not understand that one day I hope that Shenandoah will be ours and then passed onto Ann!"

Caroline was quite upset and did not give her husband a reply as she turned about to enter the house.

As Pete and Hayward approached the house, they witness the hasty departure of Caroline and the bewilderment covering Charles face. Pete began to inquire concerning the nature of the problem. It had always been Pete's desire to have a relationship with Charles, though they didn't always agree on issues, but Charles being the oldest at 31, always decline the invitation because of his pride and desired to keep his personal matters to himself.

Jokingly Pete addressed his trouble brother, "Have you been neglecting Caroline again?"

Charles snapped as he turned about to face his brother, "What happens between Caroline and myself is none of your business!"

"I know, I understand. But, you know that she is a romantic that's very much in touch with her feelings. You always give the appearance that you are to busy to give her the attention that she desires from you."

Once again, Charles felt that Pete was trying to interfere into matters that did not concern him and so he sarcastically replied, "What would you know about the needs of a woman? Well?" Charles paused waiting for an answer that didn't come, he angrily continued, "That's what I thought, your relationships with women have about as much of a future as you overseeing this Estate. And since we are on the subject little brother, we need to set the record straight about that matter. Just remember, I'm the one who has labored to make this farm as prosperous as it is, not you or anyone else. It's been my heart and soul that has gone into this place and everyone is going to have to understand and respect it, including you."

Charles changing the subject caught Pete off guard. Just as quickly and defensively, he responded to his brother's claim, "I did everything that I have been asked to do concerning the business and even the labor that goes with it. I have often worked out in the hot sun with those bucks that you see over there which is a lot more then I've seen you do." As Pete jumped down off of Victory he continued to say in a fevered tone of voice, "And I have their respect for doing it. Maybe, you need to work ten hours one day out in those fields instead of just passing instructions to that insane overseer that you hired."

Charles did not feel like quarreling with his brother after his disagreement with his wife, so after a brief pause, he half heartedly laugh and said, "I'm sorry, I was out of line with you, besides little brother to answer your question, what would you know about being married and having a relationship with a woman, especially the difficulties? You have never had one and I'm not for sure that you know how."

Pete looked at Charles' eyes and perceived what the nature of their disagreement entailed. As a smile began to appear, he answered his brother in a joking way, "One day I will, and when I do, I will not be as foolish as you and neglect such an attractive lady."

Both brothers turned and entered the house to join the rest of the family for breakfast.

Everyone was quiet as they were seated at their regular place at the table except Pete, who liked to tease Ann every morning before they ate. They could not help but smell the wonderful aroma of Pansy's sausage gravy from the kitchen as they waited on Elizabeth, Pete and Charles' Mother, to make her entrance. Elizabeth Mulligan Barker had given birth to six children, only three, the two boys and their younger sister Rebecca survived. Even after enduring the pain from such loss, still she overcame the obstacles of life to become very successful and wealthy. When it came to business transactions, she could be very stubborn and domineering. In 1835, at the age of 15, she had begun to learn the business of farming from her Father, being the only child. It wasn't until her

Father's death, that she inherited Shenandoah with its 2,500 acres. Now at 50, she had learned to be shrewd, increasing in wisdom concerning the business. Even though women were not viewed as leaders during this time, Elizabeth had gained the respect of many of prominence in the area, and was influential in business affairs throughout the lower valley.

As Ann screamed with laughter at her uncle's amusement, the family could hear Elizabeth in the next room giving orders to Matthew, the Butler of the house. Pete knowing how meticulous his Mother was concerning proper table manner, quickly repressed the fun and turned to looked at Charles who was sitting opposite him. With a mischief smile, Pete shook his head expecting her entrance into the dining room at any moment.

When Elizabeth finally entered the room, Charles stood and assisted his Mother with her seating at the head of the table, as was the custom at each meal. Caroline said cheerfully to Elizabeth as Matthew poured her coffee, "Mother Elizabeth, I really like the way that you have fixed your hair."

"Thank you Caroline for your compliment. Just this morning as I was looking in the mirror, I noticed grayer mixed in with the brown. But at my age, I know that your trying to make me feel good."

Quickly changing the subject of her appearance and turning her attention toward Charles, Elizabeth said in a calm, but authoritative voice, "Oh Charles while I am thinking about it, I want you to escort me into town this afternoon to greet Mr. Pierce, and then later after lunch, we will entertain him here at the Estate before the reception."

As Charles took one of the hot biscuits that were being served to him by Matthew, he affirmed the request, "Yes Mother, I would be honored to accompany you." He continued his conversation by giving his wife the credit for her management of the festivities that were to take place in honor of William Pierce, "I feel that I should mention that Caroline has taken the liberty of making all of the final arrangements for the reception this evening. We shall have a great feast; it will be the talk of the County. The pig that's being roasted over the open fire should be finished by that time."

Elizabeth's response was enthusiastic as she turned to look at her daughter-in-law, "Good, good. I declare, I must say Caroline, you are one of the most sociable and generous ladies living in Jefferson County. I didn't expect you to take on this task, especially after hosting the barbecue last month. Again, I would like to thank you. Your help has been much appreciated."

For the past several weeks, Charles' political ambitions had been on Elizabeth's mind. In times past this is the one subject that she was unable to agree with concerning her son's future. But after realizing that she couldn't completely control his life, Elizabeth surrendered to his cause. She felt that the time had finally arrived for Charles to pursue this goal, and it would eventually, she hoped, be to her advantage, since she was able to influence him, "This morning, I have something that I need to say. Charles, I know that it has always been your desire to enter Virginia politics, and I have tried to discourage it for my own personal reasons, which we will not discuss now. But now after great thought and with my blessing, I have changed my views and I feel that it is time for you to have the opportunity to do as you wish. I believe during William's stay, that you will be approached with an offer for your support in the up-coming campaign for the Presidency. I understand from William that there is a good possibility that Vice President John Breckinridge will be the front-runner in the national election against Abe Lincoln. I wrote him a letter last month and his reply was favorable. I feel that you should consider any offer when he approaches you."

Charles and Caroline was both full of joy and excitement as they leaped to their feet and hug each other. This was an opportunity that they had hoped would materialize. Charles has always strongly believed in the self-determination of each state and their right to govern, as they deem best for the people. This would be his chance in life to attempt to safeguard that freedom by running for political office himself, should he choose to do so.

Pete was quiet as his Mother, Caroline, and Charles rejoiced over their new endeavor. He reached across the table to congratulate his brother and sister-in-law and wished them the best on this matter.

After the small celebration and everyone was seated, the conversation changed when Elizabeth once more looked in Charles' direction and asked, "Now, have you and Pete spoken to Mr. Robinson about the property."

"No, we haven't. Though, I believe that he will sell at a price that is less then we expected."

"What information do you have to draw that assumption?"

"For sometime, Daniel and I have been spreading the word over the County and surrounding area concerning Mr. Robinson's Union sympathies. It's paying off because he hasn't been able to find a buyer for his cattle."

Elizabeth was amazed and expressed great excitement. This was the news that she had longed for and the opportunity that she had hoped would materialize. Elizabeth believed that they needed to move quickly to close a deal with the unfortunate landowner. In an excited and authoritative tone, she replied, "Now listen to me, I want to make him an offer today, but I do not want to pay the going price per acre. And I want you to close the deal as soon as possible. I believe this will work in our favor, don't you?"

Pete looked at his mother and responded loudly in anger, "Mother we should not be taking advantage of the Robinson's! I just will not agree with this. I feel we are robbing them. I want no part of this."

Elizabeth did not desire that anyone question her authority, and jeopardize her prosperity. Slowly, she rose from the table and pointed her finger in anger at Pete, crying out at the top of her voice, "Now young man you hear me out! Do not raise your voice at me! For as long as you are living here, you will respect my wishes!"

There was a silence that filled the room as every eye was upon the angry matriarch. It seemed as if minutes went by before there was a reaction. Everyone present had learned by experience not to speak when Elizabeth was angered, or to interfere when she was attempting to make a point concerning an issue. Quietly, Pete stood and defiantly looked at his Mother and murmured, "I have had enough. I'll leave."

She walked over to where Pete was standing, her composure was more subdued as she calmly spoke, "Listen to yourself, this is why I have not given you more authority over business matters, and your brother I have. Charles is temperamental and extremely intelligent. He has always been the one person that I could count on; the one who carries out my wishes and the one that I most trust. You have always lived the life of a rebel. You could never see life and business issues as I do." As she walked around to where Charles was seated and placed her hands upon his shoulders, she stopped and looked in the direction of Pete. With his feelings bruised, Pete turned abruptly and immediately left the room.

As Pete proceeded from the house to the stable, Hayward was repairing a carriage wheel. He noticed his friend and enthusiastically called out "Pete, Pete!" There was no answer. Pete ignored him. Frequently since the brothers had returned home from college, trouble had increased within the family. Hayward knew the probability of what took place, and by experience to stay out of the disagreement. He shook his head in frustration and continued with his repairs.

Once Pete was about to leave, Ann came running out of the house and waved good-bye to him. He took notice of her as he departed from the stable area and returned her gratification. She was the person that he loved the most in this life, and rewarded him with the greatest joy.

The rain shower that began during the breakfast hour had ceased as Pete made the short journey into Harpers Ferry. As he approached Shenandoah Street, he waved and smiled at Miss Jane Powers who he had recently taken out to dinner. He had enjoyed their conversation and was fond of her as a friend, but she was beginning to take their friendship too serious. His passion was quite different; he didn't have the desire to engage in a relationship that could become permanent.

Harpers Ferry was busy with activity today. The street was crowded with ladies that were going about their daily errands. Pete laughed as a merchant scolded some kids that knocked over his cart full of fresh fruit. The smell of fresh bread filled the air from the bakery. Pete noticed customers going in and out of the dry goods store and Mr. Frankel's clothing store appeared to be doing a handsome business. As he glanced toward High Street, he noticed William Tyler, whom he disliked from his youth, walking with Martha Johnson, his first lady friend.

Arriving at his destination, Whites Tavern, Pete walked into the establishment, which was nearly empty. As he approached the bar, he asked to have a beer. It was only noon, and it wasn't his custom to drink at this hour of the day. With the events that had taken place at the Estate, Pete made the exception; he needed time to ponder on the issue. Walking over to an empty table in the corner, he sat down and stared out the window as the laborers at the Armory went about their business. Occasionally, he would speak to someone sitting near by, but he preferred being alone and in fellowship with only his thoughts.

At the Estate, Charles mounted his stallion and departed for Highland, which borders Shenandoah. With his arrival, he noticed Mr. Robinson, working in a small garden in the rear of the main house. After formal greetings, Charles decided to make his intentions known and resolve their business as soon as possible. Methodically, he confronted the old landlord, and inquired, "Mr. Robinson, as I understand, Highland is up for sale, and I am here to offer you a fair price for your property."

The surprised owner was caught off guard at the proposal that was being offered to him. His response reflected his feelings, "I did not know that my farm was for sale. Besides young man, I do not know where you came across that information. I have no intentions of selling now, or at anytime in the near future."

"I won't waste your time nor mine. I will get to the point. As I understand, your unable to find a buyer for your cattle, and that your in need of the money. I am here to make an offer; that way, you will have the money that you need, and I will have the property that I want."

Mr. Robinson began to lose his patience with Charles. This information concerning his troubles had not been made public yet. His reply reflected his anger, "Like I said, I'm not going to sell now, or anytime in the future!"

"I'm just trying to be neighborly. Besides, you should have known that you couldn't compete with the Barkers. No one can, and as long as I have anything to do with it, no one will."

"You Barkers, must believe that you can run over anyone if given the chance."

"No, I wouldn't look at it that way. We just don't let anyone stand in our way."

"One of these days you'll get yours."

With his patience exhausted, Charles fully understood that the Robinson's were not going to depart with the property unless they were forced too. So, it was time for him to use the law to his advantage and bring an end to the matter. Charles responded to Mr. Robinson's anger calmly, "Well, I was hoping that it wouldn't come to this, but, as I understand from Mr. Morgan at the bank, you are not able to make your mortgage payments. And I know that they are ready to foreclose on the note. I feel that I should inform you, that if I have to, I'm going to make the bank an offer on the property when they foreclose on the debt. And when I do, I will pay off the mortgage and be the new owner. So, that means if you do not accept my offer, then unfortunately, you will be without a home, and no money. If I were you, I would consider selling the property to me, and no one else, understood. Besides, my offer is better then nothing at all. I expect to hear from you soon."

Mr. Robinson sadly acknowledged the invitation as Charles was mounting his horse for the return trip home. There was a subtle smile as Charles bade him a good day. He rode off at a slow pace, rejoicing in his victory over his prey.

It was shortly after noon at Shenandoah, and Ann was playing in the yard as her Father approached. As he rode up to where she was playing, he greeted her, and asked, "Ann have you seen Mr. Hayward?"

Ann jumped down from the swing that her uncle had constructed, and replied, "Father, he went into the stable, one of the horses seems to be afraid."

There was a concern expression upon his face as Charles walked quickly across the yard and through the stable door. He noticed Hayward stroking the mare's neck and speaking softly. Charles anxiously asked, "What's the problem?"

Looking over his left shoulder, Hayward calmly assured Charles, "Somethin' disturbed Pride, I's not sure wat. Could've been a snake or jist a strange noise."

Charles was calmer and convinced as he turned to leave. He paused and suddenly, he turned around facing the masterful employee, "Will you get the carriage ready? Mother and I will be going into town to meet Mr. Pierce. His arrival time is 1:00 p.m. on the train from Baltimore. And I want to be there in plenty of time."

Hayward nodded in acknowledgement, and proceeded to carry out the request.

On the way to the train station, Charles and his Mother began to discuss a variety of issues concerning the future of the Estate and the family business of breeding cattle and horses for the U.S. Army. His thoughts were upon the instability of the nation and how this would all play out. It had always been his vision from his youth to possess ownership of the Estate. It was his intentions to prevent interference from anyone, even his younger brother and sister. Time and again, he had proven to his Mother his loyalty in business transactions, even to the point of using unfair tactics. He was obsessed with greed, which he knew from experience provided power and authority.

Charles looked across the seat of the carriage and begin to casually address the feelings of his heart, "Its appears that it might be a beautiful day after all."

"I sure hope so. I'm expecting many guest for the reception."

"We need to enjoy more days like this. Who knows how long they will last."

Elizabeth turned and looked at him, "What do you mean?"

"Mother, I am quite concerned over the serious situation concerning the country. If Abe Lincoln is elected to the Presidency, I believe as others that I've spoken with, that South Carolina will carry through with their threats and secede from the Union. That could mean war."

Elizabeth began to laugh, repressing the reality that could take place. She spoke with a since of humor that she was known for at times, "If Mr. Lincoln is fortunate enough to be blessed with the election, then he better not hope for war, because our boys will give it to him."

"If war comes, and I believe it will, we shall all be affected by it in someway. I feel that our family as well as the business should be prepared. I am concern it will all be jeopardized if we are not ready. Mother we have to come forth with a plan in the event that Virginia secedes; we can not lose everything that we have labored all of our life for and earned."

Elizabeth paused; her keen perception knew where the conversation was leading. For sometime now, she knew of Charles' desire and intentions of owning the business. It was her wish, that in time he would oversee complete operations and have sole authority, but for now it was to complicated. Out of courtesy and devotion, her resolve was to discuss this with him, "What do you propose we should do to be prepared if Lincoln is elected, and war follows."

Charles paused for a moment and carefully chose his words, "I'll get to the point. In the family's best interest, I feel you need to consider releasing operations and authority of Shenandoah to myself until such time this potential crisis passes. Have I not been the one who has prospered the business and the most dedicated to its success?"

Elizabeth was quiet in thought and admiring the beauty of the mountains, the quiet still waters of the Shenandoah as they approached the street for which it received its name. She knew in her heart, that her intuition had served her well. There was truth in Charles' insight concerning the possibility of war and the continual existence of the Estate. Her greatest concern involved Pete and Rebecca, her only daughter. What would be their involvement in the picture, how would they accept her decision in Charles' favor? It was because of these two younger children, that it would be too complicated, but for now she would have to stall Charles in his quest for power. Although, she knew that a decision would have to be made soon; it was an experience of reality that she did not relish. As for Charles, she knew that he would pursue his quest now that the subject had been presented. The question in her mind for now was; how would she be able to approach the situation without offending him. He has always been the one that she truly confided in, and he carried out her wishes. There had to be an answer, but for now, she would avoid the decision.

In a compassionate tone, which Elizabeth seldom displayed, she replied, "Charles, you are right in your judgment, but I trust that you would accept mine and not be offended. Until we know what's going to take place with the general election, and if there is going to be war, I would like to keep control of the farm. If all of this passes, which I pray to God that it does, then I will uncontionally turn over Shenandoah to you, even though I know that Pete will have difficulty with my decision."

Charles was surprised, certain that the time was right, though he didn't express an opinion, nor did he agree with her judgment. For now, he would have to accept her decision; he would look for an opportunity in the future and press the subject. Out of respect for his Mother, he replied disappointingly, "I understand."

As they entered the main area of town Charles instructed Hayward to stop at the bank. After the horses had come to a halt, Charles walked to the opposite side of the carriage and assisted his Mother.

Mr. White, a friend of the family, called out as he approached from across the street, "Charles, Elizabeth, how good it is to see you. How are you on this lovely day?"

Charles reached forth to shake his hand, "Good, good! And I hope the same for you and your family."

Mr. White, who was known for his honesty and compulsiveness said, "Charles we have to arrange some time to get together.

Charles anxiously replied, "I agree."

Mr. White expressed his excitement, "My, my! We are going to be in a very serious crisis if Lincoln is elected. And Virginia, oh my Charles, what if the state calls a convention for the business of secession."

Charles spoke with vigor and eloquence, "Sir, at the reception for Mr. Pierce of Richmond this evening, I'm sure that we will take up the matter of Lincoln's possible election. I believe that the leadership of this County must have a strategy in place should the state be drawn into the business of secession. We must consider raising additional forces for our militia. We should draw on our consensus and strength to defend our homeland should we become united with a Confederacy. Of course, I'm sure that Mr. Pierce will be more than willing to share his insight and wisdom should Virginia need to take this important step of separation from the Union."

With a smile that covered the width of his face, Mr. White happily replied, "That's a boy Charles, that's the spirit, that's what we need to hear. I am sure that you would be willing to do your duty should you be called upon."

"Yes sir. My loyalties will always be with Virginia."

Mr. White quietly noticed the determination in Charles' eyes. As he departed their company, he tipped his John Bull hat and proceeded to cross the street.

After witnessing the conversation between Charles and Mr. White, Elizabeth knew in her heart that she no longer would be able to live in denial. As she stood silent, she was troubled and grieved over the prospect of war. What would become of her Sons? What would be their role in this conflict? Would they live to see an end? The questions were complex, when suddenly tears slowly begin to flow from her eyes. Just as quickly, she wiped them away with her hands, her sorrowful expression changed to a smile, not allowing anyone to witness the vulnerability of her heart.

CHAPTER THREE

It was an uneventful morning for William Pierce as he walked toward one of the passenger cars of the 10:15 west bound train to Harpers Ferry. As he paused for a moment, he calmly stroked his long mustache as his gray eyes scanned the headlines of the local newspaper, the Baltimore Gazette. In the distance, he listened as the conductor called out for everyone to board the train for its departure. William was so involved with reading the national news about Abe Lincoln's views for President that he had to run to catch the train as it was slowly leaving the Baltimore railroad station. William was not a fast runner, but he was able to grab the handrail and pull his short, pudgy frame up the steps of the coach. After pausing to catch his breath and at the same time rubbing the wrinkles from his black frock coat, he proceeded to enter the coach to take a seat next to the window.

As the train moved slowly through the Maryland countryside, William began to concentrate on the Democratic Convention, which had been held in this great city by the Chesapeake Bay just two months ago. He was a delegate that had been chosen to represent Virginia and one of the many who walked out in protest over the acceptance of the anti-slavery plank view that had been voted into the party's platform. This was his first visit to the city since that time. For William, it had been a strenuous weeklong meeting with Thomas Mays, an ardent supporter of slavery and state rights. Their discussions and ideas to be implemented had gone well, and on many of the perplexed issues surrounding the up coming election they vigorously agreed. William knew that there was a good chance that Lincoln could be elected because of the division within the Democratic Party. This is one of the reasons why he met with Mr. Mays, to rally the faithful that resided in that state in support of Vice President John Breckinridge for the Presidency. The state, he believed was evenly divided concerning secession, and even if there was a vote for separation, it would be difficult for the state to do so with its boundaries surrounding Washington, the Nation's capitol. In his view, William believed that the election of Breckinridge would serve the state's best interest, and the South as a whole. It was his belief that the only way the Union would be preserved would come about only with a decisive victory in November for the Vice President.

As the train slowly chugged along the countryside, William gave considerable thought concerning Elizabeth Barker's letter that he had received the previous month. In the correspondence, she requested the favor that Charles play an important part in the up-coming campaign. With only three months left before the Nation decided who their 16th President would be, William began to think of how he would be able to utilize the Barker's help.

As William pondered these thoughts, the silence was suddenly broken by the soft voice of a woman, "Excuse me sir, is someone occupying this seat?"

Instantly, William turned away from looking out the window toward the direction of the mysterious voice. The young lady, in her twenties stood patiently waiting for a reply. The amazed expression upon his face revealed a multitude of words; he could not help but to admire her perfect beauty. Finally, after regaining his composure, he answered with enthusiasm, "No, I would be honored if you would do me the pleasure of your company."

The lady took the edges of her long blue dress that covered her slim frame, and sat in the seat beside him. After a short period of time, he glanced at her, but she was involved in reading her book of poetry, The Phoenix and Turtledove, by Shakespeare. Some years past, William had read the poem and knew by the expression on her face that she was touched by the emotion of the literature.

William was speechless; his mind was consumed with many ideas concerning his business with the Barkers. All at the same time, he began to concentrate on a way to enter into a conversation with this mysterious passenger. Quickly the thought occurred that he had not introduced himself. It was not only proper etiquette, but honorable for a Virginia gentleman. He said, "Forgive me for my poor manners, I have been so involved with my personal thoughts, let me please introduce myself. I am William Pierce of Richmond. And you would be?"

The young lady looked up from her book and answered softly, "I am Katie McBride from Boston."

William was anxious to continue the conversation, "May I ask what your destination might be?"

Katie closed her book and casually replied in a tone of optimism, "I am traveling to Harpers Ferry. I have accepted a substitute position as a teacher at the Catholic School."

"I'm going to Harpers Ferry myself. I have some friends, the Barkers, that I will be visiting over the next few days."

There was a slight pause and William did not want to lose the opportunity to continue the discussion, so he began to scramble for the right words. He was a gentleman with little experience in relationships with a lady; therefore, he struggled for the right conversation. Suddenly, it came to mind to acquaint her with the area, "Miss McBride, the area that you are about to call home is one of the most beautiful places that the good Lord ever created. The mountains are so full of color, and the birds will gladly serenade you with a melody on a walk along the river. And oh, the air is so fresh; the breeze of the wind is so gentle. The town is a place where there are many different clothing shops to make choices. And there are various activities for you to be involved, if you desire. It is here where two rivers, the Potomac and Shenandoah come together. The rolling green pastures, and busy farms and the colorful countryside is an area of serenity and calm. Should my business not require me to live in Richmond, I would have to strongly consider living in the little town."

Katie was pleased to hear about the small village and the surrounding area as she smiled and enthusiastically answered, "I am looking forward to experiencing life in the south and making new friends. Though my family disagrees fearing war will happen."

"Maybe with the right choice, war will be averted."

As the train was approaching Frederick City, Katie began to admire the green sloping hills and the beautiful Catoctin Mountains. As she admired the scenic beauty, her thoughts were upon her Father, a prominent Boston banker, and a loving Mother that possessed incredible wisdom, and was her whole world. The one that she confided in the most out of a deep trust had been her brother, Seamus. He had opposed her move to Virginia fearing that the Nation was uncontrollably headed toward an all out civil war. Though she had always possessed a deep passion for educating the slaves, she believed that with a potential crisis on the horizon that her decision to come to Harpers Ferry was the right one. Katie was an intelligent lady, who loved to be in control of her life. Her responsibility and maturity for her youthful age had given her the strong initiative to pursue any challenged that was entrusted unto her, and see the matter through to a positive conclusion. She had just finished school, and this was an adventurous period in her life.

Time was beginning to run short and William knew if he did not attempt to pursue this acquaintance, the opportunity might not present its self again. The train would be arriving in Harpers Ferry within the hour and if he was going to act then he must do so now. Nervously, he cleared his throat and said, "A reception will be hosted this evening in my honor by the Barkers. They are very hospitable people, and knowing them the way that I do, I'm sure that you'll receive an invitation to attend. I know that it would be short notice, but I feel that this would give you the opportunity to meet some of the local and prominent people of this great town, and hopefully cultivate a few friends."

Katie didn't reply, even though she was sure that William was showing an interest in her. She felt that he was a polite aristocratic gentleman, but she did not desire at this time in her life to pursue a relationship with any gentleman of good standing. Romance at one time happened to pass through Katie's youthful life, but the young man, a physician, was killed in a riding accident. It was an incident that she had been recovering from, and often she had wondered if her decision to leave Boston was because of the grief that she had experience. For now, it was more important in her life to pursue her vocation, even though at her age she would be viewed in a different light by society because she had not entered into matrimony.

As the train crept through the covered bridge into the station, slowly coming to a stop, William noticed Charles standing on the station platform waiting. He quickly grabbed his luggage and Katie's for their departure from the coach.

Anxiously, William with Katie stepped down from the stairwell of the passenger car onto the platform. Charles approached and stretched forth his hand with a jovial greeting, "William, my friend, how are you doing?"

William returned the gesture, gladly replying, "Charles, its good to see you again. "How are Caroline and the family?"

"Everyone is healthy and looking forward to seeing you once again."

Charles' attention was turned towards his friend's mysterious guest. He began to curiously inquire into the mystery of the young lady that had been standing quietly by William's side, "May I ask who this beautiful young lady might be that is accompanying you?"

William was so caught up in the moment that he forgot to introduce Katie to the Barkers, "Oh, do forgive me everyone for my negligent and rude manners. This is Miss Katie McBride whom I became acquainted with on the train ride from Baltimore. She will be the new teacher at the Catholic School here in town."

Charles smiled and cordially said as he tipped the brim of his hat, "Miss McBride, on behalf of my family, I would like to welcome you to Harpers Ferry, and extend my wishes for your success."

Elizabeth wanted to investigate into William's new acquaintance. She was known to be one of the most sociable ladies in the County, and at this moment, it was her intention to harvest all of the information that she could concerning Katie's business and life. Her hazel eyes were fixed as she began to speak politely in an articulate Southern accent, "Oh! Is that so, you are the new teacher, I do declare, that is good news. Your accent tells me that you must be from one of the New England States."

Katie's first impression of Elizabeth was favorable, but cautious, because of the way Northerners were perceived in the South. Deciding to choose her words wisely and keeping it short and polite, she answered, "Yes, I am from Boston, Massachusetts, though I'm Irish."

"Irish! Well, I"….

William interrupted, he wasn't sure if Elizabeth, who was a fire-eating believer in states rights and slavery would try to crush the newcomer from the north. On many occasions, he knew that she has been out spoken and opinionated concerning the way of life in the South. He did not feel that this was the time or place for this conversation. Besides, William did not want Elizabeth to jeopardize his acquaintance with Katie so soon after meeting her.

After taking Elizabeth by the hand, William rapidly took the initiative and kissed her on the cheek.

"Elizabeth, I always save my best greeting until last. How is the finest lady in this part of the Old Dominion doing?"

The expression upon Elizabeth's face glowed, as she answered, "Oh William, I do declare, you shouldn't make such a fuss over me. But to answer your question, I have been doing just fine and looking forward to seeing you for sometime now. Besides, everyone is looking forward to the reception that we have planned for you. Just recently, several of the invited guests said that they heard you speak in Richmond City and afterwards how much they share your insight on the up-coming election and the affairs of our great state."

William paused and the expression of joy and contentment disappeared from his face; concern and despair soon ruled his expression. He desperately searched his heart for the words that he would share. Suddenly, he looked Elizabeth in the eyes and with sadness in his voice, he answered. "I feel this nation is so deeply divided, like nothing we have ever known before in history. The conflict that waits upon the horizon will be more then any family will be able to bare thanks to the events that took place ten months ago at that old engine house over in the Armory yard." William took off his hat and the wind began to blow intensely through his sandy hair as he looked in the direction of Loudoun Heights and spoke sorrowfully, "This whole area will be fought over because of its military importance, such as the railroad. This town will see no rest from the conflict. The bloodshed will be more then anyone can imagine, but we must be willing to make the sacrifice if it comes to that and fight for what we believe in, our sovereign right as a state. Oh yes, we must."

There was a moment of silence at Williams's revelation of the possible reality that awaited them. He possessed very good insight into the passions and emotions that covered this great land. He knew that it would not be a short affair, but one of length because of the pride that both the North and South shared.

After listening to his friend's views, Charles did not want Katie to feel uneasy because of the nature of the situation that could be drawing the nation toward war. Just as William had perceived, Charles extended an invitation to Katie. It was his desire that she would make a fair judgment for herself in regard to life in the south, and the reason why they were so passionate about their way of life. Then too, if she was going to call this area home, then she needed to experience Southern hospitality, and make new acquaintances. With this in mind, and in a gentleman like fashion, Charles asked the young lady, "Miss McBride, speaking on behalf of my family, we would like to extend an invitation to you to attend the reception tonight in honor of William at our home, Shenandoah. I know that it is not giving you the proper notice to prepare, but we would like to extend our welcome to you."

Elizabeth added with a subtle smile, "Oh yes my dear, you must join us."

Katie was eager to make new acquaintances and to establish her life in the area, though she was hesitant because she was from the North. Katie felt that most of the people from this area might feel uncomfortable with her presence and that she would be judged wrongly, "Thank you, but it's been such a long trip."

Elizabeth persisted as she gazed at Katie, "Oh, but you must. You may not have the opportunity to meet this many of the County's most prominent citizens for sometime."

Finally, Katie accepted their gesture of good will; the dividends of new acquaintances would be worth it. She replied, "I would be honored, thank you for your hospitality."

Charles said as he quickly glanced at his Mother, "I will send the carriage for you around 7:00 p.m. Oh, do not eat, come hungry."

Katie softly replied not revealing the nervousness that she felt, "Now if you would be gracious enough to excuse me, I must depart from you wonderful people. I must let Father Thomas know that I have arrived."

As William, Charles and his Mother stood silently looking, Katie gathered her luggage and began to depart from their company, she turned about to face them smiling and said, "Oh! And please everyone, call me Katie."

Inwardly, William was pleased that everything had worked out just as he had expected. As she continued to walk away, he watched Katie briefly and then he turned and looked at Charles commenting, "I do believe that is one nice lady that I intend on getting better acquainted with before I depart from this town."

Charles smile and suggested that they proceed to the Wager House Hotel for some lunch, and William agreed as he was still rejoicing inwardly over his new acquaintance. Charles ordered Hayward to collect the luggage and place it upon the carriage. As Hayward acknowledged and proceeded to carry out the task, he was asked to find the younger Barker and invite him to join them.

The time was 1:30 p.m. according to Pete's watch as he departed Whites Tavern. He casually proceeded toward the shop of Mr. Harding to pick up some shoes that had been repaired. As he turned the corner of Potomac and Shenandoah Street, he heard his name called. Looking about, he noticed Hayward quickly approaching from the opposite side of the street. Pete was perplexed at the urgent sound of his friend's voice. Hayward said as he attempted to catch is breath, "Mr. Pete, Mr. Charles wants yose ta come ta de Wager House ta join him and Mr. Pierce soon, dey is waitin' for ya."

As Pete continued towards the store, he replied, "Go and leave word with the hotel clerk for my brother, that I will be there as soon as I pick up my shoes from Mr. Harding."

After departing Hayward's company, Pete was approached by an acquaintance, Miss Jane Powers, whose father was a businessman with great influence in the County. Grabbing him by the arm, in her slow, calm, and seductive Southern accent, she said, "My, my! If it isn't that sweet man that I'm fond of. Where are you going in such a hurry?"

"I have business to take care of with my brother, and an out of town friend. They are waiting for me, so I need to hurry along."

"Will I see you at the reception tonight?"

Pete's response was reluctant as he answered the young lady, "Yes, you will, now if you don't mine, I must go."

He took her hand and broke the grip; and with their eyes meeting, he tipped his hat in a farewell gesture, and then departed.

After his encounter with Jane, Pete increased his pace along Shenandoah Street toward the hotel and shortly joined his brother, Mother, and Mr. Pierce. The three of them were already indulging in their lunch and jovial conversation about social life in Richmond and William's tobacco plantation on the outskirt of that famous Southern city. As Pete approached the table where everyone was seated, Charles looked up from his meal of fish and potatoes. He had an impatient expression upon his face as he addressed his younger brother; "We have been waiting almost an hour for you. I told Hayward to tell you to hurry along?"

Pete was defensive, but kept his composure as he answered his brother, "Unfortunately I was delayed. A young lady approached me and I could not be rude. The gentleman that I am, I felt that I must be polite to her."

William's grin covered his face as he stood and reached to shake Pete's hand and agreeing, "There is nothing better on this earth, then good wine and a charming lady."

Charles and Pete began to laugh in agreement with William at his joking observations.

Elizabeth had been sitting quietly observing the guests in the hotel dinning room and listening to the exchange of conversation concerning the possibility of bitter conflict upon the nation and the uncertainly of their future. Now it was time for her to change the subject that the three men had embarked on. She respected William's insight into national affairs and was interested in the political views of some of his friends that he had spoken with concerning the upcoming elections. She needed to inquire into this subject so that she would know what steps might have to be taken to insure the security of Shenandoah if war should come. The question that still concerned her the most; would it be in her best interest to allow Charles to be in complete control, or retain authority herself? She had to acquire as much knowledge as she could from the shewed politician, so that she would be able to make a good decision and profit from it in return.

With a polite smile, Elizabeth interrupted the merry conversation between the men and changed the tone to one of seriousness, "William, what do you think will take place concerning the general election?"

William took a deep sigh and paused before speaking. He turned to face the matriarch giving her his full attention, "Well Miss Elizabeth, I'm sure that many of the Southern Democrats will vote for Breckinridge. He is a very experienced politician, well liked, and has the qualities to lead the nation, but my greatest fear is that the party will remain split. There are bitter feelings within the Party over the issue of whether there can be expansion of slavery in the new territories. Personally, I believe that Virginia would be a lot better off if it wasn't a part of the Union. But lets hope that we can gain enough support for a Breckinridge victory in November and that civil war can be averted. And let us hope, that John Bell of Tennessee will not be a factor in this endeavor, because if he becomes a serious challenger, then that will cause greater concern among Southern Democrats." William's reply was with concern, and all who were present took notice of the serious expression on his face.

Charles anxiously wanted to express his views and test his friend's insight, so he asked, "That means if the Party remains divided, then Lincoln wins and South Carolina will carry through with its threat and secede as many believe?"

"You would be correct Charles, I'm sure that Lincoln will try and keep her in the Union any way that he can, even if it means war."

There was a pause as everyone began to realize the grim reality that may be coming in the near future for the nation and their state. It suddenly became quiet, each in personal thought, and how they may have to handle their own individual life, and that of family. Elizabeth became very concern at the answers that William had shared with them. She began to think of the future of her business, and if her sons would become involved in civil war.

After what seems an eternity, Charles took a sip of the red wine that he ordered and wiped his mouth on the fine white linen, "If South Carolina secedes from the Union, then I believe that most of the gulf states will do like wise."

Pete promptly proclaimed, "I agree, she will not be the only one."

Charles replied as he was lighting a cigar, "I hope that Virginia follows immediately. We can't sit ideally by and do nothing, but we will need to take a stand with our brothers in the South in maintaining our sovereignty."

Pete laughed as he listened to his brother's perception on the issue, and sarcastically answered, "Yeah, brother, I can see you in Richmond giving the speech if it comes to this."

With pride, Charles replied to his brother's comment, "When that time comes little brother, maybe I will, just maybe I will!"

Elizabeth abruptly interrupted, "Oh, dear you two. I will not have you bickering in front of Mr. Pierce, now stop acting like children. You are embarrassing me!"

There was a moment of silence, and then Charles and Pete offered their apology to William and their Mother.

After this exchange between the two brothers, William began to relax in his chair. He casually removed a pipe from his coat along with some of the tobacco that had been grown on his plantation. As he began to light it, he glowed with a smile and said in a reassuring voice, "There is nothing wrong with a little spirited debate Elizabeth, it's good for the soul."

Brandy had just been served as Hayward walked into the dinning area where the Barkers and William were seated. Making his intentions known to the waiter, he passed a message. Without hesitation, the waiter approached Pete with a message from Billy Smith to join him in the hotel lobby. Pete was not sure of the nature of the message, but he did not care for the gentleman because of his unruly nature that he possessed at times. With a puzzled expression, he quietly excused himself and followed Hayward to the lobby to inquire into Mr. Smith's request. Billy was the same age and medium height as Pete, only slightly heavier. He was standing beside of a beautiful marble stand when the young Barker walked into the lobby. It was Billy's habit before committing to a brawl to make the attempt to intimidate his foe by the anger that his dark eyes revealed. He quickly took on an aggressive nature; "I will get right to the point. I hear that you have been seeing Jane Powers. Is this information true?"

Pete refused to be dominated as he answered boldly, "I have had dinner with her on several occasions, what business is it of yours?"

"I have been very fond of Jane for some time now and I'm not about to have some two bit lady's man interfering with my relationship with her. Do you understand!"

Pete courageously replied as he approached his foe, "As I remember, she is old enough to make her own decisions."

Billy shouted in a tone of voice that attracted the attention of the guest in the hotel lobby, "Oh, I guess I was right then, you are interfering, it's about time that you Barkers realize that you can't have everything you're way all of the time."

Seizing the moment, Pete attempted to calm the instigator with an explanation, "Look Billy, I don't want any trouble from you. I asked her out to dinner as a courtesy and nothing more, and she accepted. Other then that, I have no interest in her."

As Billy approached Pete, Billy had his fist clinched and prepared for the attack. Quickly losing his composure, he yelled, "I think that you are a no good liar!"

Pete turned to walk away when Billy quickly grabbed Pete by the collar of his waistcoat. Just as swiftly, Pete pushed him away. In a fierce manner, Billy hit Pete with his left hand in the face, causing him to lose his balance and fall over a wooden chair that was behind him. Without hesitation, Pete jumped to his feet, delivering two swift blows to the troublemaker's jaw, which caused Billy to stagger. Hayward stood near by with no intentions of interfering and watched with quiet enthusiasm as the melee was taking place.

With these events unfolding, Katie McBride was approaching the hotel to have lunch after taking care of depositing some of her money at the bank. She was looking forward after her meal of having an enjoyable afternoon browsing in some of the shops along Shenandoah Street, especially to purchase a new straw hat.

As the melee progressed, Billy and Pete struggled for the upper hand. At all cost, Billy did not want to lose; therefore, he resorted to some very ungentlemanly like tactics and kicked Pete in his abdomen. Falling backwards, Pete's body momentum struck Katie, as she was about to enter the hotel, causing both of them to fall in a huge puddle of water in the street in front of the hotel entrance.

Katie's temper flared very quickly. Taking the blue parasol that was in her hand, she began to strike Pete rapidly, taking a terrible toll upon him. She struggled feverously to remove him from off of her body, all at the same time yelling, kicking, and screaming at him in her assault. Pete began to cry out with pain as the little Irish girl continued with her relentless attack.

Finally, Pete was able to escape and roll away, covering his head as he did so. As he jumped to his feet, he felt quite embarrassed over the melee that took place in front of many witnesses. Wiping the mud from his brown trousers and waistcoat, Pete offered Katie, who was still sitting in the water his hand. She screamed, swinging the parasol, "You, you bloody fool, get away from me!"

After refusing his gesture of good will, another gentleman who had been witnessing the event stepped forward and offered his help, which she accepted.

Katie was wet and her clothes were full of mud. She began to straighten her dress and was extremely angry over the event that she had been involved. Pete could not help, but to notice her angry emotions as she picked up her blue and white bonnet from the ground. He felt embarrassed and foolish. After she was composed enough, and still removing the mud from her dark auburn hair, Pete cautiously approached and said, "I am sorry for the embarrassment that I......" Katie suddenly interrupted Pete as she held the remains of the blue parasol in a threatening manner.

"I have half a mind to take what's left of this bloody parasol and hit you again." As she continued her verbal attack, she was in a state of almost uncontrolled emotion, "You, you should not cross my path again or I will certainly carry out my threat."

Katie walked away and began to cry as she wiped the mud from her face and clothing. Pete took notice of what was left of the damaged parasol that she tossed to the ground. As he walked over and retrieved it, he felt that it would not be wise for him to try and pursue her; he had had enough for one day. Even though he felt that he had no other choice in the encounter with Billy Smith, he would have to answer for his actions, and this would not be a happy affair, especially with the young lady that had just arrived in town. On more then one occasion, he had taken part in a brawl under similar circumstances, but this was the most embarrassing of them all. Now, he would have to face the wrath of his Mother and brother.

Many of the town's people had witnessed this event. They were not only laughing at the two, but also poking fun of them.

Elizabeth, Charles, and William had departed the dining room after hearing all of the commotion and witnessed the whole scene. After the melee, Charles turned about and noticed the expression of humiliation that covered his Mother's face. He angrily proclaimed, "I will deal with this matter as soon as we return home. What Pete did was disgraceful and an embarrassment to this family. His conduct is unforgivable!"

Elizabeth said in a cold and angry tone, "I have never felt so humiliated and angry as I do now. No, Charles, I will deal with him in my own way. Trust me."

As for William, he recognized Katie as the unfortunate participant of this affair, and quickly rushed off to offer his comfort and support. As he walked across the street where she was standing, his heart sank as he witnessed the tears that filled her eyes. He wanted to take and embrace Katie, but hesitated at the thought because he felt that it might frighten her more then she was already. William said in an earnest tone of voice as he approached, "Katie, Katie. Are you all right?"

After regaining her composure, Katie reassured him, "I am fine, really I am!"

Katie noticed the compassion in William's eyes as he quietly removed the handkerchief from his coat pocket. As he gave her his handkerchief to wipe her green eyes, William began to speak in an apologetic tone, "I am sorry Katie for what has just taken place, and I do not know what to say, I do not know what got into those two young men."

She was more composed, "Thank you for your kindness and generosity."

"Is there anything that I can do, or get you?"

"No, I would just like to go and rest for awhile. I do not want you to worry. I will be alright."

As much as he wanted to help Katie, William honored her request and watched as she walk slowly toward her new residence.

Slowly, Pete began to clean the dirt and mud off his clothes and inspect the bodily damage. He was concerned for his Mother as he walked toward her, but she quietly abandoned him and walked to the carriage to leave for home. As he stood in the street alone, he felt guilty and condemned. There was a strong belief in his heart, that he had done everything to avoid the fistfight. The crowd that had gathered was still laughing as they departed the area to continue their normal life, but for Pete it would be difficult.

As Pete turned about, Jane Powers was only person left standing in the street. There was a glowing expression of joy covering the width of her face as she stood clapping her hands in victory. The humiliation of the young attractive lady, who was her age from the North, was more then enough to cause Jane to be proud and to feel a sense of victory over a potential advisory.

Jane said in an exhorting manner, "Oh I must say, you handled yourself brilliantly,"

"Yeah, now I wonder why Billy and I went at it anyway,"

Jane answered shrewdly as she slowly approached, "Oh dear, I wouldn't know. I just happen to be coming this way when I saw you and that Yankee lady fighting."

"We weren't fighting. And how did you know that she was from the North?"

"In Harpers Ferry, news travels quickly."

Pete angrily asked as he continued to clean the mud from his clothing, "Did you say something to Billy about the two of us having dinner together last week?"

Jane began to answer his question, "Well, I...

Pete interupted her and said, "Forget it!"

His expression of contempt reflected the emotional pain that he was feeling from the miserable day that he was experiencing. He walked away without another word and painfully proceeded to retrieve his mare.

Jane began to laugh and called out, "I'll see you tonight."

Pete knew that she had taken pride in the brawl with Billy, and that it was probably her that had instigated the whole matter. He felt at this time that it would be best not to acknowledge her because it would only create a greater anger and he had suffered enough.

The journey back to the Estate was a slow one. His mind was on the unforgivable event and the pain that he had caused his family and the young lady. For now, the greatest question for him was, what would be the best manner of defense in giving an account of his actions once he arrived at Shenandoah? Also, how would he be able to find the young lady and apologize to her?

Finally arriving at the Estate, Pete dismounted and walked the mare slowly toward the stable. Hayward was there and opened the door for him, but said nothing. Pete remained quiet without acknowledging his friend. He placed the horse in one of the stalls and removed the saddle. Turning to one side, he placed the riding gear over the top rail of the stall where he had just lodged the animal. Feeling very frustrated, he began to brush his horse down as he looked over at Hayward, who was feeding the horses that, pulled the carriage for his Mother.

Hayward paused and turned in the direction where Pete stood and began to address him sympathetically, "I know'd dat dere Miss Jane was gonna git you in trouble."

Pete replied remorsefully as he laid his head against one of the wooden post that supported the stall, "Hayward, I know. As always, you are right."

Hayward said confidently as he went about the care of the animals, "De eyes always tell de truth, an dat girl has eyes dat lie. I know ya."

"How is it Hayward, that you are the only person that can possibly know what I am going to do?"

A smile surface revealing the mischief expression on Hayward's face, "I know how yose are with dem dere pretty womin'."

"My friend, as I was riding back to Shenandoah this afternoon, I just had a strong feeling that I must find this lady, who unfortunately ended up in the middle of this mess, and apologize to her." As he gave the thirsty mare some water, he continued to pour out his emotions, "I did not know that she was a friend of Mr. Pierce that I must also apologize to."

Hayward strongly agreed as he stared at his friend with his dark piercing eyes, "You'd be doin' de right ting, listen to ya heart."

The main concern for Pete now was how would he be able to approach his mother. It was through past experiences similar to this, that he had received her wrath. He said somberly, "Now my Mother, that's going to be a different matter,"

Hayward suggested as he was completing his chores, "Yose better go and make it right with Miss Elizabeth, she mus' be pretty upset by now."

Pete agreed and asked Hayward to finish taking care of Victory. Nervously, he began to meditate on the words that would be appropriate in defense of his actions.

On his way to confront his Mother, he decided to stop by the kitchen house to see what Pansy was cooking. As he entered, she was standing by the table preparing some potatoes for the reception. She paused, and with a stern expression on her face, she said, "Boy, you'd be in a heap of trouble." She continued the conversation as she was retrieving some fresh dill, "Lordie, Lordie, de way Miss Elizabeth come a runin' through here a wile a go, she was fit ta be tied. Umn! Umn!"

"It's that bad, huh,"

Pansy's hands moved quickly as she continued to prepare the potatoes, but suddenly stopping, she pointed her finger at Pete and said, "Its dat bad. Dem young womin' gonna git yose in all kinds of trouble, yose should know'd better by now."

Suddenly, the conversation was broken as Matthew, the servant entered. Upon the request of Elizabeth, he asked Pete to join his mother in the parlor. Pete smiled as he looked at Pansy for sympathy, which did not come. His Mother's wrath was about to be poured out upon him and there was nothing that he could do, but hope for the best and attempt to make amends for his sin.

After entering, he walked over to kiss his Mother on the cheek, which was always customary with a member of the family when returning home. His Mother turned away from him, and walked quietly over to the huge stone fireplace. Hesitating briefly, she placed her hand upon the huge wooden mantel and said to him, "Today my Son, you made a fool out of me, not only me, but you're brother and the rest of this family." Continuing in an angry tone, "I have never witness such a display of disrespect. Never!"

Pete attempted to interrupt her, "Mother all that I."

Elizabeth pointed her finger at him and began to shout, "Do not interrupt me when I am speaking to you!"

There was a silence that fell over the room. Pete waited patiently for his Mother's next response.

After walking across the large room and looking out the window at some of the stallions, Elizabeth regained her composure. In a calmer tone of voice, she pointed at the portrait of her deceased husband hanging over the fireplace mantel, "Since your Father passed away, God rest his soul, I have always tried to raise you and Charles the proper way. You have time and again rejected my authority and committed some foolish act that's brought disgrace and displeasure to this family. You and Charles are so different. He respects my wishes and tries to carry them out. He brings honor upon our good name, but you, you would rather live the life of a rebel."

"Mother, if I may, I would like to offer my apology, and I pray to God that I will not be a part of anything that will bring you or this family dishonor, but I was attacked by Billy first. I had no other choice then to defend myself."

"Why did you not walk away? You know that he is from a low class family."

Quickly and with a tone of confidence, Pete replied, "I tried."

"Well, you didn't try hard enough! Your just like your Father!"

Pete replied in a tone of anger as he began to pace about the room, "Yeah Mother, your right. I am just like my Father. I don't believe for a moment that he would have turned his back either. We both know that he was a man of principal, but Charles calls it a weakness. At least he stood by his word. Sometimes I believe that this family is hypocritical in what it says and what it does."

Disgusted with the whole matter, Elizabeth abruptly interrupted, and in an authoritative voice, "Oh dear! I have heard enough. Other then your apology to Mr. Pierce, this matter for now is closed."

Pete stood quietly by the window and kept his thoughts to himself as his Mother departed the room.

CHAPTER FOUR

The sun was a bright, glowing, red as it began to hide beneath the horizon in the hazy western sky. The evening promised to be one of excitement as the weather was cooperating. Caroline had planned on the reception for William Pierce to be held outside behind the main house instead of the ballroom so that everyone that was invited would have plenty of room to socialize and dance. As the wind began to gently blow, one could smell the barbecue pig that was still roasting over the open fire. Pansy was running to and from the house shouting orders to those servants that had been assigned with assisting her in the preparations of the dinner. She was a servant that took great pride in being a part of the family's personal staff and was meticulous in her assignments with every little detail to perfection.

Meanwhile to the rear of the house, Caroline was standing, watching and directing some of the house servants as they placed the beautiful red roses that had been grown in the garden in their proper place on the dinner tables. They would look good with the canton china that Charles and her had received as an anniversary gift from William. The string ensemble from nearby Charlestown would perform the music for this special event. As the musicians were carefully tuning their violins, and selecting their material, Elizabeth was already approaching the leader of the group with numerous request for what she hope would be a perfect evening.

It was close to 7:00 in the evening, as Pete glanced at his gold watch that he had inherited from his Father. Walking over to his mahogany chair in the bedroom, he began whistling the song, Come Where My Love Lies Dreaming as he sat and begin dressing for the reception. As he was thinking about the events that had taken place earlier in the day, there was a knock at his bedroom door. Ezekiel had just returned with Pete's shoes that he had shined for the reception. Pete quickly acknowledged the young servant. Opening the door to receive them, he thanked him for the excellent work. Placing the shoes slowly upon his feet, he removed his new black broadcloth swallowtails with bright buttons from his wardrobe. After putting it on, he quickly glanced at the mirror to make sure that it rested on his muscular medium frame. Then, he touched up his dark brown hair with a comb so that it was neat and parted on the right side. The sound of carriages arriving with the guest for this special event continued to distract him. Pete walked over to the front window of his room and watched for a short time. He listened to the jovial greetings and conversation, as everyone appeared to be looking forward to an evening filled with excitement. Suddenly, there was a knock at the door; it was Ezekiel returning on behalf of Charles to request his presence at the reception line to greet the guests. Again, Pete acknowledged him, and quickly grabbing his white gloves from his coat pocket, hurried down the long stairway of the mansion. Charles, William, and Elizabeth were already greeting the guest that had arrived in the grand ballroom. Pete's Mother had a frustrated expression upon her face, due to his tardiness, but soon it was replaced with one of joy. He quickly and apologetically took his place beside of her and began to greet the guest that proceeded through the reception line.

As Katie McBride was riding along the river road in the horse drawn carriage to the Barker Estate, she felt somewhat nervous about being with people whose acquaintance that she had just made. There were feelings of uneasiness, a restlessness because of the deep passions people from both the North and South had concerning each other, but Katie knew that she wanted to make new friends and discover the truth for herself about Southerners and their way of life. This she was excited about. It was very important for her to make a good impression upon those acquaintances that she would come into contact with evening. She did not want to be judged for where she had recently called home, but rather for the person that she portrayed.

Shortly, she arrived at the entrance to the Estate and marveled at the tall green oak trees, the freshly painted white-railed-fence, and the well manicured grounds that lined the long gravel lane that led to the main house. Off in the distance to her right, Katie could see a large red barn, partly made from stone and the rows of stables, all painted white and very well maintain. The blacksmiths shop and carpentry building that stood adjacent to the barn appeared to be busy, even at this hour of the evening. She watched with excitement, as the beautiful black mares galloped across the field with their colts following closely behind. As she approached the mansion, she noticed that it was nestled among trees of various kinds and was upon a ridge overlooking the vast lush pastureland to the west. Katie could see some distance toward a small slope. That is where the slave quarters were. They were made of stone, and very well kept. Some of the women were going about their chores and the children were helping them. On the issue of slavery, she, like the rest of her family, disapproved of the institution very strongly, but she knew that this evening she needed to remain silent concerning the subject. As they approached the main house, Katie was overwhelmed with awe at the sight that she was witnessing. Shenandoah possessed a magical beauty about it with the various green plants, especially the azaleas that surrounded the mansion and grounds. As far as the eye could see, the beauty that covered the Estate was beyond words. The house was a beautiful stone two story dwelling, with a lower and upper porch that was supported by white columns that covered the whole length of the front. In the middle of the circle in front of the house was a large rose garden of multiple colors that was well designed and manicured. There were many various kinds of maple trees to shade and offer privacy for its inhabitances.

After the carriage came to a halt, Charles, excused himself from the reception line, and with Caroline walked out to greet Katie. Smiling, he helped Katie from the carriage. Caroline was anxious to meet her and make her acquaintance.

Charles received Katie with a pleasant greeting, "Miss McBride, I am glad that you are able to join us, I hope that you will enjoy the evening that we have planned."

Katie smiled and nodded in agreement, but asked, "Again I would like to thank you and your family for your hospitality, but please call me Katie."

As Caroline was walking over and smiling, "Only if you call us Caroline and Charles."

Charles proclaimed, "Katie McBride, I would like for you to meet my lovely wife, Caroline."

"It is a pleasure to make your acquaintance." Caroline cheerfully responded as she continued to speak to Katie with excitement, "I hope that you will enjoy your visit with us on this lovely evening."

Everyone present agreed and began to laugh as they walked slowly towards the stone steps that led to the main entrance of the house.

Charles had found the events earlier in the day surrounding his brother and Miss McBride very trying, and for the better part of the afternoon this issue had been on his mind. He had spoken with his wife concerning the proper course of action that should be taken, and it was agreed by them, that the issue should be handled upon her arrival. So, before his brother would introduce himself, he believed that it would be for the best to apologize to Katie for the incident that had taken place earlier in the day at the Wagner House Hotel, and prepare her to meet him, "Katie, before we proceed into the house, there is something that I have to say to you."

"What is it?"

"I would like to extend on behalf of the family our apology for the misfortunate incident that you were involved in today in front of the hotel."

Katie expression of joy suddenly turned to one of bewilderment as she replied, "Thank you, but why should you apologize for what someone else did. Its not your fault."

"Oh, but yes it is."

He began to search for the appropriate words as he continued to explain, "Katie, my youngest brother was the one who was involved in the fight. It was he, who you tried to defend yourself against earlier today at the hotel. That is why I felt that an apology was in order, you will be seeing him shortly."

Just as quickly, Katie began to feel her temper dominate her emotions, though she knew that the feeling that was experienced needed to be repress and not express at this time. These lovely people were gracious enough to extended their hospitality to her, she would not attempt to cast a shadow on the events planned for the evening. For now, Katie would save her anger, and when the opportunity would present it self, then she would manifest it, in an appropriated, lady like manner at Charles younger brother.

As the three of them stood on the porch, Charles quickly changed the subject and put the subject of Pete behind him. As he turned to Caroline, he suggested that they enter the house where they could meet some of the prestigious citizens of the county and state that were in attendants for the reception.

Katie was very impressed with the architecture of the mansion as they entered the house. The hand carved molding along the walls and ceiling of Roman worriers was very impressive, but the long spiral staircase of hand carved oak wood was especially beautiful. Katie was amazed with its naturalistic appearance that the crafters had carved into the wood to resemble various types of fruit. Many of the rooms that she could see were large, with beautiful oak flooring, plenty of space, and with high ceilings. The mansion was decorated with brass fixtures and paintings of the mountains and family members. Most of the furniture was made of mahogany, stained a light cherry and was hand carved with decorative impressions of a lion. Katie assumed from reading books on society in the South that every piece in the mansion was manufacture on the Estate by some of the more skilled laborers. Katie knew that the Barkers were very wealthy and influential people in this area.

Many times, Caroline witnessed the amazed expression upon Katie's face as she admired the beauty of the house. She wanted Katie to feel at home, and to make a good impression on her, knowing farewell how Northerners felt about Southerners. For some unknown reason, Caroline was drawn to Katie, and it was her desire to share with her some of the history of the property, "Elizabeth's Father called this Estate, Shenandoah. It was named after the river that borders our property. She, being the only child, inherited this farm in 1839 after her Father passed away. The house as well as the slave quarters were built from stone taken from the property in 1835."

Katie replied curiously, "How much land is there with the plantation."

Caroline paused momentarily and then answered, "We have around 4,800 acres and may be purchasing more."

"Oh, I see."

"Our business is breeding horses, and raising cattle for beef. If the War Department renews our contract, which we feel confident about, then the additional acreage will be needed."

"It appears that your family has prospered with this type of business."

"Yes we have. Shenandoah is the largest farm in the lower Valley. We are in a position to provide many horses to the Army, and the government is willing to pay as much as $150.00 per horse with good quality."

Pete had just finished greeting Mr. and Mrs. Robert Crown from Shepherdstown when he noticed Katie walking with Caroline through the hallway into the ballroom, where most of the guests were present. He was surprised and became quite nervous and uncomfortable as he recognized her from earlier in the day, though he noticed that William's expression brighten with her appearance. He knew that he needed to apologize and hoped that she would not lose her temper, or make a scene.

As she approached, Elizabeth cordially extended a greeting, "Oh Katie, I'm so glad that you could join us. Charles told me that he had apologized to you on behalf of the family. My dear, I am so sorry. But for now, we will forget all about that and have a good time."

"Thank you for inviting me. But you don't have to apologize. We'll let the matter rest for now. Besides, I have looked forward to meeting some of your guest."

William began to smile as he took Katie's hand in his and kiss it. He said as he looked into her eyes, "I am so glad that you have joined us. Later if you would, I'd like to be the first to dance with you. That is, if I may?"

"Yes William, you may."

By now, Pete was standing next to William and made every attempt possible to avoid her until he had to. And just as quickly, he began rehearsing to himself the words that he would say, and how he would handle the situation. Finally, the time for reality had arrived. He made various attempts to try and hide a shameful and guilty expression, for he knew that he needed to display his best smile and hope for the best. At times he had been known to possess the boldness and confidence of a lion. This was one of those occasions, "Hello, I'm James Barker, I am glad that you could join us for the occasion this evening for Mr. Pierce."

Katie replied with a subdue smile and manner, "Thank you. I am Katie McBride, but I believe that we have met, haven't we."

Pete did not offer a reply to her question as their eyes met. Both Katie and Pete knew that they were playing a game, and that the time for the truth would come later, a lot later as far as Pete was concerned.

There were over 200 people in attendance for this event, and it was progressing just as Elizabeth had hoped. Throughout the dinner hour, she would visit each table and socialize with the guest, as was her custom; she loved to entertain and be the center of attention. The expression that covered her face was filled with the joy and excitement that comes with holding a reception and receiving guest whom she has not had the chance to socialize with in months. Barbecues, receptions, parties, and formal balls have been a tradition and a way of life at Shenandoah since the 1840's. Pansy and her staff had prepared a meal that was enjoyed greatly, and there were many comments made to the family to that effect. The atmosphere was filled with joy, as many of the guests were indulging in good sociable conversation concerning their business, or family life. For now, the thought of war and division seem so far away and forgotten. The soft ballads that were played in the distance by the string ensemble set the tone for a delightful and enjoyable evening. Charles and Caroline had ask Katie to join them at the family's table since she was not accompanied by a gentleman and had not made any acquaintances. As for Pete, he was seated at the far end of the table away from Katie and was speaking with William Pierce in length about the tobacco business and its prosperity.

Everyone had finished the meal and now it was time for Caroline, who was seated next to Katie, to become better acquainted.

Caroline was curious about life in Massachusetts and asked Katie, "I have never been to Boston, what is it like?"

"What I like the best about living in Boston is that I am close to the water. My greatest passion is to listen to the sound of the ocean and to walk alone along the shore, especially on a summer evening."

"I know how you feel. Sometimes, Charles and I will go and spend time along the river, or I will go alone, especially in the evening, as the sun is about to set. It is so quite and peaceful, maybe that's what you and I both have in common about the water, we like the tranquility."

Katie softly asked as she was taking a drink of water, "Do you and Charles have any children?"

"Yes we do," Caroline proudly replied, "Charles and I have one beautiful daughter, her name is Ann, she is 10."

"Someday, I hope to have children when the right gentleman comes along." The two ladies burst forth in laughter as Katie continued the conversation, "Charles gives the appearance of a sincere gentleman. You are fortunate to have him as your husband."

"I know. I remembered when I met him in Charlottesville in 1848; the year before he finished his law studies and our marriage he was quite the gentleman. I was attracted to him immediately; I knew that he was right for me. Everything was perfect, even when I took him to meet my parents at their home, Glenwood Estates near New Market. They were impressed with his enthusiasm and ambition."

The conversation was interrupted when Charles stood up at the table and suggested that the men retire to the drawing room to enjoy an after dinner brandy and conversation before the dance.

As the men gathered, some of the gentleman challenged each other in a game of chess, while other participated in profitable conversation and smoked their cigars or pipes. Still, some of the gentlemen congregated in the ballroom, which afforded them more room to socialize and have their brandy, which was being offered by the servants of the house. All of the gentlemen were having a pleasant time, smiling and loudly laughing. Pete and Charles separately socialized and indulged in conversation with all of the gentlemen that were present. The topic of interest to most of those in attendants was the possibility of war and the up coming election. Their anxiety was running high concerning the subject.

About thirty minutes had passed when William Pierce entered the room smiling as all of those in attendance gave him a round of applause. Acknowledging their gratitude, he began to say in a serious tone of voice, "I would like to thank you for attending this reception in my honor. I would like to also thank the Barker family for receiving me into their home ands showing us a very hospitable evening. Now, as you well know our party is very much divided. Unless John Breckinridge is elected to the Presidency, I don't feel that there will be much hope for the South and the continuation of our way of life. If Lincoln is elected."

William was suddenly interrupted by Mason Thomas, a prominent lawyer form Berkley County. As he stepped forward and spoke in a fevered tone of voice, "William there is no foreseeable way that Breckinridge is going to defeat Lincoln in the upcoming election and that will mean war."

The capable and wily politician had been caught off guard with the interruption and Mr. Masons remarks. William felt that he must some how try to calm the anxiety that most of them were feeling. Many of these men have sons that will be called upon to take up arms for Virginia and the rest of the South if there was war. William exhibited calmness, assurance, and words of encouragement, "Gentleman, calm yourselves, the election is three months away. I am a firm believer that John Breckinridge can win. And that he will have a mandate of the population that will support him. I believe that we will see a great victory in November. The North will have to accept the results, should they like it or not, that is the way freedom works."

Shelby Masters stood shaking his head in disagreement saying, "The Republicans know that the Democrats are split and I am sure that they feel they can just take complete control of the government and in doing so abolish slavery. We must have some way of reconciliation within our party if we stand a chance of winning in November."

Hearing what Masters had to say, all of the men began to speak at once. The gathering had turned into a scene of mass confusion and was rapidly racing out of control. Charles and Pete tried to calm the men, but to no avail. Quickly, William raised his hands in the air and shouted, "Gentlemen, listen to me. History has always been on the side of the South. Over the course of time, most of the Presidents of this country have been from the South, especially Virginia. I want you to ask yourself this question? How many Speakers of the House and Supreme Court Justices have we sent to Washington City? I do not believe that's going to change; the South has always controlled the government."

Nathaniel Baker, a graduate of the military academy at West Point and Lieutenant in the Jefferson Guard from Charlestown began to respond to the conversation, "William, you happen to over look one thing. The Republicans took control of the House of Representatives in the 58 election; what makes you think that they will not be able to do the same in this election." He vigorously continued in a fevered pitch, "They are against slavery and our way of life. If Lincoln is elected and they maintain control of the House, then we are in for some very serious trouble. The Republicans will try to destroy our civilization. And what about the Fugitive Slave Act that they are not willing to support? I say gentlemen; this will only be resolved with secession and war."

With those words spoken, many of the men began to cheer loudly, and then all tried to speak at once. The room was filled with words of war and peace; and still there was uncertainty from others concerning the right course of action for the nation. Charles knew that matters were quickly getting out of hand and that he must act swiftly. He stepped forward again and held up his hands and asked everyone to maintain some order and allow William to finish speaking. The men did not heed his request. Seeing that the gentlemen were in a state of division, Charles turned and looked to William for some leadership, but William could only see the hopelessness of the situation. He was speechless, because he knew that there was the possibility that they were correct, and that war could come.

Charles had been a student of politics and a participant of the gubernatorial election of 1859, in which John Letcher had been elected Governor of Virginia. He believed now, with his Mother's blessings for a political future that this would be the time for him to step forward and attempt to provide these men with some leadership and words of encouragement.

Finally, as Charles gain control of the situation, he began to address the confusion of these political matters. Meanwhile, Pete left the room and walked toward the back entrance to the house. It was time to put the subject of war and politics behind him. He had had enough of these issues and was determine that it wasn't going to destroy his evening. He had been looking forward to having a good time after what he had been through earlier in the day. The only exception to all of this would be when it came time to apologizing to Miss McBride. His eagerness to dance and socialized with some of the young ladies that were attending this affair was the only thing that was on the agenda for now.

As Pete walked out the back door and leaned against one of the porch columns, Jane Powers took notice and began to approach him. Pete saw her walking in his direction and quickly he wanted to return to the parlor to avoid conversation with the deceitful lady. He knew that ignoring Jane would not be the proper manner for a Virginia gentleman; pride prevailed. As she walked up on the porch, Pete half heartily smiled and asked, "Jane, how are you doing?"

"The question is not how I am doing, but how are you doing after that little incident that I witness in town earlier?" She continued laughing loudly wanting to attract attention from those that stood near by, and in a sarcastic voice, "Oh, yes by the way, I want to thank you personally for the reception that you gave that little Yankee girl this afternoon."

Pete did not care for the comment and answered unpleasantly, "Yeah, yeah, I guess you did like that, excuse me."

As Pete began to walk away toward the pond, Jane called out to him, "Oh Pete, I hope that you will save a dance for me."

Pete did not answer or look back. He knew that it would provoke more sarcastic remarks and he was not in the mood for it.

As he walked by the pond, the moon was rising over the mountains to the east. Occasionally, Pete paused and focused his attention towards the sky; it was clear and filled with many stars. There was a gentle breeze; the occasional sound of a fish could be heard near the surface of the water. There was a stillness and loneliness; it was peaceful and welcomed. Now it was time for him to collect his thoughts and think about how to best approach Katie. What would he say, and how would she judge him. On occasions in the past, it had been difficult for him to express his feelings and emotions towards the opposite gender. Pete and his brother had been instructed by their Father that this was not acceptable for a gentleman to practice, it showed a weakness and vulnerability, especially in public.

Pete paused by one of the wooden benches and picked up a few stones from the path that circled the pond. In the past to relieve his uneasiness, he found that it was relaxing to try and skip them across the surface of the water. As he does so with the first stone, there suddenly appears to be another stone doing likewise. Pete turned to see who else was present. Hayward began to laugh as his big deep voice carried through the stillness of the night. He knew that he had taken his friend by surprise and enjoyed the excitement.

Pete said surprisingly as he attempted to regain his calmness, "Hayward what are you trying to do to me, scare me half out of my wits."

Hayward was speechless as he continued to laugh loudly.

Pete demanded as he gazed at Hayward, "Have you been drinking some of Charles' Tennessee brandy!"

"No, I knows wat yose doin' out here." Hayward paused briefly as he walked toward Pete and noticed the concerned expression upon his face, "I knows dat yose need ta go and make tings rite with dat pretty little girl. She shows up and yose didn't 'spect it."

"I know," Pete soberly replied as he skips more stones across the surface of the water.

Hayward began to compassionately reassure him, "Yose come here ta try and find da words; yose need ta trust ya heart an go and make tings rite with her"

There was nothing that Pete could say, but just stood staring at the water and occasionally glanced at his friend. Shortly as they began walking along the path, Hayward remained silent, and didn't offer any conversation. He patiently waited for Pete to search his heart and find the words to express his feelings. Even though his friend did not choose to, he knew by the serious expression upon his face that he had made his point. From his experiences in the past with Pete, Hayward understood why the young man chose not to share his thoughts.

As they approached the area where the reception was taking place, Pete paused and thanked Hayward for his advice.

Looking at Pete and smiling, Hayward decided to break the long silenced, "I don't think dat it will be as hard 'pologizing as yose think. Maybe not at first, but she gonna accept"

Surprisingly Pete asked, "Why are you saying that. How can you be so sure? You don't even know her, and besides, how do I know that she won't attempt to carry out her threats from earlier today?"

Hayward placed his hand on the bewildered youngster's shoulder and said confidently, "I knows, I see dat little girl look at you at de dinner table when she thinkin' that ya ain't lookin'. It gonna be ok."

Hayward trusted that in time, what he had shared with Pete would help and guide him in the right way. Even though Hayward had a limited amount of education, he still possessed an unusual perception of people.

Pete could not understand the rational of Hayward's thinking, but he knew that the words that he had heard had pricked his heart. Finally, as he was walking away, he compromised these thoughts and came to the conclusion that Hayward had been sneaking some of Charles' brandy as he first suspected, or else he was confused.

As Pete approached the area of the yard where the guests were mingling, he noticed that all of the men had left the parlor and had rejoined their wives or lady friends. The string ensemble was playing, Wait For The Wagon, a song that many were dancing the Virginia reel to. All of the guests seem to be having a good time and it appeared as though Charles and William had everything under control from the heated debate over the potential crisis that faced the country. Pete began to search the guests for Miss McBride desiring to make amends for the embarrassment that he had caused earlier in the day. He felt confident and bold after speaking with Hayward, and there would be no better time then the present. After looking about, he saw her dancing with William. Once more, he tried to rehearse the words that he would say; there was uneasiness in his stomach at the thought of expressing his feelings. The music finally came to an end and Pete waited until William had escorted Miss McBride back to the table where Caroline and Charles were seated. After a brief pause, the musicians began to play the popular ballad Lorena. Pete boldly began his journey to the table to asked Katie McBride to dance.

As Katie saw Pete approaching, she hoped that William or someone would rescue her from confronting him. With little chance of that happening, Katie quickly decided the only way to handle the situation would be to depend upon the teachings that her Mother had instructed her in the conduct of being a young lady. Katie was nervous and still angry, but knew that she must control her composure. Now would not be the time to express how she truly felt. If Pete wanted to begin a conversation, he would have to be the one to initiate any discussion.

Pete asked confidently as he attracted her attention by clearing his throat, "Miss McBride, may I extend the Barker hospitality to you and request the honor of this dance."

Katie politely replied to his request, "Yes you may."

William, as well as Charles and Caroline were amazed that Pete's offer had been accepted. Under the circumstances it would have been understood and expected if she would have denied him the privilege. Charles just smiled and shook his head as Caroline turned and looked at her husband to intercede on Katie's behalf.

After witnessing her youngest sons actions, Elizabeth frantically came over to Charles and demanded, "Charles, do something, anything, but rescue that young lady from Pete before he does something else that the family will regret!"

Charles boldly replied to his Mother's demand, "Mother, Pete is old enough to handle his own affairs. And if Katie wants to slap him, then so be it, it will serve him right and I'll enjoy witnessing the scene."

Elizabeth walked away mumbling to herself and frustrated with Charles. She returned to the conversation that she was enjoying with the Russell's of Turneysville, which was located near the base of Loudoun Heights.

Pete and Katie were silent at first because each did not want to give the impression of weakness or vulnerability. The couple was exceptional dancing partners and this made an impression on all of those who observed them. As they continued to dance Pete would occasionally glance at Katie in hopes of beginning a conversation. The events in town that involved the two of them happen so quickly, that he did not have time to recognize her beauty. This evening he could not help, but to admire her. Hopefully, there would be the opportunity to apologize to her and make an effort to become friends. There was a struggle within his heart to impress her with who he really was, or should he act out another character, which in time may prove to be false. The only course of action that should be taken was to be honest with her even though this had potential risk for him.

As Katie was dancing with Pete, she began to think about the specific principles that her Mother had taught at an early age; to respect others for their beliefs, even though she did not agree, and to forgive if asked. This time it seems that she would not be able to honor these virtues that had been taught. Her anger was still burning and she was still feeling the pain of embarrassment from earlier this afternoon and desired revenge.

Soon, Katie glanced at Pete's eyes and he seized the opportunity and said, "I would like to apologize to you for the grief and embarrassment that I caused you today. The matter in which I was involved got out of hand and I could not do anything but defend myself." He continued in a remorseful tone as he sought her forgiveness "I asked you to dance, because I felt that this would be the only opportunity that I might have to dance with you. I would like for you to accept my apology."

Katie did not trust what Pete was saying. The question that was on her mind was, is he playing a game, or is he telling the truth. In her reply, she wanted to be honest with him and make sure that she would get her point across. She knew that he was patiently waiting for an answer.

William was suffering from anxiety as he watched Pete and Katie dancing. He felt that he needed to intervene into this affair. Quickly, almost in a panic, he approached the leader of the string ensemble and requested a change in the music selection. William desired to be Katie's knight in shining armor; his feelings for her were evident. William felt threaten by Pete's presence because of his flamboyant personality that attracted the young ladies, and believed in this situation that he had to compete for Katie's attention. As he quickly approached the couple, he marveled, as they were standing with their eyes consumed on each other. Katie wanted to give Pete a reply, but she was not able to do so with Williams's arrival. As the musicians began to play a waltz, which was William's favorite music to dance to, he requested that Katie join him. As she responded, Katie watched Pete as he walked away leaving the two of them alone. Katie pondered what he had just said, and she knew that if there was an invitation at another time to the Estate or if their paths were to cross in town that she would need to give him a reply. There was uncertainty in her mind, she needed time to digest the matter, but there was something about him that attracted her.

As Pete walked back to the table where Charles and Caroline were seated, his mind was preoccupied with thoughts concerning Katie. Almost immediately as he neared the couple, Charles began to laugh.

Pete was puzzled. His attention rapidly turned to his brother, "What's so funny, what are you laughing about!" Pausing and continuing in a serious tone, "I do believe that you and Hayward have had to much of that brandy."

Finally, Charles regained his composure; "I thought for sure Katie was going to slap you for the incident that took place in town earlier today. That would have been the high light of this party."

"I apologized, alright! I could not do any more then that." As Pete turned about, he replied defensively, all the time observing William and Katie dancing.

Charles could not stop laughing. Suddenly with a flare of temper, Caroline asked him to end the child's play because it was embarrassing her; she did not want to draw attention to the three of them.

Pete excused himself because his brother would not cease his laughter and walked across the yard and began to have conversation with Georgia-Ann Brooks, who was a friend from town. He had decided to put his mind to rest about the whole matter and return to his original plan of having a good time and not allowing his evening to be consumed with the whole affair.

The time had gone by quickly and it was getting late in the evening. Some of the guests that had traveled a great distance had begun to depart for their homes. Pete walked Georgia-Ann and her parents to their carriage that was waiting in the front of the house. As he was saying his farewell, he noticed Katie and William departing.

Charles and Caroline were talking with the couple as they stood on the large porch at the main entrance to the house. Charles could see how William felt about Katie and requested that William would escort her on the return trip to town.

As for Caroline, she liked Katie very much and wanted to get better acquainted with her personally. For Caroline, she didn't have very many close friends that she felt comfortable around and that were easy to engage with in conversation. For some unknown reason, she was drawn to Katie. Before Katie's departure, Caroline wanted the opportunity to cultivate their acquaintance, so she asked her new friend, "Katie, if your schedule permits, would you consider being our guest tomorrow. I would like to show you around Shenandoah and then afterwards we could have tea."

William enthusiastically endorsed the idea by adding, "It will be a great opportunity for you to see the beauty of this Estate, and begin to build a friendship with the Barkers."

Katie said as she looked at Caroline, "Oh yes, I would like that very much. I'll look forward to seeing you."

After the exchange of conversation, William assisted Katie with boarding the carriage. He took his place next to her and they both said their farewells to Charles and Caroline.

Pete had gone into the house and was standing by his bedroom window. As he watched the carriage with the couple proceeding towards the long lane, he began to think about what Katie's reply would have been, what she may have said. The greatest mystery was the look in her eyes. What was she thinking and feeling as they were dancing?

CHAPTER FIVE

The next morning was once again hazy and sunny. The birds were outside of Pete's bedroom window singing a melody of joy. All was quiet. Everyone was sleeping later then usual because of the reception for William Pierce. It had lasted longer then had been planned. As Pete awaken, he could feel the warm gentle breeze whisking through the open window across his face. He began to wipe his sleepy eyes as he glanced at his watch laying on the stand beside of the huge four-post bed. It was 6:30 in the morning, and he had overslept. Pete had promised Hayward that he would help him move some of the Morgans from the southern grazing range to the eastern grazing range where they had not been in sometime. For him it was very important to awaken and get an early start to what promise to be a long day. As Pete began to dress in a brown-checkered shirt to work in, he walked over and looked out the window to see if he could Hayward. The only activity that was taking place was Jeremiah, one of the oldest servants, busy working in the rose garden. Pete briefly watched him; Jeremiah's expression was full of joy and pride as he mastered his skill of manicuring and treating each rose as if it was a small child. As Pete continued to watch, he began to think back in time when his Father had purchased Jeremiah as a young man in Richmond and brought him to the Estate. His Father had recognized his creative ability with gardening shortly after his arrival and it was to his credit that the flower gardens and grounds were so well designed. Jeremiah had always been faithful in his service to the family and was greatly trusted.

Pete leaned from his bedroom window and made various attempts for Jeremiah's attention. He attempted to be as quiet as possible without awaking anyone. After several attempts, the old servant looked up at Pete and acknowledged him. Jeremiah asked, "Wat cans I do for yose on dis fine mornin' Mr. Pete?"

Pete was as quiet as possible, making his request known, "Have you seen Hayward?"

"He's left shortly 'fore sunrise" Jeremiah replied as he slowly rose to his feet and brushed the dirt from his dark trousers.

Pete finished dressing as quickly as possible and hurried off to the stable area to saddle his horse. Having his mare at a full gallop across the field, Pete headed south over the ridge that was a short cut in the attempt to arrive at the southern pastures as soon as possible.

On the way to his destination, Pete came across twelve of the slaves stringing a new fencerow. Daniel was pacing and shouting orders as usual and overseeing the laborers. As Pete slowed his horse down to a trot, he could hear Daniel threatening the labors verbally as they worked to accomplish the task. Suddenly, Sherman one of the huge slaves picked up one of the shovels that they were using to dig the holes for the post and charged the angry overseer. Quickly, Daniel pulled his revolver from his holster. He pulled back the hammer and was ready to fire, pointing the weapon at the aggressive slaves body.

Pete quickly intervened. He removed his pistol and fired one round into the air. Both Daniel and Sherman paused and stood still looking at the other, each dared not to make a move. Pete knew that he needed to get to the bottom of this problem quickly and try to resolve it; they did not need to have another dead slave on their hands; this would not please his Mother. Holding his gun in his hand, Pete ordered Daniel to put his revolver back in the holster, which he carefully complied.

Pete was quite disturbed at what he had just witnessed and asked the disturbed overseer in an angry voice, "Daniel, what in the world is going on out here? Have you gone insane?"

Daniel brushed his long light brown hair to the side as he replied in an uncontrollable rage, "This here darkie refused to obey me when I told him to start digging these here holes for the fence post." He maliciously continued his verbal assault upon the slave, "Ya should have let me fill his tail end with lead, that would have soon taught him who the boss was around here."

Pete looked at Sherman, "Is that true?"

The angry buck refused to answer his question. Pete could see the resentment in his eyes as he asked again of Sherman in an angry tone for a reply, "Is that true, are you refusing to obey him?"

The angry overseer pleaded and tried to convince the younger Barker to see the matter his way, "Let me shoot him and make an example of him for the others to see."

This time Sherman was more then willing to voice his feelings, because of fearing for his life, "Dis man thinks we's animals. He treat us like one. He don't want us ta stop and have rest, or water. We's been here workin' like dogs since de sun come up."

From past experience, Pete knew that this was typical of Daniel. He was a man that was hot tempered and had no feeling for anyone. The only thing that mattered to him was the monthly bonus that Charles paid him for the amount of work that he could get the slaves to accomplish. Pete had been pressuring his Mother for sometime to find another overseer. Daniel, he felt could not be trusted. It was different for Charles; he liked the overseer's tactics and on more then one occasion intervened on his behalf when other incidents had taken place. On the over hand, Pete knew that Daniel liked Charles and would do whatever it would take to make him successful. He cherished the authority and dominance over another. Pete felt that he would have to keep a closer watch on him in the future.

Pete hesitated briefly and began to choose his words with boldness and authority, "Daniel, see to it that these bucks receive water and ten minutes of rest. From this point on I will be keeping an eye on you! The slaves are the property of my Mother, not my brother. A rested slave can work, but a dead one can not!"

Pete said this to refreshed Daniels mind over the incident that took place three years ago when Daniel lost his temper and shot and killed one of the slaves as he was challenged just as Sherman had attempted. As far as Pete was concerned the matter was over with for now. He had lost time with this incident and again put his horse at a full gallop toward the southern pastures.

Angrily, Daniel watched Pete ride off until he was out of sight. He hoped somewhere to get revenge for all of the misfortune that the younger brother had caused him, and the money that he had lost for his obedience.

Back at the house, Charles and William were finishing their breakfast with

Caroline and Elizabeth. Matthew was serving them coffee as they were enjoying their conversation concerning the reception of the previous evening. It had been a very special, enthusiastic evening for Elizabeth, especially the time that she spent with the Russell's. She shared in length how this wealthy family from near by Loudoun County had accumulated all of their wealth from the wooded mountainous property that they had acquired over the many years. The family had an enormous sawmill where they produced the wood for home construction and furniture at an affordable cost.

After Elizabeth finished her conversation, William asked Charles to join him on his journey to Charlestown to visit Mr. And Mrs. Thomas Jenkins, a businessman. William had accepted their invitation the evening before at the reception. He believed that Thomas Jenkins, who was a slave owner, wanted to make a large contribution to the Breckinridge campaign for the Presidency. This would also give him an opportunity to enlist Charles's help in the campaign.

Caroline walked to the front door with Charles and William. Charles turned about, and asked his wife, "What time is Katie coming this afternoon?"

"Somewhere around three."

"Will you be here with her when I return, or have you planned something special for your guest?"

"Oh, I thought that since Katie and I enjoy the water that we could spend sometime along the river. Maybe we can become better acquaintance."

Charles smiled and said as Matthew opened the door, "Have a wonderful time along the river with Katie. She impresses me as an honest person with a proper up-bringing."

"If you would like, you and William could join us later."

"No, you have fun. I believe that our business might take sometime. But just the same, thank you." William began to walk away while Charles kissed Caroline on the cheek, adding as he looked into her eyes, "And I want you to know how much I love you."

Caroline smiled with joy at Charles' gesture of affection and possessing great hope that he would share with her more of his affection and warmth that she so greatly desired.

On the way to Charlestown, Charles began to enter into conversation with William about the prosperity of Shenandoah and their plans for the future. He shared his hopes and dreams that one day he would own the Estate and then be able to pass it down to Ann after she proved herself worthy of the honor of responsibility.

As William admired the beautiful countryside, he was listening to Charles; his mind began to wonder about the coming election and the possibility of war. He believed that Charles had high hopes that there would not be hostilities between the Northern and Southern states; that somewhere in his heart he wanted to see a resolution to the issue of slavery and state rights. Should the time come for war, William believed that it would not be a short affair as some of his friends and fellow politicians believed, but instead it would be a long drawn out conflict that would be bloody and costly. The war would destroy homes, farms, and a way of life that has always been cherished in the South. William strongly believed that the only hope that the South had was to rally enough support for John Breckinridge's candidacy for the Presidency, and for now, that was his main goal. If unable to, then war would shortly follow. His desire was for Charles to know what he believed, and to be honest, and straight forth. William was troubled in his heart as he began to search for the words to say. He did not desire war and the destruction that it would bring about, nor did he desire to place a shadow upon the hopes that Charles had shared with him, but to give him hope and confidence in a Breckinridge Presidency. In accomplishing this, he would be able to insure Charles' support for his candidate.

As the words slowly came to his mind, William began to be candied and confident, as he spoke to his close friend, "Charles, I believe the only way that the South can avoid war with the North is if John Breckinridge is elected to the Presidency. Like I said last night at the reception, the North will accept the results of a fair election. Our way of life, here in the South is in jeopardy. You know as I do, that if Lincoln is elected, the Republicans will attempt to abolish slavery. That means our economy will perish, prosperity will fade, and our society changed. This beautiful countryside that I'm admiring, I wonder how many men that it will take to protect it from invasion. In a year from now Charles, I just can't help, but to ponder on the war that probably will be taking place. All of the beauty that I can see between these mountains will be tarnished with the blood of young men who will be taking up arms to protect our rights as a sovereign state."

Charles was astonished at William's insight and perception of these possibilities. Momentarily, he thought about the drastic changes that would be imposed on his culture, traditions, and family way of life. All that he could hope for was that life, as he knew it, would remain the same. If there was a risk of it being jeopardized, then he needed to try and help in whatever way that would be the most profitable. For now, Charles continued to meditate on the words that his close friend had shared.

As William continued quietly to admire the farms and countryside on the outskirts of Charlestown, he presented Charles with an offer in the upcoming campaign, "Charles, I'm going to need your help in the up-coming campaign. You have quite a bit of influence in this part of the state. I know personally that you are well respected, and quite frankly, I will need to use you in order to achieve our purpose, if we stand a chance of winning the lower Valley. We could not have accomplished our goal in John Letcher's election to the Governorship if it would not have been for your contribution to the effort."

In his heart, Charles was overwhelmed with pride and joy. It was as though everything was beginning to fall into place politically. He believed that if Virginia would secede in the future, or if it chose not to, then he would become a powerful political figure. With the money that his family possesses, and the influence that they had acquired over the years with the many political figures in Richmond that they knew, he would be able to win any office that he sought. With vigor and confidence, he answered, "I will do what has to be done in order to preserve our way of life and to keep out government interference in our lives." With pride he continued his conversation by saying, "I have to much riding on what takes place in November."

Looking out across the fields where the farmers were laboring, William pointed in their direction, and made a profound observation that he hoped would remained engraved in his friends memories and give him the spirit and endurance to see this vision fulfilled, "See those men in the fields, they are the ones who labor from sunrise until sunset in order to have something in this life. If called upon, they will do their duty with pride and leave home and family; some will return home and others will never. Some may never see their families again, and those who survive, their way of life will change forever. Ask yourself the question if you can live with Federal dominance and authority?"

Charles realized the seriousness of this election and understood the issues a great deal more then he had revealed to William, or anyone. He wanted to keep his eagerness disguised and not give the wrong impression to William or anyone else.

The two gentlemen for the rest of the trip to Charlestown did not exchange conversation; their thoughts were on what should be accomplished to bring a victory to the Breckinridge candidacy in November. They each had their own idea for victory and the survival of life, as they knew it.

It was close to three in the afternoon when Katie arrived at the Estate to visit with Caroline as they had previously planned the evening before. As Jeremiah assisted Katie from the carriage, she proceeded to the front door and was greeted by Elizabeth. The two walked out to the gazebo that was in the back yard. Matthew was summoned to bring the ladies tea as they discussed their views from the reception.

Caroline was still in her room and had not joined Elizabeth and Katie. Opal, Elizabeth's personal servant was summoned and asked to inquire of her absence, which she did obediently. After a short period of time, she returned to inform Elizabeth that Caroline was not feeling well and must rest for now. Katie had been looking forward to her visitation with Caroline and becoming better acquainted. Now she was very disappointed as Elizabeth began to apologize for this misfortunate circumstance.

As Katie and Elizabeth were receiving the news concerning Caroline, the sound of a fast approaching horse could be heard in the distance. Opal had recognized Pete as the rider returning from the eastern range at a full gallop. She informed Elizabeth, "Misse Elizabeth, Mr. Pete is returnin'."

Elizabeth turned her attention to the servant, and replied, "Thank you Opal. You may be dismissed."

Upon his arrival, Pete noticed that Katie had arrived and was sitting with his Mother. Pete was hot, sweaty, dirty, and possessed a rugged appearance from working and felt somewhat embarrassed. As he dismounted his horse, one of the servants took the animal to the stable for feeding and watering as Pete walked towards the two ladies. He greeted his Mother with a kiss and said, "Hello Mother."

Even though Elizabeth was still angry with her son, she still returned his gesture affectionately. As she reached and gently touched his cheek, "My son."

As he turned toward Katie, he acknowledged her with a cordial greeting, "Miss McBride, I want to welcome you once more to our home."

Katie was extremely cautious and nervous of Pete, though she did not reveal it in her disposition and manner, she answered him polity, "Thank you, Mr. Barker"

He laughingly pointed to his clothing and said, "I would like to apologize to both of you for my appearance. I've been working all day in the sun and it gets very hot by this time in the afternoon."

Elizabeth agreed, "That's alright son, we understand, the work must be done."

Looking about, Pete surprisingly asked his Mother, "Where is Caroline?"

"She is not feeling well and will not be able to join us at this time."

In the South, great pride was taken in sharing hospitality with guests that were invited to ones home. Realizing that there was possibly an opportunity to be alone with Miss McBride, Pete wanted to take advantage of it. This would give him the benefit of no interruptions as William had intentionally accomplished the night before and would give Katie the chance to give an answer. At once, he turned toward Katie, who was seated and began blurting out the words without thinking, "May I, as the only gentleman present, show you around our beautiful Estate. Hopefully when we are finished, Caroline will be able to join us."

Katie was very intelligent and realized that Pete had cornered her by his boldness, unfortunate circumstances, and his Mother's presence. She knew that it would be rude of her to refuse him under these circumstances. For her, there was no other alternative in the situation; she would have to consent to his request. Katie forced a smile as she softly replied, "I would be honored to accept your hospitality."

"Good then, if you ladies would briefly excuse me, I would like to go and clean up and I will return shortly."

As Pete departed the room, Elizabeth began to share with Katie some of the family history. Listening and acknowledging her host, Katie could not keep her mind off what the afternoon might bring. She wasn't prepared for this surprise. It was not like preparing a lesson for children that were in her classrooms; she needed to think of what they could talk about that would be on neutral territory, and wouldn't present a threat. Her greatest fear would be the continuation of their conversation as they were dancing last night. Katie began to wish and hope that suddenly Caroline would come walking down the long stairway. It would please her greatly if there would be some way that she could get out of this situation and return to town.

Quickly, Pete went about cleaning up. He wanted to leave with Miss McBride as soon as possible before his brother and William returned from their business in Charlestown. As he looked out the window he once more noticed Jeremiah walking toward one of the rose gardens to pick a variety of flowers to place on the table for the evening meal. He quickly called out, "Jeremiah, find Hayward, and tell him to hitch up a team of horses to the small buggy. Oh, and pick me one of those red roses and give it to Hayward to hold for me."

As Pete hurried from his bedroom, he slowed down to an acceptable pace with his return to the gazebo where the two ladies continued to socialize. With a glowing smile that covered his face, Pete proudly said, "Miss McBride, I am ready to show you the Estate that the Barker family calls Shenandoah."

She answered as cheerfully as she could under the circumstances, "Yes I am looking forward to seeing the Estate,"

After thanking her hostess, Katie quietly walked with Pete toward the stable area. In front of the entrance to the second stable, Hayward had hitched the team of horses to the carriage for Pete as requested, and was anxiously waiting in hopes of meeting Miss McBride. As the two approached Hayward, Pete at once introduced Katie, "Miss Katie McBride, I would like for you to meet a friend and employee of the family, Hayward Cooper."

Katie responded softly, "Hayward, I am glad to make your acquaintance."

With a smile, Hayward tipped his hat in acknowledgement, saying, "I's glad to meet ya."

The gentleman that Pete was, he helped Katie into the buggy by taking her hand so that she would be able to maintain her balance with boarding. After being seated comfortably, she thanked him for his courtesy. Pete walked around to the opposite side and took the red rose that Jeremiah had given Hayward. As Pete sat closely beside Katie, he gave her the rose, "This is to friendship."

Katie acknowledged softly and with reservation, "Thank you Mr. Barker. Roses happen to be my favorite flower."

Hayward, who was smiling as usual stepped back from the pair of horses that he had been holding and waved at the two as they departed.

Caroline watched Pete and Katie from her bedroom window, which was in the back of the house as the horses increased their speed. Soon they were riding at a comfortable pace in the direction of the river. As they did so, Caroline began to smile and silently remarked to herself, "Pete, I'm doing you a favor, now lets see if you can handle this"

The couple was only a short distance from the mansion when Pete happened to glance back in that direction. He noticed a carriage arriving from the direction of Charlestown. It must be Charles and William returning from their business. Katie noticed that Pete was looking in that direction. Her heart sank. If only they would have been delayed for a brief moment, then she may have been spared this adventure with Pete. It was to late now; knowing that she had to go through with this, she finally accepted the realization of reality. Katie decided as she was thinking to herself about this situation, that she would allow Pete to be the first to open the conversation. Katie continued to feel nervous with the palms of her hands moist with perspiration. She felt the best course of action to pursue should be honesty; under no circumstances should she reveal more then what was asked and most of all do not appear to be weak.

As for Pete, he wanted to continue the conversation from the evening before concerning the incident in town. Now that the two of them were alone, with no foreseeable interruptions, Pete was determine to finally get this matter out in the open and resolved. It was time to move on as far as he was concerned, and if she didn't desire his friendship, then so be it. He would know that he had attempted his very best. Hoping to begin the conversation, Pete was the first to speak as he glanced at Katie, "That must be William and Charles returning from their business."

Katie remained silent. Pete continued with the decision that it was time to bring up the subject that they both did not want to encounter. He thought carefully for a moment and knew that he needed to choose his words carefully. It was not his intentions to try and aggravate the wound that he believed she was suffering. It was his perception that she only wanted to live her life in peace, no differently then anyone else and be accepted into the community. With growing tensions between the citizens of the North and South, he knew that it was going to be difficult for Katie to be accepted by the community. Maybe, he thought, she would be willing to accept his help, though for now, another matter must be dealt with first. Without any warning, Pete turned about to look at Katie, and began to speak earnestly, "I believe that you and I have some unfinished business that we need to discuss."

Katie's Irish temper began to flare as she boldly replied, "I know. You are right, lets get this matter out in the open!"

"As I remembered, I apologized to you last night for what happen in town earlier that afternoon. You were the victim of an unfortunate incident." Pete professed cautiously and calmly, hoping that she would see in his tone of voice that he did not want to enter into an argument.

"I'm glad that you will admit your faults! I am still angry for the embarrassment that you have caused me and the fool that you have made of me in front of all of those people!"

As Pete shrugged his shoulders, he answered her in a pitched tone, "Again, I'm sorry!"

Katie vigorously continued in a tone of anger, "Alright, alright, but I want you to understand that this does not mean that you and I shall be on friendly terms. I will not allow you to manipulate me with your words. Is that understood?"

Pete did not respond. He was feeling quite uneasy with Katie, even though he couldn't blame her for the way that she felt about him. As a role model of a Southern gentleman that displays hospitality and the salvation of his pride, he felt continued to finish the tour of Shenandoah. Maybe matters between them would improve later.

Katie quietly admired the beauty of the Estate. She was even surprised at the well-kept condition of the slave quarters that was to the rear of the house; they were built no differently then the quarters near the ridge that she noticed the previous evening. It was Kate's first exposure to the slaves, and their way of life. From her first impression, they seemed to be very friendly as they waved their hands and shouted greetings at the couple slowly passing along the dirt road. After passing out of sight of the mansion, Pete brought the horses to a pause at the peach orchard that overlooked the small valley below; there he offered Katie some of the fresh fruit, which she accepted. As Katie enjoyed the fruit, she looked across the rolling hills and mountains. The area possessed magic, contentment, and an unspeakable solitude beyond any place that she had traveled previously in her young life. This was a place, she thought, that she could easily grow to love. As Katie had already experienced in the short duration in the area, life was very laid back, the pace was slower then living in the big city, and everyone was acquainted with his or her neighbor.

Katie said very little. She continued to be cautious of him, though at times she would glance in his direction when she knew that he was not looking.

For the next hour, Pete covered much of the Estate with Katie. The couple rode to the top of Barker's ridge where Pete brought the buggy to a halt. From this area of the Estate, they could view the many stallions, morgans, and mares that made up a large part of the business. In a continual effort to ease tensions with Katie, Pete shared the different characteristics of the various horses. Katie's eyes lighted up and a smile beamed across her face as the colts tried to keep pace with their mothers galloping across the pastures. Inconspicuously, Pete took notice of the joy that she was expressing, maybe now was the right time to begin a conversation. With a tone of enthusiasm, Pete began to say as Katie gave her attention to him, "I am glad to see that you enjoy the horses. My Mother came here at times when she was a child and watched them. She spent hours here, even as an adult studying their habits. In part this is how she learned the business. Unfortunately, it's something that she doesn't do anymore. Agriculture and raising cattle was the vision that my grandfather had for the Estate, but not my Mother. Oh no, she had greater hopes and dreams of what Shenandoah could be. The prosperity was in breeding horses and cattle for the government. I have to admit, she knew what she was doing and what she wanted to accomplish."

Katie's reply was serene, "Your Mother had a vision and pursued her dreams. In my personal opinion, no one can truly experience happiness unless they are willing to take the risk and pursue the challenges that might arise. She must have felt very gratified at the success that's been accomplished. In the short time that I have been here, I am discovering in my observations and experiences that life at Shenandoah is different then what I've experienced living in the North, it's a different world."

Pete was glad that the tension had ease for now, and that the two of them could relax in each other's company.

As they were departing, Pete suggested to Kate that they take a detour on their way back to the mansion and ride by the river. Katie continued to enjoy the scenery as Pete explained some of the history of each location of the Estate. The breeze began to increase as they arrived at their destination. The area was nestled in privacy by many sycamore, maple, and white birch trees that offered plenty of shade. There were wild flowers of many colors that covered the green grass. The view of the river rapids and the sound provided comfort and tranquility to its listeners. Katie was amazed at the beauty of this area; thus far it was the highlight of her tour.

Pete asked Katie if she would like to step down from the carriage, which she did with his help. As he walked over to the rivers bank, he removed his boots and stepped into the warm water. Looking back at Katie, he extended the invitation, "Come on, the water is warm."

Katie began to laugh, and as she did, Pete was taken by the radiance of her smile. Quickly, she removed her shoes and splashing through the water, she said, "Oh, it is warm. The water feels so good on my feet, its such a joy."

After a short period of time had passed, Pete and Katie made their way toward a log near the edge of the water. As the two sat quietly, they listened to the water as it caressed the rivers bank. It brought a peaceful song of contentment and calm to a couple that had been struggling with each other's company for the better part of the afternoon.

As Pete was glancing at the water and skipping stones across its surface, he was curious why Katie had chosen this particular area to call her home instead of remaining in the North, especially with the possibility of hostile conflict upon the horizon, "I would like to ask you a question if I may?"

"What is that?"

"Why did you decide to move to Virginia? As I'm sure that you're aware of, there may be war, even by this time next year."

Katie began to search her mind for the right words to answer, and then replying, "I'm not the ordinary girl that you are accustom to find in the South. I am someone who likes to be adventurous, though I know that it is not what is expected of a young woman. There is a compelling within to experience life for myself. I have often heard from my Uncle how beautiful the Shenandoah Valley is, as he journeyed through this area years ago. You would not understand why a single lady would venture here alone, and quite frankly, I do not expect you to."

As Pete turned slowly and looked at Katie, he could feel the excitement in her voice and the desire for a future for her life. Her eyes reflected the deepest feelings that she had kept secret for many years. He wanted to give her hope and security in the desire she possessed, but he believed that reality would reflect the out come of her dreams. For now, he would not answer in a way that would cause discouragement, but create reassurance, "I am sure that if you will allow yourself time to settle into this area, you will like it. And if I may add, should you remain open-minded, you'll discover that it was the right decision for you. As for myself, I will always call this place home."

Katie glanced at the water and just began to smile. She felt that his answer, the particular words was what she needed to hear. His reply gave her confidence in her decision in moving to this area, which her parents and brother had strongly disapproved. She hoped that there would not be war. Just maybe, the citizens of the North and South would be able to resolve they're difference in a peaceful way through negotiations and avoid bloodshed. The greatest hope that she had for now, was, that it would not jeopardize her friendship with the Barkers, especially Caroline.

Pete was feeling very relax. He wasn't as cautious of Katie as he had been earlier in the day. The whole affair that had taken place in Harpers Ferry yesterday was hopefully fading in the past. He felt that it was an unfortunate incident that should not have taken place. For now, he only wanted to be friends with Katie and didn't desire for anything more, even though he found her to be of great beauty. As he glanced her way, he knew that she enjoyed the stillness and serenity of the water. He casually began to speak with emotion, "This area has always been my favorite place to come. When I was a child, my Father would often bring me here and we would spend time together fishing, tracking game, and just talking about life. It was our time to strengthen the bond of our relationship. When I think about it, I feel it was the time in that I grew to know my Father more."

There was a side of Pete's heart that she was beginning to see, whether it was intentional or not, she was impressed and touched by his emotion. Katie cautiously replied as her eyes met his, "It's calm here, this is a place that I could come to, and collect my thoughts. Most of the time when I was troubled, I'd walk along the ocean, alone, looking for the answer to a problem, trying to find a release within from the stress and emotions that I was experiencing. I'll agree with you, your Father knew how to choose the right place."

For sometime, Pete had felt trapped by the inability to open and release the emotions of his heart. There were many feelings that he wanted to share with someone, but was fearful of doing so because of the vulnerability and weakness that he had grown to know by the example of his parent's life style. Already in the short period of time that he had spent with Katie, he discovered that she was very easy to talk to. She was quite different from some of the other female acquaintances that he had met from the North on his visitations with his Father to Philadelphia, or even from this particular area. For some unknown reason, he did not feel threatened in her company.

CHAPTER SIX

As Pete and Katie continued to spend time together along the river, the hours swiftly passed. Since the couple had come to an understanding concerning the brawl outside of the Wager House Hotel, it had been an enjoyable afternoon. Even though there was communication between the two, Katie still felt cautious of Pete because she did not know him. Katie thought she like to learn more about him, but there was that hesitation that she had come to know from time to time; something that was experienced over the years and trusted.

As they were on their returned trip to the house, there was one question that had puzzled Katie over the last couple of days. Casually saying as she turn to look in his direction, "I would like to ask a question concerning your brother and yourself if I may?"

"What's that?"

Katie asked as she gazed at the mansion that was in the distance, "When the Brown raid was taking place, where was Charles and yourself? As I understand, there were those of wealth that owned slaves that were taken prisoner."

Pete began to smile as he turned about to glance at her; "I was waiting for that subject to come up. I was still in school in Charlottesville, finishing my studies in law."

Katie was surprised as she bluntly interrupted, "You're a lawyer. After what you did yesterday. I'm very surprised at this revelation."

Pete willfully ignored her comment, still feeling the embarrassment of the incident, he continued, "And as for Charles, he was in Richmond campaigning with William on behalf of John Letcher, who was running for Governor. He did return immediately when informed of the incident."

"So why didn't they try to free some of the Negro's on this plantation?"

Pete was all too familiar with the beliefs that the Northerners felt concerning the issue of slavery. Sooner or later, he was sure that this subject would surface during his conversation with Katie. She came from a state that promoted abolition. Preparation on his part had already been made when he discovered where she was from, and he was confident on handling the subject. It would be Katie's decision to agree or disagree with the slavery issue.

"No, they did not try. Before the old fool began his killing spree, Daniel recognized John Brown from several trips to Kansas. Knowing farewell the bloody mess that he caused in Kansas, Daniel was able to organize some of the neighboring farmers that owned slaves to form a small militia until the Jefferson Guard could leave a detachment here to help protect the area. Even though Daniel and I do not get along with each other, I still owe him a great deal of thanks for what he did."

As the two were approaching the house, a little Negro boy of about seven years ran out in the road in front of the buggy. Bringing the horses to a quick halt, Pete yelled at the boy, "Get out of the way! I almost hit you!"

The lad, whose name was Seth began to cry. Wiping the tears from his eyes he asked, "Has ya seen my papa?"

Seeing how upset the child was Pete's emotions became composed as he answered, "No, I have not seen him since earlier today. I'm sure that he will be home by sunset."

Seth's father happened to be Sherman. The lad and his Father enjoyed a close relationship, which everyone at the Estate often observed, and would compliment on occasions.

Katie did not agree with the way that Pete handled the situation, though she didn't want to interfere, because it could possibly cause a hindrance between Caroline and herself. So she did not say anything in the lads' defense.

Soon, Pete and Katie arrived at the back entrance to the house, where he helped her from the buggy. By now Caroline was feeling well enough to receive Katie's company, and she greeted them. Immediately, Pete returned the horses to the stable to water and feed them, and to brush the animals down, when suddenly, he noticed Daniel approaching the house at a full gallop, shouting at the top of his voice for Charles. Pete quickly paused from the chore that he was doing and ran toward the house to see what the alarm was all about. Momentarily, Charles came running out the back door with William and began to inquire as to the nature of the alarm. As Daniel dismounted from his horse, Charles began to shout at the overseer, "What's going on!"

Daniel was trying desperately to catch his breath as Pete quickly came running up to where they stood.

"Sherman has escaped! I gave them rest just as I was ordered to and when."

Daniel was quickly interrupted by Charles, who was very angry and upset over the news of the escape. Promptly, he asked Daniel, "Who gave the order for them to stop their labor."

With revenge in his eyes, Daniel replied angrily pointing his finger at Pete, "Ya brother." Continuing his verbal assault, "As usual, he couldn't keep his dang nose out of my business. He took sides with that darkie."

As Charles turned and glanced at Pete, he was out raged with the news that his brother had interfered with Daniel's authority. Briefly, Charles paused and gave the matter some thought. After breaking his silence, Charles said, "Daniel, I want you to go over to the Hoffman homestead and get some additional help."

Daniel replied as he remounted his horse, "I'll be on it now."

"Oh, be sure that Mr. Hoffman brings the hounds!"

After making the arrangements with Daniel, Charles glanced at his brother once more with an angry expression, and departed quickly to the house.

Pete raced off to the stable to saddle his horse. The race was on to find the runaway slave, which by now had gotten a two-hour start. He knew that if he did not find Sherman before Daniel and his brother, then there would be a good possibility that the runaway at Daniels persuasion would be swinging from the end of a rope or shot. As Pete was riding in the direction of the river, he noticed Daniel heading for Halltown. Pete had been taught the skill of hunting and tracking; he was an expert in the art of following a trail made by animal or man. His Father, who was an expert in this part of the County, had mentored his son to perfection in this skill. Pete began to place himself in Sherman's shoes and attempted to think like him if he were trying to escape. He believed that Sherman would not risk going into town because of the lurking danger that would await him by the townspeople. It was his belief that Sherman would wait until nightfall and attempt to cross the Potomac below the covered railroad bridge.

With haste, he arrived at the area where Sherman was last seen and began his search of the runaway slave. Pete had learned long ago to trust his instincts, which his Father had instructed him to perfection. With a strong feeling to ride along the Shenandoah and look for fresh tracks made by foot, Pete knew from earlier in the day, that Sherman was not wearing shoes. If Sherman wanted to seek shelter in the mountains and stay hidden from his pursuers, he would have to take the long way around and avoid being noticed. This would include crossing the Shenandoah, just below the bend in the river, at Keyes's Ford, where the water was shallow. From there, Sherman would have to continue to follow the Shenandoah until he came directly across from Maryland Heights. It is here that the river joins the Potomac at the covered railroad bridge. During the summer months, the water in this area was shallow, and there would be plenty of rocks within that would offer the runaway easy protection from being detected by anyone who was trying to capture him. With ease, he could cross the canal and disappear into the mountains, which would offer him plenty of cover. It would be from this point that his escape across the wooded range would almost be certain. The route had been used time and again by the Underground Railroad. Pete did not desire to harm Sherman, but to only recover the family property.

At the ford, Pete crossed the river cautiously, not knowing if Sherman would try to ambush him on the other side, or if he possessed a weapon. As Pete was nearing the opposite bank of the river that formed the back boundary of the Barker Estate, he had his pistol cocked and ready to fire. After dismounting from his horse, he began to look for clues among the trees and rocks for the slaves' whereabouts. He noticed a particular twig from a wild cherry tree branch that was broken as he walked along the riverbank. After closer examination, he observed a trace of what appeared to be blood. His hunch was correct. His intuition was serving him well. The runaway had most likely been here and the small twig had snared his clothing and scratched his skin as he was quickly fleeing. Pete looked around for more evidence. Suddenly, he noticed what appeared to be a partial footprint embedded in some mud. He was sure now that he was on the right trail. Sherman was heading toward the high ground that overlooked the river. It would be from here that he would be able to see anyone that was approaching or fording the river in search of him. Pete could only hope for now that Sherman did not see him crossing the river. The only way that Pete would be able to capture the runaway slave would be by the element of surprise.

He knew that he could not match up to Sherman's physical strength and would not be able to handle him.

Pete continued to pursue his foe with determination and earnest. He followed slowly as the sun began to set in the western sky. Pete stopped for a moment to allow his horse and himself a rest before proceeding on the hunt for Sherman. As he sat along a rock overlooking the Shenandoah and admiring the sunset, he began to think about his conversations with Katie earlier as they sat together along the rivers bank. He was intrigued with the idea that she was so different then the Southern acquaintances that he had become all too familiar with in this area and in his travels through the South. There was something very extraordinary about this lady that he did not completely understand. He felt that given time, he could figure it all out.

As Pete continued his search, daylight was fading with every passing moment. He wanted to arrive quickly and intercept Sherman before he could escape across the Potomac. As the moon was slowly rising over the Short Hill Mountain, Pete knew that he was close to his destination. He hid his mare behind some huge boulders that overlooked the river and proceeded slowly and quietly about one hundred yards closer to the rivers bank. He hid behind some rock outcroppings, which abundantly blessed the mountain. Lying low and out of sight, he waited for his prey. He kept still; the only noise was the river flowing across the rapids, which were many. An occasional rabbit would glance at Pete and then take off running for fear of its life. The town was not far from where he was located. At times, he could hear the whistle of a freight train stopping to take on water near the railroad station, and he would glance at candlelights that flickered in homes. The moon looked like it would be full and bright tonight. This would give Pete plenty of light that he could use to observe anyone that would approach the shoreline. He knew also that it gave Sherman guidance to cross the river without hindrance onto the Maryland shore and to freedom.

As Pete awaited the arrival of Sherman, he began to wonder were his brother and Daniel might be in their search for the runaway slave. Daniel was very intelligent and skilled in tracking down runaways, and thus far Pete was surprised as to why they had not caught up to him by now. Charles and Daniel would have certainly begun their search in the same area as Pete had done. It would be for the best if they did not show up because Pete felt that he would have all that he could do to handle the huge slave himself. He did not want to endanger the runaway by Daniel's aggressiveness to cause him harm. He hope to make the capture alone. Thus far, Pete's instincts had been right on target and he believed that he would not have to wait much longer.

Sherman was smart enough to know that Daniel would not give up the chase. It was just a question as to where he might have to confront him and the area in which he would be waiting. The slave had tried to escape the year before and failed in his endeavor to do so. At that time, Daniel wanted to hang him in the town park as an example to some of the other slaves. He wanted to demonstrate to them what their fate would be if they tried to do something so foolish. It was at that time that Elizabeth intervened and put a halt to Daniel's plan.

As Pete was scouting the immediate area for any sight of Sherman, he heard the crackling of a twig and the flight of a deer. Quietly cocking the hammer on his revolver, he awaited the opportunity of surprise. He knew that it was important for him to seize his family's property and to return it to them. Hopefully, he would be returned to his Mother's grace for his noble deed. As Pete's eyes were fixed on the area from where the noise had come, he noticed Sherman cautiously making his way toward the riverbank. Sherman was continuously looking about for his pursuers as he began to step into the murky water. Pete arose from behind the rocks that had given him his cover and protection and yelled, "Sherman stop, or I'll shoot."

The runaway surprisingly paused. Pete did not want to get too close to Sherman because he was sure that the huge buck would attempt to physically overcome him. The slave was twice his size, and Pete knew that he might have to shoot him, which was not the desirable situation. As Pete approached Sherman carefully, he kept a short distance, and was cautious. Standing with his pistol pointed in Sherman's direction, he ordered, "Raise your hands above your head and do not move."

As the slave complied with the command, he began to weep and nervously spoke, "I's ask for ya mercy, Mr. Pete. I's not able ta take dis life no more."

Pete reprimanded his foe as he moved closer to him, "You should not have tried to escape. It's foolish to attempt something like that, especially when you have a family that you are leaving behind."

Sherman replied confidently as he regained his composure, "My family knows what I doin', and it's alright. I want ta fight for dere freedom, and mine."

Pete began to laugh and said to him," Tonight, there will not be any freedom, not now, or in the future."

Sherman's anger was aroused. He said loudly and in a defiant tone of voice as he gazed at Pete, "I's been beatin' and abused and still ya couldn't takes my dreams of bein' free. Now's, ya tryin' ta destroy my hopes with words, but ya can't. No one can steal my hopes and dreams of bein' free. Not yose or anyone else. No one!"

"Tonight your going back to Shenandoah with me."

As Pete was speaking the last words to his captured foe, Sherman felt that he had nothing to lose, but all to gain by taking a chance. Suddenly, and with the quickness of a lion, he lunged toward his capture. Pete was taken by surprise. Sherman threw Pete up against one of the rocks and striking him with a blow to the face, he rendered him unconscious.

Sherman placed his left hand on Pete's chest searching for a pulse, as his victim laid prostrate on the ground. After being sure that Pete was not dead, Sherman searched and removed money from his pockets, but did not take the watch that his Father had given him. The runaway knew that he had to hurry and make his flight to freedom before it was to late. As he stood over Pete's body, he was sure that his hunter could have shot and killed him before he had the chance to overcome him. Knowing that if he did not attempt to leave, then he would not be as fortunate if Daniel and Charles caught up with him. Sherman was sure that it would be a death sentence for him with Pete's body lying there on the ground.

A short period of time had elapsed as Pete lie there by the rivers edge. The warm water rushed up against his face as he slowly opened his eyes. After rising, he tried to shake the cobwebs out of his painful head. He quickly glanced about him for any sight of Sherman, only to verify by his footprints in the mud, that the runaway slave had taken off across the river. As he looked and waded out into the river to the first group of rocks, he suddenly heard in the quiet of the night the multiple crackling sounds of guns being fired. As he paused, Pete was sure that Daniel and his brother had surely sent Sherman home to his maker.

CHAPTER SEVEN

In early November, the beautiful leaves of multiple colors had fallen from the tree-covered mountains that surrounded the town. After experiencing a hot and muggy summer, the rain that was received was a blessing, as autumn had fallen early upon the area. For the residents of Harpers Ferry, it was a time of uncertainty and instability not knowing who would be the next President of The United States. This subject was the main topic of discussion in the taverns, work place, churches, and most of all, at the dinner table of each family in the evening. Most of the residents of the area were sympathetic toward the Southern states, but first and foremost, their loyalty was with the Old Dominion.

Over the last couple of months, Charles Barker had spent most of his time campaigning throughout the Shenandoah Valley for Vice President Breckinridge. He had spent long hours giving speeches and attending receptions on behalf of the candidate. Charles' strong belief in slavery and states rights had kept him focus on the prize at hand, and his own political goals in life. On this day when the country was about to elect the 16th President, he knew in his heart that John Breckinridge would lose the election. With the continuation of division within the Democratic party, and two candidates running for the same office, Charles was sure that Lincoln would be elected, and that South Carolina would withdraw from the Union just as she had threaten. He was concerned over what the prospect of war would bring regarding the family business. They had been awarded the new government contract in September, and were looking forward to even a greater and prosperous future. It seemed as though everything had gone Charles' way with the purchase of the Robinson farm. The unfortunate landlord had no other choice then to succumb to the pressure that Charles had inflicted upon him, and sale of his livestock had not improved. For Charles and the rest of the family, it allowed them to monopolize this specific industry in the Old Dominion and retain their influence over their competitors. With war looming on the horizon, his hopes and dreams of being the sole owner of the Estate was in jeopardy. All of these thoughts Charles pondered upon as he was admiring the beauty of the Shenandoah River, from the window of the passenger coach aboard the East Bound Express. Within the hour, he would arrive in his hometown where everything had looked so optimistic several months ago.

As Caroline sat in their carriage listening intently for the train whistle, her heart and mind was dwelling on her own personal thoughts. Over the last couple of months, Caroline had felt the neglect and loneliness of her husband's frequent absence from her life. She was weary of Ann confronting her regarding her Father and making up excuses. Ann had been having a difficult time with the whole ordeal and had been awakening during the middle of the night after experiencing nightmares. The only conciliation over the last couple of months had been her close relationship that she had been able to develop with Katie McBride. With the campaigning coming to an end, hopefully, Charles and she would be able to pick up from where they had left off with their marriage and make an attempt to enjoy a closer relationship.

It was close to 2:00 in the afternoon when Caroline observed the passenger train from Winchester slowly approaching. She was anxious and excited about seeing her husband, whom she had not been with for over three weeks. As the train came to a halt, her eyes were full of joy and expectation as he stepped down from the passenger coach. The expression covering her face glowed brightly. In her enthusiasm Caroline embraced him, and with a joy in her voice, she said, "I am so glad that you have returned home to me. I have missed you more than words can express."

As he slowly broke their embrace, she noticed a grim look on his face and asked, "Charles, what is wrong? Why do you look so upset? Is there something wrong with what I said?"

There was a half-hearted smile that was surfaced as he answered softly, "I'm sorry dear. On the train ride home my mind was on what is taking place in this

Country. I have labored with vigor over these last couple of months. I do not believe that Mr. Breckinridge is going to win today." He was shaking his head in frustration as he continued to pour out his despair, "I really do not think so. I am afraid that our life as we know it is about to change. It may be my dear, that war will be the only thing that will help us retain our rights as a people."

Caroline was surprised by his observation. Only a few weeks ago she received a letter from him while he was in Lexington. He had seemed to be so optimistic about the way that the campaign had been progressing and the response that they had received from the residents of that area and throughout the Valley. There was a sound of bewilderment in her voice as she asked, "What happen to the campaign in the last two weeks? I was under the impression as well as the rest of the family, that Mr. Breckinridge would win the election."

Charles was looking for the right words to say as he sighed. With a soft tone, he answered his wife, "The responses in the Valley was good, but I believe that elsewhere in the state many of the voters have mixed emotions concerning our candidate. I feel that most of the residents of this state have taken a more moderate outlook to this election then what anyone had perceived or estimated, and voted for John Bell. The only thing that is left now, is to count the votes. Tomorrow, Lincoln will be the new President, and the Country will be even more divided then what it is already. You can rest assure of that."

Caroline felt sympathetic towards her husband's efforts at this endeavor, but she had not expected the cold response that she had received from him at the station. It was as if they had become strangers, and that their relationship had lost its meaning. He made her feel frighten and alienated by his actions. Her heart was filled with despair and sorrow as she attempted to contemplate his behavior toward her. Without any further discussion between the two, the couple departed and proceeded home.

For over an hour, Pete had been looking for a new frock coat and white shirt at Mr. Frankel's clothing store. He was hoping to wear the new clothes to the dance that was to be held at Carrell Hall on Friday evening. As Pete was trying on the coat and looking in the mirror, he began to think of who he might invite to this dance. Over the last couple of months, Pete had not been able to find the time to socialize with the young ladies and attend gatherings because of his commitment of attending to the business of the Estate in his brothers absence. Now, with Charles' return from the campaign trail, Pete knew that this would all change.

As Pete was leaving the store, he noticed Katie walking across the street from the bakery toward the river. Momentarily, pausing and briefly watching Katie, his thoughts returned to the afternoon during late summer when they had spent time together along the river. Pete had been so busy, that he had not been able to find the time to become better acquainted with her. Even though Katie had spent time at length with Caroline, Pete was always somewhere else in regard to the affairs of the Estate. Suddenly, a gentle smile beamed across his face at the thought of taking her to the dance. He knew that there was the chance that she would refuse, but it would not be the first time that a lady had done so. Quickly, he proceeded in her direction.

Katie had just purchased some bread at the bakery for Mrs. Stipes, who owned the boarding house where she was staying. Her thoughts were upon the letter that she had received from her family, who had been pleading with their daughter to return home before the possible outbreak of hostilities. Katie was somewhat emotional about its content and needed time to collect her thoughts, so she proceeded toward the river where it was quiet. As Katie was walking in that direction, her thoughts were on the success that she had enjoyed as a teacher at the school and its rewarding accomplishments. Most of all, the close relationship that she was enjoying with the children gave her the fulfillment of success. When it came to Caroline, their friendship had exceeded her expectations and brought her great joy. The two of them had become very close, as if they were sisters. For over the last couple of months, Katie and Caroline had found themselves almost inseparable, sharing the most secret thoughts of the heart, as well as attending social activities together. As Katie was pondering upon these thoughts, she suddenly recognized Pete near the clothing store.

As Pete approached, he wasn't for sure how Katie would respond to him, so he tipped his hat in a friendly flamboyant gesture and politely asked, "How are you doing today, Miss McBride?"

There was a generous smile that covered her expression as she replied, "I am doing fine, I guess."

"It sounds as if there is some uncertainly in your voice."

Katie shook her head in frustration replying, "Yes, I guess I am not having a very good day. I'm sorry, it has nothing to do with you."

"I noticed that you were on your way toward the river. I remember back in August, when I was showing you the Estate; the joy that you seemed to express during that time."

"Yes, I love to be near the water. I have discovered through my personal experiences that I can sort out my problems there. I guess it is the tranquility; it is easier to attempt to resolve the issues that concern me when I am alone and walking along the water."

Pete empathized with Katie because she was so far away from home, and he knew that she must miss her family. With the possibility of war, and Katie being from the North, she had not been able to make very many friends, other then Caroline. Boldly and politely, Pete said, "Miss. McBride, I know that I'm not Caroline, who I am sure that you would prefer talking to, but if I may ask, I would like to walk with you along the river? Sometimes it's just good to have someone who is willing to listen, or to be present. Though, I do not want you to feel threaten by my presence."

Suddenly, the thought came to mind as she reminisced over her experiences with him on that August afternoon, how pleasant their time with each other had been after she had expressed her feelings concerning the affair that had taken place the previous day. Now, with three months passed, it was time for her to move on with her life, and make every attempt to try and forgive, and allow a new beginning with his acquaintance. As Katie began to smile at his humble plead, she answered softly, "I will let you walk with me, only if you will stop calling me Miss McBride and call me Katie"

Pete cheerfully replied, "Thank you, I will gladly call you Katie. And you may call me Pete."

As they were walking casually along the Shenandoah, the sound of the water rolling over the rocks was like a peaceful symphony playing music. There were some areas along their journey where some of the local citizens were fishing in hope of a good catch of carp, which would be the evening meal. Then there were some of the locals who were just mingling about and talking about the election.

Soon, they came upon an area where there was a good view and would allow for some privacy. Pete asked Katie if she would like to stop and rest, and she agreed.

As they were sitting and admiring the herd of deer on the other side of the river, Pete made the comment, "When I look at those deer, I think to myself that they do not have a care in this world. I enjoy as much as possible going off alone and watching the wildlife, or just fishing. I find that it brings comfort from troubled thoughts after a days activity."

Katie glanced at him as she softly replied, "I remember you saying something to that effect, the day that you shared the area of the farm with me where you and your father use to go."

"Yeah, I guess I did." And they began to laugh as they glanced at each other.

Katie began to inquire into Caroline's activities for the day, "How was Caroline doing before you departed the Estate?"

"She was coming to town to meet Charles on his return trip from Winchester. She seemed to be very excited about his return, and glad that the campaigning was coming to an end."

"I am glad that he is returning home, I know how much she misses him." Katie answered as though she was missing something within her own life.

"I know. Sometimes I feel sorry for Caroline, because of the way that my Brother neglects her and Ann. In everything that he attempts to accomplish, it is his goal to please my Mother, and as always, he is busy trying to make his fortune off of the business."

"That's no excuse to ignore her."

"I agree. I have attempted to speak with Charles on the subject of neglecting her, but he will not have any part of it. Therefore, I can not help him, and I keep my thoughts to myself."

Katie replied in a sympathetic tone, "That is sad. I have a great amount of respect for Caroline, and I look at her as an older sister, which I never had. I wish there was something that I could do to help."

There was a brief period of silence as they continued to watch the wildlife on the opposite shore. Pete asked Katie, "How is your family doing? I assume that you have heard from them by now."

Katie's face turned from contentment to sadness as she answered, "Yes I have. I received a letter from my Mother yesterday. She, as well as the rest of my family wants me to return to Boston, before there is the possibility of war. I found what she had to say quite disturbing. I know that my parents worry about me from time to time, but I feel that I am old enough to make my own decisions, and I would like to have their support. Really, I haven't felt like myself since hearing from them. Actually, to be honest with you, I feel depressed about the issue."

"Katie, I'm sorry that you feel that way. From what you have shared with me in the past, I can certainly understand why you would want to stay in this area. You are working at a vocation that you desire to do. Though, I can understand their concern for you. It must be very difficult for them, because of these unstable times in which we live. If war comes, then maybe you should reconsider your decision and return to the North. If you decide to stay here, then you are going to be in the thick of things. I'm not to sure that living here at this time would be in your best interest."

Hastily, Katie was on her feet. She became quite emotional over the last remark, and with a flare in her voice, she said, "Thank you Mr. Barker, but I am able to make up my own mind! Hasn't anyone noticed, that I am a big girl?"

"My dear, I'm sure that they have."

After her quick out burst of temper, she paused briefly and regained her composure. As she looked into his eyes, she felt the warm compassion that flowed from them. Katie was very touched by Pete's patience and calm emotions that he displayed with her. In her heart, she did not want this moment to end, but an apology was needed, "Oh please forgive me. How rude it was of me to take my problems out on you."

As Pete looked at Katie, he noticed that the expression on her face had changed to sorrow; that her eyes were beginning to fill with tears as she began sniffling.

Katie was touched by his sensitivity as he reached out and took her by the hand, and said, "No, Katie, I'm sorry for under estimating you as a lady. I am sure that you will be able to make the readjustment with living in the area, regardless of what happens. If you run into any obstacles, well, I will try to help you as your friend."

Cautiously, Katie took comfort and reassurance in the words that Pete spoke to her as she regained her composure.

The brief period of silence was broken when Katie said to Pete, "If I may ask you, did you vote today?"

"Yes I had the chance just before going to the bank."

"I'm sure that you voted for Mr. Breckinridge."

Pete said as he began to chuckle, "How perceptive of you."

Katie replied with a pitched tone in her voice, "I wish that I could have voted."

Pete couldn't compose his behavior, and began to laugh, "Yes, and I would be willing to bet, that you would have voted for old Abe."

Katie's face turned red as she boldly proclaimed, "That's bloody right, I would have!"

After realizing that Katie was quite emotional concerning the subject, Pete replied in a mellow tone in hopes of quenching her temper, "I have to say that I respect you for your honesty."

Katie confidently replied, "I would hope that you would."

As Pete remained seated, he felt that the conversation could not be abandoned. Katie needed to know the truth why Southerners felt so strong concerning the issue of slavery, and their right of self-determination. Pete stood up and turned looking at her, and with a calm tone, he said, "Katie, I know all to well how you feel concerning slavery, and so does the rest of the family. For us that live here in the South, we have to depend on slave labor. They help to provide our way of life. We do not have the factories, manpower, and the resources such as those who live in the North. Without the slaves, our industries would fail because of the lack of productivity. As a society, our existence would parish. We do not want the government, especially Abe Lincoln telling us what we have the right to do. In this area, and as far as that goes, the whole state, we believe that we are sovereign and have rights, and there are many who do not want those rights infringed upon. Our way of life, and how we interpreted the issues is different then yours. So, if that is jeopardized, then there will be many who will bare arms to protect their rights. Personally, I hope that it does not come to that."

Katie felt that Pete was very serious and firm in his beliefs, but found it hard to compromise her own. She had witnessed the scars on the backs of escaped slaves, who made it to the North. Her family had taught her from an early age that slavery was evil and that it had to be dealt with, and that it must be abolished. Katie's hope was to try and help Pete to see her side of the issue and why Northerners believed strongly against its existence. She looked up at him and with firmness and determination said, "I know how you feel, but for myself I can not understand why one man would want to keep another man in bondage against his will. Look at what happened several months ago at your Estate, when that young slave was attempting to escape to freedom. His only crime was to try and make a life for himself, and the right to exercise his God given free will. That's all, is that too much to ask? And since we are on the subject, let me ask you, what happen to him anyway? Did he receive a beating like so many others do in the South for their disobedience?"

Pete was surprised at Katie's comments. He found her to be very opinionated, which was not acceptable behavior from a lady in the South. It would be most profitable if he gave her an explanation. If any good could come out of this, he hoped that she would respect him for his honesty. It was difficult for him to repress his temper as he spoke, "That evening, the moon was full, and there was plenty of light. As I surprised Sherman on the opposite shore of the river across from town, he jumped me and I was thrown up against a rock and fell unconscious. As I understand from Charles later, they were waiting on the Maryland side of the river. When Sherman approached the riverbank, he was ordered to surrender, but he refused. Suddenly, without warning, there was gunfire. Charles was sure that Daniel had hit him, but because of their elevated position on some rocks, they could not retrieve his body, and the swift water they believed carried him down stream. To answer your question, I don't know."

Katie replied in a frustrated tone of voice, "I don't understand how you can justify taking another."

Suddenly, Pete became angrier and interrupted Katie with a pitch tone in his voice, "You do not understand."

Katie impatiently interrupted and asked, "Pete, please, if you will let me finish!"

"I do not feel that you and I should continue this conversation!" He replied rudely as he looked at her. Without another word, Pete stood up and suggested that they leave and return to town.

It was a long and quiet walk for the two of them back to the boarding house. Katie sensed that Pete was troubled greatly by his involvement, and their discussion of the issue. She reasoned within herself that Pete felt guilty over the incident, and that he struggled within his own heart and mind over this particular social issue.

As Pete and Katie arrived at the boarding house, the street was crowded with citizens mingling outside the dry goods store waiting to cast their vote. Quietly, they prepared to depart and go their separated way. Katie felt that she would like to address this situation, and hopefully there would be no harsh feelings. Katie turned to look at Pete and said in a somber tone of voice, "I am sorry that you and I do not agree on certain issues and that you are sensitive to them. In the future, I will respect your views, but I ask that you would respect mine."

Pete was calm in his tone, and firm in his response, "I do not believe that you understand how I feel. All of my life, I was raised with the belief that each state had the right to decide for its self, whether or not it wanted to be free, or if it desired to allow slavery. As for myself, I do not agree with the issue, but my family does. The slaves that we have belong to my Mother; although Charles has the right to do what he wants with any one of them. My best friend is a darkie, a free man, and you made his acquaintance." There was a silence as Pete paused, and continued, "Now, if you will excuse me, I must go."

As Pete walked away from Katie, she stood and watched as he rounded the corner in the direction of High Street. Katie's heart was filled with sorrow over their misunderstanding, and she hoped that their friendship had not been jeopardized, or lost. Before Katie entered the house, she paused briefly, and her thoughts began to drift back to only a few hours ago, when he took her hands to his, and the sincere look that was in his eyes. She was not sure of his feelings at that time, though for her, she felt very secure, and there was that nudging in her heart that she once knew. For the rest of the evening, Katie could not get this misunderstanding, or Pete off her mind.

CHAPTER EIGHT

Later that evening at the Estate, Charles and Caroline had been sharing time alone. Elizabeth and Ann had been spending the last two weeks in Richmond with Rebecca, and Elizabeth's former sister-in-law, Daisy Burke. They were not expected to return home until sometime next week. It had been a frustrating afternoon for Caroline. She had made every attempt to enter into a profitable discussion with Charles on any subject, or issue of interest, but all he could do was complain about the rigors of the campaign trail, and the exhaustion that he had been suffering.

Shortly after 8:00 p.m., Charles wanted to be alone. It was his intention to escape a possible disagreement with Caroline, or anyone else and retreat to the sanctity of his bedroom. After excusing himself for the evening, he quickly departed and prepared to retire for the night. The stillness of his surroundings, and the loneliness was a welcomed relief from the socials and receptions that he had grown accustom to over the last couple of months. After preparing for bed, Caroline quietly entered the room. As he turned and acknowledged his wife, he continued to comb his black hair. Slowly Caroline approached him, and asked, "I feel that you have been ignoring me all evening, and I do not know why. I had been hoping that once you were home and settled in, that we could spend some time together."

Charles had finished combing his hair and took a seat in the brown chair beside the bed. There was an expression of disappointment, and emptiness in his voice as he answered, "I am troubled by what I believe the results of the election will reflect tomorrow. Our life and business could be in jeopardy. Everything that I have worked for, and hoped possible concerning the future will be lost. If there is war, then Mother will not give me sole authority over Shenandoah, and somehow I can not allow her to do that to me."

Caroline cried loudly as she slowly approached, "Is that all that you can think about Charles, is the Estate? I have supported you in your efforts to back Mr. Breckinridge, and given you up for that cause for almost three months. I have been the one who has had to deal with Ann waking up in the middle of the night and crying because of your absence! And what about me, don't you think that I have not been lonely!"

Charles replied as he laid on the bed pulling the blankets over him, "Caroline, I am to exhausted to quarrel with you tonight. Can we discuss our differences tomorrow after I have had some rest!"

Caroline replied with a quiver in her voice and tears streaming down her cheeks, "Charles, one of these days Ann will be grown. And when she is a young lady on her own, what will happen between you and I? I'll tell you. I see the two of us being older and really not knowing each other. You know why? Because you and I will have grown apart due to the apathy in our marriage. Charles, its sad that we will have allowed our life to pass us by. If we work at our relationship we will be able to survive, even should war come. It will be easier to get through the conflict if we can pull together."

Charles replied to his wife in a sarcastic tone, "Your such an optimist. If war comes, it won't be that easy for our marriage, or the future. Personally, I hope that it does not come to bloodshed. But should some of the Southern states decide to secede, then I will push for Virginia to do likewise. Just maybe, Mr. Lincoln will leave well enough alone, and accept the fact that we do not want to be part of a Union that desires to strip us of our rights."

Caroline could not believe what she was hearing her husband say. Even though Caroline believed strongly in self-determination for each state, she did not desire the course of secession from the Union. There was astonishment upon Caroline's face as she looked at her husband. Turning to leave the room, she bluntly said, "God help you and Shenandoah if Virginia does succeed from the Union."

"Rest assure my dear, you have nothing to be concerned about."

"I guess I don't, until the Yankee army comes!"

Charles began to grin, and confidently said to her, "My dear Caroline, do not underestimate our boys. Do you think for a moment that we will let Lincoln and his abolitionist army come here and just steal our way of life and the property that we have labored for? Why our boys would put the armies of the North to flight, and they'll never return."

"You better hope so, or this palace will be laid to ruin, with you in it. Then, you have to ask yourself the question. Was it worth it, and what is left!"

With that statement, Caroline quickly continued her departure from the room slamming the door.

It was late as Pete came riding along the lane to the stables. As he walked through the doorway, Pete began to feel more like himself. Hayward was sitting on a wooden barrel playing The Yellow Rose Of Texas on his banjo. Quite often he would pass the evening with a selection or two. At a young age, his Father had taught him how to play, and since that time Hayward kept up with the instrument playing it to perfection. On many occasions, he was known to sing a song or two, and as for dancing, there was no one who could keep step with him.

"Hayward, do not stop on my account. Keep playing, I like what I was listening too."

Hayward curiously asked, "Where ya bin?"

Pete replied as he was unsaddling his horse, "I have been in town."

Raising his eyes from the instrument, Hayward said, "I's bet yose seen dat little girl, huh."

"I did, but matters did not work out like I thought that they would."

Hayward answered as he plucked a string here and there, "Yose think, I's knows better. Yose can't let ya troubles over us black folk stand in ya way."

Pete defensively replied, "Who said it was over you darkies?"

"Boy, yose not foolin' any black man, dis is Hayward. I's knows how great ya troubles are over us black people. Dis war will be 'bout de black man. Yes sire, I's know." He said in a laughing tone as he ran his left hand through his hair

"I'm sorry for being less then honest with you. Your right, we did have some discussion over the issue, and I walked away from her quite angry. And I still am. I do not agree with slavery, but every time it comes up, it causes problems. There is nothing that I can do about the matter. My Mother and Charles have all of the say so when it comes to their property here at the Estate."

"I's see." Hayward answered as he began to strum the strings gently on his instrument once more. Pete was brushing down the animal as Hayward stopped playing. Slowly he walked over to where his friend was standing, and with a boldness determination, he said, "De black man gonna cause a lot of problems fore dis all over. And it won't only be for ya, but for everyone. Dis thing gonna start boilin' over with Mr. Lincoln's election, and no one gonna stop it."

Pete laid the brush on the corner post of the stall and looked at Hayward. His eyes reflected the concern that he had over this fiery issue, and what the future might bring with Abraham Lincoln becoming the next President. Somewhere in his heart, he knew that his friend couldn't be more prophetic over this issue.

CHAPTER NINE

It was 8th of November, Friday evening several days after the national election. It began to rain heavy as Charles, Caroline, and Pete had just finished their evening meal and retired to the parlor. Charles was sitting quietly in his comfortable beige chair, sipping on a Tennessee brandy, and closely examining the headlines of the local newspaper, the Virginia Free Press, that had declared Lincoln the new President. Charles had received the news through a telegraph that had been sent to him the day before from William, who was at home in Richmond, informing him that their candidate, Vice President Breckinridge had lost the election. As Charles had already determined, John Bell won the election in the state of Virginia. They did believe that Breckinridge had done extremely well in the Valley. As for Lincoln, his name didn't appear on the ballot in Virginia, though he had received some support from the northern panhandle area of the state, where union sentiment was the strongest. Although, Charles was disappointed that Douglas, instead of Breckinridge had won the majority of the votes in Harpers Ferry, he still took great pride in the fact that Breckinridge had predominantly won the South, and finished second in the national election.

It was cool this evening as Caroline was seated near the warm crackling fire in the fireplace, and quietly playing Beethoven's Missa Solemnis on her violin. She had been mastering the instrument for the past fourteen years and possessed a passion for its sound. For her, it was a means of relieving any stress that she might have incurred during the day, and a way of openly expressing her emotions. As she was slowly and softly running the bow across the strings of the instrument, she glanced at times in the direction of her husband. After their disagreement several nights before, Charles apologized to her and promised that he would place their marriage as his first priority instead of the business and politics. With this hope, there had been a renewed spirit of life in their relationship, and despite what might occur in the future there was the possibility that everything would come together as far as family life was concern.

As for Pete, he was sitting at a small cherry oak desk that was beside a window opposite the fireplace. For sometime now, he had wanted to write a letter to his older cousin, Lester Tyler, who lived in Abingdon, Virginia, and share with him all of the news concerning the family, and the available rumors that were flooding the area concerning war. As he sat quietly looking out the window, he noticed that the rain was coming down in a steady downpour. Then his thoughts returned to the family reunion that was held at the Estate three years ago. It had been a most enjoyable time for everyone in attendance, with the men competing in a fox hunt, equestrian tournaments, and the women catching up on family issues. That was the last time that he saw Lester. Lester was now a corporal in the local militia and hoping that he would be able to take part in any conflict that would take place. His religious beliefs had become the center of his life, but he was also a strong believer in state rights, and that Virginia should stand together in unity with her sister states if they seceded from the Union.

Pete's thoughts came to mind as he began to compose the next few lines of his letter. Caroline had finished playing for the evening and walked over to where Charles was seated. Quietly, she sat in the identical beige chair near him and began to read again the letter that she had received from her younger sister Mary. As she read the portion of the letter that spoke of Pete, who her sister had been fond of for sometime, Caroline knew in her heart that there could not be a relationship between Pete and Mary because of her sisters problems with her temperance, and the amount of distance between the two estates.

Suddenly, her thoughts were broken as Charles causally asked, "How is Mary?"

"She is doing fine. She cannot wait until Mother and her leave for Atlanta next week to see my Aunt Lillian. They expect to be gone for at least several weeks"

"That's good. I hope that they have an enjoyable visit."

"Oh, knowing my Mother and my sister, I'm sure that they will. As always, I'll send your love when I reply."

As Caroline stood to leave the room, there was a mischief smile that surfaced as she walked over to where Pete was seated. She asked, "I understand that you and a lady friend were along the river several days ago, and that the two of you spent a considerable amount of time together. Is that so?"

Pete politely replied as he dipped his pen in the inkwell, "Yes that is so."

She laughingly continued her teasing of Pete, "I think that I know who the mystery lady was."

"You should know. She is probably your best friend."

Charles began to openly laugh at his brother and blurted out the words, "Oh, it must be Katie!"

Pete began to speak in a more serious tone of voice, "Look Caroline, I know where this conversation is going."

She answered with an innocent smile, "You do, oh."

"Yes I do. Katie and I can only be friends, nothing more. There are to many different between the two of us, not to say that the nation is on the verge of war with Lincoln being elected. So for now, there is no time for romance."

Caroline was hoping that he would consider her plead, "Oh Pete, she is such a nice girl. I saw her yesterday and she spoke with me concerning your disagreement."

Pete slowly rose from the table where he had been seated and without contributing to the conversation, he abruptly departed the room.

Caroline was very disappointed with the outcome of the conversation. She walked back over to where Charles was seated and sadly sat down once more near him. She began to frown as she spoke somberly, "Sometimes, I guess I do not understand your brother. Someone like Katie comes along, who would be an ideal lady friend for him, and he has the nerve to use the possibility of war as an excuse."

"He does have a point you know. I'm sure that there will be a response to Lincoln's win. We will have to wait and see what takes place once our sister states begin to secede from the Union."

"I understand what you are saying Charles, but I have become better acquainted with Katie in your absence. And, I believe that she is a very loving, mature, and sincere individual. Someone, I am sure who could calm your brother down from his womanizing, and irresponsible ways."

"I do not believe that she could, but this time, I think Pete may be using good judgment. Things are about to change."

"Do you really feel that if war comes, that Pete would join the Virginia army and fight?"

"Even though he is undecided, yes, I do believe he would. My brother, I'm sure would defend his home, and I believe his way of life. Besides Caroline, mostly everyone that we know in the area would probably do likewise. It would be their responsibility, and they would take pride in doing so. It would be an honor."

Caroline gently took her husband by the hand and said in a concern tone of voice, "I would not let you march off to war."

Charles replied as he laughed, "I feel that I could be of greater use in a less combative role. I'm not as aggressive as my younger brother."

Caroline calmly answered, "I hate to see this conflict come. In my conversation with Katie, she said that her brother Seamus would be bound to take up arms and fight if called upon."

"I do not know how this matter will be resolved peacefully. There are those in the South who are delighted that Lincoln won the election, and from what I understand, South Carolina is already making preparations to secede. Caroline was surprised and suddenly interrupted Charles in an angry tone, "How can anyone in his or her right mind want to go to war?"

"It is a matter of pride and rights. The South, as a society cannot have the Northern abolitionist or Mr. Lincoln telling us what we can do as a people, such as the rights of a state, or our property. We have the right to have slaves if we chose, and to live and make decisions based on our needs as a state. The only concern for our welfare that Lincoln and the abolitionist have is to make up our minds for us and steal our slaves. Now, I am sure I know what Pete's and Katie's differences were about the other day. Caroline, everyone with this election outcome will begin to take sides. And for those who refused to choose, such as my brother, well now, he will have to make a choice. He will not be able to escape it."

Suddenly, it became quiet. Both, Caroline and Charles sat pondering what the next couple of months would bring concerning the outcome of secession and war. They both knew that it would change their life, regardless of the conclusion.

Early the next morning, Hayward asked Matthew to awaken Pete just before six o'clock with a message of urgency. Quickly, Pete hurried down the steps. As his feet touched the bottom step, he noticed Hayward pacing in the archway to the parlor with a concerned expression covering his face. Anxiously Pete asked, "What is going on, what's the problem?"

There was a tone of anxiety in Hayward's reply, "I's been down along de river. De rain has cause it to come out of de banks. I had Matthew call ya, 'cause we hav' to get de cattle from de eastern range."

Pete said with excitement in his voice as he turned to rush up the stairway, "I want you to saddle my horse, and then go and summon Daniel. Tell him what is happening, and that we are going to need additional help, or we run the risk of loosing the herd. We will meet in five minutes in front of the stables. Now hurry!"

Just as Hayward was departing to accomplish what had been requested of him, Charles came into the room and began to inquire into the nature of the disturbance this early in the morning.

"What in the world are you two doing making all of this noise this early in the morning?" He asked in a loud voice.

"Hayward has been along the river and said that it was coming out of its banks. I sent him to summons Daniel and some of the bucks for help in moving the cattle from danger."

Charles discerned the urgency in Pete's voice, "I will go and get dressed."

Within minutes the two brothers were departing the house for the stables to meet Daniel and Hayward. They began to experience the full fury and wrath of the storm that was upon them. All through the night, the rain had fallen in a great down pour with the wind blowing over some of the trees. The ground was so drenched by the amount of precipitation that had fallen, that one's boots would be covered with water in places on the property close to the house. At times as Pete struggled against the elements, he could feel the drops beating against his face with furiousness, and it was causing him some discomfort. Suddenly, Caroline came running out the back entrance of the house and cried out desperately for her husband, "Charles, Charles! Stop! Wait!"

Charles turned and took notice of Caroline's efforts to have him return to the porch where she was standing. With the rain coming down with intensity, he did not want her to pursue him. Hastily, he returned to inquire of his wife's urgency. In a concerned tone, he asked, "Caroline, why are you calling me back. We have to get a move on if we are going to save most of the herd."

"I know, but if the river is raising at the rate that Hayward has said, then I'm concerned about Katie. She lives close to the water, right where there would be severe flooding. She needs our help!"

Charles replied sympathetically, "I can not do anything to help her now. When we return, then I will go into town and find her. I would not worry."

Caroline quickly interrupted his reply. There was a flare in her voice, "Charles, if you are not going to go, then I will saddle a horse and do it myself! But someone is going to help her."

As his wife waited on his answer, he just raised his arms in the air with frustration and said, "I will have Pete go, but you must promise me that you will stay here and wait."

Caroline's eyes glowed with satisfaction as she answered, "Alright, but tell him to hurry."

As Charles departed, he kissed her on the forehead and smiled. Quickly, he ran to the stables to summon his brother for the task at hand. Without knowing how his brother would receive the request, he decided the best course of action would be deception with only a portion of the truth.

As Charles entered the stable area, Pete noticed his brother saying urgently as he mounted his horse, "Come on Charles, we have to hurry!"

"Pete, Caroline has requested that you ride into town and bring Katie back to the house."

Pete became very angry as he answered, "What! You can't be serious?"

"Oh, but I am. Caroline is very concerned over her safety, especially with the water rising at the rate in which it has. The streets could be flooded by the time that you arrive at her residence,"

The younger brother pleaded as frustration covered his expression, "Charles, we do not have the time for this horse play. I'll tell you what, let's have Hayward go in my place, he is just as competent."

Charles spoke in a commanding tone, "No, there is no time to waste. You know how Caroline feels about Katie. She considers her the same as family. And furthermore, I will not have my wife running off, and attempting to accomplish this herself."

Finally, Pete jumped from his horse and struck an empty barrel with his foot in a display of anger. After pausing, he finally surrendered to what he thought was Caroline's request. Over the years, Pete had developed a considerable amount of respect for Caroline, and would be willing to help her in any way that was within his ability. Grudgingly, he remounted and rode off toward Harpers

Ferry across the fields at a reasonable pace, occasionally glancing over his shoulder, and taking notice of everyone quickly moving toward the river. The visibility was so impaired by the fog and hazy conditions that were covering the area, that it made even the simplest task difficult. As he continued toward town, he noticed the party of workers struggling in the steady down pour. It was so destructive, that it had made the road to the river muddy and impassable, which meant that Charles and the work party would have to abandon the wagons. For now, his anger had been calmed, even though his pride had been bruised. It had been his desire to take the leadership role in this venture, but he would undertake what he felt was a minor responsibility, and let his brother resolve the situation on his own.

When he arrived in town, the first thought that crossed Pete's mind was that Katie would seek refuge at the school, or at St. Peters Catholic Church, which was next to the school. Without delay, he rode down Clay Street in time to witness the mass exodus that was taking place by the residents of the lower section of town. As he paused near the church, Pete noticed how rapidly the river was rising and beginning to move swiftly through Shenandoah Street. It was like an angry god that was about to take its vengeance out on a helpless community that could not do anything to defend itself from its wrath. After a quick inspection of the school and the church, and finding the buildings abandon, he knew that she could only be at the boarding house. Pete's only hope of accomplishing his goal of helping Katie was to act quickly and proceed ahead to the lower section of town.

As he rode to the area where High Street and Shenandoah Street form a junction, Pete noticed Father Thomas standing near the jewelry store. Jumping from his mount, he had to shout because of the noise of the wind and pouring rain, "Father Thomas, have you seen Katie!"

"No, my son. I am on my way to the boarding house now to see if she is there, but the water is rising so rapidly, I do not know if this old man will be able to make it."

Pete demanded in an urgent voice, "Father, you wait here. I will go."

Hastily, Pete remounted his horse and began the short journey to Mrs. Stipes boarding house that was beside the dry goods store. The pressure from the swiftness of the water, and the rain continuing to come down heavy impaired his movements in his attempt to continue in that direction. In his mind there was some uncertainty in accomplishing her rescue after all. For Pete, he shrugged the thought aside; failure was not an option, he must move on, even if it would be at a slow pace. Even though his mare was becoming nervous and temperamental, he was able to keep the animal under complete control as they waded through what was becoming waist deep water. After what seemed a long period of time, Pete arrived at the front entrance, and desperately attempted to open the door to the house, but was unable too. As he held onto the horses rein, he called out for Katie, hoping for a response. Just when he was about to give up because there was no answer to his cry, Katie suddenly appeared at a window on the second floor of the dwelling. The rain was falling at such a rate and with the noise of a roaring train that it made it difficult to communicate with each other. He witnessed her near panic-stricken emotions. Pete was determined as he called out, "I have come to take you to the Estate. Can you get out on the bottom floor?"

Katie nervously cried, "No! I made an attempt earlier, but I could not get the door open from the inside, and now it is flooded on the bottom floor."

"Listen, I will throw you this rope, and you will have to tie it to something that is secure and climb down. I will help you, but you must hurry, there is not much time."

The first time that Pete threw Katie the rope she missed it. On the second attempt she was able to catch it. Already thinking ahead, Katie knew that the heavy iron legs on the wood stove in the upstairs parlor would be the most secure, and would hold her weight. Wasting no time, she quickly tied a series of knots and began her journey over the second story porch and down the side of the brick wall. As she was nearing Pete, he took Katie into his arms, and helped her onto the horse. Katie became frighten for her life as she experienced the wrath of the river; Katie prayed that God would spare them from this terrifying experience, "Oh, Lord help us, I do not want to die so young!"

And Pete quickly agreed, "Neither do I."

Katie began to cry openly. For her, she had never experienced anything like this before, and it was difficult not to feel panicky.

Pete knew that he would have to calm Katie's behavior before they began the effort to escape the rushing waters. The only thing that he could think of was to make an attempt to reassure her that they would be able to make it to safety, and that there was no other recourse. Furthermore, it would be important for their success for Katie to regain her composure, and to be observant of any large obstacles that might be rushing toward them from homes that might have been destroyed.

The water continued to rush against Pete's body with intensity. He held onto the reins of the horse with one hand to control the animal. Using the rope that was still hanging from the dwelling, he held firmly to it with the other hand. With the calmness of a dove, and the boldness of a lion, Pete began to plead with Katie, "Listen, we do not have much time! The water is rising quickly! I need you to regain your composure and help me."

Katie yelled over the noise of the rushing water, "What do you want me to do?"

"I want you to watch for any empty barrels, fallen trees, or anything that might hinder our safety. If you do, then we will be able to reach safety. I'm sure of that."

Katie answered him with a tone of confidence, "I will try!"

Pete rolled his eyes at her and replied, "I hope you will."

With that assurance, Pete was able to calm Katie's emotions. Quickly, he mounted the animal. Wrapping his arms gently around Katie, Pete urged the mare forward. The animal obediently complied. Pete knew they did not have far to go, but he hoped that the strong rapid movement of the water did not overcome them and wash the two of them uncontrollably into some obstacle causing potential harm. It was a chance that they would have to take; they could not return to the boarding house, it was too late. A huge tree was moving in their direction, and Pete wanted to keep that from Katie. As he gently guided his mare and spoke to the animal, Pete directed her in a straight and lateral direction toward High Street. The water continued to rapidly rise. They could see Father Thomas standing with some of his parishioners waiting to receive them. The swiftness of the water was moving with a vengeance against them. Suddenly, the animal began to loose its balance as she struggled desperately to move forward. Katie screamed with fear, but Pete held her firm in his grasp, and continued to speak words of encouragement, "Katie, we do not have much farther to go. I'm confident that we are going to make it. Please control your composure."

After asking this, Pete seek to regain his focus on what had to be accomplished and continued looking at the fallen tree that was drawing closer. Just as they reached the safety of High Street and elevated ground, the tree slammed into a building along the corner of the street. After thanking Father Thomas, and reassuring him that they were unharmed, the two proceeded along the same street toward the upper section of town and toward the Estate.

With their arrival, Caroline thanked Pete, and embraced Katie as she walked through the door. Both Pete and Katie were cold and wet, but glad to be out of the elements. For the younger Barker, he had been out in the elements for over four hours, and was exhausted after the ordeal. After their arrival, Charles and Hayward returned along with the rest of those who had participated in helping to rescue most of the herd. They had been fortunate and were able to save all of the cattle, which they moved toward the high ground on the western range of the Estate. For now, danger had passed and everyone was safe. They were all in a joyful spirit and thankful that everything turned out better then previously expected.

During the early evening the rains ended. The nighttime sky was clear and filled with bright stars, though it remained cool. The four had a nice dinner and then retired to the ballroom, where Caroline played the violin, and was accompanied on the piano by Katie. Both Pete and Charles were impressed with the entertainment that they were receiving, and found the melodies of soft and slow music to be a blessing after their eventful day. Suddenly, the ladies struck up the tune, Oh Susanna, which everyone began to laugh as they sang along.

After about an hour of the fun and enjoyment that was taking place, Pete excused himself to take care of a few chores that needed to be completed in the stables before retiring for the evening. As he was walking back to the house and thinking about the enjoyable evening that he had been having with Katie and the rest of the family, Pete noticed that Katie was standing on the porch looking at the stars. Pete walked over to where she stood and said, "Do you think that you could possibly count all of them?"

"Oh, no." She replied laughingly. "I was just standing here thinking about how some of them are clustered together. It reminds me of how close family should be, and the value of spending time together. This evening in the ballroom, the moment reminded me of home when Mother and I would often sing and play. I guess that is what I miss the most about being away from home, that closeness."

Pete calmly replied as he gazed toward the heavens, "I wish that I was able to experience what you are saying."

Katie glanced at Pete with a surprised expression saying, "What do you mean? I was under the impression that your family is close."

"My Mother and brother, as well as Caroline are very close. But as for myself, I'm the rebel of the family, so my Mother says. I could only hope someday that all of our differences would be resolved, and that we could see eye to eye on matters. Hayward and Ann are the only two that I am really close to."

"Why would your Mother consider you some kind of a rebel? You do not give me that impression of yourself."

"When my Father passed away, my Mother felt that it would be for the best if Charles and I learned the business. She had told my brother and me that this was my Fathers wish, and she intended on seeing it fulfilled. Of course, I was close to my Father, and was willing to do anything that would have pleased him. So, my way of fulfilling his request was to work everyday, just like those who do not have their freedom. I felt that it would give me a greater appreciation for this property and business in the future when I inherit my portion."

"What about Charles? He does not work like you do. He impresses me as the one who has all of the authority."

"I know. He wants this Estate in the worst way, and will do anything to acquire it. In every decision that takes place, my Mother will always take his advice over mine. And as for myself, well, I am expected to go along with whatever Charles decides on, whether it is the right thing to do, or not. Most of the time I am in disagreement with them, and I guess I just make my life more difficult."

There was a long silence. Katie noticed the sorrow in Pete's eyes as he spoke to her concerning his family. It was not often that someone of the opposite gender shared his heart so openly with her. This was not acceptable behavior for a man to show his vulnerability in this way, not even in the North. Now that the opportunity had arrived, Katie wanted to reach out to him, and give comfort with words of encouragement, and to express her feelings, and she did so with passionate emotion, "Today when it was raining in torrents. You braved the elements and placed your life in jeopardy for me. I can never thank you enough. As I was sitting frighten in that room, I was hoping that I would see you again after our disagreement. My hope was, that in some way you would be the one who would help me. As I sat there, and prayed, I really believed that I would not see another day. And frankly, I thought that I was going to die, and you would not come in time. Yes, there were others, who thought more of saving themselves, then helping someone else, but your willingness, and effort to help someone says quite a bit concerning your character. I am grateful for your sacrifice, and if it were not for you, I might not of had the wonderful evening with you and your family, and the opportunity to view the beautiful stars."

As Katie finished speaking, she leaned forward and kissed him on the cheek. It was a time that she cherished, and hoped that it would not come to an end, but instead develop into something new and special. For Pete to open up his heart and soul, and to express his deepest emotions meant a great deal to her, and something that she hoped would not have a short life span. Since that afternoon back in August when they spent time together along the Shenandoah, she had been experiencing warmness, and a confidence in her heart concerning this new friendship. Even though they had only agreed to be friends, there was still something of greater fulfillment taking place in her heart and mind. Then when the two of them were together only several days ago, she felt that nudge in her heart that she had once known when love had blossomed like a rose in the early months of summer. Now that nudging in her heart was returning. She could only hope that in time he would respond, and turn away from the division that stood between the two of them on social issues. Such matters Katie believed should not take priority over something that only truly happens once in a lifetime.

After listening intently to what Katie had to say, Pete could not help, but noticed that she was lost in the magic of the moment. The glow, and the light that was in her eyes revealed the sincerity of her heart. Her smile and peaceful expression would comfort any heart that was in despair, but just as important, there was the quality of person that she was displaying. For Pete to have someone who would listen to his hurt and pain, and attempt not to explore his vulnerability convinced him that in the future he would be able to confide in her again, believing that Katie could truly be trusted.

As they stood there gazing at each other, Pete placed his hands upon her shoulders and shaking his head in amazement, he calmly sighed and said, "Katie McBride, if only I knew what to do with you."

With that comment, Pete and Katie began to smile as they returned to the parlor, where Charles and Caroline were still singing.

Pete and Katie knew after all they would be friends.

CHAPTER TEN

In mid April of 1861, spring had arrived early in Chesterfield County, Virginia. The weather was warm, and there had been plenty of rain to replenish the area. The tree leaves were budding with multiple green colors that reflected the season. The sparrows were singing a song of joy that revealed the area, once more, was full of life. Many of the plantation farmers were requiring their slaves to labor from dawn until dusk to get the crops into the ground, especially tobacco, with the full expectation that this would be a good year, and yield plenty when it came time for the harvest.

Charles, Caroline, and Ann were visiting William Pierce at his 2,500 acre Estate called Norfolk, which was along the banks of the James River, ten miles below the state capitol. Over the winter months, and since the campaign had ended, the couple's marriage had greatly improve, much to Caroline's satisfaction. The only political venture that Charles had engaged in was his discussions with Mr. Barbour, the Armory superintendent, who had been elected to represent Jefferson County as a delegate at the Virginia convention to vote on secession from the Union. True to his promise to Caroline, Charles had labored diligently to improve his marriage, and on several occasions, he had taken Caroline and Ann with him on business trips to Philadelphia, and Harrisburg, Pennsylvania, something that he had neglected in the past. For the family to be invited to accompany him on his visit to Richmond, it manifested greater hope in Caroline's heart, and the intentions of a sincere relationship.

There was finally happiness and contentment, something Caroline had eventually hoped and prayed for, and now it seemed that her dreams were becoming an experience of reality.

It was on this beautiful clear morning that William was excited with optimism over the possibility of Virginia leaving the Union as most of the Southern states had accomplished without any government intervention. He believed as most of his close friends, that protecting the sovereignty of the state, and the institution of slavery, would guarantee that their way of life would continue without government interference. After South Carolina seceded in December, William at various times, and as opportunity presented itself, made vigorous arguments why the state should secede from the Union. Often over the winter months, he visited the six gulf states that had followed South Carolina's lead in an attempt to position himself for a possible leadership role should Virginia secede. William was strong, and solid in his beliefs, even to the position to where he had become one of the most respected leaders among the secessionists movement, and was very influential with state legislators, and prominent politicians in the state. Now it was time to enlist Charles' help and support, and seek his efforts to bring the Commonwealth of Virginia out of the Union, and into the Confederacy.

As Charles, Caroline, and William were sitting on the huge porch of William's white colonial mansion that was inherited from a third generation of Pierces, they sipped on freshly made lemonade that was served to them by Andrew, the main servant of the house. The men enjoyed the cigars made from the tobacco that was raised on the plantation, as Caroline listened and took part in the jovial conversation, reflecting upon William's visit to Shenandoah the previous summer. As William looked out across the huge front yard that was full of sweet bay magnolia trees, and azaleas, he watched the slaves repairing the dock where the boats would take his goods to Norfolk and Richmond to be sold. Most of all, he counted his blessings over the prosperity that he was reaping from his business.

With his mind drifting back to reality, and the possibility of the Commonwealth leaving the Union, he suddenly broke the silence, and with a smile beaming from his face, he gratefully said to Charles, "I would like to thank you for your assistance in speaking with Mr. Barbour on the importance of the secessionist movement. I believe he knows what it means for the county and state. Though, I would like to know how you approached him."

Charles began to chuckle as he replied, "Most of his friends and associates had been applying a great amount of pressure on him, and making accusations that troubled him. I used a different method. I felt that his friends and their tactics would be ineffective, and wouldn't wear him down, so I approached the matter in a different gentle way, appealing to him as a son of Virginia. I explained to him the great importance to honor ones home state, since he comes from an honorable family from the Old Dominion. I found that he was in agreement with me when it came to the question; should we as a people allow the government to dictate how one should live, and what one can or cannot do. I explained to him that in this way of thinking it jeopardizes our sovereignty as a state, and freedom as a people, and our whole way of life. I really believe that influenced his passion for the state and manifested his patriotic spirit. Actually, this approach of tactics was different for me then what I've been accustomed to in the pass."

William was amazed over this brand of politics. It was an approach that he had never attempted to demonstrate. For him, the only way to compromise, or exert his views was to apply fierce pressure, and resort to less then honorable tactics, if necessary. William was very impressed and now decided that it was time to rely upon Charles, and determine a plan for Virginia's withdrawal from the Union. As this thought crossed his mind, he wanted to know from his friend his impression as to where the support would come from for secession, since Virginia had taken a moderate stand in the national election. Slowly William stood up, and walked over and placed his arm against one of the huge white columns that supported the porch, he turned, and anxiously asked Charles, "The election did not go our way in the Valley because their views were too moderated, even though I was sure that we would carry that area. Now, I am concerned over whether the citizens of the Valley will support a resolution to secede from the Union, or fight to reject it. We need their support, or we will not be able to bring Virginia out of the Union."

As William paused briefly, Charles and Caroline waited for him to continue. When William did not choose to continue the conversation, Charles felt that it was time to interject his thoughts on the subject. He meticulously chose his words, and confidently began to explain his insight on the situation, "No, quite honestly, they have not changed their views. In my county for example, you know Harpers Ferry led the way in the selection of delegates to represent the area. Most of the voters are Armory employees from the North who are working for the government. I do not see them changing their minds. Most of them are afraid of losing their jobs if Virginia secedes, and that would affect the local economy and their vote. When it comes to the rest of the Valley, except Augusta County, I believe that most of the residents are taking a wait and see approach concerning the issue of going to war, or if there will be a compromise worked out to resolve the matter. I truly feel in my conversations with most of the local leadership that I have spoken to that they are in favor of such a compromise. But I do feel, that if Lincoln places demands on the state for troops that would be needed to put down the rebellion among the Confederate States, then that would cast a different light on the whole situation. For now as you well know, it depends on what happens in South Carolina?"

"I know. I agree with you." William said as he looked once more across the yard towards the river. He continued in an optimistic tone of voice, "As I am standing here, I know that the Confederate government will wait only a matter of time before they give General Beauregard the order to force Sumter's surrender. They are growing impatient. But, I agree with you, Lincoln will most likely place demands on Virginia for troops and that will cause considerable problems for him, though Buchanan did nothing to prevent or interfere with South Carolina's withdrawal."

Charles said confidently as if he was able to see into the future, "Buchanan was a weak President. William, when it comes time, it's the only choice that Lincoln will have. He won't be able to compromise; there will be too much pressure placed on him by members of his own party and anger from the abolitionist. Besides, I do not believe that Governor Letcher will allow Virginians to fight in a Federal army against their Southern brothers. Therefore, I suggest that we pursue the issue of states rights, and on that principal we will be able to rally many to our cause."

During this exchange of conversation between William and Charles, Caroline was peacefully seated near Charles, and did not participate in any of the conversation. She was concerned that William was attempting to engage Charles in a commitment that would once more provide a strain on their marriage. Even though Caroline shared her husband's goals in life, the sacrifice that would be required of her would be a heavy burden that she would have to bare.

Suddenly, Ann came running across the yard in her blue riding dress from the stable area, and onto the porch where everyone was gathered. Out of breath and excited, as if there was not another moment to waste, she asked, "Mother

I would like to go riding along the river. Mr. Pierce said that I could ride Crimson anytime while we were visiting."

There was a gleam of joy on Caroline's face as she answered, "No, not without me."

Everyone began to laugh at Ann's innocence. Finally, Caroline wanted to change into some riding attire; and after excusing herself from William and Charles, she took Ann by the hand and went into the house.

For the past eight months, the opportunity hadn't presented itself for William to visit Shenandoah, or the valley. Even though he had a short relationship with a mistress from Richmond, his mind from time to time would return to Katie, and a desire to see her once more. It was only after Caroline and Ann was out of sight that William anxiously began to inquire of Katie, "As I understand in my conversation from yesterday evening with your wife that she and Katie have become very good friends, and that they have spent quite a bit of time with each other?"

"Yes, they have become very close. I have noticed a remarkable change in Caroline's personality since her acquaintance with Katie. She seems to be very happy with their relationship."

"When I was there at the Estate last summer, I didn't have the time that I would like to have had to become better acquainted with her. I will be leaving to visit the Edwards in Leesburg next month."

Charles was sensing where the conversation was going, so he abruptly interrupted to offer his invitation. He said, "William my friend, you can not come to Leesburg, and not visit our family. Mother, I know would like to see you."

William's face was covered with joy and excitement as he handed his friend the glass of lemonade sitting on the table, "Well, then I accept. Thank you. This will give me an opportunity to hopefully become better acquainted with Miss McBride."

The two men were laughing as Caroline and Ann came walking out the front door toward them. As the three of them were speaking, Ann happened to notice a rider on a black mare riding rapidly and shouting as he quickly approached. William did not recognize the mysterious rider, but by now, everyone's attention was focused on him. As he rode within shouting distance, one could here the joy and excitement that was in his voice, as he shouted, "Sumter has been fired on! Sumter has been fired on!" With this news, William and Charles were jubilant in their response. Caroline turned away from everyone so that no one could witness the tears that filled her eyes. Ann could not understand why her Father and Mr. Pierce could be so happy over this news, and yet her Mother's heart was filled with sorrow. All she could do was stand there and hope that someone would help her to understand the significance of this news.

At Shenandoah, it had been a peaceful and uneventful day thus far. The sun was shining brightly with a beautiful clear and blue sky, and the temperature was warmer then normal for this time of year. Pete had rode out towards School House Ridge, which borders the Barker property, and there he met Daniel and some of the laborers already working. With the introduction of spring, it was the time of the year that chores such as repairing fence posts and replacing fence railings took priority; this is what was on the agenda on this day for the laborers. As Pete sat on Victory, with his left leg across the saddle, he closely watched a herd of deer causally heading toward the Shenandoah River for water, and he listen to the laborers reverently sing their spiritual songs of praise. He smiled and marveled at the beauty of spring that was taking place over the area, and the Estate. It was with great pleasure as Pete sat on his horse on the ridge that he could see off in the distance some of the laborers planting the flower gardens under Jeremiah's direction, and plowing the land for the family's garden.

Pete was very happy, and content with the direction that his life had been taking. Over the last five months, he had become more familiar with the operations of the Estate, and since he had studied law, Pete had been asked by Charles and his Mother to be their representative in several important business negotiations concerning the Estate. Though Pete felt a sense of pride and accomplishment, even at his young age, the greatest desire was that his Mother and brother would learn to trust him and fully accept him as a responsible member of the family. The melee that had taken place with Billy Smith last August, and the disagreement over the purchase of the Robinson farm, had seemed like a bad dream that he had awaken from, and had never existed. A new attitude in the family had seeded. Now, that Pete was finally back in his Mothers good graces. He hoped not to depart, though still, he continued in his strong convictions, and would not compromised in what he believed to be truth.

Katie McBride was happy with her friendly relationship with Pete. On several occasions over the last couple of months, they had attended several social, and grand balls together that were held in Charlestown. Though, she had received requests to attend social functions with some of the bachelors in town, she always politely refused, saving her free time to spend with the Barkers, especially Caroline and Pete.

Katie was excited at receiving an invitation from Pete to join him for the afternoon. Hayward, at the request of Pete had arrived in town at Katie's residence with the carriage to bring her back to the Estate. It would be there, that the couple would go together to the river for an early afternoon picnic, and spend some time in privacy, just the two of them.

As Katie rode slowly in the carriage on her trip to the Estate, her thoughts were on the beauty of the surrounding area. Especially the way the two rivers came together in the valley between the mountains. Soon, the trees would be full of blue birds, and sparrows, which would freely give a concert to anyone who would listen. As her mind drifted back to last August when she was on the train from Boston, she had hoped that this new adventure that was embarked on would reward her with peace, joy, contentment, and most of all, a greater appreciation for life. All of these expectations had been met. For Katie, the unexpected discovery, and the greatest reward was her relationship with the Barkers. It had exceeded her expectations as to what she would experience living in the south. Though Katie was from the north and had her views on the issues of slavery, thus far, the citizens of the village did not judge her, nor brand her as an abolitionist. For this, Katie was thankful, and grateful for their friendship, and hoped that this would not be jeopardized if there were war.

As Katie arrived at the front entrance to the Estate, she noticed Pete galloping toward the carriage. Katie's heart began to flutter with excitement as she attempted to withhold the revelation of her deepest and sincerest feelings. The expectation of spending time with Pete was something that she had been thinking about for the last two weeks. She possessed high expectations of what the day would manifest, and hoped for a closer and more intimate relationship. Pete had extended the invitation when Katie spent the afternoon with Caroline, before her departure for Richmond.

Katie turned to look as Pete rode along side of the carriage and tipped his hat, asking in a flamboyant manner, "Miss McBride, how are you doing on this beautiful day?"

Katie, began to laugh as she jokingly led him on in an attempt to use a Southern accent, "Why Mr. Barker, I am doing fine."

"Well Katie with that accent of yours, it would be difficult to past you off as a Southern bell." The two of them began to laugh loudly, and even Hayward joined the couple as they laughed.

With their arrival at the front entrance to the house, Pete jumped down from his horse and extended his hand to help Katie from the carriage. They entered the house and walked toward the direction of the parlor. The couple was talking and laughing about Katie's southern impression, and how funny that it had sounded. As they entered the room, Elizabeth was entertaining Virginia Edwards and Roseanne Russell of Turneysville, who were close friends of hers. The two ladies had arrived earlier that morning to spend the afternoon and have lunch together. As Elizabeth turned and noticed the couple, she asked anxiously of her son, "What is all of the commotion about? Don't you see that Miss Virginia, and Miss Roseanne are here."

Pete soon regained his composure, and proudly replied, "Miss. McBride, and I were just."

Both Katie and Pete began to laugh once more. The scene was beginning to embarrass Elizabeth, who did not understand the outburst, and by this time was beginning to lose her patience with the couple. Suddenly as Pete saw the displeasure upon his Mothers face, he paused and apologized, "Mother. Mrs. Russell and Mrs. Edwards, I would like to apologize for my behavior."

Just as quickly, Katie regained her composure, and began to apologize, "Mrs. Barker. Mrs. Russell, I am sorry if I have been less then a lady in my conduct. Please forgive me?"

After a brief silence, Pete took the initiative, and politely introduced Katie to the elderly lady, and her daughter from Loudoun County, "Mrs. Russell and Mrs. Edwards, I would like to introduce you to a friend of mine, Katie McBride."

Roseanne was a proud Virginian from a prestigious family, who's Father, and Uncle had fought in the Revolutionary War with George Washington. Both had served with great distinction for many years in the Virginia Legislature, and had become quite influential in the area concerning states rights. At seventy-five years of age, Roseanne still, was able to move freely, and was in excellent health, and full of life, though she was an adamant secessionist, who had a vigorous dislike for Northerners. It was her belief that those who lived in the North, should not interfere with Southern society, and should mine their own affairs, and not attempt to compromise, or attempt to change the Southern way of life.

As Roseanne looked at Katie, she smiled politely and began to inquire where

Katie had previously called home. She knew that the young lady must be from New England, because the accent was prevalent. In a curious, and probing tone of voice, she addressed Katie, "My dear, it does sound to me by your accent that you are from New England?"

Katie replied as she smiled, "Yes Mam. I am from Boston."

Mrs. Russell said as her eyes gazed at Katie, "Oh dear, you are, oh, well, I do not mean to be a busy body, but if I may ask. What brings you here to Jefferson County?"

"I am the school teacher at the Catholic School in Harpers Ferry."

"Well, I guess I should have known with the name, McBride, that you were Irish, and Catholic."

Pete was quietly standing by his Mother, and sensed where this conversation was going by the deceptive, and sarcastic tone of voice that was coming from Mrs. Russell; promptly, he excused himself and proceeded from the room to the kitchen house with Katie.

After the couple was out of sight, Roseanne shook her head and asked Elizabeth in a demanding tone of voice, "What in the world is James thinking of in keeping company with a Northerner. I do declare, I don't know what he sees in her, and furthermore Elizabeth, I do not see how you can let that girl into your home! I'm sure that her views are poison."

"Oh dear Roseanne, I should have warned you that she would be visiting today. I must apologize. But I will secretly tell you; little does my son know what I have planned for him. Their friendship will not last, trust me. I do not approve of it anymore then you do. And if I have my way, it will come to an end." Elizabeth replied confidently as a smile brightly beamed across her face.

The two ladies moved on to another topic of interest as Matthew served them tea.

Pete and Katie were soon at the kitchen house where Pansy had prepared a lunch basket for the two, which included her fried chicken, and dill potatoes salad. After thanking Pansy for her effort, the two boarded the two-seat buggy for their trip to the river. Pete and Katie spoke on various subjects of interest that were none threatening as they arrived at their destination. Here where the grass was green and soft, and the area allowed for privacy nestled among maple and hickory trees, Pete spread a blanket for them to sit. In the spirit of having some fun, Pete decided that he would like to make a fisherman out of Katie. Even though Katie was reluctant at this new adventure, she made the attempt with Pete's help in placing the night crawler on the fishing pole. The two laughed as she attempted to cast the line into the water. On her first attempt, it became tangled in some brush. Within minutes, Katie felt a tug on her line, knowing that a fish was nibbling on the bait that was on the hook. As she cried out with excitement, Pete laid down his pole and came running to assist her with the catch. With a little struggle, they had the bass out of the water, and under their control. The couple laughed with joy, and momentarily paused to gaze at each other. For Katie, she was enjoying this time with him, and wanted the day to last into eternity, knowing that the flame of romance was blooming.

After building a fire, and enjoying their lunch that had been prepared for them, they sat close to each other on the blanket. Pete spoke softly as he turned to look at Katie, "You seem to be relaxed, the sound of water must agree with you."

"Yes, it does. Far off lands such as England, France, and Germany have long intrigued me. I think it would be so romantic to sail on a ship and visit a land where there are castles, and damsels in distress who need to be saved from a villain."

"Katie you are a romantic. Instead of being a teacher you should have written love stories."

"Wouldn't you like to be romantic with someone that you were attracted too? How about I write a novel about your love life? If I may ask, how would it go?"

"To answer your question honestly, it would be about someone who couldn't find the right woman with the right qualities."

"What are you looking for?"

"Someone who will accept me for who I am, even if the rest of the world thinks that I am a rebel by nature. So many times we accept someone because of their good looks, and often we refuse to search and examine the inward qualities. And then too, if one possesses a considerable amount of wealth, they can have almost anything that they want, but true happiness and contentment. You say that you would like to travel the world, but what would you have in the end if you were still alone." Pete paused and remained silent. Staring at Katie, he laughed and continued, "I just haven't found someone, and you are privileged because you're the first lady that I have shared these feelings with."

Katie remained silent as she looked toward the mountain and thought on Pete's answer. She turned about saying as she shook her head in agreement,

"Your right. Relationship is what makes one feel that their life has purpose and meaning, not so much as to what they possess of this life's abundance." Katie paused and smiled, continuing, "I must confess I really must have sound silly speaking of traveling to some far off land."

"No, not really. If you have time and the means, then it is a good thing to travel and discover what the world has to offer, but it doesn't provide everything in life."

After a short time of silence, Katie wanted to express her feelings for the family, and her new life living in the South. As she admired the beauty of the wild dogwood trees that were blooming, and the mountains that overlooked the river, she opened her heart, and began to speak with passion, "Pete, I would like to thank you and your family for your acceptance of me into your lives. As I'm sure that you know, I do not have many friends in the area, and it can be quite discouraging for a young lady. By now, if it were not for Caroline, and yourself, and the rest of the family, I would have returned to Boston. I must admit in all honesty, that I love Caroline as a sister. And as for Ann, well, I love her the same as my niece. As for yourself, I like you very much as a gentleman friend. I feel comfortable when I am with you, and I do not feel threaten that you would allow yourself to be less then a gentleman. And I am thankful for that. Also, I have enjoyed the times that we have spent together, and the discussions that we have had, even though we have not always agreed."

As Pete sat silently, and listen to her, he wanted his reply to be fair and honest. After a pause, he spoke compassionately, "Katie, we have come along way since that incident in front of the Wager House. I want you to know how greatly that I cherish your friendship; you are so different than any of the other ladies that I have known. You are honest, and open about the way that you feel, and your view of life. I cannot say that I have seen that quality in many people. I feel that it a privilege to be called your friend."

"I would not want my life to change. I am happy, and so content sitting here along the river. It is so peaceful listening to the music of spring. I hope that the winds of war blow over."

Pete said as he looked at Katie, "I am afraid that the possibility of that happening is slim, at best. As I understand, the Confederate authorities have given Fort Sumter an ultimatum to surrender, or be fired upon. If that happens, it means war. And I do not know how Virginia will sit by, and not take sides."

Katie anxiously replied, "What will you do?"

Before Pete could answer Katie's question, they heard the muffled sound of a horse with its rider in the distance. As the couple stood and waited for the arrival of the mysterious rider, they were both apprehensive over the urgency of the fast gallop. Soon, the rider was close enough that Pete recognized him to be Hayward. His heart began to pound at a fast rate with anticipation of the news that his friend carried. He sensed that his greatest fears were coming to pass. With his arrival, Pete grabbed the reins of the horse as Hayward began to speak with the sound of alarm in his voice, "Mr. Pete, dey has started war."

Pete emotions were running with excitement as he wanted more information on this news, "What do you mean war has started?"

As Hayward was regaining his breath, Katie cried out, "Oh no! Oh no!

Once more, Pete asked impatiently of his friend, "Hayward, what is going on?"

"Dis mornin', Fort Sumta was fired on."

Pete turned quickly to see how Katie was receiving the news. He noticed that she was overcome with tears and emotion. He walked over and embraced her close to his body to bring comfort. Even though this was not the perfect situation for his affection, and concern, he still wanted to reach out to her. Katie did not want him to break his embrace. She felt secure as she looked into his eyes.

As they returned to the house after receiving the news, Pete took notice that Daniel was celebrating with a liquor bottle in hand, and singing patriotic songs, but as for the slaves, and the personal staff, they remained subdued and quiet, their life as they knew it continued.

Without a word, the couple entered the house; Elizabeth and Roseanne were speaking, and celebrating with Nathaniel Baker near the piano. All of a sudden the room became quiet as everyone turned and took notice of Pete and Katie appearance. Elizabeth was the first to break the silence. It wasn't her intentions to begin a quarrel with Katie, knowing full well how she must feel. Elizabeth asked Pete in a reserve tone, "Did you here the news of the firing on Fort Sumter by Southern forces?"

Pete's tone was reserve, and subdue as he approached the guest, "Yes Mother, I did. Hayward came to the river and informed us of the news."

Nathaniel, who was a tall and opinionated individual asked Pete, "I assume that if Virginia secedes from the Union, that I will be able to count on you to fight with us."

"I'm not an infantryman."

Nathaniel replied in a prideful tone of voice as he gazed at Pete, "Where is your honor? Think of the glory. I can not believe that you would sit out the conflict and not side with your state."

Elizabeth did not want Nathaniel to feel that the Barker family was unpatriotic, and would not be willing to contribute to the effort and share the burden. Without hesitation, she proudly proclaimed, "If Virginia secedes from the Union, then I am sure that James will be the first to offer his services to defend his home, and state. Will you not!"

With this comment, Katie became emotional with fear, and said, "No! No! Please stop!"

Elizabeth demandingly yelled, "Child, stop it now! We have the right to defend our land!"

There was a sudden silence that fell on the room. With a surprised expression on Pete's face, the couple departed quickly. As for Elizabeth, Roseanne, and Nathaniel, they continued to celebrate around the piano playing and singing the victory that they believed would take place.

On the return trip to town Pete and Katie were engaged in their own personal thoughts on what would take place next with the firing on Sumter. There was no conversation between the two, only silence, which made the trip longer then usual. The only words spoken on the lonely ride to town, was to someone who was passing by, and spreading the word concerning the events in South Carolina. As they were riding along Shenandoah Street, many of the citizens were celebrating, or arguing their views over the news, though there were those few who chose not to participate. With everything that was rapidly taking place, Pete knew that the townspeople were split in their passions concerning secession or war, and that the town might not be the safest place to be.

With their arrival at Katie's residence, Pete noticed that she was having a difficult time with the Southern aggression that was taking place. More so the behavior and enthusiasm that had been displayed at the Estate by his Mother and her guests. Pete did not want Katie to feel alienated from his family, and frighten with the uncertainty of conflict, though he did not believe that they would become aggressive in their behavior toward her. With only the truest intentions in mine, Pete wanted to make every attempt to reassure and comfort her. Choosing the right words had always been a problem for him, and presented many difficulties, due to his lack of confidence in these particular situations. Now hopefully, Katie would become the exception. Causally, he placed his hand upon hers, his eyes were filled with compassion, as the sound of his voice reflected the concern in his heart, "I want to apologize to you for the behavior that my Mother, and her guests displayed. It was unacceptable as far as I am concern. Everyone thinks that this will be a short conflict, and they can celebrate Southern independence, but I have given it considerable thought over the past months since Lincoln's election. I do not think as most, that it will be a short affair. It will not end with what has taken place today, though I wish that it would. I want you to know one thing, and that is, I will not betray your friendship, regardless of your views, and I really do not think that Caroline will either." Katie wanted to trust the words that he was speaking, and take confidence in them. One of the greatest concerns that troubled her, was the knowledge that her brother would be willing to serve if called upon, and this thought tormented her greatly as well as the possibility of Pete doing like wise. It was a difficult time for Katie with the uncertainty of the events that had taken today. She feared that if the conflict continued, would one of those that she cared about be wounded, or would death be their destiny. There was great turmoil within as she agonized over the thought.

As Katie was staring in the direction of the river, Pete became concerned with her absence of a response, and he cautiously asked, "Are you alright?"

"Yes, I am sorry. I was just thinking about my brother, Seamus, who will join the army if called upon. I tremble at the thought of him going off to war, and something happening to him. I have missed his smiling face, and the jokes that he played on me from time to time. My brother is someone who I have always been able to count on, and confide in. Even though the two of you would serve on opposite sides, still I could not bare the thought of losing him, nor would I want to see anything happen to you. We have become very good friends, and I cherish our relationship more then words can describe. My sincerity is true when I tell you that I do not want it to end. As for your Mother, and what took place today, I want you to know that I understand her passion and the concern regarding your way of life in the South and wanting to protect those values. Those who live in the North feel no differently. My greatest desire is that nothing comes between you and I, and the rest of your family. You, and your family have your views on the cause of this conflict, but so do I. As for myself, I will not allow those issues to stand between us."

Pete replied in a sincere tone as he smiled, "I agree with you. I do not want anything, or anybody to come between us."

Pete stepped down from the buggy, and then assisted Katie. He still was concerned over Katie's safety with the loud celebrating, and heavy drinking of intoxicating beverages that was taking place with some of the townspeople in the area. Again, as he held her hand and asked in a concern tone, "I want you to return with me to Shenandoah and spend the night."

Katie softly replied to his request, "No, I will be alright. I would not want to intrude on the celebrating that is taking place at your home, and wear out my welcome. Besides, I would rather be alone and write a few lines to my family."

"Katie, it would be all right. I insist."

"I believe you. But, I will be fine. I just need time."

With Katie's reassurance, he kissed her on the cheek, and began to walk away. As he boarded the carriage for his trip back to the Estate, he turned and sadly watched Katie walk through the door of the boarding house where she was staying.

On Pete's return journey back to the Estate, his thoughts were on the afternoon that they had spent together. He smiled as the thought came to mind over how she made various attempts to bait the hook with night crawlers, and wanting to take on the challenge. The conversations that they had enjoyed as they sat on the blanket, and watched the water rushing freely over the rocks came to remembrance. What attracted him most of all, was her green eyes, the reflection of their sincerity, and the life that they revealed. How could the day have begun so perfectly, with so much to look forward to and now in just the span of a minute, it all seemed to have changed so differently, and the world that they lived in, changed with so much uncertainty. Sorrow and despair began to fill his heart as tears surfaced in his eyes.

It was nightfall as Pete arrived back at the Estate. There to meet him outside of the stable was his friend Hayward. Taking notice of the concern expression that was covering his face; Pete began to speak frankly, "Well, I guest you were right with the election of Lincoln. It looks as though war may come our way unless there is a quick compromise."

Hayward replied emotionally as he wiped the tears from his eyes, "Do ya think dat de black man wanna be in bondage?"

"No. But, I do not feel that it is worth starting a war over."

"Yose do not understand. I's knows wat it is like ta be a slave and not have ta freedom. We's work in de fields all day long wit somebody cursing ya and if ya don't listin', den de hit ya wit de whip and disgrace ya, or want ta shoot ya. Most of all, yose has no freedom, yose are kept from a fair chance at wat de white man has."

With a flare of anger, Hayward tore the shirt from his back, turning and revealing the scares that covered his body, he shouted, "Are ya gonna tell me dat dis is not worth fightin' over!"

Pete was stunned by his friend's actions and horrified by the covered gashes that he witnessed. Hayward turned once more toward Pete and continued in a calmer tone of voice, "I has great hope dat my people might be free. I jist don't want people ta die, but I's afraid it is 'bout ta happen, even to my own. De price of freedom comes wit a price of death."

"I know. I am sorry for being impatient with you. It can not be no easier for you then me."

There was a somber, sorrowful feeling that consumed Pete. He was quiet and somewhat emotionally shaken by the revelation of bondage that covered Hayward's body. The family didn't practice this type of cruelty because they believed that it hindered their goal of production from the slaves, even though they had to restrain Daniel on occasions. Whipping another individual was a subject that had never risen in conversation until this moment. Hayward's actions were not intended to cause the young Barker suffering and anguish, but to help him understand the horrors of slavery, and the effects that it caused for the black man. After he was sure that he had gotten his point across to Pete, Hayward changed the subject, knowing that Pete was troubled too, "How's Misse Katie. She shure did seem upset when ya left here earlier."

"She was very upset. Katie's concern is over her brother, who will probably enlist, and I believe that she is concerned over my well being in all of this mess."

"I's knows dat she likes ya a lot. Her eyes are like de sun when she is whit you'd, dey light up when yose near."

Pete insisted as he began to unhitch the buggy from the horses, "Remember Hayward, we are just friends."

Hayward laughed.

For the first time as Pete stood silently, he began to think about the effect that war would have on the area. The destruction, and death that it would bring not only to the citizens who volunteer for service, but also to the economy. Most of the slaves would attempt to escape if Union troops were in the area, and maybe even fight for them, though that did not seem logical to him. Like most of the farmers that he knew that owned slaves, they believed that their property would not take up arms in Mr. Lincoln's army. As for Katie, he would attempt to convince her to return home and be with her family throughout the length of the conflict. This area would present too many dangers to her.

In the guest bedroom at Norfolk, the flame that was upon the candle, occasionally flickered as it burned brightly on the marble stand, next to the four-poster bed with a canopy, where Charles and Caroline were sleeping. The room had a balcony with a moon light view of the river, which Charles admired while he stood by the doorway. Looking at the view was so peaceful, and for a brief moment, tranquilly had brought rest to his soul, as if he did not have a care in this world. As he looked at his watch, it was 9:30 p.m. exactly, but then as reality took hold, tranquilly disappeared as a vapor on a cold evening. There was a part of him that was excited over the future of Virginia, and if the state seceded. What role could he play in her future, and would opportunity present itself, though on the other hand it had been difficult to control his anxieties with the events that had taken place earlier today. At this hour, Sumter was still under fire from South Carolina forces and had not agreed to the terms of surrender. With these events, he began to ponder what would happen to the new government contract that had been awarded to the family back in September if Virginia seceded from the Union. Would it benefit the business to sell their horses and cattle to the Commonwealth, or honor their contract with the government of the United States? He thought certainly, that the new Confederate government would need to equip the militia, and even the many men who would take up arms in the neighboring Southern States. In an attempt to come up with a logical solution he pondered on these issues. It would be one of the first matters that he would undertake with his arrival back home, and a chance to discuss it with his Mother and Brother. Quietly, the silence was broken with Caroline opening the door. As he turned to look, he spoke to her in a soft tone, "How is Ann?"

Caroline softly replied, "She is sleeping. It was fun for her to ride along the river trail on Crimson. Our daughter had a big day."

Quietly, she was observant of her husband's restlessness, and knew that it would be good for the two of them to take advantage of the quiet evening, and talk over the day's events. In her soft manner and tone, Caroline said, "Let us take advantage of this beautiful evening and sit on the balcony."

"I would like that very much."

As the two seated themselves on the bench that was provided, Caroline laid her head on his shoulder, and softy commented, "It is so peaceful and quiet out here. It is as if there is not a care in the world." She knew when her husband was troubled, and how to provoke him into conversation.

Charles answered in a serene tone of voice, "Yes, it is quiet. Just before you came into the room, I was standing at the door and looking out across the river, and enjoying the peace and quiet."

"I knew as soon as I walked through the door, and noticed the sorrowful expression on your face, that you were troubled. And I know what concerns you."

"My love, you know me too well. I have mixed feelings over the events that have taken place today. At first I was happy, and excited over the bombardment of Sumter, and still, I believe that it was the right thing to do. That has not changed. Personally, my greatest concern is over yours and Ann's welfare. And I must confess, I'm troubled over the future of the Estate, and the business. Back last summer, Mother and I, as we were on our way into town to meet William, had a discussion over who would have sole authority over the Estate in the future. At that time, she would not commit to a decision, but we agreed to wait and see if secession and war would pass. Now, with the firing on Sumter today, and the high probability of Virginia seceding, I fear that she will not turn over control to me."

Caroline lifted her head from his shoulder and glanced his way answering in a surprising voice, "You did not tell me about that discussion."

"No, I didn't. At the time since nothing came of it, I did not feel that it was important that you should know."

Caroline gently, but firmly requested, "Charles that's not so. Anything that happens concerning our relationship, or the business, I would like to know."

"I will agree to that. I am sorry for not including you. Though we do have another problem, since you would like to be kept informed."

"What is that?"

"If Virginia secedes from the Union, we have to decide what we will do concerning our contract with the government. Are we going to honor it, or not."

"Doesn't that depend on what takes place in the next few days?"

"Yes, that is true. I have been placing much thought on the matter, but I need to be sure of the best course of action. The profitability of the business, and the survival of the Estate are all that we have. So, I will have to act accordingly and use the best judgment."

Caroline looked at Charles, and a smile beamed across her face as she placed her hands upon his cheeks. Then, she passionately kissed him, and said, "I know that you will make the right decision."

With Caroline's statement, Charles held his wife confidently in his grasp, though he continued to ponder on what might take place, and how his family would be affected by the outbreak of war.

CHAPTER ELEVEN

Four days after the opening of hostilities against Fort Sumter, Charles was sitting on the front porch of his Aunt Daisy Burke's home on Grace Street, in Richmond. Charles, Caroline, and Ann arrived at the capitol of the Commonwealth earlier in the morning amidst excitement over the events that had taken place in South Carolina. With the streets filled with citizens of that great city discussing and debating over what the state should do concerning the business of secession, Charles was sure that the delegates that had been chosen to represent each of the counties would reconvene once again to take up this important issue and vote to secede from the Union. On the previous day, Lincoln had issued a call for 75,000 volunteers to suppress the rebellion. It was a demand that Governor Letcher refused to meet. Many of the citizens of this great state waited anxiously to see what would take place over the next few days, knowing that a decision would have to be made. The course of action, in which the convention decided on, would also possibly bare severe consequences.

As Charles anxiously awaited his sister's arrival from school, he began to walk across the huge porch. There was a smile on his face as he began to enjoy the spring warmth, and the mild breeze that was blowing across his face. The peaceful and quiet surroundings reminded him of home, where his life style was serene and familiar, which was what he was accustomed to. As Charles paused and noticed the dogwoods blooming, he chuckled at the sight of an old gray hound running and barking across the yard in its attempt to catch a white cat.

Finally, he thought of these events that life had finally returned to this area along the James River after a difficult winter.

Over the last few days, Charles' thoughts were upon the decision that the family was going to have to undertake concerning their commitment with the new government contract. They would have to terminate with the army, or negotiate a new one in favor of the Confederate government. On his arrival at the Estate, he would press the family to take up the matter, and reach a decision on which course of action would serve their best interest.

With the sound of horses slowly trotting down the street, Charles' thoughts were broken. As he stood with his hand against one of the white columns that supported the porch, he took notice, and saw the carriage that carried his sister. With the horses coming to a halt in front of the residence, a glowing smile brightened his somber face. As Charles stepped down from the porch to assist his sister from the carriage, Caroline, along with Ann came walking out the front door to greet Rebecca.

Rebecca Barker was an intelligent, sixteen-year-old student, who was studying at the Richmond Female Institute. As the breeze continued to blow mildly, she held tightly to her rose colored bonnet that covered her long chestnut hair. There was a radiating smile that revealed the joy of being united with her brother, and the rest of his family as she stepped from the black carriage. After helping, Charles embraced Rebecca and took his sister by the hand. Enthusiastically, Caroline and Ann greeted Rebecca with a smile and hug.

After entering the house, the family went into the parlor and was served refreshments by the main house servant. Without anytime to loose, Charles began to inquire respectfully of his sister's life away from the valley, "I was reading one of your correspondence that Mother had recently received. You were saying that some of the acquaintances that you have as friends do not have as great amount of respect for people that live in the lower part of the Valley, as you believe that they should. I felt to some extent after speaking with Mother, that this raises some problems for you?"

Rebecca answer the question swiftly and with pride and resentment, "Yes, that is so. But, I have discovered that they are a bunch of snobs. And, personally I do not care. They are so torn with jealously over our wealth, that all they can do is be petty about matters."

Caroline surprisingly asked as she placed the glass of water on the stand, "Is that so?"

"Yes it is. Lately I have had a gentleman that has been calling on me. I have found him to be very handsome, dashing, and he is an officer with the Richmond Grays. Wait until you meet him." Rebecca said laughing and continuing in a prideful tone, "I must say, that many of my so called friends, well, they would desire him for their own, but thus far, I have been successful in keeping him away from them."

Caroline replied in a serious voice, "Well then, it sounds like you show a great deal of pride in your conversations with your friends when you speak of him."

Rebecca said with a smirk beaming across her face, "Oh, yes I do. I have gone to great lengths to show those busy bodys that I possess greater intelligent then they do, and I can be friendly with their male friends at anytime."

Caroline replied with a tone of anger in her voice, "So, this gentleman who is calling on you was an acquaintance of a friend of yours. And, you intentionally broke up their relationship to prove a point."

Rebecca snapped with a flare of anger as she gazed at Caroline, "What point!"

"That you are just as good, if not better then she, and that is what this is all about?"

Rebecca continued to make her point with a devilish laugh, "Well maybe. Though, I am very good at what I am doing. Those busy bodys will think twice when I am finished with them."

Replying in a calmer tone, Caroline said, "Rebecca, having a relationship with someone is not all about using them to make a point and destroying other individuals in the process."

Rebecca's tone changed to sarcastic, "Caroline, there is nothing wrong with teaching someone the art of respecting you, even if an individual gets hurt. Maybe, they will reconsider their ways and think twice about how they treat you."

Charles shook his head and began to laugh saying, "You are just like Mother, to much pride and stubbornness. She will not let anyone pull the wool over her eyes."

As the family was speaking, the main servant re-entered the room, and made the announcement that dinner was ready to be served. As everyone was seated, Aunt Daisy merrily joined the family. While they were being served the tempting pork roast and potatoes, she asked joyfully of Charles, "How is James doing these days? I would have thought that he would have made time to come and spend a few days with me."

"Well Aunt Daisy, Pete has been very busy learning the operations of the business since finishing his studies. I have told him time and again that he should learn from me, and that he does not have to work like the slaves do, but you know my brother, he is stubborn and chooses to do so."

"I remember when my brother and Elizabeth were first married, and she had already inherited the property. It was his belief at that time that he had to prove his worth to her family. Oh, he labored long hours in order to make a success of the business, and he succeeded in doing so. I can see where James gets it from. Charles as you well know, there is no one who can take the place of your Father; but he is just like him."

Rebecca had been silent during this time, but curiosity had begun to take hold, she began to inquire into her brother's love life, and pleasantly she asked, "Who is the lucky lady this month in my brothers life?"

Charles began to jokingly answer his sister's question, "Well lets see."

Caroline politely interrupted with her serious and soothing tone, "I believe that Pete has found someone who he has become good friends with, and hopefully she will be able to settle him down."

"Oh, considering that he has broken every available heart in Jefferson County, who is the lucky lady?"

Caroline replied cautiously, but politely, "She is a very close friend of mine from Boston, Massachusetts. Her name is Katie McBride."

"An abolitionist!" Daisy exclaimed as she struck the table with her fist.

"No Aunt Daisy." Charles replied laughingly. "She is a very attractive and nice young lady. If Katie has any views concerning slavery, she keeps them to herself, as she should."

Aunt Daisy replied in a fervent tone as she moved her dinner dish to the side, "Well! I cannot see Elizabeth allowing this to continue. Furthermore, you can tell your brother that his friend is not welcome in my home. I just cannot believe this is happening to this family. It is people such as her that is starting this crisis throughout the country."

Suddenly, Isaac the main servant came into the dinning room to summon Charles on behalf of William Pierce, who just arrived in the city. Everyone had a look of amazement at the revelation of his unexpected appearance. Curiously excusing himself, Charles slowly arose from the table and proceeded toward the parlor where his friend was waiting.

As he entered the room, he noticed William anxiously pacing the floor. He knew that there was something of great importance that was taking place to bring him to the city this late in the day, and unannounced. Cautiously and curiously Charles began to inquire into the meaning of his visit, "William it is good to see you once more. But my friend, I must say, you look somewhat excited and anxious."

"Very much so. I have been sent for by Mr. Wise."

Charles walked over to the mahogany stand by the stone fireplace to pour some whisky into a glass. He offered William a drink, but he cordially declined. Charles slowly turned toward his friend and casually said, "It's not like you to turn down good liquor." Continuing to ask as he approached his friend, "Why has he summoned you to the city at this hour of the day?"

"Actually, it is you that they want to talk to."

"Why would Governor Wise and his associates want to talk to me?"

"I can not tell you that, though I will say, that they are going to meet at the Exchange Hotel later this evening. And, before they meet, Mr. Wise's representative would like to speak with you. That is all that I can tell you."

Immediately after the exchange of conversation, Charles left the room and went to speak with Caroline before departing with William.

It was a short ride down Main Street to the hotel. On their arrival Charles and William were escorted to a private room where Mr. Thompson, who was representing the former Governor was waiting. He was seated on a chair next to the window, gazing at the street below and deep in thought as the two men entered the room. After William introduced Charles, and some informal conversation took place, Mr. Thompson came to the point of the meeting, "Gentlemen, the reason that I have called you here is one of utmost importance, and must be kept secret. It does not leave this room under any circumstances. Later this evening there will be a select committee that will be meeting with the former governor, here at the hotel. The purpose of that meeting is to design the best and most practical way of seizing the armory and arsenal at Harpers Ferry using the state militia. What I need from you, gentleman, is to accompany the committee when it approaches Governor Letcher for his approval."

Charles was not surprise at the attempt to seize the weapons and equipment. For sometime, Charles believed that the machinery was of great importance, and that the Confederate government desired the opportunity to acquire it. Charles was interested in knowing how that he might play a beneficial role as he approached Mr. Thompson, "What is it that you require of our service?"

"I understand that you gentlemen helped to get the man elected."

William replied, "That is correct."

As Mr. Thompson was puffing on his cigar, he laughingly said, "Letcher is a moderate. He'll want to wait and see what happens with the convention when it meets tomorrow. We may need your help in convincing him the importance of seizing the weapons and machinery before the Federals confiscate the goods and ship it north, or send reinforcements. And you know what that means for Virginia. We have no time to waste we need to move now."

"You can count on us." Charles replied with a confident tone as he continued, "And, we will do our best in advising the committee that the Governor will see our way of thinking."

"Like I said, you helped to get him elected. Therefore, I guess he owes you a favor, right."

William smiled and said, "Yeah, he does. But he has strong convictions. And that might be the problem."

Thompson requested in his deep voice, "I would like for you to be in the hotel lobby in an hour."

Within the hour, Charles and William returned to the hotel as requested after having a beer at a local tavern. The three members of the committee headed by John Imboden of Staunton had been appointed to meet with Governor Letcher. After a brief discussion on the proper approach to the issue, the five of them departed.

Once they arrived at Governor Letcher home, the Governor greeted the visitors, especially Charles, who had spent considerable time campaigning throughout the Valley for his election. The plan on how to seize the government property was laid before him, which he opposed, calling it treasonous. For over an hour the meeting took place with William and Charles participating in the discussions. When the Governor seemed firm in his resolve, the meeting came to an end, and everyone departed once more for the hotel to meet with former Governor Wise, and to brief him on the results.

After their arrival, Mr. Wise, and the members of the committee began to plan the best means to capture the government property at Harpers Ferry, and the most effective way to receive the Governors approval. After the plans had been laid out for the seizure of the property, one of the gentlemen who was appointed to the committee asked, "How should we approach the Governor, he was totally against the idea earlier?"

After a brief period of silence, Charles spoke up, "Gentleman, I feel as most of you, that the state will vote to secede tomorrow, especially with Lincoln demanding that Virginia furnish its quota of troops to put down the rebellion. With that happening, the Governor will have to go along with your plan. Even he confesses that he is against Lincoln's idea. There is no other choice. I suggest that you have your plans in place to seize the goverment property at Harpers Ferry, and return to him this evening. Then, I would ask for permission to have the plan carried out as soon as the state votes the ordinance of secession. Though, I would have the state militia on the move and the railroad ready for transporting them. I believe that he will see the rationale of such action that this committee is undertaking, and will be in agreement."

Later the very same evening, the committee members along with Charles and William returned to speak with the Governor Letcher. After laying out the plans with its options and the probability of secession by the state from the Union, he was still hesitant to go along with their ideas. It wasn't until Charles and William intervene and began to contribute to the negotiations that Governor Letcher gave his approval for military readiness, but only to be used if the Ordinance of Secession was passed by the convention. The next morning, the committee members went to visit Charles and William and thank them for their contribution in their endeavor. That afternoon, the Virginia convention voted 88 to 55 in favor of secession from the Union.

At Shenandoah, Pete and Daniel were riding along the property that bordered the Charlestown Pike. For sometime now, Pete had wanted some of the dead underbrush and saplings removed between the road and the fence so that the cattle would not be in danger of becoming entangled. Daniel was cooperating with him, which was not his character. Since autumn, Daniel had been very observant of the closeness of the relationship between Pete, Charles, and his Mother. For now, Daniel felt that it would be in his best interest to go along with the rest of the family, even though he still had a resentment for the younger Barker, and would still betray him if given the chance.

As Daniel and Pete were slowly riding toward the direction of Harpers Ferry, they noticed Wesley Blair from the telegraph office riding toward them. As they brought their horses to a halt, the young man rode up and handed Pete a telegram from Charles, which simply said, "Virginia has voted to secede. Will be home day after tomorrow."

"I knew that they were a gonna split from those treasonous abolitionist. If they comes down here, we gonna give them the hell that they deserve."

Pete remained silent as he looked at Daniel. Pete smacked his horse on its hindquarter, and rode quickly to tell his Mother.

Riding at a fast gallop, Pete hurried down the long lane to the house and quickly dismounted the animal, and ran into the house. His Mother was seated in the library reading a biography of Martha Washington, who she admired. As Pete ran into the room, there was a puzzlingly expression covering his Mother's face as she looked above her glasses. With a concerned sound in her voice, she asked, "Pete, what is the matter. Why are you running in here, and out of breath?"

Still breathing at a rapid pace, Pete answered with excitement, "Mother! Mother! Virginia has voted to secede from the Union."

There was an expression of amazement that covered Elizabeth's face as she laid the book on a stand beside of the chair. She asked, "Where did you hear that news?"

"I received a telegram from Charles." Pete replied as he handed her the paper containing Charles message.

After digesting the news, Elizabeth jumped to her feet with excitement and joy. This was something that she had hoped would happen. As Pete stood there and his emotions became subdue, he began to wonder if this was the right decision for the Commonwealth to pursue. Now that Virginia had taken sides, it would certainly mean all out war. The thought consumed him about the family business, what should they do concerning the government contract, especially with a delivery of horses and cattle due at the end of the month? He was sure that this would be a priority once the excitement passed, and his brother returned home. It was time for him to collect his thoughts on the matter and be prepared when the time came to discuss the issue. Quietly Pete left his Mother alone, and departed from the room.

The very next evening, Thursday the 18th, Pete mounted Victory and rode in the direction of Smallwood's Ridge. It had been a long and hectic day assisting Doc Burns with birthing several new colts into the world. Now, with everything accomplished, he needed time to collect his thoughts concerning his feelings on the business. His Mother had departed late in the afternoon to celebrate an anniversary with the Russell's, and to spend the night with them. Katie had return to Boston to visit her parents and brother.

Riding slowly, Pete ascended the heights until he reached the crest along the Charlestown Pike. As he guided Victory through an opening in the fence and into the pasture along the road, he found an ideal area where he could be alone. The moon was full and beautiful as it shined brightly on the river between the mountains.

Suddenly, the silence was broken by the muffled sound of many feet marching in the direction where he was still admiring the heavenly display. Remounting his mare, Pete rode over to where the fence bordered the road, and observed the militia, that was several hundred in strength proceeding over the crest of the ridge toward the lower portion of town. Ever since the Brown raid almost two years ago, there had been a company of U.S. Regulars stationed in town to protect the government property. It must be the intention of the militia he thought, to attempt to seize this property, and use it for the benefit of the new Confederate government. As Pete pulled his watch from his pocket, the hands revealed that it was shortly after 10:00 p.m. The men that made up the state militia were fairly young, and marched in rank quietly. Manifested upon their face was a sense of pride that could not be hidden. Pete felt that there might be a confrontation between the militia and the soldiers, and that it would be for the best not to go any closer to town. As he rode back through the opening in the fence, he heard an exuberant voice call out to him, "Pete, come and join us. We are going to whip up on some Regulars!"

After taking notice to see where the voice had come from, he recognized Nathaniel Baker. Laughing, Pete casually replied, "No, I told you last week that I am not an infantryman."

Nathaniel enthusiastically replied as he held his sword in the air with his right hand, "But you will miss out on all of the fun. Don't you want to see them blue bellies run for their lives?"

"No, I will leave that up to you."

The young officer boasted as he continued to wave his weapon, "I will cut them to shreds with this sword, chasing the whole bunch across the Potomac."

Without any warning, the ground began to shake at the loud noise, which sounded like crashing thunder from a storm on a summer evening. Every eye was looking toward the direction of the Ferry, as the darkness of the night sky was broken by a red glow that arose from the direction of the lower area of town. One of the soldiers that was near shouted, "Fire along the river!"

Everyone present, including Pete knew that the soldiers in town were attempting to destroy the government property.

Immediately, Lt. Baker gave the order for his company to quicken their pace toward the Ferry. The militia wasted no time in complying with the request, and began to hurry toward the lower part of town where the arsenal buildings were located. This was too great of an event for Pete to return to the Estate, but out of curiosty, he followed the troops at a distance, and saw how great the destruction was that had taken place by the enormous blast. The first members of the militia arrived shortly to assist some citizens with extinguishing the fire. There was a desperate attempt by the citizen soldiers to save as many muskets as possible, but the fire was roaring out of control.

From the cliffs overlooking the lower area of town, Pete listened to the crackling of the fire burning the wooden interior of the structure, and watched as the militia and the townspeople attempted vigorously to save the buildings, and their equipment. He knew that the structures were lost and many of the weapons that had been recently manufactured were destroyed by the intense heat from the flames.

After briefly watching the destruction, Pete remounted his horse to return home. The continuous loud screams, shouts of orders, and cursing from the townspeople and militia below filled the air as they attempted to dowse the flames. He attempted to calm his horse, which had become nervous, but the structure within the masonry walls gave way with a loud crash, which caused the animal to stand on his hind two legs in greater fear. After getting his horse under control, Pete turned to look back once more, glancing at the burning buildings and then slowly rode away. With the events that had taken place this evening, Pete began to give considerable thought to his future, and as a Virginian what he would do next.

It was only a short journey back to the heights where the evening had begun. Tonight, the town had been touched with the first confrontation between the North and South in the lower Valley. What future misery, destruction, and uncertainty would take place next? It was beyond his imagination. He could not comprehend what the future would hold for his family, or even the townspeople. The one thing he was certain, that his life as he knew it had changed tonight. The winds of war had finally blown home.

CHAPTER TWELVE

True to his word in the telegram that he sent several days ago to his Mother, Charles and the family returned to Shenandoah. They arrived earlier in the day from Winchester. With his arrival, it was not a surprise for him to find the town full of militia after the state had voted the ordinance of secession. Since the destruction of the Federal arsenal on April the 18th, troops had been arriving every day from all over the state to help in the removal of valuable equipment used for making weapons from the U.S. Armory, and Hall's Rifle Works, and assuming the responsibilities of securing the lower valley. Since Harpers Ferry was the northern gateway to the Shenandoah Valley, and of great military importance, it was in the interest of the Confederate government to hold this area as long as possible, and have a sizable military force present to protect it from invasion from Federal forces.

As for the many citizens who lived in the village and countryside, they were still divided over their loyalties. Most of the townspeople who sympathized with the North maintained their silence, except for a few, and they experience the wrath of citizens loyal to the Southern cause. Many of the younger men from the area shared the same passion as their fellow Virginians, and were exuberant to enlist and fight for the Old Dominion. It was just as Charles had anticipated; the citizens of the Valley would support the Southern cause with enthusiasm once the Federal government placed demands upon them for troops.

Even though the town was full of excitement and doing a bustling business,

Shenandoah was quiet and peaceful, and life was as if hostilities had not come to pass. After his quiet arrival at the Estate, Charles spent the rest of the afternoon, along with Caroline quietly resting, and meditating on the discussion concerning the government contract that the family needed to engage in as soon as possible.

Pete and his Mother had departed earlier in the afternoon on important business at the bank in Charlestown. Elizabeth had recently discovered through a friend that the McDoogles had defaulted on their mortgage. After informing her youngest son of this good and unexpected news, they immediately decided that it would be in their best interest to purchase the one hundred additional acres of property adjacent and west of their Estate. This business transaction was something that Charles agreed to the day before after receiving a telegram from his brother.

Charles was looking out the window of his bedroom when the old wooden clock chimed five times. He noticed the carriage slowly proceeding down the lane. Grabbing his gray frock coat, he rushed down the long stairway to greet his Mother and brother. Caroline and Ann met him on the porch. Stepping down from the stone steps of the mansion, Charles assisted his Mother from the carriage and greeted her with a hug and kiss on the cheek. After shaking his brothers hand, the family entered the house, and proceeded to the parlor. They intended on discussing the events that had been taking place over the last several weeks.

After everyone was seated, except for Charles, Matthew came and offered refreshments to the members of the family who desired to partake. After taking a drink of the cold water that was served, Elizabeth began to notice Charles' restlessness. She sensed that there was something of importance on the mind of her older son, he seemed to be anxious, and the expression on his face reflected a man who was greatly troubled. It was her intentions to approach this matter without asking a direct question. Jovially, she began to inquire into Charles' trip to the capitol, "I assume that you were glad to see Rebecca, and your Aunt Daisy? How are they?"

As he stood by the window, and looked in the direction of the lane leading to the Charlestown pike, Charles politely replied in a muddled tone, "I was glad to see my sister happy, and doing well in school."

Elizabeth replied confidently, "Well then, I must assume from what you are telling me that she is doing good."

In Caroline's soft spoken manner, she said, "In her studies, Rebecca is doing good. It is in her social life with her friends that she is having problems."

Elizabeth expressed a tone of concern in her voice, "Oh dear, really!"

"Yes. It is Rebecca's feeling that the girls that she has become acquainted with do not respect her, because she is from the valley. Therefore, Rebecca has taken it on herself to jeopardize, and destroy some of those relationships that she has made by allowing some of their male companions to call on her in order to teach them a lesson."

As Charles walked over to where his brother had been quietly seated, he said sarcastically, "Well, I guess our sister gets that honestly from my younger brother?"

"Wait a minute." Pete replied laughingly, as he rose from the chair that he was sitting in, and followed Charles from the room.

An expression of concern covered Elizabeth's face. She did not know what the problem was with Charles, and he did not allow her the time to inquire. The subject needed to be pursued with Caroline, and discover the truth in detail. Before Elizabeth could ask, Caroline began to earnestly speak, "I must apologize for Charles. He hasn't been himself since the start of hostilities. After he celebrated with William on receiving the news of events in South Carolina, he has been quiet, and restless. I feel that it may be over the concern that he has regarding the business of the Estate, and a conversation that you and he had last summer, concerning your approval of him having sole oversight of the business."

Smiling, Elizabeth calmly replied, "Yes, we did. I told my son that until I knew what was going to happen with the election, and if there was going to be war, then I preferred to retain authority of Shenandoah. At the time Charles accepted my decision, though I knew he was disappointed. But now, with the outbreak of hostilities, and almost a year later, well," Pausing briefly, Elizabeth continued to finish her thought, "I am not so sure that I want to retain sole authority. There have been some changes that have taken place that I do not agree with, and therefore, I am about to make a decision based on those issues and the conflict that may be upon us. I would ask for now, that you would keep this between you and me, and that it goes no further." It was with that exchange that the two ladies ended their conversation.

Sometime later, the family was enjoying a dinner of roasted chicken and baked sweet potatoes served to them by Matthew. The main conversation on this evening that sparked the family's interest was Charles and Williams's effort in advising ex-Governor Wise and his committee on their approach to Governor Letcher concerning the capture of the government property in town. Elizabeth had been full of questions concerning the affair, but Pete just listen to the exchange of conversation like Caroline, and kept silent. After everyone finished, Elizabeth asked the family to join her in the parlor in an hour. She wanted to make an important announcement regarding the Estate. Naturally, Pete thought that she wanted to discuss the business, and what course of action that the family should pursue with the outbreak of war.

For now with not much to do, Pete walked around the pond and began to ponder on the issue. To him, it was a complex subject that would not have an easy answer. He knew that they wouldn't be able to declare themselves neutral in this whole affair. His mother and brother were clearly in favor of the course of action that the Old Dominion had taken. His ideas and feelings were mixed, though he wanted to contribute to the discussions and attempt to pursue the vision for the prosperity of Shenandoah. Many thoughts surfaced concerning his life. He didn't desire that any ideas should change his life. For the first time in many years, there was a comfortable feeling in his heart, though he was not sure if this could be attribute to the presence of Katie, or that his family finally trusted him. After a time of refection, Pete concluded that it was contentment with the family, and the role he had accepted.

As Pete returned to the house, he proceeded directly to the parlor as his Mother had requested earlier; everyone was quietly seated and waiting for her. The silence was so perfect; he knew everyone present was deep into his or her own thoughts on the matter. Pete felt that it would be inconsiderate of him to make the first comment, and would allow his Mother to begin the discussion once she was ready. He quietly took a seat next to Caroline near the window that overlooked the front of the house. As he was seated, there was an unobstructed view of the beautiful green pastures, and especially, the old hickory tree that he use to climb as a young boy. It all reminded him of the quiet afternoons that he spent with his Father. If this conflict should continue, would all that the family has worked for, and the beautiful tokens of past life that he viewed be destroyed and waste.

Pete's thoughts were broken with the arrival of his Mother. With a deep sigh, Elizabeth broke the silence and softy began to speak to her family with firmness and authority, "I have ask you all to join me this evening so that I could speak with you all on some important challenges that face us as a family. For over thirty years, I have been the sole owner of Shenandoah, except for my partnership with your father. During that time, we, as a family have established our self among the most prestigious members of this state in culture, and financial wealth. No one has been able to challenge our business in the present, nor will they in the future, if we continue to make the right decisions. I do not want to see our way of life come to an end, nor do I believe that anyone seated here does. There have been many issues that have brought about changes in this family over the last year. With the outbreak of hostilities, I feel that I have been confronted with a difficult decision concerning the government contract. I have asked myself the question continually, since the outbreak of war, as to what would be best for the survival of the business. I do not know, even as I sit here before you. The war has forced us to tread on new territory, which I believe will require new leadership and vision. Therefore, I feel that I can no longer remain in control of the Estate, and the business, simply because, I do not know what will take place. So, it is with considerable thought, that I have decided to relinquish my authority, and control of Shenandoah to Charles, who is the oldest, and in my opinion is the most responsible. Pete as for you and Rebecca, I feel that I have made the best decision based on the circumstances that are present, and what I feel is best for the survival of the Estate. I will make sure that the two of you are provided for. I would ask one final thing from you, and that is, I would like for you to respect my decision, and not allow animosity to rule your heart."

The announcement had taken everyone in the room by surprise, especially Pete, who was totally unprepared for the change of events. It was with great disappointment that he received the news.

Pete, slowly and quietly departed the room, and walked out on the front porch. He was still amazed at his Mother's decision, because it was always the intentions of both parents to pass down the Estate to him and his siblings. For some reason unknown to him, his Mother was not willing to honor the plan that his Father had proposed years ago when the children were still very young.

It was quiet, except for the jubilation that was taking place between Charles and Caroline in the parlor. Since they were married and had a family, Pete attempted to understand his Mothers intentions for acting so quickly, but for some reason, there was still a barrier between him and his family that could not be penetrated and he did not know why.

Shortly it was silent. The quietness of the night was a welcome sanctuary for Pete. As he sat in one of the wooden chairs on the front porch, he began to give thought to his future with the sudden change of events that had taken place. All of his life Pete believed that he had to compete with his older brother, and at the same time please his Mother. Everything that he attempted to accomplish for the business, and all of the effort that he put forth to make the Estate more profitable, now seemed to be a waste. What would he do next now that his life had suddenly and unexpectedly changed? His only options he thought, was to either enlist in the Confederate army and leave, or work for Charles. He knew that his pride would not allow him to work for Charles.

As Pete pondered on this decision, he noticed his brother walking across the porch in his direction. With his hands in the pockets of his trousers, and a prideful expression, Charles began to speak with Pete in a calm tone of voice, "I am sorry. I know how you must feel."

"No." Pete replied slowly, and continuing in a quiet muddle voice, "You can never know how I feel."

"Look, I did not expect Mother to make a decision so soon." Charles answered firmly and continuing with authority, "It caught me by surprise the same as it did you. But, you have to understand that it is for the best with the out break of war, and the importance that is involved with having to make the decision on honoring the government contract."

With promptness Pete jumped to his feet shouting, "Charles, it is not what Father wanted. I believe that Mother is under a great deal of pressure. But, I also think that she is afraid of what is going to happen!"

Charles replied defensively, "Then you have to understand that I am the one who is the most qualified to fill that void. Besides, nobody knows how to operate this Estate better then myself. I have been the one who has made it profitable, and secured our success, not you or anyone else."

"That is not necessarily so." Pete quickly replied in a fervent voice, "I have done my share of the work around here. It has been me, who labored in the fields, not you. If it were not for me out there with Daniel, he would have killed all of the bucks by now, as crazy as he is with them, and then where would the labor have come from?" Quickly continuing his verbal defense, "If I may ask you, would you have worked all day in the hot sun, such as myself?" After there was no reply from his brother, Pete angrily said, "No! I do not think so."

Charles became very frustrated, he angrily replied, "Like always, you are to much of a hot head! I can see that this conversation is not going to go anywhere!" Charles paused, speaking in a calmer tone, "Out of concern for you, I wanted to see how you were holding up with the news. Though I understand with the anger that I hear coming from you that you're not in a very good mood. For now we will drop this conversation, but I would like to continue it in the morning, and settle matters as soon as possible. I feel that it would be best to do so for the sake of the family, and especially Mother, so we can move on."

As Pete began walking toward the main entrance to the house, he quickly turned and replied, "I understand, we will settle it!"

The next morning bright and early, the family gathered together at the table to have their breakfast, except Pete, who had left during the night, and gone to the river to fish and think. As they were eating their meal, Elizabeth's curiosity was aroused concerning Charles and Pete's conversation. Charles told her what happen, she said, "Oh dear. I was afraid of this, he just doesn't understand what is at stake." Elizabeth continued after taking a deep sigh, "I couldn't help but to noticed that you went out onto the porch and spoke with him?"

Elizabeth noticed as did Caroline at the anger in Charles' voice as he answered the question, "I did."

As Elizabeth began to speak, her voice was shaking, but the words reflected her firmness, "For months I had given this issue great thought, and I knew that it would be a blow to him, and one that was certainly not intended. It was my feeling and belief that I was acting in the right manner for this family, and for the existence of the Estate. I believe that my Father knew when he left this property to me, that I would not loose it, or sell out to someone else. Even though Pete is blinded to the reality and truth of my decision, I know that someday he will understand my actions."

Charles spoke with the reassurance that his Mother needed to hear, "Pete really believed that one day, that he and I would both own the property. It was a shock to him, that just me, and only me, would become the sole owner. I feel that it will be sometime before he really understands the wisdom of your decision, but he is very forgiving."

"I know, but this time I think that it might be too much to ask."

As they were speaking, Pete walked into the dinning area where everyone was still having their breakfast. There was a sudden silence at his presence as he walked over to the server and quietly poured himself a cup of coffee. Quietly, Pete took his seat next to Ann. Everyone could tell by the lifeless, and tired expression that was covering his features, that he still felt very emotional over the decision. The opportunity was given to him to speak, but with his silence, Charles knew that he would have to be the first to initiate a calm discussion. It was not his intentions to continue the argument, so he spoke in an easy manner, "I suppose that you were along the river throughout the night?"

Pete replied as he looked across the table at his brother, "Yes I was there. Just me and my fire along the river."

As everyone was listening, Charles began to plead with his brother, "I don't, nor does anyone else want you to take this decision personal. Everyone here knows how much effort that you have put into the success of this business. I appreciate it as well as everyone else. I just wish that I could make you understand the importance of Mothers decision with the uncertain times that we live in."

Elizabeth began to earnestly speak to Pete with calmness, "Charles is right you know. We do not know what will take place within the next year, and how we will all be affected by it. My dear, it is my desire and hope that you will forgive me. But I must stand by my decision, and do what I feel is right."

After a moment of silence, Pete quietly stood up, and walked around the table with every eye on him, and calmly said, "Mother, I respect your decision, though I do not agree with it. As I thought about your actions throughout the night, I finally realized that I couldn't compete with Charles on equal terms. I know now, that everything that I did was done so that I could be accepted by you as an equal to my brother, and to please you. But some how I failed. I know that I will never be considered an equal with Charles, and I have tried, but I must accept that as truth. Furthermore, the most puzzling thing about this subject is, I don't know what I've done to anyone of you sitting here at this table." The silence from the family members continued as Pete paused, and walked to the server to refill his cup. As he turned about to face his family, Pete continued to pour out his emotions, "There was one continuous question which haunted my mind throughout the night, and that was, what should I do with my life, now that my brother will have the desire of his heart? I guess if I wanted, I could probably stay here and work for Charles, but it wouldn't be the same. Or, I could join the Confederate army. I just do not feel that I could be of any service to this family any longer if I stayed, so I have decided to enlist in the army and fight for Virginia, if that is what it takes to get away for awhile."

Elizabeth, as well as the rest of the family was speechless over this revelation.

Without another word spoken, Pete left the room saying, "I just have to get away for awhile."

As Pete was grabbing the saddle to prepare for his journey in to town, Hayward climbed down the wooden ladder from the hayloft. He knew the somber expression on Pete's face from past experiences. This time, rather then leave it alone, and not confront him, Hayward decided to address the feelings that he felt were being reflected from his expression. In a cautious, though compassionate tone, he said to his best friend, "I's may be treadin' on troubled groun', but I's know'd ya be upset dis mornin'."

There was not a comment, or word that came from the young Barkers mouth, only silence. Hayward's concern was evident; it penetrated deep into his heart, because it was not like Pete, not to share with him his feelings when he was troubled. Even though they were of a separated race, they always enjoyed a close relationship and built a mutual trust for each other. As Pete continued to prepare the horse, he remained silent. It was only when Pete was ready to ride into town that Hayward began to press the issue. In a louder, and concerned voice, he asked as he grabbed the horse's bridle, "Speak ta me, wat's de matter wit you'd dis mornin'?"

Pete demanded, "Hayward let go of the reins, now!"

Hayward stubbornly replied, "No, I's not goin' ta do it. Yose need ta talk, and I's not gonna let go til ya talk ta me."

After pausing and sighing, Pete shook his head and then looked Hayward in the eyes and said, "My time has come to fight for my state."

"Wat!" Hayward surprisingly answered, "Yose can't do dat. I's wont my people ta have de freedom, but not at de lost of life."

"You wanted to know, now you do. So let go of the horse."

With Pete's request, Hayward's eyes began to fill with tears. He stood back and released the animal and watched his friend depart in the direction of town.

As Pete was riding toward the road that led towards the Ferry, Charles came out of the house, and walked over to where Hayward was standing. As Charles approached Hayward, he turned to face him with his teary, glassy eyes being evident, and asked in an emotional tone, "Wat dis wrong? Why is he gonna fight? Dis not his war."

"You tell that to Mr. Lincoln. I have tried to talk to Pete, but he is able to make up his own mind." After a brief pause in the conversation, Charles continued in an authoritative tone, "Oh, the reason that I came out here was to inform you that you will be working for me from now on. As of last night, I am the owner of Shenandoah."

With that statement from Charles, Hayward understood why Pete was feeling the way he did, and was sure that joining the army was his way of manifesting his rebellion instead of fighting for the preservation of slavery. Still, Hayward was sad to see these events take place. His relationship with Pete was important to him, and he did not want to see it come to an end on some battlefield somewhere in Virginia, or anywhere else in the south.

Caroline and Katie agreed to meet in front of the jewelry store on High Street at 2:00 in the afternoon, to do some shopping. They had not had the opportunity to share each others company for almost a month, and it was today that they were going to spend sometime together, and catch up on personal matters. The weather was pleasant and sunny, and there was not a rain cloud in the perfect blue sky. The two ladies wearing colorful dresses, and bonnets to match their dresses, met as planned, and then entered the store. Caroline was looking for a gold tiepin to give Charles for his birthday, which was only a few days away. With her purchase, the two proceeded in the direction of Shenandoah Street to the dry goods store to see what merchandise had arrived earlier that day. As they were walking to their destination, they noticed the many troops that were marching along Potomac Street, in the area of the armory. Some of the officers were shouting instructions to the troops, who struggled with obedience. The ladies, with colorful parasol's shading their eyes from the sun, stopped for a moment and observed the drill of the troops. Some of the soldiers had new and colorful uniforms on, but most of them only wore a shirt and trousers that was used for everyday life on the farm, or their occupation. As Katie took notice of the sorrowful expression that covered her friends face, she asked in a concerned tone, "If I may ask, why are you so sorrowful today?"

Caroline replied with a halfhearted laugh, "It shows?"

Katie was wondering if Charles and Caroline were having marital problems again, and if so, she wanted to make an attempt and help her best friend, even if it was only listening. With a concerned sound in her voice, Katie said, "Yes it does. Do you want to go somewhere, and sit and talk."

Caroline knew that she needed to be honest with Katie, and be the one to break the news to her concerning the events that took place at the Estate yesterday evening. It would only be a matter of time before Katie found out, and she wanted to be with her when she received the news. As Caroline looked at

Katie, she hesitated in answering her question. She did not want to say anything that would damage their relationship, or jeopardize the trust that they had grown to know. There was an expression of anticipation on Katie's face, and after searching her heart for the proper words, she softly spoke, "Yes lets do sit for a moment."

As the two were seated on a wooden bench at the corner of High and Shenandoah Street, Caroline began to explain all that had taken place over the last few days, "There has been some changes that have taken place since we last saw each other. Even some that have taken me by surprise."

"Caroline, what is going on? Are you alright?"

"Yes, I am fine. Though, it is very difficult for me to find the words to share with you, but let me explain."

Katie said in a concerned tone of voice, "Please tell me what is bothering you? I want to help."

In an attempt to force a smile, Caroline calmly replied, "Yesterday, after our arrival from Richmond, Mother Elizabeth wanted to speak with the family. We were sure that she wanted to speak to us about the government contract. Charles and I knew with the outbreak of hostilities, that the family was going to have to decide whether we would honor our commitment, or break it. But knowing Mother Elizabeth, who can be unpredictable, she really surprised all of us."

Katie asked anxiously, "What did she do?"

"She believed that it would in the best interest of the family, and the survival of the Estate, if Charles was awarded ownership of Shenandoah."

"Oh God. How did Pete receive the news?"

"He became very upset. This morning, after spending the night along the river, he informed the family of his intentions to enlist in the new state army. I feel that this is going to divide the family. That is why, I guess, I had a sorrowful expression on my face."

There was a long silence as Caroline saw the fearful expression on Katie's face. When there were no words to be found upon her lips, Caroline broke the silence and said compassionately, "Maybe he just wanted time to himself, and think things over in detail."

Quickly, Katie jumped up from the bench and asked in a frightful tone, "Where do you think he might have gone?"

"I wish I knew. This whole situation worries me. At first when Mother Elizabeth shared her decision with us, I was happy, because this is what we have always hoped would happen, and that someday, we would pass the Estate on to Ann. But after lying awake all night, and seeing the damage that it accomplished between Pete and Charles, I know now that it was not worth it. Oh, how I wish that Mother Elizabeth had waited until this conflict was resolved. If only there could have been another way."

Katie fearfully replied, "I must find him."

Without another word, Katie departed company with Caroline, and began to search for Pete. After frantically searching the businesses along Shenandoah Street, she began to realize that her efforts were hopeless. Suddenly, the thought came to mind, that he might be along the river. Quickly, she proceeded down Bridge Street to the banks of the Shenandoah, and began to walk in the direction of Virginius Island. As Katie neared the island, she recognized Pete's horse. Finally, Katie recognized him along the riverbank leaning against a birch tree. She felt a period of relief. His feelings must be greatly bruised she thought, from all that he has endured over the last twenty-four hours. What would be the words of reassurance that she would speak, and how should she comfort him? Shenandoah had been his whole life. The expectations, and dreams of ownership that he shared with her over their acquaintance had been promising of a continual, and prosperous future for him. Now, with Charles the only owner, Katie could not imagine the disappointment and sorrow that he must be feeling.

With the crackling sound of Katie stepping on a dead tree branch, Pete turned to see who was approaching. Almost immediately, Katie noticed the somber expression on his face. It was as if all of the life had vanished from the jovial look that she had come to know. He took her by the hand, and helped her climb over a fallen limb, and then softly asked, "Why are you out here?"

"I wanted to fine you. Caroline told me of your Mothers decision to give Charles ownership of Shenandoah."

Sighing heavily, Pete calmly answered, "It was a surprise to everyone, but most of all me."

"Why did she make a decision now with the outbreak of war? Why could she have not waited to later?"

"I'm sure that the government contract was one issue. Mother said that she did not know if we should honor it or not. Katie, I have never known my Mother to be unequal to any challenge, nor back down from any one person. And, there was some other changes that had taken place over the past year that also influenced her decision to act now. She would not elaborate on the issue."

"Pete, what changes do you believe that she was referring to?"

"I feel that it mostly has to do with the stability of Charles and Caroline's marriage. Over the past year, there has always been the question with Mother over the survival of their relationship. In the South, it is important within the community, that you are properly bonded with your wife, and family, and that no blame can be found."

Katie confidently replied, "Pete, no one can find blame with you. Just because you are not married, and do not have a family, does not mean that you are not a person of good standing in the community. I feel that you are a gentleman, and I have felt comfortable, and not threaten with you."

"No Katie. You think that you know me, but you don't. I have had a wild streak that my brother, and Mother have resented. Remember last August, in front of the hotel. That is one example, and there have been more such incidents."

Katie replied compassionately as she gazed into his eyes, "I have noticed over the past year, that you have not engaged in such activity. I guess I have seen you in a different way then everyone else."

"Thank you." Pete answered in an appreciative tone as he continued, "I am glad that someone has noticed. But that does not take away the pain that I feel. Originally, Charles and I were supposed to inherit joint ownership of the Estate. That's why I was spending so much time, and working the long hours. I was attempting to make a contribution, and secure the trust of my family. Now, all of my labor was for nothing."

Katie replied in a sympathetic tone, "I am sorry. I do not know what I can do to relieve the hurt and pain that you feel."

There was a firmness and certainty in his voice, as he said, "At this point, there is nothing that you, or anyone else can do. As for myself, I have to get away for awhile."

Those last words that he spoke were like a knife slashing deep into her heart. With more and more soldiers from the South arriving daily, Katie was afraid that there was the chance that she would not see him again. That he might lose his life far away from home, and no one would ever know. In an excited tone, she asked, "I suppose you will join the army?"

With the softness of his voice, "Yes I did, earlier this morning." She began to repress her emotions. It was difficult for her to do so, without them being noticed. She pleaded, "Why go off and fight? You do not have to."

"As I said, I feel that I need to get away. Besides, with what little honor that I have with my family, I feel that I need to leave. I've lost my pride and my desire to stay."

Katie said, gently taking his arm, "Then I don't mean that much to you."

"It's not that."

"Please, I don't want you to go."

"Katie, I have to. I do not expect you to understand. Hopefully, someday you will."

After Pete had finished speaking, Katie wanted to share her deepest feelings with him, but she did not want him to feel under any kind of obligation to her. It was with that thought that the two of them stood there hand in hand, with their eyes gazing at each other reflecting the tenderness of the moment.

CHAPTER THIRTEEN

It was a quiet afternoon along the Potomac River, near Boteler's Ford in Shepherdstown. The wind was quiet, the sun shined brightly, and a flock of wrens crossed the river flying northward. The only sound that could be heard was the drilling of a woodpecker on a tree along a cliff overlooking the river. As Pete sat on his stallion, his eyes carefully scanned the Maryland shore for any sign of approaching Federal infantry. After his enlistment with the cavalry company from Shepherdstown, he had been assign to picket duty with the men from this area of the county. Quietly and out of sight behind some of the birch trees and underbrush that surrounded the area, Pete began to think about what his future might bring should he survive this conflict. It was always his desire to own his own business and to farm a piece of property; he was much like his Father. Because of Charles' personality, and their incompatibility, Pete knew that it was only a dream that they could ever share ownership of Shenandoah for any period of time. Shenandoah was some, if not the best pasture land and soil to grow crops in the county. As Pete continued to search his heart and mind on matters in his life, he began to dwell on Katie and what she might be doing today. Even though he found it difficult to have a relationship with her, or any lady at this time in his life, there was still a special place in his heart for her. He was thankful that she was a trusted friend, whom he could share confidence and that it did not require a love-relationship of him. Almost three weeks had past since they last spoke along the river.

The crackling sound of branches that lined the narrow path leading to this area of the river suddenly broke Pete's attention. He quickly pulled the revolver from his holster before he recognized who the rider was. It was John May from his unit. As John approached Pete on his horse, John said, "The Lieutenant would like to speak with you at his headquarters. I'm supposed to relieve you."

Pete curiously asked, "Do you know what he wants?"

John answered in his slow southern draw, "No, but hurry along. He doesn't like waiting."

Without another word, Pete departed and proceeded to Lieutenant Johnson's headquarters on German Street in town. As he rode up to the front door of the red brick two-story dwelling, Pete noticed the officer standing by the doorway. Dismounting and saluting, Pete was asked by Lieutenant Johnson to enter his headquarters. As they walked down a hallway and entered a small room, there was an officer who was seated behind a desk that Pete did not recognized. After Lieutenant Johnson introduced Major Robert Smith to Pete, he said, "As I understand from Mr. Hunter of Charlestown, you know the area and its roadways better then most of the residents of this county."

Pete answered quickly, "Yes sir, I do. My Father and I use to go hunting all the time when I was a child. I know the area very well."

"Good then. Because you come highly recommended. Colonel Stuart, who is the new commander of the cavalry in Harpers Ferry has requested your services, go and get your gear, we leave within the hour for Harpers Ferry."

Pete snapped to attention, and saluted with a reply, "Yes sir."

It was 3:30 p.m., in the afternoon as the two men departed town and rode at a gallop towards the Ferry. It was their intention to arrive before sunset.

Pete and Major Smith arrived at Colonel Stuart's headquarters in Bolivar, which is adjacent to Harpers Ferry, well ahead of their anticipated time. As the two men waited for the Colonel to return from the lower part of the Ferry, Pete told Major Smith about life in the area. The Major was from Hanover, Virginia, which is located just north of Richmond and had only been in Harpers Ferry a short time. The two soldiers waited for a short period of time. Colonel Stuart entered the large room where Pete and Major Johnson were patiently seated. After formal greetings and introductions, the Colonel came directly to the nature of his business, "Barker, as I understand you are very knowledgeable with the surrounding area, including the Maryland side of the Potomac."

Pete replied, "Yes sir, I am."

Colonel Stuart, later to be known by Pete and the citizens of the South as Jeb walked over and glanced out the window at a rider that was quickly approaching. Stuart turned about to give his full attention to Pete saying confidently as he began to point to his map lying on the table, "I have received information that Federal forces may be assembling and moving in this direction. I want you to proceed toward Middletown. From there use your discretion scouting along South Mountain, near Frederick. I want to know if there is a force to contend with, numbers of men and artillery. I want you to leave immediately." As Pete was walking out of the room, the Colonel smilingly called out, "Oh Barker! By the way, you need to dress in some civilian clothes and get rid of that uniform."

After Pete acknowledged his commander, he departed and began to carry out his orders. Immediately returning to camp and boiling some beef to eat along the way, Pete gathered his gear and changed into some black trousers and a plaid shirt for his disguise. It was close to dusk as he departed from camp where some of the cavalry from Clark County had been stationed. As he rode down High Street toward the covered bridge that would take him across the Potomac into Maryland, he began to think of the easiest and quickest route to accomplish the mission that had been given to him. Soon, Pete turned the corner of High and Shenandoah Street. He heard someone shouting his name. As he stopped and glanced over his shoulder, he saw Katie standing in front of the dry goods store. He paused and turned the animal in her direction. As he dismounted, he walked to where she was standing and gestured that they sit on a wooden bench. There was a warm and gentle smile that covered her face revealing the joy at being once more united with him. Katie said with a tone of excitement in her voice, "I did not expect to see you again so soon. I thought that you were in Shepherdstown."

As Pete removed the brown hat from his head, and wiped the perspiration from his forehead, he replied, "I was, but Colonel Stuart sent for me, and for now, I will be in this area."

Katie anxiously asked, "Then hopefully I will have the chance to see you."

Pete's reply was cautious and the tone in his voice was not optimistic, "Maybe, I do not know how long I will be in town. I understand that the Colonel has a reputation for keeping his men in the saddle."

There was a disappointment in Katie's voice as she replied, "I understand."

As Katie paused and searched for the right words to say, Pete began to speak earnestly, "I'm glad that I've had the opportunity to see you and that your doing well, and I am sorry if you feel that I don't have time to spend with you, but I do have to go. Please, stay safe, and leave town if there is trouble."

With that comment, Pete placed his hat on his head and tipped it in a friendly gesture and once more mounted his horse and departed. It was not like him to break off a conversation with someone in such a short manner. His conscious condemned him for doing so, but he knew that he needed to discourage Katie from any attempt in pursuing a relationship with him. It was still his sincere belief that she should return home where she would be safe. In his heart Pete believed that staying in Harpers Ferry would not be in her best interest because the town might be difficult to defend if Federal forces occupy the surrounding mountains and placed artillery on its summit.

After crossing the river, Pete turned his horse left onto the Harpers Ferry Road that ran parallel to the C & O Canal. By this time it was dark and he hoped he would not be noticed. The only light that was noticeable was coming from the homes in town across the river and some fires from pickets along the river. It was about a six-mile ride to the old Kennedy homestead, which was where John Brown, several years ago, had launched his raid on the Armory at Harpers Ferry. From this well-known farm, Pete crossed Elk Ridge Mountain by an old logging trail that he knew from Thomas Carey, a friend. Within the hour, he arrived at the deserted infamous farmhouse and paused to allow his horse to rest. While there that he was reminded what this conflict was about and the price that would be paid, unless there was a compromise. Hopefully, it would all end soon. Remounting and continuing toward the summit of the mountain, Pete paused briefly once more to allow his horse to rest while searching the valley below for any sign of campfires. With the satisfaction of his observations, Pete mounted his horse and was on his way once more. The trip across Pleasant Valley was less then an hour and promptly without pausing, he crossed over South Mountain, at Cramptons Gap in the vicinity of Burkettsville. Thus far his journey had been uneventful, not so much seeing one enemy soldier. Pete continued to ride slowly along the base of the mountain on an old farm road toward Middletown. It was a peaceful journey with the only sounds coming from an occasional bobcat crying, or a dog barking, as he neared a homestead. It was his intentions to avoid any contact with the local residents. His mind was consumed by thoughts concerning his family and the division that was between him and his brother, and the conduct that he had displayed a few hours earlier in town with Katie.

As he approached a western ridge near Middletown, Pete began to focus more intently on his mission. The moon was full and filled with the brightness of day, which enabled him a good view from his position. After a careful inspection of the area, Pete rode northwest of the village and across a ridge, and it was there that he looked for campfires burning in the direction of Frederick City. With no enemy troops to be found, he was convinced that his mission might have been a false alarm. It was about four in the morning and he decided that it would not be profitable to precede any further. It was time for Pete to return to Harpers Ferry by taking a different route.

After his arrival at Colonel Stuart's headquarters, Pete immediately informed him of the results of his mission and then returned to camp, where he slept for the next six hours. The next day he was sent out once more to scout the same area and to remain for several days. For many weeks thereafter, Pete was continuously employed to serve in this manner.

It had been a difficult month for Pete with the long hours that he had spent in the saddle scouting the southeastern portion of Washington County, and spending time training in warfare as a cavalryman. It was not a life style which he was accustom to, and the rigors and demands that were required of him, he had discovered, had been somewhat difficult for him to make the adjustment; he continued to challenge the different type of life. Colonel Stuart knowing that Pete lived in the area allowed him to be rotated out of his duties and given time to rest before assuming them once more. Pete, like many of the soldiers had experience some homesickness, and was anxious to see his family. He decided to return to Shenandoah before assuming his next assignment.

With his approach to the Estate, Pete once more experienced the serene and peaceful life that had meant so much to him before the war. Even though there was still unresolved differences with his family, there was an excitement and joy at being reunited with them, and especially seeing Ann? When Pete arrived, he was greeted by Hayward, who was walking toward the stables to tend to some of the horses. His friend recognized the rider on the stallion as Pete, and his expression was one of joy. Taking the reins of the animal as Pete dismounted, he said gladly, "Mr. Pete how's ya doin', I's glad to see ya."

"It's good to be back. Pausing to look about to see what changes had taken place during his short absences, he said, "You know Hayward, Shenandoah is the place that I have missed the most. It was always the place that I could call home. But that is all gone now."

Shortly, Charles came walking out the door to the back porch. With a cigar in one hand and a smile, he surprisingly said, "What an unexpected surprise. I thought that you were in Shepherdstown with the cavalry company on duty there."

"I was." Pete cordially replied as he continued, "But I was transferred here a little over a month ago at Colonel Stuart's request."

"Why didn't you inform us that you were in the Ferry?"

"I did not have the time. I have been busy with matters which I am not privileged to discuss." Pete replied as he continued to look around the homestead. Then he asked, "Where is Mother and the rest of the family?"

"Oh, Mother and Caroline went to Charlestown to visit the Whites. They should be home soon. Let's go into the house and catch up on what's been happening."

Without another word spoken, the two brothers entered the house and proceeded to the parlor. After a brief silence, Charles calmly said in a cautious tone, "How is army life?"

Pete replied in a less then enthusiastic tone, "It is difficult. Lousy food, long hours, and a life that takes getting use to."

A smile appeared on Charles' face as he spoke, "I'll tell you what. I will have Matthew bring you your meals while you're in town. That way it will make life more tolerable."

Pete replied in a loud and prideful tone of voice, "No, I do not need your help. It is something that I am going to have to get use to. Furthermore, I do not know how long we will be in the area, and I still have to get use to military life."

By this time, Charles was feeling somewhat frustrated as he continued to puff on his cigar. The tone in his voice reflected his feelings as he said, "Pete you do not have to be so loud. I am just trying to help."

After a period of silence, Charles calmly said; "I know that you still are very upset with Mother and me over her decision to give me ownership of the Estate. I can do nothing about it. It is something that you will have to learn to respect. As we both know, I have always been the one that she has trusted to make the best and most profitable decisions when it comes to the operations and acquisitions that we have acquire. Besides, no one ask you to run off and join."

Pete quickly interrupted his brother and in a loud tone of voice, "You do not understand." When suddenly, there was the sound of the front door closing, indicating that Caroline and his Mother had returned. Upon seeing Pete, Elizabeth embraced him and began to inquire into his life as a soldier; Caroline did likewise. He was especially glad to see Ann; she embraced him and refused to let him go. Immediately, Elizabeth summon Hayward and sent him to bring Mr. Lilly, who lived outside of town, to come and take an image of Pete wearing his new uniform.

After enjoying the tastiest meal in a month, Pete walked out onto the front lawn with the rest of the family as Mr. Lilly was setting up his equipment for taking the image that his Mother had requested. As Pete sat down on a chair in front of the house and posed, he noticed Ann intently watching and smiling. It gave Pete so much joy to see the glowing expression covering the width of her face. As he looked at his niece and smiled, Mr. Lilly took the image. That evening Pete spent time quietly with his Mother, never once expressing his feelings over his dissatisfaction concerning her decision with the Estate.

The next morning as Pete was departing the Estate, Caroline came walking out onto the porch with Ann. As he was about to mount his horse to return to camp, Caroline asked in a curious way, "Are you coming to the Ball tonight."

Pete answered in a surprisingly tone of voice, unaware that there were festivities being held, "Caroline, I did not know that there was going to be a dance. I haven't had much time other then soldiering."

"Oh, I am glad that I told you."

"Well then, I guess if I can arrange it, then I may see you and Charles."

Caroline asked in a pleading way, "Oh, please make the attempt. Who knows when we will all be together again?" Ann added in a cheerful tone, "Yes, Uncle Pete, please do?"

As Pete turned his horse toward the direction of the lane, he tipped his hat in a departing gesture, and said, "Like I said, I will make every attempt."

As Caroline and Ann waved good-bye to him, she knew through a recent conversation with Katie, that things did not go well between the couple during their last meeting. Even though Katie had not expressed her deepest feelings for him to her, Caroline knew from the times that Katie and Pete had been together in her presence, how Katie's eyes would light up at his presence, and the beautiful glow that would radiate from her face. If at all possible, she would not allow the conflict to come between the couple, and would do everything in her power to keep the interest alive. Knowing that Katie would be at the Ball tonight, hopefully, she thought, Pete would attend and the flame that she believed existed would continue to be nurtured.

During the afternoon, Pete spent sometime thinking about attending the

Ball. His visit to Shenandoah had not been enjoyable, and was not what he had expected of a furlough. Pete knew that Charles would be present and making every attempt to look for a political advantage that would feed his pride and his demand for power and authority. It did not cross his mind that Katie would attend, since he had not asked to be her escort.

That evening, Pete decided that he would attend the Ball after all, and not allow his differences between him and his brother spoil a chance at having some fun. As he walked through the door of Carrell Hall, the same string ensemble that his family had employed last summer was performing the music. Pete glanced about the huge dance hall looking for Charles and Caroline, and taking notice who else might be attending. Glancing about, he noticed his brother sitting at a table next to the dance floor near the orchestra. As he approached the couple and sat down and began to talk, he noticed Katie approaching the table without an escort. Since the last time that they had spoken to each other, the guilt that he felt after being less then a gentleman had continued to torment him, and it increased dramatically with her presence. In an attempt to assume the responsibility that was expected of him by his brother and Caroline, he rose to his feet, and held the chair for her while she was being seated. Most of the conversation was between the two ladies, with Pete and Charles speaking to those male acquaintances that approached the table. This took place for quite some time. After Pete had invited Katie to dance a waltz, she excused herself while he signed her dance card, and walked toward the front door. The two had said very little in the way of conversation all evening, except for Pete's apology for being less then polite in front of the dry goods store. With a sigh, Pete shortly followed Katie. He found her standing and looking in the direction of the Potomac River and mountain. The night promised all the ingredients for romance, with a full moon that shined brightly and a clear star filled sky. As he approached Katie, she turned to face him, and quietly, there was a smile that covered her expression. Calmly Pete marveled at the beautiful scene that was being displayed by the instruments of the universe, as he said, "It is a beautiful night. One could not ask for more."

"Katie softly replied, "Yes it is. I wanted to come out here and enjoy some of the fresh air and the picture of beauty that the moon is providing this evening."

"One could not ask for a more romantic setting." Pete said as he continued to admire the moon's majestic reflection shining from the surface of the river through Solomon's Gap."

Katie answered him in a peaceful tone, "I have never witnessed anything quite so beautiful."

"If I may ask?" He said stumbling over his words, "Have you ever had a relationship with someone. I mean a special person."

"I was wondering when you were going to ask me that question." Katie said as the smile continued to glow brightly on her face, "Back when I was living in Boston, about four years ago, I had a serious relationship with a doctor that I loved. One day as he was riding one of his Arabians, a snake spooked the horse. He had an accident, and died within days. I grieved for sometime after his death. If he had lived, I would have been married to him by now. You would have never made my acquaintance."

Pete replied with a sympathetic voice, "I am sorry for your lost. Though I am glad that I did make your acquaintance."

After a moment of silence, Katie wanted to continue the conversation, "May I ask the same of you?"

Pete was quiet, and thought of how he could quickly ignore the request, but he knew that she had been honest with him, though trapping him in the process through his question. It was his intention not to appear vulnerable, even though he had not engaged in a serious commitment. He replied as boldly as he could under the circumstances, "I have never had a serious relationship with a lady."

"Why not?" Katie surprisingly asked as she continued with a subtle smile, "I would have felt by now, that there would have been someone who you could have loved in your life."

As Pete turned and looked at the tenderness that Katie's eyes revealed, he softly replied, "My life has always been too troubled and complex for a commitment."

Katie looked into his eyes, and the expression on his face, she felt that he was threaten, "No Pete, its fear."

Quickly interrupting her, Pete defensively replied, "Katie."

A more serious expression was covering her features. She interrupted, and said, "Love is a risk that you have to be willing to take. I did, and I lost someone, but I learned how to deal with the lost, and go on with my life. As for yourself, you are afraid to love someone. You do not know how precious a gift that it can be until you experience it for yourself. True love comes only once in a lifetime."

Before Pete could answer, Charles and Caroline walked out of the hall toward the couple. After a brief conversation between the two couples, a courier from General Johnston's headquarters came riding to the dance hall. With haste, the courier informed the officers that were present, as well as the soldiers, that the evacuation of the town would take place tomorrow, and they were ordered to return to camp immediately to prepare for their departure. Charles anxiously prodded the courier for more information, but received very little. There was an air of excitement among the townspeople that were in attendance and soldiers because they did not know if the enemy was advancing and a battle forth coming. Fear ruled many facial expressions as the inhabitance of the town departed to prepare for the uncertainty. Charles and Caroline were talking about the possibilities of such action, when Pete asked Katie for a moment of privacy. Taking Katie by the hand, he suggested that he escort her to her residence. Pete believed that the time had come to ask her to return home, something that he had determined to do if hostilities continued, and it seemed it was happening. As they were walking in the direction of the boarding house, Pete said with a determination in his voice, "With the departure of the army tomorrow, I am not sure what this means for the town. I feel that Union infantry will be arriving soon."

"Pete I will be alright." Katie replied in a reassuring voice as she smiled once more.

"Katie." He boldly said, "Maybe it would be best for you to return to Boston until the war is over. I can't help but feel that it would ease the mind of your family if you were at home with them and out of harms way."

"Or would it ease your mind?" Katie bluntly replied. "I will not return home. I have an obligation to the school and the children that attend, and I intend on fulfilling my duties."

"Yes it would make it easier on me. Who knows what kind of men are in the ranks and what they are capable of doing."

"I assure you that I'm able to take care of myself. Don't worry."

"Then promise me that you'll go to Shenandoah if you need to, at least until they leave the area."

"Remember, I'm a big girl, I can look out for myself."

Frustrated with her stubbornness and her answer to his request, Pete said his good-byes and returned to camp.

Katie was somewhat upset over this turn of events in their life. It appeared as if everything was not going to work out as she had hoped. There was a change that she had been noticing in his personality and attitude toward her, and now she feared that their friendship was in jeopardy.

After a restless night and very little sleep, Katie awakened early the next morning and decided to visit the Confederate camp where she knew Pete was staying. There was an anxiety about the thought, because she did not want him to feel an obligation toward her, nor did she want to threaten him in anyway. In her determination, Katie quickly dressed, and rented a buggy and horse from the stable down the street. Without wasting a minute, she quickly proceeded toward the camp and arrived just as many of the soldiers were dismantling their tents and packing their wagons for the departure from town. After searching the camp area and asking some of the troopers, she finally found Pete saddling his horse. Katie was not sure how she would approach him, but she needed to know in her heart that he would take their friendship with him, and that she would not be forgotten.

As Pete turned and glanced over his left shoulder, he saw Katie approaching. Quietly, she stood facing him. There was a silence as they looked sadly into each other's eyes. Pete calmly asked, "Why did you come here?"

Katie sadly replied as she approached closer, "I wanted to say good-bye to you. After you walked me home last night, I felt that you were upset with me. I just could not allow you to leave today without making an attempt to rectify the situation. I was so angry with myself that I could not sleep." Pausing and continuing in a somber tone, "And, I wanted to see you before you departed."

"I understand. I guess I should not be meddling in your affairs." There was a moment of silence as Pete continued to prepare for his departure by tightening the saddle straps of his horse. He turned about once more with his eyes fixed on Katie continuing, "It was only my intentions for you to be aware of the danger which you may incur with the town in Union possession. It will not be safe. As I understand, Union forces have crossed the Potomac near Williamsport, and we are ordered to fall back toward Winchester. It will be there, that I will be able to report to Colonel Stuart for duty."

There conversation was interrupted by a loud explosion taking place in the direction of the railroad depot. Frighten with the unexpected noise, Katie screamed and quickly embraced Pete. As he held her tightly, she remained silent. As she looked at him, their eyes met once more, the sadness of their hearts was revealed, and they knew that their separation was impending. Words were difficult to express, though she prayed that her actions would give him a revelation of her heart. Impulsively, Katie placed her hand upon his cheek and caressing, she passionately kissed him on his lips. Slowly, she broke their embrace, and sorrowfully turned and walked toward the buggy. Pete knew that she was crying as he watched her take a handkerchief and wiped the tears from her eyes.

CHAPTER FOURTEEN

A month had passed since Pete returned to duty with Colonel Stuart near Winchester. He had been vigorously engaged in a program of training in cavalry tactics, and when called upon, scouting along the Potomac. During the minor skirmish near Falling Waters on the 2nd of July, he did not participate, but instead, continued observation activities along the Virginia side of the river until the Confederate cavalry and the rest of the army under General Johnston pulled back closer to Winchester. After Federal forces advanced to Darksville, a little more then ten miles from the Confederate army, they suddenly withdrew to Charlestown. With this maneuvering of forces, Pete was assigned to observe their movements and to report to Colonel Stuart if there was any change toward Winchester.

After being rotated from duty near Charlestown, Pete rode into the cavalry camp on the outskirts of Winchester City. It had been a humid afternoon, and the perspiration continued to cover his fair complexion. As he entered the camp, he noticed some of the men casually stretched out on their blankets playing a friendly game of poker and making merry conversation. It had been several days since Pete had eaten a hot meal and it was difficult for him to resist the smell of fresh beef that had been prepared by the servants, who had followed to attend to their masters needs. He could hear in the distance the beautiful sound of the Yellow Rose Of Texas being played on the banjo by a corporal from one of the units in the upper Valley. Pete began to smile because it reminded him of the many times that Hayward would sit in the stables, or along the river and play and sing many of his favorite selections. In another area of the camp, soldiers gathered about several regimental standards laughing loudly, attracting Pete's attention. He had been told several days before that Lester's company had arrived from Richmond, and would become part of the 1st Virginia Cavalry. As Pete came closer to the area where he believed that his cousin was camped, he noticed some of the men from the Washington Mounted Infantry mingling about in conversation and smoking their pipes. After inquiring into where his cousin might be, Pete proceeded in the direction, finding the area blessed with many trees for shade. As Pete glanced around the camp, he saw Lester sitting on a wooden crate speaking with another trooper.

Without wasting time, Pete approached and dismounted, Lester recognized his cousin from Jefferson County, and quickly jumped from his seat, and embraced him. Lester's hazel eyes revealed the joy at being united with Pete once again. As Pete observed him, he noticed that his cousin had not changed much in his appearance, though he still wore a shabby mustache and beard to cover the scars that covered his face from an attempt to master a horse that was pulling a buggy for a young lady. The animal had been frightened by a pack of wild dogs that made various attempts of attack. In a jovial tone, Lester said, "Cousin Pete. How are you?"

"Lester, it is good to see you once more."

"How are Aunt Elizabeth, Charles and the rest of the family doing?"

For now, Pete repressed his feelings of sorrow and frustration over family issues and answered, "Oh, everyone is doing well."

In a joking way, Lester replied, "I don't believe that for one moment. I know you well enough to know when things are not right. Now, what is going on back at Shenandoah?"

"Lester, I guess I still haven't gotten over the shock of my Mother turning the property over to Charles."

"Oh no, this can't be true. I never thought that she would part with the Estate." Lester replied disappointingly and continuing in a sympathetic tone, "You know your Mother always did favor him."

"True. But there is nothing that I can do to change matters."

"Well, that's no reason to join the army"

"Yeah I know. I guess I just needed to get away. Besides, I don't want the good people of Harpers Ferry to think that I'm some kind of a coward either."

Sitting with Lester and sharing some of the cheese and crackers was a slender individual, who appeared to be of small statue. As the young soldier overheard the conversation that was taking place between the two cousins, he stood and walked over and with a smile, he introduced himself, "Hi, my name is Mosby."

Lester quickly apologized for neglecting to introduce his friend to Pete, "Oh, I am sorry, bad manners I guess. Pete, I would like for you to meet a friend of mine that I have known for sometime, John Mosby."

Pete cordially replied as he shook the soldiers hand, "Pete Barker."

Mosby curiously replied, "Lester has told me a great deal about you. We were hoping to see you before now, but I understand that you have been scouting and watching the enemies' movements.

Pete confidently replied as he slowly ate the cheese and crackers, "Yeah, they are out there, but cautious. They seem to be content with protecting their supply lines and not desiring a good fight."

Mosby asked as he took his cup of coffee and began to take a sip, "As I understand from Lester, your family owns quite a spread near Harpers Ferry?"

"Well as you may have overheard, my brother owns the property now." Pete said with sadness in his voice, though he continued in an optimistic tone, "For now, until I figure out what I should do with my life." Pausing and nodding his head in pride, he said in confidence, "I will lend my services to the army."

"That a boy." Lester replied laughingly as he jokingly slapped his cousin on the arm.

Mosby said in an inquiring tone of voice, "Lester was telling me just yesterday, that you are very skillful at hunting and tracking."

Pete began to reminisce about a special time in his life with his Father, "I have done my fair share of hunting with my Father, who taught me. He began by teaching me how to track deer, and then bobcat." He continued in a subdued tone, "I still remember the day when he felt that I was confident enough in this skill. It was on a bright and sunny morning during the fall. Without any warning, he had me track him with only giving him an hour's start. From our property, across the Shenandoah, and over the mountain to a place called Loudoun Heights, that overlooks the town of Harpers Ferry, I slowly followed his trail. At times it was difficult because he engineered the disguise of his tracks so well. But in the end, there he was, sitting on a rock overlooking the river when I arrived."

As Pete spoke with Mosby and Lester, they were attracted by the clanging sound of sabers. It was coming from the direction where six members of the mounted infantry were walking in their direction and talking about possible orders to move in support of the Confederate army under General Beauregard at Manassas. Filled with anticipation, Pete and his companions approached the troopers asking about the rumor. Within minutes, an officer who noticed many of the men that had by now gathered quickly verified it. As the news quickly spread throughout the camp, there was a stir of excitement as many of the men cheered in unison for a fight with the Northern soldiers. Most Southerners believed that the war would come to a quick end with the Union army defeated and demoralized, and that they would all be able to return home as conquerors and heroes. With the great confidence that was displayed by the men, even Pete began to feel increasingly bold in the Southern ability and determination to quickly bring an end to the conflict.

Later that afternoon, the 1st Virginia received their orders that they were chosen to screen the movement of the forces under General Johnston. It was the Confederate army's intentions to elude the Federal forces under General Patterson and escape to Manassas.

For over the next twenty-four hours, the men of the 1st Virginia Cavalry found themselves in the saddle carrying out orders, protecting Johnston's movements and eventually heading for Manassas to assist General Beauregard's army along a creek called Bull Run. Pete found the route to Piedmont Station to be somewhat difficult with the roads congested with soldiers, artillery pieces, and supply wagons. In an attempt to avoid the congestion by the main body of troops, Colonel Stuart commanded the cavalry to cross the fields that ran adjacent to the road in order to avoid injury to the infantryman who might be sleeping in their path from the exhaustion of marching at a quick rate.

With the cavalry's arrival at Manassas, the 1st was instructed to bivouac near Bull Run Creek not far from a stone bridge. Most of the soldiers were hungry and weary from their ordeal. After receiving plenty to eat, many of the exhausted troopers laid their blankets on the green pastures, and fell asleep.

The next morning, Sunday, the 21st of July, near sunrise, the sound of musketry and artillery firing in the distance signaled movement by the Union forces. Pete along with everyone else in the 1st had been awakened by the sound of the weapons and officers of the regiment shouting for all to arise. Rubbing his eyes, Pete heard the bugler sound assembly as he quickly jumped to his feet with the realization of what the noise and the commotion proclaimed. As he was saddling his horse for the short trip toward the area where Colonel Stuart bivouac the previous evening, he heard one of the privates from the regiment enthusiastically proclaim, "If we will put those Yanks to death, they'll think twice before coming to old Virginey again."

His comrade added, "Yeah, we'll teach them a lesson they'll never forget."

Moving with haste, Pete approached the camp and noticed that the Colonel and a detachment where preparing to depart. The camp was full of excitement and confusion when Pete rode up to his commanding officer. The Colonel spoke with a flare of excitement in his voice as he grabbed the reins of Pete's horse, "Barker, I want you to go along with the scouting party across the creek and attempt to locate the enemies position. I want you to make every attempt to stay out of sight and report back to me directly."

Pete acknowledged as he saluted, "Yes sir."

The adrenaline was flowing like a river and the enthusiasm for battle was rapidly taking place in Pete's mind. Amidst all the drama, Pete quickly proceeded to carry out his commanding officers request, along with another scout that had been assigned to do likewise. The two men crossed Bull Run Creek and rode with haste toward the sound of the firing of weapons. After reaching the ridge, the two scouts stopped. Pete dismounted from his horse and the second scout did likewise. Approaching the summit alone, Pete was cautious to stay out of sight. As inconspicuous as possible, he gestured to the other scout that it was safe to join him. Soon, they noticed in the woods to their front the enemy's sentries. After watching the Yankees for sometime to determine their intentions, the other scout spoke with a joy in his voice, "Oh, I thought before we shoot at those fellows over there, that I might as well introduce myself. I'm Jonathan, Jonathan Collins."

As the two were lying on the ground, out of sight from the enemy, Pete turned and looked at him. He was amazed and could not understand how anyone could have a jovial expression that dominated his facial features, when he was about to enter into the madness of battle. But it was true; Jonathan's piercing blue eyes radiated a calm and confidence that Pete could not understand for this kind of deadly work. After hesitating, he replied, "Pete Barker."

"Where ya from Pete?" Jonathan curiously asked as he spit some of the tobacco juice from his mouth.

"I'm from Harpers Ferry." Pete answered as he noticed the continuous smile covering Jonathan's face that was beginning to annoy him.

As Jonathan wiped the tobacco residue from his mouth, he said, "I'm from Highland County. Ya probably don't know where that's at."

Pete answered rudely, "Shut up, we have work to do. If you continue talking, you might get us shot at by those Yankees."

Jonathan remained silent and just smiled and removed his black hat, brushing aside his long sandy brown hair. It wasn't ten minutes later when an officer from the scouting detachment joined the two Confederates. Both Jonathan and Pete contemplated taking a shot at the Union soldiers before departing, but were ordered by the officer not to expose their position along the ridge. After being ordered by the Lieutenant to return to Colonel Stuart with the information on the enemy position, the reconnaissance party returned back across the Bull Run, and Colonel Stuart reported their findings to General Johnston.

Sometime had past and the 1st had not been involved in the fighting. The regiment could hear the noise of cannon and musketry taking place to the west of their position near the Warrenton Turnpike. The sound of battle continued to grow closer as every man in the unit began to experience some anxiety at the possible chance of seeing action. It had been difficult to see what was taking place from the woods in the unit's front. Colonel Stuart had been restless since the first sound of action had commenced, even to the point that couriers had been dispatched to inquire of the cavalry's possible service in the Confederate effort.

It was close to 1:00 in the afternoon., and the regiment still had not been called into action. Colonel Stuart had summoned Pete to report to the area where he was waiting. As Pete rapidly rode toward the area where he could locate his commanding officer, a shell exploded near by discharging its shrapnel in every direction. Without breaking a stride, his horse was not affected by the concussion from the blast as he continued toward headquarters. With his arrival, Pete noticed Colonel Stuart pacing and speaking with some of his staff officers. As the young Barker was about to dismount, the Colonel quickly commanded, "Find General Johnston and tell him my cavalry is ready for a fight and where should we come into the action."

After Pete acknowledged Stuart, he slapped his horse on its hindquarter and proceeded in the direction of the firing. At times, the smoke impaired his vision with the heavy clouds that covered the field. Pete was sure that he would be able to find the General Johnston in the area of the field where the most intense fighting was taking place. As he approached the pasture near the backside of Henry's Hill, he received his first experience of the heavy fighting that covered the region. Before his eyes, he witnessed an area where many of the soldiers had fallen in rank that had once stood proudly in a line of battle. Laying on the green pastureland in their new uniforms of various colors saturated with blood, both blue and gray rested. The warriors had fallen in battle believing that they had sacrificed their lives for a glorious cause, and that their life had not been given in vain. Many appeared to Pete to be sleeping peacefully and it seemed that they would awaken at any moment, rather than the eternal rest that comes with death. One brave Southern comrade in particular caught Pete's attention. He was lying prostrated with his left hand gripping the field grass. Pete knew that his death wasn't without anguish and great pain. Already, the scene along the battlefield was more horrible then what Pete had imagined. As he temporarily halted, Pete looked down on the ground nearby and witnessed men crying from wounds that they had received, especially a young boy to be no more then sixteen in age was suffering from an abdominal wound caused by canister fired from an artillery piece. Some of the wounded, one elderly soldier in particular captured Pete's attention cried, "Please someone, give me a drink of water." A soldier that was attached to the Medical Corps graciously met his need. Pete was stunned as he continued to glance about the many soldiers, both blue and gray that covered the field. He was touched with their suffering from the horrifying gashly wounds to their body, and the agony it caused. The echo of their cries for the mercy of death to relieve them of their tribulation was unbearable. Although, Pete knew on this hot and humid historical day that he could not tarry, and needed to carry out his orders, even though he wanted to render assistance to the helpless. It was easy for him to be confused by all of the different colored uniforms that both the Northern and Southern regiments wore for this battle. As Pete approached some of the regiments and officers along the battle line firing their muskets, the only sign of enemy or friend he discovered was the flag that the unit displayed. Pete knew it could be very hectic, or even costly at times if he did not exercise caution. There were no intentions, he thought, of becoming a prisoner of war so soon in the conflict. The smoke from the massive cannon and musket fire blinded him at times as he attempted to look for General Johnston's headquarters flag that a member of his staff would have been carrying as they rode across different portions of the field while directing the battle.

Once Pete was told of General Johnston's whereabouts from an officer of a Virginia regiment, Pete rode with haste about a mile southeast of their position to Portico, the Lewis house. When he arrived, Pete saw the headquarters flag in front of the white frame dwelling and knew that the General was present. As he dismounted from his horse, Pete asked an officer who stood near by shouting orders to some of the couriers, "Sir I am Private Barker, 1st Virginia Cavalry. Colonel Stuart is requesting orders from the commanding General where he should enter the engagement."

The officer asked Pete to wait while he made the inquiry from the General. Pete walked over to a tree and placed the canteen to his mouth and began to drink the warm water. The wet drops felt good on his dry lips, washing away the dust that had been stirred up from all the activity. His dusty uniform was wet with perspiration as he listened to the battle rage on in the direction of Henry's Hill from where he had just been; the battle seemed to be at a stand still. For now, the Confederate forces where holding the hill and plateau.

After what seemed an eternity, the Captain returned and said, "The General informed me that the orders have already been given to Colonel Stuart. A courier sent from General Beauregard dispatched them. But I will repeat them in case that courier didn't get through. Tell Stuart that he should enter where the fighting is the hottest."

"Yes sir." Pete answered anxiously as he quickly departed to rejoin his regiment.

As he was riding in the area of the battlefield where there was some woodland, Pete noticed the Colonel riding at the head of the column of troops. Stuart gestured for him to join the unit and Pete fell in with the Loudoun Company. The smoke by this time was so thick, that it made the visibility on the field very difficult for the cavalrymen to see. Pete noticed that they were on the left flank of the Confederate battle line near a North Carolina regiment of infantry. One of the members of the Loudoun Company began to say laughingly at a young comrade, "We gonna give dem Yankees what for and return home heroes and have our pick of the ladies. Ain't we boy?" Many of the men agreed heartily and began to laugh, though Pete had heard similar statements over the last couple of days, and believed that most of the troopers where caught up in the romance of war. Although, some of the men didn't share the same enthusiasm as their comrades, they kept their thoughts hidden within their heart. A certain number of cavalrymen became so emotional over the pending combat that they emptied the contents of their stomach over the animals they sat upon and themselves, knowing soon they would have their first real baptism of conflict.

As the 1st emerged from the woods, the heavy cloud of white smoke from the firing of weapons began to lift with a mild breeze. Pete watched with excitement as Colonel Stuart observed a regiment of Zouaves dressed in blue jackets and red trousers moving along the dusty Sudley Road. Pete noticed the excitement and anticipation that covered the Colonels face. The brightness of his eyes and the adrenaline that flowed from his behavior told the story that an attack was eminent. It was with Pete's observation that he noticed the prideful and excited expression on many of his comrades' faces, though there were some of the soldiers that expressed in words an uncertainty of their fate in this engagement. One of the troopers who was impatient was within earshot of Pete saying as he stroked the neck of his horse, "Come on dang it, lets go and get the killin' over with."

As the Colonel led the men through a gap in a fence, the wind blew once more clearing away more of the smoke from the field. After carefully observing the Zouaves in an attempt to determine there identity, the Colonel noticed the stars and stripes after the unit emerged from a cut in the road. The enemy was less then one hundred yards away. The bold and flamboyant Stuart moved to the front of the 1st, and ordered the troops to form columns of four. After the troops moved into line of battle as Colonel Stuart directed, Pete watched him wave his French sword above his head and without hesitation, he commanded, "Charge boys."

Pete and the rest of the Virginia cavalrymen moved swiftly toward the Zouaves, yelling and shouting as they charged. Suddenly, the Zouvaes fired their muskets at the cavalry, unleashing a cloud of fire and smoke. The first volley from the Zouvaves took a terrible toll on the cavalrymen. Some of the cavalrymen fell from their horses with wounds or sudden death. Those soldiers who had horses shot from under them and survived the fall, screamed with agony as the troopers in the following columns struck them accidentally with their animals.

As Pete rode across the field toward the enemy, he frightfully heard the missiles of death whizzing by his body from the volley. He laid his head close to the horse's neck for protection with his revolver in the other hand. The Zouvaes were frantically attempting to load their muskets as the 1st charged into their ranks. Pete was full of anger over the enemy's volley that killed and wounded some of his comrades that he had known. As Pete and the 1st penetrated deeper into the line of Zouvaes, there was screaming and yelling as the regiments clashed. Pete took his pistol and deliberately aimed it at a Zouvae and fired. The soldier grabbed his chest, right above the left side of the heart and fell to the ground shouting with pain and bleeding profusely. Pete knew that the wound for the Zouvae was mortal and that he probably would not live to see that evening's sunset. Still, he felt his anger burn within and his judgment of the individual from the North was justification for the death of his comrades. As he rode totally through the Zouvae line of battle, his heart was beating rapidly and he was thankful to God for sparing him the fate of death. With the command from an officer, Pete reformed with the rest of the 1st and charged toward the Yankees once more. This time a Zouvae took a jab at Pete with his bayonet, but missed his body and struck the lower part of his saddle. Pete's horse was frightened and stood upon its hind legs. By instinct, Pete discharged his weapon once more, hitting the Zouvae in the left shoulder. There was confusion between both regiments and the air was filled with men shouting screams as they were being inflicted with pain from the wounds they were receiving. Many, on both sides were yelling, cussing and there were commands of surrender from both blue and gray. It was confusing for the participants, every man seem to be for himself, with Confederates discharging shotguns, sabers slashing, striking their foe with screams of anguish. Blood from the wounds inflicted upon soldiers stained the new uniforms and dirty faces. During the melee, Pete found himself almost surrounded by the enemy. He knew that he would have to ride through some of the Zouvaes and possibly run the risk of being wounded, which was better then being captured. As he made the attempt to move forward, he once again discharged his weapon. A Yankee private seeing Pete, yelled, "Surrender, you dang rebel or I'll shoot." Then another Zouvae soldier lifted his musket to shoot the young Barker from behind. With a shout and the discharge of the Zouvae's weapon, the Yankee fell dead being struck in the head by a saber blow from Jonathan Collins, while Pete shot the second Yankee to death. There appeared an expression of relief on Pete's face as he glanced at Jonathan and noticed his jovial expression. The two of them continued to fight along side of the other as the Zouvaes began to flee in confusion and fear while some of the 1st gave pursuit.

After returning to the woods, where the attack began, Pete and some of his comrades followed the Colonel in his effort to support an artillery unit. As they were riding in that direction, Pete found Jonathan and cordially said, "I want to thank you for saving my life back there."

"I figured that I best look out for ya." Jonathan smilingly replied as he spit out some tobacco juice and wiped his mouth with his hand.

"Again, thank you." Pete replied as he slapped his horse on the rear quarter of its body and proceeded toward the front of the unit with the Colonel.

Around 4:00 in the afternoon, the Union forces began to flee from the battlefield. Colonel Stuart asked for permission to pursue the enemy, and before receiving his instructions, he ordered the 1st to proceed with haste after the panic stricken Yankees. As Pete rode with the 1st, they inflicted terror on their defeated foe. Many of the Yankees threw down their weapons and ran like scared rabbits. The Union soldiers and the civilians from Washington City that had followed today littered the road from the stone bridge with army wagons and buggies that they had deserted. With the defeat of the Union army, Pete had hopes that this would be the end of hostilities and that the war would come to a peaceful conclusion. Then maybe, he could return to Harpers Ferry and pick up the pieces of his life. Somewhere within his heart, he perceived that this battle would only be the beginning and that more bloodshed would take place before the nation was purged of Civil War.

CHAPTER FIFTEEN

As the battle of Bull Run raged back and forth in the early afternoon between the soldiers of the North and South, Katie was visiting with Caroline at the Estate. The word of the first great conflict of the war had not been received, and life was going on as usual. Caroline had invited Katie to Shenandoah to give her riding instructions and help her to prevail over the fear of horses. The two ladies, along with Ann were proceeding to the stable area, where Hayward stood waiting with their horses that he had saddled. Caroline was in a humorous mood on this historic day as was Katie. They knew that the armies had been concentrating around Manassas, but no one knew of Pete's whereabouts. As they arrived near the stable area, Caroline said to Katie, "Now remember what I have told you about Happy. He is a Morgan, and has good temperance. I love to ride him along the river in the evening, he is so obedient."

Katie smiled as she nervously replied, "I hope today that he is in the mood that you have describe. As I was telling you last week, I have never ridden a horse before, and I am still somewhat apprehensive about the idea."

Caroline began to laugh with an answer of reassurance as she was preparing to mount the animal, "Oh, come on. I will be there with you all of the way."

With a glowing smile, Ann said in agreement, "Yes, Miss Katie, we will be there with you all of the way." As Hayward acknowledged the ladies, Caroline instructed Katie to rub the horses face and speak to him. When she had done so, Hayward helped Katie, along with Ann mount their horses. He held the reins of

Katie's horse until she felt comfortable sitting on the left side of the saddle. Slowly, Katie and Caroline left the stable area with Ann following closely behind. The road toward the river was in the greatest condition and Caroline decided that this would be the best route for them to take, until Katie had received more instruction and had greater confidence in what she was doing. The horses were moving at a very slow pace. Caroline wanted Katie to get use to the feel of the animal. Caroline said confidently to Katie as she rode along side of her on Angel, "I want you to feel in command of the horse, and when you do, the confidence will follow. That is why I had you rub the animal and speak to him. I wanted you to become acquainted with each other."

Katie surprisingly replied, "Oh, I see."

As they continued to ride slowly in the direction of the Shenandoah River, Caroline was confident that Katie and she knew each other well enough that she could feel free to ask of her best friend some very personal questions that had been constantly on her mind. She glanced in Katie's direction and asked in a soft tone, "Katie, I do not mean to be nosey concerning your life, but I have noticed an emptiness in your heart lately. Is there something wrong that you would like to talk about? Are you concerned about your brother joining the army?"

Katie's reply was spoken very softly, "Yes I am concerned over his safety. When I was home in April, he was thinking about enlisting at that time. I've always been close to him."

Caroline seeking to know if her intuition was serving her well concerning Katie and Pete casually asked her friend, "If I may be so bold to ask, is he the only person that you are worried about?"

Katie answered in a frustrated tone of voice as she turned about to glance at Caroline, "No. I am concern over Pete's safety also. I just began to feel like I was really getting to know him when this whole thing started. He was just beginning to open up to me, and share his feelings concerning his life."

Caroline smiled with Katie's reply and joyfully reminisced, "I remember when I first realized that I loved Charles, when he was in Charlottesville. I had a good friend tell me that there was always brightness in my expression and a glow in my eyes when he was around. I see the same thing with you, when you are with Pete."

"I am very fond of him, I admit, but."

Katie was politely interrupted by Ann, who laughingly said, "You love him, don't you?"

Caroline laughingly replied, "Out of the mouth of babes comes the truth."

As Caroline glanced at Katie, she ended her laughing. Katie looked at Caroline with a serious expression that her friend had not known up until this time. Katie's voice reflected her emotion, "I am in love with him, but I do not believe that he feels the same about me."

Caroline promptly replied, "Oh my dear, give him time."

Katie continued to express her feelings, "You were right when you said that there was an emptiness in my life. I feel the loss of his absence and warmness of his companionship. I worry over his welfare and if I will ever see him again. At times, my heart hurts with pain, especially when I want to tell him how I feel. It is painful for me when I share my feelings with you about the loss that I feel. Please, I would only ask that you not share this revelation with anyone, especially Pete. He needs to discover for himself his feelings for me."

Caroline agreed, "It is our secret, I promise."

Without warning, Caroline grabbed the reins of the horse to control the animal as Ann slapped the Morgan on its hindquarter. The three of them were off at a moderate gallop, laughing and for now forgetting about the war.

On this hazy afternoon, Charles was speaking with his Mother on the front porch. She had been drinking lemonade and using her palm-leaf fan in an attempt to break up the stagnation of the air. They had been discussing the events that had just recently taken place in the area. With Union General Patterson establishing his headquarters in Harpers Ferry, it was very difficult for Charles to carry out any transactions with the new Confederate government for the future purchase of his horses. After the first month of the war, Charles felt that he could not continue to sell his horses to the U.S. Army. With his loyalties dedicated to the state of Virginia and the Southern cause for independence, he broke his contract with the government. It was his decision alone, to hold on to his stable of animals until the new government in Richmond was in need of horses. It had been a difficult decision for him because they were not making any money, though Pete had warned him of a possible loss to his business if the war continued and the area was under Federal control.

After a brief period of time, Charles decided to go to the library, when he noticed a cloud of dust at the far end of the lane. At first, he thought that it might be a cavalry patrol from the Federal forces that had occupied the town. As the horses and carriage quickly approached the house, he recognized William Pierce, who he had been expecting. William was scheduled for a visit in May, but delayed it because of the Union blockade. He had been vigorously attempting to export his products with blockade-runners so that the effects of the blockade would not tarnish his business. With William's arrival, Charles and Elizabeth greeted him, "William it is good to see you once more. Did you have much difficultly?"

"I had to secure a pass." And continuing with a smile, he said to Elizabeth, "And, Elizabeth, how are you?"

Elizabeth answered in a disappointing tone of voice, "Well William, I do declare, I would be doing a lot better if those Yankees in town would leave. I swear, I do not know of General Johnston's whereabouts. He would have put them to flight by now."

As William turned to look at Charles, he replied, "Several days ago when I was in Winchester, visiting Henry Wiles, I watched thousands of our troops moving through the city. It appeared that Johnston was moving to possibly reinforce Beauregard at Manassas."

Charles surprisingly answered as he was seated, "I thought they were still in the Valley?"

William confidently replied as he took a seat beside Charles, "No, I am sure that it was Johnston."

"Oh dear, my son. What about Pete? I did not think that this matter would go this far after the fall of Sumter." Elizabeth said with a distressful voice, knowing that her conscious was condemning her with guilt over the decision that she had made in releasing ownership of the Estate to her oldest son. If she hadn't acted so hastily she thought, then Pete would have been here at the Estate today.

Charles reassured his Mother, "If I know my brother, he will survive anything that happens. Father taught him well."

Elizabeth replied slowly in a concerned tone, "Yes, he did. Yes, he did, but this is war. It is much different this time."

Charles asked one of the servants to take William's bags to the guest bedroom, and then he invited his friend to the parlor for refreshments. After taking a seat near the window and lighting up his pipe, William asked Charles casually, "Where are Caroline and your daughter if I may ask?"

As he began to sit in one of the chairs by the porch swing, Charles replied, "Oh, Caroline is giving Katie McBride some riding instructions. They should be returning soon."

"Charles, if you do not care." William asked boldly, "While I am visiting Shenandoah, I would like to get to know Miss McBride in a more personal way. Of course, if that is agreeable with you."

Charles cordially replied, "Oh yes, by all means."

William continued saying as he puffed on his pipe, smiling, "I just felt that the last time that I paid you good people a visit, your brother had her in an emotional frizzy, and it made it very difficult for me to get to know her."

Charles merrily added to his friend's request, "William, I was sort of hoping that you and Katie would get together on this trip. Knowing my wife as I do, I am sure that she will invite her to stay the evening and dine with us. Afterwards, I will make sure that you have time alone with her if you so desire."

"Charles, I am blessed to have you as a friend." William said as the two gentlemen began to openly laugh.

Within the hour, Caroline, Ann, and Katie returned from riding along the river. As the ladies entered the parlor where Charles and William where seated, Katie had a surprise expression on her face after witnessing William's presence. Elizabeth entered the room with Matthew while he offered the ladies something cold to drink. Before anyone could begin a conversation, Ann was standing on the front porch, and noticed a rider galloping at a quick pace over the ridge to the east of the house. With a cry of excitement, she began to sound the alarm. Everyone was quickly on their feet and heading for the front door to see what the urgency was all about. Ann quickly recognized the man on the horse as Daniel. With quickness, Daniel dismounted his horse upon arrival, and said to Charles with great excitement in his voice, "We have whipped the Yanks at Manassas. We sent them a runin' back to Washington City like a pack of scared hounds with their tail between their legs."

Charles, William, and Elizabeth suddenly broke forth with a roar of jubilation.

Elizabeth began to shout, "The war is over. The war is over."

Caroline watched her Mother-in-law and husband celebrate, but she was sorrowful like Katie over the news. Both of the ladies knew that there had to have been casualties, though at the moment it didn't seem to be of any concern to those who surrounded them.

Later that evening at dinner, everyone was excited and talking about the great Confederate victory at Manassas except Katie who had been very quiet since receiving the news earlier in the afternoon. She could not understand why

Charles, William, and Elizabeth could be so jubilant, knowing that there was probably many causalities, and that a member of their family, Pete could have been one of them. After the meal, everyone retired to the parlor to continue the discussion over what the potential victory might bring for Southern independence. An hour had passed, and Katie was restless with the discussion. After excusing herself from their company, she walked outside on to the front porch to be alone. Katie had listened to enough about the battle that took place, and needed to have time to collect her thoughts. As she stood with her hands wrapped around her arms, William soon followed. She was standing along the corner of the porch and gazing at the beautiful sunset as William approached. Katie perceived that he still held an interest for her, though she did not feel the same. If the matter presented itself, she would be honest and inform him of her feelings. Her only hope was, that they would be able to be friends; again Katie did not want anything to hinder or jeopardize her relationship with the Barkers.

As she turned to look at William, there was a peaceful expression that consumed his face as if he had already won her love. He softy said to her, "You have not been very sociable on this magnificent evening. Actually, you have been very quiet. And, I think I know what the problem is."

"You do?" Katie asked in a whispering tone as she looked into his sensitive eyes.

"I do." He affirmed, "I believe that you have a difficult time with accepting the outcome of the victory today. Oh, I can understand how you must feel, being from the North. But, with this victory, hopefully, the North will want to negotiate a peaceful settlement, and we can all continue our life."

"Is that all that you can think about, William?" Katie replied angrily and continuing in that tone of voice, "How about the men that lost their life on the battlefield today? Do you think that it will be easy for their families to go on with their lives?"

William realizing that she was quite emotional over the events of the day, gently replied, "No, I do not think so. Those boys that met death on that field of glory for our cause, performed a noble deed that will not be forgotten."

"Oh, William," Katie replied, in a voice of frustration, "You sound like a politician." As she continued in a more mellow voice, she said, "I have listen to you and Charles, and his Mother all afternoon, and into this evening boasting about the great victory at Manassas. No one at anytime made any mention of Pete's fate in this conflict. No one!"

"I see." William softly said as he placed his arm against one of the huge columns and continued in a tone of disappointment, "You are concerned over his well being, and if he survived."

"Yes William, I am very concern. Now if you will excuse me, I would like to return to the parlor and speak with Caroline."

William sadly noticed the tears that began to fill her eyes as she departed his company, and walked across the porch to re-enter the house. William displayed his anger by making a fist and hitting the column. His disappointment in the outcome of their conversation, and the expectations that he had dreamed for this evening had damaged his pride as a Southern cavalier. The quest for Katie's love and affection would continue, even if he had to contend with the younger Barker on the issue. Maybe, he thought, it would be for the best to use whatever influence in Richmond that he could exert, in order to keep Pete on the front lines of battle, and thus keep the couple apart from the others company.

Later that same evening, Daniel was sitting on his horse along a ridge overlooking the Shenandoah. He was admiring the reddish glow from the full moon as it shined brightly on the river's surface. As he was thinking of the possibility that the war might come to a quick end, he noticed that the light of the moon revealed some people moving along the riverbank. Daniel decided to cautiously approach in that direction and investigate what might be happening. Earlier in the day on his trip into town, Daniel was informed that some of Mr. Emerson's slaves had disappeared. It was with this thought that he believed that the figures he was witnessing along the river just might be the slave owner's missing property. If it were as he suspected, Daniel would capture the slaves and return them before they could escape into the Ferry, and possibly receive help from the Federal troops that were stationed there.

Within minutes, Daniel was riding along the river. As he approached the area where Pete and Hayward would often fish, he noticed a man quietly standing along the river's bank. Tying his horse to one of the birch trees that covered the area, Daniel slowly and methodically proceeded on foot with his pistol drawn. The figure along the riverbank continued to sit on a rock and look in the direction of the mountain, as the wily hunter, Daniel continued to quietly stalk his prey. After carefully observing the man for a short time, Daniel approached the mysterious individual, and demanded that he not move, or be shot to death. Approaching with caution, Daniel asked the man to turn and face him. As the command was complied with, the overseer was surprised to recognize that it was Hayward.

After noticing that Hayward did not have a weapon of any kind, Daniel placed his pistol in his holster. He asked Hayward in a suspicious tone, "What are you doin' out here?"

Hayward answered boldly, "I's come out 'ere ta have time 'lone."

Daniel began to snarl as he walked around the immediate area looking for any evidence of the fugitive slaves that belonged to the Emerson's. Hayward did not reveal in his behavior to Daniel the nervousness that he was feeling. He cautiously asked, "What yose lookin' for?"

Daniel quickly replied, "Uh, nothin', nothin' at all."

Hayward said in hopes that Daniel would leave the area, "Den I's like to be left alone, so I's can pray."

Once more, Daniel snarled at Hayward, and was frustrated that he had failed to catch him with the runaway slaves that he believed Hayward was helping in their flight to freedom. As Daniel angrily departed the area, he heard Hayward singing the hymn, Amazing Grace.

Daniel quickly rode back to inform Charles of his suspicions concerning Hayward and his possible participation in the Underground Railroad. As he walked up to the back entrance to the mansion, Matthew greeted him. Daniel immediately requested to speak with Charles.

As he was restlessly waiting, Opal walked into the library to look for a book for Elizabeth. Daniel did not notice her, but she knew that he was standing in the hallway. After finding the literature that was requested, Opal heard Charles' voice coming in her direction. Sensing that Daniel had some information of interest, she remained silent and out of sight, but within listening range.

Charles abruptly asked as he approached the overseer, "What is wrong?"

Daniel answered with a serious expression, "You know those runaways that I was tellin' you about earlier?"

"Yes." Charles answered quickly.

"Well, I think I may have known what happen to them," Daniel confidently answered as he continued, "I think Hayward is behind their escape."

The sound of Charles' voice reflected his interest, "How do you know?"

"As I was near the river tonight checkin' on some of the herd after this hot day, I noticed what looked like six people movin' along the river bank in the direction of Keyes's Ford. After I was able to git a little closer, they suddenly disappeared. The only one left was Hayward. I looked around when I spoke with him, but saw nothin'. I think he's up to no good."

Daniel could tell by the surprised expression that covered Charles' face, that he did not expect to receive this information. The overseer wanted to pursue this opportunity to get rid of Hayward, who he despised. He asked with an inquiring tone in his voice, "What do ya want to do with him?"

There was a moment of silence as Charles thought about the situation. Then he answered as if he was sure that his orders were the right thing to do under the circumstances, "If you catch him with just one runaway." He angrily said as he continued in an authoritative tone, "I want you to shoot him and the slave that he's attempting to free. Bury their bodies along the river. Understood?" As Charles was returning to the parlor, where the family, Katie, and William were being entertained, he slowly turned and called to Daniel, "Oh, by the way, keep this conversation between you and me."

"Yes sir. I understand fully." Daniel replied as he said goodnight to Charles.

Opal was grieved with Charles' decision. She was sure that Daniel would be more then willing to carry out the order with the presentation of the first opportunity. She must find Hayward and alert him to the revelation of his possible destiny.

CHAPTER SIXTEEN

As Pete was returning from the pursuit of the Federal forces across Bull Run Creek, he noticed Confederate soldiers taking possession of wagons, cannons and camp gear that had been left behind by the fleeing Union troops in their haste to escape the pursuing Confederate army. What attracted him most of all, was the abundant of food and delicacies that had been left by the panic stricken civilians that accompanied the Federal army. He glanced at some of the cavalrymen laughing and commenting, "This is shor good eatin', thanks to dem Yanks," they said as they feasted on the beef that had been left behind. It was near the Sudley farm, that he found the remainder of his regiment and began to welcome the rest from the heat and battle. His lips were dry as he took a drink of water from his canteen. The gray jacket that he wore today was covered with dust, as was his brown hat. Pete watched intently as a man tall in stature, dressed in black attire rode along side of some of the infantrymen and was speaking with them. He over heard one of the cavalry officers' comments to a fellow officer that this individual was President Davis. Taking a few minutes to rest, he decided to look for his cousin Lester.

After searching for Lester, he found him drawing water from the well. Pete had a difficult time recognizing him with the grimy black gunpowder that covered his freckled face and flaming red hair. His uniform was covered from head to toe with dust and dirt, but in spite of his appearance, Pete was able to manage a smile. Pete hugged his cousin and rejoiced that they had survived the first great conflict that had taken place.

In the lateness of the evening as Pete and Lester were by the fire, enjoying some coffee and talking about the events of the day, Jonathan Collins appeared. As the two cousins looked up from the crates that provided a seat, Pete noticed the glowing smile that was quickly becoming his trademark being displayed. Jonathan politely said, "Ya mine if I have some of that coffee?"

Pete replied politely as he handed him a cup, "No, have some."

"We really tore into those Yanks today, didn't we?" Laughing as he continued his conversation, "I'd never seen such a skiddaddle. They ran faster then the rabbits back home when old Boss chases them. Ya see that's my hunt'n dog."

Pete looked at the jovial individual and bluntly answered, "Today, I shot and killed one of those Yanks. How many did you kill today?"

"Well, not enough." Jonathan angrily replied as he smiled.

Pete replied with sadness in his voice, "Jonathan, the man that I shot will never go home to his family. How do you think they are going to feel once they receive the news of his death?"

"Those Yanks should have stayed home. They didn't have any business coming on Virginia soil," Jonathan loudly answered as he drew the attention from some of the other soldiers that were sitting nearby around their campfires. They all gave a shout and agreed with Jonathan. With their approval, the jolly fellow began to smile and laugh once more.

Pete shook his head and said, "I still have a difficult time of taking another mans life, regardless of how you feel. But for now, sit and have some more of Lester's terrible coffee."

Jonathan quickly pulled up a wooden crate and the three of them began to talk about the battle that took place today, and about their own individual life. Lester causally asked Jonathan, "Do you have a family and young ones?"

Proudly pulling an image from his pocket, he allowed Pete and Lester the opportunity to look at his wife and two children. He said as Lester passed the image to Pete, "This is my wife, Martha, and my two sons, John and Joseph.

Jonathan asked with a tone of expectation as he returned the image to his coat pocket, "How about ya fellas?"

Lester replied, "No, I am not married, though I have a sweetheart, Mary Ann."

After a moment of silence, Jonathan asked Pete, "How about ya?"

"No, I do not have a family with kids, or a sweetheart," Pete softly replied as he began to write home to inform his Mother that he had survived the battle.

Although, he knew at times during the battle, that his mind had been on Katie McBride, Pete still did not accept her in a romantic way. As Lester and Jonathan continued their conversation about their families and love ones that they had left behind to serve the Southern cause, Pete quietly excused himself and walked over to the edge of the camp. Looking at the star filled sky and listening to the conversation and music that was being played in the camp, he began to reflect on his life. He knew that he could have been one of the killed or wounded from this battle. At one point today, as he crossed the field, he noticed the surgeons busy at amputating legs and arms from those who had been severely wounded. At times the screams from those poor men could be heard above the cannons and muskets. At least they would be able to return to their families and pick up the pieces of their life, instead of those who had been captured. Then Pete thought about the dead that he saw today, how they laid where they had fallen, never to return home and share life with their love ones. The thought of this happening was too unbearable to continue to dwell upon. Even though the Southern army had won a great victory, he knew that there would be more scenes such as this as he had experience today.

It was almost 10:00 in the evening at Shenandoah. The Barker family and William Pierce had retired for the evening after the eventful day. Katie had returned to town. As Caroline was preparing for bed, she casually said to Charles, "I could not help, but to noticed all evening William's interest in Katie. Especially, when she left the parlor and went out onto the porch to get away from the conversation. He had to be near her."

Charles replied in a humorous tone of voice as he climbed into bed, "My love, Katie is a very attractive young lady, and who would not follow her around like a lost puppy dog."

Caroline was looking in the mirror and combing her hair. Turning about to face her husband, she replied in a soft voice, "To be honest with you my love, I do not think that she is interested in William, and he is only wasting his time."

Charles suddenly rose from bed, and quietly walked over and stood behind his wife as she continued to comb her hair. Placing his arms around her, he passionately said, "Maybe you and I should make the attempt to flame a spark of interest." He romantically said as he kissed her neck.

She suddenly broke his embraced and walked over to the bed and answered with a determination in her voice, "No, I want nothing to do with the matter. Katie is old enough to make up her own mine."

With her reply, Caroline laid down on the bed to go to sleep, leaving her husband thinking of what attempt could be made in the future, since his wife was not willing to cooperate with him in playing the match maker on behalf of William.

In their cabin, Opal was discussing the conversation between Daniel and Charles with her husband Matthew, the main servant of the house. After considerable debate over the subject, it was decided between the two that Hayward must know that his life was in jeopardy, and make an escape before Daniel took advantage of the situation. Opal quietly peered out the cabin door and looked about, to make sure that she would not be noticed in her attempt to find Hayward. The house was totally dark as was many of the slave's quarters that covered the area. As quickly as possible, she ran in the direction of the first stable. Opal believed that Hayward would be in that particular area of the property. As she was nearing the stable, she heard a noise, like the sound of a horse coming from the direction of the river.

Immediately, Opal hid behind some water barrels by the first stable where she believed Hayward was still tending to the animals. She recognized Daniel, who had apparently had too much whiskey to drink. He was singing to himself, something he would not do unless he had had too much of the spirits. She cautiously waited and quietly stayed out of sight and watched him to see what he was going to do. Opal knew that if he found her and told Charles, she would loose her privileges in serving Elizabeth. It was not her intentions to be returned to hard labor working in the heat on humid summer afternoons.

As Daniel staggered and open the door, he entered the stable where Hayward was working. Opal waited patiently for him to leave and retire for the evening. After a short time, she heard the overseer depart the stable, laughing and cussing her friend. Daniel began to speak about the joy of the victory that was won today in hopes of tempting Hayward in to a brawl. Opal knew that Hayward was too smart and patient in character to allow that to happen. As the angry overseer walked by where Opal was hiding, she overheard him say in a whispering voice, how he hoped to take advantage of the opportunity of ending Hayward's life as soon as possible. When it seemed that the area was all clear, Opal made her flight through the stable door. After entering, she quietly called out for Hayward. There was only silence. Just as she was about to leave and return to her cabin, Hayward called her name. Opal turned in the direction of the voice and soon saw the light from the lantern. As she was breathing a sigh of relief, he calmly said, "Opal, what you'd doin' out here dis time of night?"

"I's come to warn ya."

"Yose warn me 'bout wat, woman?" He surprisingly asked as he approached one of the animals to rub it down from pulling the carriage from town.

"Deys knows 'bout what yose doin'. 'Bout helpin' our people to escape." Opal replied and continuing in a serious tone, "Yose need to leave. Mr. Daniel is goin' a shoot ya, if he catches you'd helpin' our people. He's told Mr. Charles, I's overheard dem."

Hayward was not caught off guard by the news that Opal had brought him. Instead, he expected after the confrontation with Daniel by the river earlier in the evening that the overseer suspected that he had been helping runaway slaves to escape to the North. He said in a sincere and calm tone of voice, "Opal, I's been helpin' runaways for over two years now, and I's not 'bout to stop. It is my way of helpin'. I can't see my people in de bondage sufferin' anymore like my papa."

Opal began to express frustration with Hayward's stubbornness and unwillingness to listen to what she had to say, "Well, what yose gonna do? Stay here and git shot. Mr. Charles told Mr. Daniel to kill ya, and bury ya along de river."

The uncertainty that covered Hayward's face told the story of his sudden silence. He was not sure what would be the most profitable course of action, since he had aroused Charles' suspicion. After considerable reflection on the matter, he did not believe that the time had come for him to make his escape. His intentions were to take advantage of every opportunity that manifested its self in helping his people to seek their freedom. It was worth the risk.

CHAPTER SEVENTEEN

Toward the end of June in 1862, Federal forces continued its occupation of the town of Harpers Ferry, and most of the immediate area with a new commander, Colonel Dixon Miles, a veteran of the United States Army. Thus far during the conflict, the town had changed hands six times between Union and Confederate forces. Many of the citizens that lived in the village departed when conflict was near and returned when there was no longer a threat. The complete destruction of the Armory and Arsenal the previous year had left the economy of the town in shambles, and with the lack of employment, the town population had decreased.

At Shenandoah, Charles still had not been able to negotiate a contract with the Confederate government due to the continual Federal presence in the surrounding area. The family was very wealthy from its previous years of abundant business with the U.S. Army and was not in need of monetary funds right now. With the occupation of Federal troops in the area, some of the slaves from the Estate had managed to escape to safety that meant a greater workload on those laborers that remained. Under the authority that Charles had given Daniel last summer, he captured a family that had escaped and executed them near the mountains on the opposite side of the Shenandoah. He committed this treachery in order to instill fear among those slaves that remained. Many of the slaves had not received their liberation from the Federal forces in the area and were still in the possession of their owners, unless they escaped. The main focus of General McClellan, who was appointed General-in-Chief of the Federal forces, was to defeat the rebel army and reunite the country. Once the war was concluded, McClellan believed, that the Lincoln administration could attempt to deal with the social issues, particularly slavery.

Early on Monday morning, Charles was walking through some of the beautiful flower and shrub gardens that surrounded the property of the Estate near the mansion. He admired the crafty work that had been performed by the laborers under Jeremiah's supervision. Even Charles was impressed with Jeremiah's vision of creativity. As Charles walked from the flowerbed that surrounded the gazebo, he noticed Ann swinging and decided to join her. He intended to speak with Ann regarding her Mother's birthday, which was only a week away. Suddenly, with haste, Matthew came from the house and requested Charles' presence in the parlor. There the main servant told him he would find a messenger from Charlestown with a telegram from Richmond. Charles' first thought as he proceeded toward the house, was that Pete was sending the family a message. Charles believed that his brother was in Richmond, since it was known that General Johnston had removed his army from Manassas to Richmond because of the threat from the Union army under McClellan. As Charles entered the parlor, the messenger handed him the telegram that he opened. Immediately, much to his surprise, it was from President Davis. The President was requesting Charles' presence in Richmond as soon as possible. After dismissing the courier, he excitingly called for his Mother and Caroline.

The first to arrive was Elizabeth. She said with anticipation as she entered the room, "Charles, what is wrong?"

"Wait until Caroline arrives, I have some news to share with you."

At the completion of his reply, Caroline entered the room and asked in a concerned tone the same question. With the telegram in his hand, Charles confidently broke the news, "I have received a telegram from President Davis, requesting that I come to Richmond."

The ladies were taken by surprise. The first to react verbally was Elizabeth. Holding her hand against her cheek, she asked Charles, "Well I declare, why does President Davis want you to come to Richmond? I don't understand."

Caroline enthusiastically replied as she held her hands together, "Maybe the government wants to purchase some of the cattle, or horses."

"No, I don't think so." Charles answered in a cautious tone. Though, he continued optimistically, "I feel that it has to do with the war effort. I'm sure that it has nothing to do with buying of any of the livestock."

Walking over to the stand to take a drink of water from her glass, Elizabeth disagreed and said, "I think you might be wrong on this issue. The army, especially the cavalry will need new mounts. The war has gone on longer then anyone had anticipated, and horses have been lost in battle."

Caroline excitingly interrupted, "Not to say that the army needs the cattle for beef to feed the soldiers."

There was a moment of silence as the two ladies watched for a reaction from Charles, who was standing by the fireplace. He seemed to be in deep thought; the joy had vanished from his face and was replaced with uncertainty. Caroline quickly picked up on her husbands mood change and asked with a concerned tone, "What is wrong, Charles?" As she slowly approached him, "Please tell me?"

Charles replied confidently as he gazed at his wife, "I do not know what this is all about. Though, I am sure of one thing, and that is, the government does not want to purchase cattle and horses at this time."

"How can you be so sure?"

"They know that the lower part of the Valley is not under Confederate control. Do you think that Dixon Miles would allow us to sell our livestock to his enemy? No, I don't think so."

Elizabeth had been impatiently standing and listening to the conversation, she asked, "Then Charles, what could the President want with you?"

As Charles walked over to the front window to look out toward the Charlestown Pike, he said with a tone of astonishment, "I really don't know, but I will find out shortly. I must leave as soon as possible."

Caroline said in a tone of excitement as she approached her husband, "But what about the Yankees. Do you think they're going to give you a pass? I don't think so."

"My love, Daniel and I, months ago, worked out the arrangements if I needed to leave the area." Charles said in a tone of reassurance to Caroline and cautiously reminding, "Although, more importantly, I asked that whatever you do, keep quiet about the telegram and its contents. If you don't, we may have a price to pay at the hands of the Federals."

After the agreement between the three of them, the discussion came to an end. They separately continued to ponder on this important message, especially Charles.

Early the next morning, several hours before sunrise, Hayward was waiting to help a family of four escape from the Jones farm near Charlestown. He had been told by a Northern sympathizer, who was involved with the Underground Railroad to meet the family near a grove of trees in the vicinity of the Bloomery Mill. From there, he would be their guide and place them in contact with the Archers of Sandy Hook, across the Potomac River below Harpers Ferry.

The attempt to escape had not gone well for David and his family. The foreman of the farm, Robert Carleton had kept the slaves working long after sunset into the evening cleaning out the barn and the adjacent buildings. This was unexpected by David and his family. They found that it was not safe to make the attempt to freedom until well after midnight. As soon as it was safe to do so, the slaves made their getaway, and hoped to make contact with Hayward at the designated area.

Hayward knew that there was little time before the first rays of the sun would appear over the mountain. After anxiously awaiting for several hours, he noticed the approach of the escaping slaves, and urged them to hasten. He knew at sunrise, the foreman would be looking for David and his family with help from town. If he was caught with the fugitives, Hayward knew they would be killed along with those he was attempting to smuggle. It was his belief that time was running short and not on their side. It was a good three to four miles through fallen trees, thickets, and underbrush from the area where Hayward had met the runaway slaves to Keys Ford. As the gleaming rays of sunlight began to appear, Hayward and his party were still quite some distance from their destination. Hayward did not reveal his anxiety to David and his family because he already knew that they were frightened. By now Hayward knew Daniel was on his way with some of the laborers to begin the necessary work that he had overheard the overseer and Charles discussing the previous evening.

As Hayward and the escape slaves approached the area of the Estate where Pete and he had spent their leisure time together, the sun had risen high enough over the mountain to where there was enough light to reveal their presence. From there position, they were easily exposed to Daniel and the work party coming from the direction of the barn. Hayward attempted to hasten David and his family. As they were going along, David's wife fell over a tree limb and cried out with pain. Looking back, Hayward noticed that she had injured her right ankle. As David attended to his wife's injury, Hayward watched for any sign of Daniel. He knew by now that Mr. Jones must have sounded the alarm for help.

The thought crossed Hayward's mind, that it would only be a matter of time before Daniel would make haste for the river because of his suspicion, and knowing that along the river was the best possible escape route. It was all that Hayward could do to repress his fear of discovery, while urging David to hurry as he continued to attend to his wife needs. Time was running out, and Hayward knew that he had to come up with an alternative plan for their escape. Hayward was sure that Daniel knew of Mr. Jones's missing property and burning within at the opportunity to carry out his threats against him. Daniel was a very good hunter and could follow a trail with superb skill. Hayward decided the first course of action would be to cover up their trail. He anxiously said to David, "I's gonna cover de trail. Yose need to hurry."

David replied with a fearful tone as he hastened to make a splint, "I's tryin', I's tryin'."

Hayward took a small branch from one of the trees along the riverbank and began to sweep their footprints clean. He lay some of the loose brush along the way from the direction that they came. Soon, David's wife was ready to be moved. David carried her and along with his sons proceeded toward the direction of Harpers Ferry. Hayward followed closely behind covering their trail as quickly as they fled. After a short distance, David had to stop and rest from carrying his wife. By now she was crying with intense pain. David was out of breath and attempted to communicate with Hayward, "I's don't think I's can go on. Take my sons."

He was immediately interrupted by Hayward who had noticed Daniel on the ridge looking in their direction. Hayward called out, "Dey's seen us."

Quickly Hayward's eyes scanned the immediate area for shelter and a place to hide. As he was doing so, Daniel was quickly approaching the escape party at a fast gallop. The area was filled with an outcropping of rocks and underbrush. He noticed several huge rocks that were formed together along a small hill that allowed them shelter. It was their only hope. Hayward pointing to the rocks and said to David, "Go dere, under de rocks. Hurry!"

As David and his family complied with the command, Hayward watched Daniel cautiously approaching the area. When Hayward knew that the fugitives were safe, he quickly disappeared from Daniel's sight and covered the shelter with underbrush and fallen limbs, and destroyed their footprints with the branch that was still in his hand. Now, he knew that he had to hide or the overseer would shoot him. Hayward's time had run out. Daniel was in the area where Hayward had first noticed him. Daniel had not seen Hayward yet. As the overseer began to look around the riverbank for any sign of the escape slaves, he did so with his pistol in hand. As Hayward hid behind some of the rocks and watched Daniel, he observed him standing and looking in the area where David and his family were hiding. Daniel walked along the riverbank looking for footprints. He walked up the small hill and stood directly in front of the hideaway, and began to look in the area for evidence of their existence. As Daniel walked among the rocks, Hayward began to think of what he should do. If he ambushed Daniel, he knew that he had the advantage in physical strength, but Daniel was taller and more agile. Still, there was the chance that the angry overseer would kill him, though David and his family would be able to escape. Should this happen, then David and his family would not know who their contact would be, once they were near town. The thought came to mind, should they stay where they were hidden, then there was the possibility that once the hounds arrived, then they would be discovered and all of them would be put to death. Hayward believed the odds were on his side. There was no other alternative. As Hayward watched Daniel for the element of surprise and the opportunity to overpower him, he heard a soft sound coming from the direction of where the fugitives were hiding. It must be David's wife crying with pain. Daniel also heard the noise and cautiously approached the area where the sound was heard. As Daniel began to investigate near David and his family's hideaway, Hayward meticulously stalked his prey. He felt confident in this skill that Pete had taught him over the last few years when they were hunting game. Patiently, he pursued his foe. After continuing to hear groans of pain, Daniel found where the runaways were hiding. He loudly gave David and his family an order, "Come out you darkies or I'll shoot ya."

"Don't shoot." Came the shout from the brush.

As David crawled out from under the huge rock, he began to help his wife. Daniel pushed him to the side. In an aggressive manner, Daniel reached out with his hand and pulled David's wife from the brush by her hair. David was enraged with anger over the act of violence committed by Daniel, but he could not do anything with the gun pointed in his direction. Hayward acted impulsively, and without any warning he lunged like a lion from the brush for the slender overseer. Daniel's gun fired making a noise that seemed to echo along the river and broke the peaceful silence. The two men fell back against a rock where Hayward took Daniel and delivered a blow to the side of his foes head. As the overseer fell to the ground unconscious, David yelled, "Dey's comin', dey's comin! Dey's know we's here!"

Hayward quickly glanced in the direction of the ridge where Daniel had been previously, knowing that the gunshot had been heard. There he saw seven men with their barking hounds moving slowly in their direction. Hayward looked at Daniel lying on the ground to make sure that he was still unconscious and would not pose a threat to them in making their escape. Grabbing the reins of Daniel's horse, Hayward commanded David to assist his wife in mounting the animal as he kept a close eye on the men. When David was ready, Hayward grabbed Daniel's pistol from the ground and the fugitives began to flee from their pursuers. The band of men had not seen Hayward and the runaways yet. Pete had taught Hayward the best way to elude pursuit, was to destroy any clues, such as footprints and a hound's ability to pick up ones scent. The best way to accomplish this was to continue toward the Ferry by walking in shallow water. This was possible for their escape since the river had receded after the flooding at the beginning of the month. He knew that they would stop and attend to the unconscious overseer and the cut above his left eye before continuing. There was a cave along the river a short distance from their presence location that Hayward knew about. Hayward had used it on several occasions when he was helping runaways in the past as they were being pursued. He believed that it would provide sanctuary for the fugitives.

As they came to a bend in the river, several miles from town, Hayward knew that they were close to the shelter. Soon, the fugitives were in the area of the hideaway that no one, not even Pete knew about. Only Hayward knew of its existence, location, and the landmarks used to discover its location. Along the way of escape, Hayward had thought of a plan for their safety. The runaway slaves, along with him would stay for several days until Daniel and his friends ended the pursuit. From there by night, they would cross the river and once again ford the Potomac near Sandy Hook, their destination.

It was only a thirty-minute journey from where they had confronted Daniel to where they would come close to the hideaway. Hayward paused and quietly looked about before leaving the water. They climbed a steep embankment, and there, a small white dogwood tree with one drooping limb on the left side was used as a landmark. From there, the runaways crossed over a shallow ridge among a heavy grove of trees filled with thickets and underbrush to the cave. Hayward had disguised the small entrance with some of the underbrush and two pointed black slate rocks stacked to resemble a V. As they crawled through the small entrance into the cave, they entered into a large chamber. Hayward secured David and his family's safety He then returned to the river and covered their trail and disguised their scent. He accomplished this with laying some honeysuckle mixed with underbrush, thickets, and briers that were growing among the trees that lined the riverbank. After he finished, he returned to the cave with the fugitives. As he sat down on a small rock near a fire, David approached him and asked, "Wat's you'd gonna do now. Dey's sure to shoot ya if ya go's back."

"I's know, I's know." Hayward sorrowfully replied and continued in the same tone, "Is's time dat I's leave too. I's can never go back, never."

There were tears that filled Hayward's eyes as he thought about what he had just said to David. The only place that he had called home was Shenandoah. It grieved him deeply that he could never return to the place that he had learned to love, knowing that his life was in jeopardy. Now, Hayward must make his escape to Pennsylvania along with David and his family and pursue a new beginning in a strange and unfamiliar area. Hayward held his hands to his face and openly wept at the thought of not seeing his friends at the Estate again, especially Pete.

On the following day in Richmond, Pete, Lester, and Jonathan were riding along Main Street after receiving a one-day furlough. For most of the month of June it had been rainy, though this afternoon was sunny and clear. It was a welcomed relief. Over the last eleven months, the three cavalrymen had been riding together continuously, especially Jonathan and Pete. It was through the tragedy of war and conflict that the two men became close friends. The troopers had fought together at Eltham's Landing, Williamsburg, and though not engaged at the battle of Seven Pines, their regiment did support the infantry. The greatest adventure that the threesome shared was being chosen along with nearly 1,200 cavalrymen in a raid around the whole Union army along the peninsula. General Stuart had captured many supplies and prisoners, not to mention horses and mules. His cavalrymen were viewed by the people of Richmond and the Confederate government as heroes.

As Pete, Jonathan, and Lester were slowly riding toward Pete's aunt's home, they took particular noticed of the residents milling along the street, or going about their business. The three cavalrymen noticed infantry marching towards the front to join General Robert E. Lee, the new Confederate commander of the army as they prepared to do battle with Union forces on the outskirts of the city.

At this moment, more importantly, special attention was given to the pretty girls dressed in colorful attire, waving and smiling as the three cavalrymen passed their way. Occasionally, they would witness some of the wounded soldiers sitting along the street speaking with the older gentlemen from the city. Then there was the creaking sound of wheels, as convoys of wagons were taking supplies to the army, which was station a short distance outside of the city. What attracted the three soldiers the most, was the smell that was coming from the silver platters decorated with yellow roses, which three Negro's dressed in their fine white jackets were carrying. The aroma was tempting as the hungry troopers with the exception of Jonathan continued toward their destination. Jonathan brought his mare to a halt in front of the lead servant and politely said, "Where's ya goin' with that food."

One of the servants kindly replied as he gazed at the soldier, "We's bin ordered by Misse Abigail ta take de food ta de hospital for de wounded."

Jonathan looked at the three servants with his trademark smile and demanded, "Ya can just leave that there chicken here with me. I'll take it to the hospital."

The lead servant shook his head in disagreement, and politely replied, "Nos, we can't do dat. Yose gonna git us in all kinds of trouble."

The answer that Jonathan received, and coming from the disobedient Negro made him angry. After noticing that Jonathan was missing, Pete and Lester returned in time to witness him pulling his pistol to cause possible harm to the servants. Pete rode along side of Jonathan and grabbed the barrel of his pistol saying angrily, "What are you doing?"

Jonathan replied angrily as he turned about to look at his friend, "These darkies won't give me deir food."

Lester asked one of the servants, "Where are you going with all of that chicken?"

The lead servant said, "As we's told him." Pointing to Jonathan, "To de hospital. Dis chicken for de wounded and he's not gonna git it."

Pete quickly apologized to the three servants and sent them on their way. Since Pete had been promoted to Sergeant in the early spring, he held rank over Jonathan and Lester. They were both corporals.

Pete and his companions soon arrived at his aunt's home and were warmly greeted by her. Aunt Daisy happily said to her nephew as she hugged him, "Oh, I am so glad to see you. I felt like you had forgotten about me, but when I heard that your regiment was near the city, I just knew that you would come and see me."

Pete replied in a remorseful tone with sorrowful eyes, "I must confess I have procrastinated, and I am sorry."

"That's alright, I'm just glad you are here and well."

Pete did not see his sister, Rebecca, so he began to inquire where she was, "Aunt Daisy, is my sister home?"

His aunt took him by the hand and smiled as she jovially answered, "No, she is with a friend. She should be home by supper time."

"It's been a long time, and I am anxious to see her."

Standing quietly and feeling somewhat ignored, Jonathan began to clear his throat. As Pete turned to look at Jonathan and Lester, he once again, as many times over the last year, noticed Jonathan's grin. Pete knew why his friend had interrupted his conversation with his aunt; he had not properly introduced them. After their introduction, Pete noticed his brother Charles and William Pierce walking out onto the porch to greet them. Pete was surprised, he had not expected his brother to visit his aunt, and began to wonder why he was in the city. He believed with the continuation of the war, that Charles would have stayed in the Valley and attempt to profit from the cause in some way. After introductions, Pete curiously asked, "Charles, I'm surprised to see you here. What brings you to Richmond?"

A prideful expression glowed across Charles' face and with a boastful tone of voice, he said, "Yesterday, I received a telegram from President Davis requesting that I come to Richmond. It was a matter of service to the Confederate government."

Puzzled by the news and his brother's answer, Pete replied, "Oh, I see."

An equally boastful William Pierce said, "We have been invited to the President's residence tomorrow afternoon."

"What service could you contribute to the cause? You are not willing to fight like us."

Charles walked over and put his arm around his little brother and continuing to boast, he said, "Whatever it might be, it will exalt me higher among those of prominence in the Confederate government. I do not need to be on the battlefield."

William proudly added, "Whatever the President desires of us, it will add to the overall effort. Some of us make a contribution by fighting and giving up ones life for this noble and glorious cause, while others excel on the political front."

With William's comments, he entered the house with Charles and Aunt Daisy. Lester walked over to where Pete was quietly standing and placed his arm around his shoulder. He began to comment on his thoughts concerning the matter, "Well, that's Charles alright. His head is always bigger then the rest of him. He thinks that he's a big dog among a bunch of little pups."

Jonathan boldly added, "He should come with us and get himself in a good scrap with dem Yanks, then he would sing another tune. Ya know Pete, not to hurt ya feelings, but I don't like him, or that other fella."

Jonathan and Pete began to walk toward the front door, and as they did Jonathan asked in a jovial tone, "By the way, what does that long word mean that ya said when ya were talking to ya aunt?"

"Oh, procrastination."

"Ya, ya. That word." Jonathan eagerly replied.

"It means I was lazy."

Jonathan said as he began to openly laugh, "Sometime, I'd like for ya to teach me sum of those fancy words."

Pete grinned as he answered, "Alright, I promised."

As Pete was standing in one of the guest bedrooms in front of the large mirror that was in the corner of the room, he began to rub the whiskers that covered his chin. For over a year, he had been absent from the Valley, and thoughts of home and friends filled his mind, but most of all, his times of solitude along the river at Shenandoah. Momentarily, his thoughts returned to reality, and the war. Many of his friends that had enlisted in the military, he was not able to keep in contact with due to the infrequency of mail delivery. The question that lingered the most was, how many of them were alive, or returned home with serious wounds that incapacitated them for life? Hopefully, he thought, this war will end with a few more victories. Then, his thoughts drifted in a different direction. As Pete walked slowly over to the front window, he began to ponder on the advice that he had given Katie before leaving home. It had been several months since receiving a correspondence from her, and naturally he assumed that she had returned to Boston just as he had advised.

His concentrations on these concerns were broken with a knock at the door by one of the servants. Quickly, Pete finished tying his tie, and acknowledged the servants request to join the family for dinner. Pete was walking down the long stairway, when he saw his sister and her male friend enter through the front door of the house. Rebecca was surprised to see her brother and was speechless, though thankful that he was still alive. She had not seen him, or spoken to him in over a year.

As Pete walked over to where Rebecca stood smiling, he hugged and embraced her short frame. Rebecca surprisingly said, "Pete, Pete. I did not know that you were arriving today." Pausing and gazing at her older brother, she continued, "I am so thankful to see you."

Pete was feeling somewhat guilty over the fact that he had not seen his sister in sometime, nor had corresponded with her in months. Out of the love and respect that he felt for his sister, an apology was in order, "Rebecca, I'm sorry that I have not kept in touch with you. I guess I could have made up many excuses, but the fact is, I have not taken the time. I'm sorry."

"The only way that I knew of your welfare was through my correspondence with Mother."

Pete was still feeling the condemnation of his error as he brushed his hair straight back with his hand. Once more, he remorsefully said, "I am sorry for my lack of responsibility."

Rebecca answered with a smile as she took her brother's hand, "That is alright, but in the future, I want you to keep in touch. I will not worry so often over you, if I know that you are all right. By the way, how long are you going to be with us?"

"My regiment the 1st, is camped outside of the city, so the three of us were allowed a one day furlough."

Rebecca's brown eyes glowed as she laughed and said, "Oh, I do declare, forgive me of my bad manners. Pete I would like for you to meet a friend of mine, Thomas Monroe."

Immediately, Thomas reached to shake Pete's hand and in doing so, he said, "Pete, I'm glad to make your acquaintance. I have heard many good things about you from Rebecca."

Rebecca had a mischief glow that covered her attractive features as she asked, "As I understand from Caroline, we may be attending a wedding before long."

"What?" Pete shouted as everyone took notice of the couple.

"Yes, you and Miss McBride."

Lester said as he continued to laugh with Rebecca, "Cousin what a surprise, you didn't tell us that you had a sweetheart. huh?"

Very quickly, Pete was on the defensive, and it reflected in his tone of voice, "Oh, now wait a minute. You have this all wrong. I am not getting married to her or anyone else for that matter."

William was within a short distance and overheard the conversation. He had been speaking with Charles about the series of victories and successes that Stonewall Jackson had been enjoying in the Shenandoah Valley. From what he had just heard Pete say, he knew that it was only Katie who had the sincere feelings. It was still his intentions on keeping them separated.

During the dinner hour there were many question about Stuart's great triumphed raid around the Federal army. The first to bring up the subject was William. He was anxious to know the details and how this was accomplished with little loss of men. With a tone of excitement in his voice, William asked, "I am amazed at how General Stuart was able to plan and pull off such a stunning victory. How did he do it?"

Lester was one who was always ready to tell a good story and with confidence and jubilation in his voice, he said, "We were chosen to take part in a scouting expedition around the Union army's right flank. After we were satisfied that it was protected by a small number of cavalry, we immediately returned and informed General Stuart."

William urged Lester, "Go on."

"Jeb, that's General Stuart you see, went to inform General Lee with this information. The General asked and was given permission to raid McClellan's supply lines and communications. We left camp on the thirteenth with my old friend Lieutenant Mosby, who was leading the scouting party and proceeded to Hanover Court House. We were about"

Jonathan laughing with excitement interrupted Lester and added, "Ya all should have seen dem Yanks run. They'd didn't want to fight."

Aunt Daisy said to Lester, "Please continue, we would like to hear more."

Lester continued with a prideful and patriotic tone in his voice, "Well, we had a few scrapes with the Yanks along the way. D company got into a pretty good brawl with a Yankee company. It happens that we were also in the area and took part in the skirmish. Pete and Jonathan were the first to charge the Yanks with the rest of the company following. They reminded me of a couple of warriors that I have read about in past history. I've never seen such boldness from an individual."

Charles looked at his brother and surprisingly said, "I knew that you were daring, but I didn't think that you would take that kind of a chance."

Jonathan added, "He fought like the devil at Manassas."

Charles was amazed and asked his brother, "Is that how you were promoted."

With a serious expression covering his face, Pete said, "Charles, I do not like war. I fight to stay alive."

Charles excitingly said as he gestured for the main servant to pour his water, "But you received a promotion. Is that not worth something?"

"No one here knows but us three soldiers what the horror of war is like." Pete continued in a subdued voice, "The next day after the engagement at Manassas, I rode across the field. I noticed that some of the dead had a peaceful expression upon their face; they appeared to be sleeping like angels and were very content. But then, I witnessed the torment of a painful death that covered the faces of many others that had fallen in combat. One of those was the private that I killed. He was probably no older then me. You don't forget those images. They'll always stay in my mind all of the days of my life, I'll never forget as long as I live."

Lester added to his cousin's explanation, "Not to say the cries of the wounded that lie on the dirt ground, crying in pain from their injuries. You want to help, but one thinks twice before he runs to help someone in need, fearing for his own life."

There was a silence that filled the room. For now, the family had heard enough testimony of the troubles and tribulations that resulted from conflict.

After the meal, the men retired to the parlor. As they were seated near the fireplace, the conversation took a different direction. Charles was totally surprised that his brother had not made any inquires into life at Shenandoah since his arrival in Richmond. The question would present its self, Charles was sure, and at that time he would inform his brother of the recent events that had taken place at the Estate concerning Hayward. He knew that Pete and Hayward had been very close friends, but he did not believe that his brother had any part in helping slaves escape to the North. Charles was under the impression that Hayward used his friendship with Pete as a cover up to the reality that was taking place. It would be shocking news to Pete, though he would wait until the right time to break the news to him.

An hour had passed since dinner and just as Charles had expected, his brother began to inquire of life at the Estate, "I have not had the opportunity to ask you how matters are at Shenandoah and in the lower valley?" Pete asked, as he took a drink of the brandy that had been served.

Charles slowly answered, "Oh, they are doing fine. Thus far, the Yanks have left us alone. As for Mother, she keeps you in her prayers." After a brief silence, he felt that Pete must have been feeling guilty because of his lack of communication with the family. Charles became aggressive in his tone of voice and said, "You should write more correspondence and not keep the family worried about your safety. If you had, you would have known what your friend Hayward had been up too."

Pete anxiously asked, "What do you mean?"

"I have some shocking news for you." Charles said in a serious tone as he continued to unfold the events, "Hayward has been helping runaways."

Pete quickly and angrily interrupted knowing Charles' feelings concerning Hayward, "I do not believe for a moment what you are saying! What proof do you have?"

Charles knew that his brother was angry and he could use this situation to make Pete appear weak in front of William and his comrades. It was his intentions to undermine his brother whenever opportunity presented its self. Charles raised his hands into the air and with a calm voice he began to explain, "If you would let me continue? Last July, Daniel, was checking on the herd. After noticing some people walking along the river, he decided to investigate. By the time he arrived, Hayward, was the only one left."

Pete jumped to his feet and shouted, "Charles, I don't believe this!"

"If you would please let me continue, I'll finish." After a moment of silence and gazing at his brother, Charles continued to speak, "For sometime now, we have watch Hayward very carefully, and I believe he knew that we suspected him of helping the darkies to get away. Several days ago, we were informed that Mr. Jones was missing some of his slaves and right away we suspected Hayward. Daniel saw them along the river and made the attempt to recapture the runaways. When Daniel was about to apprehend them, he was attacked by Hayward."

Pete was surprised, and if the information that he was receiving was true, then he felt betrayed by his friend. He slowly asked, "Are you sure?"

Charles replied with confidence, "Yes, he is missing. He must have escaped."

For the rest of the evening, Pete didn't participate in the conversation. He felt grieved over this new revelation concerning his trusted friend. How could Hayward have been helping slaves escape to freedom without him knowing or even suspecting his friend of doing such a thing? With all of the time that they had spent together, never once was there the slightest suspicion, or impression given by Hayward that he was a participant of such an illegal scheme.

As the clock chimed nine times, Pete stood up and said, "If you all will excuse me, I am going to retire for the evening. I'm very tired and must be up very early in the morning to return to the regiment. Lester, Jonathan, maybe you should consider likewise."

There was a puzzled expression upon Lester and Jonathan's face. Jonathan quickly jumped up from his chair and replied, "Yeah, sure, come on Lester, he's right you know!"

CHAPTER EIGHTEEN

Early the next afternoon, Charles and William were in a pleasant and jovial mood as they proceeded down Grace Street toward the residence of President Davis. The two gentlemen discussed their business prospects and if there was to be a peaceful solution to the war. Charles hoped to supply a new Confederate States Army with all of the horses and cattle that they would need, which meant purchasing additional acreage. William also wanted to increase the size of his tobacco plantation and expand his business abroad. Most importantly, both of the gentlemen hoped that there would be a political future for them in this newfound nation.

As their carriage made its turn onto Clay Street, the coachman brought the horses to a halt. Charles and William took particular notice of a soldier's funeral with the regimental band playing as it proceeded slowly toward Hollywood Cemetery. Out of respect, the two gentlemen removed their hats in tribute to the fallen worrier, as his flag draped coffin, and the rider less horse followed with boots fixed in the stirrups of the saddle. Their hearts were filled with pride believing that the warrior had died for a just and noble cause. As the procession proceeded toward its destination, Charles and William continued the journey to the Executive Mansion.

Within minutes, the carriage was within sight of the President's residence; Charles was impressed with the exterior view of the mansion. It was a large three-story, gray stucco house that had trees in the front and sentries posted near by. Flying over the portico was the physical symbol of a new nation, the Confederate flag.

As the carriage came to a halt, the main servant of the house greeted the gentleman. With excitement they entered the mansion, and looked forward to meeting President Davis. They had heard many good reports from associates who personally knew him. Charles began to take notice of the interior of the mansion as they momentarily stood in the doorway. He was impressed with the marble looking wall covering, and the chandelier that hung from the ceiling; it resembled the one at Shenandoah. The main servant told the two gentlemen that he would escort them to the gardens, where President Davis was located. Charles began to be caught up in the romance of royalty as he observed the plush interior of the mansion as they walked through the house. Someday he hoped, the blessings of God would be upon him and he would inherit this kind of power and authority that President Davis possessed.

Charles noticed as he walked down the steps of the mansion, the President standing along the stone walkway observing the gardener using his skills in tending to a rose bush. The gardens were well kept and the flowers and plants revealed their magnificent beauty of multiple colors. As the two gentlemen approached the President, he turned to greet them, "Gentlemen, I have been looking forward to meeting you."

William and Charles simultaneously replied, "Mr. President."

Charles noticed energy in the President's tone of voice as the President said, "I am glad that you have answered your country's call, and have acted swiftly to her plead. There is much to do and little time to accomplish it." President Davis pointed with his hand in the direction of the gardener gazing and reminiscing as he continued his conversation with Charles and William in a more passionate tone, "I want you to take notice of the skillful dedication that this man is committed too. See how he loosens the soil around the bottom of the tree. He knows that the roots need to breathe; weeds need to be pulled to allow the bush to remain healthy, and the tree gets water when it rains. I have stood here and observed for sometime his labors. This gentleman's patience and dedicated effort will bring about a desirable result. I remember the day when I was informed that I was elected to the Presidency. I was working in my flower garden at Brierfield in Mississippi, and laboring the same as this gardener is doing. When I was called upon by the people of this youthful nation to serve in the capacity of the Presidency, I committed myself to do so with all of the strength and ability that I possessed. Since taking the office of the Presidency, I have given all of the energy that I possess to see to this new country's success. Just like you see that this labor is committed to taking care of this rose bush; I have the same dedication to this nation. The people are depending on me, and I do not intend on disappointing them."

Charles noticed the determination that glowed from the President's expression and felt inspired by the Southern leaders confidence and faith in the cause that they were fighting. William confidently replied, "It is a privilege and honor to serve one's country and to hold the admiration of its people."

"Very true, and remember it. What I am about to ask of the two of you, if successful, you will also earn the admiration of the people." The President reassured them as he continued to explain their mission and observed the gardener's skill, "The Union fleet has blocked all of our seaports, and they are slowly destroying our economy. And I don't have to tell you what that means to this young nation?"

For nearly a year, William had been experiencing difficulties in shipping his tobacco to England because of the blockade. He somberly replied as he gazed at the President, "Yes sir, I personally know."

The President continued in an optimistic tone, "It will slowly destroy the cotton industry and everything that we have struggled to achieve. We have to consider a different course of action in the way we deal with the enemy fleet."

Charles curiously inquired, "What is that, if I may ask?"

"In March we had great success with the Virginia at Hampton Roads."

"Yes, we did. As I remember, she was reconstructed with metal and had great success with destroying some of the wooden vessels."

"The Confederacy needs more ships like the Virginia to break the strong-hold the Union fleet is placing on our ports. Gentlemen, this is why I have asked that you come to Richmond. And, this is how you can serve this young nation." Charles and William were surprised, but excited to be chosen by the Confederate government for this task. After allowing the two gentlemen to digest the news, President Davis continued, "As I understand from the Governor, You two are very good at negotiations and your reputation precedes you in this skill."

Charles wanted to impress the President and take every opportunity that became available. His political future depended upon his willingness to prove his ability to Mr. Davis and the rest of the Confederate government. He was confident of handling any business affairs that he might be asked to undertake and it was evident in his voice, "Yes sir. A little more then a year ago, I re-negotiated a new contract with the army for the purchase of our cattle and horses. Instead of receiving the customary fee for each head of cattle and for each mount, I was able to negotiate for ten percent more."

"How did you accomplish that?"

"For one, my family's history and reputation for quality with delivery on time, and our ability to meet their demand. Secondly, for sometime, the army has been constantly complaining about their horses and cattle that they had been receiving from other breeders. It happens that their mounts were undesirable and didn't meet standards, or the livestock was of poor quality. I believed that my asking price was more than fair. And, if the requirements weren't acceptable, then I was willing to take the risk and take my business elsewhere. I might also add, our business has expanded so rapidly, that we had to purchase a small farm adjacent to our property. We were able to make the acquisition for next to nothing."

"Really." The President replied in a tone of amazement, and continued to curiously inquire into Charles' skill, "If you do not mine me saying, you must have a way of negotiating that I have not learned yet. You'll have to teach me so that I can, lets say, negotiate peace with Mr. Lincoln."

Charles was smiling as he looked at the President and said, "Lets just say for now, that I acquired one of my Mother's good traits, persistence."

"I see, or maybe a little ruthlessness at your approach?" The President replied as he gestured for Charles and William to walk with him toward the Executive Mansion. As they stood on the portico, the President waved at some of the citizens that were passing by the mansion. As he did so, he continued to explain what the two gentlemen's mission would be, and what he hoped would be accomplished, "By now, your probably really curious why I have summoned you gentlemen. I have called you here to help us negotiate a deal to construct several ironclad ships to be used to challenge the Federal fleet and to destroy her ships."

William enthusiastically asked, "Who shall we be dealing with?"

The answer came swiftly from the President, "You will be advising Captain Bulloch, our agent who lives in England."

Charles asked, "When shall we leave?"

The president's eyes were fixed on their expression of excitement as he answered, "Within the week, hopefully. We are secretly in the process of making the arrangements for your departure."

William proudly replied, "Mr. President, we are honored as Virginians and as citizens of this new country to serve in this noble effort."

The President cheerfully said, "Mr. Pierce, I like to work with men who have a zeal about them, and believe in the cause that they represent." He continued in an optimistic tone of voice as they began to enter the mansion, "I would like you gentlemen to stay in the city for the next several days so that you can meet with Secretary Mallory and Secretary Randolph to work out the details before leaving."

Late in the afternoon, Charles returned to his Aunt Daisy's house to see if Caroline and Ann had arrived from the Valley. He requested that his family follow him as soon as possible, provided they could secure a travel pass from the Federal Provost Marshall. He knew that Caroline would be excited at the opportunity to visit Richmond once more. Furthermore, he did not have any knowledge how long his business would keep him in the capitol and away from the Estate. With these events, it was his intentions to spend as much time as possible with his family.

Charles' eyes shined brightly as he stepped down from the carriage and embraced Caroline and Ann, who had arrived safely from Harpers Ferry. As they walked into the house, Caroline began to inquire into the meeting that her husband had earlier in the day with the President, "Charles, why did President Davis ask you to come to Richmond on such short notice?"

Just as Charles was beginning to answer his wife, Aunt Daisy and Rebecca walked into the parlor with the same question. In an attempt to be as polite as possible, he began to smile and holding his hands in the air for silence, he said, "I know that everyone is curious to know what took place today in my meeting with the President, but quite frankly, I can not discuss the matter with you."

Rebecca anxiously replied, "Oh dear, why? What is going on that you can't share with your family?"

"It is government business, and at this time I can't share with you our discussions. Eventually, you shall all know." Charles replied as he placed his hand around Caroline's waist. The room was filled with awe as everyone glanced at each other and respected his wishes. Quietly, he excused himself, and along with his wife, they retired to the guest bedroom.

As they were walking up the stairs, Caroline anxiously asked her husband, "What is going on?"

Charles replied as he glanced about to see who was within the sound of their voice, "Please wait until we have some privacy?"

Before Charles and William had departed the Executive Mansion, President Davis had requested their secrecy on the subject because of possible spies in the city. When he was sure that none of the servants were outside the bedroom door and they were alone, he allowed Caroline to speak freely. Without hesitation, she began to inquire, "If I may ask, now, that we are alone, why did the President want you to come to Richmond?"

Charles confidently answered as he changed his shirt and tie, "It is his request that William and I travel to England and assist Captain Bulloch in his negotiations with a British contractor for the construction of two new ironclad ships to be used against the Union blockade."

Caroline asked surprisingly, "What? You can't go abroad and leave Ann and me."

Charles began to laugh as he turned from the mirror that stood in the corner and placed his hands on his wife's shoulders. He said in a smiling and reassuring tone, "I can not take you and Ann with me. First of all, I don't know how long my business will keep me abroad. Secondly, if you haven't forgotten, there is a war going on, not just on land, but also by sea."

"I can not let you go. I am afraid something may happen to you!"

The smile disappeared as Charles replied with a tone of seriousness, "Caroline, nothing is going to happen to me. I'm going to come home to you and Ann."

There was persistence in her voice, "It is too much of a risk! Mr. Mason and Mr. Slidell were captured and sent to prison in their efforts last year when they attempted to go to England on government business."

"Yes, and they finally made it."

"Well, if something happens to you; what will become of Ann and me?"

"Caroline, Caroline my love." He said as he held her close to his body and caressing her long blond hair. "This trip is too important for our young nation and its citizens." As he continued to speak passionately, "This is my way of contributing to the cause, just as my brother is contributing by serving with General Stuart. This is very important to me, very important. I don't expect you to understand; I just ask that you will accept my judgment in this matter. In the future, I could prosper from this service."

Caroline earnestly said as she gazed into his eyes, "My love, I don't care if your political ambitions prosper or not. I would rather have nothing in this life, then to lose you."

As she continued to gaze into his eyes, he did not answer. She only saw the determination and will to go forth with the President's request. Caroline had been filled with anxiety and fear since Charles had received the telegram from the President several days ago. At night, sleep had escaped her grasp, and tears had filled her eyes as she laid upon her pillow with premonitions of what the future might bring for the couple. It was tempting for Caroline to share these feelings with her husband as he held her, but she repressed them knowing that it would grieve him, and possibly show a mistrust in his judgments. She knew that he was a prideful and stubborn man who would not turn down the President's request, even against her wishes.

After six that evening, William joined Charles and his family for dinner on their request. It was a delightful hour as they reminisced in times past before the war. They had just finished their meal when Caroline softly asked her husband, "Charles, has anyone seen or heard from Pete?"

"Oh yes." Charles cordially replied as he wiped his mouth with the fine white linen after taking a sip of the black coffee that had been served to him by one of the servants. "His regiment was camped outside the city, and he was able to acquire a one day furlough. Lester and a friend that he met from the Valley, I believe his name was Jonathan were with him."

Caroline replied in a disappointing tone, "I wish that I would have arrived in time to see him. I miss him so."

With the same expression of feelings, Ann added, "I would have like to seen him also, Father. Why didn't you tell him to wait for us?"

In a serious tone of voice, Charles said to his daughter as she began to wipe a tear from her eyes, "Ann, your Uncle Pete had to return to his regiment. He has responsibilities. Do you remember what I taught you about that subject?"

Ann promptly replied sniffling, "Yes, Father."

"Oh, that reminds me," Caroline said, remembering something of value she was carrying for Pete, "Charles, I have a letter for Pete from Katie. She was going to send it, but when I told her that I was coming to Richmond, she asked me if I would bring it with me.

Charles replied ignorantly, "I do not know where his regiment is located. When I spoke with him yesterday, he did not know where the 1st would be moving next."

There was a concern in Caroline's voice as she asked, "How will I be able to deliver Katie's letter?"

During this exchange of conversation, William had remained silent and listened carefully to every word. He had been curious about the relationship between Katie and Pete, but did not want to be so bold as to make any inquiries. On several occasions since the beginning of the war, he had had the privilege of visiting Charles and his family at the Estate. When he saw Katie on those particular visits, he was cordial toward her, though he knew that she desired a relationship with Pete. Still, there was a strong determination to win her love. He believed that would be possible with persistence, and Pete's willingness to show a lack of interest in a relationship with her. It would be to his advantage, as long as the war continued, that they would remain separated. William had heard from one of General Stuart's adjutants that furloughs were hard to come by with the army under going such important operations; and he did not foresee any in the near future. This was a joyful tiding to William's ears. Now, if possible, he wanted to get his hands on the letter that was intended for Pete from Katie. Politely, William intervened, "If I may, I know of a dear friend here in the city who may help. I just might be able to get Katie's letter to him."

"Thank you. I am sure that Katie will appreciate your generosity." Caroline gladly replied, as she handed him the sealed envelope.

Rebecca asked, as she glanced in Caroline's direction with a tone of deceitfulness, "Oh, maybe there will be a wedding after all." Giggling and continuing, "I wonder if my brother was fibbing to me about Miss McBride?"

Caroline's expression turned from contentment to one of seriousness as she swiftly replied, "Rebecca, what did you say to him?"

As Rebecca replied, she had a mischief smile that covered her face, "Oh, Caroline, as I recall, on your last visit you said something to the effect that Miss McBride was showing an interest in my brother, and that there was hope of a permanent relationship between them. Is that not true?"

Caroline paused momentarily and then she chose her words wisely, "Yes, I remember the conversation. But Rebecca, as I recall, what I said was something entirely different from what you have insinuated. As I recall, I said that hopefully Pete and Katie would begin to have a relationship. I said nothing about the existence of one already. Now, if you will answer my question, what was his response?"

Rebecca looked in the direction of her older brother for his deliverance from his wife's question. She did not want to seem foolish in front of Mr. Pierce and her aunt. When no one was willing to come to her salvation, she answered in a mellow tone, "He became very defensive and I believe a little angry at me, though he did not show it. Caroline I am so sorry. I just wanted to have some fun with him. You know how he is with the ladies."

"Yes, I do." Caroline answered as she continued in a serious tone, "But I do not feel that it was your place to bring up the subject of marriage to him."

"Oh, Caroline." Charles said with laughter in his tone of voice, "You know how my brother is. He is a ladies man. Matrimony will never be an option for him in his life."

Caroline was beginning to defend Pete when Aunt Daisy abruptly said, "What James sees in an abolitionist I will never know."

Caroline cried out, "Please Aunt Daisy, she is my friend."

"I do not care! She is an abolitionist!" Aunt Daisy replied angrily and continued to display her feelings with a pitched tone, "This war that our boys are fighting is because of people like her, they just can't keep their nose out of our affairs. If they did so, we would not be fighting a war. Now would we?"

Caroline cried out, "That is not so! That is not so!"

Charles shouted, "Caroline, that is enough!"

Caroline began to weep and said to everyone that was present, "You all do not understand, she is like a sister to me."

Ann became very emotional as her Father attempted to calm her. She was granted permission from him to leave the room, and was escorted by Trudy, Caroline's personal servant.

Rebecca was always ready for an argument and loved the challenge that it could bring. She said to Caroline in a nasty manner, "But she is from the North. Why do you think those Yankees are at the doorstep of the capital? They have invaded our homes and our way of life, and bring destruction. Caroline, have you ever thought that one of them might be her brother pointing a gun at the gentleman that I have become fond of, not to mention my brother. Besides Caroline, you are from the Valley. I just can't imagine you wanting to be friends with a Yankee girl any more then I could see my brother married to one."

William began to smile and kindly said to everyone, "Well, one day this conflict will come to an end, and I guess we will see how strong of a friendship these two ladies have. If this war does not destroy it, then nothing will."

Charles calmly said, "William is that your feelings on the matter?"

Rebecca did not allow William time to answer Charles' question, instead she rose from her chair and angrily replied, "Caroline, you have betrayed your family and your husband."

Caroline verbally fired back, "How can you say that, Rebecca?"

Charles shouted as he waved his hands in the air for everyone to be silent, "Ladies, that is enough!

Caroline excused herself from the table and quickly departed to the privacy of her room.

Charles stood and shook his head in frustration as he took a drink of water. Then he said in the same manner of voice, "No one in this room wanted to see war with the North no more then I did. I didn't want my life to change and had hoped that there would have been a peaceful resolution to this matter, but unfortunately, that did not happen. Now we must see this conflict to its conclusion and hope and pray that our life as we know it continues. As for Caroline and her relationship to Katie McBride, well, I have felt for sometime that they had become too close in their relationship. Mother didn't like the idea from the beginning, and with the outbreak of conflict, I really didn't attempt to promote it. But on the other hand, I didn't do anything to discourage it."

"Why Charles?" Rebecca angrily replied. "If you knew how Mother felt about Miss McBride, why were you so passive?"

"Charles, Charles." Aunt Daisy added as she shook her head in disappointment.

Charles was frustrated and disappointed with himself because he had not addressed the subject with Caroline before now. It was a matter that he had been contemplating for sometime, but because of Katie and his wife's close relationship, he had desired not to hinder it in anyway. Since Katie and Caroline had become close friends he had noticed a difference in her disposition and attitude toward life. It was as if there had been a void that had been filled within her heart. She was more jovial and sociable, and her moods of depression had long vanished. With no end to the conflict in sight, it would become a risk for them to continue a relationship, especially now that Charles was going abroad and involved in secret government matters. He became more determine in his tone of voice as he answered, "No, Rebecca is right. I have been too passive on the matter. I need to speak with Caroline about Katie as soon as there is an opportunity. Their relationship can not continue with the continuation of the conflict."

William agreed, "Yes Charles. You would be doing the right thing, the sooner the better for everyone that is involved."

As Charles and William were exchanging conversation, Caroline had quietly walked down the stairs to return to the dinning room to apologize for her actions. As she was about to enter, she overheard the two gentlemen talking about her relationship with Katie. Caroline was shocked and grieved by what transpired. Taking her handkerchief, she held it against her face and silently began to weep. Quickly and without drawing attention to herself, she returned to her room.

Caroline was sitting by the window that overlooked Grace Street and began to think of what she had overheard her husband discussing. Caroline was still in disbelief. She began to ponder on her friendship with Katie McBride. It had grown immensely over the pass year and a half. The two of them had become almost inseparable and shared a love and trust for one another. Even though Katie was from a state that strongly supported abolishment of slavery, they still respected one another's views on the subject, and did not allow it to hinder their loyalty. Caroline gradually began to feel depressed over her husband's intentions. As she stood and walked over to the mirror, she glanced at the somber expression that covered her face. There was a sorrow that ruled her heart. What would she say and do when her husband approached her concerning this issue. How would she react? For now she hoped, he would not return to the room. With feelings and emotions of being caught off guard, Caroline needed time to concentrate on her response. As she returned to the window and glanced at some of the citizens walking casually in front of the mansion, she became fearful at the thought of separation from her closest friend.

After dinner, William and Charles retired to the library, where in privacy they discussed their meeting with the President earlier in the day. They shared their views and the best approach for negotiating an agreement to have the ironclad ships constructed. After a few brandies, they broke off the discussion. With the hour late and everyone having retired for the evening, William and Charles decided to do likewise.

As William entered his room, he removed his gray frock coat and began to loosen his black tie, when he remembered the letter that Caroline had entrusted to him from Katie. He took a sip of the brandy that he had carried to his room and contemplated opening the letter. It was difficult for him to overcome the temptation. He laid it on the stand next to the chair while he continued to prepare for bed, occasionally glancing at it and wondering about its contents.

After washing his face, he wiped with the towel that had been provided. As he did so, William decided that the letter could not be delivered to Pete as originally promised. Instead, he would read Katie's correspondences and then destroy it. Slowly, he walked over and picked up the letter; he didn't feel guilty at the thought of looking at its contents. He knew from what he read, that Katie was making every attempt to keep the lines of communications open with Pete. It was his intentions to keep that from happening. William removed a match from his pocket and lit it. As the flame flickered and burned brightly, he held the letter in his left hand. Igniting the letter, he watched the flames as they begin to consume the paper that contained its valuable wording. He began to think to himself; there will never be a union between the two as long as I live. With that thought, he began to softly laugh, believing that Pete would never know the words that had been written to him.

CHAPTER NINETEEN

Very early the next morning, the birds were singing outside of Caroline's window. She quietly dressed and walked out into the garden that was to the rear of the mansion. It was quiet in the capital of the Confederacy, and at sunrise the city still appeared to be sleeping even though Federal troops were within a short distance. It had been a restless night for Caroline; sleep had escaped her weary eyes. She felt exhausted from contemplating her options concerning the course of action to pursue once Charles confronted the question about her relationship with Katie McBride. Surely her husband would present the subject before he departed for the Executive Mansion and his meeting with Secretary Mallory and President Davis. As she sat on the wooden bench along the pathway, she admired Aunt Daisy's gray cat taking care of its kittens. For a short of time, Caroline observed the mothers behavior and smiled as she attended to their needs. It was the first time in many hours that she allowed her mind to rest from pondering on the war and the future of her relationship with Katie. There would not be an easy answer to the problem; soon she must determine what her response will be when Charles confronts her. If she allows some separation in the friendship with Katie, then her marriage would continue to be a relationship of harmony and contentment that she had enjoyed for the past year. But also, she never experienced the joy of fellowship with her younger sister like she had with Katie McBride. Caroline was torn within her heart. If she weren't obedient to her husband's request, then the matter would cause a possible division and destruction of her marriage to Charles. One of the many thoughts that troubled her mind was the commitment that her husband was making to the Confederate government, and the secrecy that it demanded of him and the family. What would happen if she accidentally shared some of the information with Katie? Would she pass it on to Union authorities since they still controlled the Ferry? Almost immediately, Caroline shrugged the thought, she didn't believe that Katie would jeopardize the trust and love that they shared. The challenge for Caroline would be convincing her husband of Katie's trust. If she were not able to do so, then there would be no other alternative but to end her relationship with Katie. There was a special commitment concerning their friendship, and the thought of making this difficult choice made her feel nauseous and anxious. As she thought on these matters, there was the sound of a voice from behind, "Caroline, you have awakened early." Charles said as he placed his hand on her shoulder.

As she turned and touched his hand, she softly replied, "Yes, I couldn't sleep, so I came to the garden."

Charles sat next to her and gently held her hand. She anxiously waited for him to continue the conversation, but he just gazed in the direction where the capitol building was located. Caroline inquired, "Your quiet. Is there something wrong?"

There was calmness as he looked into her eyes, replying, "I guess I'm troubled with leaving you and Ann."

"I was awake all night, concerned about your safety traveling to Europe. I was thinking that if for some reason your intentions were discovered, then the Union fleet will make an attempt to stop your ship, and if your vessel resist, then it will be fired upon. I could not bear the thought of losing you, or you being in a Federal prisoner-of-war camp, "She said with a tone of anxiety. As she continued, she desperately pleaded with him, "I wish that you would reconsider the President's request and return to Shenandoah with Ann and me. We could leave today."

There was brightness in Charles' eyes as he spoke with earnest, "Caroline, sometimes in life you have to be willing to assume a risk in order to get what you desire. In this case, it isn't a political future, but the survival of a way of life. Ours. If the North wins this conflict then the equation will change, and once more we will have to submit to Union authority."

"What? What are you saying Charles?"

He sighed and took a deep breath, "What I am saying my love is simply this, should Lincoln win this war, then slavery will be abolished. Do you have any idea what it would cost us to hire laborers to work 4,800 acres? Quite a bit. With slave labor it cost nothing."

"Well Charles, some of the slaves have already escaped."

"I know. But if we win this war, or compromise, then we can retain the institution of slavery," Charles confidently replied and continued to speak with his wife in the same tone of voice, "My love, this is what I am fighting for, this cause for independence is what means the most to me, and I hope for you. Our way of life is our future, and Ann's. I cannot bare the thought of it changing. It is such a small price that I would pay for making every attempt to serve when called upon."

Caroline was silent, but filled with admiration for her husband's commitment to the new Confederate government, and his willingness to risk his life for a more promising future for the family. She softly said as she placed her hand upon his, "I'm touched by your spirit of patriotism and dedication to the cause for Southern independence. I just want you to promise me that you will come home when your business abroad is finished."

Charles said as he leaned forward and kissed her lips, "I will."

After his show of affection toward his wife, Charles, turned once more and gazed in the direction of the capitol building. As he did so, he began to share with Caroline some of the conversation that President Davis had shared with him the previous afternoon, "The President said something to William and me yesterday at the Executive Mansion that left an impression on me."

"What's that dear?"

Charles continued in a humble tone, "He told us that when he accepted the Presidency, he committed all of his strength and ability to the effort. By his determination he would not fail the citizens of this youthful nation. His faith and commitment to his office and responsibility to the Country amazes me. The zeal that he possesses intrigues me even with his bad health. I hope that you and I might acquire that kind of dedication to this campaign."

Caroline spoke swiftly with a sound of assurance in her voice, "Oh, but I do. I agree whole heartily with your views. I do not want my way of life to change anymore then you do. I have a great desire and hope that the Union forces will leave Virginia."

Charles turned once more and looked into her eyes, "Well my love, if you are as sincere with your feelings on these issues as I am, then we have something that we need to discuss before I leave for England and you return to the Valley."

Caroline asked, with a cautious tone knowing the issue her husband was about to ask, "What is that my love?"

As Charles continued to gaze into his wife's eyes and with a passionate sound in his voice, he said, "Caroline, there is not a word on God's earth that could describe my love and admiration for you. But what I have to ask of you causes me much grief and sorrow. For you, it will be a great sacrifice, I know, but our future and Ann's depends on what happens with the out come of this war. Therefore, we have to do what ever it takes to protect our survival as well as our family." Charles sighed deeply and with a painful expression on his face, he continued to speak to his wife, "What I'm asking you is this." He paused briefly and momentarily looked away, then once more he turned and gazed into her eyes, continuing, "Caroline, my love, you should end your friendship with Katie McBride." As Caroline began to speak, Charles held up his hands and asked, "Wait my love, allow me to finish. I know how close your relationship is with Katie, but Caroline she is from the North. Her views and values are so different from ours. How do we know that she could be trusted, especially with the task that I have been entrusted to do?"

Caroline's behavior was calm, though there was a defensive tone in her voice, "Charles, we have known from the outset Katie's feelings concerning slavery and our way of life. And never once in our conversations has she ever condemned the way in which we have lived our lives. As you well know, she is like a sister to me; she is even closer to me then my own flesh and blood." Caroline said with a quiver in her voice as she continued to speak, "I have a very difficult time with your request of me. I had a premonition of this and I was afraid that eventually you would ask this of me."

Charles noticed the tears that began to fill his wife's eyes. Taking a handkerchief from his coat pocket, he gently wiped them away and once again spoke in a passionate tone, "I knew that this would cause you much distress. I've noticed the behavior in which your life has changed with your acquaintance with Katie; you have been a totally different person. But I am fearful that somewhere along the way she might get a hold of some important information and betray us. It may cause casualties for our side, and one of them just might be my brother."

Caroline became frustrated and said, "Charles, Charles how can you say that about her. She has the highest regards for you and your Mother. Katie respects you. And when it comes to Pete, well, there is nothing that she would do to cause him injury. What do you think it going to do to her if I tell her we can not be friends any longer because of this war? How do you think she is going to feel?"

Charles replied with a flare in his tone of voice, "Hopefully, she will understand!"

Caroline quickly cried out, "No Charles she will not understand! She will feel betrayed and deeply hurt by our actions. Wouldn't you, if the roles were reversed?"

Charles was silent and allowed Caroline's emotions to calm. He stood and looked toward the northeast, and calmly said as he pointed in that direction, "Not too far outside of the city, the Confederate army is about to do battle with General McClellan. As I understand, his army is over a 100,000 men, who are better equipped, then our men. And even though my brother and I do not see eye to eye on matters, I know that he is out there doing his duty to God and our Country, as I'm sure that Katie's brother is doing likewise. Caroline we owe it to Pete, and every able body man who is fighting for the Confederacy to be given the chance to win."

"I know."

Charles turned and placed his hands on her shoulders, looking into her teary eyes, he said, "I respect your feelings in regards to Katie, but I feel that it would be for the best if you sever your friendship with her as soon as possible. As your husband, I must insist upon this request."

Caroline noticed the sincerity in his eyes and the determination in his voice. She knew that it wouldn't be wise to be disobedient to his demands for fear that it would jeopardize her marriage. Caroline responded, "If this is what you demand of me, even though I strongly disagree, then I guest I have no other choice in the matter. Do I?"

"Charles shook his head and softly said, "No, there is no other way. For now, I would just ask that you trust my judgment on this matter."

Caroline began to openly weep and clinched her hands tightly in frustration and anger. She swiftly ran into the house without saying a word to Aunt Daisy, who was walking from the drawing room. Caroline proceeded toward the bedroom. Charles followed and called out, "Caroline! Caroline!" But she would not stop and answer.

Aunt Daisy, taking notice of her nephew, as he was about to pursue his wife up the long stairway quickly called out to him, "Charles, Charles, wait!" He paused in his efforts and looked in his aunt's direction. Slowly he turned and walked back down the few steps towards her. There was a pleading sound in her voice as she said, "Charles do not be hard on her. Give her sometime to be alone and think. By the end of the day she will see the wisdom in your decision."

As Charles looked in the direction of the bedroom, he answered his aunt, "I hope so."

Still feeling greatly frustrated over the disagreement, Charles walked out on to the front porch of the house. There he noticed William smoking a cigar and sitting in one of the many wooden chairs that covered the porch. He slowly walked over to where William was, and leaning against one of the white columns that supported the upper porch, Charles noticed some of the citizens passing by in their coaches and carriages.

William knew that the discussion between Charles and Caroline had taken place just as his friend had promised the previous evening. As William remained silent, he began to ponder upon the advantages that this decision would have for him in his efforts to win Katie's love. Surely, with any visitations in the future to the Estate, it would be an imposition of him to invite Katie to any of the functions that the Barker's might have. Also, with the amount of dedication that Charles felt toward his commitment to the Confederate government, he would frown upon any communications with Katie. Whatever contact he wished to make with Katie would have to be done secretly. Though, without any friends in town, would she return to Boston? He did not think so. With Caroline's revelation that her family had pleaded with her on more then one occasion to do so, Katie would have acted by now. As for Pete, William did not believe as long as the war continued that he would be a factor. Fighting with the 1st Virginia would keep him busy for now, and the couple would be separated. William was positive of that. As soon as his business abroad was accomplished, he would depart for the Valley, and visit with the Barker's as long as it was safe to do so. It was his belief that by the time he returns from England, Katie will have felt the effects of the alienation of Caroline's companionship. If this happens, the way that he has imagined, then it would be the ideal time for him to take advantage of her vulnerability and make various attempts to win her affection and devotion. For now, he thought, the attempt should be made to comfort his friend's pain; William calmly said, "Charles, you are quiet. I assume that you have spoken with Caroline about Katie, and apparently, it did not go well?"

Charles replied with a sound of frustration in his voice, "No William, it didn't."

William puffed on his cigar and looked in Charles' direction as he continued to express words of reassurance, "I didn't feel that it would go well. Caroline and Katie became too close at the wrong time in their life. It's too bad they didn't meet each other somewhere down the road. Unfortunately, there is a war going on, and at this time no one knows who their friend or foe might be."

William made this statement to give Charles the confidence that the action he was demanding of his wife was the right course to follow. As Charles stood and slowly walked toward the front door of the mansion, he said with conviction, "I do believe that I made the right decision for my family and myself. As difficult as it may be for Caroline, I know that she will honor my request. Hopefully, when all of this is over with, then, maybe Katie and Caroline will be able to salvage, or pick up from where they left off."

William shook his head in disagreement, and said, "No Charles, I don't think so. Once you have broken the trust between two people it becomes very difficult to rebuild a relationship all over again."

As he patted his friend on the shoulder, William proceeded into the house, leaving Charles with his thoughts concerning the actions and the consequences that were sure to follow his request of Caroline.

It was still early in the morning as Charles and William arrived to attend their meeting at the President's office that was to be held on the second floor of the Executive Mansion. Those present for these discussions besides Charles and William were President Davis, Secretary Mallory, Secretary Randolph, Colonel Preston Johnston, and Captain Moss, a secret agent for the Confederacy. During the meeting, various ideas had been presented by the Secretary of the Navy concerning the acquisition of the ironclad ships, but how to pay for their construction presented a problem. Charles and William had suggested payment should be made with products produced in the South, such as cotton, but the President rejected the idea. As they continued, Charles noticed that President Davis seemed to be restless; it appeared to him that his mind was not on the business at hand. The President would occasionally stand behind his desk and then he would walk over to glance out the window. As the conversation continued Charles asked Captain Moss when they would be leaving for England. He was informed that it would be by the end of the week. Charles again took notice of the President by the window; it was though, he thought, that the

President was waiting on something to take place. Time had quickly passed; they were concluding the business that brought them to the Executive Mansion. There was a knock at the door. Captain Moss walked over and opened the door. It was a messenger from General Lee informing the President that there would be an assault on the Union forces near the Chickahominy River in the vicinity of Mechanicsville. Charles noticed that the President was standing straight like a soldier at attention while receiving the news; the fiery-glow that was in the President's eyes revealed his determination for success in this conflict. He gave Charles the impression of a warrior, who was ready to do battle, a Roman leader who was ready to conquer and lead his nation to victory. At once the President asked that his horse be saddled and invited Charles and William to join him.

Secretary of War Randolph joined the President, Charles, and William for the short journey toward Mechanicsville. As they hastily proceeded along the road toward the sound of battle, they forded the Chickahominy River and passed the troops of Major-General D. H. Hill's division. Some of the soldiers came to a halt and cheered as the Presidential party passed by, others just continued to proceed toward the rumble of musketry and the thunder of artillery. It left an impression upon Charles at the positive attitude and confidence of the ordinary soldier in the Confederate army. As William and Charles were riding side by side on their horses, Charles made the remark, "The troops seem to be in fine spirits and itching for a fight."

William answered with excitement as he listened to the increasing crescendo of musketry in their front, "Yes my friend, they are showing confidence and determination."

Charles was curious and asked, "I wonder where my brother might be?"

"I don't know. As I understand from Captain Moss the 1st was somewhere in the vicinity with General Jackson," William replied, as he observed some Confederate officers mounted on their horses in the middle of the road directly in front of them. Shells went screaming overhead and occasionally, one would explode near the officers, but they were not hindered in their direction of the engagement. It was not the environment that Charles and William were accustomed to, and they were somewhat frightened by it all. Off to the east of the road in the field, they noticed a Confederate brigade in battle formation with flags fluttering in the air. Charles noticed an officer looking in their direction as they approached, then he turned his back to them to speak with a fellow officer before turning once more in their direction. He naturally assumed that this important officer must be General Lee. Charles was riding directly behind the President, when the party came to a halt. He noticed the disturbed expression that covered General Lee's face as he frigidly saluted President Davis. General Lee was not moved by the Presidential party, and once again turned his attention toward the battle that was taking place. There was an irritating tone in his voice as he asked the President, "Who is this army of people with you, and what are they doing here?"

There was complete silence as everyone waited for a response from President Davis. It did not come. Both Charles and William glanced at each other with a surprised expression, knowing that the General was speaking to the President about the presence of those who accompanied him on this journey to witness the engagement. In his attempt to ignore the situation between the two leaders, Charles continued to observe the steady flow of troops that were arriving.

Charles noticed the President turning in his saddle to look at the General. From the cold expression that covered the President's face, Charles knew that he was quite upset with the chilly reception from General Lee. Charles could tell by the General's demeanor, that he was not intimidated by President Davis' presence. At times while General Lee was seated on his mount, he would glance at the President and his party of followers with an expression of dissatisfaction. After pausing, President Davis said to General Lee in response to his question, "It is not my army, General."

General Lee replied with promptness, as he looked through his field glasses at the Union position, "It certainly is not my army, Mr. President." Continuing in a commanding tone of voice, he glanced at President Davis, "This is no place for these people. They may become injured if they stay."

The President was stunned by the reception from General Lee that his party had received. After he regained his composure, he bluntly said, "Well, General, if I withdraw, perhaps they will follow."

William was sure that if the President and those who accompanied him didn't leave soon, then General Lee might have them removed by force in order to protect them.

President Davis turned his horse's head, and saluted General Lee. He proceeded slowly with the party toward the bridge. As they complied, Charles was stunned when a soldier fell dead near the President, as Union artillery began to pound the road that they were traveling. He was terrified at the sight of blood pouring from the trooper's upper body. Bringing his horse to a halt, Charles gazed at the horrified expression that covered the soldier's face. Then quickly, he crossed the stream with President Davis and William. On a high bank behind some bushes and trees, they continued to observe the battle that raged.

The Confederate batteries and infantry had already silenced the Federal artillery and had driven their forces about a mile to some fortifications along a creek with a high bank overlooking it. From his position, Charles observed the Federal infantry entrenched in large numbers and in a strong position of defense along with the artillery support. As the Confederate infantry prepared to storm across an open area, Charles continued to observe the troop movements with the anticipation of the outcome. He took pride in what he witnessed. There were many in the Confederate ranks that were very young, but Charles noticed that some of the soldiers were more then old enough to be their fathers.

With the field officers giving the command, Confederate infantry with their battle flags blowing in the breeze rapidly began its assault on the Union lines. As the Confederate skirmishers rapidly moved toward the Union battle line, the fire from the Union artillery and infantry became intense. The skirmishers retreated under the Federal borough. Within minutes, the main column of Confederate infantry advanced in force under the cover of heavy artillery fire from behind their battle line. The sound from the rebel's cannons was deafening. Charles watched as a murderous volley of musketry killed or wounded many of the men in the front ranks of the attacking regiments as they approached the Union fortifications. The fighting appeared to Charles to be at a close range. As the assault continued, Charles, reposition himself on his saddle, looking in William's direction. He yelled, as the Confederate batteries continued to fire shot and shell with fury, "The Yanks are well protected. It's going to be difficult to defeat them in such a defensive position."

William promptly replied, as he pointed in the direction of the Confederates regiments from Georgia and Louisiana as they waded in the water to assault the Union flank, "Charles, I am confident that the assault will be successful. Our boys can take those entrenchments."

As the Confederate regiments proceeded into the wooded area to attack the Union flank, Charles glanced at President Davis to see what his reaction was to the events that were unfolding. He was surprised as he looked to see that he was not troubled at the amount of life that was being lost from the assault on the Union position. President Davis appeared to have an expression of pride and resolve as he sat motionless and straight in his saddle. It was then, that Charles remembered that the President was a graduate of West Point and a veteran from the Mexican War. This incident explained to Charles, why at the onset of this engagement, he showed no emotion when the Confederate soldier was killed near him earlier as they departed General Lee's company near the bridge.

Quickly, Charles' concentration was broken with the sound of gun and cannon fire, as some of the Union troops were pouring volley after volley of heavy musket fire and canister from the artillery pieces into the Confederate regiments that were attempting to turn their flank. As he noticed the grim expression on William's face at the onslaught of life, he knew that his friend was having difficulty with the events he was witnessing. Charles kept his silence.

By now, it appeared to Charles, that the Federal forces were as determined to hold their position as the Confederate forces were to take it. Both Charles and William witnessed the hand-to-hand combat that was taking place, and struggled to hold their composure at the brutality of this type of warfare. At times during the engagement, the firing was so intense, that the field was covered with thick white clouds of smoke that impaired their view of the battle. It was with great difficulty before Charles could determine the outcome of the assault; all he could hear was the constant crashing thunder of the weapons releasing their missiles of death. The struggle had been going on for sometime. Grudgingly, the Confederate regiments began to retreat back across the field of battle. As the rebels did so, the Union forces were relentless in their attack as they kept up their murderous fire. Everywhere the eye could see, Charles thought, the carnage was beyond anything that he could have imagined. There was not an area of the battlefield that was not covered with the dead and wounded. After the attempt by the Confederate regiments, there was a lull in the engagement.

It was near dusk, and another assault was going to be attempted by the Confederate troops. After the furious frontal assault, Charles could not believe that there would be another attempt. Charles observed the brigade as they stormed gallantly and heroically across the field in another charge on the Union fortifications. He gazed at the horrible death that came to many of the officers and enlisted men, as their bodies became human sacrifices in the charge. The explosion of shell and canisters had a devastating affect on the charging Confederate ranks as they fell by the dozens shrieking with pain. Courageously, the soldiers continued forward. On more then one occasion, a soldier carrying the flag fell, but gallantly, another courageous soldier retrieved the colors and continued the charge at the head of his regiment. The moans and cries of the wounded attracted Charles and William's attention as the medical personal carried them on litters toward a field hospital for medical care. Charles could not imagine the pain and suffering that the soldiers were experiencing, but his attention always returned to the outcome of the conflict. The Federal forces had been successful once more in their attempt to hold the position as the Confederates retreated across the field to safety. After the smoke from the battle had settled, Charles' eyes scanned the field. His heart was filled with sorrow as he looked at the many soldiers that laid motionless from the Confederate efforts. He watched as comrades from various Confederate regiments that fought in this engagement offer assistance to the wounded. His ears could not escape the sounds of the dying and the wounded that pleaded for help. Or those looking for relief from death for the terrible pain that they suffered. The battle had ended and Charles found himself without words that expressed his feelings and emotions. The images today, he thought, would linger in his mind for the rest of his life. Though it appeared to be such a waste of life, Charles believed that the men, who sacrificed their life at Mechanicsville, had not done so in vain, but for a noble and just cause. With these feelings he found comfort and justification in his pride for the Southern cause for independence.

CHAPTER TWENTY

By the first of July the Union garrison stationed at Harpers Ferry was still under the command of Colonel Miles. General Wool was in charge of the Middle Department in Baltimore and argued to Secretary of War Stanton, that the defenses of the town were not adequate to meet any Confederate threat. The General's recommendation was to send additional regiments and artillery to the area to bolster its defenses, and be placed under Colonel Miles command. For some months, the town had been vacated by many of its citizens due to the continuous threat of conflict and campaigning. Now, with the increased infantry and artillery presence, many of the civilians returned to the town and attempted once again, to live a normal life.

At Shenandoah, it was a quiet and peaceful day. Elizabeth was alone and eating some fresh fish that had been caught earlier from the river for her afternoon meal. As she quietly sat at the table, she was lost in her thoughts about Charles and the nature of his business with President Davis. She had received very little word from Charles, and as a loving mother; she was concerned for his safety. Elizabeth, as well as many in the area knew of the on going Northern campaign against the Confederate capitol by General McClellan and she was quite concern. Elizabeth had been very careful not to reveal Charles and Caroline's business to Daniel, or even their absence to her close friends in the area. Life had been somewhat stressful for Elizabeth. She had discovered that the war was affecting her quality of life; still, she made the attempt to live life normally under the circumstances that war produces. For the past several months, the family had been under scrutiny from Union authorities because of their Southern passions, opinions, and political views on the issues of slavery and states rights. Periodically, over the last two weeks, Federal patrols visited the Estate and inquired into where Charles might be. With the increased number of slaves that were escaping from the Estate, this also added to the family's difficulties. It had been a time of tribulation for Elizabeth, but because of her strong ability to prevail, she was willing to endure any hardships and sacrifices that were needed to be successful.

As Elizabeth was finishing her meal, Matthew came into the dinning room and informed her that there was a coach approaching the house. Elizabeth had not extended an invitation to any of her friends today; therefore, she began to wonder who might be paying an unexpected visit this afternoon. Without hesitation, Elizabeth got up from the table with Matthew's assistance, and walked out onto the front porch to see who it might be. As the coachman brought the horses to a halt, Ann began to wave from the window in the door of the coach. There was a glowing smile that covered Elizabeth's face with the arrival of her family. Maybe, now, she could find out some news about Charles' meeting with President Davis. Elizabeth was excited and anxious as the coachman opened the door of the coach and began to help Ann and Caroline. Charles was not with them, and immediately, Elizabeth became somewhat concerned. Quickly, she placed a hand on her cheek and despair replaced her smile. Caroline took notice of her mother-in-law's expression of fear and moved with speed to bring words of reassurance, "Mother Elizabeth, Charles is fine."

Ann added, as she hugged her grandmother, "Father is fine, he had to stay behind. He sends his love and he will be home soon."

Elizabeth found comfort in their words and her emotions began to calm as she held her hands together. Elizabeth anxiously asked, "Caroline, why didn't Charles return with you and Ann?"

Caroline was prompt with her answer as she gestured for her personal servant, "His business will require him to be absent for awhile longer."

"What kind of business would keep him away from home?"

Caroline knew that she must tell Elizabeth the truth about what had taken place with Charles' meeting with the President, but it would not be until they were in a place of privacy. For now, she needed to protect the information that her husband had shared, and stall Elizabeth's efforts. She began to smile as she asked Trudy to attend to Ann. Then Caroline paused and said to Elizabeth in an optimistic tone, "You know how it can be when you are operating a business."

Elizabeth was persistent in knowing the truth, "Does this mean the sale of some of the livestock?"

"Hopefully." Caroline replied with a halfhearted smile and continuing her answer said, "I will share with you what I know as soon as Ann and I get settled."

With the end to the conversation, Caroline entered the house and proceeded to the bedroom to clean up from the long trip from Richmond. Elizabeth, was still curious about Caroline's reply. Elizabeth felt that Caroline was hiding something.

As Caroline was sitting in the bedroom, she began to think about her husband and where he might be. The following Saturday after the battle of Mechanicsville, he departed for his trip abroad with William. Charles did not share any of his travel arrangements and or by what port his departure would be. In the quiet of the afternoon, she remembered some of the details that he had witness from the battle of that day and how they had affected him; he had nightmares and tossed and turned throughout that night. She stood and slowly walked over to the front window. There she pulled the curtain to one side and allowed the gentle breeze to blow through her hair. As Caroline gazed in the direction of the long lane that led to the road to town, she began to wonder. Should the war continue, how long would the family be spared the bad news about a love one? She glanced toward the direction of Harpers Ferry and began to think about the grim reality of ending her friendship with Katie. It was an ordeal that she didn't want to face, and constantly over the last few days she struggled within her mind. For her, it was the most difficult request that Charles had asked in the life of their marriage, and her feelings had been mixed over the right course of action to pursue. She knew that Charles was probably correct in his feelings that the friendship should be severed. He had been placed in a vulnerable situation and entrusted with sensitive information that needed to be protected. The last thing that Caroline wanted was the capture of her husband by Union authorities, or perishing in some kind of conflict. No matter how difficult the task would be, she felt, there was no other alternative. It gave her a nauseous feeling to end a relationship with Katie McBride. She had been so trustworthy and honest. It was evident, that her greatest fear was, if the war came to an end soon, then there might not be the opportunity to mend their friendship; Katie might decide to return to Boston feeling the alienation being too great. For Caroline, the bottom line was, Charles' safety and her marriage, this must come first.

Within the hour, Caroline slowly walked down the stairs to speak with Elizabeth. The continuous thought that dominated her mind was how much information should she share with Elizabeth. It was her intentions to protect Charles and only allow her mother-in-law to know a certain amount of information. As Caroline walked toward the parlor she saw Matthew coming from the dining room and asked, "Matthew, do you know where Mother Elizabeth might be?"

"Yes, mam. She be in de libary."

As Caroline proceeded in that direction, she knew that she would have to choose her words wisely because of possibly alarming Elizabeth. Slowly, Caroline walked into the library where she noticed Elizabeth looking through a book on colonial history.

Elizabeth turned and looked surprisingly at Caroline. She removed her glasses and said jovially as she walked toward her, "Caroline, is everything alright?

Caroline replied with a cautious tone, "Oh, yes, everything is fine."

Elizabeth wasn't convinced that her daughter-in-law was telling the truth. She had perceived that there was something troubling Caroline from the very first moment that she laid eyes on her upon her arrival earlier. Elizabeth began to open her heart and speak in a mellow manner, "I was just looking through one of my books about the great rebellion against England in the 1700s. I always find encouragement in the sacrifice that they endured during the struggle for independence. Our forefathers were willing to take a risk and fight for the cause in what they believed to be true. The patriots that fought for independence reminds me of what we are facing with those tyrants from the North and the cause which my sons bravely fight to preserve."

Caroline had been caught off guard by Elizabeth's observations and could not find the words to say. She attempted to answer in a nervous tone, but Elizabeth interrupted and continued her conversation as she laid the book down on the stand that was near, "Somewhere in my heart, I feel that you are being less then honest with me. I have known since your arrival earlier that there was something troubling you. I just felt that you would have told me by now." As Caroline was given the option to answer, she instead remained silent. Suddenly, Elizabeth began to lose her composure and angrily shouted, "Caroline, Charles is my son. I have a right to know!"

Caroline turned and closed the doors to the room and noticing the angry expression on Elizabeth's face, she answered calmly, "I don't know how to tell you this, but Charles will not be coming home for sometime."

"Why?" Elizabeth commanded and continuing, "What is going on that I do not know about. I'm sure that as urgent as President Davis' request was it must be of the utmost importance."

Caroline sighed as she walked over to the window and began to watch Jeremiah manicuring the roses in the garden in front of the house. As she scrambled to collect her thoughts, she turned toward Elizabeth and noticed the determination in her eyes to discover the truth. Maybe it would be for the best to be as honest with Elizabeth as she could, without giving her all the details. Caroline began to softly speak as she approached Elizabeth, "What I will share with you will go no further then this room, that must be understood. Charles did not return with me because he was asked by President Davis to represent the Confederate government on business somewhere in Europe."

"In Europe!" Elizabeth screamed and continued to express her excitement, "What kind of business?

Caroline cautioned her, "You must keep your voice down, or the servants are going to hear you and so will Ann."

Elizabeth held her hand across her mouth and surprisingly said, "Ann doesn't know?"

"No." Caroline promptly replied. "Charles and I agreed not to tell her for fear that she would accidentally allow the information to slip. We were afraid that if the information was received into the wrong hands, then there might be retribution against us and the Estate."

"Well if I may ask, what did you tell her?"

"For now, I have told her that her father would not be coming home with us. I told Ann that it was important that her father stay behind and escort Aunt Rebecca home next month. She is such a sensitive child and I hated to be less then honest with her, but circumstances at the last moment dictated it."

Elizabeth knew that Caroline was feeling guilty and she wanted to give reassurance, "Your intentions were for Ann's' best interest, but what about my son? Where is he going in Europe?"

The conversation came to an end with the sound of galloping horses approaching the house. Caroline and Elizabeth walked out onto the porch and watched as a Union cavalry patrol came to a halt near them. The ladies were quiet as an officer dismounted and approached. He nodded in respect, and politely said, "Ladies, I am Lieutenant Roland Payne of the 1st Maryland Cavalry. I am here to speak with a Mr. Charles Barker. If I may ask, is he available?"

Once more, Caroline felt that the Union army was intruding on their privacy. It was her belief that these unexpected visits that were taking place on a frequent schedule was meant to harass and spy on their private lives and business. She felt an anger burn within, but guarded her resentment. As a Southern lady, who understood the social graces, she calmly answered the officer, "Sir, he is not home."

"Oh, I see. When do you expect him to return?" Lieutenant Payne asked in a suspicious tone as his eyes glanced about the property observing the gardeners at work in the flowerbeds.

Caroline promptly fired back, "I am not sure. He is away on business."

The officer turned and focused on Caroline with his expression turning to one of sternness, and with a tone of firmness, "Is he away on business for the rebel government?"

Caroline answered in a defensive manner, "No, he is not away on business for any government. If you haven't noticed, we breed horses for a living."

"Yes, I have noticed." The officer replied and continued to pursue the subject, "I have also noticed that your husband owns more slaves then anyone in this area, or at least he did. I also understand that your Southern passions are well known throughout the state." The Lieutenant said sarcastically.

Suddenly, Elizabeth angrily said, "I have had enough of these Yankee insults and insinuations. Please excuse me, I'm going into the house."

The officer tipped his hat in respect as Elizabeth swiftly departed his company. Caroline looked at the officer and said angrily, "If your business is finished, I would like for you to leave now."

"Alright Mrs. Barker, I will leave for now, but I must warn you, that in the future if your husband is found to be working for the Confederate government, you could lose everything that you own. Yeah, it sure would be a shame to see such a beautiful place destroyed."

Caroline was silent, though she held the utmost contempt for the officer. As he mounted his mare, Lt. Payne was still suspicious of the family's intentions and spoke once more in an authoritative tone, "Also, I should warn you, that if anyone of you is caught spying for the rebels, then you could be hung without mercy." Swiftly, the officer tipped his hat, "Good day mam."

Glancing once at the activity around the Estate, he gave the command for the unit to move out. Caroline's resolve intensified for the Southern cause as the Federals rode toward the Charlestown Pike.

Caroline stood watching the Federal cavalry until they were out of sight. Then she asked Jeremiah to go and get the carriage for the trip to town. As he went about the task that was requested of him, Caroline went into the house to make sure that Elizabeth and Ann were all right before departing. After receiving assurances by her mother-in-law, she departed for town alone.

On the way to the Ferry, Caroline thought about buying material to have some new clothing made for Ann. From her daughter's infancy until the present, Caroline created new fashions for her to wear, receiving the child's gratitude as her reward.

As the carriage proceeded along Shenandoah Street, Caroline noticed the Union infantry that filled the streets of the village. Their presence caused her anger to resurface, especially after the visit that the family had received earlier. While she was passing a company of the 3rd Maryland Infantry marching in the direction of the Baltimore and Ohio railroad depot, she thought about complaining to Colonel Miles concerning Lieutenant Payne's conduct at the Estate.

The coachman brought the coach to a halt in front of the dry goods store. Caroline noticed as she entered the store some of the Federal soldiers purchasing tobacco and paper to write home. Many of them were polite to her, but she still regarded the Federals as intruders and invaders of her home and state. After purchasing some blue and green material, she walked outside to where the coachman was waiting to take her back to the Estate. For a brief moment, Caroline paused and thought of Charles, wondering where he might be. The loneliness had been bearable for her, but she greatly felt the absence of his presence from her life.

As Caroline gave the packages to the coachman, he began to help her board the coach to return home. Suddenly, she heard her name called. Turning to see who it was, she recognized Katie McBride walking in her direction.

There was a coldness in Caroline's voice as she stepped down from the coach, "Katie, how are you?"

The two ladies had not seen each other for almost a month. There was a joyful sound in Katie's voice as she spoke, "I'm doing fine. Oh, I have missed you; I am so glad that you have returned. Do you have time to have some dinner and visit?"

"No." Caroline sharply replied. "I have to return home and tend to Ann. Now, if you will excuse me!"

As she boarded the coach, Katie was puzzled by Caroline's attitude toward her. It appeared that Caroline had something dramatic happen to her and the family. The woman that she had been acquainted with for the past two years, she thought, would never have been so rude and impolite to someone. It caused great concern for Katie, and she wondered what was going on with the Barkers.

The matter dominated Katie's mind the rest of the afternoon. Around five that evening, Katie compulsively decided to rent a buggy and horse from the stables and travel to Shenandoah. She felt strongly the need to visit with Caroline to see if there was something that she could do for her friend. It was apparent to Katie that Caroline was in pain over an issue that must have recently taken place in her life. On the trip to the Estate, Katie began to ponder on words of encouragement that she could say. Katie believed that Caroline and her were close enough in their friendship to have the freedom to express their feelings, and the privacy that they shared would be respected.

It was quiet at the Estate when Katie arrived. Matthew answered the door and immediately proceeded to Caroline's sitting room to summon her. As Katie stood in the parlor by the fireplace waiting for Caroline's arrival, she began to think about her own life. For several years now, she thought, her life had changed dramatically. She had left home to pursue a life and a new beginning as a teacher. That had been rewarding. For the first time in four years, she found fulfillment and contentment, but then there is a promising relationship with a gentleman. Now, war breaks out and there is separation and concern. It also appears the conflict might be taking its toll on the relationship that she has enjoyed with Caroline. Katie concluded that something must have happened while Caroline was in Richmond to cause her to be so distant earlier in the afternoon.

Katie turned to look at the images on the marble stand in the corner. There she saw one of Pete and the family. As she looked at Pete, she held back the tears, and began to wonder where her relationship would have been by now if it were not for this conflict. In her life, she continued to feel the abandonment of his presence and the loneliness that would often be experience with separation. It had been months since she had heard from him and constantly she thought of him. Katie could not understand why the people of this great land could not have continued to compromise their differences peacefully on the social issues that divided them. Her life had suddenly taken a wrong direction, and she was witnessing the changes that the war was bringing upon everyone, both North and South.

Caroline quietly walked into the room and observed Katie looking at the image of the family. She spoke in her usual manner, "Yes Katie, he is still alive."

"Oh." Katie was startled as she turned to face Caroline. Katie smiled and softly said, "I was standing here thinking about him and the changes that our families are experiencing with this conflict. I think about the effects that it must have with my family, especially my brother who is serving with the 1st Massachusetts Cavalry. Oh, and knowing my Father," She said tearfully, "His nights must be sleepless with worry. He and my brother are very close in their relationship."

Caroline replied pridefully, as she starred at Katie, "Yes, I agree. The war is having an effect on society, particularly here in the South. Many of the families in this area alone have been called upon to pay the ultimate sacrifice of life by sending their sons to die for our cause."

Katie began to notice the sharpness in her friends voice once more, "Why is there such a change in your attitude?"

"As I said, the war has affected us here in the South."

Katie cried out, "I don't understand Caroline. You were fine before you left for Richmond. Now, it appears, your attitude and personality have changed and I don't know why. You are so cold toward me, will you please talk to me?"

"Katie." Caroline fired back, "I see my way of life changing and my families survival to cling to it. I don't like war no more than you do. Pete, who, I dearly love in spite of his faults, at this very moment, might be fighting for his life, and my husband cannot return home because the Union scrutiny that he must endure. Katie, you don't understand how I feel right now. I am separated from the family that I love. Besides, that doesn't take into account the way that this war might cause us to suffer financially. Many of the slaves have escaped with all of the Yankees that are garrisoned in the area. Why don't they just go home and leave us alone?"

Katie replied with a flare in her voice, "Caroline, do you think that this war only affects you? You're bloody wrong if that is what you believe. I am just as concerned about Pete as I am my own brother. I pray daily that the two of them return home safely and that this war will end soon. For me, it's not just about a bloody business, but it concerns the value of a human being."

Caroline promptly replied shouting, "No Katie, you do not understand what is at risk here. You don't know everything, and I'm not privileged to tell you what is going on. There is more at risk for me then just the Estate! It's my family!"

The two ladies emotions had calmed somewhat after a few moments of silence. They just stared at one another. Caroline continued coldly, "Katie this war has even affected our relationship. Apparently, both of us are under too much strain with what is happening in our personal lives to continue to be as close as we have been. I have my views on this conflict, and you have yours and we don't agree. For now, it would be best for you to leave."

With that statement, Caroline promptly left the room and returned to her sitting room. There, she began to cry uncontrollably in privacy, knowing that she had honored her husband's request, but quite possibly lost the best friend that she had ever had. Caroline attempted desperately to reason within her heart the rationale of her actions, but she knew that she couldn't. Her family would have to come first, even though the guilt was consuming her conscious. Ever since Caroline left Richmond, there had been a battle-taking place within her heart and a struggle over destroying a relationship that had been built on trust and love. For the sake of the war this had been one more costly sacrifice.

Katie departed quietly and emotionally drained. As she returned to town in the buggy, Katie hoped that the disagreement would not end her friendship with Caroline. She tried to reason in her mind the suffering the family was enduring and the sacrifices they had to pay. The war was being fought on their territory. She also thought Caroline was thinking of her own interest. Everyone was suffering as far as Katie was concerned. Even though her family was in Boston, that didn't mean they were not affected by the war with her brother's involvement. Everyone would have a price to pay in some way if this war continued. The disagreement and the possible end of their friendship was just one of the casualties of war that had taken place. For now, Katie would honor Caroline's request and keep her distance. Hopefully, once everything was concluded, maybe, just maybe, they could pick up the pieces and resolve their differences.

CHAPTER TWENTY-ONE

For most of 1862, the Confederate army had been successful in defeating the Union forces in the eastern theater of the war. The success was largely due to the brilliant Shenandoah Valley campaign that General Stonewall Jackson fought over a six-week period. During that time, he simultaneously defeated three Federal armies, and then joined forces with the Confederate army under General Robert E. Lee near Richmond. Over the seven-day period, the Confederate army fought five engagements against the Army of the Potomac under General McClellan and turned back their efforts to capture the Confederate capitol. With the completion of their success, General Lee and the Army of Northern Virginia were challenged once more in their efforts to protect Richmond from the Union invaders. A new Federal force that was recently organized under the command of Major General John Pope, was moving against the Confederate capitol from the North by way of Culpepper County. Once more, Stonewall Jackson was called upon to engage his forces against the foe, and did so successfully at the battle of Cedar Mountain. It was not Lee's intentions to allow the Federal army under Pope to escape without its possible destruction. Lee had been quite angry over the destruction of private property and scrutiny that the civilian population in that area of Virginia had to endure under Federal occupation. General Lee divided his army and sent General Jackson on a series of maneuvers gaining the rear of Pope's army. It was by the brilliance of Robert E. Lee and Pope's own arrogance that brought about the battle of Second Manassas. There, Lee crushed the Army of Virginia and sent it fleeing back to the fortifications of the Union capitol of Washington. Now, with the high spirits and confidence of success among the Confederate leadership on the field and in Richmond, it was time to cross the Potomac and launch a raid into Maryland. It was Lee's goal to possibly enable the citizens of that great state the opportunity to be liberated from Union control, and at the same time a chance to replenish the ranks of the Confederate army with men from the region. Another benefit of the invasion, Lee's army could enjoy supplies of food from the abundant harvest.

On the 5th of September, the Confederate forces crossed the Potomac at White's Ford a few miles from Leesburg. The 1st Virginia had been assigned the task of being the first regiment to advance into Maryland. After some skirmishing with Federal cavalry, the regiment pushed forward to Urbana with a squadron picketing near New Market, Maryland. The 1st Virginia was assigned to General Fitz Lee's brigade. They made various attempts to probe the Union army that was moving under the command of General McClellan from Washington City and was attempting to intercept Lee's army near Frederick, Maryland. Lee divided his army, giving General Longstreet Corps orders to move his corps in the direction of Hagerstown. Lee then gave D. H. Hills Corps the task of defending the gaps along South Mountain that led to the Potomac River. General Jackson was to cross the Potomac at Williamsport and capture Martinsburg and the large Federal force at Harpers Ferry. After accomplishing his mission, Jackson was to reunite with General Longstreet.

The first rays of sunlight were beaming brightly on the horizon of the eastern sky in Frederick County, Maryland on Sunday, the fourteenth of September. Pete Barker and Jonathan Collins were mounted on their horses along the ridgeline of the Catoctin Mountain, scouting the Union armies' position for most of the early morning. They had returned to the area after skirmishing with Federal cavalry from the previous day. The two Confederates were patiently observing the slow moving columns of Federal infantry moving from the vicinity of Buckeystown toward the gap near Jefferson. Jonathan was quiet and intensely watching the enemy as he smoked his pipe, while holding the reins of his horse. As Jonathan removed his pipe, he pointed in the direction of the Federals and commented, "It looks ta me like dem Yanks could be headed our way. Yep, that's what it looks like, possibly a brigade."

Pete was observing the enemy, just as his friend was, though he did not choose to speak. He silently wrote down his observations and gave the note to another scout who was near by and asked him to take the message at once to General Stuart, or Colonel Munford near Crampton's Gap. Jonathan was curious, "What ya say in the message?"

Pete turned in his saddle and broke his silence, "I told the General exactly what you said."

Jonathan surprisingly replied, "Na, ya didn't."

Pete smiled at his friend, who by now was grinning from ear to ear, "As surely as I'm sitting on this horse, I sure did."

Jonathan's grin soon disappeared and the sound in his voice became more serious in its tone, "Have ya ever thought that ya might not see your family again?"

Pete began to reflect on his feelings, "Yes, on several occasions, like the engagement at Manassas a little over a year ago. Remember how you saved my life?"

"Yep, I sure do." Jonathan replied, and continued to reminisce, "We gave those Yanks a terrible beating. I'd really did hope we'd end the war dat day, but they keep comin' and more blood continues to spill.

Pete smiled, saying, "I know. When we charged those red leg soldiers and that fire fight got hot, it was a that time that I thought I would never see home again, nor my family."

Jonathan asked, as he cleaned the tobacco from his pipe, "How 'bout your sweetheart?"

"Well, Jonathan, she is not my sweetheart. Though, I must admit that I think of her on occasions. And, sometimes I wonder what she is doing. But, she is only a close friend."

Jonathan was grinning when he asked, "Have ya gotten real close to her yet?"

Pete loudly replied, "No, like I said, we are just friends."

"Well......"

He was angrily interrupted, "Jonathan, I don't want to discuss this any longer."

After a moment of silence, Pete turned in his saddle and noticed the glassy appearance of Jonathan's eyes. He listened carefully to the quiver in his voice, "The thing dat I hate the most about this war is not seeing my wife and two sons. God, I miss dem. They's all dat I have, and my little farm. Ya know, I don't think I'll see the end of this war."

Pete quickly attempted to reassure to his friend, "Oh come on Jonathan." He placed his hand on his friend's shoulder, and continued with a smile, "You'll be going home just like the rest of us when this war comes to an end. You have proven time and again that you know how to survive."

Jonathan began to shake his head in disagreement as he continued to observe the Union brigade slowly moving in their direction, "Na, I don't think so. I just feel it."

As Jonathan turned about to look at Pete, there was a popping noise at the base of the ridge. Pete turned in his saddle and quickly recognized a Federal cavalry patrol shooting at them. As the Federals advanced at a gallop in their direction, Jonathan and Pete promptly pulled their revolvers and returned fire, hitting two of the Yanks. Pete yelled at Jonathan, "Let's get out of here before we get hit."

The popping sound from the Yankee revolvers continued as the two Confederates retreated toward the little hamlet of Jefferson. The Union cavalry patrol followed closely in hot pursuit. As Jonathan and Pete entered the town along the main street, they immediately turned their horses and began to fire rapidly at the Federal patrol in an attempt to slow their pursuit. The Federal cavalry came to a quick halt with some of the soldiers dismounting and taking cover among the brick and stone dwellings. The sound of missiles were whizzing through the air, with one removing Pete's hat from his head. Pete became furious and shouted to Jonathan, "Did you see what those Yankees did. Lets charge them."

Jonathan warned his friend, "If we do, dey gonna fill us with lead. I don't know about you'd. But I'm a runnin' like a rabbit, and gettin' out of here."

By this time, the Federals were working their way closer to Pete and Jonathan's position, firing as they advanced. Pete slapped his mare on its hindquarter and turned in haste with Jonathan toward the direction of Burkittsville. As they proceeded at a fast gallop toward the road that led to the little village, Jonathan and Pete simultaneously jumped a stonewall fence. The Union cavalry continued to pursue the two rebels, firing their revolvers as opportunity presented itself. Pete and Jonathan laid low against the neck of their horses to avoid the flying missiles of death; they were only several hundred yards in front of the Federals. Without allowing their horses time to break stride, the two rebels rode down into a gully and crossed Catoctin Creek and as quickly as possible, they ascended the steep ridge that guards the creek. Bringing their horses to a halt, Pete turned and fired several rounds at the Federals along the road. The squadron of Union cavalry came to a halt at the base of the ridge opposite the creek and returned the fire, taking cover in the heavy underbrush and thickets that covered the area. Once Pete and Jonathan were sure they had their advisories penned down with gunfire, they fled the area before the Federal cavalrymen could surround them and take the two prisoners.

While Pete was skirmishing with Federal cavalry near Burkittsville, Charles was approaching Shenandoah after a two and one half month absence from his family. Caroline had previously warned him of the frequent visitations from the Union authorities, so he chose not to return home immediately after his arrival in Richmond. It was not until he had received news of the Confederate occupation of the lower Valley that he decided it was safe to return to the Estate. Before leaving Richmond, he had thought about sending Caroline a telegram informing her of his pending arrival. After thinking about this, he decided against it for fear that Federal authorities in the area would intercept it, and possibly harass his wife and family.

After the long journey from the Confederate capitol, it was a relief for Charles to once more see Shenandoah. As he approached the entrance to the Estate, he wasn't surprised by all of the military activity in the area. President Davis had informed him during their meeting on the ninth of September, that General Lee had crossed the Potomac and was near Frederick.

Slowly, he made his turn onto the long lane that led to the mansion; he paused briefly and watched a regiment, the 42nd Virginia with its musicians playing "The Bonnie Blue Flag" march quietly toward the Ferry. As he continued to ride in his carriage, he thought of the peacefulness today. How the war had interfered with such tranquility and his homecoming. He turned once more in the direction of Harpers Ferry and noticed Confederate soldiers of General Trimble's brigade massed upon the crest of School House Ridge along with General Lawton's Georgians. The line officers of the various regiments caught his eye while they were directing their companies into the appropriate position to defend the ridge. The appearance of the ordinarily foot soldiers left a lot to be desired. They had long straggle hair. Some were toothless, and had ragged looking clothing. Most were crusted with dirt, and were cursing quite frequently. He looked upon them as bold knights about to give battle to the enemy and save the kingdom from harm. His mind returned once again to the horrible effects of combat at Mechanicsville. It was an experience, he hoped, that would not take place on his family's property, and that his prayers would be answered sparing them the tragedy of war and the memories that it brings with its eternal scars and images. For now, the winds of war would be swept away and the anticipation of being reunited with Caroline consumed him. The thoughts of holding and kissing her caused him to be excited in the mist of adversity.

After stepping from the carriage, Charles walked the four levels of steps to the entrance of the house and slowly entered. It was quiet, almost too quiet. After a few moments, Caroline appeared at the top of the stairway, and with a sigh of relief, he began to smile. With the joy and excitement of a child, she ran down the long stairway with her arms open and embraced him with affection and tears. It was as though she had been separated from him for an eternity; time and war was not of importance as they shared this intimate moment of love and privacy together. As Charles gazed into his wife's eyes, he passionately spoke of his love for her, "More then anything in this world, I have greatly missed you. There were nights when I was abroad that I had dreams of what this moment would be like, then there were times that I thought I would never see you again."

"What do you mean my love?"

It was not Charles' desire to tarnish the bliss of the moment, instead he placed his finger on her lips, and softly said, "And it doesn't matter now my love. We are together again, that is what is important."

Caroline cherished and savored this moment of intimacy with her husband. Her eyes brightly glowed with serenity as she caressed his cheek with her hands and softy said, "My love all of my fears can be laid to rest with your return. My heart can no longer experience the loneliness and void of the absence of your presence."

Soon, Ann appeared at the top of the stairway with a yellow rose. She quickly ran down the steps to embraced her Father with a kiss, and then present her gift to him, "Father, I'm so happy to see you."

As he received her love, the smile that covered his face was as the radiance of the sun. Charles joyfully said, "Ann my child, I have missed you so much. I have counted the days until I could see your smile once more."

Ann asked innocently, "Where is Aunt Rebecca? I thought she was coming home with you."

With Caroline and Charles being caught up in the bliss of their reunion, it didn't occur to Caroline to ask of Rebecca's whereabouts. It was with an astonishing look that she waited on her husband's answer, "Ann, Aunt Rebecca will be coming with Mr. Pierce shortly."

"Charles," Caroline regretfully said, "I forgot to ask about Rebecca. I......."

Charles quickly interrupted and said in a reassuring tone of voice, "It's fine. The only thing that matters is that we are together as a family."

Charles suggested they retire to the parlor where they could share the events that were taking place in their lives. Charles removed his frock coat and gave it to Matthew. He was seated beside his wife and once more expressed his joy at being reunited with his family. Then he began to inquire where his Mother was, "Caroline, I have not seen Mother. Where could she be today with all of the military activity that is taking place?"

Caroline reassured her husband, "She is safe. With so many hostilities in the area, I had Daniel take her to Charlestown to spend sometime with the Whites. As soon as things are settled, she will return home."

With a sigh of relief in Charles' voice he said, "Good, I'm glad that she is safe and away from potential harm. I noticed all the troops on the ridge as I approached the lane."

"Yes." Caroline agreed, and continued to explain what had been taking place during her husbands absence, "Several days ago, an aide to General Jackson requested that troops be allowed to cross the property and use it to do battle with the Federal forces in town. I agreed. Since you have been gone, Union cavalry patrols have been constantly harassing us concerning your whereabouts. They have relentlessly threatened us with the destruction of our property if they discover your involvement with the Confederate government. I am so tired and angry at living under such scrutiny. I hope that our boys deliver a decisive blow against them and that some normalcy will return to our lives."

There was a sadness and disappointment in Charles' voice, "Well, I don't think it's going to be that simple. Furthermore, I don't know how long I will be able to stay with you. The President has asked me to return to Richmond at the earliest convenience and continue to be an advisor on some of the political disagreements and issues that have resulted between him and our sister states in this conflict."

Caroline asked in a concern tone, "What about Ann and me?"

"For now, I would like for you and Ann to stay here in the Valley with Mother and take charge of the Estate in my absence. Besides, as I have given the matter some thought, I really don't believe that the Federals would destroy the Estate. They are probably just bluffing in an attempt to intimidate us."

Caroline replied with a flare of emotion in her voice, "No Charles! I will not do that! Ann and I should be with you. Now is not the time for our family to be divided, nor to be concerned with the Estate."

Charles argued, "The safest place for you and Ann will be here at Shenandoah. They will not bring harm to the family, but it's not safe for me."

"Caroline was persistent in pressing the issue, "Charles, I do not want to"
. . . .

She was interrupted as Charles stubbornly pleaded, "Caroline, you have always trusted me in the past, please do so now. I found out before leaving Richmond that it is quite possible that if our success continues in defeating the Union army, maybe, just maybe, there might be some kind of intervention by England, or hopefully France. Should this occur, the war would come to an end."

There was a calm between the couple as Charles walked over to the window and watched the Confederate soldiers along the road to Charlestown. He softly spoke, "It all depends on that raggedy bunch of men out there and what they can accomplish in the next couple of days."

It was late morning along the crest of Crampton's Gap; Pete had just awakened from several hours of sleep after the ordeal Jonathan and he had with the Union squadron of cavalry. As he glanced about the area, cavalrymen from the 2nd and 12th Virginia were about to take up a defensive position along a stonewall fence on the outskirts of the village at the base of the mountain gap. He didn't know how, but Jonathan was still sleeping amid the skirmishing and occasional firing of artillery. Pete gazed off into the direction of Harpers Ferry, and began to concentrate on his family's welfare. Less then ten miles away lies what was once his paradise and the property that he hoped to inherit with his brother. Now, his way of life had drastically changed from a wealthy son of the influential Barker family to that of a ragged and dirty soldier with hardly anything to eat. He felt as though he had nothing of importance to show for his life and no place that could be called home. Other then his Southern pride, he felt degraded. The many hopes and dreams that he once envisioned of prosperity and life had become as a vapor evaporating, disappearing so quickly on a cold winter night.

Then Pete thought of Katie McBride. It was known, that the town would have to be reduced by force unless the Union garrison there surrendered. He hoped that Katie had left the village and was seeking refuge with Caroline and the family at Shenandoah. Many months had past since Pete had received a correspondence from Katie informing him of her welfare. At times he was concerned. Pete shook his head and laughed as he recalled the incident in front of the Wager House Hotel when Katie and he fell in the mud puddle after his melee with Billy Smith. Oh, what temper and stubborn determination Katie possessed. He felt saddened as he remembered that particular evening at the reception for William Pierce. The two of them were alone, dancing to the music. The look that was in her eyes on that special occasion still remained a mystery to him, now two years later.

Suddenly, Pete heard the popping of gunfire to his front. As he shook Jonathan, the two of them ran quickly to the cover of the stonewall fence. Union artillery to the east of town was beginning to increase their fire. The shot and shell from the Union cannons were thudding and bursting behind the line of defense where Pete and Jonathan were seeking refuge, causing a terrifying effect of terror on some of the new recruits. As the green soldiers began to make haste for the rear and toward the wooded slopes, one of the line officers commanded, "Stop at once you cowards and return or be shot." The officer fired his revolver into the air, but the recruits took their chances anyway hoping for the best as they fled. Pete watched and laughed as the officer began to swear with various kinds of cursing. After two years of hell, Pete was a well-seasoned veteran of many battles and skirmishes with the invaders, cheating death on more then one occasion.

As the firing from the Union forces continued, Pete cautiously raised his head above the protection of the stonewall fence and peered across the corn stubble field in the direction of the road that led to Middletown. There he noticed the Yankees taking what cover they could, and keeping up a continuous fire; this action kept up for sometime. After several hours of skirmishing, the Union soldiers began to form a battle formation that covered the whole length of the field. Pete raised his head and counted five regimental flags fluttering in the mild breeze, occasionally ducking with the thudding of an artillery shell passing overhead. He knew that the Confederate forces had the advantage of cover with the wooded ridges and the stonewall fence, though it would only be a matter of time before the Federal forces, who greatly out numbered the Confederates would capture their position. Recognizing this danger, Pete wanted to protect his friend, and guard him against the premonition of earlier announcing his death. Pete turned and looked at Jonathan who was grinning from ear to ear and whispered with frustration, "Do you always smile when you are about to kill someone, or possibly get killed yourself?"

Jonathan's expression changed to a hollow appearance as he somberly answered, "Sometimes that smile hides my real feelin'. If I live or die, I'm gonna make the most of it."

Pete whispered, "Well then good! Listen to me. We can't hold this position against these odds." The pinging sound from the guns of the Union skirmishers chipped the stone to pieces above them, and the fragments of rock stung their faces.

Pete listened to an officer commanding the Southern forces, "Boys, hold your fire until those Yanks get closer. Fire low."

As they waited, Pete frantically said once more to his friend, "If we retreat, I want you to go first. I will give you cover fire."

An angry expression covered Jonathan's features, as he firmly replied, "No!"

With Pete's comment to his friend, the command came for the rebels to open fire. They did in unison, aiming low as commanded and firing deliberately at the advancing Union columns of infantry as they approached their position. It appeared to Pete that many Yankee invaders fell with the first rebel volley. Still, the Federal infantry continued its advance, yelling defiant words in hopes of intimidating their foe. Meanwhile, the Union artillery from the eastern side of the village began to fire with intensity, their shells exploding with a loud concussion behind the Confederates at the stonewall fence taking down trees and limbs with every round. Some of the Union artillery shells fell in front of the Confederates at the stonewall fence, spraying the area with shrapnel, but few casualties resulted. The rebel defenders kept up a steady fire causing many of the Federal attackers to fall wounded and dead; still the Union lines would not waver. After climbing a wooden fence that crossed the length of the field, and pausing to realign their formation, the invaders continued to steadily advance. By this time a Confederate soldier who was standing and firing grasped his face with his hands and yelled with pain. As he fell over Jonathan, Pete noticed the terrified expression of anguish that covered the troopers face as he gasped to breathe. When Jonathan pulled him to the side, he noticed the tears filling the soldiers eyes and heard him groaning with pain. The soldier mumbled, "My family, oh, my poor family. Please take the image of my love one's from my pocket."

Jonathan sorrowfully answered, "Yeah, sure."

As Jonathan complied with the trooper's last request, he gazed momentarily at the lovely woman and three sons. There were tears that filled his eyes as he once more thought of his loved ones that he had left behind in the upper Valley to fight for the Southern cause. Jonathan took the image and handed it to the dying warrior and observed the painful smile that covered his face. Once satisfied that he could touch and hold his family near his chest, the soldier peacefully took his last breath of life, clutching his family tightly. Jonathan was somewhat shaken by this event, it traumatized him momentarily.

By this time, Pete had emptied the chamber of his revolver and was in the process of reloading with another magazine of ammunition when he noticed Jonathan's eyes fixed in a startled gaze. Seeing that many of the Confederates were beginning to flee from their position behind the stonewall fence, Pete yelled to Jonathan, "Get out of here now!"

Jonathan shouted, "No!"

Over the loud noise of the battle, Pete shouted the command, "That's an order! Move it!"

There was an expression of anger that covered Jonathan's face as he reluctantly obeyed. With the Union soldiers moving at a steady pace and closer to the stonewall fence, Pete turned around and kept firing as fast as he could. Pete did not want to be captured, so he decided to make haste for the woods nearby and take his chances of being shot from behind. As he made his escape, Pete could hear the Union victors cheering as they captured the position that the rebels once held. Almost immediately, there was a pinging noise striking the tree limbs, fallen timber, and rocks around him. It was from some of the Federals that noticed him. Fortunately, they missed their mark. He scrambled like a scared rabbit in his attempt to escape from his pursuers, fighting the concentrated thick underbrush and thickets that populated the steep slopes, but his persistence and determination, he believed, would reward him. As opportunity presented itself, Pete took shelter behind a tree. From there, he watched several of the Federal soldiers detach from the main body as they scaled the ridge. He crouched low behind some underbrush attached to the tree and when the soldiers were close at hand, he fired. One of the soldiers fell on the ground. The other Federal lifted his musket and fired. Pete heard the missile from the Yanks gun hit the front of the tree causing the bark to fly. Promptly, Pete fired his revolver, blood covered the soldiers face, and Pete knew he had struck the Yank in the head. Quickly, he began to retreat toward the crest of the ridge knowing that the firing of weapons would bring additional help for the fallen soldiers.

By the time he reached the crest of the ridge, he was out of breath, but could only pause briefly; his enemy was close behind in their pursuit. As he quickly glanced about, Pete noticed some of the Confederate infantry along the crest of the gap taking a position of defense in an attempt to halt the Union assault. In the mist of all the confusion, Confederate officers attempted to rally the retreating defenders of the stone wall, using profanity and swinging their sabers in acts of desperation, but it was to no avail. The Federals continued their attack on the retreating rebel forces, but Pete knew that the battle was lost. After a few volleys, the Confederate infantry retreated in disorder, though attempts were also made to rally them. Jonathan was mounted and waiting for Pete with his horse so that they could report to General Stuart. Grabbing the reins of his mount, Pete and Jonathan retreated with the infantry columns that were beginning to do likewise.

By mid afternoon, Caroline was standing alone on the porch looking toward the direction of the Ferry. She laid her head against one of the support columns and began to wonder if Katie was safe with the town under siege from the Confederate troops. Over the last two and a half months, Caroline had experience guilt and difficulty within her heart for the abandonment of her friend. Even though she had made various attempts to repress her feelings by justifying her actions, she still had been unable to quench the feelings of her conscious.

As Caroline was pondering on her relationship with Katie, Charles interrupted her thoughts. He had summoned one of the servants with the carriage to take Caroline and Ann to Charlestown to stay with his Mother and the Whites. He believed the danger of pending hostilities in the area warranted his family's safety. In the distance, the quiet was broken with the sound of battle. There was a tiresome and worried expression that covered Charles' face. Caroline began to inquire from what area the muffled sound of battle was coming, "Charles, it sounds like there is an engagement taking place across the river once more."

Charles confidently answered as he gazed in that direction, "Yes, it sounds like it might be beyond the mountain."

The humility had returned to Caroline's spirit and voice, "Yesterday as I stood here, I heard the sound of battle taking place toward the same area. I couldn't help, but think about the men that were taking part in the engagement, and how some wouldn't return home to their families. The one good thing that I have learned through this war, and that is, life is precious and should be lived to its fullest. Oh, how I wish that this war would come to an end and the killing would cease."

As Caroline was speaking with Charles the carriage pulled up to the front entrance to the mansion. Charles took Caroline's hand and walked her over to the stone steps, where Ann and Trudy joined them. After embracing Ann, Charles gave her reassurance and said, "Ann, everything is going to be fine. I promise as soon as possible, I will send for you and your Mother."

Ann tearfully replied, "Father, I don't want to leave you."

In a hesitant manner, Charles allowed one of the servants to assist Ann and Trudy into the carriage. Then Charles turned about and held Caroline close to him and passionately said, "I will send for you when it is safe to return. My love and heart go with you." Then he kissed her and assisted his wife into the carriage beside Ann.

As they departed, Ann waved and smiled at her Father. He stood by the flower garden in front of the entrance to the mansion and returned her gesture of love. As she continued to look in his direction, the hollow and sorrowful expression that she witnessed upon his face would remain within her heart all the days of her life.

Charles turned and walked back to the area of the porch where Caroline and he had been standing. He was lost in his thoughts when a loud booming noise came from the direction of Loudoun Heights. Loudoun Heights is a high elevation that towers above the Shenandoah River and Harpers Ferry. It was shortly after two o'clock by his watch. As he looked up to witness the cloudy haze from the cannons on the heights, he noticed Daniel riding his thoroughbred at a fast gallop from the direction of the river toward the mansion. By this time, the artillery on School House Ridge began to open with all of its fury, rattling the glass windows, shaking the ground like an earthquake beneath his feet. As he waited for Daniel's arrival, he intensely observed the artillerymen manning their pieces with precision. He was proud of the discipline, which the artillerymen displayed and the courage that he witnessed.

Suddenly, Charles heard the sound of a fast galloping horse coming from a different direction. Turning to see who it was, he noticed a Confederate officer approaching the mansion along the lane that led to the Charlestown Pike. The officer promptly dismounted and introduced himself, "Mr. Barker, sir, I'm Captain Smith of General Jackson's staff. On behalf of the General, he sends his respects to you and your family." Charles nodded in acknowledgement as the officer continued by pointing in the direction where the Confederate artillery was firing, "Sir, we would like to move some of our infantry across your property, using the ridge to disguise their movements from the Yankees along Bolivar Heights."

"Whatever General Jackson needs to capture the town, he shall have."

Swiftly, the officer thanked Charles and hastily proceeded back down the lane leaving a cloud of dust behind him.

Charles turned his attention to Daniel, who had just arrived. He asked the overseer, "What is going on toward the river?"

Daniel promptly answered as he pointed in the direction of the lane that lead to the river, "There are some scouts lookin' for a way to get at the Yanks from the river. I heard all of the shootin', so I followed the sound from where it came."

Charles was optimistic in his observations, "I see. That is apparently why General Jackson's staff officer was asking permission to cross the property. They want to try and find a way along the river to get to the Ferry to attack the Yankees."

With a serious expression covering his face and a humble tone of voice, Daniel asked, "Mr. Charles, if them Rebs try to get at those Yanks from the river, then I'd like to go along?"

Charles surprisingly asked, "Why Daniel? What do you hope to accomplish, you're not a soldier anymore."

Daniel paused for a moment; there was a wild glare in his eyes, a look of revenge, something that Charles had witnessed only once. Daniel began to speak with a tone of anger in his slow manner, "Well, while you were gone, I had several of the darkies escape into town lookin' for safety amongst those darn Yanks. Well to make a long story short, some of those boys from New York threaten to shoot me if I didn't leave them darkies alone. Now, as far as I'm concern, those slaves belong to you. I have a score to settle with them New Yorkers."

Charles knew that he had been losing slaves with Union control over most of the area. He began to inquire into his loss, "Yes, you are right. Many have escaped? How many exactly?"

Since the beginning of the war, Daniel had never relinquished his taste for killing. Over the last several months, he continued his skill by killing an additional three slaves, who attempted their flight to freedom. Daniel paused once more because he knew that Charles would not be happy with the information. Cautiously, he tallied Charles' lost and replied, "I figure over the last three months we have lost a total of thirty."

Charles began to shout loudly with anger, "What! I can't afford that kind of loss. Who is going to keep up the property?

"I know." Daniel replied, "But I can't keep up with them runnin' off like they do."

After pausing and allowing his temper to calm, he gave Daniel his answer, "Yes, by all means, kill every damn Yankee you can find."

Daniel quietly placed his gray hat upon his head, and returned by the route that he had arrived. The artillery fire from the heights across the river and on the ridge to his front was increasing with every passing moment. It appeared to have all of the makings of a major engagement. Charles promptly went to his bedroom and began the task of packing his important papers for a possible evacuation from Shenandoah.

CHAPTER TWENTY-TWO

Over the last couple of months, Katie McBride's life had become so miserable with all of the prostitutes living in the lower section of town that she gave up her residency at Mrs. Stipes boarding house, and took a new residence along Washington Street. After seeing the young lady's need, Mrs. McDonald, a parishioner at the Church extended the invitation to Katie to reside at her home. Today, the landlord was visiting with a sister in Winchester, Virginia.

As the very first bombardment of shells that fell upon the town from the artillery on Loudoun Heights, Katie rendered it too dangerous for her to remain in the house. She decided to take refuge alone in the wet cellar beneath the structure. The only light that she possessed came from the candles that were lying on the table she had recently made. With the sound of shells bursting with such terrible noise, in her haste, Katie didn't have time to grab a shawl to ward off the coolness, nor dampness of the cellar. As she glanced around in her place of refuge, she noticed a freshly dug pit full of potatoes in the middle of the dirt floor. After continuing her investigation with the candle holding the candle, she paused to examine the goods that were on the shelf in the corner that had been preserved by her new landlord. Nearby was a huge rock that had not been removed when the house was constructed many years ago; it was flat on the top and provided a seat for her comfort. Katie placed the candle on a wooden crate and began to ponder on her life. Katie was still teaching at the school, though the towns' population had fallen dramatically with the hostilities and uncertainty of the war. At times during the conflict, Katie had wondered why the school and church continued to open its doors with the absence of many of the students and parishioners. With much thought, she concluded it was due to the commitment of the priest and Church to continue to hold services and remain open for those who desired prayer during this time of tribulation. As she continued to quietly meditate on her life, the thought began to surface concerning the circumstances surrounding her friendship with Caroline. She was greatly concerned that a friend had been lost because of the conflict. When she was a young child, Katie's Mother taught her by word and example that relationships were to be nurtured and built upon a foundation of honesty, trust, and love. In some respects, she felt betrayed by Caroline and the Barkers, feeling that their relationship was without substance; the only exception was Pete. Somewhere within her deepest being, she believed that Caroline might have been placed under extreme pressure from Charles and Elizabeth because of their firm stand on slavery and states rights to end the friendship. Even though these were important social issues and the cause of the war, Katie strongly believed that these matters shouldn't play a role in a sincere relationship with Caroline, or anyone else for that matter. She could not help, but to dwell on this subject, deeply bruised by it all. In time, she would attempt once more to contact Caroline, and re-establish their relationship.

As for Pete, Katie felt the void of his absence, the emptiness that it created, and it was more then she could bear at times. Her concern for his safety and welfare was constantly an issue, even to the point that she would awaken at night screaming and crying from a bad dream that involved his death. Somewhere in her heart, Katie knew that he must be in the area; would she see him once more, and share his fellowship and comfort?

At times her thoughts were broken by the loud crashing sound of the bombardment taking place on the outside, but she would always return to thoughts of romance with Pete and hold the beautiful dreams and memories of her life with him close to her heart.

Suddenly, there was a sound outside of the wooden door that led to the cellar. Katie jumped to her feet and quickly glanced about for a place to hide. There were some old wooden barrels that were in the corner near the shelf that had contained some of the jelly that Mrs. McDonald had preserved. With promptness, Katie hid and blew out the light of the candle. Katie heard the creaking of the door as it slowly opened. Katie began to breathe heavy, her heart racing as she heard the sound of footsteps. As Katie laid low near the ground, she peered through an opening to see who the intruder might be. She could tell by the light of the sun that was gleaming through the doorway, that he was a Union soldier. Still, she didn't know if he was friend or foe, but continued her silence. After looking at the items near the steps, the Union soldier moved toward the far end of the cellar in his investigation of the premise. As he did so, Katie quietly arose from her position behind the crates and made haste for the open doorway. Immediately, a hand grabbed her arm, she screamed, but to no avail. The soldier cried out, "I'm friendly."

Katie recognized the sound of his New England accent. As she turned about to look at the Union soldier, she noticed he was frail in appearance and had dark eyes to match his olive complexion. There appeared to be blood on his blue and red shell jacket from a wound to his right forearm. As Katie was relighting her candle and placing it on one of the crates, she said in a concerned tone of voice, "You are wounded, let me take care of that injury."

Quickly, Katie tore a piece of her petticoat and began to gently wrap his wound. She began to inquired into his injury, "How did this happen?"

The soldier grimed with pain as he hastily answered, "I'm with the 5th New York Artillery. As I was loading the cannon in an attempt to return fire on some of the rebel infantry across the river, a shell from one of their artillery pieces exploded in front of me. I got hit by some of the shrapnel that flew through the air. Immediately, I asked for help. I was directed by one of the officers of my unit to move to the rear, when suddenly shells began to burst all around. I made haste for a shelter."

Katie knew that the soldier was less then honest with his story. It was her belief that the information that he shared with her was partially true, but there was more to it, something was missing, so she persisted in her efforts for the truth and was blunt with the question, "Where is your regiment?"

The soldier said as he observed Katie tending to the wound, "Near the cliffs, overlooking the river."

As Katie turned her attention from tending to the injury, she looked the soldier in the eyes and replied in a suspicious tone, "This home is a little ways away from your regiment. Isn't they're a surgeon with your unit, or did you become frighten by the intensity of battle and run?"

There was a smirk, and then a smile on the soldiers face as he earnestly replied, "A little bit of both I guess. Yes, I should have gone and received help from one of the physicians. But this is my first engagement and I was afraid of being killed by the next exploding shell, or perhaps of being finished off if the rebels invaded the town. I admit it, I ran at the first opportunity, but I'm not ashamed. There is no way on the face of the earth that we can win this engagement with all of the Johnnies that surround us."

"I know, I know." Katie agreed as she continued to tend to the wound.

The soldier continued frantically, "They are on the heights across the Potomac and Shenandoah, as well as the ridge to the west of town. This morning we were told that General McClellan would battle the Johnnies across the Potomac. I don't believe that help will reach us in time, so why should I sacrifice my life in a losing cause?"

There was a sigh of discomfort, when Katie gently touched the wound. He carefully observed her tender methods that she used in ministering to his needs. Her beauty attracted him; it was beyond anything that he had seen in a young lady. Sensing by her soft accent, he, too, thought that it was probable that she was from his area of the North, so in an investigative manner he said, "Are you from New England? What's your name?"

Katie answered as she continued to mend the wound, "I am from Boston, Massachusetts. My name is Katie McBride."

There was a pause and then the soldier politely said, "I am Bradford Westgate, I was born in Lexington, Massachusetts."

"What brought you to New York?"

"My Father was a professional soldier; an instructor in engineering at West Point. When he received his appointment, I was eleven years old, so at that time my family moved to New York."

Katie said as she finished wrapping the wound, "Oh, I see."

After tasting the awe of conflict, a gentle grin was resurrected upon the soldiers face, and softly he reminisced about the past, "I remember when I was a child, especially the summer months when all of the family would get together at my Auntie Martha's home in Plymouth for some of her delicious chowder. After eating our fill, all the kids would walk along the water for hours at a time, or just sit on the rocks listening to the sound of the ocean beating mightily against the rocks and spraying us with the cool mist. Maybe if we were lucky, we would see a ship cross the horizon." The soldier shook his head in an attempt to hold back the tears as he looked at Katie for her empathy, "That was when life was so different. Now, I have no idea what will face me tomorrow, or the next day if this war continues. Oh, what I wouldn't give to be on those sandy shores with my family and far away from the blood and misery of war."

Katie agreed in some respect, though she desired to shame him with words for his cowardly attitude, "I also have a brother who is fighting for the Union army with the 1st Massachusetts Cavalry. Many months have passed since I've heard from him, and I must admit, I wish the war would end the same as you. But knowing my brother as I do, I'm sure that he is ready to exchange his uniform for his civilian attire. I'm positive he'll do his duty with honor until it is complete. He is one of the most prideful and courageous men I have ever known. Still, there is a tenderness revealed within his heart."

As Katie and Bradford continued their conversation, the sounds of battle were increasing; the crashing noise from the Confederate bombardment was deafening. At times Katie feared the structure would be struck by one of the shells and the house would collapse around them.

Bradford noticed the terrified expression that covered Katie's face, and even though he desired to physically comfort her and speak words of encouragement, he felt that it was for the best to keep his distance. The one thought that crossed his mind, was she married? Throughout the whole ordeal, he had been glancing at her left hand; he did not notice a wedding ring, or any other symbol of matrimony, but in her haste to flee from the Confederate bombardment, maybe she left it somewhere in the house. They had been in the cellar for over an hour and yet she had made no mention of her husband. If he existed, where was he? Who lived in the house with her? Maybe her husband was fighting for the preservation of the Union. Bradford could not imagine Katie married to someone who was fighting for the Southern cause. Katie impressed him as a very sociable, prime, and proper individual who liked sincere and intelligent conversation, and possessed greater standing in class then most of the citizens in the area. It could not be possible for such a lady to be interested in some tyrants from the South. Maybe if he asks some questions, he could learn more about the lady and if there was someone special in her life.

As he turned his attention away from the flickering flame of the candle, he noticed that she was feeling the effects of the coolness and dampness in the cellar. He stood and removed his jacket and offered, "I can't help but notice that you are shivering from the chill that fills the air. Here, allow me to give you my coat to keep warm."

"No, no." Katie replied, "You need to stay warm. If you don't, infection might result from your wound."

With an expression of discomfort on his face, Bradford stood, and slowly removed his jacket. As he placed the jacket around Katie's arms and shoulders, he eloquently asked, "How can I witness the sacrifice of such beauty after you have been so kind to me? Your husband would never forgive me."

"Bradford." Katie asked, "Where did you get the idea that I have a husband?"

Bradford began to chuckle, "I just assumed."

Katie became angry and sternly replied, "Never, just bloody, never assume anything in life."

Soon, the smile disappeared from his face and the conversation between the two took a serious turn. Bradford began to speak, "Katie...."

Katie quickly held her hands up for him to stop speaking, and straight forward implied, "Bradford, I know the direction this conversation is taking, I know what you are about to say."

Bradford defensively replied, "How do you know. You didn't let me finish."

Katie saw the disappointment and the emotions in his expression and eyes as though he knew what she was going to say. Still, Katie was determine to get her point across with honestly and he needed to hear the words, "Bradford, for most of the afternoon, I've noticed you staring at me when you thought my attention was elsewhere. Sometimes when a woman looks into the eyes of a man she gets the feeling if there is an interest on his part. You can call it woman's intuition, or a feeling. At times, it's the brightness, joy, that is in his eyes, that gives him away when he sees that special someone."

Bradford silently walked over to the shelves that contained Mrs. McDonald's jellies. He picked up one of the jars and returned to his seat and began to remove the wax covering with his knife. After he sighed, he admitted the truth in part to Katie, "Yes, I'll be honest with you. I have found your beauty very irresistible. But then, I have always found it difficult to win the affection of someone that I was attracted to. Why should this moment be any different?"

Katie refused Bradford's gesture of some of the grape jelly; hunger was the furthermost thing from her mind as the sound of battle raged forth. She began to wonder if Pete was in the area with the Confederate army, and if he were, would he return to Shenandoah once more. Her heart yearned to see him and to touch his body, but most of all, to tell him the deepest feelings that have consumed her for the last two years. The time had come and the risk would be worth the gamble. As she continued to ponder on these thoughts, the brightly burning flame in the center of the wooden crate attracted her attention. It resembled the deep and sincere love that burned within her heart for Pete Barker. The flame was the perfect analogy to illustrate to Bradford her commitment and devotion for Pete. After a long silence and much meditation on the subject, she softly said, "Bradford, has there ever been anyone in your life that you have been truly committed to, such as being in love?"

As Katie's attention turned from the burning flame, she could tell by the glare in Bradford's eyes that he was surprised by the question. He didn't say a word, but looked at the dirt floor in shame and shook his head no.

Katie promptly spoke with firmness in her voice, "I didn't think so. Maybe if you would make an attempt to be honest with someone, then your chances of success might be much greater.

Bradford replied in a repentant tone, "I can tell by your answer that you appear to be wiser then what I thought. I sincerely apologize to you for my dishonesty concerning my inability to win a woman's affection.

Katie began to use her teaching skills, pointing at the candle, she calmly said, "As I have sat here, I've been observing the candle that is burning. Do you see how the brightly burning flame stands tall and straight, and never flickers, not even for a moment?"

"Yes," he reluctantly replied.

Now that Katie had his full attention and he was curious to know the meaning of her lesson, she continued with an undying confidence that reflected in her sincere tone of voice, "The flame that you are watching at this moment, illustrates the love and commitment that I have for someone else. I'm not about to betray, or compromise the deepest feelings of my heart. If I attempted to, happiness would elude me."

"I see. Is he fighting?"

"Yes, he is. I hope to see him soon."

Bradford calmly said as he stared at her, "I hope for your sake that he returns safely. Katie McBride, you are a strong willed individual, and you have a gentle and compassionate heart."

Katie remained silent, hoping soon that they could go their separated ways; the conflict continued with no end in sight.

After relinquishing his responsibilities to an assistant by the name of Marcus, Daniel reported to the first regiment that he came into contact with moving along the backside of School House Ridge. It was Colonel Lane's 7th North Caroline Infantry, of General Branch's brigade. Immediately, he offered his services for this particular engagement, and after informing the Colonel that he was familiar with the area, he was promptly dispatched with Captain Lewis of Branch's staff to General Hill. The General was riding his horse and was distinguishable by his red shirt. As Daniel and Captain Lewis rode up to the General, the Captain saluted and introduce Daniel, "Sir, this is Daniel Johnson, the overseer for this Estate."

General Hill said as he continued to look in the direction of the heights, "Mr. Johnson."

Captain Lewis continued to speak with optimism, "Mr. Johnson is a veteran of the war of '46 and he has volunteered his services."

The General said as he looked in Daniel's direction, "Good, good. Sir, how well do you know this area, especially along the river?"

Daniel spoke confidently of his abilities, "Nobody in this dang area knows the Shenandoah like me. I've lived in these parts all of my days, and God willing, I will always continue to do so."

General Hill laughed and replied, "That's good, because I need you as a guide." The General brought his mount to a halt and turned and faced School House Ridge. Pointing in the direction of the wooded heights beyond the ridge, he began to explain to Daniel their objective, "Mr. Johnson, all along this section of the heights toward the river is Colonel Mile's left flank. If all possible, General Jackson desires that I gain access to the enemies rear and flank without being discovered. We believed that the best approach in accomplishing our mission would be to move our forces along the river, and through that wooded area undetected if possible and strike the enemy a blow. And if everything goes as planned, we will be able to lay down fire along the river."

Pausing momentarily in his answer, Daniel removed his gray hat and wiped the perspiration from his brow. He replied in his rough voice, "The only problem is, we'd be box in between the river and the steep slopes. If the Yanks don't hear us, yeah, we could gain their rear, and lick them. But if they know we are comin' and decide to fight, well......."

The General was determined as he leaned forth in his saddle pointing at the heights, "My division can take that hill, yanks or no yanks. If the enemy remains there, we'll drive them from that position."

Without another word, Daniel departed with Captain Lewis and proceeded to guide Hill's division southward in the direction of the river, using the wooded area beyond the ridge to shelter their movement. When the Confederates arrived near the river, the brigades moved eastward at a slow pace following the river's shoreline and the Winchester and Potomac Railroad toward town. It was a treacherous endeavor fighting the thickets, vines, and undergrowth that populated the terrain along the railroad. Many of the soldiers were barefooted and suffered greatly from the rough stony ground and dense underbrush that would often rip open their skin, causing them to bleed. Occasionally, they would stop and tend to their injured feet, but they obediently kept their silence and resumed the march toward their destination. Off in the distance, one could hear the intense thundering sound of artillery as some of the Confederate brigades were making a demonstration of force against the Federal soldiers on Bolivar Heights. It had been General Jackson's strategy in an attempt to distract the Union forces long enough for Hill to have the element of surprise, and not be caught with his forces backed up against the river.

As the soldiers moved along the steep slopes, they came upon a bend in the river with a hill that ascended to a plateau above the slopes. As Daniel glanced about for landmarks, he was confident that the division was somewhere near the Chamber's farm, and hopefully against the Federals left flank. After informing the General of the Yankees proximity, it was agreed on that the Confederate troops would climb the hill and prepare for battle.

Shortly before dusk, three of the brigades fanned out across the ridge and began their movement toward the crest. Daniel noticed that the hill was absent of any type of fortifications and troops. The only obstacle appeared to be, fallen trees, vines, and underbrush full of thickets. Should the Federals discover their presence; then it could be a disastrous situation for the Confederates with little room to maneuver. As the soldiers steadily began their movements toward the crest of the hill, Federal soldiers appeared and fired several volleys at the advancing Confederates. By instincts, Daniel quickly fell to the ground and drew his revolver from his holster and returned the fire. Just as swiftly as the musketry began, it came to a halt, the Federals had retreated. Now, with the discovery of the Confederate presence, Daniel believed that the Union forces would be waiting as General Hill's troops reached the crest of the hill and try to attack them while they were still advancing through the thickets and entanglement of fallen trees.

After reaching the crest of the hill, the Confederate soldiers were forced to surrender to the darkness of night. Any attempts to attack the Federal troops that protected the left line of their defense were useless. Instead the Confederate division spent the night placing artillery on the hill that they had gained, and prepared for an all out assault on the Federals at first light.

At dawn the next morning, there was a thick, heavy fog and mist that covered the heights and valley. A. P. Hill's division laid in the forest along the fields that shadowed the Chamber's house ready for the signal to begin the assault on the Union left flank and rear.

During the night Daniel found General Pender. Daniel had met the General while guiding the division on this flanking maneuver, and requested that he be allowed to take part in the assault against the Federal units positioned to the brigade's front. After receiving permission from the General, Daniel quietly waited along the tree line with the 16th North Carolina Infantry. Hill's artillery began to belch its fire and shell at the Union soldiers to their front. Daniel's adrenaline began to flow; he was ready to move and take his part in sweeping the Federals from the field. As he stood anxiously waiting for the word from the line officers to move forward, his mind returned to the Mexican War. For a moment, he recalled the carnage and the miserable devastation of war that he had experienced, and trauma that resulted from his experience. Since the war of '46, he discovered the only remedy to soothe the ugly painful visions of night and the images of war that haunted him was at the end of a whisky bottle, which he gladly indulged in, when given the chance. He silently glanced about the faces of the young men that were called upon to do battle on this dreary morning, and was amazed at the expressions that he witnessed. Many of the soldiers had that hollow, somber, expressionless appearance that carries with a veteran of many conflicts. A soldier knows what is expected of him, and will carry out his duty to God and Country. As Daniel continued to glance about, he noticed some of the soldiers appeared to be frightened with the sound of artillery shells exploding; these he assumed must be new recruits. There was one soldier that appeared to be no older then fifteen or sixteen years of age, that drew his attention. The lad began to tremble. A fearful expression masked his face with each crashing and thudding sound of a passing artillery shell from one of the Federal guns. Daniel knew what the youngster was experiencing, he, too, had such feelings when he entered his first engagement along the Rio Grande. The sound of battle didn't faze Daniel as he left his position in line. He said to the lad, "Ya not thinkin' of runnin' are ya?"

The young soldier mumbled, "No."

Daniel attempted to reassure the lad, "I recall the first time that I fought any kind of battle. I was a young soldier, such as ya self scoutin' along the Rio Grande in Texas with the 2nd Dragoons. Sum of us were waterin' our mounts when a Mexican company of regulars started shootin'. As they crossed the river, they attempted to surround my party. We quickly mounted our horses and returned the fire. I'm not going to tell ya that I wasn't scared. I almost peed myself with fright; I thought that my life was comin' to an end. I could have run like a scared rabbit like the rest, but I didn't. Ya know what I did?" The young soldier remained silent maintaining his fearful expression. Daniel continued to boast, "See this scar on the right side of my neck. I got it when I pulled my saber and charged them. The others rallied and followed. Not only was I decorated there, but at Chapultepec, too. I received several field promotions for bravery."

The soldier rubbed his eyes and somberly said, "I didn't know that my feelin's showed that well."

"Yeah, they sure did. Once ya get out there in the thick of things, then ya will be to busy tryin' to survive rather then gettin' scared. Now I'll tell ya what I'm gonna do. When things start gettin' hot, I'll fight right along side of ya."

As Daniel stared at the youth and waited for a reply, he wondered if the youngster had a premonition of impending death. With hesitation, the soldier softly replied, "Alright, I'll do my killin' along side of ya."

With the heavy fog lifting, there was a lull in the firing from the Union guns. The order was immediately given for the advance to begin on the Union left flank. The regiments moved swiftly toward a Union battery that was placed along the Charlestown Pike. Daniel kept an eye on the Confederate soldier that moved along side of him. The regiments moved with haste towards the silent guns that stood less then a thousand yards in front of them. Suddenly, the Federal cannons unleashed a storm of shrapnel that bounced off of the ground to their front, striking some of the troops on the front line. As the Confederate regiments began to return fire, Daniel yelled to the lad, "Pick a target and fire!"

The soldier didn't respond. Daniel turned and shouted, "What's the matter with ya! I want ya to fire now, or I'll shoot ya myself."

The lad dropped to his knees and began to cry. Daniel exhibited his frustration with the lad, "Ya dang coward, I hope the Yanks shoot ya before I do."

Daniel allowed the lad to cry and proceeded further with the line of battle, firing and loading as fast as possible. The canister fire from the Union guns became too intense for the Confederates, so they began to withdraw across the field to the wooded area. As Daniel was returning, he noticed the lad lying in a fetal position on the ground. He stopped and knelt down along side of him. After shaking the boy on the shoulder, Daniel turned the lad over on to his back, only to witness the miserable and agonizing expression of death that covered his face.

Daniel murmured as he wiped the perspiration from his forehead, "Dang fool of a kid. He got what he deserved for not listenin' to me."

Daniel stood up on his feet, and walked away, though he made various attempts to hide and repress the guilt that consumed him. As always in past situations, Daniel reasoned within his heart to quench the fire of his conscious that had made various attempts to trap him so many times in his life.

Within the hour, the bombardment of the town and Bolivar Heights ceased. The conflict at Harpers Ferry came to an end with the garrison and its supplies being surrendered to General Jackson. At the very end of the bombardment, Colonel Miles was mortally wounded and died a short time later.

After receiving the good news of the towns surrender, Daniel returned to the Estate to share the tidings of victory with Charles. At once Charles sent for his family in Charlestown and was thankful that they were spared the terrible ordeal of the misery and trauma that he witnessed at Mechanicsville. For the second time during the war, Shenandoah wasn't used as a battlefield between the blue and gray bringing its destruction and damnation, though, Charles pondered how long before his family would be affected by the horrors of war.

CHAPTER TWENTY-THREE

After the engagement on the fourteenth of September, at Crampton's Gap, Pete and Jonathan were reassigned to duty once more with the 1st Virginia Cavalry. With the defeat of D. H. Hill's division at the gaps, the 1st along with the rest of Fitz Lee's brigade were dispatched, attempting to delay the Federal Army as they advanced from the mountain passes along South Mountain. All of the cavalrymen possible would be needed to retard the Federal effort, and give the retreating Confederate infantry time to reunite with Longstreet's Corp. The skirmishing had been heavy at times between the cavalry units of both the blue and gray on the outer perimeter of Boonsboro. As the Confederate cavalry passed through the village, the streets were so narrow that the brigade had to move in columns of four. The 9th Virginia covered the retreat, as the intensity of battle increased. As the Confederates struggled to go through the town, not only did they have the Federal troops to contend with, but citizens who were loyal to the Union. They kept up a steady volley of fire from windows and trees along the way, hampering Confederate efforts. Once the Confederate brigade of cavalry was on the outskirts of town, they reformed their ranks and encountered the enemy at the little hamlet of Keedysville. Skirmishing between Lee's brigade of cavalry and the Federals continued periodically throughout the day. Once Fitz Lee felt secure that he wasn't being pursued any longer, the command moved to Sharpsburg, only several miles from the Potomac River. There the brigade was placed on the left flank of the Confederate battle line.

Later that same afternoon, Lester Tyler was standing along the Boonsboro turnpike with General Lee and his staff. The commanding officer was intensely studying the countryside from where the Union forces were positioning to do battle. Lester had been on courier duty since the beginning of the campaign and was about to be relieved to return to the regiment. He admired the beauty of the well-kept farms and homesteads that surrounded the area even though it had been a dry summer. Everywhere Lester looked, he noticed the abundance of prosperity. The area he observed was far from the devastation and destruction that he had witnessed in his home state. Now, Lester thought, it was time for the citizens that were sympathetic to the North to receive a taste of what Virginians had experienced over the last two years.

As Lester continued to watch the commander-in-chief, he heard the approaching sound of horses. He turned in his saddle and saw General Stuart approaching their position along the high grounds that overlooked the Antietam. As the cavalry General rode up, General Lee turned in Stuart's direction. The commanding General returned the cavalry commanders salute, and said, "General Stuart, what information can you give me on the surrender of the garrison at Harpers Ferry?"

Lester listened as Stuart spoke to the commanding General, "General Hill is writing the paroles of the Federal troops as we speak. We have captured a great deal of ammunition and artillery pieces."

"What else?" General Lee asked as his eyes continued to survey the area across the creek.

General Stuart replied optimistically, "We captured many stores of supplies, but from what I understand, General Jackson's troops pretty much helped themselves to the spoils."

As General Lee was asking General Stuart about shoes for the soldiers, Lester departed.

Confederate troop movements were taking place as Lester rode slowly along the turnpike toward Sharpsburg. There he saw a company of North Carolina Cavalry near the intersection of Main Street and the road that led to Hagerstown. Some of the troopers were mounted and holding the reins of horses for their comrades while they searched for something to eat for the rest of the company. Lester brought his stallion to a halt and noticed a private chosen for such duty, Lester had to shout because of the loud rumbling sound of the passing batteries, "Hey, have you seen the 1st Virginia Cavalry?"

The private yelled, "What ya say?"

Seeing that his efforts were futile because of the noise, Lester waited until the last limber past and slowly approached the private. This time without shouting, he asked, "Do you know where the 1ˢᵗ Virginia might be."

"Well." The cavalryman paused scratching his black hair and then continued in his Southern drawl, "I think they's on da left of da line towards da river."

The private slowly turned in his saddle and pointing in the direction to Hagerstown saying, "Out yonder dat way."

As the private turned once more and faced Lester, he asked, "Where ya from?"

"I'm from Washington County, the southern part of Virginia."

The private replied as he spit out some tobacco juice and wiped his mouth with his dirty hands, "I'm from Boone County, North Carolina."

Lester was rubbing the neck of his horse as he spoke, "I guess in the next few days we will be fighting the Yanks."

The North Carolinian shook his head in agreement and sadly commented, "Yeah. I always think dat the next battle is gonna be de last one. But they keep a comin'. Ya know I'd like to go home. I'd not been dere since this foolishness started. My wife, my little ones, I miss 'em."

After agreeing and wishing the trooper his best, Lester proceeded along the road to Hagerstown. As he slowly moved toward the area where the North Carolinian had told him the 1ˢᵗ might be located, he began to gaze about in hopes of finding the regiment, so he could inform Pete of the news concerning Harpers Ferry.

As Lester maneuvered his stallion across a farm lane, he came upon pickets from Fitz Lee's brigade. After inquiring the whereabouts of the 1ˢᵗ, Lester made haste in a westward direction. He found the regiment on the backside of a ridge that overlooked the Hagerstown Pike and about a quarter of a mile southwest. Lester found the ridge to be of strategic advantage with its rock-outcroppings. It provided a commanding position that overlooked the road to its front as well as good visibility across the cornfields and wooded area on the opposite side of the road. From here he thought, the brigade could protect the Confederate army from the Federals gaining their rear and cutting off a possible escape should the Confederate's not be successful against the Yankees.

Lester didn't have to look for long in his search for Pete. He was sitting on the opposite side of the ridge on some outcroppings under a grove of trees playing cards with Jonathan, and several other members of the 1ˢᵗ.

After dismounting, Lester slowly and quietly walked in the direction toward the soldiers playing poker; some of them noticed his approach. He gestured to the soldiers by pointing to his cousin and placing his finger to his mouth for silence. He did not want them to reveal his presence to his cousin. Lester noticed the familiar grin on Jonathan's face as he put down his cards on the blanket before them. Suddenly, without warning, Lester grabbed Pete from behind. As Pete jumped to his feet and attempted to defend himself, Lester made his presence known, "Its your old cousin, Lester."

Both of the cousins along with Jonathan and the other members of the unit began to laugh. Pete was surprised to see his cousin and expressed it in his tone of voice, "Lester, I thought you were still assigned to General Lee's staff. What are you doing here?"

There was a grin that covered the width of Lester's face as he replied, "Well cousin. General Lee sent me back to the regiment knowing that you needed someone to look out for you."

In a humorous manner, Pete took his hand and slapped Lester on his back as they walked over to the smoldering fire, "Come on, have some coffee, we don't have much left."

Lester noticed Pete's dirty and famished appearance, "You look like you haven't eaten in sometime. At least I got something to eat on courier duty."

"No, I haven't eaten. We have been on the move so much. The only thing that has satisfied me over the last three days is a piece of wormless hardtack and a moldy biscuit I found going through a dead Yankee's possessions near South Mountain. Its nothing compared to the goods at Catlett's Station last month."

Jonathan said, as he handed Lester the coffee, "Hell, we'd be so hungry, anythin' be tasty, right boys? Some of the boys are chewin' on straw because they have nothin'.

Lester attempted to reassure his comrades, "The commissary trains had to go by a different route, so they are going to be late in arriving with rations."

Jonathan was disappointed and expressed his feelings by kicking some dirt on the fire, "I don't know about ya-all, but I'm hungry. I hate to steal from these good folks, the good book preaches against it."

As Jonathan rode away with his fellow comrades, Pete turned to Lester as they began to walk along the tall brown grass in the field. Pete desiring information asked, "Have you heard any additional news concerning the capture of Harpers Ferry?"

"Yes, just as I was being relieved from duty. General Stuart carried information to General Lee from a courier that arrived from the Ferry. He told the General that we captured a large amount of supplies and artillery."

Pete said sadly with a quiver in his voice, "When I was at Crampton's Gap the other day, I thought about the family's welfare and the possible chance to return home since we were so close. Its been over a year since I have seen my love ones, I'm sure things have changed in my absence. If I could return, just for a moment, that would satisfy me."

Lester asked, as he sipped the coffee, "What about your lady friend? Didn't she live in town?"

As the two soldiers stood on the crest of the ridge, Pete momentarily paused. He removed his hat and allowed the breeze to blow freely through his hair. Turning about and facing his cousin, Pete finally replied, "The last that I heard from Katie was during the latter part of winter. I'm sure that if she stayed in the area, Caroline gave her refuge at Shenandoah before all this began. But hopefully, she received my advice and returned to Boston."

As Lester emptied the rest of the contents from the cup and gazed in the direction of the cornfield and farm that ran parallel to the Hagerstown Road, he said with earnest, "You know, a lot of good men in the next few days won't be leaving this area to return home. I'm convinced General Lee will fight on this ground. As I look out across this beautiful countryside, I have a difficult time thinking of the destruction that will come to it with an engagement. The many years that it has taken for the farmers to build the homes, barns, and the possessions they have accumulated will be gone. Although, on the other hand, I couldn't help but think about what two years of war has done to the citizens of Virginia and their homesteads."

Both Pete and Lester knew that a major confrontation with the Army of the Potomac would soon be unavoidable as they were continuing to approach the Antietam.

The next evening at Shenandoah, the Barkers were celebrating the homecoming of Rebecca. After completing her education at the Richmond Institute for Females, she decided that it was time to return to the area she called home. Rebecca was accompanied from Richmond by William. William made good his promise to spend sometime at the Barker's after tending to affairs at his estate in Norfolk.

With the conflict recently ending in Harpers Ferry, and troops converging on Sharpsburg, Elizabeth decided against having a reception. Instead, the family would just have a quiet dinner and invite guests at another time should the area remain under control of the Confederacy. As they were seated enjoying the roasted chicken that Pansy had prepared, and toasting with their glasses of white wine, they indulged in optimistic conversation concerning the prospect of peace. Elizabeth curiously asked William, "During my stay in Charlestown several days ago, I had a conversation with the friends that I was visiting, and it was Mr. Whites perception that the governments of France and England might become actively involved. Have you heard any news concerning their possible involvement?"

William was optimistic in his tone as he replied, "As I understand in Britain, the unemployment is very high. And, in many cases, the textile industry is suffering greatly causing worries to soar to an all time high for fear that cotton will become scarce. Also, there is a strong resentment growing among the British for the North, especially among those in power because of the deliberate act of the seizure of the Trent on the high seas. With several more victories, Britain may recognize the Confederacy as a nation, which would apply pressure on Lincoln to give up this struggle."

Caroline spoke as she was cutting her chicken, "William, I hope that you are correct."

Charles added his observations to the conversation, "When I was in town earlier this morning, I was speaking with Major Ford of General Hill's staff and he tells me that General Jackson's troops had been departing to join the Confederate forces around Sharpsburg. He went on to say that Hill's division was to join them at that location after paroling the Union soldiers captured in town. They do expect to fight McClellan in the area. I understand McClellan moved forces through the gaps of South Mountain and he is moving in Lee's direction."

Caroline replied in a concerned tone, "I see."

"Remember, my love, what I told you the day before yesterday?"

Caroline looked up from her dinner toward her husband and answered, "Yes, I do."

Charles continued as he gestured with his hands, "Everything depends on what those dirty ragged soldiers that are on our property can do. If we defeat McClellan, then maybe the victory will convince Britain to join us in our effort to achieve independence."

Elizabeth was somewhat puzzled, "Oh dear, I don't understand what you are saying."

William said jovially as he wiped his mouth with the fine linen cloth, "If Lee isn't defeated by McClellan, it will place greater pressure on Lincoln with the anti-war sentiment that is growing in the North. And then too, maybe members of Lincolns own party might demand a peaceful compromise to the end the war."

Rebecca added optimistically, "I hope so, the gentleman that I'm fond of is with the 1ˢᵗ Virginia Infantry. Thomas has seen some intense fighting with Longstreets Corps. Hopefully, Mother, you will meet him soon." Placing her white handkerchief to her cheek, Rebecca continued, "Oh, how I miss his companionship."

Caroline looked up from her meal and surprisingly said, "Wait a minute, when I was visiting with you and Aunt Daisy last spring, I thought this gentleman was someone you were using as a gopher to punish some of your friends. I was under the impression that there wasn't any kind of a commitment."

Rebecca had just finished eating and Matthew was removing her plate. She paused and wiped her mouth with the white linen and methodically answered, "Oh, dear, Caroline, you take life so seriously."

Caroline turned about with an angry expression and snapped, "And you don't!"

Charles pleaded as he gestured with his hands, "Ladies, ladies."

Rebecca did not desire to share her feelings and deepest thoughts concerning her relationship with Thomas Monroe at this time because she didn't know if there would be a commitment in a relationship on his behalf. It was with a defensive tone that she replied to Caroline, "Oh Caroline, I do not feel at this time that it is appropriate for a young lady, such as myself to indulge in ones privacy, especially in front of a guest. Matters between a man and woman should be kept between the couple and not for the whole world to know. Don't you agree?"

Elizabeth broke her silence and demanded, "Speaking for this family Rebecca, I feel that Caroline is asking a legitimate question. Are you or are you not taking advantage of Mr. Monroe feelings."

Rebecca answered promptly in a snippy tone, "No Mother, I am a lady. I just feel that there are some things that should be left sacred, such as a man and woman's relationship."

After remaining silent, Charles began to take sides with his younger sister, "I agree with Rebecca. What is between a man and a woman should remain confidential." After pausing, Charles continued to defend his sister, "And if she doesn't want to share this area of her life, then that's her privilege. Besides, I believe that Rebecca knows the importance of protecting the family's honor."

Caroline was firm in her resolve, "I just do not agree with using another human being as a pawn, such as your sister did with this individual when we were in Richmond."

Rebecca threw her handkerchief on the floor and with a flare in her tone, "Who says that I'm using him for a pawn."

Elizabeth commanded in a loud voice as she stood, "Young lady don't you display that kind of behavior in this house in the presence of a guest. Now, I expect you to apologize to Mr. Pierce."

Rebecca shamefully and reluctantly turned to William who was sitting beside her and calmly said, "Mr. Pierce, I ask that you would accept my apologies."

William replied, with a cordial smile, "Rebecca, that is quite alright."

Rebecca said in a humble tone, "I would like to apologize to everyone for my actions. I would ask for your forgiveness. As for Thomas, I would like for Mother to have the privilege of meeting him, when that opportunity comes. Furthermore, I hope to marry him one day."

Everyone at the table began to glance at each other pondering on the revelation Rebecca was sharing with them. In the past on various occasions, Rebecca had been known to be dishonest in order to protect her pride. Each member of the family, as well as William, kept their personal thoughts to themselves concerning the subject and did not want to pursue the issue.

For Pete Barker, it had been a long and restless night. Like most soldiers in the Confederate ranks, he thought about home and when the opportunity presented itself, to see his family. At times over the past year, he had thought about desertion, but he believed that men only resorted to those types of actions out of desperation to rejoin their families, or they are cowards. In any case, he knew that his conscious would pour out condemnation for such actions.

Pete pulled the blanket away from his body and looked at his watch. The black hands on the watch indicated that it was shortly after four in the morning on the seventeenth of September. The air was filled with a mist and dampness as Pete began to prepare for the confrontation that was sure to take place today.

Pulling his revolver from his holster, he checked the magazine to make sure it was full of bullets and that extra magazines of ammunition were on hand for quick reloading of the weapon. By now, most of the men of the 1st were up and doing the same thing. As the first gray rays of morning appeared, Pete noticed the artillerymen on the crest of the ridge that were assigned to the cavalry and three additional batteries in position near by. He noticed the artillerymen laboring about their guns making sure that the cannon tube had the correct elevation before firing, and examined some of the ammunition.

As Pete walked over to where a fire had been burning the previous evening, he discovered there wasn't any coffee left; the last of it had been used yesterday. As he stood by what use to be a campfire, Pete became frustrated and kicked some dirt into the smoldering cinders. His actions were observed by Jonathan, who began to openly laugh at his friend's temperament and said at the same time, "There's nothin' worst then wakin' up in the mornin' without hot coffee."

Pete snapped as he looked at his friend, "Jonathan, its not funny. If this continues to happen, then I'm going to have to resort to stealing from civilians, which I hate; it would make me feel guilty."

Jonathan began to speak as he began to light his pipe, "Ya think so huh?"

Pete laughed and replied, "Yes, I do."

Without warning, there was a loud crashing thunder that came from one of the Confederate artillery pieces positioned along the line of defense, where the cavalry was positioned. Within moments, artillery across the crest of the ridge where Pete, Jonathan, and most of Fitz Lee's brigade were positioned began to fire with intensity. As assembly was sounding, Pete, along with Jonathan, mounted their horses and fell into rank with members of their regiment. Within minutes, Confederate artillery massed on a plateau near a small white building along the Hagerstown Road and joined in on the attack against the Union artillery, that by now had answered the call. After a sharp encounter the evening before, the Federals had taken position in a wooded area toward the east of the Confederate line of defense, and in the vicinity of a farm that ran adjacent to the road on the northern side. At once with the bombardment beginning, General Jackson sent a brigade of infantry to support the artillery on the ridge, which is called Nicodemus. Pete and the 1st were positioned there. It was here, that the Confederate leadership feared that the Federals would attempt an attack to turn the Confederate armies' left flank, driving them toward the river. Thus, cutting off their route of retreat, and possible destruction.

As the cavalrymen of the 1ˢᵗ prepared to defend the artillery guns, Union artillery shells came crashing by and exploding to the rear of the regiment. Pete and Jonathan observed some of the women and children fleeing from a stone farmhouse terrified with their hands in the air screaming with fear. It appeared to Pete that the civilians were running toward the Confederate lines to seek refuge. Some of the soldiers of the 1ˢᵗ began to laugh, but Jonathan pointing in their direction said, "Look at those dang fools. What is they tryin' to do, get killed?"

Immediately, an officer from the 1ˢᵗ galloped into the cornfield to assist the women and children. The Union gunners ceased firing while the rescue was taking place and the officer guided the victims to safety.

Brigades of Union infantry from Hooker's Corps moved from the cover of the woods toward the Confederate infantry that were laying in the pastureland, behind fence rails and a wooded area near the Dunker Meeting House. As the Federal troops advanced in battle formation, Pete calmly said to Jonathan, "My friend, we are in for a real fire fight. Things are going to get hot shortly."

"I know." Jonathan said, as he dismounted from his mare along with Pete. Jonathan continued to say with confidence, as they move to a position along side the cannons, "There most be over 10,000 of them dang Yanks comin' across that field."

As the Federals approached the Confederate infantry line of defense, the defenders rose and unleashed a terrible volley of musketry at the Federals. Yankees fell in great numbers with the destructive fire from the rebel artillery and infantry. Immediately, the field of battle, like so many in the past was covered with a white cloud of haze on a windless morning. Pete watched as both blue and gray artillery shells exploded above their foes, lighting up the sky. The battle raged on with the Federal advance stalling near the fence that bordered the road to Hagerstown. A great number of the Yankees were shot to death as they climbed the fence, and in some instances the Union soldiers tore down sections of the fence. Still, the Union continued to screamed obscenities at the Rebels and loading their muskets. They were persistent in continuing the advancement of their battle line, yelling along the way.

Many of the men both blue and gray fired volley after volley and fell in the ranks never to rise again. The ground was covered with the dead stacked upon one another, falling where struck by the missiles of death. The killing and maiming of soldiers continued without either side giving ground. Pete was anxiously waiting for the word to be passed down by General Stuart for some sort of advance by the cavalry, since they were on the right flank of the Federal battle lines, but it didn't come. Suddenly, Jonathan let out a shout of victory, and pointed toward the Smoketown Road saying with great excitement, "General Hood's Texan boys are comin', look at them fellas movin' across that field."

Pete began to hope for a quick victory with the Yankees retreat across the cornfield. Hood's Texans reformed their line of battle and proceeded to counterattack the Federals pushing them into the cornfield. The fighting that took place in that small area was some of the most savage and ruthless that Pete and Jonathan had witnessed thus far in the war. Continuous volleys were poured unmercifully into the ranks of Confederates and Yankees alike. Union and Confederate artillery were unable to render assistance to their comrades because the fighting was too close. At times, it appeared to Pete that the Rebels and Yankees were using the butt of their weapons to club their opponents into submission. Still, many were engaged in hand-to-hand combat. It appeared to Pete to be almost inhuman with the carnage, which was taking place; the sacrifice of life and the shedding of blood between the soldiers were freely poured today. One could hear even at Pete's position, the screams of agony and terrifying death that the soldiers from both sides were experiencing. What were once full regiments of soldiers among the Texans quickly dwindled in strength, some unit's, only the size of several companies. Pete turned and glanced at Jonathan, but kept his silence when he witnessed the horrified expression that ruled his features. After what seemed an eternity of killing, the Texans had to retreat to their former battle lines.

By seven o'clock, the Confederate forces retreated back to an area around the Dunker Meeting House that stood along the Hagerstown Road. As Pete and the rest of the regiment anxiously watched the Confederate infantry surrender the ground to the Yankees, he heard General Stuart give the command, "Prepare to move out by the left flank."

Jonathan overheard one of the officers nearby say to another officer, "It looks like we are going to move back to our original position."

Jonathan turned about in his saddle and facing Pete anxiously said, "Did ya hear that."

"Yes, I sure did."

"Well, what ya think?" Jonathan whispered as if he didn't desire to be overheard.

Pete shrugged his shoulders, "I guess there is a reason for it."

General Stuart brought his horse, Virginia, to a halt near the two officers and commanded, "I want this column moved to the extreme left of the line."

With obedience, the two officers complied with the General's command. As he turned in the saddle and looked in Pete and Jonathan's direction, he shouted, "Quickly, come with me."

With the retreat of Hood's division, the Rebels began to prepare for another Union offensive. At this time General Stuart ordered some of the batteries on Nicodemus Hill to limber up and follow him to Hauser's Ridge, directly behind a wooded area west of the Hagerstown Road. From this position, the batteries would have commanding advantage over the Union forces advancing upon that area of the battlefield near the Dunker Meeting House. General Stuart directed the cavalry company that Pete was riding with, to support the artillery. As the batteries unlimbered and began firing at the Yankees who were moving quickly toward the road, the General shouted, "Barker, you come with me."

In the distance, but within a good area behind the batteries, General Stuart observed the intense firing from his guns on the Federals. Pete once again as in Manassas the year before, noticed the brightness that battle brought to the General's expression. As for Pete, it was a different feeling. Over the last several hours, he witnessed enough bloodshed to last him a lifetime, but it appeared that the slaughter and torment of conflict would continue for a while longer.

CHAPTER TWENTY-FOUR

It was during mid-morning and the battle at Sharpsburg continued without either side willing to give ground. Both the Federals and the Confederates had suffered enormous causalities with just the fighting that had taken place along the Hagerstown Road and the cornfield. With a lull in the battle, General Lee requested of General Jackson a plan of operation that would relieve the growing force of opposition against General Hill's division, which was positioned in a farmer's sunken lane.

General Jackson outlined a plan that included the cavalry gaining the rear of the Federals along the left flank of the Confederate line of defense. Walker's Confederate division of infantry, positioned in a wooded area, west of the Hagerstown Road, would cooperate with the cavalry in a frontal assault at the sound of Stuart's artillery.

Pete remained with General Stuart and members of his staff as they moved backward and forward among the artillery units along Hauser's Ridge and Nicodemus Hill. Sitting on his mare looking in the direction of the cornfield where some of the most deadly and destructive combat had taken place, Pete began to ponder if he would see the end of this conflict. He was not optimistic with the outcome for the Confederate armies' chances of success because they appeared to be outnumbered by the Federals. The silence of Pete's thoughts was broken by the rapid gallop of a courier from headquarters. He presumed that the courier carried a message for General Stuart. As the officer brought his horse to a halt, the courier informed the General after saluting, "Sir, General Jackson request that you would accompany me immediately."

General Stuart gave some instructions to several of the couriers that rode along with the staff, and departed toward the woods where General Jackson was located. Since the Federals showed no threat of advancing, Pete dismounted from his horse, and seized the opportunity to walk into a wooded area behind the artillery line and rest. As he sat alone on an old oak tree that had fallen, he heard a shuffling sound in the underbrush. Quietly, Pete pulled his revolver from its holster and listened intently for the sound once more. Again there was a crackling noise as he quickly and quietly jumped to his feet. Slowly, Pete walked toward the direction of the thickets and vines with his pistol ready to discharge. Pulling back some of the underbrush and vines, he saw a Confederate soldier badly mangled from a ghastly wound to the abdomen groaning with pain. Pete stared at the soldier's face. It was covered with gunpowder and grime from the deadly work that he had participated today. With further inspection of the soldier's identity, Pete realized that it was someone that he knew from Harpers Ferry, his old nemesis Billy Smith. Pete knew that even though Billy and he had been enemies, he couldn't abandon the wounded trooper, though he felt like he should after all the difficulty that Billy had caused him. Billy's eyes gazed at Pete and the young Barker was sure that he recognized him. Billy continued to groan with a whispering sound and Pete looked as the wounded soldier motioned with his left hand for him to kneel down so he could speak. Pete removed his hat and complied with Billy's request. Gasping for air, Billy murmured, "I guess it is only fitting that you and I should be together when death is at the door."

Pete placed his finger to his mouth and whispered, "You need to be quiet and save your strength. I will go for help."

"Nah, nah, it's too late for that. I won't be alive by the time you return." Billy replied and continuing his attempt to speak, he said as he gasped, "I know you and I have always had our differences, but I must ask, as a fellow comrade in arms, for a favor."

Pete asked, as he pulled the cork from his canteen, "What can I do for you?"

Billy replied as he gritted his teeth from the intense pain, "If you are able to return home, I want you to take something for me, will you, please?"

"Yes, sure, whatever I can do for you."

Billy removed a letter from the pocket of his gray coat and asked, "Will you see that the recipient receives this at your first convenience? With the army on the move, I didn't have time…" Billy paused and began to cough, "to deliver it."

"Billy," Pete somberly replied as he held the wounded soldiers head to give him water, "I promise you."

"Thank you," Came the dying soldiers feeble reply. Finally, Billy spoke his last words, "I am sorry for the problems I caused you."

Almost immediately the sound of life departed from the young soldier. Pete examined Billy for any sign of life, but his chest was not expanding with air and he was totally motionless with his eyes staring at the heavens. Convinced that Billy's agony and tribulation was concluded, Pete slowly stood to his feet, glancing once more at the corpse, he left the wooded area.

Pete was curious and about to open the correspondence that he received from Billy, when General Stuart returned with an expression of confidence covering his features. Over the last two years before a cavalry engagement, Pete had become familiar with Stuart's expression in the heat of conflict. Pete knew that the regiment was finally going to see some action, so he placed the letter in his pocket for safekeeping. Immediately, he grasped the reins of his horse and mounted. There was a tone of excitement in the General's voice, "Boys, we are going to see some action. It is General Jackson's desire that we make an attempt to gain the Federals flank and rear. If we are successful, then there will be an assault by Walker's division from the front along the Hagerstown Road."

The first order the General gave in preparing for the attack was to Pete, "Barker, I want you to scout a way for us between here and the river and see if we can accomplish this with an element of surprise. Report directly to me and make it quick, time is not on our side."

"Yes sir," Saluting the General, Pete departed.

As Pete rode behind the ridge, he turned in the direction of the Potomac River. From there he passed the Cox homestead and proceeded with caution toward Mercersville, a little village to the north. Pete was well beyond the Confederate line of defense, riding at a brisk pace behind a ridge that parallel the river and the canal. He knew if he was detected by the Federals, then it would jeopardize his mission and Stuart's chances of gaining the surprise attack against the enemy. It didn't take Pete long to cross a fork in the road. If he continued north, then the road would take him on to the village, or he could attempt to probe for the enemy traveling the short distance east in the vicinity of the Hagerstown Road. Pete quickly ruled out the latter for reason of easy detection by the Yankees. The only option left was to continue toward the village along the east side of the road. Sheltered by a wooded area, Pete cautiously dismounted from his horse. As quietly as possible, he led the animal into the woods. From his concealed position, he proceeded carefully by foot up a slope and to the edge of the trees and thickets that populated the area. Peering through his field glasses, Pete observed the Federals placing many artillery pieces and strengthening their flank and rear with infantry. Pete thought this was going to present major problems for the rebels with such a powerful concentration of men and weapons. The terrain would make it difficult for cavalry operations with the heavy amount of rock outcroppings that covered the fields and slopes. This effort might only be made possible if the cavalry fought dismounted. Swiftly, Pete returned by the same route that he came.

As the young Barker rode with haste across Hauser's Ridge, he noticed General Stuart finalizing details of his plans with one of the officers from an artillery unit. Slowing his mounts gallop, Pete rode to where the General was sitting on his horse and saluted. General Stuart asked, "Well Barker, what news do you bring me?"

Pete wasn't optimistic about the Confederates plan to dislodge the Yankee from their position and the preparations that he had witnessed on his reconnaissance. He said in a tone of doubt, "Sir, there is a road that runs parallel to the river." Pete continued as he turned in the saddle and pointed in a westerly direction, "We might not have enough room to maneuver between the river and the rough slopes, besides, the Federals are strengthening their position along the Hagerstown Road as I'm speaking. I noticed that they are placing cannons on the high ground to lay down a heavy fire on any approach with at least a brigade of infantry for support. Not only that, but the way of approach is filled with rock outcroppings."

Pete noticed by the General's serious expression that he wasn't discouraged by the report, "Well done, Barker. I want you to stay near."

Soon the preparations for the assault were completed. The cavalry and infantry began the movement with the artillery units. The column moved toward the direction of the river and into position west of a farm near a wooded area close to the fork in the road, where Pete had been previously. It was just as Pete had witnessed, the Federals had massed artillery in great number along with infantry in the attempt to protect the Union armies flank and rear. At once the order was given to unlimber some of the artillery and make the necessary preparations to open on the Federal defenses. Pete calmly gazed at the gun crew as their cannons unleashed their missiles of death. Once more, the Federals outnumbered the Confederates in artillery guns and the massive number of infantry, which supported them. After a short artillery duel, Stuart realized that the cavalry losses would be too great against the Federal defenses; the Confederate effort was abandon.

It was late in the afternoon; the battle on the Confederate left flank had completely ended except for some sporadic firing from the opposing troops. As Pete was seated on a rock, he heard the sound of anguish and torment coming from the thousands of soldiers that had been wounded on this bloody day. The burning stench of flesh filled the air as the sound of battle filled the air toward the far right of the Confederate line. The smell of gunpowder lingered across the ridge, and many somber faces masked the features of the cavalrymen of the brigade. Pete wondered if the army would stay and fight again tomorrow, or if they would gather their wounded and retreat across the river to fight another day. If General Lee decides to cross the Potomac into Virginia, Pete thought, then the general order would come immediately and it would have to take place under the cover of darkness. Surely, General McClellan and the Union army would not allow the Confederates to retreat without making the attempt to destroy Lee's army. The thought crossed Pete's mind that the war could be over within a few days if the Federals take advantage of the possible opportunity. Time was so precious and he was fatigued from the combat, yet Pete was grateful that his life had been spared by Providence.

The next day, a truce was declared between the Federals and Confederates to minister to the wounded on the battlefield and to bury the dead. For now, Pete remained on duty with General Stuart's staff and had been given permission from his superiors to locate Thomas Monroe, Rebecca's gentleman friend from the 1st Virginia Infantry. As Pete rode along the Hagerstown Road, he witnessed the carnage from the previous days combat. Union and Confederate soldiers lay motionless along the fence rail of the road that led to Hagerstown, their bodies darkening and beginning to bloat from death. Limbs on some of the soldiers were missing from the devastating use of canister fire by the artillery pieces. Still, other combatants were so disfigured from wounds that they were unrecognizable. The intensity and desperation of combat was revealed the greatest in the cornfield. It was there, that Pete brought his mount to a halt and observed the corn that had been ready to be harvest the day before and now totally destroyed and cut to ground level in most areas by the heavy fighting. The field was covered with the gruesome sight of war with bodies lying on top of bodies. Many of the soldiers that met their fate in that bloody area of the battlefield were still clinging to their weapons with unspeakable expressions of death covering their face. It grieved Pete to witness the vultures of the air feasting on the remains of the dead as they lay east of the Hagerstown Road on a small slope across from the Dunker Meeting House. The building was full of holes, drilled by the intense musketry and artillery projectiles that struck it, but now, it was a haven for the infirmed. Soldiers from both sides had been formed as burial details to tend to the task of interment for the deceased; still many of the civilians assisted the Medical Corp to transport the wounded to the nearest field hospital. Some of the Confederate soldiers, kneeling beside their dead comrades openly wept with emotion. As Pete glanced about, he noticed a Confederate soldier carrying his musket over his shoulder and with the other hand; he began to plunder a wounded Yankee. The Yankee cried out with the greatest sound of pain that Pete had ever witnessed. The Confederate soldier showed no mercy for the defenseless individual. He began to confiscate some of the wounded soldiers personal possessions, especially the small gold frame that contained the image of his family. The Yankee held tightly to the precious possession, and yelling, the Confederate said in a threatening tone, "Ya dang Yankee, if ya don't shut up, I'll put ya miserable life to an end."

The Yankee soldier was in such terrific pain that he wasn't able to comply with the Confederates demand. Suddenly, the rebel began to loudly curse the dying Yankee, taking his weapon and placing the bayonet on the end of the barrel, he lifted the gun to strike the Yankee and end his suffering prematurely. Promptly, Pete pulled his revolver and shouted, "Stop, or I'll shoot!"

The Confederate lowered his weapon, and with a look of defiance he said, "Boy, whose side are ya on anyway?"

Pete angrily replied as he slowly approached the Confederate, "The Yankee is unarmed, he can't defend himself."

As the Confederate soldier complied with the order and departed cursing, Pete dismounted and walked over to where the Yankee was laying. Kneeling beside him, Pete gave the soldier some water from his canteen. The soldier continued to cling to the image that was so precious. With tears streaming from his eyes, the Yankee spoke in a quivering tone of voice, "My Mother is all that I have. What will be come of her with my death."

Pete was speechless; he didn't have the words to say that would comfort the Yankee's heart. It caused Pete to ponder on his own mortality. It appeared that the battles were becoming more deadly and savage with each passing engagement. If the war continued, he thought, the odds of his survival were against him. His concentration was broken by the arrival of the angels of mercy from the Medical Corp, who attended to the Yankee soldier. Slowly, Pete stood to his feet and mounted his horse for the short journey into town.

In Sharpsburg, the town had been turned into massive turmoil with congestion from wagons carrying the wounded and supplies. Some of the artillery units moved causally toward the front after refilling their limbers with ammunition. The village had been turned into a hospital for the wounded soldiers, both Union and Confederate. Everywhere the eye could see, civilians were helping the surgeons attending to the loud unbearable cries of the casualties. Pete began to inquire into the position of Kempers brigade of Longstreet's Corp. After being informed that the Confederates had been involved in the fighting on the right flank of the army's battle line, Pete proceeded in that direction.

Pete turned his mount and headed along the Boonsboro Pike to the crest of the ridge. There, a short distance eastward, he witnessed some Confederates and Federals exchanging tobacco for coffee, and indulging in friendly conversation. After the terrible battle that took place yesterday and the carnage in its aftermath, it was difficult for Pete to understand the friendly feelings the soldiers could share toward each other so soon after the conflict. Quite possibly, he thought, all hell could break loose again today or tomorrow, and more bloodshed and lives would be poured out on the field of combat. For now, he was without provision and would take advantage of the truce and attempt to trade his birthstone that his mother had given him. Casually, he dismounted and approached the soldiers standing along the road. Pete removed the ruby from around his neck and held it in his left hand. There was a Union cavalryman who noticed Pete carrying the precious commodity in his hand and quickly seized the opportunity to trade. The Lieutenant of the 1st Massachusetts Cavalry asked in his deep sounding voice, "Hey Johnnie, what do you have there?"

As the officer caught Pete's attention, he turned around and walked over to where the Yankee stood. The Union officer inquire into the jewel, "Is that a ruby that you have there?"

"Yes, my Mother gave it to me when I finished school several years ago."

In a sarcastic voice, the Yankee said, "Oh, is that so. I didn't think you Johnnies went to school down here in the south."

Pete and some of the Confederates that were continuing to trade paused because of the insult. A rebel officer was quick to reply, "Yank, if it were not for this truce, I'd kill ya now and take your possessions, instead of trading. And, I'd leave ya for the buzzards to devour."

The Yankee officer laughed and was quick to reply, "Sorry, sorry, I didn't mean to be offensive." The Yankee turned about and said to Pete, "Well Johnnie lets conclude our business. You have something that I want and I'm sure that I have something that you want. Lets deal, do you want food, coffee, or money, green backs of course."

Pete replied as he looked at the officer with a defiant expression, "Coffee and food."

The Yankee began to open his saddlebag and remove the coffee, bacon, and flour that he had brought along to trade. As Pete handed him the ruby, he asked, "Yank, what's your name?"

The Yankee continued in a sarcastic tone, "Why Reb? It doesn't make a bloody difference. You are going to go your way and I'm going to go my way."

"Pete replied in a calm and threaten tone, "Well yank, there's going to be a time and place where we will meet again. I just want to know who I might be engaging."

The officer began to openly laugh at Pete's continued defiance, "Seamus, Seamus McBride from Boston. You better bloody remember that when you come after me, right Johnnie?"

The first thought that crossed Pete's mind, was this Seamus McBride that was Katie's brother. Pete couldn't believe that someone who was so eccentric, conceded, and prideful could be the sibling of a lady who showed so much humility. As Pete stood motionless in thought, he noticed that the Yankee had red hair only it was lighter then Katie's. He remembered in a conversation with Katie at the Estate one evening, before the war how she described her brother. She said he was of average height and build, though very muscular, and wore a red beard. His eyes were hazel and they appeared to have a piercing effect when he stared at someone. The soldier possessed the same appearance and description that Katie had revealed about her older brother. Before Pete departed, he needed to know the truth concerning any relationship between

Seamus and Katie. Slowly, Seamus mounted his horse for the short journey across Antietam Creek. Pete said in a curious tone, "McBride, I think you and I might have a mutual acquaintance."

Seamus turned about and answered with confidence, "No Johnnie, I don't think so."

As Seamus turned his horse about toward the Federal lines, Pete loudly said, "Katie, Katie McBride."

Instantly, Seamus turned about in the saddle and surprisingly gazed at Pete, inquiringly, "Are you Pete Barker from Harpers Ferry?"

"Yes I am."

Seamus began to laugh sarcastically and shaking his head, he sighed and said, "Well, Barker, we finally meet. I have heard some interesting things concerning you from my sister. Have you seen her?"

"No, I haven't. I have not heard from her in months. I thought that she might have returned to Boston."

"My sister? She is too bloody stubborn to listen to her family. I'm sure she was in that hellhole of a town that you come from when it was blown to pieces several days ago. When we regain possession of that town from you Johnnies, I'm going to make a point of hopefully seeing her, and when I do, I'm going to put her on a train for Boston."

"Yeah, I hope you do."

Seamus concluded as he rubbed the neck of his horse, "Hopefully for her sake, I don't kill you before then."

Pete angrily replied, "Don't count on it."

With a smirk coving his face, Seamus departed with haste. It had been an interesting afternoon for Pete. He had finally met Katie's brother, and someone he didn't care for, and hoped not to see anytime in the future. Placing his brown hat on his head, Pete rode across the ridge in his continual effort to locate the 1st Virginia infantry.

Within the hour, he found the 1st near the Harpers Ferry Road. Many of the soldiers were resting, some sleeping, and others mingling in conversation. There was a Captain sitting in the grass playing cards with some of the men from his company that attracted Pete's attention. Pete dismounted and slowly approached asking, "I am looking for an acquaintance of mine, a Captain Thomas Monroe of the Richmond Grays. Do you know his whereabouts?"

Without turning to look at Pete, the captain answered the question as he laid down another king of spades from his hand, "Yeah, he was wounded yesterday afternoon."

"Well, where is he? Where did they take him?"

The officer looked up and snapped, "I don't know, one of the field hospitals, or into town I guess."

Pete silently walked away. The captain stood and walked over to where the young Barker remounted his horse. Apologetically, he said, "I'm sorry. All of us have been under a lot of strain, and still, we are on edge."

"Yeah, we all have been at that place recently."

The Captain said as he turned and walked away, "I wish I could be of more help."

Evening was finally upon the battlefield as Pete diligently sought the location where Thomas may have been taken for medical attention. He came to a field hospital near the village where the surgeons' worked by light provided by lanterns. In his observations, Pete noticed the surgeon's assistant placing a cone-like devise over the patient's face. The injured soldier moaned with discomfort until the assistant poured some chloroform into the funnel of the cone. Slowly, the soldier was motionless and the surgeon began to remove the left leg from the knee down. After packing the stump, the surgeon threw the limb over into a pit where many amputated arms, legs, and feet would be buried. The surgeon's expression was void of emotion. As Pete continued, he glanced in the direction where many of the civilian women were quietly stirring linen in a huge black kettle of boiling water, while others cut bandages from old dresses, tablecloths to wrap wounds. Still many of the men from the town removed the wounded from the wagons that had just arrived from various areas of the battlefield.

As Pete rode into town, the Confederate army was beginning its retreat across the Potomac into Virginia. The street was jammed with infantrymen and walking wounded moving toward the direction of Shepherdstown. After searching for the past two hours for Thomas, he came on a church along Main Street, which was being used as a hospital. The sound of anguish, the name of a love one cried out sent chills down Pete's spine when he entered the building. The nurses with their somber expressions labored reverently to comfort the soldiers. One lady in particular, prayed with a Minister for a wounded Confederate soldier who was apparently clinging to his last moments of life. With time running against him, Pete's eyes scanned every area of the church looking for Thomas. A man quietly lying in the corner with his head placed on his balled up uniform coat caught Pete's attention. Pete moved for a closer examination. The soldiers face was covered with the grime of black gunpowder and dirt. His hands and white blouse were covered with blood from the wound that he had received to the abdomen. He murmured with pain, the blood still oozing from the wound. As Pete kneeled and leaned over to listen, he noticed that the officer was Thomas. Pete somberly said, "Thomas, it's Pete."

Thomas slowly and softly said, "Its good to see that you survived. I know that I won't."

Pete attempted to reassure him, "Yeah, you will."

"I'm not a fool. I realize the seriousness of my wound." As Pete began to speak, Thomas interrupted him, "No, no, listen to me. I want you to give Rebecca a message. Tell her that I couldn't commit myself to the relationship." Thomas began to cough up blood and gasp for air. Pete wiped the wounded soldiers mouth with a handkerchief from his pocket. In spite of his pain and anguish, Thomas, attempted to cling to life and finish his message for Pete's sister, "I have always had the fondest feelings for her from the very first time that we met at Richmond's Grand Ball. If I had lived to see an end to this war, I would have married her and loved her all the days of my life. I swear to God. Tell Rebecca, please, she doesn't know my feelings for her."

As quickly as Thomas finished his last words, he stopped breathing. Pete laid Thomas' head once more on his uniform coat. There were many thoughts of despair racing through his mind. After pausing briefly and saying a short prayer, Pete departed. Many frustrations, anger, and pain caused by the torment of war began to surface as Pete walked to the rear of the church, away from the presence of the medical personnel. There he fell prostrated on the floor and began to openly weep with sorrow. For two years he had withheld his feelings and emotions with the destruction of human life, the tribulation, despair, and grief that the war had caused. If he should be fortunate to return home, the tidings of sorrow that he would share with his sister, the expectations of a life with Thomas would be shattered forever. How could he possibly break this tragic news to Rebecca?

CHAPTER TWENTY-FIVE

Several days after the battle of Sharpsburg, the Confederate army had returned to the Shenandoah Valley beyond Martinsburg. Once more, the Confederate cavalry was picketing along the Potomac River to observe McClellan, and warn General Lee if the Union army crossed the river. With the temporarily suspension of hostiles, Pete received a furlough to return home and visit his family. It was a short journey from the Potomac River to Shenandoah Estate. Before leaving Sharpsburg, Pete had learned from a North Carolinian of A.P. Hill's division about the fighting that had taken place around Harpers Ferry. His thoughts were upon the tribulations of the civilian population during that period of the campaign and what they might have experienced. In the same conversation with the soldier, Pete learned of the Confederate army's flanking maneuver against the Federals, and Daniel's help, and how he had guided the division across some of the Estate toward the river. It greatly concerned Pete about his family's welfare and what scars that it might have imprinted upon their heart and mind. As Pete had experienced over the last year, war wasn't an acceptable way to resolve ones differences, nor its results easy to digest. The thought crossed his mind, what about Katie, did she have time to escape the conflict before it all began, or was some wet cellar in town her only refuge. Maybe, she had return to Massachusetts, or sought refuge at the Estate.

It was late in the afternoon when Pete arrived at the little hamlet of Halltown. From there, it was only a very short distance to Shenandoah. As Pete rode along the Charlestown Road, he noticed the familiar maple trees surrounding the property that he had come to love and cherish. After a fourteen month absence, it was still difficult for him to accept the reality that Charles, and not his Mother was the landlord of the Estate. Still, it refreshed him and replenished his soul to be reunited with his family once more. As he approached the main entrance to the Estate, it appeared that war had not wasted and tarnished the property thus far. The tall oak trees still towered along the roadway. The stables and barns remained intact, but there wasn't any livestock and only a few horses that were visible. As he rode along the lane, some of the slaves were singing and going about their chores of chopping wood as the children gave assistance to their parents needs by carrying and stacking the kindling. A few of the slaves, and servants recognized Pete and with expressions of joy, they waved, and some shouted, "Mr. Pete." Pete returned their respect by removing his hat and waving. It was the young Barker that the slaves had learned through his fair, plain demeanor to surrender their respect. For Pete, the most gracious sight was the mansion along the ridge still standing with all of its majesties and beauty. When Pete arrived, his Mother was standing on the front porch to greet him. As Pete dismounted, one of the servants took his horse as he ran up the steps to embrace his Mother.

For Elizabeth, it made no difference concerning the dirty, ragged appearance of her youngest son, he was safe and in her arms. The guilt and fire of Elizabeth's conscious had condemned her for the deeds and trespasses against Pete during his absence resulting from the transfer of ownership of the Estate to Charles. Elizabeth knew if she hadn't sinned against Pete, he might not have joined the army. Now with her prayers answered by Providence, she must attempt to persuade him to give up a soldier's life and remain home. As they broke their embrace, she gazed at him, her expression glowed brightly and she said with a joy in her voice, "Oh dear, let me look at you." As she noticed his thin appearance, she said, "I swear it does appear that you have lost weight. This army life can't be agreeing with you, but we'll take care of that quickly." Immediately, she shouted for Matthew. Immediately, the servant answered the call. As soon as Matthew recognized Pete, his face was covered with happiness. Before Matthew had time to speak, Elizabeth commanded, "Matthew, I want you to go to the kitchen house and have Pansy prepare something for Pete." The servant wanted to speak to Pete, but Elizabeth commanded once more, "Now you hear me, go on!"

As Pete and his Mother walked through the front entrance to the mansion,

Pete noticed Ann running through the hallway. With all of her strength, she embraced her uncle and kissed him on the cheek. Pete was glad to see her and it reflected in his voice, "My little Ann, you are safe. I was worried about you when I heard about all the soldiers in the area."

"That's alright, Uncle Pete. My Mother, Grandmother, and myself went to Charlestown to stay with the Whites."

"Good, good, I'm glad to hear that."

Pete raised his head to look at his Mother, and with a sigh of relief he was glad that the family had been spared the ordeal of war, and not witnessed the carnage and agony such as he had experienced at Sharpsburg. It didn't come to mind at first about Katie McBride's welfare; it was overshadowed with the good news about the family's salvation. Pete stood to his feet and the thought crossed his mind about Katie's safety during the siege of the Ferry. As he was about to address the matter, Charles and Caroline entered the entrance area to the mansion from the drawing room. Charles was surprised to see his brother and it reflected in his tone of voice, "Pete, I wasn't expecting you home with the possible continuation of hostilities."

"I know." Pete replied, and continued to say, "I was granted a short furlough of a couple of days by General Stuart. He knew that I wanted to see the family, and since we were so close and behind Confederate lines, he was gracious enough to see to my needs."

Pete walked over to Caroline and held her hand, being dirty and having an odor about him, he was embarrassed and apologized, "I'm sorry for my appearance. It's not what you are use to, I know."

"Caroline's smile reflected her happiness that Pete was home, even at his undesirable appearance, she still insisted, "You may greet me in the manner you have always been accustom to."

Within minutes, Rebecca and William walked through the hallway to greet Pete. As Pete noticed the joyful expression that covered his sister's face, though glad to see her in their reunion, he knew that it would only be temporary, for the realities of war was about to be engaged. After Pete and Rebecca exchanged greetings, she asked with the excitement of an anxious child, "Did Thomas come with you?" There was a silence as Rebecca walked over to the window near the door and glanced about to see if he was still outside. Without seeing him, immediately she turned about with a fearful expression and asked, "Why didn't he come with you?"

Everyone gazed at the somber expression that covered Pete's face, the tears that filled his eyes. The room was so quiet that you could have heard a pin drop. The first casualties of the war had knocked at the family's door; they all knew the meaning of Pete's silence. Rebecca began to scream with grief and shock as she kneeled down weeping uncontrollably. Elizabeth and Caroline seek to comfort Rebecca as she cried, "Oh no, oh no. My life can't go on without him. What will I do, what will I do?"

Charles was greatly shaken by the tragic news, and witnessing his sister's emotions caused him much distress. There was somberness as Charles softly asked, "What happen?"

"Thomas was wounded on the seventeenth of September as the 1st was attempting to hold back the Federals. They were outnumbered. A small brigade on a hill overlooking a bridge that crossed Antietam Creek attempted to beat back repeated attempts; the Federals broke their lines. After reforming, the Federals once more continued their attack against General Longstreet's right line of defense. I understand that the fighting was heavy. It was there that Thomas was wounded."

As Elizabeth shouted for Rebecca's personal servant to assist them, she sent Matthew, who was standing near by into town to bring Dr. Robertson to the Estate. Charles desired knowledge of the battle at Sharpsburg and suggested that the men retire to the parlor while his Mother and Caroline escorted Rebecca to her bedroom to await the physician's arrival.

After pouring a much needed brandy, the men were seated near the window. William said, as he sipped the applejack, "Pete, as I understand from Daniel, General Lee has crossed the Potomac with heavy casualties."

Pete softly replied as he sipped the liquor, "Yes, you're correct. The Yankees had us outnumbered throughout the day. We held our own, but it was costly in lives, and nothing gained."

Charles shook his head in despair and said, "This war is bringing tribulations on many families. Just yesterday, when I was in Charlestown, I was told by Eugene McCoy at the bank about the death of Nathaniel Baker and William Tyler at the battle of Gaines Mills."

William added, "And don't forget about Colonel Allen, perishing while leading Nathaniel's regiment."

Pete began to reflect on the battle that recently took place in Sharpsburg, "The engagement along the Antietam was the worst and most savage of the war that I have experienced thus far. I witnessed men that were dead lying on top of their comrades, many without limbs due to artillery fire, and even one soldier's head had been removed from his body, probably by a cannon ball. The vultures swarmed the carcasses and devoured the corpses as opportunity was presented. Along the left flank of the Confederate line of defense, regiments lost many of their line officers and even some of their general officers. A cornfield with its abundant harvest that once stood along the road that led to Hagerstown, was totally devastated from the heavy fighting that had taken place in that small area. There was nothing left. The blood of the men that fell there flowed and dried in puddles. As I understand from an officer with the 1st cavalry, the fighting in the center of the Confederate defenses was just as savage. He said that the dead were piled on top of each other in such a small space that you could walk the length of the lane and never touch the ground. He went on to say that the smell of the dead was extremely offense."

Charles said with a tone of humility, "I just can't imagine that kind of devastation. It concerned me greatly when I arrived home to witness the military presence on the property."

Pete said with a sound of frustration, "You can't even begin to fathom the reality until you have experienced the death of a friend, and the cries of the wounded for yourself. It's hell to live life like that, and I've had enough of killing and watching good men die, to last me a life time."

The conversation was beginning to depress Pete. He excused himself to bathe. He walked quietly and slowly up the stairway to his bedroom, still able to hear the cries of his grieving sister. Exhausted from war and the tragedy that he shared with Rebecca, he dropped to his bed, and there, he began to dwell on life before the war. Memories of foxhunts, ring tournaments, and family gatherings briefly resurrected the radiance of a smile, which was seldom with the growing months and years of war. Occasionally, he thought of the receptions and balls that were held at the Estate and the many times that he participated in the hat dance. Now, the memories were replaced with the agonizing cry of the wounded, the dying, and images of battle and carnage. Slowly he stood to undress, remembering the correspondence that Billy Smith had asked him to deliver once he returned home. He removed the contents from his dirty-checkered shirt. Pete had no previous knowledge that the identity of the recipient of the correspondence might be. When he opened the envelope, he was surprised, it read: "My Dearest Jane. I write you somewhere near Manassas

Junction. It has been a humid, hot, and almost unbearable afternoon. We have covered many miles of marching, and I suspect that soon we will give battle to General Pope's Army. Each conflict that we are involved in becomes more brutal and savage with no end in sight. I know that your heart is devoted to another, but my love remains steadfast and committed to only you. I pray in time that you will see my devotion and receive my affection. The thought of your smile, glowing expression is the only consolation that I possess. At night as I think of you, the war and its horrors fade away, if only briefly, I find comfort. We are being ordered to assemble I must go. Your devoted and loyal servant, Billy."

Pete was touched by the sincerity and commitment that Billy showed for Jane Powers as he laid the letter on a stand.

After reading Billy's correspondence, Pete lost his appetite. He got out of his dirty clothes, bathed and put on clean clothes. Since he wasn't hungry, he decided to journey down to the river.

For Pete, the stillness of the Shenandoah was peaceful, and was always good medicine to relieve the anxieties, tensions, and cares of this world. Its quiet surroundings only broken by the splashing sound of an occasional fish near the surface, and the singing of the birds nesting in the trees caused the battle at Antietam to temporarily fade. It was now that Pete had the fullest understanding why his Father and he spent so much time in this area of the Estate. Then his thoughts shifted to Hayward. Where was he? What was he doing? He was a freed man and not considered in the chains of bondage. Why risk so much and flee to the North. Pete began to wonder if he would see him again. Hopefully, Lincoln would not allow the slaves that have escaped to the North to fight. If so, Pete dreaded the thought of meeting Hayward on the field of battle.

It was late in the afternoon as Pete mounted his horse for the ride to the western area of the Estate. There, he noticed the presence of a limited number of horses and less then a dozen of the Black Angus Cattle. At first, he didn't realize why his brother hadn't said anything to him about the possible sell of the animals, but with the tragic news that was shared with his sister; he understood that wasn't the time. Still, not fully adjusted to the change in ownership, he quickly rode with haste for the mansion to inquire on these matters of business.

As Pete arrived and walked into the house, he found Charles and William in the drawing room finishing a friendly game of chess. The two gentlemen were laughing as if they didn't have a care in the world, when Pete made his appearance. He bluntly asked with a tone of anger, "Charles, where is all the horses and cattle? Did you sell them?"

Charles replied with confidence as he looked at his brother, "Calm down, calm down! I sold the morgans and stallions to Robert Lowe, of Frederick City, who is also a breeder. The cattle was sold to John Crim over in Washington County. Only for U. S. greenbacks, of course. With the money that I received, I invested it in promissory notes issued by the Confederate Treasury to finance the war. The note will be paid with interest at the conclusion of the war." Pete attempted to speak, but Charles continued," I know what you are thinking, trust me, I gave the matter considerable thought, and with the area continuing to switch hands, we couldn't have held on to the animals much longer without them being seized by the Yanks."

Pete replied in a calmer tone, "You know the Yankees are going to end up with some of those horses. Oh…. I see, you are playing both sides of the game, when it is to your advantage. Yet, there are civilians being stripped of everything of value in Culpepper County. They willingly make the sacrifice for the cause."

Charles in a friendly voice attempted to reprimand his younger brother, "Pete, I have been at this business for sometime now. I feel confident in my judgments, and the rest of the family, including Mother, feel that I do a pretty good job of it."

Charles ignoring his brother turned his attention to William and continued the game. Pete was puzzled by his brother's explanation. It wasn't like Charles not to make the attempt to receive as much as possible when it came to money and power.

As Pete was leaving the drawing room, he noticed Caroline walking slowly down the long stairway toward him. With a tone of concern, Pete said, "Rebecca, how is she?"

Caroline said with reassurance as she paused at the bottom of the stairway, "She is resting. It was a great shock to her. The evening before his death, she had expressed her affections for Thomas and the hope of marriage. Now, all of her dreams and expectations of a life with him have been shattered."

Pete said as he looked in the direction of Rebecca's bedroom, "Well if she is resting, I will leave her alone. Before Thomas passed on, I was with him and he gave me a message for her."

Caroline was curious, "What did he say?"

Pete politely said as he looked in Caroline's direction, "I do not want to be rude, but I'd rather wait and speak with Rebecca. Then, if she desires to inform the rest of the family, then that will be her decision."

Elizabeth was just entering the hallway when Caroline replied, "I understand."

Elizabeth's expression was somber and hollow, her red eyes revealed the secret of sorrow and despair that ruled her heart. It had been Elizabeth's desire that her daughter would possess the attributes that she had established among the community. That was one of the reasons why she had sent Rebecca to Richmond to be educated, and secondly, that she would marry into a Southern family of wealth, influence, and power. Thomas had come from such a family. His father owned one of the largest tobacco plantations along the James River, and was a gentleman of influence abroad in England. Rebecca's dreams were not only destroyed, but Elizabeth's also. Pete's Mother softly said to Caroline, "How is she?"

"Resting for now."

"Good." Elizabeth continued, by reflecting on the past, "It is such a devastating blow when you love someone and all of a sudden the news comes of their death. I know that feeling all to well. It's something that you always remember."

As the two ladies departed for the dinning area, Caroline placed her arms around Elizabeth to comfort her grief.

Pete leaned against the stairway banisters and began to think about all that had transpired today. He paused and his thoughts momentarily returned to the night that the Federals had burned the arsenal in April of 61. In his remembrance, the thought concerning the tragedy of war, the misery, destruction, and how it would affect the family consumed his mind. Now, with experiencing the first tragic blow, reality had sunken its claws deep into Pete's heart by witnessing its terrible affect on his sister. He knew all too well, and by many experiences could identify with the sorrow and horror of this tragedy that his family was experiencing.

CHAPTER TWENTY-SIX

That same evening it was calm with a gentle breeze blowing among the trees. The red-glowing sun was setting in the western sky, and the wrens were swarming old Isabella, the gray cat owned by Matthew. Rebecca was still resting and continued her seclusion in the bedroom, while Charles and William embarked on a stroll along the pond to discuss the political affairs of the Confederate government. Caroline and Elizabeth were seated on the front porch speaking of merrier days as Ann joyfully brushed her horse Buttercup. Occasionally Ann asked her Mother one of those curious questions that she was known for asking concerning the adult life. With everyone finding the time to relax and allowing emotions to rest, Pete walked onto the porch. He brought with him a shawl for Caroline and his Mother in the event they began to feel a chill in the air. After giving the ladies their possessions, he leaned against one of the white columns and glanced in the direction of the Charlestown Pike. He turned about to face Caroline and casually asked, "I haven't received a correspondence from Katie since the latter part of winter. By chance did she return home?"

Caroline knew the subject of Katie McBride would be a topic of conversation. She had given the matter considerable thought and was prepared with words of determination to justify her actions and support for her husband. Caroline knew that Pete wouldn't be happy with the news of their broken relationship, and he would most likely be displeased and angry. Caroline said as she looked at him, "Katie and I haven't seen each other since I returned from Richmond late last spring."

The revelation caught Pete by surprise and Caroline knew by the reflection in his tone of voice, "What! What is wrong! What happen?"

Caroline's reply was quick, "Pete, please, calm down."

Pete said angrily as he approached her, "Will someone please tell me what is going on?"

Elizabeth spoke sharply while rising to her feet demanding, "James Barker, you have no business yelling at your brother's wife in this manner. Do you hear me? I did not raise you to be like some of the lower class in town."

Ann pleaded as she grabbed her uncle's hand, "Uncle Pete, please listen to Grandmother."

Pete took several deep breaths and sighed as he gazed at his mother. After a brief pause, he calmly apologized, "Sorry, Mother." Turning his attention to Caroline, he said, "Caroline, please accept my apology." Almost with the next breath, Pete impatiently asked, "What about Katie?"

"Last spring when Charles was asked by President Davis to journey to England with William, I felt that it was best considering the nature of Charles' business abroad, that Katie and I should end our friendship. At the time, Charles' business was very sensitive, and if the information was revealed by a mistake, then it could have meant that my husband might have ended up sitting in a Yankee prisoner-of-war camp somewhere in the North."

"I see." Pete softly replied and allowed his deepest feeling to be spoken, "Caroline, I guess that I underestimated your relationship with Katie. I thought that I knew you better then what you portrayed."

"I'm not some villain you know. My first priority is to my husband who I love, and I'll do what ever it takes to protect my marriage and family."

Elizabeth added in a pitched tone, "Pete, sometimes I don't understand you. How can you expect our family to trust someone from the North when they are our enemy? You are in the Confederate army serving a glorious cause and I'm proud of your accomplishment, but son you shouldn't be keeping company, nor should any of us at this time with Miss McBride. It is to dangerous."

"But Mother." Pete pleaded, "We accepted Katie into our home. She had dinner with us on many occasions and frequently we invited her to visit. I remember when she first came to the Estate, how everyone went out of their way to make her feel at home." Pete turned from facing his Mother to defend his case to his sister-in-law, "Caroline, you wanted Katie to be your friend, you encouraged her company and visitations to the Estate. And what about the many times that you confided in her trust? But now, you and everyone in this family have decided to betray her and treat her as the enemy, not to say that she had to endure that hellhole of a town while it was under a bombardment. She isn't fighting for the North, no more then that old gray cat."

Upon hearing the loud sound of voices and commotion coming from the house, Charles and William immediately proceeded in that direction. Charles, overhearing Pete's last statement began to defend the family's position concerning Katie, "Pete, times have changed. The war has caused the family to see Northerners in a much different light."

"How is that Charles?"

Charles believed his younger brother to be naïve about Katie's life in the South, laughingly he expounded, "Well, I have it from very good sources in Richmond, that before the war, the Federal government sent spies posing as residents to live in the South when the fear of an all out civil war was inevitable. It might be that Katie was such an agent. After all, she wanted to venture from home, which you have to admit, does not happen with a lady of honor, unless there is a reason."

Pete became very angry and shouted defensively, "No, Charles. I do not believe for one moment that Katie McBride is a spy for the North. She is a victim of this family's imagination."

"Well, little brother, we don't know that to be true, do we, huh?"

William had been standing near by quietly, but with matters getting out of control; he believed that there should be intervention on behalf of the family. He began to motion with his arms and boldly stepped between Pete and Charles saying calmly, "Gentleman, gentleman, please let us regain our composure."

Everyone was silent, waiting for William to continue, which he did with a passionate sound in his voice, "I have known this family for many years. Yes, you have had your disagreements, but you've been able to resolve your differences. I know under the circumstances, which we live under, in defending our freedom, it is stressful and the times are trying, but as it says in the good book, we must run the race, and not be distracted from the goal. And that goal is to win this war as soon as possible and then, hopefully, we can all rebuild our nations and learn to respect each other's social views in a civilized society. At that time, maybe we can be civil toward one another once more."

Pete continued his anger in a loud tone, "William, this is not some kind of a political rally where we need a speech of exhortations. We are dealing with a human being with feelings and emotions!"

Elizabeth became angrier, "Pete, Pete, stop it right now! You have said enough!"

"Yes, Mother, your right. I've said enough and I have had enough, I'm leaving."

The young Barker began to walk away toward the stable area to saddle his horse when Elizabeth angrily asked, "Where are you going?"

Pete said as he turned around, "I'm going to look for Katie."

Elizabeth was furious and yelled, "Young man, don't you dare bring her here, do you understand me?"

Without acknowledging his Mother's comments, Pete continued toward the stables at a brisk pace.

Elizabeth's face was blood red, and she was so angry that she abruptly ran into the house without further comment to anyone. As for Charles, he looked at his wife and shrugged his shoulders. He knew that this rebellious behavior was typical of his younger brother, and inwardly, he was sure that his Mother would not second guess her decision in the future concerning releasing her ownership of the Estate to him. As William stood quietly by Charles, his heart was racing with intensity. Katie and Pete's reunion was the last thing that he wanted to happen. It had been his intentions to pay Katie a visit on this journey to the area; he hadn't expected Pete to receive a furlough and return home. For Caroline, there was an expression of concern that covered her features. She wasn't happy that this verbal war had taken place in the presence of Ann, nor that the family was torn by indifferences. In her heart, she rejoiced in the thought that Pete must have sincere feelings for Katie, or he wouldn't have become so emotional about the whole affair and race to search for her. Even though she had not spoken to Katie nor seen her over the last couple of months, she knew where Katie was and her welfare by secretly sending Jeremiah into town periodically to keep a watch over her. Ann was somewhat shaken by the whole affair. She was confused and terrified over conflict between family members. Ann was accustomed to deeds of love, which provided her with security and a close family bond of togetherness.

Pete wasn't sure if Katie was still living at Mrs. Stipes boarding house, or if she had returned to the North. It grieved him deeply with the family's behavior, their change in attitude and actions that they displayed toward his friend. His temper began to subside, the tense pressure of conflict eased; he released several deep sighs and began to focus his thoughts on seeing his lady friend from New England.

Pete was riding along Shenandoah Street like so many times in past years. This time it was quite different; he didn't know what to expect. As he neared his destination, Pete noticed Confederate soldiers along the street, loading some of the military supplies into wagons that had been captured when the Union garrison surrendered less then a week ago. Some of the soldiers were whooping it up after polishing off some of the whiskey that they had confiscated. The effects of the war had devastated the armory, mills, and the rifle factory, all that were symbolic of a thriving economy. Pete knew that the Confederate forces had no intentions of holding the village, and that his reunion with Katie would not last long. The greatest change in the towns' appearance was the absence of so many of its citizens. Without the presence of the townspeople, he thought, the village possessed no life.

The appearance of the boarding house hadn't changed. The iron porch rails that covered the length of the upper portion of the dwelling reminded Pete of the afternoon when he rescued Katie from the wrath of the mighty Shenandoah. After dismounting his horse, he saw Father Thomas walking from Frankel's clothing store, just across the street from the boarding house. He called out to the Priest, "Father, Father, wait!"

Father Thomas stopped and turned to see who was calling. Noticing that it was Pete, he smiled and said, "My son, how are you doing? I am so glad to see you."

Pete replied cordially as he approached the Priest, "With what I have been through since I've left the area, Father, you don't know how good it is to see you."

"Son, I've lost many of the young men that attended my Parrish. Oh, this is such a dark era in our history. I pray constantly to God for the end of this horrible war, and that he would grant me the desire of my heart that many of my people would return to the town."

"I agree with you." Pete commented and inquiringly asked, "Father, do you know if Katie is still living at the boarding house, or did she return to Boston?"

"Pete, Mrs. McDonald is in Winchester taking care of her ailing sister. Katie agreed to live in the residence and take care of the property."

"Thank you Father."

As Pete turned to proceed across the street to remount his horse, Father Thomas shouted, "Pete, Pete."

As the young Barker turned about, Father Thomas jovially said, "Katie comes to the church at about this time every evening and lights a candle for you."

With this information Pete turned and proceeded toward the church. The glowing red moon was beginning to peer between the mountains in Solomon's Gap as Pete arrived at the house of worship. As he opened one of the huge wooden doors, the only glow of light came from the many candles that burned brightly for the prayers of loved ones who had needs. Pete noticed the shadow of a figure kneeling in front of the area where the candles were placed. As Pete proceeded slowly to the alter in the front of the church, he attempted to identify the lone person. Quietly, he waited, noticing that it was Katie saying her prayers. As she raised and made the sign of the cross, she turned toward Pete and the sad, somber, hollow facial features that ruled her expression, suddenly changed with his presence. Tears of joy and reprieve flowed freely like the mighty waters of the Shenandoah from her eyes. Pete and Katie immediately embraced and held each other tightly. Katie kissed his cheeks; he felt the warmth of her tears cover his face. She began to caress his face with her hand; both were speechless with their eyes fixed on each other. Pete raised his hands to grip hers, and held them tightly against his chest. For the moment, the couple remained silent; no words could be found to describe the emotions of their heart. Katie cried, "I'm sorry; my heart has been sorrowful and filled with despair. I haven't heard from you for sometime, and I didn't know if you were dead or in some prisoner-of-war camp."

"No, no. I have been all right. I guess God has been good to me, thus far. Lighting those candles and your prayers have helped to see me through this struggle."

As Pete and Katie sat closely on one of the wooden pew benches in the front of the church, Katie asked, "Why have you not written me? I sent a correspondence with Caroline last spring when she came to Richmond. I was so disappointed when you didn't reply."

"I'm sorry, I didn't receive it. Matter of fact, I haven't received anything from you since the latter part of last winter."

"It wasn't until the last time that I visited with her at the Estate, that she reassured me you were well. Since that time, I haven't seen nor spoken with Caroline, so I didn't know of your welfare. I spent many a restless nights thinking of you. I just didn't know what to think concerning your safety, but I refused to give up hope."

Katie was surprised to hear that her correspondence had not reached Pete, it was apparent that he didn't know its contents. As she silently thought for a moment, Pete placed his arm around her shoulder. Katie's insecurities vanished with his embrace as she reached to hold his hand. He was puzzled by the distance relationship between Katie and Caroline; there was a concern and still a burning anger for his family's attitude toward Katie. Pete believed that he should apologize for the family's conduct and said, "Katie, I'm sorry for the way that my family has treated you. I guess the war and the hardship that it produces have caused their heart to become calloused toward you, and most Northerners. But most of all, I am especially surprised with Caroline. You two appeared to be so close, just like sisters, I don't understand what happen."

Katie softly replied as she looked into his eyes, "I don't either. When she returned from Richmond last spring, she was a different person. It was like the Caroline that I once knew and loved had died and no longer existed."

Pete was astonished and it reflected in his words, "I agree. She is not the loving person that we trusted. I just arrived today and she gave the appearance of someone who has withdrawn from life, and when she spoke, it was easy to discern the tone of resentment in her voice."

Katie shook her head in an act of frustration concerning the subject and added, "Caroline needs to understand that it is not only the citizens living in the South that has been affected by the war, but also, many who live in the North. I have given my relationship with her considerable thought, and I don't know what, but something had to have taken place in Richmond when she joined Charles at your aunts."

Pete was silent and remembered that Caroline had mention something in their disagreement earlier at the Estate concerning Charles' trip abroad for the new Confederate government. He began to share his thoughts, "Today when Caroline was attempting to explain why she didn't desire to continue a friendship with you, she mentioned something about Charles' involvement with a business transaction. She said that his trip was sensitive in nature, and that was why she needed to end the relationship. Apparently, she didn't trust you enough as a friend. She thought that you would not keep matters to yourself."

"That hurts me deeply."

"I'm willing to lay odds, that Charles has applied pressure to Caroline to end the relationship with you. Yes, that would be so characteristic of my brother."

"But Pete, he appeared to be so different. He was the one who invited me to come to the Estate in the first place."

"No Katie, he is the same person. This has a Charles smell all over it."

Katie replied with a tone of anger in her voice, "He would suppress Caroline into some kind of bondage for his own personal gain?"

There was a small glimmer of a smile that covered Pete's face as he replied, "Yeah, I'm afraid so. He was attempting to persuade me that you could possibly be a spy or some sort of agent, sent here before the war."

Katie was alarmed by the information that Pete had shared with her. She remained expressionless and silent.

CHAPTER TWENTY-SEVEN

Time was a precious commodity to Pete and Katie as they departed the church and proceeded toward the Shenandoah River. As they walked along High Street through the lower village, they noticed some of the Confederates departing for Winchester with the supply wagons carrying the remainder of the spoils of war. Pete knew that his time with Katie would be limited, due to the rebels' departure. The village was quiet, dark, and lifeless of civilian population at this hour of the evening; it wasn't the thriving town that Pete remembered when he departed over two years ago.

Pete and Katie came to the river's shoreline and there, Pete built a small fire to comfort them from the autumn chill. Katie was clinging to her gray shawl that was wrapped around her shoulders. Pete sat beside Katie on an old walnut tree log near the rivers edge. The only sound was the water rolling gently over the rock like rapids, and gently caressing the shoreline.

As Pete gazed at the fire and listened to its crackling sound, he turned about and said, "This evening when I was riding into town, I noticed the different changes that two years of war has cost this community. I must admit that it was difficult for me to see that the rifle factory and Mr. Herr's mill on the island destroyed, but the town seems so deserted, lifeless. The village has been put to death by this conflict."

Katie softly replied as she tossed some dry branches on the fire, "The citizens come and go, and those who stay, well, they live in fear. I know some of the townspeople have been shot and killed from across the Maryland side of the Potomac. Many of my students are gone and I sometimes wonder why we keep the school open for classes. Father Thomas refuses to close the church, though there are only a few that attend mass."

"I remembered when I first enlisted with the 1st Virginia, I thought the war would end quickly if we defeated the Federals at Manassas. The romance, the confidence of being a soldier and coming home as a victorious warrior appealed to me, but for some reason after we managed to win, all of that faded. Afterwards, I just felt confident that this war would continue."

Katie shook her head as she empathized, "I can't imagine the horror of battle, the pain and agony that you have experienced. I have had just a small taste of what it is like. Just last week, when the town was being bombarded from the heights, the sound of the exploding shells reminded me of thunder, and it felt like the ground was shaking when they exploded. I had to seek refuge in Mrs. McDonald's cellar; it was quite a different experience."

As Pete tossed stones into the water, he continued to reflect on the sorrow of war, "Katie, in the last two years, I've witnessed and experienced fighting in the most savaged way. I have seen men screaming in pain from a ghastly wound, the dying calling out for a love one, and I have even had to take the life of another in self-defense. They will never go home to their family. Sometimes at night when I'm sleeping, I can still visualize the agonizing expression of death that covered the soldier's face. It is very difficult for me to share with you my emotions concerning that type of experience."

"Pete, you need to release your feelings. Please get it out in the open and share your hurt and pain with me."

"I remember last week after the confrontation at Sharpsburg. Instead of fighting the enemy, I rescued a Yankee from the clutches of a rebel soldier. It happen when both sides agreed to a truce to remove the wounded from the field. The soldier was going to steal some valuables from a dying Yankee. The Yank was defenseless, I challenged the Rebel and he moved on. But nothing is more undesirable then to bring sorrowful tidings home to a family member."

"Oh my God, Pete, what happen, tell me."

Pete's eyes began to tear as he continued to share his sorrowful experience at the Estate, "For sometime now, my sister, Rebecca, has had an interest in a gentleman soldier from Richmond. It was in late spring that I made his acquaintance while on furlough. As fate would have it, we fought together at

Sharpsburg. In the battle that took place, his regiment was attempting to defeat the Union forces near the town, and he was seriously wounded. The next day, after the battle, I was given the time to locate him. I had no idea of what had taken place. After discovering his fate, I found him in a church in the village. I felt helpless, I wanted to render assistance, but there was nothing I could do, only listen to him speak his feelings for my sister. Afterward, I broke down with sorrow. I felt guilty because I was spared his terrible fate. It was difficult for me to return home because I wanted to take his place. As I was retuning to Shenandoah, I knew from speaking with him previously at Manassas, that Rebecca, was planning at this time to visit the Estate. He had hoped to join her there for a couple of days, and tell her how much he was committed to her love. When I arrived home, Rebecca wanted to know where Thomas was. I couldn't speak the words. I didn't know what to say. I guess everyone knew by my silence and sorrowful expression of Thomas' fate. My sister began to cry uncontrollably; now she mourns with a heavy heart."

Pete's eyes were fixed on Katie as she placed her hand once more in his and spoke words with strength, "You had no choice in the matter, there was nothing that you could do for Thomas. Our lives on this earth are difficult. Sometimes we are helpless, we attempt to search for the right answers, and hope that we make the right choices in life, but it doesn't always work that way. More then anything, you felt that you should have been able to save Thomas' life and bring him home to your sister. You've always felt like you were the protector of your family. But you can't, and you couldn't be to Thomas. And now you feel that you're the blame for her sorrow. Pete, you have something precious to give Rebecca."

"What can I give my grieving sister?"

Katie said with a passion in her eyes as they were fixed upon his, "Share with Rebecca the words that Thomas spoke to you. Give her the truth; she needs to hear his words. It won't bring him back, but it will give her the understanding of the truth that she was on his mind and in his heart when he met death. I remembered when my suitor, Edward, was thrown from his horse while competing in an equestrian tournament. He lingered unconscious for several days after the accident. A friend of his informed me, that just before the event, Edward shared with him his love and affection for me, and his plans of marriage. Knowing the truth about Edward's intentions and feelings gave me a sense of comfort and release, a healing within my heart. It did not remove the grief and anguish that I experienced, but it helped me to move on with my life. I personally know what Rebecca is going through, and she needs to know that Thomas loved her." Katie paused and continued softly saying, "Just as I love you."

Pete was astonished and stunned at Katie's last comment, "Katie, what did you say?"

Katie looked at Pete, her love and passion for him was revealed in the bright glow of her eyes; her expression surrendered to tranquility. The secret of her heart had finally been revealed. She took the risk and prayed to God that he would receive all that she had to offer, her heart and love.

Pete was speechless. There wasn't a thought that he could express, or word that could be spoken, he could only gaze in amazement.

After a moment of silence, Katie continued to hold his hand; "I can see by the expression on your face that I caught you by surprise. I'm sorry that it came out that way; it wasn't the way that I intended to express my feelings for you. I wanted you to discover your feelings for me, but with your absence and the pain and void that it has left me, I took the risk of telling you because I don't want you to return to the army. Now, you know after almost two years how I have felt about you."

Pete quickly stood on his feet and replied with passionate emotion, "Katie, quite often there have been times since the war began that I have thought of you, laying by a campfire, sitting on my horse on a dark and quiet night doing picket duty, and always before we entered a fight, I wondered if I would see you again. I have always known from the very beginning that there was something different and special about you, more so then the other ladies that I have known in my life. I believe your feelings to be sincere, and your trust unchallenged. But there is a war going on, and who knows if I will live to see its conclusion. Now, is not the time to fall in love with someone."

Katie became emotional with fear, "Pete, please don't say that. I know that you feel the same as I do. Only, I'm no longer afraid to tell you that I love you."

Pete pleaded with emotion, "Katie, you don't understand. I am very fond of you, but I don't know that I'm in love with you. I have seen so much with this conflict that I feel that I've changed since we last spent time together."

Katie softly asked, "Is there someone else that you love?"

"No, no. It's nothing like that. My heart belongs to no one."

"I know that you can't fully understand how difficult my life has been over the last year. The war is becoming more brutal with thousands of men becoming casualties in one battle, many soldiers fall by the dozens in battle formation where they stand and fight. In many of the engagements that I've been involved in, we are always outnumbered by the Yankees." Pete continued by saying out of pride, "If I continue to fight, the odds are against me that I won't survive the end of this conflict, and if I don't, it will be worth the effort that I have put forth. One day, hopefully, Ann and her family will have the life that I enjoyed before this all began."

"Is that all that you are bothered about, your way of life? Pete Barker what about your own personal life, don't you care? Doesn't it have any value? Don't you want to be with someone who truly loves you?"

"Katie, now is not the time for me to become involved with you. I know that you don't understand, and its not expected of you to do so."

Katie jumped up from the log and grabbed Pete by the arm as he began to walk away. Pete turned around to face her as she continued to plead with him, "You wouldn't have to return to the army and fight. We could leave tonight and travel north to Boston. We would be safe with my parents."

With a flare of anger, Pete cried, "No Katie, I can't do as you have requested. What about my comrades that are depending on me? What would they say, or how would they feel about me. They would think of me as some kind of a coward, the same as my family. I could never return home. I have more honor then to run and escape my commitments."

"Why do you use the war and your honor as an excuse and continuously run from me! Why!" Katie pleaded tearfully.

Pete turned and embraced Katie firmly; in return she held tightly to him. As Pete held her, he softly said, "Katie, tomorrow the remaining Confederate forces will depart from the Ferry and the cavalry pickets along the Potomac will most likely do the same. I assume Federal forces will re-occupy the town as soon as possible. That means I will have to leave also and rejoin my regiment."

"But you just arrived. You can't leave yet."

"I'm sorry. If I'm captured, it means a Union prison camp somewhere in the north. From what I understand from some of the prisoners that were exchanged and rejoined the regiment, they said the treatment was horrible, it's worst then being wounded in battle. They tell me that many of the men die slow deaths from various types of diseases. Katie, I don't plan to be one of them."

Then, he gazed into her eyes. She refused to break their embrace. The two of them were silently lost in the moment. They knew their union couldn't last; once more their separation was inevitable.

It was near midnight as Pete returned to the Estate after escorting Katie to her residence. After bedding down his mare in the stable, Pete walked quietly through the back door of the mansion. The house was quiet and he naturally assumed at this hour of the night that everyone was asleep. As he walked through the hallway to the long stairway, he noticed a light coming from the library. He overheard the sound of conversation between William and his brother concerning the possible formation of a new state from many of the western counties in Virginia. Pete walked toward the doorway to the room, and noticed his brother seated behind the huge mahogany desk that had belong to their Father, looking through some of his business statements as he spoke to his friend. Pete slowly entered the library as William turned about in the chair where he was seated. Charles turned his attention to his younger brothers appearance; an expression of amazement covered his features. William, sensing that the two brothers should have sometime alone, said, "Well gentleman, it is way past my hour for bedtime. I will see you both in the morning at breakfast."

As William walked from the room, Pete desiring to know of his sister's condition asked, "How is Rebecca?"

Charles stood and spoke as he walked over to a safe in the corner of the room, "Considering the shocking news, she is doing about as well as can be expected. Mother spent sometime with her earlier. As I understand, Rebecca wouldn't speak, or eat. Mother said that she is taking Thomas' death very hard."

As Pete stood and looked at his sister's portrait hanging on the wall over the fireplace, "Before I leave in the morning, I must speak to her."

Charles walked back over to the desk and once more was seated. As he shuffled some papers to return them to the proper order, he spoke as he examined some of them, "Oh, I see. I'm sure that your presence will mean a great deal to her." Pausing briefly, Charles inquired, "Are you returning to your command?"

"Yes." Pete answered, and continued, "I noticed that most of the Confederate forces that were left behind to finish loading up the supplies in town were leaving for Winchester. The Federals will most likely occupy the town shortly after their departure."

Charles' work came to an immediate halt. He looked at Pete and said surprisingly, "I really thought that I would be spending more time with Caroline and Ann, but I guess I won't being doing that after all."

"Why do you have to leave so soon? You're a civilian, not a soldier."

Charles stood and walked over to where his brother was standing and leaning his body against the desk with his arms folded, proudly said, "No, I'm not a soldier such as yourself, though in another way, I guess you could say that I am."

"How is that?"

"Little brother last spring when I was in Richmond at the President's invitation, I was asked by President Davis to go abroad to England and help Captain Bulloch negotiate a contract to construct two new ironclad vessels for the navy. I spent several months abroad and returned home only a week ago, just before General Jackson began the bombardment of the town. So I guess to answer your question, some of us are called upon to fight this war in various ways."

"So that was why you were there. Your visit to the capitol had my curiosity aroused." Pete laughingly said.

Charles spoke with a sound of concern in the tone of his voice, "Yes, and I have to return. It's not safe for me to be here anymore then it is for you. I will need to return tomorrow, also. I'm sure that it will upset Caroline and Ann."

Pete poured some of the water from the silver pitcher that was sitting on the desk into a glass, "I'm sure they will be." Pete continued to speak with boldness and a flare of anger, "And now I fully understand after speaking with Katie this evening why Caroline has been so cold toward her."

"The only thing that I know about their relationship is that Caroline felt it would be for the best to end it for now! There is nothing wrong with loving your family enough to protect them, and placing those that you value first." Charles snapped.

Pete said with defiance in his tone, "Is that what your love for Caroline is all about, pressuring her to end a friendship with someone that can be trusted? It would appear to me that you need a few lessons on this because this kind of love is sick and is only one way. Yours."

Suddenly, Charles lost his composure and knocked the cup from his brother's hand, and grabbed him by the coat collar. Immediately, Pete shouted, "Go on hit me, see if I care."

Charles released his brother and Pete continued to speak, "The type of war that I wage isn't like serving with the President's administration, or for power, nor enticing your wife to destroy a friendship. It is totally different. Maybe before this struggle ends you'll receive a taste of what I have gone through. It will change your thinking on a lot of different matters concerning life."

As Pete departed from the room, he turned about and pointed, "I don't believe that Caroline wanted to end her relationship with Katie." He continued with an emotional tone, "And if my convictions are correct, then I'm coming after you."

Charles shook his head and watched as his brother disappeared. In frustration, he turned toward the fireplace and hit his fist in the palm of his other hand. Charles attempted to repress the condemnation and guilt that he was experiencing.

Charles calmed his emotions and proceeded to retire for the evening. As he entered the bedroom and prepared to dress for bed, he stood by his dresser removing his tiepin, he thought about the confrontation with Pete. Despite his brother's insinuations, he believed that the actions that he had requested of his wife were for the best, not only for the new nation, but also for the family. If this war came to a successful conclusion, he thought, then his loyalties to the President would pay great dividends and he would possess power and authority in a new government.

Caroline had been lying awake for sometime reading a book of poetry that Katie had given her last year for her birthday. Since their bedroom was at the top of the stairway overlooking the library, Caroline heard the commotion that had taken place between the two brothers. She was curious as to the nature of the indifferences between Pete and her husband. Laying the book in her lap, she began to inquire, "Charles, what was all of the noise between you and Pete? I'm surprise that the whole house wasn't awaken by you two."

There was a reserve tone as Charles looked in the direction of his wife; "My brother feels that I am the blame that you decided to end your relationship with Katie."

Caroline promptly answered hoping to make her husband feel guilty about his request of her, "Well, aren't you?"

Charles silently walked over to the bed and pulled back the bedspread and laid next to his wife. After taking a deep sigh, he answered, "I just felt that it would be for the best all around, if your relationship with Katie came to an end. With the war going on and the sensitive nature of my business abroad, I felt that too much was at risk. As I said earlier this evening, it is believed that the Federal government placed spies in various locations knowing that war was inevitable. Harpers Ferry is a prime location for that type of individual."

Caroline held her hands over her mouth and laughed, the serious expression that covered Charles' face turned to one of bewilderment. He was puzzled by his wife's behavior and asked, "Caroline, what is so funny?"

Caroline regained her composure and said, "I have to agree with Pete on this one. I don't think that Katie McBride is a spy anymore than I believe that you do. Besides, breaking off my friendship with Katie was out of my love and devotion to you."

Caroline's answer greatly pleased Charles and he rewarded her with an affectionate kiss. He passionately said, "My love, I will always reverence the ground you walk on and my devotion to you is without question."

Caroline replied as she caressed his cheeks, "And my love is unchallenged for you."

As Charles gazed into her glowing eyes he knew that he needed to inform his wife about his possible departure tomorrow. It grieved him once more to experience the pain of separation, and the loneliness that her absence would bring. He would have void feelings within, and the intimacy that they had learned to share over the past two years would be challenged once more. As he kept his silence, Caroline discerned by the somber expression that ruled his features that he was withholding something from her. The tone in her voice reflected the concern in her heart, "Charles, what is wrong, please tell me?"

Charles' voice was soft as he spoke, "Pete informed me that the Confederate forces in the Ferry are leaving."

Caroline interrupted, "tonight?"

"Yes even as we speak. Pete will be leaving tomorrow as well as myself for fear that Federal cavalry will re-occupy the town as soon as the last of the Confederate forces are gone."

Tears began to fill Caroline's eyes as she spoke with emotion, "Charles, you just arrived."

"I know I hadn't plan for things to happen this way. I had high hopes that the Confederate forces would hold the area for a while. I'm just as disappointed as you are."

Caroline anxiously continued, "I had made plans for us to spend sometime together with Ann. How do you think she is going to react to the news?"

Charles was speechless, the words couldn't be found within his heart to comfort his wife. He knew through Confederate agents, that the Federals had information of his involvement with the Confederate government. Charles was informed by agents while in England of the Federal spy network in place concerning his many meetings with Captain Bulloch. Staying at Shenandoah posed too many risks for him, especially since he was suspicious of Katie, who probably knew of his visitation. If he stayed, he probably would be in a prisoner-of-war camp in the North. He knew that he would have to return to Richmond; he gave his word to the President. For the rest of the night, he spent with his wife, not knowing once he departed when they would share such a moment again.

CHAPTER TWENTY-EIGHT

Shortly after sunrise the next morning, the bright rays of the sun peering through the window awakened Pete. At once, he prepared for his departure by packing the rest of his personal belongings in a carpetbag that belonged to his Father. Afterward, he walked down the stairway to the dinning room, where his brother and Caroline were already having hot tea. As Pete allowed Matthew to pour his coffee, he noticed that Charles and Caroline were subdued in their demeanor. Pete knew that his brother had broken the news to Caroline of his impending departure today, and this was the reason for their mood.

Pete's thoughts were broken when William and Elizabeth entered the dinning room. William assisted Elizabeth as she sat at the head of the table. Matthew began to serve the family and guest some of Pansy's blueberry buckwheat cakes and scrambled eggs. As Elizabeth glanced around the table, she noticed Charles and Caroline's expressions, and being unaware of events that were leading to the departure of her sons on this morning, she asked in an investigative manner, "Good morning everyone, I see that we are still rightfully concerned for Rebecca."

Pete asked as he placed some butter on his cakes, "How is she?"

Elizabeth answered as she glanced in his direction; "She was still sleeping when I looked in on her about an hour ago. It has been a terrible ordeal that she has experienced, and at such an early age."

Pete said as he wiped his mouth with the fine white napkin, "I would like to see her before I depart this morning."

Elizabeth was surprised and it reflected in her voice, "Young man, where do you think that you're going?"

Pete answered as he sipped his black coffee, "I'm returning to the regiment this morning. Last night when I was in town, I noticed that many of the supply wagons were departing for Winchester. That means, the Federal cavalry will re-occupy the Ferry as soon as our forces depart."

Caroline broke her silence and said with a sorrowful voice, "It also means that Charles will have to leave and return to Richmond."

Elizabeth's expression quickly turned to despair and sorrow. She wiped her mouth with the linen and momentarily hung her head, hiding her face with her hands so that no one could witness the tears that filled her eyes. After a moment of silence, she raised her head and regaining her composure, she spoke with the authority that she was accustomed, "Pete, with your brother being in such a sensitive position with the government, I do not know why you have to leave. I feel that you should be the one to stay behind and help run the Estate until it is safe for Charles to return. Besides, if you would do the family this favor, then it would be possible for Caroline to return to Richmond with him, and they could be together." Elizabeth said this in hopes of persuading her son to leave the army and stay at home, and to protect Charles and his family.

"Mother, as much as I don't like the fighting and the risk of some prisoner-of-war camp, I have a duty to my fellow comrades in arms." Pete, with his eyes fixed on his Mother continued to express his convictions, "Two years ago you gave Charles the ownership of the Estate. If anyone stays here and works the property, then it should be the owner. I have no place here any longer. This house and property are no longer my home."

"Please Pete, don't feel that away."

Charles added as he looked at his mother lifting his hands in a gesture of frustration, "No, No Mother. It's fine. Let him go."

After his Mother's plead, Pete stood and excused himself from their presence, and returned to his room to collect his bags. As he walked through the long hallway towards the stairway, he paused in front of his sister's bedroom door. He listened for any sounds that would indicate that she had awakened; there was an on going debate within his heart if he should knock on her door. As much as he desired to speak with Rebecca, he thought that it might be for the best after all, if he spoke with Caroline and revealed the contents of Thomas' last words to be deliver to his sister. After pausing, he remembered the testimony that Katie had shared with him the evening before as they sat along the river. Pete softly knocked and waited for an answer. He heard a soft voice within the room, "Who is it?"

Pete spoke softly, "It's Pete."

Rebecca came to the door and opened it. Pete noticed her red, swollen eyes from weeping. The exhausted pale appearance of her features broke his heart. He began to identify with Rebecca's emotions as he had done so many times with his comrades after losing a fellow friend in battle. As he entered the room, he hugged her and sat in a chair near a table opposite his sister. The words were difficult to find. He opened his heart, and began to express his feelings, "Rebecca, is there anything that I can do for you?"

Rebecca spoke in a soft whisper, "No. Thank you Pete, but I don't think anyone can help me."

Pete passionately said, "I wanted to see you before I departed to rejoin General Stuart. There is something that I need to tell you, and I wanted to speak to you in private."

Rebecca began to weep, "Oh, what could anyone say that would relieve the pain that I'm experiencing."

Pete continued to speak words of comfort, "The pain is something that is going to take time to recover from. I remembered when Father passed away; it was the most difficult tribulation that I had ever experienced. All that I could think of was our times along the river fishing, hunting, or just riding across the property, and occasionally watching the wildlife. If you remember, shortly after his death, I became angry and resentful for quite a long period of time. It was because I really believed all of the expectations, the many plans for the future with him, were gone. That companionship was abruptly taken from me. I know all of us suffered, especially Mother, but eventually we managed to go on with our life."

Rebecca took the handkerchief that was in her hand and began to wipe the tears away while Pete handed her a glass of water. After she had regained her composure, she glanced at the image of her deceased suitor on the table near her seat, as Pete continued, "I wanted to tell you that I spoke with Thomas just before he passed away."

Rebecca's attention returned to the conversation with her brother, "You did. What did he say?"

"The day after the battle at Sharpsburg, I spent most of the afternoon looking for Thomas. I found him in a church on Main Street that was being used as a hospital. He was quietly lying in the corner of the building toward the back. I kneeled over so I could speak with him and he asked me to tell you that he has always had the fondest feelings for you since the very first time that he met you at the Grand Ball in Richmond. Thomas went on to say that if he had lived to see an end to the war, he would have asked you to marry him. That was his last statement before his passing. I wanted you to hear this from me, before I departed."

Rebecca softly said, as she fought back the anguish, which she was experiencing, "Thank you. I can't express the words that consume my heart. What this means to me. I was looking forward to Thomas meeting Mother and my spending some time alone with him. For some unexplained reason, I don't know why, I felt within my heart that something was wrong; there was something that was going to happen. I just didn't know what to expect."

"Rebecca, are you planning to stay with Mother for now?"

Rebecca shook her head to indicate to her brother that she would. Pete sadly said, "It might be for the best if you did." After pausing and standing, he continued with a sigh, "Well, I must go now."

Pete hugged his sister, kissed her on the cheek, and turned about and quietly departed the room. As Pete walked down the stairway, Elizabeth noticed her son and asked, "How is your sister."

"She is grieving," Pete said as he glanced once more toward the upstairs area.

Elizabeth continued in a concerned tone, "Well, in a little bit, I'll have Matthew take her some breakfast and we'll see if she feels like eating."

Pete believed that he needed to apologize to his Mother for his anger the evening before, "Mother, about last night."

Elizabeth interrupted her son and said graciously, "Pete, let it rest. The matter will settle itself."

Pete said with a quiet tone of emotion in his voice, "Mother, I just have a strong conviction that Katie is a decent person. She isn't like some of the young ladies that I've brought home in the past. Katie is much different."

Elizabeth took a deep sigh and expressed her feelings, "My son, please understand the position that this war has caused the family to undertake. You are fighting for the Southern cause as a soldier, and your brother's sensitive involvement with the Confederate government must be protected. Katie is from the North; she struggles for their cause. Charles made a valid point concerning her possible involvement as a spy with the Federal government. Even now, she could be relaying information of Charles' whereabouts, even as we speak."

"And if that was so, what about myself? I have served with General Stuart in various capacities."

"All she wants to do is attempt to extract information from you by any means," Elizabeth said with an emotional tone.

Pete became angry and it reflected in his voice, "What is that suppose to mean, huh. Mother for your information, I haven't gotten that close to her yet."

Pete grabbed his bag and departed through the hallway to the back entrance.

William had been standing in the library glancing through a book of short stories and listening to Pete and Elizabeth speaking. He was sure that Pete and Katie were together last night, and now he was infuriated. William knew with the words that he had heard that he must make the attempt to see Katie before Charles and he leave the Estate.

After saying his farewell to Charles, and Ann, Pete requested of Caroline that she would deliver the correspondence from Billy Smith to Jane Powers. Caroline promptly agreed that she would.

Charles was speaking with his family as the clock in the parlor chime ten times. William briefly interrupted, "Charles please excuse me, but I must run into town briefly on a personal matter. If I may, I'd rather take one of the horses then the carriage, it will be quicker that way."

Charles smiled, "By all means. I will have Matthew summon one of the servants to saddle you a mount."

It was a warm morning as William walked out onto the porch in the rear of the mansion and quickly mounted the animal. With haste, he headed for town. As he neared the village, he passed the last of the Confederate forces leaving the village along the Charlestown Road. He knew that his time was precious if Pete's theory about the Federal cavalry was true. Surely by now, they have been scouting the town from the Maryland side of the Potomac and might even cross the river and occupy the village today.

As William entered the village, the town was quiet, and almost empty of its occupants. After inquiring of Katie's residence at the church from the Priest, he quickly proceeded to Mrs. McDonalds. On his arrival, he knocked several times on the door. It appeared to him that no one was at home. As he walked away to mount his horse, Katie answered the door and called, "William."

At once, William dismounted and returned to the porch. Katie was suspicious of his appearance and began to investigate the nature of his visitation, "William, what brings you to town?"

There was a laugh, and a smile on William's face as he began to speak, "Katie, I have been visiting with the Barkers over the past several days and I thought that I would pay my respects since I haven't seen you at the Estate."

"Thank you. That was thoughtful of you."

William continued speaking in a friendly tone, "Actually, my visit is more then just paying my respects. I would like to speak with you, if I may."

Katie was somewhat puzzled, "About what?"

"About Caroline and Pete."

As William was seated in one of the wooden chairs on the long front porch, Katie walked from the doorway and sat in the swing. William had Katie's curiosity aroused, and she asked, "What about Caroline and Pete?"

William had finished lighting a cigar when he answered, "Katie, I'm here because I'm tired of Pete and Caroline trying to play you for some kind of a fool."

Katie cried, "Oh my God, William. What are you trying to tell me?"

Sensing the emotion in her voice, William held his hand in the air and gestured for Katie to remain calm, "Katie, I know the reason why Caroline has broken off her relationship with you." Katie was silent and anxiously awaiting his revelation. William confidently continued as his eyes were seriously fixed upon hers, "It has always been evident to me that you have been very fond of Pete."

"How have you drawn that conclusion?"

William chuckled and said, "It shows in your expression when you are near him. For example the evening that the Barkers held the reception in my honor at the Estate before the general election of 1860, there was a sparkle that filled your eyes. Also, what about the evening after the battle at Manassas, as I remember, you were quite concerned over his welfare that evening and close to tears on that occasion."

Katie confessed, "I must admit, I am fond of him."

"Well, if I were you, I'd give up on that notion and I would be searching for someone else to keep company with, just as Pete has been doing."

Katie was surprised and stunned by the revelation. It reflected in her voice, "William, what do you mean? Please tell me, what is going on?"

William continued with words of despair, "Well, it happen that several days ago as I was walking around the pond and admiring some of the beautiful flowers that surrounded the pathway, I noticed Pete entering the stable area. Oh, it was less then five minutes later, I noticed Caroline enter the same stable. At first, I thought nothing of it. But then, I must say my curiosity got the best of me." William, with a half-hearted chuckle continued to speak boldly, "I have always been a person that has possessed keen intuition, very seldom have I been proven to be wrong. Slowly, I walked to where there was a side entrance to the stable, out of sight, of course. And there, I watched Pete and Caroline speaking, when suddenly the two of them embraced. I thought nothing of the affair until Pete and Caroline began to passionately kiss, and then one thing led to another. I thought to myself, how can I be a witness to such an act of aggression against my best friend, Charles."

Katie promptly stood and replied, "No, William, it can't be true. I just don't believe that Pete and Caroline are that type of people. It wouldn't be characteristic of Caroline to jeopardize her respect and honor in this way."

"I didn't either, but I was just as surprised as I know that you must be. I can plainly see why Caroline wanted to break off her relationship with you; she didn't want you to stand between Pete and the feelings that she has for him. Katie you became a threat to her little fling that she was enjoying with Pete, and you had to be removed from the picture. As I gave the matter more thought, I felt that there were some flirtations taking place last spring when Caroline and Pete were together in Richmond." Katie was silent, stunned, and experiencing emotional pain as William continued to speak, "Now look Katie, I have known the Barkers for quite sometime. Pete has always possessed an admiration for the ladies in the area. At one time, Elizabeth confided in me that her greatest concern was that Pete was giving the family a bad reputation for his frequent womanizing. And as I understand from his Mother, she has gotten him out of a fix more then once. The young Barker just doesn't know how to have a meaningful relationship with a young lady of your standing."

Katie calmly asked, "And what about Charles. Have you spoken with him about this matter?"

"No, I haven't. I have decided to tell him once we leave later this afternoon." Katie was quiet and expressionless as William express his feelings, "Katie, you are an attractive, intelligent, and a sociable young lady. If I were you, I'd forget about Pete and move on with your life. I don't believe that it would be in your best interest to waste anymore of your precious time worrying about him."

As William was finishing his statement, he noticed a squadron of Federal cavalry on the opposite side of the Potomac along the towpath of the C & O Canal. As he gazed in the Federals direction, he said, "Well Katie, it appears that the Yankees are about to re-occupy the town. It won't be safe for me to stay any longer. As always, it's been a pleasure seeing you, I just wished that I could have given you greater tidings of joy. I must say my farewell and depart and warn Charles."

William tipped his hat, and with a cordial smile, he mounted his horse and departed for the Estate.

Katie watched as William rode out of sight at a gallop. She was shocked at the revelation that William presented. As she sat on the swing, she began to intensely ponder the subject. To Katie, it was logical by Caroline's behavior towards her that she could be truly involved with Pete. After all, he admitted the previous evening that he hadn't received the correspondence that she had entrusted to Caroline when she went to Richmond the previous spring. Then Katie remembered last night along the river, Pete had revealed to her that he wasn't in love with her, and the thought grieved her. Although, when asked if there was another lady of interest, he assured her that there wasn't anyone special to him. The one thought that concerned Katie the most was, Pete had always been honest with her and his intentions. Maybe, she thought, Pete needed a lady friend, such as herself to keep Charles and his Mother blinded by the truth. As Katie attempted to sort out the facts, the confusion was more then she could endure.

William slowed his horse down to a trot as he neared Bolivar Heights. There was a devilish laugh at the thought of damaged that he had just incurred upon the lives of the Barkers with his fabrication concerning Caroline and Pete having an affair, and too, the misery that it caused Katie. Hopefully, he thought, this little lie would settle the romantic ideas that Katie was consumed with for Pete, and just maybe, it would give William the chance somewhere in the near future for an opportunity to share Miss McBride's company. William had not been convinced that the friendship between Katie and Caroline was totally severed. William couldn't be sure, but Caroline's words and actions in Richmond last spring led him to believe that she was just playing along with her husband for now. Though, William was confident that the revelation he shared with Katie would continue to manifest a great amount of damage to the separation that already existed between the ladies. If everything played out as he intended, William knew that there would be great dividends for him and his pursuit of Katie. Also, the division that Caroline had initiated would keep Katie in the dark concerning the sensitive nature of his and Charles' service to the Confederacy. In order to insure the two gentleman's protection on these matters, and to keep him abreast on Katie's personal life he would have to trust someone. This person would have to keep him informed of Katie's whereabouts, who she kept company with, and if she was to visit the Estate, and the nature of her visitation. William needed to know this information. Immediately, Daniel's name came to mind.

As William arrived at the Estate, he rode to the rear of the mansion and dismounted. Handing the reins of the animal to a servant that was standing near by, he noticed Daniel coming from the carpenter's shop. William walked in the direction of the overseer, and shook his hand saying, "You are just the man I want to see."

Daniel answered in a suspicious tone, "Oh, really."

William said with boldness, "Yes, I have some work for you that will pay a very handsome fee, if you're interested, of course."

Daniel was cautious in his answer, "What do I have to do to earn this money?"

William said, as he folded his arms and leaned against the fence railing and looked in the direction of the Ferry, "Daniel, since it's origin, I've worked for the Confederate Secret Service."

Daniel interrupted, "Mr. Charles said nothin' of this."

William promptly replied, as he glanced at the overseer, "Charles doesn't know anything about the nature of my business with the agency. And it must be kept that away. Just between you and me. Understand?"

Daniel said obediently, "Oh yeah, I understand."

William aggressively continued, "I want you to listen to me, this is how I desire to employ your service. I have every reason to believe that Miss McBride is spying for the Yankees." William turned about and noticed the surprised expression covering the overseers face. Pausing to light a cigar that had been taken from his coat pocket, he continued with Daniels full attention, "Oh yeah, and don't ask me why. I need for you to keep me abreast of everything that she does. I want to know if she visit's the family, who she keeps company with, and most of all, I want to be informed immediately if Pete returns to the Estate. Its imperative that I keep those two separated, or she might attempt to extract information from him regarding troop movements by any means at her disposal. Do you understand the seriousness of this request?"

Daniel shook his head in acknowledgement as William removed a considerable sum of money from his possession.

William warned Daniel by saying, "Remember, it is of the greatest importance that this mission remains between you and me. If for some reason, you were to reveal this meeting between us to anyone, especially the Barkers, it could mean that your life would be in jeopardy."

Daniel spoke with assurance, "Mr. William, ya can trust me. I won't let ya down."

William turned about and proceeded toward the house to inform Charles that the Federals were lurking along the Potomac. As he did so, William's thoughts were upon the outcome of his visit with Katie and how soon he would be able to collect on his investment.

CHAPTER TWENTY-NINE

In the spring of 1863, the war for the Confederacy in the western theater wasn't producing victories. The Federal army had been victorious against the Confederate forces at Stone River and Port Gibson. For the past several months, the Union forces under the command of General Ulysses S. Grant had been attempting to defeat the Confederate army at Vicksburg, Mississippi. If Grant could defeat the army that held the fortifications around the city, then Union forces would control the river, thus splitting the Confederacy in two. With victories over the Confederate forces under General Joseph Johnston at Raymond, Jackson, and Champion Hill, Grant and the Union army controlled the western half of Mississippi with the exception of Vicksburg. During the end of May, Grant was pressuring the outer defenses of the city with infantry assaults, while the Union Navy under Admiral David Porter was bombarding the Confederate fortifications along the river.

In the eastern theater of the war, the struggle on the battlefield was favoring the Confederacy. With victories at Fredericksburg in December of 1862, and at Chancellorsville in May of 1863, the success was tarnished by the death of General Thomas (Stonewall) Jackson. Still, there was great hope of Southern independence among the government officials in Richmond. General Robert E. Lee conceived a plan of invading the North just before the Chancellorsville campaign, but with the Federal forces crossing the Rappahannock River, he wasn't able to implicate his vision. Now, later in the month, Lee had returned to the Confederate capitol upon President Davis' request to present his plan before the President's cabinet.

It was mid-afternoon in Richmond, on May 26th 1863. Charles Barker was quietly sitting at a desk in the library of his Aunt Daisy's home finishing a correspondence to Caroline. The last time that Charles and his family spent time together was over the Christmas season, some four months ago when the family, including his Mother and sister came to the city. It was painful for Charles to endure the separation from his loved ones, but he believed that the sacrifice for Southern independence would be worth his effort. Over the past months of serving the President, he had strived to keep stability between some of the legislators of various Southern states, and the Confederate government. It had been a tedious and sometimes difficult task, especially when the issues involved the President and Governor Brown of Georgia.

As he was signing his name to the letter, Amos the servant came into the room and said in his graveled voice, "Mr. Charles, Capt.'s Moss would like to speak with yose in the parlor."

Charles replied as he sealed the envelope, "Tell the Captain that I will be there shortly."

Immediately, Amos departed. Charles began to ponder on the nature of the officer's visitation as he arose from the desk.

As Charles walked into the parlor, he noticed Captain Moss looking at the image on the fireplace mantel of Caroline, Ann, and himself posing on the front porch of Shenandoah. The Captain turned to face Charles and said, "Sir, I hope you didn't mine me taking the liberty of admiring your family. With all due respect, it brings warm memories of joyful days in Rockingham County before the war."

Charles smiled as he lit a cigar and optimistically replied, "Captain, hopefully with more victories such as we have recently enjoyed, this war will come to a conclusion in our favor, and those fond memories will continue."

"That is why I'm here. President Davis has requested that you accompany me to the Executive Mansion."

"Do you know what the President is requesting of me?"

"Yes sir, but I'm under strict orders to remain silent."

Charles was puzzled as he walked from the room with Captain Moss. As Amos handed Charles his black hat, William appeared at the front door. By his expression, Charles knew that William was taken by surprise with the Captain's visitation. William inquired into the nature of the Captain's visit, "Captain Moss, I'm surprise to see you here. If I may ask, what is going on?"

Captain Moss promptly replied, "Sir with all due respect, I'm under orders to remain silent."

Charles gazed at William and said, "I have been sent for by the President. That is all I know."

William smilingly said, "Then I will join you."

Captain Moss said in a cordial tone, "Sir, only Mr. Barker is to accompany me to the Executive Mansion."

William disappointingly replied, "Oh, I see."

As Charles and Captain Moss boarded the carriage that was waiting, William stood at the doorway bewildered over the nature of Charles' business with the President; jealousy was conceived in his heart.

It was a short journey to the Executive Mansion from Grace Street. The area around the mansion was bustling with activity as Charles and the Captain arrived. Charles noticed a small escort of cavalry near the front of the mansion and naturally assumed that an officer of high rank was with the President. The butler of the Executive Mansion met Charles and the Captain at the front door and escorted them to the second floor where the President was expecting their arrival. As Charles walked into the room, he was surprised to see not only the President's cabinet, but General Lee seated around a huge table speaking. After introductions, Charles sat near the President. Charles listened intently as General Lee continued to present his vision for an invasion of Maryland and Pennsylvania. The General optimistically continued, "I am sure that once my army crosses the Potomac, General Hooker will quickly follow. If I have a large enough force for this endeavor, I believe that the Lincoln administration will be inclined to reinforce Hooker with troops from along the Mississippi, and Tennessee, thus relieving General Pemberton and Bragg. Instead of Vicksburg being under siege, by the actions of our army, the major cities and industries of the North will be threatened."

One of the cabinet members asked, "General Lee, how many soldiers will this invasion require? After all, we must consider the safety of the capitol if Hooker doesn't swallow the bait, but instead proceeds south."

The General paused for a moment, and then confidently replied, "An invasion of this magnitude would require as many brigades as I could muster. It's my intentions to guard my lines of communication with Richmond once the army has crossed the Potomac. Hopefully, some of those reinforcements to help in this task will come from the soldiers stationed in North Carolina. And as for Hooker, I sincerely believe that he'll follow. For some reason, the Federals are ridiculously afraid of us capturing Washington,"

President Davis said, as he looked across the table at the General, "With all due respect, General Lee, I still believe that it would be beneficial to send a Corps of troops from your forces to relieve General Pemberton at Vicksburg. Between Grant and the Union Navy, General Pemberton is surrounded and is rationing provisions among his soldiers. Those poor boys as well as the civilian population are starving. I know that the Confederacy cannot afford to lose Vicksburg. With Union control of the Mississippi, our young nation will be divided."

With the exchange of strategic opinions between General Lee and President Davis, Charles perceived that the cabinet was favoring General Lee's plan of invasion of the North. Many times in previous meetings with cabinet members, only the President, secretaries of each department, and military advisors would exchange conversation concerning government business and military strategies. Charles knew that the hopes and dreams of Southern independence could very well depend on this military campaign. Immediately, Charles asked, "Gentleman, if I may impose upon you, I would like to speak with the President in private for a moment?"

The expression upon the President's face confirmed his astonishment at the request, since he was an individual and leader that dominated many of the cabinet meetings. Quietly, he rose from his chair and walked into the hall with Charles. As he gazed at Charles with a somber expression, he asked, "Charles, I know what you are going to say, but I trust my judgment in this matter. I'm quite hesitant of an invasion."

"I understand Mr. President, though I'm convinced that if we proceed with General Lee's plan, this time we might do enough damage in the Northern states that the peace movement will press for an end to hostilities, not to say that a victory on Northern soil could still possibly bring about foreign intervention from France or Britain."

The President was emphatic with his reply, "No, Charles. There are thousands of our men in that besieged city waiting for relief. There isn't time to organize an invasion of Maryland, or Pennsylvania."

"Mr. President neither is there time to relieve Vicksburg." Pausing and continuing, Charles said boldly, "At least with General Lee's plan we have an opportunity to accomplish the goal of foreign intervention, and just maybe, the conclusion of this war."

The President was quietly pondering Charles' perception of events as the two of them re-entered the room where the cabinet and General were seated.

During the final week of May, the town of Harpers Ferry was once more bustling with activity under Federal occupation. The Baltimore and Ohio Railroad Bridge had been rebuilt as well as many of the damaged structures that had been destroyed in the lower area of the town. Many of the town's citizens had returned with the attitude of making an attempt to continue their life. The residents of the town along with the rest of the citizens from Jefferson County were about to cast their ballots for possible admission to the new state of West Virginia. Union officers and soldiers were monitoring the polling facilities so that citizens loyal to the Confederacy wouldn't intimidate voters. During this time, Seamus McBride, was finishing a ten-day furlough after spending time with his sister Katie, whom he hadn't seen since the beginning of the war. As Katie was walking along Shenandoah Street, and holding the arm of her brother, she said as she noticed some of the townspeople entering the polling facility, "Seamus, it doesn't appear that the turn out for the election will be significant?"

Seamus glanced at his sister and replied, "No, I don't think so. I believe that most of the men from this bloody area that could have voted are fighting with the rebels, like that bloody Johnnie that you call your friend."

Katie jerked her brother's arm, and came to a halt, angrily she replied, "Look here Seamus McBride, I am bloody old enough to decide for myself who I want to call a friend."

Seamus fired-back angrily, "Katie out of all of the men on this earth that you could have been married to, or called a friend, why did you have to come down to this bloody hell hole to meet someone that's a bloody rebel?"

Katie's emotions had calmed and she was quietly watching a young boy attempting to manage an unruly team of mules pulling a small wagon. Her mind was on the sincere relationship that she had always enjoyed with her brother. Even though he would disagree with her on the subject of Pete Barker, and most likely continue his anger, she knew that it wasn't the time to display any dishonestly with him and jeopardize the trust that they shared. Katie methodically chose her words and illustration, "Seamus, do you remember when you were fond of Maggie Adair?"

A smile that covered Seamus' face brought forth his reflection of the affair, "Oh yes." Pausing and continuing to answer his sister's question, "I do. I remembered how I made Father angry by sneaking out the upstairs window and climbing down from the porch to run off and meet her at the park. Maggie was my first love, you know."

Katie knew that she had trapped her brother, but she needed to do so in order to make her point. She wisely said, "Do you remember how father felt when he came looking for you and found the two of you together."

"Yes, I do. Father spoke with me on the way home and expressed his disappointed in my behavior. I made every attempt to persuade him to see the subject my way, but he refused."

Katie was willing to demonstrate her intentions concerning the friendship that she shared with Pete, and that the situation wasn't any different then what Seamus had experienced at that particular time in his life. Katie promptly asked, "Why? What did he say?"

Seamus knew by this time that his sister had used her teaching ability to deceive him into admitting the truth concerning his feelings for Maggie Adair. Out of his love and respect for Katie, he would be fair and truthful. Seamus shook his head in frustration and said, "I was told by Father that Maggie came from a family of disputable reputation. Maggie's Father was a drunkard and had spent time in prison, and while he was in confinement, her Mother resorted to prostitution to make ends meet. Father felt that if I continued to keep company with Maggie, that it would give our family an undesirable name in the community. He threaten to send me to a military school if I continued my association with her."

Katie said in a serious tone, "Seamus, don't you see my point? You are attempting to treat me the same, as Father demanded of you. Yes, Pete is fighting for a different cause then you, but because you two disagree on issues concerning the way that society should function doesn't necessarily give you the right to pass judgment on his character and heart. Seamus, what you see is someone wearing a gray uniform. You have judged him outwardly without knowing him. I judge him inwardly. I have listened to him share his heart and mind and I know how he feels about life. I see his character in action, and his treatment in relationship with those around him."

Seamus became defensive; "This bloody war has made matters different. That bloody Johnnie friend of yours is my enemy. I met him at Antietam Creek last September and he threatened to harm me if we met again."

Katie's eyes were fixed on her brothers' with a piercing effect. She demanded, "Seamus, how did you meet Pete."

Seamus remained silent and refused to allow his eyes to meet hers. Katie raised her voice and demanded, "Seamus McBride, tell me. How did you meet him?"

Seamus shook his head in frustration and shouted, "What's the bloody use." Pausing, turning to glance at the soldiers marching down Shenandoah Street toward the railroad platform, he turned around and continued, "After we whipped the bloody Johnnies, we agreed on a truce to remove the wounded and dead from the battlefield. As usual, many of the soldiers from both sides gathered to exchange goods such as food and tobacco. Shortly after my arrival on a ridge outside of town, I noticed a rebel approaching, carrying a beautiful ruby that he had removed from around his neck." As Katie continued to listen to her brother the thought crossed her mind that Pete never parted with the valuable jewel, it must have been him. Her focus returned as he was saying, "I wasn't about to allow the opportunity to pass me by, so I called out to the Johnnie to work out an exchange. Afterwards, he began to inquire into my identity. I asked him why, and he verbally threatened me. I must admit he was surprised to discover who I was."

"Please, Seamus, I know your temper. I beg of you not to harm him."

"Katie, he is my enemy."

Katie caught her brother by surprise saying, "And, he is the man that I love."

Seamus was shocked, a sadden expression covered his face; he was quiet and emotionally disturbed by the revelation. He asked, "Does Mother know?"

"No, and I would ask that you keep this matter to yourself. When I feel that the time is right, then I will be the one to break the news to her."

Earlier in the afternoon, Daniel Johnson had arrived in town to cast his vote. After doing so, he went to Whites Tavern to quench his thirst. After enjoying a fifth of applejack whiskey and sharing the latest news concerning the war, he departed from the establishment. As he looked in the direction of the ruins of the Armory, he lit a cigar and walked the short distance to the corner of Potomac and Shenandoah Street. Daniel was about to turn and proceed in the direction of the dry goods store, when he noticed Katie walking down the street with a

Union officer. For fear of being recognized, Daniel quickly turned about and walked toward the tavern from where he came. As Katie and her brother proceeded in the direction of the railroad depot, Daniel's curiosity was aroused. After receiving a handsome bounty and his pledge to William Pierce, Daniel was going to make every attempt to discover Miss McBride's business. At a distance, Daniel kept her under surveillance.

It was 3:00 in the afternoon and the eastbound passenger train from Martinsburg was behind schedule. Katie sat on one of the wooden benches along the platform watching some of the Union soldiers waiting for the train's arrival. She couldn't help, but to overhear one of the Federals speaking to a comrade about a Private John Berry from up-state New York who was engaged to be married next week. The Federal soldier expressed his sorrow at breaking the news to the bride-to-be concerning her groom's tragic death at the hands of Confederate raiders that had been harassing the railroad line between Harpers Ferry and Martinsburg. Katie was grieved to overhear such tragic tidings. It was unbearable for her to think that this type of news could reach her before the end of this conflict.

Suddenly, her thoughts were broken with the sound of the whistle from the locomotive pulling the train that would take her brother to Washington City. As the train came to a halt, Katie quietly walked with Seamus to the coach that he was going to board for the trip. Seamus turned to face his younger sister and sadly said as he pulled the ticket from his coat pocket, "Katie, I wish that you would return to Boston. This is no place for a young woman such as yourself."

Katie said in a confident voice, "Seamus, I can't leave at this time. I know that you will never understand, but for now, I have to stay."

As the whistle sounded for the passengers to board, Seamus replied, "No, I don't understand why you would want to expose yourself to such a danger and this way of living. There is a better life waiting for you in Boston, if you would just return. I'm very concerned for your safety here in this desolated place. Why do you stay?"

"My feelings hold me captive to another."

As Katie kissed her brother on the cheek and embraced him, Daniel was standing in the area of the old armory warehouse observing these actions as they transpired.

CHAPTER THIRTY

The month of June had provided Jeb Stuart's Confederate Cavalry with intense campaigning. On the ninth of June, the Confederate horsemen were suddenly surprised when the Federal Cavalry under General Pleasanton crossed the Rappahannock River at Kelly's Ford near a place called Brandy Station. Both sides battled throughout the day to a stand off. The Federals retreated across the river. With the Federal withdrawal, the Army of Northern Virginia's II Corps, now under the command of Lt. General Richard Ewell, moved slowly into the Shenandoah Valley toward the Potomac River. Stuart's cavalry was given the responsibility of screening the Confederate movements by guarding the gaps along the Blue Ridge Mountains, and thus, keeping the Army of The Potomac under General Joseph Hooker from discovering the large invasion force that was moving toward the river, and on to Pennsylvania.

Pete Barker had received orders by a courier from General Stuart to report to the General's headquarters near Rector's Cross Roads. It was early on the morning of the eighteenth of June when Pete rode into the General's camp. As Pete dismounted, he noticed that many of the men were busy cooking their breakfast and boiling coffee. The smell of bacon frying over an open fire was tempting, but after being awake throughout the night scouting near Mountsville, Pete's greatest desire was to partake of the coffee. With a smile, he walked over to a fire where two Confederate cavalrymen were seated on wooden crates enjoying their meal. Pete boldly asked the older of the two soldiers, "Do you mine sharing some of your coffee. I've been on duty for quite sometime without anything to eat or drink."

The older soldier looked up from his meal and jovially replied, "Shou're fella, pull up one of those crates and help ya self."

The younger soldier asked as he glanced in Pete's direction, "What regiment are ya with?"

"Pete replied as he filled his cup with the coffee, "I'm with the 1ˢᵗ Virginia."

The older of the two Confederates said, "The last that I heard the 1ˢᵗ was somewhere near Middleburg."

Pete said, as he took a sip from the cup, "That's right."

As Pete rose to his feet, the younger Confederate soldier said, "What brings ya here?"

With a puzzled expression covering his face, Pete replied, "I really don't know until I speak with General Stuart."

As Pete left the two soldiers and walked the short distance to the General's headquarters, he noticed a rider approaching in the far distance. Giving the matter of little concern, Pete asked the sentry to announce his presence to the General. The guard complied with the request. After entering General Stuart's tent, Pete saluted his commanding officer and respectfully said, "General Stuart, I have reported just as you have requested."

Pausing as he sorted through some papers, the General replied, "Thank you, Barker, for being so expedient in my orders. I have called you for an important task."

As the General laid before the young Barker a map of Loudoun County, he pointed with his index finger in the area of Middleburg. Almost immediately, the sentry announced the mysterious rider that Pete had witnessed earlier approaching the camp. The guard said, "General Stuart, Major Mosby has arrived and requests to see you."

The General turned his attention to the sentry and gave his consent for the Major to enter and join them. Pete was surprised; this was the first time since the campaign around Richmond in 1862 that he had seen Mosby. Now, he was the leader of a group of partisans from the area. As the young Major entered the tent, General Stuart's eyes glowed and his voice reflected the enthusiasm of seeing Mosby, his trusted comrade, "John, how are you?"

The Major promptly replied, "I'm doing fine."

Major Mosby turned and smilingly said to Pete as he reached to shake the young Barker's hand, "Pete, its been what, a year since we last saw each other?"

Pete returned the friendly gesture, saying as he shook Mosby's hand, "Yeah, something like that."

Stuart said as he looked at Mosby, "Hey, you know Barker?"

Mosby said as he glanced at General Stuart, "Yes, yes, I would like to have this man transferred to my command."

"No, John, I need him. I am about to send him to scout on Pleasanton's activities."

Mosby replied as he walked over to the map that was laid out on a small table, "There will be no need to do that. Although, there may be something of greater importance for him to do."

General Stuart appeared surprise and said with a sense of urgency in his voice, "John, you must have a good reason for your last statement."

Mosby laughingly said as he removed some papers from his shirt, "I do. Late last night, I chose three of my men to accompany me on a raid near Fairfax Station. Our effort was rewarded with the capture of important documents confiscated from a courier. The papers were from General Hooker to General Pleasonton." Mosby laid the papers out on the lower portion of the map and continued explaining, "Gentleman, these papers outline the movement of Hooker's army, the disposition of each Corps and their objective."

Pete knew by the wide grin that dominated the General's expression that he was greatly pleased by what Mosby had captured for him. General Stuart remained silent as he studied the map and the contents of the papers. He was optimistic and jubilant in his reply, "According to these documents, most of the Federals are camped along the Orange and Alexandria Railroad. Apparently, once Pleasanton discovers General Lee's intentions, he is to communicate with Hooker at Fairfax Court House. That means he will be using maximum force in an attempt to penetrate our cover. Also, De Forest's cavalry is moving toward Warrenton in an attempt to locate our position. I must warn General Hampton of De Forest's move so he will have time to prepared to engage him there and protect our flanks."

General Stuart at once called the sentry, "Brown, come here now!"

As Private Brown entered the tent, the General commanded, "Send at once for Major McClellan."

Turning toward a small desk in the rear of the tent, quickly, he began to scribble some thoughts on a piece of paper. Afterward, he rose and faced Major

Mosby and Pete and said with a tone of urgency, "Barker, as soon as I prepare a dispatch for General Lee, I want you to ride immediately to the General's headquarters near Berryville and deliver these papers to him, then return. For now, rest, you'll probably be up most of the night."

As Pete turned to leave, Mosby said to him, "How is Lester?"

Pete answered with a tone of concern, "Lately he has been depressed. He would like to return home to see his sweetheart and family."

Mosby shook his head in agreement, "Don't we all."

Pete silently shook his head in agreement and departed, leaving Mosby in privacy with General Stuart.

With a limited amount of time to spare before departing for the Valley, Pete found himself a place of comfort near the General's tent under a tree. Once more, he asked and received some coffee, and to pass the time, he felt that it would be wise to write a correspondence home to the family. Pete borrowed a wooden crate to use for a desk, and removing some paper from his saddlebags, he wrote a few lines to his Mother informing her of his welfare. After finishing and sealing the contents, he began to write to Katie. As he penned the first words, he couldn't help hearing the echo of the beautiful tenor voice throughout the camp, accompanied by a guitarist singing the ballad Lorena.

Pete paused and listened to the vocalist as he sang, "Yes, those were the words of thine, Lorena. They are within my memory yet. They touch some tender chords, Lorena, 'twas not the woman's heart which spoke. Thy heart was always true to me."

The verse from the song caused Pete to reflect on the last visit to Harpers Ferry and that particular evening at the church where he found Katie. Somewhere in his heart, he knew the true nature of her affections for him. Although for some unknown reason, he wasn't capable of returning her affection. At times over the past nine months, the thoughts and words of her heart had resurfaced time and again, but there was always some reason to repress those thoughts from his mind, still again, a song resurrected them.

As Pete finished writing the correspondence to Katie, Major McClellan came from the area of the General's tent. He called out to Pete, "Barker, General Stuart will see you now."

Pete rose to his feet and brushed the dust and dead grass from his torn trousers. Quickly, he returned his personal items to the saddlebags that was near his side and followed the officer. After being announced, Pete entered the tent and saluted the commanding officer. General Stuart waste little time, he said as he handed Pete a pouch containing the papers, "Barker, its imperative that General Lee receives these documents along with my letter."

Pete replied as he placed the documents inside of his blouse, "I will see that they are delivered."

It was with a look of confidence, Stuart commanded, "Now hurry."

Without hesitation, Pete left the General and mounted his mare and galloped away, heading westward toward the Blue Ridge Mountains and into the Shenandoah Valley.

At Shenandoah Estates, it was a gray, cloudy, and misty afternoon. The residents of the Estate bored somber expressions on their faces. Many mourners had gathered to pay their last respects to Charles Barker, and to console Caroline, Elizabeth, and the rest of the family who were stricken with grief. It had been told to his associates and friends by Caroline, that Charles had bravely fought along side of his brother and had died from gunshot wounds at the battle of Brandy Station.

The eulogy in the ballroom by Pastor Morton was somber with a closed coffin. The Pastor spoke eloquently of the decease. The service lasted for an hour or more praising the many accomplishments of Charles' public service. Some of the mourners openly cried in an expression of their sorrow and despair, while many kept silent, still in disbelief. As for Daniel, he stood near the entrance to the ballroom burning with anger, and swearing within his heart revenge against any Federal soldier, or slave. Shortly, the procession of mourners, servants, and slaves proceeded toward the cemetery slowly behind the coffin singing the spiritual Swing Low Sweet Chariot. Soon, they came to an open grave in the family cemetery near a grove of trees about one hundred yards from the main house. There the pallbearers quietly placed the coffin on some wooden planks and rope to be lowered into the grave. Caroline gently held Ann's hand as she took her place along side of her husband's coffin, while Elizabeth wept uncontrollably supported and comforted by her personal servant. Rebecca was numb with anger and anguish, still not having fully recovered from the death of her suitor, Thomas Monroe.

Pastor Morton opened his small black King James Bible to the New Testament, the Gospel of John, third chapter, sixteenth verse and read, "For

God so loved the world that he gave his only begotten Son, that whosoever would believe in him would not parish, but have everlasting life." As the Minister continued his words of strength, the sound of galloping horses could be heard quickly approaching in the direction of the main house. The attention of some of the mourners was compromised by curiosity as they glanced in the direction of the mansion to observe the Union cavalry patrol.

The Federals had returned to the area from shadowing General Ewell's II Corps as it forded the Potomac River near Williamsport, Maryland. Captain Joshua Link rode at the front of the twenty-man unit as it galloped down the long lane to the mansion. As the cavalrymen came to a halt at the front entrance of the mansion, the house and the grounds around the immediate area appeared to be lifeless of its inhabitants. This raised the suspicions of the military officer, who turned about in his saddle and commanded, "Squadron, dismount."

As the soldiers of the unit complied with the order, Captain Link turned and walked about saying, "Search the grounds, and do not harm civilians. Understood!"

Immediately, the Federals began walking toward the stables, barn, and slave quarters with their weapons ready to fire if needed. Captain Link detained some of the soldiers to search the grounds around the mansion while a few stayed with the horses. As Captain Link began to knock on the front door, one of the privates that had been searching in the stable area came running toward the officer shouting, "Captain, Captain!"

Captain Link turned about along with Corporeal Hayes and quickly intercepted the soldier as he approached the stairs to the porch of the house. Captain Link promptly asked, "My God soldier, what is the matter?"

The private pointed in the direction of the barn, "There is a large gathering of mourners at a cemetery about one hundred yards in that direction."

Captain Link gave the command, "Mount up!"

The Federals rode in formation two by two with the officer in the front as they approached the area of the funeral. Slowly, the cavalrymen came to a halt. Captain Link dismounted along with Corporal Hayes and quietly walked toward Caroline, who was dressed in black. The mourners remained quiet, though many believed that the Union intrusion could have been avoided while respects were being paid to the decease and family. Daniel was among some of the mourners, holding tightly to the butt of his revolver, which was hidden under his black frock coat. As Captain Link began to speak, he removed his blue kepi in respect for the widow, and softly said, "Madam, I am sorry for the lost of your love one."

Caroline repressed the anger that consumed her heart, and said as she held a handkerchief toward her face, "Thank you Captain."

The Captain asked suspiciously as he glanced about the mourners, "If I may ask, who is in the coffin?"

Caroline answered with a quiver in her voice, "It is my husband Charles."

Captain Link was surprised to receive the news of Charles Barker's death. For sometime, the Union authorities had been raiding the Estate on a frequent basis hoping to capture Barker and imprison him for his role with Jefferson Davis, and the Confederate government. Captain Link's voice reflected the astonishment that he felt, "I am most surprised to hear this news. When did your husband die?"

"Several weeks ago at Brandy Station. He was killed by Yankee scum, who were no more then cowards."

As the Captain continued to glance about the mourners, he quietly gazed at the coffin; his suspicion continued in the sound of his voice, "For some reason, I find that hard to believe."

Many of the mourners were shocked and angry at Captain Links answer. Caroline removed the handkerchief from her mouth and said in defiance, "Then Captain, I guess you will have to open the coffin and identify the remains for yourself."

Captain Link was a soldier of pride, whose principals were against waging war among civilians. In this particular situation, Charles was not considered a civilian, but a combatant; therefore, the Federals were within their authority to inspect the coffin.

The order went forth from the Captain, "Corporal, open the coffin!"

Corporal Hayes moved toward the coffin as Daniel began to quietly pull the revolver from his holster. Suddenly, Pastor Morton stepped forward and cried, "Captain, please think of the family, especially their daughter. Don't you have any respect for the grieving, and those who came to pay their final respects to the decease and family?"

The Captain gazed at Ann sobbing, and then he raised his hand in the air and shouted, "Corporal Hayes, wait!"

Without saying another word, or command, the Captain gestured for the Corporal to mount his horse. Still with an expression covering his face that continued to reveal his suspicions, he glanced once more in Caroline's direction, and gave the order to depart. Captain Link and the cavalrymen rode toward the direction of Harpers Ferry.

The services continued without further interruption, though Caroline believed that the Federal intrusions might come to an end with her husband's death.

After a reception for the family's friends in the ballroom, and everyone had departed, Caroline walked briefly onto the front porch to have sometime to rest and collect her thoughts. With the many friends and neighbors that had turned out to express their condolences to the family, the emotion had mentally and physically taken its toll on her. Looking off in the direction of the Ferry, she noticed a lone rider making the turn down the lane toward the mansion. She began to wonder who might be paying the family a visit at this hour in the afternoon. Patiently she waited, focused totally on the approaching visitor. As the rider cleared the shadows of the tall oak trees that garnished the long lane, she realized that it was Katie McBride.

Katie had overheard Corporal Hayes speaking with some of the citizens in the dry goods store concerning the events surrounding the death of Charles Barker. The news surprised the young lady. She was shocked and stunned, but most of all concern for Caroline and her family's lost. It must be devastating beyond words to Caroline, and the rest of the family, she thought. This war continues to affect the lives of families from the area. Her first impulse was to make the attempt to visit Caroline and to bring comfort even though she was still experiencing emotional pain from William Pierce's revelation concerning a relationship between Pete and Caroline. She didn't know how the Barkers would receive her. Regardless, Katie knew the effort had to be made.

As Katie dismounted from her horse, Caroline said, "I see that you have learned how to ride with confidence."

Katie replied softly as she handed the reins of the animal to one of the servants, "I had a good teacher."

Caroline said, as Katie approached the top of the stone steps, "What brings you to Shenandoah at this hour in the afternoon?"

"I couldn't help but to overhear a Federal cavalrymen in town say that Charles had been killed."

Caroline wasn't able to look Katie in the eyes. She turned and stared at the multiple colored roses that filled the garden alongside of the house.

Katie said in a tone of compassion, "Caroline, I'm sorry for the lost of Charles, it is difficult, I know. When I heard the news, my first thought was to make every effort to comfort you and the family. I came not knowing how you would receive me, but I was compelled to act upon the feelings that I have for your family. The emotion that I'm experiencing for the family's lost doesn't acknowledge the division that exist between us over this conflict."

The words that Katie spoke to Caroline, penetrated her heart with guilt, conviction, and brought unspeakable sorrow. Caroline repressed these feelings, turned and said, "I appreciate your concern, but you have to understand the anger and resentment that I feel over the circumstances of Charles' death. Because of some Yankee's bullet, Charles is gone. I have lost the only man that I have truly loved in this life," Caroline emotionally continued, as she broke forth in tears, "And Ann will be deprived of a relationship with her Father."

Katie answered with a quiver in her voice, "You don't know how often that I've prayed to God that this war would come to an end. I, too, am fearful for my brother, but also for Pete. My feelings for him have not changed. Often when the casualty list is posted on the bulletin board at the telegraph office, I, like others examine it. Its a horrifying experience to have a queasy stomach out of fear that the name of someone that you love might be posted under the dead."

Caroline promptly replied, "Maybe you'll be seeing Charles' name among them."

Katie's expression reflected the pain she was experiencing as she pleaded, "Again, I'm sorry. Please let me help."

With Katie's statement, Caroline turned and said as she walked toward the front door of the residence, "Katie, if you'll excuse me, I'd like to be alone. Good day."

As Caroline disappeared through the front door, Katie slowly walked down the stone steps to mount her horse. She took the reins from the servant and paused and gazed in the direction of the house. Katie's mind continued to be trouble by Caroline's coldness and reserved demeanor toward her. Maybe, she thought, there was some truth to William Pierce's confession concerning Pete and Caroline. It was beginning to make sense with Caroline making every attempt to exclude Katie from her life. With Charles deceased, there wouldn't be any obstacles that would stand in the way of Pete and Caroline being united. Katie rode slowly down the lane and then onto the Charlestown Pike toward the Ferry, continuously pondering her personal life.

After riding a short distance, Katie approached the crest of School House Ridge. It was such a lovely afternoon and there wasn't any rush to return to town. The sun was beginning to set beyond the horizon, producing a red-bluish glow in the western sky. Katie thought that she would be able to admire the scene and have a greater appreciation of nature from an area along the southern ridge that overlooked the Estate. At once, Katie turned her mount toward the area, and she attempted to sort out the confusion that had dominated her life.

A period of time had lapse as Katie noticed off in the distance Caroline leaving the mansion by the back entrance. It appeared that she was walking at a brisk pace toward the stable area. Katie continued to observe when suddenly, Caroline came bolting out of the stable mounted on her favorite stallion heading toward the river. Katie's curiosity was aroused, and she was suspicious of Caroline's intentions. With Caroline leaving at such haste, the question arose in Katie's mind that a reunion might be in the making between Pete and Caroline, since Confederate forces were in the area. Katie had to resolve the suspicions that she felt. Inconspicuously, she followed Caroline at a safe distance.

Caroline rode over Barker's ridge, south toward the river and then turning westward, riding along the trail that led in the direction of Kabletown. Shortly, Caroline came to the Robinson homestead that the Barkers had purchased before the war. The small farm was abandoned and had only been used to graze cattle and horses. Katie came to a grove of trees that offered her seclusion and a good view of the farmhouse, where Caroline was dismounting. Katie tied the reins of her horse to a small tree branch. Under the cover of increasing darkness, she quietly maneuvered her way, using some of the shrubs, underbrush, and out buildings to shelter her from detection by Caroline. There was a candlelight that appeared in the back window of the cabin. Katie was cautious and fearful of what she might discover when she looked through the small window. Katie's heart raced with anxiety, anticipation ruled, and the palms of her hands were moist from perspiration. Kneeling beneath the window ledge, Katie rose slowly to her feet. As Katie glanced through the window, there was surprise and relief at the scene she was witnessing. Charles wasn't dead as everyone was led to believe, but at this moment, he was embracing his wife. Katie inwardly rejoiced that Caroline was reunited with Charles instead of Pete. The only mystery that puzzled Katie was why did Caroline fabricate Charles' death. What was the couple up to, and whom were they attempting to deceive. Then once more as she kneeled beneath the window, the thought crossed her mind concerning William's visit. Katie began to wonder if he wasn't trying to deceive her for his own personal interest.

In a grove of underbrush and trees, Daniel quietly stood observing Katie.

CHAPTER THIRTY-ONE

Under the cover of darkness shortly before midnight on the 27th of June, Jeb Stuart's Confederate Cavalry crossed the Potomac River at Rower's Ford, about twenty miles west of Washington City. Once on the Maryland side of the river, Stuart's men destroyed boats, barges, and a portion of the Chesapeake and Ohio Canal, along with the capture of three hundred Federal soldiers. Near Rockville, the raiders surprised a large wagon train headed for Hookers Army, capturing most of the teamsters and the supplies they were transporting; the cavalrymen seized a total of 900 mules and 125 wagons. As the 6,000 Confederate cavalrymen moved into Pennsylvania, their pace was hampered by the captured wagons and animals that they were transporting for use by General Lee's forces. Since his departure from Virginia, Stuart had not been able to keep his line of communications open with the commanding general. The only means available to the cavalry leader in his attempt to verify the location of the main body of Confederate forces was his reliance on the information from his scouts, and the local newspapers.

As the Confederate cavalry moved into Pennsylvania, the rebels fought numerous engagements; the most significant was at Hanover. It wasn't until the afternoon of the 2nd of July, that Stuart opened communications with General Lee, and reported to the General's headquarters at a small village in Adams County called Gettysburg. It was there that many in Stuart's ranks discovered that the Army of the Potomac had received a new commander by the name of George Meade.

Near Carlisle, General Fitz Lee's brigade had been lobbing artillery shells into the town. With the knowledge of the fighting in Adams County, Lee received orders from Stuart for the brigade to withdraw, and protect the rear of the main cavalry columns, arriving late in the afternoon near Gettysburg. That evening, the men of the 1st Virginia, which belonged to Lee's brigade were allowed to rest after intense campaigning. News spread quickly through the ranks of the regiment concerning the bloody, and intensity of the fighting that had taken place around the village for the last two days. On the morning of the 3rd of July, it appeared that there would be another day of bloodshed and carnage. The men of the 1st Virginia were ordered to replenish their ammunition, and secure supplies in expectation of conflict that would take place today. It had been rumored that the cavalrymen would attempt to gain the flank and rear of the Union forces holding the ridges and hills around the village.

Pete Barker had only one magazine with six rounds of ammunition left when he rode the short distance with Jonathan and Lester to the supply wagons. Many of the cavalrymen were jovial as they mixed conversation; others shared humor as they filled their saddlebags. Some of the soldiers as in many engagements before preferred to remain silent, carrying somber expressions, though maliciously preparing for any event that confronted them. As the young Barker dismounted with his comrades, he removed his hat and wiped the perspiration from the brow of his forehead. Looking toward the heavens, Pete said to Jonathan, "With that bright red sun, the heat is sure to be unbearable today."

Jonathan replied as he spit some of the tobacco juice from his mouth, "Yeah, but I'd rather be home workin' them fields then out hear spendin' another day of killin'."

Lester sadly added as he rubbed the neck of his mare, "If I could just return home for a day, I would be satisfied. I haven't been home and seen Grace and my family since I departed three years ago."

Jonathan nodded in agreement as he replaced a magazine with rounds of ammunition in his revolver.

Pete was sure that the work ahead today would be deadly. He knew that Lester needed to get his mind off home and his love ones, and concentrate on the Confederate effort today. If Lester didn't, then he could easily become prey to a Yankee soldier's wrath. Pete walked over to Lester and reprimanded his cousin, "I know how you feel. It appears that today will be no different then the ones in the past. There is going to be fighting and bloodshed. But you need to remain alert and put home to the side for now."

Lester snapped as he turned about to face his cousin, "No, you don't know how I feel. Haven't you been home on different occasions? That is more then I have received."

Pete replied with calmness, though firm with his tone of voice, "Lester, that's enough. If you don't get your mind on what lies ahead of us today, you might go home in a way that you don't want."

Jonathan noticed that there was a glassy appearance in Lester's eyes. He quietly walked over to where Lester stood, placing his arm around him saying, "Ya better listen to ya cousin. He's only lookin' out for ya best interest. Just as you'd, I'm a hurtin' for my family."

By this time, many of the men of the first regiment were mounting and preparing to move into position. Pete said as he mounted his horse, "Let's go and hope that we can be successful today. And maybe, just maybe the Yanks will be willing to end their efforts of keeping us in the Union, then we can all return home."

Shortly, the main column of the Confederate cavalry was mounted, and moving along York Road, east of Gettysburg. As the men traveled toward their destination, they were especially quiet. It wasn't like previous occasions when the soldiers would sing songs, talk of home, or share some humorous stories. It was the first time since the invasion began, that it was quiet and the regiment wasn't engaging in battle with the enemy. Pete took advantage of the leisure to appreciate the beautiful farms and homesteads that covered the area. As in times past over the last three years, the fruit orchards, the grazing cattle, running horses, and most of all, the peace and serenity reminded him of his life at Shenandoah that he enjoyed before the war. He knew all to well the lost, loneliness, and sadness that his cousin was experiencing; it, too, had been a real difficult struggle for him. As Pete observed some of the cavalrymen riding toward their destination, he pondered the fate of some of his comrades like Ben Evans from Clarke County. Ben was a farmer, owning a small homestead overlooking the Shenandoah, a man of strong religious convictions, with a family of six children. Would Providence grant him the blessing of surviving this day without injury, Pete thought, or would Ben find a place on the casualty list in Berryville? Also, his concern turned toward his cousin Lester who was having extreme difficulty focusing on the reality of what was ahead. Pete thought, if he could help Lester through this campaign, then maybe he could intercede with their superiors on his behalf for a short furlough to return home.

As Pete continued to ponder on the issues in his cousin's life, there was a crashing roar from an artillery gun. Glancing in the direction of the noise, Pete determined that the gun was fired from a ridge southeast of the brigade's location. He looked at Jonathan, whose grin covered the width of his face, but remained silent. Lester appeared to show considerable concern.

With the sound of battle, Fitz Lee hastened his cavalrymen. In view of the brigade as they approached the area from where the artillery gun was fired, there was a ridge that was heavily populated with trees and thick undergrowth. There was an old dirt road that led to the crest of the ridge, which the brigade was instructed to use by their guide. As Lee's brigade arrived, every soldier knew that the fighting had commenced. Some of the dismounted Confederate cavalrymen, used as skirmishers were retreating toward the safety of the ridge after already battling dismounted Union cavalrymen. With an apparent lull in the battle, and the arrival of the full brigade, General Fitz Lee gave the order to advance toward the Federals. In a line of battle with sabers drawn, glisten in the bright sun, the brigade moved towards the enemy. The Federal artillery began to open a furious fire upon the brigade as the Confederates moved in perfect formation. In a short amount of time, the fire from the Federal cannons overwhelmed many of the troopers, and due to the Union gunners good aim and wrath, the Confederate cavalrymen began to retreat to an area along the left flank of Stuart's main forces. Along the ridge, a dense population of trees shielded the brigade with the 1st Virginia in the front, and on the left of Lee's brigade.

For the present, the men were relieved that they were not ordered to pursue the enemy, and given time to reorganize. Many of the cavalrymen began to light their pipes and casually open conversation to pass the time. Lester was mounted alongside of Pete in formation. Lester turned about in his saddle and said with a tone of remorse, "Pete, you were right about me not having my mind on my job."

Pete was rubbing the neck of his horse. Turning with a somber expression, he said, "Lester, I really do know how you feel, it's not easy living the way that we have chosen. Even though I can't call Shenandoah my home any more, for some reason I want to return. I have missed the life I once enjoyed, the barbecues, dances, but most of all, the tranquility of living along the river. I've been thinking that someday when this war is concluded, I'm going to purchase some of the property from Charles."

"When I return home, I am going to ask Grace to marry me, then hopefully, we can begin that family that I've been dreaming about for so long," replied Lester.

"I didn't know that you were that fond of her."

Lester removed his blue kepi, placing it over his heart saying in a Shakespearean tone, as he smiled, "Cousin, I didn't either, but being away from her for this amount of time has caused me to reflect on our relationship." Changing his tone to one of serious expression, Lester continued, "I have missed Grace more then I can find words to express."

After pausing and waiting for a response that didn't come from his cousin, Lester broke the silence and said, "What about your lady friend, don't you miss her?"

Pete remained quiet as he gazed at some of the dismounted Confederate cavalrymen to his front that were behind a fence near a white barn. Finally, Pete turned around facing his cousin and replied, "I have to admit, there are times that I think of her, especially at this moment."

Lester's curiosity compelled him to say, "You didn't answer my question. Don't you miss her?"

Pete shrugged his shoulders and replied with earnest, "There is something different about Katie. I guess for one thing, I have learned through different experiences that I can trust her. And I can speak my heart with her, without fearing judgment, if I'm wrong. You don't know how much I miss that."

A subtle grin covered Pete's expression as he quietly looked once more in the area of the homestead. Once more Lester became curious and pursued the subject by saying, "If I may ask, as I observe your grin, are you thinking about settling down with her."

"No, Lester. It's out of the question. Katie and I are from two different worlds, a different society with opposite views." Pete said, as he continued to observe the Confederate cavalrymen around the white barn opening fire against the enemy."

Lester desiring to continue the conversation, "You said that you've learned to trust her. If I may ask, what has happen in your life to cause you to feel this way?"

Pete answered as he observed General Stuart along the crest of the ridge directing the movements of his troops, "I've learned over the last three years that Katie McBride is a lady who is very much in touch with her feelings. She is firm and persistent in what she believes to be the truth. As I have enjoyed her company during our acquaintance, I've been open with her concerning my hurt and pain that I've experienced in my dealings with my family. She is sincere and confidential in her conversation and possesses strength in her words. Her word is reliable and unchallenged. And I know that she has sincere feelings for me. I just can't return them."

Lester smiled and said, "Does Katie presented a challenge for you? Maybe you love her, that's what your experiencing at this moment."

Pete promptly replied with a tone of defensiveness, "No, I don't think so."

Lester said as he removed his canteen from his mouth, "I know how your life is with the ladies. From correspondences received by my Mother from yours, she revealed how many hearts that you've broken in Jefferson County. Now someone has pierced yours, and you are not gentleman enough to admit it."

Pete glanced at his cousin with a defiant expression and said in the same tone of voice, "Lester, she is only a friend, nothing more. I can't allow myself to be bonded with anyone at this moment with a war taking place."

Lester said as he placed the cork on the mouth of the canteen, "That's no excuse. Pete, all jokes to the side, it makes no difference if Katie is from the North or elsewhere. The only thing that matters is if there is a love between you two."

Pete did not desire to share with his cousin the conversation that had taken place between him and Katie on his last visit to Harpers Ferry. He became defensive in tone, "Katie is just a friend that I can confide in, that's it, alright."

Lester gazed at the troublesome expression that ruled his cousin's features. He knew that the words that were spoken had penetrated his cousin's heart, and the reflection from Pete's heart was taking its toll, or else he wouldn't be so disturbed. Lester decided against pursuing the subject any further; Pete was too prideful to admit his feelings; something that he considered a weakness, and then too, maybe he didn't recognize his emotions for Katie. Hopefully, in the future the time would come when Pete wouldn't be able to secure any peace concerning her, or that some situation would occur that would enlighten him.

As Pete glanced at the white smoke and thundering sound of artillery that was rising in the distance toward Gettysburg, there were many thoughts that raced through his mind concerning Katie and the family. Then Pete's attention was focused upon his cousin. For some unknown reason, he felt queasiness in his stomach concerning Lester's fate.

Pete intensely observed a Confederate cavalry regiment begin an attack against the Union soldiers that were hidden behind a post-and-rail fence. The fire from the Federal riflemen was intense, but soon began to slacken. With this change of event, General Lee ordered the 1st Virginia forward. From the shelter of the trees, the Confederate cavalry moved forward slowly in parade like fashion with the battle flag and the regimental standard fluttering in the breeze. The men removed their sabers from their scabbards and placed the blunt end along their right shoulder. There was a reflection of pride that covered the face of the men of the regiment, more so Pete thought, then in times past. Pete glanced at his cousin and said, "Lester, this may be the most intense fighting that we've experienced thus far in this war. Remember, the fire is going to get heavy, keep your mind on what's going on!"

With a tone of reassurance in his voice, Lester replied, "Don't worry, we are going to make short work of these Yanks like times in the past. Watch them skiddadle as we approach their lines."

As Pete glanced about, he noticed dismounted cavalrymen from some of the other regiments of the brigade moving alongside them to provide support for the attack. The Virginians continued their approach, when suddenly, the Federals that were behind the fence opened a weathering fire at the cavalrymen from various directions. The 1st promptly responded with some of the soldiers dismounting and returning an intense volley of deadly missiles from behind a fence. Pete glanced at Lester, who was unnecessarily exposing himself to gain a greater aim and accuracy in discharging his weapon. Pete shouted, "What are you doing, trying to get yourself killed!"

With the loud noise caused by the firing of weapons during the engagement, Lester didn't hear Pete and wasn't able to respond. Bullets were whizzing and making a thudding sound as they struck the wooden fence that protected the cavalrymen. Without considering his own safety, Pete boldly leaped to his feet and grabbed his cousin by his blouse and pulled him to the ground.

Lester yelled as he looked up, "What are you doing?"

Pete snapped as he held him to the ground, "I'm trying to save your life. You are needlessly exposing yourself and placing your life in jeopardy."

As Pete glanced about to survey the fighting between the rebels and their foe, it appeared that the casualties would be high. Near the area where Pete was shielded by the fence, he heard the anguish of the wounded, and noticed several of the men rolling about with members of their abdomen hanging freely from their body. Pete heard the warning cry of Jonathan, "A body of horsemen approachin' to the right."

Immediately, Pete replaced the empty magazine in his revolver. At the head of the approaching Union cavalry formation, an officer was waving his saber and exhorting his troops forward. Momentarily, Pete watched the Federal cavalry regiment as they slashed their way through the first Confederate defenders on the right flank of the 1st Virginia. As some of the Federals rode through the Confederate ranks, Pete rose to his feet, aiming with his revolver at the Federal officer that continued to shout commands; he pulled the trigger of his pistol. The weapon misfired. Pete was sure that if the revolver had functioned properly, he would have wounded the Federal officer, thus, discouraging any further advance by the attacking columns.

The Federal cavalry, and the dismounted Federal troopers to the front of the Confederates began to withdraw. Pete and Lester remounted their horses, and with the rest of the regiment, charged the Federals. Within minutes, the Confederate horsemen clashed with the mounted Federals. Pete, like many of the other riders, both blue and gray toppled to the ground from the enormous impact of the collision caused by the horses. As Pete rolled free from the wounded animal, he removed the second pistol that he was carrying and began to fire at the enemy. The cavalrymen from both sides created much confusion, inter-mingled in combat. As Pete kept up a steady fire, he glanced about. Some of the soldier's sabers produced a crashing sound as one warrior attempted to thrust the other with his weapon. There was the intense popping sound of pistols being fired between the combatants at close range, and both blue and gray shouted curses for their foe to surrender. A Yankee came from behind Pete, jumping from his horse, he wrestled the young Barker to the ground. As the two combatants rolled among the fallen horses, each man attempted to gain the upper hand. The Yankee placed one hand around Pete's throat, and used a knife in the other hand in an attempt to stab Pete in his chest. Both of the worriers had a desperate expression covering their face as they attempted to subdue the other. Pete held the wrist of the Yankee's hand that contained the weapon, and with his right hand, he struck his enemy with a large rock. The Yankee rolled from Pete unconscious. As Pete lay on the ground in an attempt to regain his breath, he glanced about to witness the confusion, cursing, and shouts of intimidation between the combatants. Frantically, his eyes searched the grounds for Lester. He noticed his cousin about twenty yards to his left dismounted, shooting at some Federals as they raced toward him on their mounts. Quickly, Pete rose to his feet. Grabbing a pistol from the ground, he rushed to his cousin's aide. Pete witness Lester attempting to discharge his pistol, but it too, misfired. Pete's expression revealed the fear that he had conceived earlier for Lester's life, knowing that he was easy prey for the oncoming enemy. As one of the Federals approached, he raised his left arm, with saber in hand, and delivered a slashing movement at Lester, but he quickly ducked the blow. Swiftly, Pete began to discharge his weapon, killing the Federal as he rode by. Turning his attention once more in an attempt to aide his cousin, Pete witnesses the second Yankee rider thrust Lester across the back of his neck, causing him to drop his saber and pistol. As Lester cried with pain and began to slump toward the ground wounded, the Yankee raised his saber toward the sky; he stood in his saddle lowering the weapon across the side of Lester's head. The blood from his cousin's wound splattered across Pete's face as he approached. Instantly, Pete raised the weapon and pulled the trigger, but the weapon wouldn't discharge its missile. Immediately, the Yankee turned his attention toward Pete, gritting his teeth in a display of anger. The Yankee yelled, "Burn in hell Johnnie," thrusting his saber at Pete's upper body piercing his blouse. As the Yankee prepared for another assault, Pete grabbed Lester's saber from the ground, raising it above his head to protect against the next thrust, which was being delivered by his foe. As Pete and the Yankee battled to gain the upper hand, Ben Evans rode alongside of the Yankee and shot him in the head. The Yankee soldier fell from his horse to the ground holding his face with his hands, and cursing the two rebels. The struggle between the combatants was ending with cavalrymen from both sides returning to their lines of defense. Pete looked in Lester's direction. He was laying on the ground crying in unbearable agony, "Oh God, help me please, please." With Lester's saber still in his hand, Pete rushed at the sound of his cousin's plead. As he knelt by Lester's side, he was shocked and horrified with unbelief at the amount of blood that was pouring from the ghastly head wound. Anger and rage surfaced within Pete's heart as he quickly jumped to his feet. Rushing over to where the Yankee was continuing to suffer from his wound, Pete raised the sword to thrust it through the Yankee's body in an attempt to quench his emotions. Suddenly, Jonathan grabbed the weapon from his hand.

Pete continued to manifest his anger saying as he attempted to break free from his comrade, "I want to kill him. He doesn't deserve to live."

Jonathan shouted loudly, "That's not for ya to decide. Killin' that Yank, as he lays there defenseless would be murder. Remember last year at Sharpsburg when ya stood between the dying Yank, and a Reb that was about to steal from him."

Pete's anger began to subside, "Yes. Yes I do."

Jonathan said assuredly, as he knelt beside the wounded Yankee and removed the pistol that was lying near him, "Besides, he'll be dead by sundown."

Pete returned the saber to the scabbard and walked with Jonathan to where Ben Evans was tending to Lester's wound. By now, Lester was unconscious and breathing heavy. Ben looked up at Pete and sadly said, "It looks deep. I don't think he is going to make it."

Tears began to fill Pete and Jonathan's eyes. They had become very close over the last three years, just like brothers. Ben suggested as he looked about the battlefield, "I think we better git Lester out of here before we discover what the inside of a Yankee prisoner-of-war camp looks like."

With Jonathan covering Pete and Ben, they placed Lester on a horse and swiftly proceeded toward the ridge. There, to receive Lester and attend to his injuries was several members of the Medical Corps. As they placed Lester on a litter, the soldier appeared lifeless. Pete was quite shaken by the intensity of the engagement, and the suffering that his cousin had experienced. Pete had to have time for himself. Inconspicuously, he walked into the woods and emptied the contents of his stomach. As he stared into the sunny-blue sky, he could only hope that Providence would give Lester the will to live.

CHAPTER THIRTY-TWO

For the 1ˢᵗ Virginia Cavalry, it had been a difficult, tedious, and costly mission since their departure from the outskirts of Gettysburg on the morning of the 5th of July. The regiment, along with the rest of General Fitz Lee's brigade had been assigned to protect the rear and flank of the retreating wagon train that carried the wounded toward the Potomac River across the rugged roads of Pennsylvania and Maryland. Throughout the journey, the Federal cavalry had been harassing the wagon train with hit and run raids that had cost the Confederates in artillery guns, wagons, and soldiers captured, either wounded or in combat, not to say, the struggle with the muddy roads caused by heavy rains. As the long train neared the river, Federal cavalry attacked the Confederates. The battle was continuing when the 1ˢᵗ Virginia arrived to help repulse the Federal advance on the wagon train, capturing over 100 prisoners that were not able to reach their horses in time.

After the engagement, Pete Barker was anxious to know Lester's welfare. When the wagon train departed Gettysburg, late on the afternoon of the 4th of July, his cousin was still clinging to life. From his experience of riding within a close distance of the wagons, Pete could only imagine the suffering that the wounded soldiers endured, especially his cousin. At one time during the slow journey, he heard the cries of a wounded Confederate soldier pleading for someone to have mercy, and to relieve him of his misery by shooting him; allowing death to relieve the agony that he experienced. Still, some of the wounded soldiers cursed, and pleaded for the wagon masters to stop the wagons and allow them to die along the side of the road. Constantly, during the rugged trip, almost all of the suffering cried, or spoke of a loved one. Pete discovered, as he had approached one wagon that there wasn't anything of comfort for the wounded soldiers to rest their bodies on, only the wooden boards that made up the floor of the wagon.

Because of the heavy rainfall over the last several days, the Potomac had risen rapidly, and the wagon train carrying the wounded was unable to cross the deep waters. It was late in the afternoon, and all of the fighting had ceased with the Federals retreating toward Boonsboro. With time to rest, Pete and Jonathan were given the opportunity to locate Lester. On the journey from Pennsylvania, Pete hadn't received any information concerning his cousin's fate. He was very anxious to know of his welfare.

As the two cavalrymen neared the area where some of the wagons were located, Jonathan noticed surgeons laboring feverishly to preserve a life. Many of the wounded laid in rows groaning with pain waiting for medical attention; still, some of the Confederates had departed this world through death, their misery concluded. At times, Pete and Jonathan held handkerchiefs against their face because of the dreadful smell that some of the wounds produced because of the lack of medical attention on the journey from Gettysburg. Finally, Jonathan grabbed Pete by the arm and pointed in the direction of a wagon that was near a tree. The two cavalrymen walked toward the area, and there, they found Lester lying beside of the wheel of the wagon on his coat. Pete was somber and quiet as he glanced at the appearance of his cousin. Lester's wound was slowly oozing. There was dried blood covering his black and gold-checkered blouse; his red hair matted against the wound. Pete knelt along the side of Lester, placing his hand on his chest. He remained unconscious, and his breathing appeared to be shallow. Fearing that Lester's death was pending, Pete said as he covered his face with his dirty hands, "It's my fault, it's all my fault."

Jonathan knelt along the side of Pete, placing his hand around his friend's shoulders. He calmly spoke slowly as he gazed at his wounded friend, "Pete, there was a lot of confusion. It's every man for himself when ya in the middle of the enemy a fightin' like we did. There's no way that ya could have known, specially with ya horse rollin' over on ya."

Pete replied angrily, "If I would have been by his side, the odds against him wouldn't have prevailed. Jonathan, throughout the morning I had a premonition that something was going to happen to him. But I didn't know how I was going to prevent it from coming to pass."

Jonathan answered as he took some of the water from his canteen and placed it on his handkerchief to moisten Lester's dry lips, and to clean the blood from around the area of Lester's wound, "Sometimes things are just meant to be, and ya can't do anything to keep it from happenin'."

Pete turned and gazed at Jonathan with a puzzled expression on his face. He wasn't certain of the meaning of his friend's statement. Apparently Pete concluded Jonathan believed everything in life was predestine to happen, and there wasn't anything that one could do to control the issue.

The next afternoon, Pete and Jonathan were ordered by General Stuart to take part in a reconnaissance with two other scouts toward Boonsboro. As the scouting party approached the outskirts of Funkstown, the Confederates came to a pause. The Lieutenant in command studied the roads that led to Boonsboro, and another toward the Potomac River. The officer's silence was broken as he shared his thoughts, "Barker, I think that this road to my right cuts back to the river. If the Yanks are to our front, then I feel that it is important that we are certain that our flank is protected, and they don't maneuver into our rear. I want you and Collins to take that road."

Pete and Jonathan saluted as they replied, "Yes, sir."

The two cavalrymen traveled about a mile, when they came upon the rear of a Federal cavalry patrol. Quietly, Pete and Jonathan left the road and took cover behind some out buildings. As the two Confederates observed the Federal cavalrymen, Jonathan said, "What do ya think that they are up to?"

Pete replied as he intensely observed the enemy, "I don't know, but I feel that we should follow them and try to get a better look."

Jonathan disagreed as he turned to look at his friend, "I don't think so. Maybe we should just rest here for a spell and see if dey return."

Pete turned in his saddle and commanded, "No, we need to get a better look. I want to know what they are up to."

The two Confederates cautiously rode along the road with their revolvers ready. As they approached an area along the road that was covered with trees and underbrush, they came to a halt and paused for a moment. For Pete it was very quiet, almost too quiet, he felt that something was wrong. Pete and Jonathan's eyes peered through the heavily wooded landscape, and across some of the open fields that were to their rear. As Pete turned to speak to his friend, a single shot rang out, he felt an excruciating pain in his right side. The blow felt like someone hit him with a clinch fist; he began to breathe heavy.

Immediately, Jonathan returned fire in the direction from where the shot came; the Yankee was silenced with Jonathan's perfect aim. There was a fearful expression that covered his face as he witnessed Pete removing his hand from the area of the lower abdomen; Pete was covered with blood. As Pete leaned forth in the saddle, looking in Jonathan's direction, he said, "I'm hit! I think it's bad."

Jonathan said as he heard the sound of horses approaching, "I will cover ya while ya get away."

Pete shouted as he held his hand against his side in an attempt to retard the bleeding, "No, you must leave, too. Someone must warn…."

In an attempt to remain conscious, Pete shook his head. Just as the Federals appeared along the road to their front, Jonathan turned Pete's mount, and struck the hindquarter, causing the animal to gallop toward Funkstown. Jonathan dismounted and opened an intense fire on the approaching enemy, using an old log on a small slope that bordered the dirt road. As Pete's horse proceeded at a fast gallop, he turned to witness Jonathan waving a white handkerchief, symbolizing his surrender to the Federals.

Along the dirt road, there was a wooded bend that obstructed Pete's view from determining if he was being followed by the Federals. Pete knew that the Federals would be searching for him once they had secured his friend as their prisoner. As Pete approached the homestead where Jonathan and he had observed the Federals earlier, he noticed a white weatherboard farmhouse sitting on a knoll surrounded by some trees. It was difficult for the young Barker to remain conscious, laying his head on the neck of his horse and continuing to apply pressure to his side. After easing himself to the ground, he noticed that the house and the surroundings appeared to be deserted. Using a carbine rifle as a crutch, he slowly, painfully, and gradually made his way to the front entrance of the house. The door was unlocked when Pete opened it. As he stumbled through the opening, he saw a young woman standing by a stone fireplace. He softly pleaded, "Please help me." Afterward, Pete lost consciousness and fell on the wooden floor.

The young woman was terrified at the sight of the wounded Confederate. It was the first time that she had witnessed the devastation and horrors that war can cause. She cautiously approached the injured soldier. After searching his haversack, she recognized him to be a Confederate soldier. He must be one of the cavalrymen that she recognized behind the out buildings earlier. As the lady was attending to Pete, she heard the muffled sound of horses approaching. She glanced out the front window, noticing Federal cavalry along the road near the entrance to the farm. Knowing that they were probably looking for the wounded Confederate, the young lady briefly thought of what her next move would be. Should she surrender the Confederate to them, or shield him to fight another day? There had been rumors in the community concerning the horrors of various diseases and death that confinement brought by being a prisoner-of-war, still as she glanced at the rebel, there wasn't the greatest hope that he would live to witness another sunrise.

The Federals soon paused at the entrance to the farm. The lady glanced over at the motionless body of the Confederate, and then once more turned her attention toward the Federals. Some of the troopers continued toward the village, while four of the Yankees cautiously made their approach to the house. The young lady had heard of executions, by both the blue and gray of prisoners from various local individuals living in the area. It was her fear that the Federal troopers may remove the Confederate to the front of the property and deprive him of life in that fashion. Even though she was sympathetic to the Northern cause, this kind of action, she thought, would bring unbearable condemnation and guilt upon her. Quickly, she decided to hide him. In one area of the house in the dinning room, there were some loose floorboards in the corner of the room near a window where a small four-legged table stood. Before the war, Hannah and her husband used the hiding place under the floor to conceal runaway slaves that were fleeing to freedom in the North. By the sound of the horse's hooves pounding the dirt lane to the front of the house, she knew that the Federal cavalrymen were near. The young lady was small in statue and petite in weight, making it difficult to move Pete from the parlor to the hiding place under the floor. She wasn't willing to surrender to the advantage of size, but scrambled with haste to accomplish the challenge, occasionally removing her long dark hair from shielding her gray eyes. About the time that she placed his body in the trench under the flooring, there was a loud knock at the front door. Promptly, she returned the table to its rightful place, and with gaining a normal breathing pattern; the lady opened the front door. There on the front porch stood three Yankee cavalrymen covered with dirt and dust with a fourth holding the reins of the horses. One of the Federals, a Sergeant tipped the bill of his blue kepi and said in a graveled voice, "Madam, I'm Sergeant Barnes with the 18th Pennsylvania Cavalry."

The lady replied as she gazed at the soldier, "Sergeant, I'm Hannah Graceham. What brings you to my home?"

As several of the soldiers glanced about the property looking for the fugitive, the Sergeant fixed his eyes on Hannah and said, "A mile or so back down the road, some of my men fire on several rebels. We were able to capture one, the other we believe has been seriously injured by our gun fire."

Hannah cautiously answered knowing that the penalty for protecting the enemy could be imprisonment, confiscation of her property, or the farm being destroyed by fire. "Oh, I see. I remembered earlier two Confederates snooping around the outbuildings about an hour ago. I didn't dare approach them for fear that they would harm me."

With a half-hearted laugh, the soldier said, as he made a gestured with his hand for several of his comrades toward the buildings, "Well just the same, if you don't mine, we'd like to look around to satisfy ourselves on this matter." The soldier paused and then continued as he removed his revolver, "And that includes the house.

Hannah was flushed; she answered fearfully, "Sergeant, why would I help a rebel, especially since my husband David is serving with the 5th Maryland. My loyalty is with the Union."

The Sergeant answered sternly, "Now, if you don't mine, I would like to search the house."

Hannah softly said, as she stepped to the side of the entrance, "Go ahead."

With his pistol ready, the Sergeant entered the parlor, looking about for any clues of the fugitive. From the parlor, the soldier walked slowly into the dinning room. There, he walked and stood in the area of the floor that concealed Pete's body. Without showing any fear, Hannah, walked quietly behind the Federal soldier. In the area where the hideaway had been constructed, there was a window that had given Hannah and her husband an unobstructed view of the property coming from the direction of the village. From this vantage point, the couple could notice anyone approaching the residence and have ample warning to conceal the runaway slaves. It also provided them with a view of the property in the area of the barn, which provided for a rapid escape. As the Sergeant glanced through the window, he noticed his comrades diligently searching the premises. He turned to move away from the window and heard the flooring creak under his weight. The Yankee said, "The floor has a noisy creaking sound to it. You must have some loose floor boards."

Hannah answered as she attempted to repress the nervousness that she was experiencing, "It's been difficult trying to keep up the property by myself during my husband's absence."

Sergeant Barnes replied as he kneeled down to check the flooring, "Then I assume that you're the only occupant on the premise."

"Yes, that's correct."

Being content that the lady had nothing to hide on the lower level, the Federal slowly walked up the creaky stairway that led to the bedrooms on the second floor. Hannah didn't follow him, but could hear the Yankee walking around from room to room. As he made his way down the short stairway, Hannah noticed that there was still some blood covering the wooden floor near a chair where Pete had fallen unconscious. Acting quickly, Hannah moved inconspicuously to the area, and stood, concealing the evidence from Sergeant Barnes. Finally after being convinced, the Sergeant said, "Madam, I apologize for any inconvenience that we may have caused you. My men and I will be leaving."

Hannah remained quiet as Sergeant Barnes departed. She briefly watched the troopers disappear heading in the direction of the village. When she knew that it was safe, Hannah removed the floorboards and kneeled, gazing upon Pete's motionless body looking for signs of life.

CHAPTER THIRTY-THREE

After a rainy week, the sun peered its glowing bright rays through Solomon's Gap; the sunlight reflecting had a glossing effect on the Potomac River. The beautiful cloudless Tuesday morning promised to be a typical summer day. With Lee's invasion of the northern territory, many of the citizens had vacated Harpers Ferry, but still, the few that lived in the village had begun their labor and activities for the morning. They were not the only ones who were busy this early in the dawn hours. The Federal Armies' Engineering Corp was busily repairing the bridge that had been damaged for their infantry to cross in an attempt to intercept the Confederate forces fording the river near Williamsport. After two weeks, the residences of the town had been unaware of the major engagement that had taken place on Northern soil. It wasn't until several days previous that the townspeople had learned from a Federal officer the devastation and carnage that had taken place. Like many, Katie McBride was among those who had received the news of the thousands of causalities that covered the fields surrounding the village of Gettysburg.

For the first time since the outbreak of hostilities, Katie hadn't only experienced fear, but a premonition of Pete Barker's fate. She had known for several days that something was terribly wrong. Katie spent the nights tossing and turning, but when her mind would rest, she found sleep, only to be awakened by a bad dream. The turmoil taking place in Katie's heart and mind was unbearable, even to the point of helpless frustration.

On this morning, Katie was abruptly awakened by such a dream. Her heart was racing with intensity, and Katie's body was clammy with perspiration. Anxiety ruled Katie's emotions, fright filled her heart, and tears flowed from her tired blood-shot eyes. The dream that Katie experienced was so vivid and real. It was as if she had actually been there as a by-stander and witnessed the whole event. The picture was so clear, her memory alert to the horrors of the experience. As she sat alongside of the bed, Katie thought about what she had seen in the dream. She recalled sitting on a beautiful hill that overlooked a valley covered with lush green meadows, multiple colored wild flowers, and a small stream where the water was so clear that one could see the fish freely swimming beneath it's surface. The birds were serenading in a perfect concert of harmony, and there were no pressing matters in life to fear. It was so peaceful and serene, and tranquilly was easily found, no money could purchase the bliss. As Katie glanced at the perfect blue sky, she observed the horizon that was changing with every passing moment; the sky began to darken until it became frightful. In the distance the peace, serenity, and tranquility was broken by the cries of pain, anguish, and agony. The words of many voices were so clear and articulate pleading in unison for a family member. Thunder-like roar, many reddish glows of flashes, bellows of white smoke, and the smell of powder from the many cannons and musketry filled the air. As her attention returned to the valley below, she witnessed thousands of warriors dressed in blue and gray uniforms engaged in the fury, wrath, and deadly destruction of war. In the mist of the fighting, Katie was attracted to one of the gray warriors, who stood out among the rest of the army engaging an enemy warrior in hand-to-hand combat. After the gray warrior subdued his enemy, he fought boldly with furiousness against another, and still many more, striking them with his sword. The fighting appeared to increase with many more warriors dressed in blue reinforcing their comrades. Within little time, the gray warrior and his comrades were outnumbered, though they bravely continued the contest, until suddenly, the gray warrior fell by the sword.

Katie continued to be horrified and distressed as her mind returned to reality. With haste, Katie dressed and ran to the telegraph office where the casualty list was posted daily on the bulletin board. She noticed upon her arrival that many of the townspeople were present, and examining the names of soldiers wounded, missing, and killed in battle at Gettysburg. Katie cried impatiently for the crowd to step aside, allowing her to maneuver toward the front. Frantically gazing across the list of names, Katie noticed that Lester had been wounded and Jonathan captured. It was known by Katie from conversation with Pete that these two men were either related to him or a good friend. With her eyes moving as quickly as her fingers scouring the list, Katie finally found Pete's name under the combatants that were deceased. The tears flowed intensely from her eyes. As some of the female citizens of the town grieved and expressed their sorrow concerning a love one, Katie walked slowly to a wooden bench near the entranceway to the depot, and nearly collapsed from the horror and shock that she was experiencing. In the twenty-three years of her life, Katie had not known this kind of grief and pain. As Katie glanced toward the direction of Maryland Heights, the thought continually tormented the young lady of life without Pete Barker. Even though Pete and Katie had not seen each other since last September, Katie still felt closeness to Pete, always keeping him near her heart.

After walking along the river, Katie returned to her residence where Mrs. McDonald was standing near the front door to meet her. Katie was looking down at the ground as she approached the wooden steps that led to the porch, deep in thought over the unexpected change that was taking place in her life concerning Pete.

Mrs. McDonald, quietly noticed Katie as she slowly made her way up the long flight of steps. As Katie lifted her head and looked at her landlord, Mrs. McDonald immediately recognized the troubled expression and red-glassy eyes that consumed Katie's features. Mrs. McDonald knew that the young lady had received troubling news. Always with a heart of compassion, the elderly lady reached out to individuals in need, regardless of their passions concerning the Northern, or Southern cause. Mrs. McDonald's compassion compelled her to comfort Katie, "Oh dear child. What is the matter?"

As Katie began to openly weep, Mrs. McDonald immediately embraced the young lady, who continued to cry as a child on her shoulders. Mrs. McDonald knew from her many years of experience in dealing with such tragedy among parishioner from the Church, how to comfort, and the words to speak in these particular situations. It was without bias that Katie wouldn't be an exception since she was from Massachusetts. After allowing Katie time to weep, Mrs. McDonald sat her gently on the swing and gave her water to drink. Finding that Katie was somewhat more composed, Mrs. McDonald asked, "My dear child, what troubles your heart today."

Katie was holding a white handkerchief to her face when she replied in a murmur, "This morning, I went to the telegraph office after having another bad dream, to look at the casualty list from Gettysburg." Katie continued as she wiped the tears from her eyes, and sniffling, she said, "I was frantic with anxiety because I knew that something had happen to my friend Pete Barker. For sometime now, I have had this premonition in my heart that something was going to happen to him."

Mrs. McDonald finished Katie's reply when the young lady was unable, "And you found his name on the casualty list?"

Katie murmured softly as she wept, "Yes, I did. I was so shocked that I thought that I might faint. Oh, I just can't imagine my life without him."

For some unknown reason to Katie, there was a gentle smile, like an angel that covered Mrs. McDonald's face. The words that this woman of wisdom shared with Katie penetrated her heart and mind, and she needed to hear, "My child, tragedy is something that we all experience in this life, and it seems to strike us when we least expect it to happen. This war has taken a terrible toll on families' both from the Northern states as well as the Southern. Today, many such as yourself grieve with pain over a loved one that will never come home." Mrs. McDonald glanced at the beautiful red roses that were blooming on the bush in front of her residence. Pausing momentarily, it reminded her of an incident that had taken place in her life many years ago, which she felt at this time would be appropriate to share with Katie, "Many years ago when I was living in the southwestern area of Virginia, I was very young such as yourself, and so deeply in love with a gentleman, who was a blacksmith. Constantly, my Mason was in my thoughts and heart. I remember on many occasions when he wasn't with me, how that I would dwell on the words that he had spoken the day before, or just maybe, the quietness of the evening when he would hold me in his arms. Then the war with England began, and Mason volunteered for service. And then one day as I was tending to my rose garden, a neighbor informed me that he had been killed in a battle near Baltimore. At the time of Mason's death, I was stricken with all the same shock and grief that you, my child are experiencing. I believed that my love was like a rose that was trampled upon by death. My life had been robbed and stripped of the only thing that had any meaning or purpose. If you will look," Mrs. McDonald continued, as Katie looked in the direction of the flowers, "Just as you can see those beautiful roses that are full of life this morning, I have discovered that ones life must continue, and no matter how difficult the tragedy that you've endured. Oh yes, it is difficult, you'll feel that your unable to function, but you'll learn to, and in time find love once more."

Katie sighed and said softly, "At one time, I did love someone back home. Unfortunately, he met death in an accident. But what I felt for him, and the depth of my love that I've experienced for Pete is much different."

Mrs. McDonald gazed at Katie with a soft and warm expression covering her face and replied, "I have discovered that it is the life that we have planned to live and share with that special someone; the expectations of a future and having a family one day, which vanishes from us. Sometimes during the evening when I'm alone, I reach into the memories of my heart and see Mason and joyfully remember the times that we spent together, whether they were good, or difficult. I will always hold to those pictures in my heart for as long as I live. It doesn't cause the pain to vanish, but it does make my life easier, even after all of these years." Pausing and softly continuing with a smile, Mrs. McDonald said, "And still after all of these years, when I smell the fragrant of those roses, I am reminded of the love which Mason and I shared together." Pausing and turning about with her eyes fixed upon Katie, "My dear child, I will always eternally love him and hold his life with reverence in my heart."

In the early afternoon, once Katie was composed, she traveled to Shenandoah to pay her respects to Elizabeth and Caroline. As Katie approached the Estate, she was reminded of joyful times from the past when Pete was present, especially, the afternoon when she was invited by him to partake of a picnic along the river. Within her heart and mind, Katie thought about the excitement as she watched Pete approaching from the ridge to greet her and the joyful smile that covered his face. The occasion along the river was unexpected for both Pete and Katie as they opened their hearts and revealed many intimate passions concerning their personal lives. It was the first time, she thought, that Pete was attempting to be open with his life, and share with her the many pains that he had experienced, without feeling threaten, or vulnerable. If only the news of the bombardment of Fort Sumter hadn't been received that afternoon, and war wouldn't have commenced, then maybe the couple would have been together today. Again as Katie approached the mansion, it was difficult for her to withhold the grief and tears from her eyes.

It was very quiet as Katie dismounted from the stallion that she was riding. Katie noticed that many of the slaves that would be laboring around the premises had disappeared. Naturally, she assumed that they had escaped during Federal occupation of the area, and with the Emancipation that Lincoln had issued earlier in the year, giving them their freedom by law. As Katie stood at the entrance to the mansion, her eyes glanced about the property; her heart was burden with grief. Everywhere Katie glanced, she could see Pete with Hayward going about the chores, or speaking with some of the slaves, but most of all, his jovial smile and innocent expression.

Turning once more toward the door, Katie began to think of the words that she would say. Still, she and Caroline were experiencing strain relations over the war. Katie hoped that with the death of Pete, the bitterness that the family must be experiencing might be expressed toward her. With the compassion and humbleness that was her virtue, she fully understood and was mentally prepared for any event.

After knocking twice on the huge wooden door, there was no answer. Finally the third time, Matthew slowly opened the door. There was a somber expression that covered his features; he was quiet as she walked through the doorway. Matthew closed the door as Katie glanced about the lifeless dwelling. As Katie turned to face the servant, she softly asked, "Matthew, is Caroline at home?"

"No mam. Miss Caroline, she is visitin' with her family. Wes' spect her to return dis day."

"Then I must assume that Miss Elizabeth is with her?"

From the distance hallway came a soft, broken sounding voice, "No, Katie. I am here."

As Katie approached Elizabeth, her features appeared tired, lifeless, and aged. Katie looked at the red swollen eyes of the matriarch and could tell that she was broken in spirit. Katie softly said, "You know about Pete?"

As Elizabeth held a white handkerchief to her face, she softly replied, "Yes, I received the news this morning from Daniel."

"I came because I wanted to pay my respects to you and Caroline."

"Thank you for your consideration to the family." Elizabeth paused momentarily, and continued to softly speak, "It must have been difficult for you to receive the news."

"It was. And I will continue to experience difficulty with his death for sometime. My life will never be the same without him."

Elizabeth promptly answered as she looked at Katie, "I know. It was apparent to the family that you had acquired feelings for him."

With boldness and confidence, Katie replied as she approached Elizabeth, "Do you mean that I was in love with him? Yes, I was. And I will always love him until the day that I die. I really don't believe that there will ever be another to take his place."

Elizabeth wasn't only experiencing grief and sorrow over the death of her son, but too, the condemnation and guilt over the trespasses that were committed against him. With two sons lost to the cause, Elizabeth did not believe that she should withhold the revelation and truth concerning her actions against Pete, and the decision on ownership of the Estate. Elizabeth needed to purge her heart and mind of this fiery issue, beginning with Katie. As Elizabeth glanced at the sorrowful, innocent eyes of Katie McBride, she invited the young lady to join her in the parlor. After asking Matthew that the two of them not be disturbed, Elizabeth began to confess, "Katie, as I have journeyed through this life, I have experienced many blows. Most of them, I survived, or learn to deal with the issue. But one never can deal with the death of a loved one, especially two sons in such a short period of time. As I sit here looking at you, I have always believed that I loved Charles as much as I loved Pete. Though, by my actions of giving Charles the ownership of the Estate at the beginning of the war, you probably don't agree that my love was just as equal toward one, as the other."

Katie gazed at Elizabeth, pausing momentarily, and methodically choosing her words, "No, I don't. It was difficult for me to understand why you could hold one son in such high esteem, and reward him, while the other son you took and cast off. In my discussions with Pete, I knew that he was deeply hurt and troubled by your actions. He believed that it was always your intentions to hand down the Estate to Charles and him. When he told me of your actions, I must confess, I was surprised and troubled knowing that it was going to cause division and strife within your family." Elizabeth remained silent as Katie continued with a tone of anger in her voice, "When I arrived earlier, the property appeared to be lifeless, and its prosperity vanished like a vapor on a cold winter evening. I guess now neither son will reap the benefit of ownership."

Elizabeth wept momentarily as Katie withheld her anger. Afterward, Elizabeth said, "You are justified in being angry with me."

Katie was shocked and stunned by the revelation, "How could you do something like this? I can't believe that someone would stoop so low in an attempt to destroy another human being, especially your own flesh and blood?"

After regaining her composure, Elizabeth continued to explain her actions,

"Katie, it was my intentions of protecting my family and our way of life. I knew that with Charles, I could control his decisions and actions, and in reality still remain in control of the Estate, still allowing him the feeling of ownership and accomplishing something in his life. Katie, Charles has always been loyal to me, and in every situation he has regarded my wishes in the highest. As for Pete, he was always in total opposition to Charles and myself and our vision. In almost every issue and business dealing that this family embarked on, Pete was in disagreement, with the idea of having a more prosperous, and most of the time, a more honorable way of doing business. He was very much like his Father in his ways, a rebel."

"No, Pete wasn't a rebel. His desire was to just be himself and to make his own decisions. And just because you couldn't master him, he rebelled and you took your anger and dissatisfaction out on him. I believe after listening to you, that it was your intentions to use the Estate to reward Charles for his obedience, and at the same time, it was your punishment upon Pete."

Elizabeth's voice began to quiver as she answered, "Yes Katie. You are correct in your observations. I'm so sorry."

Katie stood on her feet saying as she placed her gloves on her hands for the return journey to town, "Also Miss Elizabeth, it wouldn't surprise me in the least if your actions didn't reveal the animosity that you felt, I'm so sure against me too, since I'm from the North and our views are different. Actually, the real fear that I believe that you experienced was the reality that Pete and I would have continued to experience a relationship that may have led to marriage. Most likely, you experienced so much distrust for me, that I was the real threat to your way of life, not Mr. Lincoln, nor the Yankees."

Immediately, without another word, Katie turned and walked away from Elizabeth's presence believing that the matriarch's actions reflected the hatred that she felt for her. On the return trip to Harpers Ferry, Katie's anger wasn't overshadowing her grief and sorrow, but the hurt and pain concerning Elizabeth's revelation was more then she could bear. It was because of Elizabeth's words, that Katie began to feel that she was the blame for Pete Barkers death. Along the road at the crest of Bolivar Heights, Katie brought her mount to a halt and began to experience new emotions of guilt over his death.

Katie arrived at her residence, and there lying on the bed was a correspondence addressed to her. In many ways, Katie was uncertain as to who would be sending her a letter, but slowly as she began to open it, she realized that

Pete must have written it before his death. Slowly, her eyes began to scan the contents of the correspondence. Her heart was deeply troubled, sorrow ruled her features, and tears filled her eyes as she attempted to bring her emotions under control. Finally, in the last paragraph, Pete said, "My heart longs for your companionship, the comfort of your words, and the memories we shared, these blessings I will always hold close to my heart." Pete continued in the last sentence, "I will always hold your feelings with the utmost respect, and will forever be in debt to you."

Katie laid her head down on the pillow, crying and holding his letter against her breast, she softly said, "And my love, I will always hold you close to my heart."

CHAPTER THIRTY-FOUR

As Pete Barker awakened, he could hear the birds singing outside of his bedroom window. Even though it was a humid afternoon, the smell of fresh cut roses filled the room and reminded him of home. His eyes were blurry as he glanced about the room; the discomfort in his right side reminded him of the wound that was inflicted upon him. It was quiet. His surroundings appeared to be peaceful. As he raised his head and looked about for his weapon, a woman entered the room and said frantically, "No, no. You must be still and lie down. If you don't, then your wound will open once more."

As Pete gazed at the mysterious lady, he asked, "Who are you? Where am I?"

The lady said as she sat along side of the bed, "I am Hannah. Hannah Graceham. Don't you remember me?"

Pete was puzzled and attempted to regain his memory, "No, I am afraid that I do not."

Hannah took the cloth that was in her hand, placing it in some cold water, she moisten his lips and asked, "What is your name?"

"It's Pete Barker."

Hannah said, as she continued to wipe his forehead, "I didn't know. I must confess that I searched your belongings for some type of identification, but there wasn't any."

"I must have lost some of my possessions."

"I noticed that you are a Confederate. Where are you from?"

"I'm from Harpers Ferry."

Hannah said, as she rose to her feet, "I want you to rest for now. Shortly, I'll return and give you something to eat."

As Pete observed the flames dancing about in the fireplace where Hannah's meal was simmering, he began to think of the incident surrounding his injury, and his life. He knew that he was fortunate to be alive and recovering from a serious gunshot wound. Again, he thought, his friend Jonathan had saved his life as he did several years ago at Manassas. Still, he believed, if he continued to fight, the odds of his survival would be against him. As for Jonathan, he hoped that he was still alive, although he knew that his friend was probably headed for some prisoner-of-war camp even at this very moment. His concern turned toward his cousin Lester's welfare, was he still alive and safe, or did he succumb to his wounds. As he thought on these matters, his heart was filled with despair, and he grieved. Suddenly, troublesome thoughts of his family surfaced. With the war continuing longer then had been anticipated, Pete feared that the family was beginning to suffer and feel the effects of the longevity of the conflict. He knew that many of the slaves had escaped from his previous visit before the Gettysburg campaign, but with their absence and without production from the business it would only be a matter of time before the family would be financially ruined. As for Charles, he thought, probably his brother was safe in Richmond; maybe even Ann and Caroline were with him. Hopefully, his Mother joined them.

Pete took his hand and rubbed the stubble whiskers that filled his face. He had lost track of time; Pete began to wonder how long he had been lying in this bed recovering from his wound. His thoughts continued with the return to his personal life concerning Katie McBride. By now, Katie must have read the local newspaper knowing that a great battle was fought north of the Mason Dixon Line. Knowing her deepest feelings for him, Pete was sure that she was worrying and concerned for his welfare. Yet, there was nothing that he could do to inform her of his safety. As his thoughts returned to Katie's love for him, he began to examine his own heart concerning any feelings that he might have for her. At times in the past, he had felt closeness, comfort, and a bond that was strongly committed to a friendly relationship. Most of all, they shared a trust that was unbroken and had stood the fire of trials and thus far, the tribulations of the conflict. Once more, Pete thought about the last time that they were together at the church, the night that Katie expressed her deepest feelings for him. It was a moment in which he felt so close to her as if they were one instead of two. Although he knew that as the evening progressed, he was feeling frighten by the risk that was tempting him, his commitment to her. Was Katie correct when she challenged him during their conversation along the river? Was he really using the war as a way to avoid his feelings for her, or was she wrong? Pete had known Katie long enough to know that she possessed a keen perception of people, and was very much in touch with the feelings of other individuals. Still, as Pete thought on these matters, he attempted to reason his actions for resisting the young lady from New England. As he did so, his heart and mind were filled with confusion.

Pete's thoughts were suddenly broken as Hannah returned as previously promised with something to eat. As she sat once more alongside the bed, she took the spoon and stirred the stew. Placing some of the meal on the spoon, she began to quietly and slowly feed Pete from the bowl. The meal taste good, and he was thankful for her sacrifice. After he had eaten his fill, Pete was curious and began to speak, "How long have I been here?"

Hannah replied as she laid the bowl on the stand next to the bed, "For a week."

"A week?"

"Yes," Hannah replied as she gazed at Pete. After a pause, she continued in a soft tone of voice, "It was the seventh of July that you were wounded, today is the fourteenth of July."

Pete was somewhat bewildered as he continued, "Was I unconscious the whole time?"

"Periodically, you would awaken, but you were too weak from the lost of so much blood, and to complicate things, you had a fever. I must admit I took some risk in removing the bullet. I'm not a doctor by any means, but I would say that if the bullet that was lodged against your ribs would have continued to penetrate your body, you probably wouldn't be alive today."

Pete sighed as he replied, "I want to thank you not for only tending to me medically, but you risked your life. If the Yankees would have known that you were helping a rebel, then they would have possibly destroyed your property."

Hannah paused, gazing at Pete, and then replying, "Shortly after you passed out, the Yankees did arrive. They insisted on searching the property, even though my husband is fighting for the Union cause. I pleaded with them, but to no avail."

Pete continued the conversation by asking, "Hannah, if I loss consciousness, why didn't they find me."

Hannah smiled as she answered, "I hid you under the floor."

"Under the floor, I don't understand."

"Before the war, my husband and I built a trench under the floor in the dinning room for the purpose of hiding runaway slaves."

Pete was amazed and answered in a surprising tone, "You were part of the Underground Railroad?"

"Yes we were. Since the spring of 1858, we've been helping slaves in their efforts to escape to the North and experience freedom."

Pete's amazement continued, as he gazed at the young lady, "If you feel that strong in your convictions, then why didn't you turn me over to the Yankees. I don't understand."

"I guess I hoped that if my husband who is with the 5th Maryland were in the same situation, that someone would be as generous."

Hannah stood momentarily and looked out the window and watched the cattle grazing near the barn. Shortly, her silence was broken as she turned about and faced Pete. As she stood near the bed, she said, "I guess like many, I'm tired of the continuation of this war. Some of my best friends have either lost their husbands, brothers, or good family friends. I've seen the suffering that they have endured and been very touched by the experience. I'm sure that it is no different in Virginia."

"No, it isn't. After Antietam, I had to be the one to break the news to my sister that her gentleman friend had lost his life. It was a very difficult moment for me to see her grief and anguish. I will always remember that moment as long as I live. And then at Gettysburg, my cousin was severely wounded. Even at this moment as we speak, I don't know if he is alive."

There was a glimmer of a smile as Hannah spoke, "I heard from my husband David two weeks ago. At that time he was doing fine. There isn't a day that goes by that I don't pray for his safety. I'm tired of the killing; I just want him to return home." Hannah paused and looked out the window for what seemed a long time, and then, she gazed at Pete once more and said in a somber tone of voice, "I too pray to God that he survived the fight at Gettysburg. He might even be close. From what I understand, the Confederates have been unable to cross the river due to the heavy rains of the past couple of days."

Pete said softly as he looked into Hannah's eyes, "I know how you must feel to be separated from someone who is close."

Pete paused as Hannah continued the conversation, "I know that there must be someone at home waiting for you. I couldn't help but feel if the Union soldiers would have taken you prisoner, then probably you would have died from your wound. For you, the gift of life has been restored. Somewhere in my heart, I hope that you will return home and give up your effort to fight in this miserable war. I know someone must be anxiously waiting for news of your whereabouts."

Pete replied in a somber tone, "Yes, your right. I'm sure that my Mother and family must know by now that I'm missing. And there is a lady friend that I'm concerned about also."

"I figured that out already."

Once more, Pete expressed a look of amazement, "How?"

"At times you called out for Katie. I figured that was her name. Personally, I feel that as soon as you're well enough to travel, you need to return to her."

Pete was surprised at Hannah's revelation. Silence ruled as he gazed at the young lady. There wasn't a word that could be found to reveal his inner, deepest feelings.

Along Shenandoah Street, Katie McBride was slowly walking near her former residence toward the river with her head bowed. It was her intentions of remaining unnoticed to those that passed by so they wouldn't notice her red eyes. One Union soldier in particular did make the observation. As he tipped his hat in a gentlemanly gesture, he said, "Madam."

But Katie was so stricken with grief that she continued toward her destination without acknowledging the soldiers courtesy. As she came upon the area where Pete and she had spent sometime together on his last visit home, Katie began to dwell on their conversation concerning him leaving the army and returning home with her to Massachusetts. If only he hadn't been so stubborn and prideful, then he still would have been alive, she thought. The notion crossed her mind about returning to Boston anyway. Harpers Ferry was no longer the town that she had envisioned upon her arrival three years ago. Most of the citizens were gone, few students remained to teach, and the village possessed only memories of her relationship with Pete and the rest of the Barker family. Maybe it was time for her to accept her brother's advice that he was so animate about on his last visit. As Katie removed the image of Pete from her purse, she kissed it and clutched it tightly against her chest and wept. After a few quiet moments, the silence was broken by a voice, "I loved him too."

The sound of the voice was familiar as Katie turned about. Caroline slowly approached and continued, "I wanted to see you as soon as I received the news. All to well, I know what you are feeling." Katie didn't reply, and after a moment of silence, which the two continued to gaze at the other, Caroline softly continued to express her emotions, "It's difficult losing someone that you love, and being alone without someone to share your grief with, it makes things even worse."

Katie began to wonder what kind of game Caroline was playing with her. With Charles being alive and well, who was she attempting to deceive, and why? For now under the circumstances, Katie wouldn't pursue the issue. In her heart, there were distrusting emotions that had developed for Caroline; something that she had never imagined could result from their relationship. Katie softly replied as she continued to hold onto the image, "Yes, it is very difficult."

"If I may ask, what will you do now?"

"I really don't know. Maybe I'll return to Boston." Katie paused and sighed as she continued, "Caroline, there really isn't a reason for me to stay in the area any longer. There is a lot of truth in what you say; it will be too difficult for me. Even now as I glance about, I'm constantly reminded of memories that Pete and I shared. The pain and anguish is more then I can bare."

"He died for a cause that he strongly believed in."

"And so hasn't many." Katie cried. The redness in her face revealed the anger that she was experiencing. Katie continued with a flare in her tone of voice, "I'm not too bloody sure of that. After speaking with your mother-in-law, she revealed to me her bloody scheme that ignited a controversy in your family, and drove her son away."

Caroline was astonished at Katie's attitude, "Katie McBride, what are you insinuating?"

"After receiving the news earlier this morning concerning Pete, I rode to the Estate to see you and Miss Elizabeth. In our conversation, she justified her decision to turn Shenandoah over to Charles. And it was because she could in a subtle and deceptive manner control and influence your husband's actions."

Caroline screamed, as she held her hands to her face, "That is not so. It's all a lie."

"Oh, I'm not questioning Pete's loyalties to the Confederacy. But you know what terrified me the most? It was her blatant actions in this manner that Pete decided to join the army. Caroline, everything that she did was to punish him because of his friendship with me and he wouldn't play her game of lies and mistrust. She was afraid that we would marry one day, and that life would change at the Estate with me living around her family."

An angry expression consumed Caroline's features as she snapped, "Yes, maybe you have done enough to separate this family."

With that statement, Caroline abruptly turned about and walked away. She was still consumed with anger. It was her intentions upon her arrival at Shenandoah to confront Elizabeth with this revelation.

As Katie watched her once close friend depart, she finally realized that a friendship between them could never exist, nor be resurrected. Too many social issues, loss of property, financial debt, and the death of a family member, all caused by the war would continue too manifested many emotions that would only construct a wider gap between them. It wouldn't be her intentions to visit Shenandoah anytime in the future under any circumstances; she must make the attempt to find healing for her wounds, and to deal with the loss of Pete Barker in her life.

CHAPTER THIRTY-FIVE

After her encounter with Katie McBride along the river, Caroline quickly mounted her stallion and departed. As her horse raced with haste toward Shenandoah, Caroline continued to feel the anger over Katie's revelation concerning Elizabeth's true intentions of why she transferred ownership of the Estate to Charles. Caroline always believed that she knew her mother-in-law well enough to know that she was an honest individual, and enjoyed the respect of citizens in the community for her integrity. Though now, she began to wonder how many times in previous events and business affairs had she been ruthless and dishonest in her transactions using Charles as a pawn.

The time passed rapidly as she approached the entrance to the Estate. With her arrival, the area surrounding the house was quiet. Caroline quickly dismounted, and ran up the steps and through the front door, slamming it as she entered. Matthew quickly approached, "Mrs. Caroline, is ya alright?"

"Where is Miss Elizabeth?"

"She's in de back sittin' in de gazebo. Does ya want me to git her?"

Without replying to the bewildered servant, Caroline raced by him and ran out the back entrance of the mansion. As she approached the gazebo, Caroline noticed that Elizabeth was quietly sitting and looking off toward the direction of Barker's Ridge, and watching the group of fawns peacefully standing and gazing in her direction.

Elizabeth turned to notice Caroline's rapid pace toward the gazebo, and naturally assumed that something had happened to bring the family more anguish and pain. With an expression that was filled with fear, Elizabeth asked, "Oh, dear, my child what is your hurry? What is wrong?"

Momentarily, Caroline paused gazing at her mother-in-law. Elizabeth noticed the anger that filled her eyes and the tense expression that covered her features. Once more, Elizabeth asked, "My dear Caroline, what troubles you?"

Caroline replied with a flare in her voice, "How dare you ask me what troubles me."

By now, Elizabeth perceived the nature of Caroline's anger, knowing that she had rushed off earlier to find Katie and to comfort her concerns over Pete's death. Elizabeth was most certain that Katie had shared with Caroline the conversation from earlier in the afternoon between the two of them when she visited the Estate. In her attempt to suppress Caroline, "Why are you so upset with me?"

"How could you betray your son's trust?"

"My child, what do you mean?"

"You know very well what I mean. You betrayed Charles, your own son. You used him for your benefit."

Elizabeth attempted to betray Caroline with an expression of astonishment as she answered, "Have you been speaking with Katie?"

"Yes I did. Katie told me about the conversation that she had with you earlier before I arrived. I'm shocked and appalled by the revelation that she shared with me."

"Since you've made your insinuation, please tell me what she said so at least I can defend myself."

"Katie spoke of your conversation with her this morning. In her despair, she revealed that the only intentions you had in releasing the ownership of the Estate to Charles was so that you could indiscriminately control his actions, and decisions by your influence. You abused his trust and love for you to gain your results, like influencing him to sell the cattle and horses and using the money to invest in promissory notes with the Confederacy. With the turn the war is taking, they'll probably be worthless before too long."

"Now Caroline, Charles made that decision on his own accord. He felt that it would be for the best to make the investment."

Caroline walked over to the edge of the gazebo and glanced toward the river. Turning about once more and facing Elizabeth, she said, "No, I disagree.

Several weeks before the cattle and horses were sold I noticed that you and Charles were in the parlor discussing matters in a soft voice. I have to admit, I was curious. Later that same evening, I noticed as I have done so many times in the past, his reserve demeanor and troubled expression. As any concerned wife would, I asked him the nature of the discussion. He was quite frank and told me that he had reservations about selling the cattle and horses at that time. He believed that it would have been for the best if we waited longer. It was his convictions that the livestock would have been of greater value. Instead, we sold out to a private owner and ended up with a Confederate promissory note instead of gold. Charles was very hesitant about this deal, more so then the other transactions that you and he had discussed. I was just too naïve to realize what your truest intentions were."

Elizabeth said in a soft and confident voice, "Alright, I admit, I played a part when I knew that he might make an error. We couldn't have kept the herd without the Yankees confiscating them, or for that matter, the Confederacy. It would have only been a matter of time and we would have lost everything. I had to intervene."

Caroline replied in a blunt tone, "It appeared that you intervene often. For sometime now, I have sensed a change in Charles' behavior. Now I know, he was questioning your confidence in his ability to act on his own. No wonder he was questioning his own decisions."

Once more, Elizabeth attempted to convince Caroline that her intentions were honorable, "Caroline, I had to act quickly in order to save a life's worth of hard labor. For one moment, do you think that it's easy building a business such as the magnitude of Shenandoah?" Caroline remained silent though Elizabeth's facial features expressed a sincerity, but Caroline wouldn't be deceived. Elizabeth continued, "No, it isn't. My Father labored day and night, investing long hours, seven days a week and learning by his experiences in farming, raising cattle, and breeding horses to prosper this Estate. Now, unfortunately, the war has cost us, but we haven't lost everything yet, and I don't intend to."

Caroline angrily replied as she began to weep, "But, you led Charles to believe that you trusted him to make all of the right decisions. Actually, you led both of us to trust you. Now as far as I'm concern, it was all a lie, a well planned out deception. How do you feel that this is going to affect Charles when he discovers the truth?"

Elizabeth was stunned, amazed, and momentarily speechless. Her emotions were mixed between happiness that her son was yet alive, and anger over Caroline's deception. Finally, there was coldness in her eyes as she began to speak, "Why did you deceive me and cause such terrible anguish. Why! Tell me now!"

Caroline knew that the words that she had spoken had trapped her. It wasn't her intention of revealing information to Elizabeth concerning Charles. The couple had vowed to keep their knowledge a secret until the right opportunity presented itself. Caroline began to calmly share with Elizabeth their reasons for secrecy, "It was to protect him." Elizabeth remained silent waiting patiently for Caroline to find the right words to continue, "As you well know, the Yankee cavalry's intrusions had become frequent and without warning. Charles had revealed to me that Federal spies in Richmond knew of his involvement with the Davis administration, and his business abroad in England. We were both afraid that he would be captured if he returned to Shenandoah. So, I conceived the plan to falsify his death in hopes that the Yankees would leave us alone, and spare the Estate from possible destruction from the hands of Yankee raiders."

The sound of a voice rejoicing could be heard, "Mother, do you mean that father is alive?"

As Caroline and Elizabeth turned about in the direction of the voice, they noticed Ann, speechless and gazing in astonishment. Immediately, Caroline approached her daughter and began to explain and apologize, "Ann, I'm sorry for being dishonest with you, and the pain that I put you through, but I had no other choice then to keep it from you."

"Why Mother?" Ann asked as tears filled her eyes.

"It was something that your Father and I felt for now would be for the best with the continuation of this war."

"Didn't you trust me? Were you and Father afraid that I would say something."

Caroline said tearfully, feeling the guilt and condemnation of her dishonesty, "We were afraid that it might accidentally slip while in town, and be overheard by one of the Yankees. That's why we kept it a secret; it could have greatly damaged our family. Please understand."

"Its funny, Mother, how life works."

Caroline was astonished as she answered her daughter, "What do you mean?"

"Today is my thirteenth birthday. I receive sad news this morning that my Uncle is dead, and very good news this afternoon that my Father is alive."

Caroline embraced her daughter and asked as Elizabeth stood nearby and anxiously looked on, "Who told you?"

"No one, I overheard Mr. Daniel tell Grandmother."

Elizabeth held her hands to her face and cried, "Oh dear child, I'm so sorry. Together, your Mother and I were going to tell you after she returned from town."

Ann replied with a soft tone of voice as she gazed at her Mother and Grandmother, "You'll never know how greatly I will miss him. The moments of teasing that we enjoyed at the dinner table, the quiet conversations, especially when I was troubled, and his bright smiles, even during difficult times."

Elizabeth wiped the tears from her eyes as she spoke, "Ann, I always want you to remember that your Uncle Pete fought for a noble and bold cause. He sacrificed his life so that your way of life wouldn't change, and that you would always continue to enjoy life as you have known it."

"I know, but like many, even at my age, I read the newspapers, listen to the conversations here at home and in town, and somewhere in my heart I don't think that we can win the war. It's been difficult for me to witness the events that have affected our family, such as the unexpected visits from the Yankees, and Aunt Rebecca losing someone that she hoped to marry. In my own way, I've suffered greatly with my Father unable to return home and once more living as a family. Now, my uncle has lost his life. Already, I feel that my family has given so much. I hope that it all ends before too much longer."

Ann quietly turned about and walked slowly toward the house. Elizabeth was amazed at Ann's observations and feelings concerning her life. Since her birth, Elizabeth possessed the ability to protect Ann from harm and protect her emotions. With the war being raged about them, Elizabeth realized the toll that the conflict had produced, and conceded that it would be impossible to protect her from the fruit of pain and anguish. It grieved her deeply, though she hoped that once the war concluded that Ann's life would return, as she had always known.

For the first time since the beginning of the war, this was the first time that Ann spoke her truest feelings of her heart. In a way, Caroline was impressed with Ann's openness, but sorrowful that she had to experience the events. Within her heart, Caroline agreed with her daughter that it would be difficult for the South to win the war.

CHAPTER THIRTY-SIX

In the aftermath of the Gettysburg campaign, the war began to go against the South, and their cause for independence. By the spring of 1864, President Lincoln was gratified with General Ulysses S. Grant's success in the western theater along the Mississippi River and promoted him to Commander-In-Chief over all of the Union forces. Grant's successor, Major-General William T. Sherman continued the quest in the western theater by defeating the Confederate forces in a succession of victories at Resaca and Dallas in northwestern Georgia. Now Sherman was in the process of driving toward Atlanta, the major industrial center of the Deep South. In the eastern theater, the Confederate forces had succeeded in battling the Union army to a stand off. With Grant in command, the Federals didn't retreat as in previous encounters, but continued to attempt to out-flank and out-maneuver the Confederate forces still under the command of General Robert E. Lee. After a series of bloody battles near Richmond, the war continued with heavy casualties at places called the Wilderness, Spotsylvania Court House, and Cold Harbor. During the heavy campaigning against Richmond, the Confederacy was once more plagued with the loss of one of its greatest Generals, Jeb Stuart. On May 12th he died in Richmond of a gunshot wound suffered at the battle of Yellow Tavern.

As the blue and gray continued to battle around Richmond, General Lee sent General Jubal Early with the Armies II Corps into the lower Shenandoah Valley with hopes of threatening Washington. It was General Lee's desire that the

Federals would reinforce the city with troops from Grant's army, thus relieving pressure on the Confederate capitol. After defeating a small Union force near Frederick, Maryland, Early's seasoned veterans continued marching to the outskirts of the Union capitol, only to retreat toward the Valley once more after a brief skirmish.

During this bloody summer season on a humid July afternoon, Pete Barker was mounted on his horse along a ridge overlooking the Water's farm. After traveling at a steady pace from the Hillsborough area, Pete wanted to give his mare a rest. Still experiencing some tenderness from the wound that he received a year ago, Pete had returned to Virginia once more to fight for the Confederacy with his friend Colonel Mosby, and his small force of partisans. As his horse grazed on some of the grass along the crest of a ridge near the Methodist Church, Pete laid on a blanket near a grove of trees along a dirt lane. He began to ponder on the conversations that he and Hannah experienced during his period of convalescence. Since his return to duty, the words that she had spoken concerning the restoration of his life and given the second chance to live had constantly been on his mind. His near death experience on the outskirts of Funkstown had been a close one, and he knew he had been fortunate. More then once during his recovery, Pete had given considerable thought about returning to Harpers Ferry and Shenandoah. He was thinking of surrendering the fight that was beginning to feel useless. The war and the bloodshed had affected his emotions considerably. With the carnage that he had experienced in the three years of fighting, the war had engraved horrible images of death and maiming within his mind that he believed would impart many scars.

As his eyes gazed across the beautiful valley, his thoughts turned to Katie McBride and his family. It had been a year since he had seen or heard from Katie and his love ones. For months during his recovery from the injuries he suffered, he had been too weak to correspond with Katie to inform her of his welfare. He knew that if discovered by Federal authorities that he might be placing Hannah in jeopardy for sheltering a Confederate fugitive. Everything that she had worked for could be destroyed, or seized by the government. As he gazed in the direction of Loudoun Heights, he knew that the life he once lived was still at Shenandoah, and there was a burning desire to subdue his pride and return.

Often during his stay at Hannah's homestead, the continuous thought remained within his mind concerning Katie. Did she return to Boston, or was she still a resident of Harpers Ferry. By now, he was sure that Katie and his family believed that he had perished at Gettysburg with so many other soldiers. Katie's heart must be broken, he thought; they had become very close in their relationship to be just friends, but he wasn't able to give more to someone he knew that deserved so much. If Katie was still in town, he contemplated compromising his mission in the Ferry to see her, and to inform her of his welfare. Then the thought crossed his mind that maybe she had found someone special and had continued to live her life. The thought of this happening began to tear at his heart and mind.

Rising to his feet, Pete remounted his mare and rode the short distance to the Russell homestead where he was sure to find a place to rest and enjoy a hot meal. Most of the residences that lived in the area were sympathetic to the Union and couldn't be trusted. As he rode along the road that led to Harpers Ferry, he came to the Russell's lane. Turning his mount toward the house, he noticed the abundant grape vineyard that was sheltered by several tall oak trees. An abundant garden of every kind of vegetation appeared between the house and a peach orchard. Slowly, Pete approached the two story stone dwelling that rested on a ridge. In Pete's observation of the property, he noticed that many of the slaves had disappeared, though still a few remained loyal to the family, and were about accomplishing their task. One of the servants was drawing water from the well, and returned through the side entrance to the house. Once Pete dismounted his horse, Miss Virginia appeared on the side porch and observed his appearance. Finally, she continued in his direction, and continued to determine his identity, "James. James Barker, is that you?"

A grin broke forth that dominated their expression as Pete replied, "Yes, Miss Virginia, it's me."

"My goodness James, you are suppose to be dead."

"I figured by now that everyone had reached that conclusion."

"Did you give up soldiering?"

"No mam. I didn't give up military life."

Pete knew that Miss Virginia was puzzled with his appearance by her bewildered expression. Before he could explain, she fired off several quick questions, "Why are you wearing black trousers, and a black coat? Have you taken up preaching?"

Pete laughed as he tied his horse to a post near an old walnut tree, "I have some business to take care of in town. I just prefer not to be recognized."

As she continued to examine Pete's appearance with a serious expression, she said, "Well, with that long shabby beard you don't have to worry. That's for sure."

After a moment of silence and giving up the quest to gain information concerning his mysterious disguise, Miss Virginia offered, "Come on in to the house. I'll have Ester fix you some of her country ham and fried potatoes."

As Pete and Miss Virginia entered the parlor and were seated, Pete opened the conversation by anxiously inquiring information regarding his family, "Miss Virginia, with the intense campaigning that I have experienced, and uncontrollable circumstances, I wasn't able to communicate with my family to inform them of my welfare. I don't know what is going on."

Miss Virginia said in a serious tone, "Then you don't know about Charles?"

An anxious expression covered Pete's shallow face as he answered in an urgent tone, "What about my brother?"

"He died several days after the fight at Brandy Station."

Pete knew there wasn't any truth in her statement because he wasn't involved in the engagement. Furthermore, he didn't quite understand why Miss Virginia and probably many of the family's friends had been deceived. For some unexplained reason, he believed that someone had a very good reason to plot such a fabrication. With the knowledge that his brother had been secretly involved in business for the Confederate government, he knew in time, that he would discover the truth. For now, he would concede and play along with the conversation. Acting as though his heart was grieved and full of despair, "I didn't know the extent of his injuries, we had to move on."

Pete continued his sorrowful expression as Miss Virginia gazed at him and continued to smiled and speak, "Oh James, you would have been proud of the send-off that your Mother and Caroline gave him. I believe that everyone of prominence in Jefferson County attended the funeral. Congressman Boteler, Andrew Hunter, and the Whites attended. And all of them were visibly shaken by Charles' death."

Pete's concern turned toward his family, "What about my Mother?"

"Your brothers death was a devastating shock to her. It was unexpected. Oh, what tribulation for poor Elizabeth," Miss Virginia said in a somber tone, shaking her head in despair, and continuing, "I have never seen such a display of grief for someone. Oh James, you would have been proud of Caroline, she contained her composure, and was very strong, but my heart goes out to Ann. She ran to the coffin as they were lowering it into the ground and wept uncontrollably."

Pete continued in a somber tone of voice as sorrow ruled his expression, "With the heavy fighting and constantly on the move, I didn't receive any mail, so I didn't know. And when I was wounded near Funkstown on the retreat from Gettysburg, it was impossible to communicate with the family. I spent the last six months recovering from a wound that almost cost me my life."

"Just recently, I spent the afternoon with your mother and tried my best to bring her some cheer, but she is so disheartened from Charles' death and yours. She believes that she has lost both of her sons to this cause."

With a tone of determination, Pete replied, "I must see her as soon as possible."

Miss Virginia replied with a tone of caution, "You must watch yourself, Yankees have been moving along this road for most of the afternoon."

"I know, I noticed some of them camped near Hillsbourgh."

As Miss Virginia walked Pete toward the entrance to the house, she replied sorrowfully, "I wish that your mother would have accepted my invitation and spent sometime with me so that we could talk about the grief that she has endured. But knowing her, as I do, she is a very proud lady and doesn't like to reveal her weakness."

"I know. Sometime this evening, after dark, I intend on seeing her."

"I'm sorry that you didn't have time to stay and have something to eat."

Pete anxiously replied, "Really, I must go."

"May God's speed be with you, James?"

Within the hour after leaving Miss Virginia's, Pete was riding along Shenandoah Street, portraying the role of a Methodist minister. After participating in a raid with Colonel Mosby near Seneca Mills, Maryland, the partisan commander instructed Pete to leave immediately for the town and surrounding area. Orders were given to him to gain information regarding troop strength, location of defenses, and possible weaknesses for raids on the railroad, especially their time schedules.

As he glanced about the once bustling business area of the town, he noticed that the war had ravaged many of the shops and stores of their prosperity; they were closed for business. Many of the shopkeepers and citizens of the once friendly village had departed for safer haven elsewhere, leaving the town nearly empty. It grieved Pete to witness such a scene of desolation. As he dismounted near the dry goods store, he removed his white haversack and bible to reduce suspicion of his real purpose, and to give him the appropriate identity. Pete turned and entered the store and noticed several Union soldiers at the counter purchasing writing material. Pete walked inconspicuously as possible toward the rear of the building and examined some cups on the upper shelf. Acting as though he was interested in purchasing, he listened to the conversation between the soldiers and the proprietor. One of the Federals said as he removed some money from his possession, "I will take these items."

The proprietor was stocking a shelf nearby as he turned his attention to the soldier, "That will be 25 cents."

The soldiers were quiet as the good-natured proprietor attempted to extract a conversation from the Federals, "I understand from one of your officers that Mosby's band of partisans are far from here."

One of the Federal soldiers said in a sarcastic tone of voice, "We wouldn't know that. Though, if we catch any of them murderers, we'll hang their hide from the highest tree that we can find."

Without another word, the soldiers turned about and proceeded to leave the store. As Pete approached the proprietor, the old gentleman commented, "Sorry Reverend."

"That's quite alright." Pete replied as he looked down at the money that he was counting.

The proprietor momentarily gazed at Pete and said, "You must be new around these parts. I don't believe that I have seen you before?"

Pete handed the proprietor the money and answered, "No you haven't. I hope to hold revival services tomorrow for the troops in town."

The proprietor answered with a grin that covered his expression, "With some of the gambling, drinking, and prostitution that goes on around here, a little religion wouldn't hurt."

"No, it wouldn't." Pete replied to the proprietor as he departed the store waving in a friendly gesture.

Pete stood along the street and observed some of the Federals marching toward the platoon bridge that crossed the Potomac. His focus was broken by the sound of many horses. Turning about and looking toward the direction of the old bakery, he noticed a company of Federal cavalry trotting towards him. He quietly watched as they silently rode by listening to their commander ordering them to come to a halt. As many of the soldiers dismounted, Pete remained calm placing the cup that he had purchased in his saddlebag.

With calmness, Pete mounted his horse and rode up the hill to the Catholic

School. He was anxious and interested to see if Katie was still in the area or if she had returned to Boston. As he stayed saddled, out of sight, behind some trees on his horse along the small slope that overlooked the church and school, he noticed Katie with the Priest walking toward the church. The strong breeze was blowing her hair about as she brushed it from her face. Pete noticed that she appeared to be tired and troubled. Her expression was somber, and lacked the glow of life that once filled it. He wanted to approach Katie and reassure her of his welfare, but he knew how she would react to his presence. It might jeopardize his work and he would be hung for spying. He couldn't imagine how she must feel, the pain, sorrow, and depression that she experienced over the past months. Now as he watched her, he wondered if Katie's feelings of love were still as strong for him. As Katie entered the church, Pete slowly rode away toward a Federal camp near Bolivar Heights. Thus far, he hadn't been recognized by any of the citizens that he knew personally that were still residing in the village.

Near the base of the heights, the Federal camp that Pete had been searching for was along a cliff overlooking the river. As he dismounted once more, he glanced across the Potomac in the direction of Maryland Heights. Slowly, he removed his haversack, which contained his bible while he observed the Federal camps that populated the crest and slope of the Maryland Mountain. He walked casually in the direction of the camp, where a sentry allowed him to pass after speaking with him. To his left, he noticed a group of soldiers sitting around a fire cursing, laughing, and playing a friendly game of poker. Directly to his front, there was a tent with a cross to indicate that a regimental chaplain was present. As he approached the Chaplin's quarters, he overheard a conversation-taking place in an officer's tent between two participants. Pausing and kneeling to tie his shoes near their tent, he listened, "Well Harry I see it this way. If we continue to receive the kind of information from this informant that General Lockwood spoke of this morning, then maybe the war will end quicker in this area then what we thought."

Both men laughed as Pete continued to listen to a different voice reply, "I wonder what old Jeff Davis would say if he knew a snitch was going to possibly cost him the war in the lower valley?"

Pete had possibly stumbled onto information that he hadn't expected to receive. Who was the identity of the mysterious individual? They must live in the area he thought. Katie's name suddenly crossed his mind. He knew that Charles and William had been suspicious of her true intentions of living so far from home. He just couldn't believe that she possessed that type of character. For the duration of the afternoon, he remained in camp with the chaplain and soldiers. After dark, he would make the attempt to see his family, and then pay Katie a visit to assure her of his safety.

CHAPTER THIRTY-SEVEN

After finishing most of his chores, Daniel was sent into town by Elizabeth to purchase several bags of flour. It was close to four in the afternoon as he was riding along Shenandoah Street in a wagon that was pulled by two mules. As he blotted out the rickety sound of the wagon wheels, he thought about the many slaves that once belonged to the Barkers, but now, had escaped to freedom in the North. The Yankees confiscation of the remaining livestock, including their prize horses such as Pete's mare, Victory, fueled his hatred. With these events caused by the conflict, this left Daniel in a position of laboring late hours with little help, something that he wasn't accustomed to doing He disliked and resented his way of life, and appeared to many of his friends to be increasingly unhappy.

As Daniel brought the mules to a halt in front of the dry goods store, the sound of a train whistle caught his attention. It was the afternoon passenger train arriving from Washington City. Turning about in the wagon seat, he glanced off in the direction of the train depot, and noticed Katie McBride anxiously heading towards that destination. Once more his curiosity had been aroused. For nearly a year, he had been true to his promise to William Pierce, observing and informing him of her activities in the area, especially around town. Daniel calmly rubbed his chin as he decided to follow the young lady and intently watch her. As he stood at a distance, he noticed a young Union officer step from the coach carrying a dark satchel. It appeared to Daniel that the officer and Katie knew each other by their warmness toward each other. After exchanging what appeared to be cordials, Katie and the officer walked to the buggy and departed toward High Street. Daniel decided to follow at a distance and investigate their intentions. Slowly, he proceeded toward the upper area of town, which in the past had been mostly occupied by Federal camps. Their buggy made a left turn onto Columbia Street, and then a left proceeding east on Fillmore Street. Daniel continued to maintain a safe distance keeping his presence as inconspicuous as possible. Within minutes, Katie and the officer reached their destination at a redbrick, two-story dwelling at the top of a ridge. This building was known by the citizens of the community as the Armory paymaster's quarters and grounds. Daniel knew that the Federal government owned the residence, and that General Howe, who was commanding the Union forces in town, had taken the privilege of using the house as his headquarters.

As Daniel maintained a safe distance from the grounds, he observed Katie and the officer entering the front entrance. He was suspicious, wondering if Katie had passed information on to the officer. On a regular basis for the last several months, Katie had been absent from the area, and Daniel was knowledgeable of this, though, ignorant of her whereabouts. He believed that she had received information concerning General Early's troops along with partisan raiders in their effort to wage war against the railroad, and now, she was informing General Howe with the intelligence. Daniel believed that the visit was used by Katie and the officer to pass along names and locations of citizens in the area that were sheltering some of the Confederate raiders.

After an hour of watching the residence from his shelter among the brush that covered the cliffs overlooking the Ferry, Daniel noticed Katie and the General walk onto the huge front porch. There, another officer joined them in conversation. Immediately, the same officer mounted his horse and rode with haste down Fillmore Street. Daniel suspected that the courier was dispatched with the important information to General Hunter's headquarters. It was near sunset when Daniel departed for Charlestown to inform his contact with the information to be passed on to William Pierce.

For most of the early evening, the servants, along with Caroline and Ann, spent time packing their clothing for a visit to Richmond where she would be with Charles. Caroline was feeling very depressed over the continuation of the war and the enormous effect of long separations from her husband. As she paused to look out the bedroom window, she was reminded of the desolation that the conflict had imparted upon the family and their business. The property that was once kept immaculate with fresh gardens of roses and vegetation had all but disappeared. The stables and barn that once were occupied by cattle and horses was lifeless of their inhabitances. The dwellings were depleted and in desperate need of repair. As she glanced in the direction of Harpers Ferry, most of the wood used for the fence that ran along the boundary of the property had vanished. The wood was used by Confederate and Union troops for firewood when they previously occupied the property. Quietly, Caroline walked toward another window at the opposite side of the room and gazed in the distance at the empty slave quarters. The only inhabitance that still occupied the Estate at the present was the family, and a few servants along with Daniel. For the last three years the family had been unable to effectively operate the business and was financially ruined. Caroline knew that it would only be a matter of time before they would lose the Estate, especially, if the North wins the war.

Caroline's silence was broken with a knock at the door. She turned and answered, "Who is it?"

"It's Elizabeth."

Caroline walked over to the door and opened it, "Please, come in."

Elizabeth walked into the room and stood by a marble top table that she had given Charles and Caroline as an anniversary gift after one of her trips to France. She turned and there was a grim expression that ruled her features. Caroline knew that something was terribly wrong, "What is the matter? What's wrong?"

Elizabeth appeared to be tensed, concerned, and replied in an angry tone, "Daniel just came from town with some grim news."

"What did he say?"

"He saw Katie meeting a Federal officer at the train depot. From there, they paid General Howe a visit at his headquarters."

"So, what is wrong with that? She is from the North, you know."

"Caroline, I'm surprise at you. What do you mean, what is wrong with that? Apparently, she was there to give the General information regarding names and locations of safety for some of the partisans that have operated in the area. Have we not opened our home and offered such help?"

Caroline was quiet. She began to express her deepest fear, "Maybe, they know that Charles is alive."

"Oh dear. What shall we do now?"

Caroline and Elizabeth's conversation was interrupted by Ann running into the room and shouting, "The Yankees are coming! The Yankees are coming!"

As Caroline glanced out the front window, she was surprised that the Federals had returned to the Estate. For the past year, the Federals had ceased their harassment of the family. She turned to Elizabeth and said, "I wonder what they want?"

"Maybe we are about to be confronted with our deepest fear."

Caroline abruptly left the room with Ann and Elizabeth following her down the stairway to the front entrance. A Federal officer was dismounting as the ladies walked onto the porch. The ladies remained silent as the officer climbed the stone steps to speak with them. There was an expression of defiance that covered Caroline and Elizabeth's faces. Ann was nervous and fearful that the soldiers might harm them.

As the officer approached the ladies, he expressed confident in his demeanor by saying calmly, "Ladies, I am Captain William Marcel of the 1st New York Cavalry."

Elizabeth answered the officer with a steadiness and politeness in her voice, "What brings you to Shenandoah this evening?"

"Madam, with all due respect, I'm here on business."

Caroline asked as she stepped forward, "What business do you have with us?"

As Captain Marcel turned to face Caroline, she noticed the coldness in his eyes. He promptly answered, "I have received orders from General Hunter to burn your property, including the house."

Ann began to cry, "Oh no. Oh no."

Elizabeth was enraged with anger, and Caroline began to scream loudly, "No, there must be some mistake. You can't destroy property belonging to civilians. We are alone. We are innocent women."

Captain Marcel replied with firmness in his tone of voice, "No mam. We have information that your husband is still very much alive and still very much a participant with the Confederate government. Therefore, he is considered an enemy of the United States and the property can be destroyed."

There was a cold glare in Caroline's eyes as she pleaded in a angry tone of voice, "You can tell General Hunter that it doesn't take much of a man to wage war on innocent civilians, especially when they are women."

Captain Marcel quietly stared at the ladies, and then turned about and commanded with a shout, "Sergeant Hayes, put the torch to it. All of it, including the house!"

As some of the soldiers entered the house to prepare it for its destruction, Elizabeth clinched her fist and struck the officer in his chest crying, "This house has been in my family for generations. Why! Why are you doing this to me!" Quickly, Caroline stepped forward to join in the attack. After putting up a desperate struggle, several soldiers subdued Elizabeth and Caroline. Ann stood nearby under a tree crying, and soon was escorted quietly along with her Mother and Grandmother to a safe distance from the dwelling. Seeing the hopelessness of the situation, Caroline placed her arms around Ann's shoulders to comfort her. As she angrily watched some of the cavalrymen light their torches and dashed off on their horses to the stable area, she began to weep. After removing the remaining animals, the soldiers yelled with joy and made offensive remarks concerning the family as they threw the torches of fire into the stables. The fire roared forth quickly through the roof and the many windows within the dwelling. Helplessly, Caroline watched the destruction take place. Through the tears that filled her eyes, she watched as the soldiers set fire to the hay in the barn, causing the flames to shoot toward the heavens. Then they ignited the outbuildings without removing the contents and tools within. Soon, all of the structures except the main house were burning. As four of the dismounted soldiers raced up the stone steps to the entrance of the mansion with torches ablaze, Caroline turned her attention toward Elizabeth, who once more had to be restrained by the soldiers that were guarding them. She couldn't imagine the pain and agony that she was experiencing. The property had been in her family's possession for over fifty years. She was born near the house in a little log cabin that her Father had built. It was the only place that she had ever known as home. In a short period of time, the fond memories of earlier years would be the only thing untouched. It was the one precious possession that the fire and war couldn't deprive her. As Caroline walked toward Elizabeth, she turned to receive her embrace. Soon, they noticed the fire lighting up the interior of the house. Just as quickly, the flames were shooting with vengeance through the windows. The immediate area around them was glowing brightly with the destruction of their property. Elizabeth cried as she witnessed the horror of the reality, "Oh dear God, my father's portrait, my family's heirlooms. They are all gone! Vanished! I will never be able to replace the years of memories."

Caroline attempted to console her with words of encouragement, "But thank God, our life has been spared. They will be repaid for what they have done, and we will recover."

As the fire continued to crackle and race throughout the dwellings, Caroline watched as the roof began to collapse. Once satisfied that the mission had been carried out as ordered, Captain Marcel, and his company of cavalrymen quietly remounted their horses and slowly departed the Estate.

Pete Barker had just finished dinner with Chaplain Barnes when he heard the sound of cheering coming from the direction of the pickets stationed along the crest of the heights. There was an expression of amazement that covered Pete and the Chaplain's face as the commotion continued. Chaplain Barnes turned and said, "I wonder what all of the cheering is about?"

Desiring to know more information about the Federals activity, Pete replied, "I don't know. Let's go and see for ourselves."

With haste, the two men mounted their horses and rode toward the crest of the heights. On their arrival, Pete was amazed to see the darkness of the southeastern sky toward the river filled with a bright reddish glow. Immediately, perspiration broke forth above the brow of his eyes, his heart began to race with fear. He knew that the fire was coming from the direction of Shenandoah. The Chaplain glanced at Pete and commented, "I was afraid that something like this would happen."

As Pete repressed and disguised the fear that filled his heart, he calmly answered, "What do you mean?"

The Chaplain took a deep breath and sigh, "Somehow, I feared that we would retaliate against the rebels and their sympathizers after General Early destroyed the railroad tracks near Martinsburg. Although, there are many who would disagree with me, I hate to see war waged against civilians."

One of the Union officers standing near Pete and Chaplain Barnes overheard the conversation and said as he turned and glanced at the two men, "As I understand, that's not some civilians home that is going up in flames, but its Charles Barkers."

Chaplain Barnes surprisingly said, "I thought he was dead."

"No sir. As I understand he is still very much alive and in Richmond."

Pete interrupted and asked as he approached the officer, "How can you be so sure."

Once more, the officer turned with a grin that covered the width of his face and replied, "As I understand, their friends may not be as loyal to them as they believed."

As Pete excused himself and slowly walked away, he was concerned for his family's welfare. He knew that they must be terrified and in shock, especially, his Mother. As he once more turned and glanced at the bright sky, his heart was filled with anger at the aggressive tactics that the Federals were pursuing. Turning to mount his horse, he paused, still looking in the direction of Shenandoah. The greatest mystery that puzzled him was, who is the person's identity that is passing the information.

After ascending the crest of the heights along the road to Charlestown, Pete prodded his mount at a full gallop until he reached the entrance to Shenandoah. He wasn't sure if the Federals were still at the Estate, so with caution he proceeded along the lane. As he slowly approached the house, Pete paused and watched the barn collapsed making a terrible crashing sound as it fell to the ground. The fire crackled and danced, as its flames were shooting skyward. The out buildings, carpentry shop, carriage house, and blacksmiths shop were smoldering and had completely vanished. As he looked in the direction of the mansion, his heart was filled with despair as the flames were still belching forth toward the sky, the roof of the dwelling being totally destroyed. As he paused and watched the huge porch that crossed the length of the house crash against some tall trees, he thought about some of the joyful memories of his youth. All that remained of the mansion was the exterior stone walls; blacken by the heat of the fire.

Pete looked about for any sign of his family, shouting, "Mother! Caroline!" He repeatedly called their names. Caroline, Ann, and Elizabeth appeared from their place of refuge near the family cemetery. Quickly, they tearfully raced toward Pete as he dismounted. Elizabeth cried loudly, "Pete my son, is that you?"

"Yes, Mother, it's me." Pete replied as he joyfully embraced her.

"I thought you were dead."

"I was seriously wounded, but I'm fine thanks to a lady who lived in the area."

"I am so glad that you are alive. When I received the news from Daniel, I constantly grieved for you. I have so much that I want to tell you."

Caroline and Ann both embraced Pete as Ann cried, "Look what the Yankees did. They have destroyed our home and all of our family valuables."

Pete said as he turned and watched the second floor interior of the house collapse, "I know." Pete paused and turned once more toward his Mother and Caroline, and said, "I just came from the Union camp along the heights. As I saw the fire, a Federal officer said that one of our friends might have betrayed us."

Elizabeth replied in an outburst of anger, "But who would do something this terrible to us. Who!"

"Mother, I don't know."

"Well I do." Elizabeth replied in a flare of anger, "Only, Katie McBride could have brought this evil upon us."

"I'm not to sure of that."

Caroline broke her silence and said, "I agree with Pete. Even though Katie and I are not the best of friends, I really don't believe that Katie is a spy, and capable of doing something like this."

Pete asked, as he looked at Caroline, "Then who knew that Charles was still alive. As I understand from Miss Virginia, everyone believes that he is dead."

"No one, but Ann and Mother Elizabeth."

Suddenly, Pete and Caroline's conversation was interrupted by the approaching sound of a horse. Pete walked over to his horse and removed a revolver from his saddlebags. With the bright sky providing light, Pete recognized the rider as Daniel. Pete lowered his weapon as the overseer dismounted.

As Daniel approached Pete, there was an expression of amazement that covered his face. He was surprise to see that the young Barker was still alive. Daniel promptly said, "I thought you were dead. I was the one who broke the news to Miss Elizabeth."

Pete answered coldly, as he stared at Daniel, "I guess you were wrong."

Daniel turned away from Pete and began to watch the flames continue to dance within the structure. After a minute or so had past, Pete turned and noticed the expression of anger that covered Daniel's features. Pete knew that the overseer felt the indignation just as the rest of the family by the events that had taken place. Silently, Daniel stood by Pete and watched as the flames continued to roar throughout the dwelling. In an angry tone of voice, Daniel said, "I knew that something like this was going to happen." Pete was amazed, as he turned to look at Daniel. Striking his fist against a fence rail in a near rage of temper, the overseer continued, "I just came from Charlestown where Federal cavalry destroyed the home of Mr. Andrew Hunter in the same manner as they did this home. The General hasn't even spared his own cousin's property."

"Caroline held her hand to her mouth and cried, "Oh no. Please, dear God, let it not be so.""

Elizabeth said, as she continued to display her anger and despair, "The Yankees told us that since Charles' continuous involvement with the Confederate government, they still had the right to destroy our home and property. But everyone knows that he is dead.""

Daniel knew that Charles was still alive, but he hadn't, nor would he reveal this knowledge to anyone. Elizabeth continued to release her frustration and indignation, "Someone betrayed us. Someone who claims that Charles is still alive."

"Well, I may know who that might be."

Caroline turned and gazed at Daniel asking, "Who Daniel? What do you know?"

"Well Mam, earlier this afternoon when I went into town to pick up some supplies, I noticed Katie McBride at the train depot meeting a Yankee officer. I guess I was just being snoopy, but I followed them to General Howe's headquarters on Fillmore Street. After about an hour had passed, I noticed her and the officer speaking with the General on the front porch. Shortly, a courier, departed in a big hurry carrying I'm sure a message for General Hunter. Several hours later, the torch was put to the Congressman's home." Pete remained silent as the middle-aged overseer continued to taunt, "I don't have much education such as yourself, but what does all of this tell ya?"

Pete promptly said, as his eyes gazed at Daniel, "That still doesn't mean that she is responsible for what has taken place."

"Well then you tell me why she didn't move out of the widow Stipes boarding house when some of those Yankee officers moved in. And why over the last two years has she disappeared at times from the Ferry, huh."

"How do you know?"

"I know. Trust me, I know."

Pete turned and looked at the expression of amazement that covered Caroline's face. The information that Daniel was sharing was difficult for him to accept. For the last four years he had come to trust Katie with his whole heart and believed that she always, unconditionally, shared the truth with him. Now, he struggled too fight off the doubt. It was to painful to imagine that she was the one, who betrayed him and the family, causing this tribulation to befall them. He must be certain. He must make the attempt to see her this very night. Pete knew that he must keep his intentions to see Katie a secret. After briefly speaking with

Caroline and his Mother concerning his return to Colonel Mosby, he made a request of Daniel to escort the ladies to the Whites in Charlestown.

As the evening hours crept by, Pete rode along the Shenandoah toward the Ferry. He knew he must attempt to avoid Union pickets stationed in the area. Under the cover of darkness, Pete arrived at Katie's residence and slowly walked up the steps. He noticed that the house was dark and quiet. There was no answer after he knocked at the door several times. He attempted to open the door, but it was locked. After walking around the perimeter of the house, he was convinced that Katie wasn't there. Where could she be, he thought? It was late, very late. She had completely vanished.

CHAPTER THIRTY-EIGHT

By the end of August of 1864, General Jubal Early's Confederate troops had driven the Union forces from Winchester, Virginia, and were in complete control of the city and the surrounding area. Katie McBride had accompanied Mrs. Polly McDonald to the city to visit with her ailing sister Martha, and to help with her medical needs. In the five weeks that the two ladies had been present in the city, they had experienced once more the sound of battle and the anger of war. For Katie, it had been a very difficult year, still without the knowledge that Pete Barker was alive and fighting with Mosby's command. Over the past six months, Katie had struggled with the anger and depression that one experiences over the loss of someone that they have love and known. Her life in many ways with Pete's absence had lost its meaning and the void that filled her heart was unbearable at times. Often, during the quiet of the evening, she wept and spent restless nights tossing and turning attempting to find peace and acceptance of the lost of Pete. On many occasions over the past year, some of the Federal officers in the Ferry had exhibited an interest in her, inviting her to social functions, but she always refused the invitation, desiring to be alone. Katie's life was one of seclusion. Happiness had lost its meaning. All of her visions and dreams of life had vanished, even to the point of resigning her teaching position at the school. On one occasion, she returned home to visit with her parents, even pondering the idea of staying in Boston for good and attempting a fresh beginning with life, but for some unknown reason, she returned to Harpers Ferry against the wishes of her family. As the war raged on, her brother Seamus had maintain very little in the way of correspondence with her, still angered over her love for Pete. The only knowledge that Katie had of Seamus' welfare was from her Mother, who informed her that he was still fighting with the 1st Massachusetts Cavalry somewhere in Virginia. Like many, Katie, was becoming weary of the conflict and desired for its conclusion.

There was a gentle morning breeze blowing through the open window where Katie slept. After experiencing a restless night filled with bad dreams of the war, Katie was aroused by the sound of many footsteps pounding the pavement. As she slowly rose from the huge mahogany bed and walked over to the front window, which provided her with a perfect view of Braddock Street, she intensely watched Confederate soldiers marching Federal prisoners to an area of confinement. Her mind dwelled upon these particular soldiers and the horrors that they would face in some prisoner-of-war camp in the south. Maybe, some would return home to be with a loved one, but she knew that many would die in confinement. Out there somewhere, a family member, or sweetheart would experience the same feelings and emotions that she had gone through over the previous months. After dressing, she slowly walked down the stairway to the dining room. Before she entered, Katie listen to Martha share her feelings with her sister, "Polly, I'm so darn glad that our boys have regain the city. It does my heart good to see them."

There was a pessimistic tone in Polly's voice as she looked at her sister, "Oh, Martha. Do you really think that we are going to win this war? Our men are starving, and General Lee is in a stand off with Grant below Richmond."

Martha was persistent in her tone of voice, "Our boys have a strong will, they'll keep fighting for as long as General Lee tells them."

"Let's just change the subject, I don't feel like arguing this morning with you concerning the war." After pausing, Polly's face brighten and in a tone of excitement, "Oh, Martha. Do you know who I ran into yesterday?'

"No Polly, I don't. Who?"

"Emily Todd. She is going to hold a tea and we are invited. I was planning on asking Katie if she would like to attend. Would you like to go?"

"No, I don't believe so, I'm still not feeling all that well. Besides, do you really feel that the ladies of Winchester would feel comfortable with a Yankee lady attending one of their functions?"

Katie walked into the dining room with a smile on her face saying, "No Miss Martha, I really don't think that they would."

Polly said in a pleading tone as she watched Katie take her seat, "Oh child, please make an effort, there needs to be reconciliation in this wretched society?"

Katie said, as she stirred the sugar and cream in her cup of tea, "No Mrs. McDonald, I wouldn't want anyone to feel uncomfortable with my presence. I will stay here this afternoon and keep Miss Martha company while you go."

"Well, then I won't go either." Polly said, as there was a loud knock at the front door.

Martha said, with a tone of amazement, as she looked in Katie and her sister direction, "Oh dear, I wonder who that might be this early in the morning?"

As Polly rose from the chair to answer the door, she replied, "I don't know, but we are going to find out."

As Polly opened the door, she was surprised to see a young Confederate officer accompanied by several privates holding their muskets. After briefly pausing and finding the words, she said in a nervous tone of voice, "Lieutenant, what brings you to our home this early in the morning?"

The officer replied by introduction and tipping his hat, "Madam, I'm Lieutenant Arnold of the provost guard. May we come in?"

There was an expression of concern that covered Polly's face, and it reflected in her voice as she answered, "Is there something wrong?"

The officer replied as he looked through the door to the entrance into the room, "Madam, if we may enter?"

As she stepped aside to allow them to enter, she cordially answered, "Yes, by all means."

The officer turned about to face Polly, "Is there a Miss McBride staying with you?"

After hearing the officer speaking with Polly, Katie stood and walked toward the front entrance saying in a soft, calm voice as she approached, "Yes, I'm Miss McBride. How can I help you?"

The officer turned about and said as he tipped his hat in a friendly gesture, "Miss McBride, I have orders from Colonel Moore to escort you to his headquarters."

There was an expression of astonishment as Katie answered, "Why? What does the Colonel want with me?"

The officer politely said as he gestured for her to walk toward the door,

"That will all be explained to you once you see the Colonel. Please Miss McBride, if you will?"

"I don't understand." Katie replied as she slowly proceeded with the soldiers toward the front entrance and placed her bonnet on her head.

Polly McDonald grabbed the officer by his right arm and pleaded, "What has she done?" The officer was silent as Polly continued, "Please sir, there must be some mistake."

As the soldiers and Katie walked toward a carriage that was waiting in front of the residence, Martha joined her sister at the front door and said as they watched the soldiers helped Katie into the seat, "I believe that young girl is in a lot of trouble. A lot of trouble."

Polly said in a concern tone, "Later, I'll make the attempt to find out what is going on. I can't believe that she is in some kind of trouble. Katie is such an innocent girl."

"Well sister, there may be things about that young lady that you and I don't know about."

As the carriage slowly proceeded to the provost officer's headquarters, Katie remained calm thinking about her life. She was reminded of pleasant thoughts with Pete that night in the church over a year ago, it resurrected a subtle smile on her face. She didn't have any regrets of revealing her deepest feelings for him, nor pleading with him to return to Boston with her. Now at this very moment, she desired his touch, his embrace, the security that he gave her, and the warm compassion that flowed from his eyes. It was times such as this, that she needed his comfort and reassuring words of wisdom. If only he was alive, she knew he would not hesitate to render her assistance in this time of need.

Katie's thoughts were interrupted by the sudden jerk of the carriage coming to a halt. The officer that was seated opposite Katie stepped down from the carriage and rendered assistance to her. As she looked about, Katie noticed that she was being taken into a brick house somewhere along Loudoun Street. Katie glanced at a regiment of cavalry as it passed the carriage, hoping that everyone was wrong and that Pete would be riding with them, but she was sadly disappointed.

As the officer and two guards escorted her, Katie entered the residence and was immediately taken to Colonel Moore, who was seated in a chair near a table in the library. Upon her entrance, Colonel Moore stood and politely said, "Miss McBride, please come in and be seated."

Bluntly and angrily, Katie asked, "What is the bloody meaning of this? Why did you embarrass me and bring me here? Why!"

The Colonel was quiet as he removed a cigar from a box on the table. After lighting it, he calmly replied, "Miss McBride, you should calm yourself. You and I are going to have a friendly little chat. Just the two of us."

Katie remained silent as the Colonel ordered the officer and the two guards to leave the room. Once more, he turned his attention to Katie and after being seated, he continued to speak, "As I understand, yesterday evening you were visiting the camp of the 1st Virginia Cavalry on the edge of town."

"Yes that is correct. Is there something wrong with that?"

"Madam, that depends on the nature of your business."

Katie replied in a defensive tone, "I did nothing wrong."

"Miss McBride, I'm not too sure of that." The Colonel lifted his hands, gesturing after seeing that Katie was going to interrupt. He knew that Katie was still angry and defiant. The officer continued in a polite tone of voice, "If I may, let me ask you a question? Why would a pretty girl like you be visiting with a regiment of cavalrymen? I'm sure that you weren't there to socialize, and you don't appear to be, let's say, someone of questionable nature."

"I was looking for information concerning an acquaintance, someone I knew personally who fought with the regiment."

The Colonel grinned as he spoke, "Oh, is that so? Or let's say, that you were looking for information to pass to the Yankees?"

Katie promptly replied as she continued to stand with her eyes fixed on the officer, "Like I said Colonel, I was looking for someone who could tell me how my friend gave his life for this bloody, miserable, cause."

"Miss McBride, I don't for one moment believe a word that comes from the mouth of a Yankee. Especially, someone who wears a dress and can impress soldiers who haven't been home for quite sometime, nor been with a lady in an intimate way. Those cavalrymen are vulnerable, and you knew it."

Once more Katie became angry and it reflected in her tone of voice, "Well, you can bloody believe anything that you like, but it's not what you are insinuating. Like many of the people that live in this area, I've had enough of this bloody war."

The Colonel lost his patience with Katie and shouted, "I feel that after a night of confinement, maybe you will be more cooperative." Pausing and pointing his finger in her direction, he continued in a calmer tone of voice, "You and I will resume this discussion tomorrow, and hopefully, you will be more willing to cooperate with me."

Without hesitation, Colonel Moore called out for the guard, who was posted outside of the door to the room. The sentry opened the door, and as he did so, Colonel Moore shouted, "Take Miss McBride and confine her until further notice."

As the guard took Katie by the arm, she turned about and shouted, "You can't do this. You're making a bloody mistake."

The guard escorted Katie to the city jail. She was walked to a cell in the back of the building. As one of the guards opened the door to the cell, she noticed that there was a window with bars, but too high for her to look out into the ally behind the building, or attempt an escape. She stood at the entrance to the cell glancing about and noticing that the only furnishings was an old rusty-iron frame cot with grimy linen for bedding, and a wooden stand with a pitcher and bowl for bathing. As Katie was ordered to step into the cell, tears began to fill her eyes. After the guard locked the cell door, reality and the seriousness of the situation began to surface within her heart. She began to fear for her life. Katie knew that she was being accused of spying for the government of the United States and was sure that if convicted, she could be put to death by hanging, or by a firing squad. What could she do? What could she say in the morning when she confronted Colonel Moore once again? Her intentions had been honorable in visiting the camp of the 1st Virginia and seeking information regarding Pete's death. In her desperation, she didn't give consideration concerning the consequences of her presence in the camp, especially being from the North. Quietly, she passed the afternoon pondering on her defense and innocence.

After seven that evening, her thoughts were broken by the loud sound of the huge wooden door that led to the cellblock. As she looked about, she was surprise to see William Pierce walking toward her cell. Katie began to wonder what business might have brought him to the city, but most of all, how he knew about her dilemma. With a cigar in his hand, William stepped to the cell and ordered the guard to open the door allowing him to enter. Without a word, the guard complied with the order. By now, Katie's expression had turned to one of seriousness as she asked, "William, what are you doing here?"

William, politely and calmly answered, "I came here to see my cousin, Colonel Moore. But briefly after speaking with him, he informed me of your apprehension. So, I came to see you, and to speak with you concerning your problem. As I'm sure you well know, you are in some serious trouble."

"William, I didn't do anything. Please, believe me."

William was silent as he gazed at Katie. He knew that he still possessed strong feelings for her, and hadn't given up his quest for her love and devotion. It was his intentions by his actions to gain her loyalty by making certain promises for her freedom in exchange for information on her spying activities. William was sure that Katie had been carrying out such activities for the Federals since the beginning of the war, and that her periodical absence from Harpers Ferry, such as now, was to gain information and intelligence to pass across Federal lines to her superiors. William methodically chose his words and spoke with caution, "Katie, I'm here to help you, but it's important that you cooperate with me, or else there is nothing that I can do for you."

Katie pleaded as she approached William, "This is all a bad mistake. I've done nothing wrong."

"Then what were you doing in the camp of the 1st Virginia? And not only their camp, but also several other regiments that were positioned near by?"

"I was looking for information about Pete's death. Maybe someone could have told me something, or they saw him, or spoke with him before he was killed. I just wanted to know if there were any last words. That's all."

Within his heart, William was furious that Katie could be holding on to feelings for Pete, especially after being dead for over a year. Still, he believed that if he could help her, that she would feel indebted to him, and he would be able to manipulate her for his own purpose.

"Katie, trust me, that's going to be difficult for anyone to believe. I certainly don't accept your explanation. I believe that you were looking for information to pass to the Federals and just using the death of a brave warrior for your own purpose. How can you do that to someone that you claimed to have feelings for? After all of this time, how?"

"But its true. I came with Mrs. McDonald to assist her with her ailing sister. Just recently, I saw the 1st Virginia camped near the edge of town and I knew that they had been engaged at Gettysburg. It was my only chance of gaining information about Pete."

"Then you are telling me that you don't know that the Barker Estate was put to the torch by the Yankees as well as several other homes in the area? Totally destroyed! Everything completely gone! Those villains left nothing! The Barkers are homeless because of you."

Katie was caught off guard by Williams's accusations. Katie was surprised and stunned by the news of the devastation of Shenandoah. She was silent, her expression turned to grief, her eyes appeared glassy from the tears that filled them. Her thoughts turned to Caroline and Ann, she promptly asked, "What about Caroline and Ann? Where are they?"

"At the moment, they are in Richmond. See Katie, I know everything you have been up to."

"William, what are you talking about?"

William continued as he paced from one side of the cell to the other, refusing to look at Katie, "I know about your visit to General Howe's headquarters the day that Shenandoah was destroyed, as well as the other homes. Also, I know that you know that Charles Barker is alive and in Richmond. You were spying on him and Caroline, and informed Union authorities of his existence. You just played along and kept it all a secret and acted as if he didn't exist anymore. Why Katie, why?"

"How did you know?"

"I've been at this business a lot longer then you or anyone else. Really, no one knows, but you and a few others. Even the Barkers are in the dark concerning my activity. And we'll keep it that way. Understand."

Katie remained silent as she noticed the coldness that filled his eyes and expression that ruled his features. Now, too, she feared William and what he might attempt to do to bring her harm. It was apparent that he had an informant and spy that had been watching her every move. Katie knew that she could expect little in the way of help from him unless it came with a price. She broke her silence and asked, "What now?"

"In the morning, you and I will leave for Richmond. There, I will speak with President Davis concerning your fate. Hopefully, you'll be imprisoned for the duration of the war. Maybe, you'll only be banished to the North."

Katie softly replied as she gazed at him, "If that happens, then I guess I will owe you a great deal of gratitude." After pausing and waiting for a reaction from him, which didn't come, Katie continued with these calm words of defiance, "But, not my love."

William lost his temper and physically grabbed Katie by the arm. Katie screamed, "William, let go of me. Please, your hurting me."

William yelled at Katie, "You are so ungrateful. Don't you understand? I'm the only one that can save your life and deliver you from this mess!"

"You want more then that. You want what I can't give you, my love."

In a continuous rage of anger, William knocked the washbowl from the wooden stand and yelled, "If I can't have you, then no one can!"

"William, you can't make someone love you."

"Then so be it. But, if I have anything to do with this matter, you'll never see the light of day again! Ever! Do you understand me?"

As William increased the pressure on Katie's arm, once more she loudly pleaded, "You are mad! Please let go, I beg you!"

Without saying another word, William slapped Katie across her face with the palm of his hand. Katie lost her balance and fell on the floor striking her head against the iron cot. As she touched her lip, she noticed the blood that was trickling from her hand. Immediately, Katie looked at William and noticed the wild glare that was in his eyes, the tense expression that covered his face. She didn't know if he would continue to punish her, or if his aggression would come to a halt. Katie began to loudly cry, "Help me! Please someone help me." No one came to her assistance.

Finally, William walked over to where she was still lying. He stood over his prey as a lion does its victim. Inwardly, Katie began to tremble with fear, though outwardly, she didn't reveal her feelings. William began to speak angrily, "Tomorrow, bright and early, you and I will leave for Richmond whether you like it or not. Understood!"

Katie remained silent as she helplessly looked up at him. Once more William said as he knelt beside her, "I said do you understand?"

Katie's appearance was cold as she answered in a whisper, "Yes, I understand."

Slowly, William rose to his feet. Once more, his cold eyes glanced at Katie as she laid helplessly on the floor. He turned about and called for a guard. As the sentry approached the jail cell, he was stunned to see Katie lying on the floor still bleeding from her injuries. William commanded to the sentry as he stepped from the cell, "Remember one thing, you didn't see anything. Do you understand?"

"Yes sir."

William said in an authoritative and intimidating tone of voice, "If you do, I'll have you shot. Understand?"

Once more the sentry answered, "Yes sir, Mr. Pierce."

Again, William quietly turned about glaring at Katie. Quickly, he departed with the sentry warning the guard once more about the consequences if he revealed what he had witnessed.

In the twenty-four years of her life, no man had ever handled her in such a physical way. Katie was very angry, shocked, and stunned by William's behavior. In many ways Katie felt betrayed by William, who she knew for the last four years and believed was friendly toward her. Even though they shared differences concerning the social issues, which was what this war was all about, Katie didn't believe until now, that William was capable of such anger and violence. As she thought about all that had just transpired between them, she knew that William possessed more influence in Richmond then originally believed. She must come up with a plan of escape before morning. Her freedom and life depended upon it.

CHAPTER THIRTY-NINE

As Pete Barker sat on his mare along the Blue Ridge Mountains near Snicker's Gap, he observed the sun's bright glow, as it was beginnng to set along the western horizon of the Allegheny Mountain range that borders the Shenandoah Valley. He had been ordered by Colonel Mosby to carry a sealed dispatch to General Early concerning their endeavors against the Federal cavalry raids. It had been a difficult six weeks for Pete, still sadden by the loss of his home, and concern for his family. He wondered how much longer the war would continue. The conflict had brought much sorrow and despair upon the citizens of the Valley with the devastation of mills, the destruction of farms, crops, and the senseless killing of soldiers. The local home guard was not displaying any mercy either toward sympathizers who showed charity to deserters, but even placed some under scrutiny. As Pete thought about the situation, it was obvious that the Union armies' gains in Virginia and the rest of the lower South was a crushing blow to the Confederacy. There wasn't any way that the South could win the war. Like many of his comrades still engaged in combat, Pete knew the only way that there could be peace would be if Lincoln lost the up coming election in November. Many times since he received his wound near Funkstown, the words that Hannah had spoken to him continued to resurface within his heart, and it caused him to give great thought as to why he continued the struggle, and what could be possibly gained by it's continuation. On more then one occasion, he had thought about desertion, but his pride still ruled in favor of honor. Pete knew the possible embarrassment that it would cause his family.

Before dark, he discovered a trail that slanted in a southwestern direction from the crest of the mountain that he slowly followed. At a plateau along the mountain not far from the river, he came upon a stone house. As he cautiously approached, he noticed an elderly gentleman standing on the front porch with his right hand stroking his long gray beard carefully observing him. Pete wasn't wearing a soldier's uniform. Instead he wore civilian clothing such as that of a farmer. With his revolver concealed in his saddlebags, he rode to where the gentleman was standing. In a friendly and polite tone of voice, he said, "Howdy."

The old man had a cold and suspicious appearance about him. He remained silent as he nodded in a friendly gesture. It wasn't Pete's intentions to stay any longer then necessary. He got straight to the point of his business, "Where can I cross the river."

The old man turned and pointed, saying, "Straight through them there trees, and down the slope. Go up stream, oh I say about a hundred yards or so and you will see a tall lone sycamore tree near some rock. You can cross there. You can't miss it."

As Pete thanked the old gentleman, he proceeded in the direction shared with him, to find that the way was just as he was told. Once on the opposite side of the river, he noticed a young boy fishing. Briefly pausing, he reflected on the days of his youth at the Estate when he, too, would spend a leisurely day along the river. As he turned his horse westward, his mind returned to reality and he knew that he must find his way around the Federal cavalry patrols that were roaming the area.

It was after dark when he arrived in Winchester. Immediately, he delivered the dispatch as ordered, only to discover from one of the soldiers at headquarters that his old cavalry regiment was positioned on the road toward Berryville. Over the past year, he had often thought of his good friend Jonathan Collins and his welfare. On more then one occasion, he owed Jonathan his life for protecting him during combat. With the exchange of prisoners being halted by the Federals, he often wondered if his friend was released before the practice began. He was curious to know.

Pete proceeded with haste and found the 1st Virginia in camp along the Opequon Creek, a short distance from the city. As he dismounted and allowed his horse to roam freely, Jacob Smith approached and recognized him, "Pete? Pete Barker, how ya doin'?"

Pete turned and said enthusiastically, calling him by his nickname, "Smitty. The question is how are you doing. I understand from the newspapers that the 1st has been doing a lot of fighting?"

"Yeah, too much. We've been sufferin' mostly from the lack of new recruits. It's difficult to replace dose good men that has fallen."

"I don't know how much longer that we can hold out."

Quickly, Jacob changed the subject and asked, "Hey, rumor has it that ya are ridin' with Mosby?"

"Yeah, for about the last nine months. It's a different type of fighting. Usually, we hit and run." After a moment of silence, Pete asked, "Have you seen Jonathan Collins?"

"We've had some men return to the regiment, but I don't know that he's one of them."

After speaking with the soldier for a short time and catching up on the activities of the regiment, Pete continued to search for his friend. Pete knew that it was common practice for a soldier to return home, if possible, after leaving prison rather then return to duty. Pete decided to visit their old company and begin his search there.

As he walked through the camp, he noticed that some of the soldiers cherished the time alone writing correspondence to a love one, a friend, or even maybe the hometown newspaper. Some of the men appeared to be cooking their supper, as others sat around the campfire smoking their pipes and speaking of merrier days. Still, a group of the soldiers laughed loudly and humored themselves by telling friendly jokes, yet a few passed the leisurely time with their hats covering their face napping. Off in the distance, Pete paused to listen to a soldier playing a banjo and entertaining some of his comrades singing Jine The Cavalry. It brought back pleasant memories of the days when he rode with General Stuart and the regiment.

Pete continued to walk slowly through camp; he paused when he heard a deep, loud, and over bearing laugh that was prevalent over the sounds of the other soldiers that were present. He began to smile; he recognized the sound as coming from his good friend, Jonathan. Pete walked between the tents to find his friend playing cards with five other soldiers. Jonathan was laughing because he had just won the round of poker and was in the process of poking fun at the losers. Quietly, Pete walked over to where the soldiers were seated on crates. Jonathan looked up from his hand, and immediately, a surprised and relieved expression covered the width of his face. Jonathan jumped to his feet laughing with joy, and embraced Pete saying, "I knew ya wasn't gonna die."

Pete replied, as he laughed with his friend, "It was close, too close. After the war ends, I need to return to Maryland and thank the lady who saved me from death."

Jonathan turned quickly about and said to his comrades, "This is my friend, Pete Barker." As he once more focused his attention on Pete, Jonathan continued with enthusiasm, "I knew that ya wounds was serious, that's why I kept fightin' to give ya the chance to git away. But, I killed two of them before I gave up."

Pete placed his hand on Jonathan's shoulder and seriously said, "Jonathan, thank you for your sacrifice. You could have gotten away and have been spared the torture of a prisoner-of-war camp."

"Yeah, I know. That place was some stink hole. It was hell on earth the way that we were treated. They gave us hardly anything to eat, almost no shelter from the rain. I saw a many good man die from disease. But ya want to know what burns me up the most?"

Pete remained silent as he continued to listen to his friend speak of the horrors that he had endured, "At anytime they felt like it, the Yanks would shoot our men for no reason at all." Jonathan lowered his head in despair continuing, "Even now, it makes me mad to think about it."

"Say no more. Hopefully, the war will be over with, and we can all go home, and someday forget."

"Why don't ya sit a spell and I'll fetch ya some coffee. There's not much left, but ya's welcome."

"I can't stay long, I have to return to Colonel Mosby."

"So that's who your ridin' with. I remember him from 1862, a little sort of fella."

"Yeah." Pete said as he laughed shaking his head and continuing, "But he is a fighter."

As Pete sat on one of the crates, Jonathan handed him the coffee that he had just poured. Pete took a sip and said, "Have you heard any word concerning Lester."

"I know that he made it back to Virginia, but other then that, I don't know."

As Pete paused and reflected on his cousin, he continued by asking, "How about your family? Are they alright?"

"I don't know, I haven't heard. Ya know I haven't seen them in four years. At times, I git some word from home, but seldom. What bothers me more then anythin' with this war is not knowin' 'bout my family."

"Fortunately, I've had the opportunity. It gave me great relief, but the Yankees burned Shenandoah and destroyed everything. For now, my family is in Richmond."

Jonathan said angrily as he threw the rest of his coffee on the ground, "The blasted Yankees are tryin' to take everythin'. Every time we go somewhere different, we see the mills, barns, and homes that they have burned. Our people are homeless, 'specially the kids." Pete remained silent gazing at his friend as Jonathan continued to release his anger, "I heard earlier from Carl Smith of H Company, that we caught a female Yankee spy right here in town."

With a reply of astonishment, Pete said, "Really. Did Carl say what she looked like?"

Jonathan began to laugh as he rubbed his chin, "Yeah. Matter of fact, he did. He said she sure had beautiful dark red hair and the expression of an angel. But, that's it."

As Pete looked at Jonathan, he knew that the description could possibly be Katie. With the information that Daniel had shared with him and the family regarding Katie's visit to General Howe's headquarters last month, by that very act alone, she raised suspicion, especially with the destruction of homes of prominent Southern sympathizers. If she was being detained, Katie could be transferred to Richmond. Even with the devastation of homes and property in Jefferson County, Pete had a difficult time believing that Katie was supplying the Federals with information concerning Confederate activity in the area. Even if she was guilty of such crimes, he couldn't allow her to remained imprisoned for spying, knowing that the punishment could be harsh if convicted. It wasn't a chance that he could take. He had to do something. He needed to discover if the prisoner was really Katie, or someone else. Immediately, he enlisted the help of his friend, "Jonathan, can you spare a few hours to help me?"

Jonathan possessed a mischief grin saying as he looked at Pete, "Sure, what ya need?"

"You may not like it, but here it goes anyway. I believe that the lady that's being held in town may very well be my friend, Katie. Matter of fact, the more that I think about it, the more that I am convinced."

"She's ya lady friend that Lester and I use to tease ya 'bout."

"Yeah. Your right."

Jonathan's demeanor turned to one of seriousness, "What ya want me to do?"

"We need to borrow a few things before we go into town. Come on, I'll tell you what I have in mind."

Without wasting another minute, Pete and Jonathan were secretly busy about seeking those items that would be needed for the task.

It was late in the evening as Pete and Jonathan rode slowly into the city. Pete was wearing the uniform of a Confederate Major that the two of them stole from Major Clark's tent. They brought their horses to a halt in front of the jail and dismounted. With confidence and boldness, they walked toward the front entrance of the building. Pete gave particular attention to where the guards were posted in case their plan failed. He noticed one standing near the outside door, which saluted him as he passed, and two more as they walked through the entrance. Jonathan quietly stayed close to Pete's side as they entered the dwelling. Once on the inside, Pete was confronted by one of the guards, "Sir, if I may ask your business?"

"I'm here to escort a prisoner to Richmond." Pete replied as he continued to look about the premise.

"Sir, I will escort you to Captain Massey's quarters. He is the officer in charge of the prisoners."

The prison was dirty, dark, and dungy as Pete and Jonathan followed the guard down the long hallway. It was quiet, the only sound coming from the soldier's boots tapping against the wooden floors. The sentry halted and knocked on the door. Immediately, a graveled voice came from the opposite side of the door commanding them to enter. The officer looked up from his desk as Pete, Jonathan, and one of the guards entered the room. After noticing Pete's rank, the captain promptly asked, "Yes Major, what brings you here this late in the evening?"

"I'm here on orders from President Davis to escort the lady that you are holding for spying, back to Richmond."

"Sir, if I may see your orders?"

Pete was prepared for such a request. He removed the papers, which he forged from his coat and handed the order to the captain. Silently, the officer began to read, "Major Thompson, you will proceed directly to Winchester, and if found, escort Miss Katie McBride to Richmond without hesitation."

The order was signed, "Your obedient servant, Jefferson Davis."

After reading the order, the officer looked at Pete sighing, "There has already been a gentleman here earlier with orders to escort her to Richmond."

Pete said in a firm and authoritative manner, "Are you refusing the President's order?"

"No sir, I wouldn't refuse the President's orders, it carries more authority then Secretary Seddon's request. But I have to clear up this matter."

"There isn't much time. Besides, it's too late in the evening to telegraph the Secretary of War. He is probably sleeping and would only be angry if you awaken him. You can inform him in the morning."

"But sir?"

"That's an order Captain. Now, have the prisoner brought to me." The officer paused momentarily with perplexity covering his wrinkled features. Once more Pete commanded, "Now captain!"

The captain glanced at the guard and nodded his approval. Slowly, the guard turned about and proceeded toward the cellblock. Pete's hands began to perspire, his stomach felt queasy from the uncertainty of the moment. He began to give considerable thought concerning the course of action that they would undertake if discovered. He knew that Jonathan and him could be imprisoned, or hung if their identity was disclosed by an unexpected visit to the jail by William Pierce, or anyone else that might recognize them. They would have to make their escape as quickly as possible without raising any suspicion. After leaving the city, Pete knew that they would have to avoid Federal cavalry patrol as well as the possibility of Confederate agents attempting to track them down once their deception was known. Too add to his difficulties, he hoped that Katie would withhold her emotions once she recognized him and until after they were out of the city. He was sure that she still believed that he was dead.

As Pete reminisced on happier days before the war with the captain, he heard the sound of footsteps approaching the office. Jonathan remained silent, but inconspicuously with his hand near the revolver that he carried. Pete's heart began to race with anxiety, but as many times in the past, he didn't reveal his fears. There was the sound of the door opening, and then all conversation ceased. Pete turned about, and for the first time in over a year, he saw Katie standing by the guard. Her face was pale, and her hair needed grooming. She remained quiet with a calm expression covering her features. Pete knew that she was surprised to see him and that it was all that she could do to withhold her emotions. It was difficult as well for him. Pete knew that he wanted to embrace her and reassure her that everything would be all right, but he must remain focused on their flight to safety. He was angered and concerned by her appearance, especially the bruised wound that was on her lower lip. Still, he remained silent and didn't make the attempt to question the officer concerning the injury.

Katie was very reserve in her demeanor as her eyes were fixed upon Pete. Inwardly, she was joyful, relieved, and the depression that imprisoned her began to subside and release her from the inward prison that she had endured for so long. Her heart raced with anticipation, she was tantalized by his presence, and she repressed the temptation of touching him, and being near his side. She was thankful to God that he was still alive her prayers were answered. Within her heart, she was convinced that he must feel something for her, far deeper and stronger then he had previously led her to believe, and was willing to reveal. The stroke of his boldness amazed her, but it confirmed her beliefs regarding his loyalty and word. Katie remembered the words of reassurance that he spoke at the beginning of the war, "I will never betray our friendship regardless of your beliefs and views concerning our social differences." Suddenly, Pete ordered the guard, "Bound the prisoner," broke her thoughts.

Katie was surprised, but knew that she must play the role and remained silent as the guard complied with the order. As soon as the guard finished, Jonathan gestured for Katie to depart with him as he walked by her side. After mounting their horses, the trio headed south, and then along Loudoun Street toward the outskirts of town.

For most of the evening, William Pierce had reservations about leaving early the next morning, but instead, he decided to move up his departure with Katie tonight. According to Confederate scouting reports on the Federal army's activities east of the city, General Crook's division was in the vicinity of Berryville, while General Sheridan's forces were moving from Harpers Ferry toward Charlestown. He knew that there would be a general advance by the Union forces to regain the city and eventually move through the Valley to drive out its defenders. William was filled with fear and doubt in the Confederate army's ability to hold the city, and thus mistakenly leave Katie behind to be rescued by the Yankees. He must move rapidly, he thought. After packing his belongings and requesting an orderly to bring him his horse and a mare for Miss McBride, he quickly departed for the jail. As he arrived at the prison, he could barely make out the three riders that were proceeding in a southerly direction toward Kernstown. Quickly, he dismounted and entered the jailhouse, proceeding directly to Captain Massey's office. William knocked loudly and without waiting for an answer, opened the door, and demanded, "Captain, I want you to bring me Miss McBride!"

The surprised captain answered as he rose from his chair, "Mr. Pierce, I received orders from President Davis to release her to the custody of Major Thompson of the President's personal staff."

As the officer handed William the order, his eyes quickly scanned the contents. He shouted as he struck the desk with his fist, "You fool, there is no Major Thompson on the President's personal staff, or for the matter anyone else. Do you know what you have done?"

The captain replied with a quiver in his voice, "No sir. No sir, I don't."

"Most likely, you have just released a Union spy to the Yankees, an agent."

The officer pleaded with William as he came from behind the desk, "Sir, if you'd let me explain."

As the captain came within arms length, William grabbed him by his white shirt and shouted, "There is no time to explain! I want them pursued now. Do you hear me Captain!"

"Yes sir. I will get right to it."

"And Captain, if you don't bring her back to me," William paused and the officer noticed the cold, wild, and ruthless glare in his eyes, "Trust me, you'll swing at the end of a rope."

With haste, the officer called several of the guards to go for help in an attempt to carry out William Pierce's command. William sent for a courier to carry a message to Daniel, who he knew had just arrived in the city. Once more, William had requested his service to assist in escorting Katie and him to Richmond. With the family business shattered by the war, he was no longer needed by the Barkers to oversee the Estate.

As Pete, Jonathan, and Katie disappeared into the night, they came upon a lane about a mile outside of the city. Quickly, the threesome turned their mounts due east. After about a mile, they brought their horses to a halt within view of a farmhouse. Under a grove of trees out of sight of the owners of the homestead,

Pete dismounted and requested Katie to do likewise. As Katie glanced at Pete, she noticed that he was removing some men's clothing from his saddlebags. With the clothing bundled under his arm, Pete approached Katie. There was an expression of relief on her face as he walked over to her. Immediately, Katie dismounted and embraced him, caressing his face with her hand saying, "Thank God, I am so thankful that you are alive. Pete, I have many questions to ask you." Just as quickly as Katie spoke the first word, Pete broke their embrace, placing his finger on her lips in a gesture for her to remain silence. He didn't want to give away their position because he knew they were fugitives subject to harsh punishment if captured by the Confederate provost officer. They were enemies of the Federal army. Softly, he said pointing, "Katie go behind those trees over there, and put these clothes on. They are for riding. You must hurry. We don't have much time."

As Pete removed his finger from her lips, she replied, "But Pete."

Once more, Pete interrupted and said as he handed her the garments, "We will speak later. There's not much time. Hurry."

Katie took the clothing and proceeded to do what had been requested of her. Pete watched as she disappeared. As he approached Jonathan, who was still in the saddle, Jonathan said as he smiled, "Yes sir, she shor' is pretty. Yes sir."

"Jonathan, you better get away while you still can. You need to go home and be with your family. There is no way that we can win the war. Just several days ago, I was in Harpers Ferry and witnessed reinforcements arriving daily to increase the size of Sheridan's army. It's over Jonathan. To continue this war is useless."

Jonathan's expression turned to one of seriousness as he answered his friend, "What are ya gonna do?"

"I'm going to help Katie escape. After that, I really don't know."

There was a somber expression that covered Jonathan's face as he answered, "Ya know it would be good to see my family. But, on the other hand, I'm not ready to give up fightin'."

"I can understand how you feel. Your going to have to do what you feel is right." Pete stretched forth his hand to shake Jonathan's saying, "I can never find the words to express my gratification for all that you've done for me. What I'm going to say is from the bottom of my heart." Jonathan continued to quietly look at Pete as Pete spoke, "Over the last four years, you and I have become very close, just as brothers, and I mean that. You're just like the brother that I've always hoped to have in life, but unfortunately, I didn't. Charles and I aren't close, and we never have been, unless it was something that was going to benefit him. As for you and me, on more then one occasion we have suffered lost, hunger, and humiliation. From Manassas to Winchester, we've rode together and been through hell. And if I have had any good fortune that has come from this conflict, it was knowing you, and that you were a part of my life. As surely as there is a God in heaven, I'll never forget you."

Jonathan quietly rode a few paces, paused, and turned in his saddle saying, "What does that word grat-i-fi-cation mean anyway?" A grin broke forth over the width of his face as he waved and continued, "Well there's no time for that now. Maybe, one of these days ya can teach me some of those fancy words."

As Pete quietly watched Jonathan ride in a westward direction, Katie returned to his side. Without a word, he helped her mount her horse and the two of them continued to ride east toward the Shenandoah River.

William Pierce was pacing impatiently at the entrance to the jail as Daniel arrived. Daniel noticed the harden expression that covered William's face as he said in a tone of anger, "Katie McBride has escaped. I want you to find her, and when you do." William momentarily paused as he stared, "Kill her and those that you find accompanying her."

Without a word, Daniel mounted his horse and rode in the direction that Pete and Katie were last seen.

CHAPTER FORTY

Pete and Katie had been riding for a little over an hour in their attempt to escape Confederate pursuit, and avoid Union cavalry patrols that were roaming the area. They passed unnoticed through the Confederate lines of defense, but they weren't beyond the point of safety; danger still lurked around them. The moon that glowed earlier in the evening was now obscured by clouds, and lightning could be seen streaking across the western sky. As Pete and Katie brought their horses to a halt along a ridge that overlooked the Shenandoah, Pete could here the muffled sound of thunder in the distance. Pointing in the direction of the river, he said with a tone of urgency in his voice, "If it pours, the river is going to rise quickly. It will prevent us from making our escape."

Katie turned in her saddle and said, "You and I have been through this before."

Pete shouted as he smacked his horse on the hind quarter, "Yeah, let's go!"

Quickly, they rode side by side to the riverbank, and there, they crossed the shallow area of the river that the old farmer had told Pete about earlier in the evening. Once on the opposite side, Pete and Katie dismounted near an old tree log and allowed their horses time to rest. As Pete approached the water to wash the dirt and dust from his face and hands, Katie joined him. Pete removed an old handkerchief from his pocket and dipped it into the warm water. After removing the excess water, he quietly looked at Katie with compassion and began to wipe away some of the dry blood clots that was still on her lip. Once satisfied, he asked, "How did that happen?"

Katie said as she bowed her head in despair and turning away, "I don't want to talk about it."

Pete remained silent as he touched her shoulders. As she turned to face him, he gently touched her cheek and lifted her chin with his finger. His heart sank with sorrow as he noticed the somber expression that covered her face, and the tears that began to fill her eyes. Once more, he softly asked, "Katie, what happen? Did someone do this to you?"

Katie began to openly weep as she spoke slowly in a whispering sound of voice, "It was William, William Pierce."

Pete said with a tone of anger as he embraced her in his arms, "He hit you? Why? Why in the name of heaven would he do something like that?"

Katie looked into Pete's eyes and said, "I was taken by surprise when I saw William enter the cellblock. I really thought that he was coming to help me, not expecting something of me that I could never give him."

"What did he want?"

As the sound of thunder continued to roar, Katie continued to answer Pete's question, "He wanted information about my visit to the camp of the 1st Virginia. I was honest with him, but he couldn't accept my answer. Then he attempted to make a deal with me in return for leniency. He wanted something that I couldn't give him in return for his intervention. My love. When I refused him and without any warning, he went into a furious rage. I would have never known that he was capable of displaying that type of behavior. In the past he has always been a gentleman to me."

Pete's body immediately tensed with the words that she spoke. He was angry and it reflected in his tone of voice, "When I see him, he'll pay for what he has done to you. I promise."

Katie replied, as Pete stroked her hair, "No, please, I don't want you to go after him. The whole episode is not worth you risking your life. I did something that was foolish of me, but in desperation." Pete remained silent as Katie continued to speak, "After learning of your death last July, it was important for me to find out any information surrounding your death. The opportunity was there when I came to Winchester with Mrs. McDonald. I knew that the 1st Virginia was camped near Winchester after seeing them riding through the city."

Pete broke their embrace and started to walk toward the river, and then turning, he said, "Katie, that wasn't the smartest thing to do, especially with you being from Boston. This is why you were in confinement. They were led to believe by your presence in the camp that you were looking for information to pass across Union lines."

"I know, I was careless, but all that I was looking for was information concerning your death. I wanted to know if there was someone with you that heard you say something about me. Us."

Once more, Pete approached Katie and gently placed his hands on her shoulders saying as his eyes were on hers, "After I had been shot, you're the only one that I thought about. I didn't know if I would see you again, and that frighten me."

"Katie's eyes glowed with the brightness of life as she replied, "Then you do care, more then you're willing to admit?"

As Pete's eyes were fixed upon Katie's, she noticed the sincere compassion that flowed as he spoke from his heart, "I was willing to risk my life for you."

Katie challenged him and asked, "Why Pete, why?"

"I guess," Pete paused as his eyes continued to meet hers; his expression of words was with passionate emotion. "I really don't feel that I want to run from my feelings for you any longer."

In the distance, the muffled sound of horses caught Pete's attention. He knew that they needed to seek shelter along the rocks and growth that populated the hillside overlooking the river. From there, he thought, they would remain until the possible existence of danger past. Pete gestured to Katie to remain silent as they led their horses to an area that was filled with rocks, undergrowth, and various trees. With haste, Pete covered their tracks with a branch containing leaves as Katie led the horses toward the hillside. As they knelt behind some rocks, Pete's eyes were fixed on the riders approaching on the opposite side of the river. In the darkness of the night, it was difficult to determine if it was a Union cavalry patrol, or some Confederate's dressed as civilians in pursuit of them. After pausing the riders crossed the river at the same shallow area previously used by Pete and Katie. As Pete held his revolver, Katie whispered, "Maybe, we should make a run for it?"

Pete placed his hand on her mouth and said, "Hush."

As Pete observed the riders looking around the area where they had been previously, he quietly watched as several of the riders dismounted. They walked around the area. One of them knelt and examined the area for evidence of Pete and Katie's presence. Finally, the second rider stood and appeared to be speaking as they continued to search the area near an old log. Pete knew that they were apparently looking for tracks. Pete remembered in their haste to hide, that he had left behind the bloodstain handkerchief that he used to tend to Katie's wound. His heart began to race. Pete noticed that the wind had increased with intensity causing the mysterious riders horses to become frighten. Before the riders were able to complete their examination of the area where Pete and Katie had been, they were forced by the weather related elements to give up their efforts and remount their horses. Instead of re-crossing the river, they continued in a southern direction along the river at a gallop.

From the crescendo sound of the crashing thunder, and constant streaks of lightning, Pete knew that the storm was near with all of its fury. As he gazed at the sky, Katie said with a tone of concern in her voice, "What are we going to do? We have to find some shelter before it rains." Katie paused and said once more in a tone of urgency, "Pete, what are we going to do?"

As Pete turned his attention to Katie, he said, "I feel that we have two options. This afternoon as I was passing near this area, there was an old farmer who lived over the hillside not very far from here. It would seem to be the best place to seek shelter, but for some unknown reason, I don't trust him. It might not be safe for us to stay there. Then too, the most risky might be the best option."

There was fear in Katie's eyes as she touched his arm. In an anxious tone of voice, "What is that?"

"I believe that if we continue to follow the river in a northern direction, we could pass by the Federal cavalry picket that I saw earlier this afternoon at Snicker's Gap. If the storm produces heavy downpours then hopefully they will seek shelter and we can slip by undetected."

"I would rather suffer the elements of weather then be captured."

The wind continued to gust with intensity as Pete and Katie mounted their horses and proceeded in the direction of the gap. The rain began to fall lightly, and then later, it fell in a heavy downpour. As Pete and Katie battled the elements, the wind blew the rain in torrents against their faces and bodies. The bright flashes of lightning continued to provide them light along the river trail. Before long, the ground became very muddy, the horses sinking at times in the soft earth, causing Pete and Katie to dismount and lead their horses by foot. The short journey was slow and tedious. As the couple neared Snicker's Gap, Pete proceeded on foot a short distance to observe the road that led to Berryville for any activity by Yankee cavalry. After being satisfied that there weren't any Federals in the immediate vicinity, he returned to Katie, who was waiting with the horses. The rain continued to pour with force as Pete and Katie continued along the base of Snicker's Gap, still following the river. Pete noticed that the Shenandoah was beginning to rise quickly, still they diligently continued.

By early morning the rain had come to an end. It was humid and the glowing red sun was shining as Pete and Katie were close to the vicinity of Vestal's Gap, which overlooked Shenandoah Estate. Even though there was the temptation of riding to see what remained of the homestead, Pete believed that it would be too dangerous for them. Throughout the night as they rode in the rain, the words about Katie's involvement, and Daniel's apparent spying activities near General Howe's headquarters continued to resurface in his mind. The question that continued to puzzle him was, who hired Daniel to spy on Katie. He didn't believe for one moment that it was Charles, even though he had his suspicions concerning her. It was out of the question that any of the remaining family members, including his Mother would commit themselves to such a deadly game. The Barker's had many close friends, but he believed in their loyalty, especially since they were sympathizers to the cause. Pete's thoughts were broken by the sound of gunfire coming from the same direction that they were proceeding toward. He turned in the saddle and said to Katie, "I want you to stay here while I go and see what is going on."

"No, I'm coming too."

As Pete and Katie arrived at the road that ran through Vestal's Gap, they noticed four Union cavalrymen lying quietly, and motionless on the ground. With his revolver in his hand, Pete turned each of the Federals face up to see if they were dead or alive. After being satisfied that they were dead, Pete began to go through their personal belongings. Katie dismounted and became quite angry saying as she approached, "What are you bloody doing?"

Pete replied as he continued to rapidly look through the Yankees saddlebags, "I'm looking for money and food. We need to eat, and we're going to need the money."

Katie continued to protest as she witnessed Pete's actions, "I'm appalled at such bloody action. Don't you have any respect for the dead?"

Pete turned and angrily said, "Katie this is war. I've spent the last four years surviving this way. It has become a way of life in the Confederate army. You get use to it." Katie remained silent as Pete continued, "Besides, we need their horses, ours are too exhausted and won't make the rest of the journey." Katie continued her protest of silence as Pete began to make the exchange of mounts. Once more he commanded, "Come on and help me. We need to get out of here before this place is swarming with Yankees."

As Katie heard the sound of horses approaching from the river, she quickly complied with Pete's request. With haste, she saddled her mount and exchanged saddlebags, continuing to glance in the direction of the river for the approach of the mysterious riders. Katie mounted her horse and said, "I want you to know that I'm bloody mad about this whole affair."

With a concerned expression, Pete said as he glanced at Katie, "If those riders discover us with these dead Yanks, then we'll both be swinging from the end of a rope."

With haste, the two were on their way continuing in a northern direction. Once they arrived at Bear Pond Gap, they proceeded east into a narrow valley, which was known by the locals as Between the Hills. Pete knew that they weren't far from the Russell homestead, but he believed that it wouldn't be safe for Katie because of the possibility that Miss Virginia was sheltering Confederate partisans. By now, he thought, the alarm had been sounded by the Confederate authorities in Winchester concerning her flight to freedom.

The humidity was becoming oppressive as Pete and Katie reached the road that led to Harpers Ferry. In order to continue their escape, Pete was reminded of a trail that crossed Short Hill Mountain. For many years, it had been used by the locals who lived on the opposite side of the mountain to bring their crops and eggs to Harpers Ferry to sell. Pete thought that by using this trail, they would be able to continue to avoid detection by Confederate agents, who he was sure would be in Harpers Ferry watching for Katie. After riding at a gallop for about a mile, Pete found the lane that led to the trail. On this particular morning, many of the farmers that use the trail were absent, leaving Pete and Katie the ability to ascend the mountain at an easier pace.

As they were slowly riding side by side, the only sound that they heard was the horse's hooves striking the ground. The two of them had not spoken since the incident at Vestal's Gap, though by now, Katie had calmed her emotions and was anxious to apologize and carry on a conversation with Pete. Katie was observing a squirrel swinging from one tree limb to another when she began to giggle. Pete was curious and asked, "Why are you giggling? What's so funny?"

Katie was relieved that Pete had broken the silence that had reined for so long between them. Promptly, she turned her attention to Pete and said, "I was watching a squirrel swinging among the trees."

"So. What's funny about that?"

"It just reminded me of an incident in my life when I was nine years old. There were many trees that were nestled together at our old home outside of Boston. I remember Seamus and myself attempting to pass the time of day and trying to do something similar, such as that squirrel. Only for us, we landed on our bottoms. If you could have seen the exasperated expression on my brother's face. At first, we both laughed over the foolish incident, but then, he began to cry."

"If you were just having fun, then why did he get so upset?"

Katie said in a tone of seriousness, "You don't know my brother. Seamus doesn't like to fail or lose at something that he puts his heart into. When we were children, he had to win at everything or he would just quit and become angry. For instance, I'm a much better swimmer then what he is, but that's difficult for him to accept."

"Yes, and many times at Shenandoah, Caroline Barker could out ride me and handle a horse better then me."

Katie wanted to continue the subject about Caroline. She said in a soft tone of voice, "I miss her. I miss her more then you could ever know."

Pete glanced at Katie, "I know. Somewhere, I believe that the feeling is mutual."

"Really, I mean Caroline thinks that I'm a spy and that I caused her grief and loss. I'm sure that she must have a great deal of bitterness toward me."

Pete reached for his canteen and pulled the cork and took a drink. He offered Katie, but she refused wanting to know why he sounded so sure about her friend, "The night of the fire at the Estate, my Mother and Daniel were quick to accuse you of the family's misfortune. Caroline didn't believe that you were capable of such hatred and malice. Besides, for many months when the two of you weren't speaking, she had old Jeremiah keeping an eye on you to insure your safety and security."

Katie was surprised and moved with emotion as she replied, "I didn't realize that she still cared. I thought that our relationship had been destroyed because of this conflict. Now, you have given me hope in what you have revealed."

Once they arrived upon the mountain's crest, Pete and Katie departed from the trail and found an area near a huge crop of rocks that overlooked the Potomac River. After being constantly in the saddle for the past thirteen hours with little rest and no sleep, they decided to rest.

Several hours had gone by when Pete awaken. Katie was still sleeping as Pete quietly observed the view of Solomon's Gap and listened to the birds, and the sound of the river rushing over the rocks below. As he looked through the gap, he saw off in the distance his home, Harpers Ferry. On the Maryland side of the river, he could see the Union forces on the heights. His mind was on the possibility of the family losing Shenandoah once the war concluded. He knew that financially they had lost everything, and would probably lose the Estate. His thoughts were interrupted as Katie awakened from her sleep. As she rubbed her eyes, she said, "How long have you been awake?"

"Not long."

As Katie glanced about and marveled at the scenery, she said, "It's a beautiful view. Here, one can momentarily escape the tragedy of war."

Pete said, as he turned and glanced at her, "Yeah, they can. But it will be a long time before I'll ever be able to."

"I can't begin to imagine the horrors that you've seen, and the experiences that you've been through over the last four years."

Pete said somberly as he began to recall events, "No Katie, you can't even begin. Over the past three and a half years, I've walked across many fields where battles have been waged. It's not an easy thing to watch a man crying in agony and knowing that he'll die. I have often thought about the family that he's leaving behind, what it will be like for them without him being a part of their life. And the thoughts that must have crossed his mind that he'll never see them again. At times, I've seen soldiers who had just met death with tears still wet on their cheeks holding an image of their loved one close to their body. What were they feeling or thinking about that person? On many occasions the wounded asked for mercy, help, or just plead for death to arrive and relieve them of their misery. As long as I live, I'll always remember the different expressions upon the faces of the dead. I remember at Gettysburg, my brigade was heavily involved in the conflict. I watched helplessly as my revolver misfired and a Yankee slashed part of my cousin's scalp away. No Katie, you don't know what I've been through. The images will haunt me for the rest of my life."

Katie said as she moved closer to his side and rested her hand on his arm,

"The war is over for you. When we reach safety we'll stay until there is some sort of peace agreement between the two sides."

Pete remained silent in thought. His demeanor puzzled Katie. She said in a concerned tone of voice fearing rejection, "Why are you suddenly so quiet? Don't you agree with me?"

Pete turned away, he couldn't look Katie in the eyes when he spoke, "Katie, I've been thinking that it would be for the best that you return home to Boston. I'm going to take you as far as Frederick City where I'll put you on a train to Baltimore. That's why we are going this way."

Katie became angry and said in a pitched tone, "Mr. Barker, as I've bloody said before, I am a grown lady, not a child who needs to be taken care of."

Pete promptly replied angrily as he jumped to his feet, "I'm not going to argue with you." As he gazed at her sitting, he continued to speak in a calmer tone of voice, "It's not going to be safe anywhere around here for you. I really don't think that you understand the danger that you might possibly face if you remain. Confederate agents will track you down like a dog and kill you." As Pete paused, Katie took particular notice of the serious expression that covered his features, "And me too, if I'm found with you. I've thought about it all night and I'm convinced that William is acting as an agent for the Confederate spy ring, or agency. And from what I know of the man, he is very persistent. He'll have us tracked down like animals until we are found. I don't care how far we try to run."

Katie stood to her feet and said in a calm tone of voice, "I believe you. Last night when he came to the jail, and began to interrogate me for information, I became very suspicious of him. Like I said earlier, he was a different person then the one that I knew previously before all of this began. I wondered all along if he used our friendship in the hopes of extracting information from me. He really thought that I was spying and just playing some charade with him. He actually thought that I would unintentionally pass information to him for the rebel's use."

Pete gazed at Katie as he held his hands on her shoulders, "Are you spying?"

"Would it make any difference between us if I was?"

CHAPTER FORTY-ONE

Frederick City was bustling with activity by Federal troops as Pete and Katie rode along Market Street looking for lodging. The two were filled with fatigue and hunger after battling once more the inclement weather throughout the night. The marching sound of many feet, and the creaking sound of wooden wheels drew Pete's attention. He noticed a company of Federal soldiers marching with a four-gun artillery battery followed by some supply wagons moving in the opposite direction toward the outskirts of town. As he observed some of the citizens of the community, life for the locals appeared to be going about in a normal fashion. All the shops along the street were open for business. The ladies were shaded by their colorful parasols, smiling and chatting with the gentlemen that were accompanying them. Most of all, the city gave the appearance of security from the war that continued to rage in Virginia. Several months ago, a major engagement was fought along the Monocacy River that was several miles east of town. Pete knew that this was one of the reasons for the Federal troops presence, the other being, to protect the Baltimore and Ohio Railroad.

As Pete continued to look about, Katie pointed to an establishment where they could have breakfast. After dismounting, Pete noticed an elderly gentleman sitting on a wooden bench in front of the dwelling whittling a piece of wood with a knife, and humming sad songs to himself. His appearance was filled with sorrow as he somberly continued about his woodwork. He gave Pete the impression that he was caught up in a world of his own and could care less of those around him. Many thoughts crossed Pete's mind concerning his own family's welfare in Richmond as he observed the old fellows mood. His thoughts turned to the elderly man's dilemma. Maybe the old gentleman was a refugee, such as his family from across the river in Virginia. Maybe the old man had lost his home and possessions in the conflict, such as his family. Maybe, he had lost a son or two at some point in the conflict and was still grieving. Pete's thoughts were suddenly broken by Katie's words as he turned to look at her, "Pete what is wrong?"

The old man's situation had manifested feelings of guilt within Pete's heart due to his inability to prevent the grief and anguish that his family was experiencing with the destruction of Shenandoah. In an attempt to keep his emotions subdued and avoid the question, Pete replied, "Nothing, nothing at all."

Katie was puzzled by his actions, though she remained silent, but wasn't convinced of the truth as they entered the establishment.

As Pete was assisting Katie with seating at the table, he noticed a group of Federal soldiers sitting at the far end of the tavern exchanging jovial conversation. It was difficult for him to repress the resentment that he felt toward the men who wore blue, and the damage that their kind had caused his family. The question that concerned him was, would it be worth the effort to return to fight against them knowing that it was only a matter of time before the Confederacy collapsed. He concluded, that it would only be revenge.

After being seated and requesting a meal of eggs and bacon, Katie noticed the angry expression that covered Pete's face as he continued to quietly observe the soldiers. Katie knew within her heart that he was thinking of his family as he watched the old gentleman earlier at the entrance to the establishment. She placed the coffee cup on the saucer and took Pete by the hand. As he gazed at her, she said with a soft voice, "I know that it hurts, but you have to let it go. There is nothing that you can do."

Pete replied in a tone of anger, "It's because of them, that my family is homeless. If the Yanks had stayed out of Virginia, then this whole thing wouldn't have happen. But no, they had to come and impose their way of life on us."

Katie knew that he had been repressing his feelings since the destruction of the Estate and the displacement of his loved ones. Now, she thought, she must make the attempt to reason with him and that it was useless for him to continue to hold onto his feelings of anger and possible revenge. Katie gently touched his hands. Once she received his attention, she said, gazing straight into his eyes, "For now, your Mother and family are safe. That alone is much to be thankful. Like many who have endured this horrible war, you and your family have lost everything, but you still have each other. Once the war is concluded, hopefully, you'll be able to pick up the pieces and rebuild your life as well as the Estate."

"It will be difficult because we are ruined financially. Also, my brother was a member of the Confederate government, which means that he will suffer harsh treatment once captured as well as his family. And to make things worst, the Lincoln government may allow Shenandoah to be taken from us."

"If it's an issue of money, my family might be willing to help you."

"Oh yeah, I don't think that they would be so generous after having their son shot at by us rebels. Harsh feelings between Northerners and Southerners will continue long after the fighting has ended."

Katie knew that the war hadn't affected Pete's pride and stubbornness. She had learned from living in the south, that every gentleman valued pride and honor, and that it was cherished among Southerners. Somehow, she needed to find the words that would penetrate his heart for him to realize that there wasn't any shame in asking for assistance. After all, she thought, there would need to be reconciliation and healing between the two different societies once the war was concluded. Katie softly and confidently replied, as she continued to gaze at him, "Pete, don't let your pride continue to inflame the problems that you are facing, and that will be challenging you once the war has ended. There is no shame in losing the war. You only fought for what you believed to be right, as many on both sides have done. But if you allow your pride to blind you, then you won't be successful when you begin to rebuild your life as well as Shenandoah. Hatred will rob you of every opportunity and relationship that you can have."

Pete shook his head and smiled as he glanced out the window at the old gentleman, who was still at his woodwork. Turning about once more, silently his eyes were fixed on Katie. He knew in his heart that she was correct in her perception of him. He cleared his throat and softly admitted, "Yeah, your right. It's difficult when you are raised with everything in life such as an education, a nice home, and plenty of money and possessions. Then, all of a sudden, it vanishes; it's been totally destroyed and taken from you. For me, I've found that it is a humbling experience, and it takes some getting use to. I always thought that regardless of the hardships that I must endure as a soldier, that I would always have Shenandoah to come home to, even though I didn't feel that way when I left home. Yeah, I was hurt by my Mothers actions, but it's the only place that I've ever known as home."

Katie replied as a smile beamed across her face, "And it still can be your home."

After finishing their breakfast, Pete and Katie found the lodging at the National Hotel. Pete had learned from the inn keeper that the train to Baltimore wouldn't be leaving until four o'clock that afternoon, so for now, they had time to rest and spend together before she began her journey home.

As they were sitting quietly in the room, Pete was reading the local newspaper, the Frederick Examiner and occasionally glanced at Katie. He knew that he was going to miss her and lose her once more to the circumstances surrounding the war as had happened so many times over the last four years. Somewhere in his heart, he had hoped that matters would have changed and that they could have been released from the burden of separation. For the first time in many years, Pete did not feel the void that had dominated his heart and life. When he was with Katie McBride, he felt that closeness that comes only once in a lifetime. As Katie walked over to the window that overlooked the street to listen to the church bells, there was a breeze that caressed her face and blew through her hair that drew his attention.

For Katie, many thoughts resurfaced within her heart concerning their conversation along the river after escaping from Winchester. The subject hadn't surfaced since that evening, and before she departed his company, she needed to know what the future might hold for them. Katie began to comment as she continued to hear the sound of the bells, "Pete, do you hear the bells?"

Pete folded the paper and said as he laid it on a stand by the chair, "Yes, I do."

Katie turned about to face him and said with a serious expression covering her features, "Do you think that some couple might be getting married?"

"I don't know. I suppose that they could be."

Katie was agonizing within her heart to know the truth of Pete's true feelings and emotions for her. As she continued to gaze at him, she approached asking boldly, "Did you really think of me when you were gone, and care for me as you said along the river?"

There was a serious expression that covered Pete's face as he answered, "Yes, I was honest and sincere with you."

As Katie approached him, she continued to express her feelings, "Do you love me as I love you?"

Pete was silent as he chose his words, "Katie, I've had so much happen to me over the last four years. The killing, destruction, the emotions that I've attempted to deal with from those experiences, and the guilt that I bare for taking another person's life." Pete paused briefly and looking into her eyes, he said, "I really don't know who I am anymore. At times it's difficult for me to discern what my deepest feelings are about anything." Pete paused as he noticed the disappointment that covered her face, the sorrow that filled her eyes. He continued to speak as he reached forth and took her by the hand, "I risked my life for you. But, I just don't know if I'm in love with you."

Katie was quiet. She turned away from Pete in an attempt to hide her emotions. After quickly regaining her composure, she turned once more and said in a calm tone of voice, "I guess now I understand why you could never commit yourself to someone else in the past. Why your life has been so complex. Now I know from my own experience with you. You have always used some excuse and reason to escape the bondage of your feelings. This time it is the war."

"Katie." Lowering his head, Pete paused as he methodically chose his words. Once more he raised his head and continued to speak, "It's not just the war. It's me. Maybe, you and I crossed paths too soon in life, I don't know."

As Pete and Katie were discussing their relationship, there was a loud knock at the door. Pete was quiet, his eyes continued to be fixed on Katie. There was a second loud knock. Katie broke the silence, "I wonder who that might be."

"I don't know."

Walking over and opening his saddlebags, Pete grabbed his revolver and cautiously opened the door. As he did so, Daniel pushed the door open with his pistol drawn, knocking Pete to the floor. Swiftly, Pete reached for his weapon that had dropped from his hand when he fell, only to have Daniel kick it from his reach. Katie was terrified and began to speak, but Daniel shouted, "Shut up, woman!" Then he looked at Pete, who was still lying on the floor, and commanded, "I should have known that ya would try somethin' this stupid. Git up and git over to her side."

As Pete rose slowly from the floor, Daniel closed the door to the room, but it still remained open slightly without his knowledge. Then he approached the couple grinning with delight and satisfaction that he had finally made his capture and would receive his reward. Katie asked as she held to Pete's arm, "What do you want with us?"

Daniel began to grin, saying in a confident tone as he gestured with his pistol for them to move back near the wall, "I want to have a friendly little talk. Just the three of us."

Pete replied as he moved Katie closer to his side, "Daniel, who put you up to this? Was it William?"

Daniel raised his pistol and pointing the barrel at Pete, he snapped, "It makes no difference does it? You're a deserter from the Confederate army, and ya help free a spy. It appears to me that ya sin is the worst between the two."

Pete answered angrily as he broke Katie's embrace and took a step forward toward Daniel, "Your mad. Katie's isn't a spy."

Daniel promptly cocked the hammer on the weapon and shouted; "Git back or I'll kill ya now and be done with it."

Pete refused to take his eyes off of the angry overseer as he stepped back, complying with the order and embracing Katie once more. Daniel continued to allow his emotions to rule him. He asked Pete in a demanding tone, "If she isn't spyin', then ya tell me why she was at General Howe's headquarters just hours before yer Mother's home was burnt to the ground."

"I can answer that." Katie said as she broke Pete's embrace, "Before the war, General Howe and my father were close friends. They fought together in the war of 1846, and have continued their relationship since that time. Many times in the past, Mr. Howe was the guest of my family. Naturally, when I heard that he was the new commander of the forces at Harpers Ferry, I wanted to see him."

Daniel turned the weapon toward Katie and shouted, "Do ya think that I'm that big of a fool to believe that story? I don't believe it for one moment. Nope, not for one moment."

Pete said in a tone of frustration, "Charles should have gotten rid of you years ago. You've been nothing but trouble since you came to Shenandoah."

Daniel paused and began to stare coldly at Pete. Silently, he nodded his head saying as he continued to point the pistol at Pete, "I've been waitin' a long time to settle a score with ya. When I think of all those times that ya interfered with me tryin' to git work out of those blasted bucks, and the times that ya tried to humiliate me in front of Miss Elizabeth and the rest of the family. Not to say, the many times ya wanted me fired. Ya don't know the hate and anger that I have for ya. Naw, it's time to end this and to shut ya up for good. And, I have the legal right to do just that. Ya never will bother me again."

After seeing the irritation that was coming from the former overseer, Pete attempted to reason with him and hopefully secure Katie's freedom, and said, "Daniel if I am guilty of the greater sin, then let Katie go and I'll return with you to Virginia and receive my just punishment for deserting and helping her to escape."

"No, I can't do that, she has to die also."

Katie said defiantly in a loud tone of voice, "Well, then may your bloody soul be punished in hell."

There was a wild glare in Daniel's eyes, which Pete had only witnessed once before when Sherman escaped from the Estate. There was a grin of joy that covered his face as his finger snuggled the trigger. Suddenly, there was a single popping sound that came from the direction of the door. Immediately, Daniel gasped for air, dropping his revolver, he fell prostrated to the floor. Without hesitation, Pete kicked the weapon away from his body and cautiously turned the body over facing up. After inspecting him for any signs of life, Pete was convinced that Daniel was dead. Pete turned to look at Katie, and both were astonished by the intervention that had taken place.

Simultaneously, Pete and Katie turned to look in the direction of the door. There appeared Hayward, quietly standing with a small pistol in his right hand. Pete slowly stood to his feet and said with a surprising tone of voice, "Hayward." Pete was silent, still attempting to find the words to overcome his amazement. After pausing briefly, he continued to speak with a tone of astonishment, "I thought I would never see you again."

Hayward placed the small pistol to his side, "I's know. I's felt de same."

"How did you know that we were here?"

Hayward entered the room, shutting the door behind him, "I's didn't. For sumtime now, I's been helpin' my people to git away to freedom even though Mr. Lincoln says that de have deir liberty. I's was to meet sum folks who's stayin' here who's been helpin' me. When I's saw Mr. Daniel enter de hotel, I's thought dat he was here to bring harm to those good folks. I's followed. And den when I's seen him pull his gun from under his coat, I's knew dat he was up to no good."

"I must confess that for all of these years I didn't know or even suspect that you were smuggling slaves North. When I was in Richmond several years ago, Charles and Daniel suspected you of helping runaways in their attempt to escape, but I refused to believe in your involvement."

Hayward said as his eyes were fixed upon Pete, "I's been helpin' my people for de pass ten years. I's has no regrets."

Katie interrupted the conversation saying as she approached Hayward, "Personally, I would like to thank you for your intervention into our lives. You saved us from sure death."

"Yes'im. Mr. Daniel was an evil man. He's deservin' of what he git." Once more Hayward turned his attention to Pete and said, "Does it change things now dat ya know?"

"No, it doesn't. You have been too loyal of a friend that I should have differences with you over this matter."

There was some noise coming from the hallway. Pete said, as he turned about to look at Katie, "If we don't get out of here, we are all going to end up in jail."

Hayward knelt by Daniel's body preparing him to be moved from the room. He looked up at Pete and said, "Ya all go while I git rid of de body."

"No, Hayward, that's not fair."

"I's will decide dat. Now go!"

As quietly as possible, Pete slightly opened the door to investigate the noise. It appeared that a constable was speaking with a hotel guest down the hallway near the corner of the building. Pete closed the door and turned about and said, "There is a constable several doors down. Apparently, someone heard the gunshot." After pausing and quickly pondering on the situation, Pete said, "We need to hide the body."

Hayward said, as he kneeled to help Pete, "But where?"

"Let's hide the body under the bed until he leaves."

Katie said, as she approached the huge bed, "No, he might look under there." Pointing in the direction of the back wall, she continued, "Let's take our chances that he won't look in the wardrobe."

Pete and Hayward moved the body and placed it in the huge wardrobe in the room. Katie cleaned the bloodstain wooden floor with a towel and then hid it under the pillows. Almost immediately, there was a loud knock at the door. Pete gestured for Hayward to leave by the window overlooking the street. There was a second knock on the door. This time Pete responded. As he opened the door, he noticed the cold stare in the constable's eyes. The policeman said in a firm and abrupt tone of voice, "One of the hotel guests reported to the desk clerk that they heard the sound of a gunshot on this floor coming from somewhere around this area. Did you hear anything?"

"No. No, I didn't."

"If you don't mind, may I have a look around?"

In an attempt to delay the officer from entering the room and giving Hayward sufficient time to hide on the porch roof, Pete asked, "Before you enter, I'd like to make sure that my wife is dressed."

There was a hard appearance that covered the constable's features as he nodded in agreement. After closing the door most of the way, Pete turned and looked at Katie, who was placing a rug over the area where some of the blood remained on the floor. As She looked at him and nodded in the affirmative, she sat on the edge of the bed where she hid the bloodstain towel under the pillow. Once more, Pete opened the door and allowed the officer to enter the room. Pete quickly introduced Katie as his wife. The constable remained silent as he looked about. As he approached the wardrobe where Daniel's body was hidden, Katie fired a question at the officer, "Sir, wouldn't a gentleman give considerable thought before searching an area where lady's apparel would be hanging?"

The officer turned and with a smug expression answered Katie, "Oh, I'm sorry madam. I guess so."

As the constable approached Pete, he was quiet and still possessed the cold appearance in his eyes. He paused and then turned and tipped his hat in a friendly gesture to Katie saying, "Madam, have a good day."

After closing the door behind the policeman, Katie informed Hayward that it was safe to re-enter the room. Pete walked over to the window and pulling the curtain to the side, he watched the Constable leave the hotel. Again, Hayward demanded, "I's will take care of de body. Yose must leave now."

Katie agreed, as Pete turned to look at her, "We must go before it is too late."

Pete made arrangements to meet Hayward on the outskirts of town after Katie departed the city. Hayward reassured him that he would be there and that he had friends that would give them refuge for as long as it would be required.

Quickly and as inconspicuously as possible, Pete and Katie departed the hotel for the short walk to the railroad depot. They remained silent, still surprised at the events that had unfolded.

As they arrived at the railroad depot, Pete purchased Katie's ticket with some of the money taken from the dead Yankee soldiers found in the gap several days ago. There were some wooden benches along the depot platform where Pete and Katie waited for the train that was due to arrive within the hour. Katie asked as she was being seated next to Pete, "Now that I'm going home, what will you do? Will you go and fight another day?"

With his arms crossed, Pete turned and said, "No, for me the war is over. It's useless to continue to fight for a cause that I don't feel that we can win. I've given it some thought, and I'll return to Shenandoah and make the attempt to rebuild my life and home." After pausing briefly, Pete asked as he handed Katie the remaining money, "What about you?

"Oh, I guess I'll spend sometime with my family and try to make amends with Seamus when he returns home. We had quite an argument over you. And then hopefully, I'll find a position teaching in Boston and start my life anew."

Pete laughed as he recalled his encounter with Seamus. I remembered when I met him during a truce after the fighting at Sharpsburg; he impressed me as being very eccentric in his demeanor. At that time he was very frustrated with you because you continued to live in Harpers Ferry instead of returning home. Even, I must admit, I was quite disturbed with you for the same reasons."

Katie answered in a soft tone of voice, "I didn't return because I felt like I was with family. I remember the first time that I met Caroline. I was drawn to her, and after all of the difficulty and division that we've experienced, I still don't know why? As for you, my feelings and emotions grew even though there were times that I tried to repress them or deny that they were real."

"Yeah, I agree with you about Caroline. She has always attracted her admirers with her personality and ways. As for the rest of my family, they have their faults. I just didn't realize, I guess that you felt that close to them even though I did suspect your feelings for me."

"Before the war, I was drawn to the warmness, concern, and openness of your family."

Pete was puzzled. He didn't know that much about Katie's family because she had said very little since their acquaintance. After pausing, he said, "I take it that you're not very close to your family, only your brother. That's why you came south to Harpers Ferry."

Katie was unable to look at Pete. She said as she glanced in the direction of some Yankee cavalry moving along the street, "You finally figured it out?"

"No, I've known for sometime. I just felt that it was an uncomfortable subject for you."

Katie turned to face Pete, "How? How could you have known?"

"Do you remember just before the election of 1860 when I walked with you along the Shenandoah, the emotions that you were experiencing that day?"

"Yes I do, I was quite upset with my parents because of their demands that I return to Boston. They have never been able to accept the fact that I am a grown woman."

Pete began to probe the subject with persistence, "I believe that you were going through the same experience in life that I was going through with my family. Attempting to be your own person with your own separate identity. Maybe we are both considered rebels by our family. In your case I'm convince somewhere in my heart that they gave you the alternative to stay in Boston, or if you came south, that you weren't allowed to return home."

Katie was silent and stunned by Pete's revelation. She asked in a soft, calm voice, "How did you know?"

Pete answered Katie in a serene tone of voice as his eyes were looking into her eyes, "I know how you feel about me. Although, I just don't believe that with all of the opportunities that you had to return home that you would continue to stay in an area that was so engulfed in conflict and destruction. I mean Boston is totally untouched by this war. The citizens that live there only know the devastation by what they read in the newspapers. They haven't the slightest idea of what it's been like for the good people that have lived in Virginia, Georgia, and the rest of the South. This is an opportunity for you to make things right between you and your family. I'm sure that they probably have seen matters in a different light by now and are anxious to be reunited with you."

Pete noticed the passion that glowed in Katie's eyes as she spoke earnestly, "It will be difficult enough for me to return home to an uncertain future, but leaving you touches me in a way that surpasses any word that I could describe. My feelings for you are so deep. I could never love another as I love you."

In the distance, the couple could hear the sound of the approaching train that would take Katie to Baltimore. Pete said, as he took Katie by the hand with their eyes on each other, "I am going to miss you more then I can ever express in words. Maybe, someday our paths will cross again in times that aren't so troubled."

Katie replied with a quiver in her voice, "And again, I want to thank you for placing your life at such a high risk to free me from prison."

"I didn't know if you were spying or not, and at this point, I really don't care, but I couldn't leave you there."

"I can never find the words to express my gratitude, and my loyalty to you. It will always be unchallenged. I'm just sorry that it didn't work out between us."

There was a deep, troubled expression that covered Pete's features. He answered somberly, "Too much has happened. I'm just not the same person that I was before the war began. As I said earlier, I am part of the problem. I'm going to need the time to re-establish my life and re-discover who I am, and that takes time."

As the train came to a halt at the depot, Pete walked Katie to the passenger coach. As she was about to be assisted to the coach by the conductor, she turned and leaned forward and kissed Pete on the cheek, saying, "And I will always love you. Maybe someday, you'll come to realize the truth. And when you do, I'll be waiting. I promise."

Pete replied sorrowfully as he held her hand, "I don't expect you to. I want you to go on without me and begin a new life."

Katie said, as she caressed his cheek with her fingers, "Again, I can never love another as I love you. Never."

There was a sorrowful expression that covered Pete's face; he was without words to give an answer. He continued to remain silent as Katie climbed the stairway of the coach. As the train began to slowly pull away from the station with the whistle blowing, Katie turned. There was a somber expression that covered her features, she resisted the tears that filled her eyes, but allowed a smile to surface as she waved farewell.

As Pete quietly watched the train disappear, many mixed emotions began to surface within his heart about Katie. He was reminded of a verse from the ballad Lorena, which described his feelings at the present, "The story of the past, Lorena, Alas! I care not repeat; they touched some tender chords, Lorena, they lived, but only lived to cheat. I would not cause even one regret to rankle in your bosom now. For if we try we may forget."

CHAPTER FORTY-TWO

By the first of April 1865, the Confederacy was on the verge of collapsing. With the defeat of the Democratic nominee General George McClellan in November, Abraham Lincoln won re-election to the Presidency of the United States and began to serve his second term. It was with this major blow that Southern hopes for independence had vanished. In the effort to preserve the Union, Federal forces had captured many of the largest cities in the South including Charleston, South Carolina and Atlanta, Georgia. With the lost of these major Southern cities, the Confederate army and government was incapacitated to continue the war. With the destruction of its major industries in these particular cities to manufacture war material and also the destruction of the rich agriculture prosperity in the Shenandoah Valley, the end of the war was in sight. In the western theater of the war, The Army of Tennessee had been badly defeated at Franklin and Nashville the previous December, losing many of its fighting men. With only a remnant of that famous force remaining along with the addition of coastal forces from the Carolinas and General Hardee's small army, this was the only formal opposition left for the Union forces beyond the borders of Virginia. Joseph Johnston was placed in command of this small army. In early April, his 35,000-man force was battling General Sherman's much larger army near Bentonville, North Carolina.

Near Richmond, General Robert E. Lee's Confederates continued to struggle with General Grant's forces near Petersburg, Virginia, which was about twenty-five miles southwest of the Confederate capitol. On March 25th, Lee made the attempt to break the siege by using half of his available force to attack the left flank of the Union forces at Fort Stedman. At first, it appeared that the Confederate's were going to be successful, but with Union forces counter-attacking, the Confederate's were unsuccessful in their effort. Grant took the initiative and attacked the Confederate Army's right flank at Five Forks. After a crushing defeat, the Confederate's supply line was threaten, and Lee extended his forces, which by now were heavily outnumbered to the point of breaking. Other then Montgomery and Mobile, Alabama, Richmond was the only major city that hadn't been captured.

It was the first Sunday in April. Many of the citizen's of Richmond were preparing to go to Church and acting as though all was normal in their lives. It was a warm, quiet, serene, beautiful morning as Charles Barker was standing on the front porch of his Aunt Daisy's residence smoking a cigar and waiting for his Mother and family to join him so that they could attend services at the Centenary Methodist Church. With admiration, he gazed at the blossoms of spring as a mild breeze stirred them from side to side. He could not escape the thoughts of the conference at Hampton Roads in February where he was a participant. Upon request from President Davis, he had accompanied and advised Vice President Stephens, R. M. T. Hunter of the Confederate Senate, and the Assistant Secretary of War, John Campbell in their discussions with President Lincoln and General Grant to find a peaceful solution to end the war. The conference failed because the Confederate government insisted on separate Unions, and the Lincoln government desired that the rebellious eleven states would without condition rejoin the Union. Until this occurred, Lincoln made it clear that there couldn't be any peace between the warring factions. After this event, Charles knew there wouldn't be any hope that the Confederacy could win the war, though President Davis was determined that the struggle should continue. He, like most in the Confederate government desired a peaceful conclusion of hostilities and the most generous terms possible with amnesty toward the government leaders. With the lost at Five Forks yesterday, he knew that General Lee wouldn't have the ability and resources to hold the Petersburg line. The evacuation of Richmond was inevitable.

Charles turned his thoughts to the recent act of desperation that Congress had undertaken. They had voted to use Negro's as soldiers in return for their freedom, but even this idea, Charles opposed because he didn't believe that they could be trusted to fight. Over the last three years of service with the Confederate government, he had witnessed a continuous struggle in ideology between the President and his political enemies in the Senate and among the Delegates. He firmly believed that the leaders were too divided in their vision and views, and that the problem had hampered their efforts to the point that it was difficult for them to agree on much of anything.

The war had been costly for Charles. With Shenandoah in ruins, the slaves and servants gone, and his family's prosperity vanished; Charles was very depressed, but still loyal to President Davis. His hopes and dreams of a position of power and authority within the new nation had perished. All that was left was a rapidly dying and fading dream. He was grateful that his family had been spared injury and death thus far in the conflict, and was relieved when he discovered that his younger brother, Pete was still alive. As he thought about Caroline, memories arose concerning Katie McBride. On many occasions over the past year, the subject of Katie's participation as an informant for the Federal forces near Harpers Ferry had been the spark for great disagreements between them. Somewhere, should Caroline admit it or not, he knew that she still, within the deepest part of her heart was protective of Katie, and her love was still intact. Maybe, he thought, there was a burning desire on his wife's behalf to renew the relationship.

The sound of Church bells ringing throughout the Confederate capitol broke Charles' thoughts. They were late for services as he turned to re-enter the house. As the door opened, there appeared Caroline, Ann, and Elizabeth at the huge front entrance. They were dressed in their most appropriate dresses. It gave Charles the impression that they believed that all was well, but somewhere deep within his heart and mind, he knew that it was only a matter of time before reality would take it's place within their lives and that he must be prepared for it. With a smile that covered her face, Caroline asked in a joyful tone of voice as she turned a full circle, "How do we look?"

Charles had just finished removing the cigar from his mouth. A small grin appeared as he spoke, "You ladies look lovely. By the way, where is Rebecca?"

Elizabeth answered in a concerned tone, "She wants to stay with your Aunt. She is complaining of those nagging headaches again."

As the family was walking along the walkway to the carriage that was waiting for them, there attention turned toward the buggy that was rapidly approaching from the direction of Capitol Square. Charles immediately recognized William.

As the buggy came to a halt in front of their carriage, William quickly stepped from it and said with excitement, "Charles, we have received a telegram at the War Department from General Lee informing us that he will have to abandon his defenses. That means Richmond will have to be evacuated!"

Charles removed the cigar from his mouth saying, as he looked at William with a determined expression covering his features, "Does Secretary Breckinridge know?"

"Yes, he was there when we received the message. A courier has been sent to inform President Davis of the news."

Without hesitation, Charles turned around, only to witness the grim and somber expressions that covered his wife's face and that of his Mother and daughter. Before Charles could speak another word, a courier appeared. Without dismounting, he said, "President Davis desires to see you at once."

Immediately, Charles turned once more facing Caroline and the family and said as he held his hands on her shoulders, "I want you to pack a few things. As soon as I return, you'll need to leave the city along with the rest of the family."

As Charles began to walk away, Caroline became frighten and cried, "Charles, please!"

Charles turned as he continued to walk toward the buggy, "Please, Caroline, hurry!"

Quickly, Charles and William departed to meet with the President at the executive offices between Franklin and Main. On their arrival, they noticed that the President's cabinet along with Governor Smith and the Mayor of the city, John Mayo were present. Charles noticed that some of the members of the cabinet were quiet and somber as they were being seated, with the exception of Secretary Benjamin, who disguised his feelings with a smile, already being shaken by the disastrous news. Charles and William remained standing near the entrance to the room as the President entered. Without informal discussion and reminiscence, which the President was known for before each meeting, he came straight to the point of business, "As you already know, General Grant launched an assault on our troops this morning along the Petersburg defenses and has broken through our lines. General Lee fears that his remaining route of escape across the Appomattox will be severed unless he pulls back. Let me read you what he said." The President read Lee's telegram to the members of the cabinet and afterward, continued to say, "At best, the army might be able to hold out until after dark, and then, they must pull back. Gentleman, the government must be prepared to abandon Richmond this evening for Danville."

At first, some of the members of the cabinet were shocked and silent, though there were others that expected the sadden news from General Lee. William spoke with a tone of anxiety in his voice, "Mr. President, what should we remove, and how do you want this accomplished."

"I would like the rest of the most vital archives and papers that are in our possession loaded onto wagons as well as the treasury removed south toward Danville. There, the government can continue to function until we are in a better position to know what will take place with General Lee's forces. Also, arrangements for the transfer of the deposits from the Virginia banks must be made as well."

Secretary Mallory said, as he looked at the President, "I will volunteer the services of the midshipman at the Naval Academy for this duty. They can act as escorts." As he scribbled on some paper, he continued to say, "I will immediately send the order by courier for them to meet us at the Danville depot by 6 p.m."

Charles approached the President and cabinet members and said, "Sir, with all due respect, the city is going to be in a state of panic and turmoil when they realize that Richmond must be abandoned. By now, they have noticed the piles of documents in front of the auditor's office being consumed in flames. My concern is that it is going to get worst, a lot worst before it is over with. What is going to happen with the break down in civil authority once the troops have departed."

There was a concerned expression that covered the width of the President's face. Softly, he replied with a question that reflected his concern, "Do you still have family within the city?"

"Yes sir, I do."

The President paused, and then he looked down at the table, lifting his head once more, he confidently answered, "Then they need to leave immediately." He continued to turn his attention toward the rest of the members of the cabinet and said, "After the troops depart the city, civil authority and looting will be the responsibility of the home guard. They'll have to do the best that they can with what they have."

Charles was greatly concerned for the welfare of his family. They had to leave Richmond immediately before the whole city knew that the government officials and troops would be leaving. After Secretary Breckinridge finished with the details of the plan to evacuate Richmond, Charles departed with haste to warn his family. As he left the executive offices, he borrowed a horse from a Confederate officer instead of using the carriage. Many of the citizens that knew that the President and cabinet were in a special meeting were milling about in conversation in front of the building. The expressions of bewilderment, somberness, and sadness were evident on the faces of men and women alike. Once they noticed Charles leaving through the front entrance, they shouted, "Sir, can you tell us what is going on?"

Charles quickly hastened by some of the anxious citizens without replying. Already, some of the citizens were crowding the streets in wagons in an attempt to cross the James River using the Mayo Bridge for their escape southward. As he turned the corner to Grace Street he whipped his mount into a gallop. With his arrival, he saw Caroline and Amos loading a trunk on the back of an old buckboard wagon. Quickly, he dismounted and approached Caroline. The grim, somber expression that covered her face revealed to him that she knew the worst. He knew that for her sake as well as the rest of the family that he needed to remain calm and composed so that he wouldn't alarm her and the rest of the family of the seriousness of the situation. Caroline turned about waiting for Charles to speak. Finally, he said with a gentle, but serious tone of voice, "Caroline." Charles found the words difficult to express because he never really believed that the war and his life would turn out this way.

Caroline reached for his hand and said, "We must leave. Isn't that what you have to tell me?"

"Yes, I'm afraid so. President Davis and the cabinet are going to do likewise later this evening." As he paused momentarily, Charles' eyes were fixed on Caroline as if it might be the last time that they would see each other. There was a compassion that glowed in his eyes, as he just remained silent speaking not a word. Then, he broke his silence and continued to speak, "I must go with them." Caroline remained silent, but the disappointment and sorrow that ruled her expression revealed the feelings of her heart. Charles continued speaking softly, "When the war broke out, I really thought that we would win within the first year. Once we established our independence, I believed with all of my heart that there would be a place in the new government for me." Tears began to fall from his eyes and down his cheeks as he spoke his heart, "Oh, did I have high hopes and dreams. Now, I have to run like some kind of a fugitive, a criminal."

Caroline attempted to reassure him as she brushed the tears from his cheek, "No my love. It will be safe for you and me with my family at Glenwood. They will shelter us and we can remain together until it is safe for us to go abroad."

Charles was amazed at Caroline's strength. He momentarily allowed his eyes to meet hers. He caressed her hands and said in serene tone, "I can't run the risk of placing you and the family in harms way. Caroline, I love you so much, that if anything happens to you, it would destroy me. I can't, and I won't take that chance. I have Ann and Mother to think about as well."

"Where will you go? How will we remain in contact?"

"All that I know is that I'm to leave this evening for Danville with the President and his cabinet. I really believe that President Davis feels that our stay there will only be temporary. He has high hopes that Lee and Johnston's armies will be able to unite and crush Sherman's forces, and then turn northward and defeat Grant's forces. But I can clearly see the handwriting on the wall. We can't win; there is just no way that it is possible. I've seen the demoralized expressions on the faces of our soldiers; their pride has vanished. I really don't believe that they want to continue the struggle anymore then many of the members of the government."

As Charles and Caroline continued to speak, Ann, Rebecca, and Elizabeth along with their personal servants appeared on the porch carrying personal possessions to take on the trip. Charles and Caroline approached them to break the tragic news together, "Mother, I have come to say farewell."

A troubled expression ruled Elizabeth's features as she asked, "Oh no my son, where are you going? Tell me please!"

Charles broke the news, "Richmond is going to be evacuated this evening. I will be traveling with the President and the cabinet at least to Danville. Hopefully, we won't have to go any further, but I can't promise that either."

There was a terrified expression that covered Elizabeth's features as her voice reflected her fears, "Oh dear. No, my son, you must leave with us. It will be too dangerous for you to remain with the President. You have done enough to serve your Country. Now, it's time for you to give up the struggle. All is lost."

Again Charles gave reassurance that it would be to their benefit to travel without him, "I wish that I could. I wish that all of this was a bad dream and that I could wake up from it all, but I can't. Union authorities will be anxious to capture members of the Davis government, which I'm a part of. I promise that as soon as I can, I will make the attempt to communicate with Caroline and you."

Ann looked at her Father and said, "We will be safe, but promise me that you'll take care of yourself.'

Charles smiled, as he looked at Ann, "I will. I will."

After hugging Ann, Charles stood and quietly turned around and walked to the wagons. Without a spoken word, he finished helping the servants load the few remaining trunks when he asked, "Amos, where is Rebecca's trunk?'

Amos replied in his low gravel sounding voice, "Mr. Charles, Misse Rebecca says dat she's not gonna go. She's told us to leave her things in her room. So we's obey her."

Without another word to the servants, Charles quickly entered the house shouting for his sister. Shortly, Rebecca appeared with her Mother. Charles said with a tone of anger, "Rebecca, you have to leave with the rest of the family. It's not going to be safe for you here. I'm going to have Amos load your belongings on the wagon."

Rebecca answered with a determination and firmness, "No Charles, I'm staying with Aunt Daisy. She is too sick to travel."

"Rosy can stay, but you have to leave."

Elizabeth said as she looked at her daughter, "I agree with your brother, it's going to be to dangerous. Besides, the Yankees will not harm Rosy."

Rebecca was persistent and determined in her answer; "I will not leave my Aunt with someone else. No! I will not leave and that is final."

Charles began to lose control of his emotions. He grabbed Rebecca by the arm and shouted, "Your going to go if I have to tie you and put you in that carriage myself."

Rebecca began to scream as Charles removed her physically from the house. Elizabeth shouted as she followed, "Charles, please let her go. She can stay if she wants."

Charles paused and released his sister. Then he began to speak in a tone of frustration, "Mother, you all have no idea what is about to take place. All hell will fall upon this city within the next few hours after the word spreads that the troops and the government is leaving. You have no idea the danger that will fall on the inhabitants that stay behind."

"I know. But I have to learn to trust my daughter, something that I've been unable to do. If she will give me her word that she will follow as soon as possible, then I will have to accept it."

Promptly, Rebecca answered, as she moved away from her brother, "I will Mother. As soon as I know that Aunt Daisy is recovering."

Charles said, as he pointed his finger at Rebecca, "Alright, but you must stay inside and keep the doors locked until I return. Do you understand me?"

"Yes, I do."

Charles walked away to give strict orders to Amos and the few male servants that would travel with them.

Elizabeth hugged and kissed her daughter. She caressed her cheek and said, "I want to say something before I leave."

"What's that, Mother?"

"You are just like your Pete. Both of you are rebels, and it's caused differences between us, and divided us from sharing a meaningful relationship. I intend on speaking with Pete as soon as I see him. For now, I pray that you will forgive me for the way that I've been in the past. I guess I've never been able to accept the rebellious nature that you two have displayed in life. You have always desired to do the opposite of what I asked, and expected from you, but that doesn't mean for one moment that I haven't loved you. Your nineteen now, and I guess that I have to let you be the lady that you desire, just as I have to allow Pete to be the man he desires. It's difficult for me to let go. In the future, I will make the vigorous attempt to allow you that freedom."

Rebecca hugged her Mother and said in a compassionate tone of voice, with tears filling her eyes, "My life has changed considerably since I've lived here in Richmond. After losing Thomas, and for a while believing that my brother was dead, it made me think. It made me see that my life could end suddenly and leave so many relationships destroyed, or unfulfilled. No, I want to live my life to the fullest. I have something to give, and that's my love. It's a side of me that the family hasn't really seen that often. But for now, I want to thank you. I've waited a long time to hear you say that you love me. You'll never know how much those words mean to me, and I'll always cherish this moment."

As they were ready to depart, Elizabeth once more pleaded with her son as he helped her into the carriage, "Charles will you please reconsider your decision and leave with us?"

"No Mother, I can't. I just can't. You'll be safe, and that gives me peace of mind."

Elizabeth began to weep as Charles hugged Ann once more and assisted her into the carriage. He struggled with a smile. It had always been his practice never to show any displeasing emotions around her, but this time it was different. Again, there was a sound of despair in his voice, "I'm going to miss you. But the most important thing to me is to protect the one that I love, and that's you. My prayers will be with you, and I'll see you again. I promise."

In an attempt to control her composure and to act as a young lady, Ann withheld her deepest sorrow and grief. Like the other members of her family, she feared for her father's life. She answered in a calm and composed tone of voice, "I know that you will, Father. You've always kept your word to me."

Caroline was able to manage a smile as she allowed her husband to assist her into the carriage. She gently touched his hand and said, "I will be waiting for you."

Charles silently gazed at her, not knowing when they would be united once more. He heard the commotion from some of the crowd that had gathered down the street. He gave the command to Amos to leave immediately. As the carriage and wagon departed in a westward direction toward the Shenandoah Valley, Charles stood silently, motionless, and with an expression of sorrow covering his features. In his heart and mind, he didn't know when and if he would have the blessings of God to embrace, touch, speak, and enjoy his family again. For now, he knew that his own life would be in danger if Federal troops and authorities captured him and tried him for the crime of treason. The only hope that he had was that the Presidential party and members of the Cabinet would be able to seek shelter while General Lee's army continued to struggle with Grant's Federals. He knew that there wasn't much time left for them to stay in Richmond. The Federal cavalry could attempt another raid on the city as was attempted back in the fall. Even though that mission failed, still, the next one might prove to be fruitful. Charles didn't desire to be captured, and he knew that government officials wouldn't receive the same treatment as soldiers. As he watched the carriage disappear, he began to experience the sorrow, emptiness, and grief that accompanied any separation. Only this time, Charles didn't know how long his separation would be, or if it would be permanent.

CHAPTER FORTY-THREE

By now, word was rapidly spreading throughout Richmond of the impending evacuation of the remaining Confederate troops, President Davis, his staff, and members of the Cabinet. Charles had armed himself with a revolver and extra ammunition that he kept at his aunt's residence for his protection as well as his sister's. Before leaving Rebecca, he gave her strict instructions not to leave the premise and he promised to return as soon as he could. Then as quickly as possible, Charles returned to the President's office to collect important papers that belonged to the Chief Executive. Along with several of the President's closest aides, he helped to remove the important items to President Davis' residence to be packed in a trunk for shipment to Danville.

When Charles arrived at the President's home, he found the house to be bustling with activity. Servants were packing some of the most valuable possessions that the family owned, such as silverware and family heirlooms. Yet there were a few of the President's acquaintances enjoying the brandy, wine, and other alcoholic beverages that were still available. After about an hour, the President arrived from his office. As he walked about the mansion, he noticed Charles quietly packing a few remaining documents in one of the upstairs rooms. President Davis slowly approached him, placing his hand on his shoulder, he said, "Charles, I want to thank you personally for your loyalty, commitment, and zeal for the Southern cause for independence. It's been a long and difficult road with many challenges and uncertainties, but together we faced them and did the best that we could." Charles continued to listen as he noticed the President's calm and dignified demeanor. He noticed the determination and fire that still burned in the President's eyes, even as he had witnessed on so many occasions in the past when there was disappointment over what should have been an opportunity to win an engagement, or failure in members of the Confederate government embracing an idea or vision. Charles marveled at his commitment and zeal even when it appeared that the days of the Confederacy were numbered. His emotions were just as strong as they were when William and he had first met him in 1862. Charles continued to listen as the President continued to pour out his feelings, "Tomorrow, Richmond will be occupied by Union forces, but I still firmly believe that we can win this war. If we can rally those troops that have deserted to return to their regiments, and fight with Lee and Johnston combine forces, then there is still hope. That is our challenge, to give our boys encouragement. Losing Richmond is only a minor discouragement. That's all."

Charles said, as he picked up a bundle of papers and began sorting through them, "Mr. President, if everyone possessed the determination and strength that you exhibit, then it would be impossible to fail. My concern is that the vision of an independent nation has vanished."

President Davis was determined in the sound of his voice as he placed his hand on Charles' forearm, "No Charles, the South can never give up hope and submit to subjugation by the North. We must continue our struggle until we force the leadership of the North to the peace table, and only be willing to negotiate and settle on our terms."

Charles marveled at President Davis vision, but thoughts were nestled in the back of his mind as to the President's ability to reason between reality, and living in a false hope that had snared him. Charles suggested, as he turned around and gave his full attention, "Mr. President, maybe you should rest before your departure this evening. It's going to be a long night."

The President silently turned around and glanced at the image of his family. He reached forward and gently held the image. As he continued to gaze at his wife and children, he asked, "I assume that your family has departed the city to some place of security?"

"Yes sir, they left this morning for the Shenandoah Valley. My wife's family lives near New Market. They will be safe there."

The President returned the image to the table and turned and calmly said, "Has the thought crossed your mind when you may see them again?"

"I can only hope soon, that it will be safe for them to join me."

"Lately, I've wondered how soon that I'll see my Varina." The President paused and remained silent. Gazing once more at the image, and touching his wife's face, he continued to speak with confidence, "Charles when my wife and I are united once more, we will never be separated again. Never again."

"I believe that sir."

The President didn't answer, but instead, he cleared his throat and changed the subject and said, "There's much to do." The President paused, scribbled a few lines on some paper, sealed it in an envelope and handed it to Charles continuing, "I want you to go and see if you can be of any assistance to Secretary Breckinridge with the travel arrangements, and to carry this message to him."

Charles softly said as he packed the last few documents lying on the table, "Yes sir, however I can be of service to you."

At once Charles left for the War Department. He noticed the continuing exit from the Capitol by some of the citizens riding in their wagons and carriages. They were heading south, across the bridges carrying many of their possessions and valuables. With his arrival, he found Secretary Breckinridge in a meeting with General Ewell, Brigadier General Gorgas of the Ordnance Department, and Mayor Mayo. As Charles walked into the room, they were in the middle of discussing the impending evacuation and what they should do with all of the military supplies that filled the warehouses. General Ewell was speaking and suggested, "Gentleman, it's always been our policy to destroy stores that would be useful to the enemy. I can't see any reason why that should be changed at this point."

General Gorgas immediately protested, "Mr. Secretary, as I have said before, if we light fires to all of the warehouses that contain tobacco and other stores, then I'm concerned that the fires will spread and cause wide spread damage to other dwellings in the city. I don't believe that this is the best course of action to pursue. If we are going to destroy the supplies, then we should pursue the method that I spoke to General Ewell about earlier, and that would be to pour turpentine on the supplies."

Secretary Breckinridge said with confidence and firmness, "I know and I understand, and that might be the best course of action. As for the bridges, they will have to be destroyed in order to slow down any pursuit from Federal cavalry. Therefore, I will give the order here and now that the bridges across the James River be burned once the evacuation has taken place."

"But General," Gorgas pleaded, "We run the risk of destroying the whole city. We won't be able to control the fires once they begin to spread."

"Mayor Mayo added his voice to the opposition, "I agree strongly with General Gorgas. We jeopardize too much."

Finally, Secretary Breckinridge said after sighing, "For now, we will withhold destroying the warehouses. It would be disgraceful of the Confederate government to endanger the destruction of the entire city. But as for the bridges, the order is to be carried out."

The meeting adjourned and the participants departed with only Charles remaining. He slowly approached Secretary Breckinridge, removing the envelope from his coat pocket, he said, "Mr. Secretary, I have a message for you from President Davis."

Secretary Breckinridge silently opened the envelope and quietly read the contents. He looked at Charles and without revealing the confidentiality of the message, he said, "For now, I want you to remain with me."

For the remainder of the afternoon, Charles helped in packing the remaining archives to be removed to the train depot.

After 6:00 in the evening., Charles and Secretary Breckinridge arrived at the train depot on 14th Street. Already, there was a large crowd that had assembled. Many were in a state of confusion and turmoil, while still others were angry, noisy, and demanding to gain entrance. Confederate troops had arrived to instill order and safety for the President and the members of his staff and Cabinet. None of the Cabinet had arrived yet, but the one hundred midshipmen were there to protect the treasury as ordered. There were two trains that had been assembled, one for the Presidential party, and the other for the treasury.

Within the hour, the President's carriage arrived with William and a military staff member. Confederate soldiers immediately moved forth to protect and to escort them into the train depot. There he saw Secretary Breckinridge continuing to oversee the evacuation with Charles' assistance. As the President approached, the Secretary excused himself, and walked with the President to his coach.

Lighting a cigar and disposing of the match, William walked to where Charles stood and asked, "Were you able to see the family off to safety?"

Charles said, as he watched President Davis and Secretary Breckinridge standing at the foot of the steps of the railroad car, "Yes, thank God. I feel that the city is about to come apart at the seams. I couldn't imagine Caroline being caught up in all of the turmoil."

"The President is quite concern over the lost of the city, even though he won't admit it."

"I agree. Earlier this afternoon, he told me that it was just a minor set back, but he couldn't hide the somber expression on his face."

For months, William had withheld information concerning Katie's escape from confinement with Pete's assistance. Now he believed that he should inform Charles of the events that had taken place in Frederick, Maryland even though at this time it would make no difference, "Charles, there is some information that I've been keeping from you for sometime concerning your brother."

Charles turned and gazed at William. In an authoritative and firm tone he said, "What about my brother?"

"There was an incident that involved Katie McBride and your brother that carries considerable and serious circumstances if they are captured."

"What about Katie and Pete?"

William dropped the cigar to his side as a subtle expression covered his face. He spoke with a tone of confidence as he answered, "Charles, Pete posed as an impostor and helped Katie escape from confinement."

Charles was surprised and without words. Finally after gathering his thoughts, he said, "How can you be sure? What proof do you have?"

William's words were preplanned and methodically chosen for this moment as he began to share his information, "Sometime ago, I enlisted the help of Daniel to keep an eye on Katie."

"Why?" Charles promptly snapped.

"Didn't we suspect her of spying on our activities and passing the information on across the Potomac to Union authorities?"

"Yes, but after giving it considerable thought, and after speaking with Caroline, I really felt that out beliefs were speculative, and that's all."

William shook his head in frustration and began to become persistent in his presentation, "Listen to me Charles, there were periods of time when she disappeared. I know that for a fact. Just before we captured her, she was visiting with General Howe who was in charge of the garrison at Harpers Ferry."

"That doesn't mean anything."

"Then you explain how Shenandoah was torched?" William's frustration continued with his friend as he attempted to make his point, "Do you remember the 63 invasion?"

"Yes, I returned home briefly only to discover that my wife had deceived our friends and neighbors into believing that I was dead."

"Well she may have deceived many, but not all. Caroline was being followed the evening of that great event to the Robinson homestead where you were hiding."

William noticed the angry expression that was covering Charles' face. It reflected in the sound of his voice as he spoke, "How do you know that?"

"Daniel. When he left that evening to check on the few horses that you had left, he noticed Katie following Caroline at a distance. Charles, Katie was watching through the window. She knew that you weren't dead. Now you know why Caroline and your family were still being watched by the Federals and why Shenandoah was destroyed. The only way they could have known was by her information. That alone was enough to convince me."

Charles said as he continued to gaze at William, "So how does my brother fit into all of this?"

"Katie was in Winchester with her landlord from Harpers Ferry. One evening, she was in the camp of the 1st Virginia cavalry asking and posing like she was looking for your brother, but for the most part, probably counting the number of soldiers in the regiment. The next day she was arrested and imprisoned. Somehow, your brother got wind of what had taken place. Well, anyway to make a long story short, another soldier and Pete posed as an officer from the President's staff that was dispatched to escort Katie back to Richmond. The Provost guard released her on the authority of the forged documents that Pete presented to him. Finally during the pursuit to capture them, we found out that they had crossed the river on a ferry near Berlin, Maryland. Daniel continued to follow them to Frederick where he was killed in his attempt to capture them." Charles lowered his head in frustration and disgust as William continued, "We know that it was them by the vivid description given by the clerk at the hotel. Also, Pete was reported to be missing after he failed to return to General Early's headquarters. He had been ordered to carry a reply to a dispatch that he had been entrusted with, from Colonel Mosby."

Charles was angry, but withheld his temper knowing that there wasn't anything at this time that he could do about his brother. For now, he knew that he had to escape and at a later time he would deal with his brother in his own way.

Hours continued to go by. The Presidential party had not departed. Finally, Charles was summoned by the President to return to the Executive Mansion to retrieve some personal items that had been forgotten. As Charles was given a fresh horse, he said his farewell to William and proceeded to the mansion to accomplish the President's request. On his journey, he witnessed some of the men, women, and even children of the city milling about the gutters in their attempt to salvage the whisky that had been poured into the streets by the Provost guards. There was the crashing sound of glass breaking as widespread looting of businesses occurred without intervention by the authorities. Charles knew the city had erupted into turmoil, commotion, and chaos. In his journey, he had to immediately bring his mount to a halt near Main Street to allow a fire brigade to go by.

Suddenly, a drunken soldier grabbed the bridle of his horse and demanded, "Git off that dar horse boy, before I pull ya off." As the soldier began to pull his knife from his belt, Charles quickly pulled his revolver and struck the soldier across his forehead. As the soldier fell backward holding his injured head, Charles rode off continuing to the mansion. In the distance toward the river he heard a loud crashing explosion that shook the city. He didn't look back, although, he knew from the discussions that took place earlier at the War Department, that the Navy might be destroying its ships. The citizens that were in the street broke forth in panic with the sound of the explosion. Just hours ago, the city was calm and peaceful, but now, it was rapidly moving out of control. As he briefly paused, he saw some Confederate soldiers marching to the river, and he assumed that they were on their way to link up with General Lee's forces. Off in the distance toward the river, he watched the flames shoot up in the nighttime sky. They were coming from the location of a larger warehouse. Charles knew that many of the cities scoundrels were going to turn out once law and order would cease to prevail, but he was very surprised when he witnessed some of the cities most prodigious ladies running with goods that they had stolen from some of the vacant businesses. As he turned his mount to continue, there was a large explosion coming from one of the powder magazines that startle the animal into rebellion. The glass from several of the businesses that had been shattered by the thundering sound and blast, sprayed Charles and his horse with small pieces. Unhurt, he quickly brought his frighten animal under control and rapidly spurred the animal to continue their progress. Soon, Charles arrived at the mansion to find the house in darkness. Upon entering, he found some of the servants that were left behind frighten and hiding for fear of their life from the drunken mob that was roaming the city. After retrieving the items that was requested, he knew that the President's train should have departed for Danville. With all of the confusion and lawlessness that was spreading throughout Richmond, he feared for his Aunt Daisy's, and Rebecca's lives. After packing the items in his saddlebags, he hurried to Grace Street. In the background, he could hear cannon shells, rifle cartridges popping and exploding, lighting up the sky. By now, the city was in complete terror. When he brought his horse to a halt in front of the Grace Street residence, he noticed like many homes in the city that it was totally dark. As he entered the house, he called out, "Rebecca, Rebecca, where are you?" Without hesitation she answered from the second floor, "I'm up here with Aunt Daisy."

Charles ran up the long flight of stairs to the second level, where he found his sister sitting at her Aunt's bedside with Rosey. Rebecca calmly said as Charles pulled a small chair to sit next to her, "Charles, I'm terrified. With all of the explosions and the sky lit up from the many fires, it's frightening. What's going on?"

"It's anticipated that the Federals will occupy the city tomorrow, Confederate authorities are destroying the warehouses and anything that might be of use to them. In doing so, lawlessness among the citizens has taken over. On my way here, I witnessed many of them looting and stealing from businesses that they had broken into."

Rebecca said in a somber tone of voice as she glanced at her brother, "I really didn't think that it would come to this. The war has changed so many things in our life. For instance, the people that we love, and those that are no longer with us. I've never recovered fully from Thomas' death."

Charles placed his hand on his sister's and said, "You really did love him."

Rebecca said as she turned her attention to her sleeping Aunt, "Yes, I did. At first he was just another conquest in the life of Rebecca Barker. But there was something different about him. His manner, his way of looking at life, and most of all the security of his affections." Rebecca changed the subject as she heard her Aunt's restlessness and sigh, "I wish that we could move Aunt Daisy, but I'm afraid that her medical condition is worst then what we expected. She hasn't eaten anything thus far today, and at times cries with pain."

"Well, it's still not to late too get you away from here."

Once more, Rebecca was firm in her resolve, "No Charles, I'm not leaving her."

"I know that you feel obligated to her, but at this point, you have to think about your own welfare."

"That would be quite selfish of me, wouldn't it?"

"Yes, but."…

Charles was interrupted by his sister, who passionately said, "Aunt Daisy has devoted her life to me. For most of the time that I have lived with her, I was rebellious, conceited, and malicious in my attitude and behavior, especially after I returned to her after Thomas was killed at Sharpsburg. She was understanding and helped me through my struggle to recover from the tragic experience and trauma that had befallen me. And then, she helped me to see and understand the anger that I felt toward Mother and you. She made me deal with the problems in my life."

Charles was surprised and asked, "Why, what did we do to you? I don't understand."

Rebecca said in a soft and calm tone as her eyes were fixed on him, "Of course not, let me explain. During the years that I lived at Shenandoah, everything in life centered around one person. You. Here I was looking for attention, I'm sure that Pete was also, and all that Mother continued to do was to give her affection and time to you. After Father passed away, I felt like some kind of an orphan. Aunt Daisy filled that void in my life. Now that she is very ill, the least that I can do is to minister to her while she is sick and remain faithful as she did for me."

Charles quietly stood and slowly walked from the room. He disagreed with his sister, but wouldn't acknowledge any fault of his own. He didn't desire to debate their differences on this issue, instead, he walked down the stairway to the den, where he took some paper and began to write Caroline a correspondence before departing. It had been a long, tiring, busy, and exhausting day for Charles. By now his mind was confused with the revelation that his sister had shared with him, and the continual thought of a safe escape from the capitol. Charles became frustrated destroying some of the paper that he had began to write on. He struggled to find the words to write. After he wrote a few meaningful lines, Charles laid his head on the desk and closed his eyes, even with the loud explosions that were still taking place throughout the city, he fell asleep.

Hours had gone by. Charles awakened. It was quiet throughout the house. He stood and looked at his watch. It was 3 a.m. in the morning. Secretary

Breckinridge must be wondering where he was. As he walked into the hallway, he heard a noise coming from the second floor. At first, he thought that it might be Rosey. Then he walked to the foot of the stairway and paused, thinking that it might be Rebecca assisting his Aunt. Charles was surprised. The noise came from a Confederate soldier who appeared at the doorway after searching the rooms on the second floor. Upon noticing Charles, the soldier immediately lifted his pistol. Charles reacted quickly and did likewise. Charles and the soldier fired a single shot each simultaneously. The soldier dropped his weapon and fell down the stairway dead. Charles was uninjured by the confrontation. Without hesitation, though quite anxious, he raced to the second floor. There, he found his Aunt with Rebecca slumped over her body still lying in the bed. As he examined his Aunt, she was already deceased from a knife wound to the chest. Rebecca had suffered a similar wound, but she was still breathing heavily. Charles cried, "Oh no, dear God, oh no. Please don't let this happen."

Rosey appeared at the doorway speaking words similar to Charles'. Immediately, Charles gently lifted his sister into his arms, and removed her to the next bedroom. Rebecca was holding her chest with her hands as Rosey examined the wound. Rebecca briefly opened her eyes and said, as she gasped and struggled to breathe, "How is Aunt Daisy?"

Charles answered in a sadden tone of voice as his eyes looked at her, "She's gone."

Rebecca was silent. As she touched her brother's hand, she softly said in a whisper, "Charles, I'm sorry. I'm sorry for everything."

Charles said as he gently brushed away the hair from her face, "It's alright, I understand. You did the right thing by staying. I was the one who was wrong and inconsiderate."

With a terrified expression on his face, Charles glanced at Rosey, who shook her head as a gesture that Rebecca's wound was mortal. Once more, Rebecca looked into her older brother's eyes, and compassionately said, "In spite of our differences, I have always loved you. I just wished that we had been closer in life. But it gives me great comfort to know that you're here with me in my last moment."

As Charles began to reply, Rebecca took a deep breath, and peacefully closed her eyes. Charles put his head down and began to weep. He continued to stroke Rebecca's hair, and said, "Oh dear Lord, please no."

Rosey stepped forward and placed her hands on his shoulders and said, "Mr. Charles, yose must leave da city before de Yankees fine you."

As Charles attempted to regain his composure, he turned and looked at the servant and replied, "It makes no difference now if I'm captured or killed. I must do the right thing and bury my sister and aunt."

"No, I's will tend to dat. I's will do everythin' properly."

"I can't leave them."

Rosey replied with a firmness in her voice, "You'd must think 'bout yours wife and child now. How is dey gonna git along if yose not dere with dem. Who's gonna look out for dem if yose go and git yourself killed or captured by dem Yankees?"

Charles looked at Rosey and nodded his head in agreement. Charles knew that Rosey was right, but the guilt of his failure to protect Rebecca and Aunt Daisy was consuming him. It gave him some comfort to know that his Rebecca loved him, though he had always been distant with her. Rebecca and Pete had always been the closest.

After kissing Rebecca's forehead, Charles departed to find Secretary Breckinridge and the other staff members that had stayed behind to conclude the government's business before evacuation of the city.

It was near sunrise as he rode his horse slowly through the city streets amidst the angry, riotous crowd; his mind was consumed with the events surrounding his sister's death and the conversation that they embarked on earlier in the evening.

As Charles turned his mount toward the direction of the river, he found soldiers from the 7th South Carolina Cavalry sweeping the city for stragglers. As he rode with them to cross the Mayo Bridge, he noticed Secretary Breckinridge waiting along with additional staff members. Charles remained silent, still stunned by the events of the day and the tragedy that occurred with his family. As everyone assembled to cross the James River, the remaining guards torched the bridge.

On the opposite side of the river, Charles paused momentarily as everyone else did likewise. The mood was somber and calm as various conversation and comments were taking place among the soldiers and the Secretary and staff. The winds swept across the water as Charles sadly glanced at the flames continuing to dance toward the sky. Much of the downtown business district and all along the waterfront was roaring with fire. Clouds of dense smoke continued to rise over the city. As Charles looked at the reflection of the flames and destruction beaming from the surface of the river, he finally accepted after so many years that his life had changed. As the massive fire went higher in to the heavens any hope of Southern independence had vanished. Now, he would be no more then a wanted fugitive as well as the rest of the Confederate government. He didn't know if he would ever see his wife and child again, nor his family. Maybe, he would never be able to return to Shenandoah, the only place that he called home.

CHAPTER FORTY-FOUR

One week after the last Confederate forces and President Davis and his Cabinet evacuated Richmond, General Lee and the Army of Northern Virginia surrendered to General Grant's Army of the Potomac. After the Confederate forces were surrounded at a place called Appomattox Court House, Virginia, General Lee believed that it would be in the best interest of his men to give up the struggle, and bring an end to the useless shedding of blood. After all the Confederate soldiers surrendered their arms, they were paroled and allowed to return to their homes. Several weeks later, General Johnston surrendered his Confederate forces according to the same terms of surrender to General Sherman at Durham Station, North Carolina. After the two major Confederate armies had discontinued the struggle, the rest of the Confederate forces east of the Mississippi River did the same. The War Between the States had ended.

As for Confederate President Jefferson Davis, he still continued to elude his Union pursuers in hopes of escaping and continuing the struggle west of the Mississippi River. President Lincoln was tragically assassinated on April 14th while attending a play, Our American Cousin at Ford's Theater in Washington City. Within the next twelve days, his assassin, John Wilkes Booth, a prominent actor, along with a fellow conspirator, David Herold were trapped in a tobacco barn near Bowling Green, Virginia. After resisting the Federal cavalry's demands for surrender, Booth was shot and killed by one of the soldiers while the other conspirator surrendered to the Federals. There were three other conspirators, one a female that had been accused of playing a role in the crime. They were captured and being held in prison in Washington City awaiting trail. During this time, Lincoln's Vice President, Andrew Johnson of Tennessee, succeeded the slain leader to become the seventeenth President of the United States.

Six weeks had gone by since the conclusion of the war. It was Pete Barker's intention to return to Harpers Ferry after staying with some friends of Hayward's near Mechanicsville, Maryland. He had been fearful of returning home until the war concluded because of several reasons. The first involved his role in Katie's escape from Winchester, and eluding Confederate agents, who still might be in the area continuing their espionage activities, and secondly, his service under Colonel John Mosby. For his involvement with Mosby, he feared that he would be perceived as a fugitive by Union authorities, and subjected to harsh punishment for the type of unconventional style of warfare that they had waged. After learning that he would be eligible for the same conditions of surrender that Lee's men had received, he immediately departed for Frederick to receive his parole and then onto Harpers Ferry.

It was a cool, brisk, morning as Pete and Hayward rode along Shenandoah Street after crossing the Potomac River. It had rained the previous evening and the street was covered with mud and puddles of water. Pete gave particular attention to the Union soldiers standing along the street engaging in merry conversation with expressions of relief that the conflict was concluded. The war was over and the soldiers knew that they would soon be reunited with their loved ones in the North, and have the opportunity to continue their life. The loud noise of shuffling feet from several infantry companies marching with drums beating the cadence and fifes playing patriotic music, caught Pete and Hayward's attention as they proceeded down Potomac Street. After receiving their freedom, some of the Negro's were loitering about the street with little to do. The Negros were watching the activity of the Federal soldiers. There were others that were sharing their hopes for a future now that they had received their liberty. Pete had even recognized several that had been the property of his family, but didn't approach them. With there deliverance, they were able to come and go as they pleased. They were free and given the chance at a new beginning in life. Pete knew that slavery was forever dead and it would never be resurrected again. From the conflict, a new state had been born into the Union. Harpers Ferry, Jefferson County, wasn't any longer within the territorial boundaries of Virginia, but a new state, West Virginia.

As Pete approached the Provost Marshall's Office, he noticed that many of the buildings had suffered some destruction, and there were a few that had their roofs damaged from artillery shells, but most remained intact. The village was dirty and tarnished from years of neglect. Harpers Ferry was far from the bustling village that it once was known to be. Now there was the destruction of industries and mills. Many of the citizens that had filled the streets had vanished and moved from harms way. The town was barren of its businesses, it wasn't the same joyful village that Pete had once known and remembered, but just a mere skeleton of existence.

There were several Union soldiers standing guard near the Provost Marshal's office. As Pete dismounted and entered the dwelling, Hayward remained mounted glancing around the surroundings. For him, it was difficult to accept what had taken place over the last four years. In his heart, he believed that the town would once more prosper. He turned in his saddle and was surprised to see a new hotel built on the same foundation as the Wager House. He chuckled as the thought crossed his mind of the time when Pete and Katie fell into the mud puddle in front of the structure. Today, there was water in the same mud hole. His concentration was broken by a deep and familiar voice, "Hayward. Hayward what's ya doin in this hole of a place."

Hayward turned in the saddle and recognized one of the former slaves that the Barker's owned by the name of Samuel. Hayward joyfully said, "I's thought dat yose was in Chambersburg. Wat are ya doin' back here?"

"Well's after ya help us to escape, we's stayed dere for awhile, but once de rebs com north, we's fled to Harrisburg until de war ended. We's thought dat we's return and maybe git sum of de property. Dis is home."

"Dere's no work here."

Samuel answered just as promptly with a smile, "Well, dere's no work dere either. Dey's don't want to hire de black man."

Hayward asked the middle aged man as he turned to glanced in the direction of the entrance to the Marshall's office, "What yose gonna do now?

Samuel said as he shook his head in frustration, "I's don't know, I's really don't."

Samuel looked up at Hayward and asked, "What 'bout ya"

Hayward said with a smile that covered the width of his face and speaking with a firm confidence in his voice, "I's gonna help Mr. Pete rebuild his home. We's gonna git the place up and runnin' again."

Samuel's demeanor turned to defiance and anger. He rebuked his friend, "What's wrong with ya'. You'd don't have to work for dem people. Dey's kept us in bondage, we's owe dem nothin'."

Hayward turned once more toward Samuel. He was calm and dignified as he answered his friend, "Now yose look here. Mr. Pete, he's always treated me kindly, and done good by me. I's not gonna be like you people who want to keep de anger a goin'. No, it's time dat we move on. It's time dat yose move on. Dis war is over. Yose have ya freedom."

Samuel's expression revealed his anger. He spat on the ground and walked away saying, "I's should of spit on ya'. You'd no better den dey are."

Hayward turned around shaking his head in frustration and at the same time taking notice of Pete leaving the Provost office. After mounting, they continued along Shenandoah Street. Pete was quiet, more reserve then usual. Hayward said as he continued to look about and pointing in the direction of the river, "Dat bridge is gone like many of de places. I see many changes."

"Yeah, Hayward. Many things have changed since the war began. Many lives have been changed, and life will never be the same. I will always see things differently."

"How's dat?"

"For one thing, I don't think that you can take life for granted. I remember before going into battle wondering if I would be fortunate enough to see its conclusion. Afterward, once the smoke settled and I was spared by Providence, I glanced about the battlefield wondering of the poor souls that lay lifeless. Whom did they leave behind?" Did they leave a wife, how many children, or maybe a sweetheart? Did they have a close relationship with someone that they loved? When you are separated from the ones that you love in this life, its difficult. I've seen men openly cry before going into battle because they believed that they might not see their family again. The possessions that we have in this life mean nothing when it comes to being separated from a family that you love. Sometimes you learn the hard way to have a greater appreciation for them."

Hayward was surprised at the revelation that Pete had shared with him. He knew the bitterness that the young Barker felt and how emotional that he was over his Mother giving the Estate to Charles. Hayward boldly said as he turned to glance at Pete, "Den yose tellin' me dat yose see things in a different way with de family?"

"I guess I have. Do you remember when I was upset with my Mother and brother when I left home for depriving me of my rightful inheritance? At the time, maybe I wasn't responsible enough to be trusted, but I really thought that I was. Still, I felt cheated and betrayed. I had to get away from the area, and refused to be persuaded by family or friend. After awhile, like many others that left their homes, I actually began to be caught up in the romance of war and returning as some great hero. Then, too, I strongly believed that our rights as citizens of this state, and our way of life were being treaded on. Until the battle at Manassas, I, like many thought the war would be quick and easy. Maybe, just maybe, Charles would give me a piece of the property for my services to the state with my return home from a quick war. But, after that first great battle, I realized that the war would last for sometime, I just really didn't realize how long. It wasn't until the experiences that I went through, the lonesome moments during battle laying among the dead on some battlefield, and the quiet nights under the star filled sky that I began to think of my life and family. I prayed that I would be able to see them again and make things right between us. Truly, that's all that I thought about. Yes Hayward, war and death will change the way that you think and the way that you perceive different situations in your life. And, when you have lost everything and have nothing but your life, one becomes more grateful and thankful for what they may have. I will never be the same as before since all of this happen."

"In our own way, I's don't think either of us will be."

Pete and Hayward paused along School House Ridge. There Pete's eyes scanned the family's property. It was in ruin and almost unrecognizable with weeds, tall grass, thickets, and undergrowth from the neglect. Some of the tall oak trees that graciously hovered above the lane had fallen or been chopped down and used for firewood by some of the soldiers that camped on the property at one time. In many areas surrounding the immediate area, the beautiful white fence that covered the property line had vanished, and what remained, was in need of repair. All that was left of the old and valuable beautiful mansion that Pete called home was the stone exterior, and that was badly tarnished with black soot from the damaging fire. All of the out buildings, the beautifully design roman style carriage house that was constructed a year before the war, the stone kitchen house, and smokehouse existed no longer. The only semblance of the barn was the lower stone walls, and there wasn't even that much that remained of the stable area. As Pete continued to quietly stare at the premises, he was reminded of the pleasant days of years gone by, when the family was together enjoying a barbecue, entertaining friends, and participating in a ring tournament with his friends, or just jumping hurdles with Ann. It was depressing to witness such destruction though there was hope that Shenandoah could become prosperous once more.

As Pete continued to look about, Hayward broke the silence and spoke with confidence, "We's can build this place back up. I's know's dat we can."

After reviewing the shambled estate, Pete answered in a somber and sad tone of voice, "I'm glad of your confidence, but it's going to take money, and plenty of it, which we don't have."

"It cou've been a lot worst."

"How is that?"

"Squatters cou've been on de property."

Pete struggled with a smiled and said, "Yeah, I didn't think of that, but your right."

"I's know dat de government has allowed dem to do so. Sum of de men from town had return to find dat dey were livin' in dere homes."

"Then I guess we need to get started and hope for the best."

As Pete and Hayward rode across one of the fields toward the ruins of the mansion, they had to watch where they were riding due to the pits that soldiers had dug to build fires during their occupation of the property. The warmth of the sun began to penetrate through the dreary morning promising a pleasant day. A breeze gently blew causing the branches of the trees that were filled with the greenness of spring to toss carelessly to and fro as Pete and Hayward dismounted and allowed their horses to roam freely. The two men walked to the back of the mansion and there the blossoms began to bloom on the apple trees in the orchard along the lane that went to the river. Hayward recognized all of these natural events and said in a tone of reassurance, "See, jest look at de new growth. It's jest now beginnin'. Life is springin' forth as I's speak."

Pete smiled and nodded in agreement as Hayward and he cautiously entered the remains of the structure to begin the task of cleaning out the debris. As Pete examined the interior of the remains, there was nothing of its prior existence that remained, but still, it was home.

After about an hour, Hayward came upon a metal box that he had found under some wooden beams. It had been blacken by the fire, but without any other damage. He called out to Pete with a tone of joy in his voice, "Mr. Pete, Mr. Pete."

Pete threw the remains of a heavy wooden beam that had been partially destroyed in the fire to the side and immediately climbed over the rubble to where his friend was standing. Hayward held the box for Pete to see. He recognized it by the flowers that were engraved on the cover as belonging to his sister Rebecca. Hayward handed the precious item to Pete, who slowly opened it to see what it contained. In the metal box, there was an image of the family taken the same year that their father had died. Pete's heart was pricked with emotion as he gazed at the image. A note was included, written in Rebecca's handwriting. She wrote each members name, the date, and continued with a saying, "My heart burns within that they might know the seed that blossomed, and the flower that was created from deep within the soil, and may they accept the rose for it's color, fragrance, and beauty."

This riddle puzzled Pete. He was closer to Rebecca then the rest of the family, but still he lacked the understanding of her heart. During the afternoon, the riddle continued to trouble him as he gave thought to its meaning.

After many hours had gone by, Pete paused to rest with Hayward. As they sat on a rock opposite of what use to be the front entrance to the mansion, Pete noticed a lone red rose growing from one of the bushes that use to be in the garden circle. He was amazed, because roses didn't bloom this early in the spring. It usually wasn't until summer in this area that they revealed their majesties. He silently stood and walked to the bush and with his eyes fixed on the rose; the meaning of the riddle came to mind. He remembered, even at an early age, that Rebecca experienced a difficult time with expressing her feelings and emotion, with the exception of her occasional outburst of anger. On more then one occasion, she sought the attention and affection of her Mother, only to be told that there wasn't the time. It always appeared that their Mother was to busy with other obligations and left the issues of raising the children to one of the personal servants. When their Mother did have time and showed any affection to one of them, Charles was always the recipient of her love. He remembered how Rebecca would run behind the barn and cry because of the pain that would strike her heart due to her Mother's neglect. Even if the rest of the family ignored her, it was difficult because she desired to be the center of attention. Pete knew from his own experiences that it not only caused difficulty for him, but division and strife among his siblings. That is why when Rebecca reached a certain age, that the quarrels that his Mother and sister were having had reached its plateau. It was then that Charles suggested to their Mother that she send

Rebecca to a finishing school in Richmond. Now for the first time, Pete really believed that his sister truly loved Thomas and was expecting to live the rest of her life with him because he unconditionally loved her and she responded to his affection and devotion. The riddle was Rebecca's way of saying that she had something special to give, her love, and that it would multiply, and continue if given the chance and was accepted by the recipient. He believed even at her young and tender age that she was trying to tell someone that when they display their love, it is like a light that burns brightly for all to see, or like the sweet smelling fragrance for all to enjoy. This particular rose that Pete was admiring possessed a special deep color. To him, she was revealing to her admirer the significance of the depth and sincerity of her heart. He was amazed at the tenderness of her heart. Now he knew that over the years that her love had been smothered and trampled on, and that this was the reason that she rebelled in order to gain the family's attention. Pete felt guilty because he knew at times that he had failed to recognize the symptoms of her erratic behavior, yet he occasionally ignored her.

Pete removed a knife from his belt and cut the rose from the bush. Somewhere in his heart of wisdom, Hayward knew by Pete's glowing expression that his friend had received a revelation about the flower. Hayward looked and smiled when Pete said, "I want to go to the river and be alone."

"I's be here when yose return."

Pete mounted his horse with the rose in his hand and departed for his special area along the Shenandoah. With his arrival, he once more allowed his horse to roam freely as he sat along the riverbank. He noticed the reflection of the trees on the surface of the water and listened to the multitudes of birds singing. The trees were green with their blossoms. Occasionally, a rabbit would leap to and fro among the weeds and underbrush breaking the silence. This appeared to be the only place on the property that was unchanged by the war. It was peaceful and serene as though nothing had ever interrupted its solitude. As Pete sat and quietly gazed at the water, he thought of Jonathan. Now that the war was over, did he safely return to Augusta County? On more then one occasion, Pete hoped that after the evening in Winchester when Jonathan helped in Katie's escape, that he would have heeded Pete's advice and Jonathan would return home to his wife and sons. Then Pete's thoughts turned to Lester. The last time that he saw his cousin was after Gettysburg. Though he understood from his Mother who had received a correspondence about a year after the great invasion of the North from his aunt, that Lester was totally disabled and lived his life confined to a bed without the ability to communicate. The war had been a dreadful, tragic, and agonizing experience for Pete. He had been compelled to act in ways that he had never thought imaginable. In his mind, he could still recall the afternoon at first Manassas when he took the life of another human being. The first time he didn't glory in the act such as some of the soldiers that he had fought with on that day, but instead, it depressed him. He knew there was no other alternative; he was compelled to act in order to survive the battle. As the war raged on, it became a way of life and nature. The war had made his heart calloused. As for the particular soldier at Manassas, and the other engagements where he had been compelled to take a life, his thoughts turned toward their family. Their loved one would not return. What would their life be like with the absence of that husband or sweetheart? He could only imagine what his family experienced with his supposed death, the grief, trauma, and the void that fills one's heart due to an unexpected separation. Now, with the end to the conflict, his heart began to soften, tears began to flow down his cheeks. He began to weep from the guilt that consumed him for the lives that he had taken, and the pain that he had inflicted on their loved ones. Yet the war experiences that he endured, the hardships and the suffering that he was afflicted with during the four long years had caused him to see the value of life in a different perspective. The benefit of living the life of a soldier in a losing cause, gave him the perseverance and endurance to prevail in all situations. Quite different from the way that he lived his life before the war, when everything that he desired was there for his enjoyment. He had learned a difficult lesson of appreciating life and being thankful for the little that even now he possessed. The life-threatening wound that he had suffered two years ago still reminded him occasionally of the second chance that he was given on life by a gracious Providence. Was there a divine reason for the intervention? Was it to rebuild Shenandoah for his family, or to make amends for their indifferences? Pete didn't know.

With the end of hostilities, the thought of being united with his family excited him. After such a long separation with hardship, maybe everyone would be willing to begin his or her relationships anew. After reading a Frederick newspaper, Pete was sure that Charles had fled with President Davis and his Cabinet in their efforts to elude the pursuit of Union authorities. He didn't know when he would see Charles, but hoped for his safety.

Again as many times during the war, pleasant thoughts surfaced concerning Katie McBride. Often, he would pause during his daily routine as a soldier and give thought as to what she might be doing with her life, though it didn't end there. Katie continued to be constantly on his mind. Earlier today as he entered Harpers Ferry, he glanced in the direction of the Catholic School and smiled as he thought of the days, which they had shared together. The most memorable was the evening when Katie told him that she loved him. At first, it frightened him. He wasn't prepared for the commitment that love requires, and wasn't willing to embark upon the risk that was involved, even though he was tempted. It was difficult to say farewell to her at the train depot in Frederick, though he still considered his actions of sending her home being the right thing to do considering the danger that awaited her if she stayed in the area. Pete wasn't sure if they would ever see each other again unless he made the trip to Boston. He gave Katie the impression upon her departure for home that there couldn't be any type of commitment between them.

Pete slowly walked along the riverbank occasionally halting to skip some stones across the surface of the water, something that he hadn't done for sometime. As he continued to think of Katie, his thoughts were interrupted by the muffled sound of an approaching horse from the direction of Barker's Ridge. At first, he thought that it might be Hayward coming to warn him of impending troubles. Patiently he continued to watch as the rider rapidly approached. He noticed the rider wasn't Hayward, but it was Katie. Pete marveled and commented in astonishment, "I can't believe it. What is that fool girl doing back here?"

Pete was thrilled and excited to see Katie, although he withheld his emotions as she brought the animal to a halt. After dismounting, she turned around to face him. They silently gazed at each other. Katie broke the silence and said in her soft, calm manner, "I had to come back. The suspense and anticipation was greater then I could bear. Somewhere in my heart, I hoped and prayed that I would hear from you. I couldn't wait any longer. I had to see you."

Pete was relieved, though he remained silent as he gazed at her. He noticed the glow that filled her eyes, much the same as it did in 1860 when they danced together at the reception that his family hosted for William Pierce. Pete softly said as he continued to allow his eyes to meet hers, "I remember the first time that you came to Shenandoah at William's reception. I wanted to dance with you in order to apologize for the incident that had taken place earlier in the afternoon. When we were together, I was drawn by the bright glow in your eyes, such as this very moment. It has always remained a mystery to me."

"I was once taught by my grandmother that the eyes are the door to ones heart. She said, your eyes tell many stories about you and your life. They reveal who you are, and what you feel. One can know if there is sorrow, anger, but then, too, peace." Katie paused and then continued, "And most of all love."

Pete was content with her answer and replied, "Now I know what they might have been expressing on that night. I know now that your feelings must be sincere and committed to have waited for me this long, especially not knowing if I would be fortunate to return to you."

Katie's heart was jubilant, her expression continued to brightened, and her eye's twinkling with joy. She knew that she had made the correct decision in returning to Harpers Ferry. This was truly home and she didn't want to venture away in the future. Shenandoah filled all of her expectations and dreams of raising a family. She fell in love with the area the very first time that she rode in the carriage along the lane the evening of William Pierces' reception. Although, she knew her vision and dreams couldn't be fulfilled without Pete's love for her. She said with deep passion as she continued to allow her eyes to meet his, "Pete, I love you with all of my heart, and I don't want to be separated from you ever again. When I left you in Frederick, I really believed that you would return to the army and continue to fight to the end." Tears began to fill Katie's eyes as she continued to express her emotions, "I must say this. There is a void that fills my heart, which can only be satisfied when we are together. I've never experienced such emptiness than when we are separated. It's like bearing anguish, an emotional pain that continues; there is no peace that can be found within. For me it's been difficult to deal with the loneliness. When I returned to Boston, I spent long evenings along the ocean, thinking of the times that we spent together, especially the afternoon that Hayward informed us of the bombardment of Fort Sumter. I really believed that you and I were becoming close in our relationship. I witnessed the warmth that filled your eyes as we shared those intimate moments concerning our life and our dreams. I agree with you that had the timing been different, then you and I could have experienced a different relationship."

A gentle smile filled Pete's expression as he removed the red rose from his checkered shirt saying, "Now, the timing is different."

Pete handed the flower to Katie. She rubbed the tears from her eyes. A glowing smile covered her features as she passionately and surprisingly said, "A red rose means romance. It's an expression of commitment."

Pete answered with sincerity in his tone, as his eyes continued to look into hers, "I know. The rose also means affection and love to someone that is very special." Pete paused briefly to allow Katie to regain her composure." Katie, I'm going to say something to you that I've never said to another lady."

Katie's heart was racing, as she remained silent. She believed that Pete embraced and cherished this moment as much as she did. Pete continued in a soft, peaceful, and humble tone of voice. The words confidently and without hesitation came slowly from his lips, "I love you. Truly, I can say without reservation that I love you." Pete placed his hands on her shoulders as he continued to express his feelings, "At first, I thought that you and I would only be the best of friends, and that was mostly because of the complications surrounding our different social views. But all of that changed for me when I was recovering from my near death experience after Gettysburg. As I was in bed suffering from my wound, the only thing that filled my mind was you, and how was all of this going to affect you once you found out that I was missing. Katie, you were constantly on my mind. I saw you everywhere that I turned. In my heart, I wanted you to be with me, and if it was my time to die, I wanted just to see your face and embrace you once more. When I was away from home, I had a lot of time to think on matters. It was through my experiences with my family and the challenge of survival that caused me to examine my priorities. What is the most important thing in life? Is it power such as Charles desired, or is it possessions such as we all desire, or is it receiving and returning the love that one experiences with someone. I've known for sometime how you have felt, but I was afraid of returning my feelings because of the risk involved. You're right when you say that I used the war, not only to escape from my family, but too, to escape from my feelings for you. Deep within my heart, the thought of you with someone else tortured me to the extreme, though I kept everything built up within. When I knew that you were in prison for spying, I had to come. I was fearful for your life and I was willing to give mine in return for your freedom and safety."

"Why didn't you tell me how you felt before I left for home?"

"If you knew how I felt about you, I feared that you would have refused to go."

"Then everything that you said at the train depot about going on with my life was to push me into returning to Boston?"

Pete said as he took her by the hands, "Yes, you are right. Katie, I didn't want to let you go, though, because of the dangerous circumstances, I had to. I'm old fashion I guess, but I believe that if you really and truly love someone, then it takes a greater love to let them go then to hold onto them."

Katie said as she gently rubbed her fingers across the back of his hands, "The war is over with. We needn't be separated again."

Pete embraced Katie and remained silent. As he gazed into her eyes, he said, "Yes the war is over, and we'll never be separated again. Never, I promise."

With his embrace, Pete brushed his fingers across the softness of Katie's face, and then he passionately and affectionately kissed her. As he gazed into her eyes, she smiled and said softly and passionately, "Through Sabers and Roses, our love was born."

Epilogue

There was a loud-crashing sound of musketry that echoed through the park along Washington Street in a salute to the soldiers that gave their life during the Civil War. As Danny's eyes gazed at Miss Ann, he noticed that she jerked and began to tremble with fear. Ann's hand rested on her cheek and tears flowed from her eyes as she suddenly began to withdraw from the story on her family and life. Immediately, Danny jumped from his seat and slowly approached Miss Ann. He placed his arm around her shoulders and said in a calm reassuring tone of voice, "Miss Ann, its ok. The war is over."

Ann slowly spoke as she looked at the lad, "The war will never be over for me. I will always have moments of despair as I think of what life was like before the war. As I look back on those days, it was a time of happiness, gatherings, and socials that we as a family enjoyed with friends we loved. It was a time of gaiety and building relationships that meant something in life. In the morning when I arise from my sleep, I can still see me as a young child, such as you on a crisp, sunny morning riding my horse Buttercup across Shenandoah with my Mother, and occasionally with Miss Katie. I loved Katie McBride with all of my heart. She was so gentle and such a pleasant person. Even in the most adverse situations, I can still hear her soft and gentle voice. I can still visualize her on the day that my Mother and I gave her the first experience at sidesaddle riding. If you could have seen her face and witnessed the overwhelming expression, then you would have laughed just as my Mother and I did. By the third year of the war, Katie had become very proficient at horse back riding. Katie was such an optimist concerning life, even in the most difficult situations.

As Ann paused, a gentle, peaceful smile covered her expression. Ann's eyes glowed with a bright radiance as she spoke of her Mother, "Oh, how I miss my Mother, you'll never know. We were so close. We did everything together. During my time, it was customary for the children to have a personal servant to tend to and help in raising the children. My Mother was the exception; she gave me the proper instruction and discipline that was required, always showing her love and affection for me. I could confide in her about anything that troubled me, and never would she judge me, nor say anything that would cause me pain. Unfortunately because of some physical problems during my birth, my Mother was never able to bare any more children. I have felt her loss beyond anything that I could possibly put into words.

Ann continued after taking a handkerchief and wiping the tears from her cheeks. Once more, she managed a smile for her guests as she continued to speak in a calm tone of voice, "After learning of my Aunt Rebecca's fate, I grieved over the lost. Prayerfully, I had hoped that someday she would return to Shenandoah with us. I know that she had her faults as we all do, but sometime during the last year of the war there was a remarkable change that took place in her life. To this day, I don't know what took place in her heart to cause her to make such a rapid change in her attitude. She became so loving and affectionate to me. I felt like I was really getting to know her personally, and I wanted to have more of the love and peace that she expressed in her character. I remembered when my grandmother received the news of her death; we were still in New Market. It was a rainy afternoon and she was still very concerned because we didn't know of my Father's fate. My Mother was the one who broke the tragic news of Rebecca's death; my grandmother Elizabeth wept uncontrollably. It was the most disheartening experience that I witnessed as a youngster. My grandmother was never the same after my Aunt Rebecca's death. She grieved for years to come. On many occasions and without any warning, grandmother would begin to weep over the despair and the unfair hand that life had dealt my Aunt Rebecca. I know that in part, my grandmother had expected that my Aunt Rebecca and she would have the relationship that they allowed to elude them all of those years. And when you expect to spend the rest of your life with someone and they all of a sudden leave you, then its difficult to accept. It takes time, though some people can never fully accept the reality. Unfortunately, my grandmother was one of those people.

Ann's mood and emotions began to change to frustration and anger, "As I look back during those times, I still feel an unforgiving anger. Sometimes I feel that if it were not for the hot-tempered political minds that failed to reason and compromise over the issue of slavery and states rights, then maybe, the war wouldn't have come about."

Jason abruptly interrupted and interjected, "But Miss Ann, many of the good soldiers, both blue and gray shed their blood for what they believed so strongly."

Ann paused and silently reminded herself of the commitment that she made to herself at the turn of the century. With the conclusion of the war not only did the weapons of destruction have to be laid down, but too, the weapons of bitter resentment, hatred, and division. The Northerners were dedicated to a cause to preserve the Union, and the Southerners to defend their rights as citizens of sovereign states. Ann decided for once and all to put the matter to rest. She said to the lads in a gentle tone of voice, "Yes, your right. I've promised myself over and over that I would stop fighting the war and like others, I could live the rest of my days in peace. It's been difficult with the strong convictions and passions that we experienced during those times. It has been so much a part of my life and being for all of these years that the emotions have become normal. As my mind occasionally returns to those dark days, I promised myself that all of my loyalties and passions would remain with the Southern way of life. But now, I guess it's finally time to make the effort and move on with my life and realize that the sword was laid to rest many years ago. I guess that the good that came from the war is that we have become a richer, stronger, and prosperous nation. As I once heard the famous female Confederate spy, Belle Boyd say at the conclusion of her recital in Front Royal, Virginia, One God, One Flag, One People Forever."

Once more, Danny wanted to investigate into the lives of some of the rest of the family. He said as he turned about from glancing out the window, "What happen to the rest of your family?"

"After the war ended, we stayed with my Mother's parents for the summer. I can still see my Mother sitting patiently and quietly by the front window of their brick house looking for my Father to arrive. I knew that something terrible had happen, we all did, but we held to our belief that he couldn't come to us because the surrender terms didn't apply to him since he wasn't a soldier. He had no other alternative but to escape the Union authorities."

"What about the young man in the picture, your uncle?"

"After the war, he received the news of Aunt Rebecca's death. It was difficult for him to accept, but with the help and love of Katie McBride, he came to grips and learned to accept the tragedy. As far as actual military life and battles, he spoke very little to the family about what he saw and experienced. He would just say when asked, that it was too painful to speak about, and the memories were too terrifying to recall. My uncle learned to be the type of person that didn't look back in life, but always ahead attempting to live a more prosperous life finding peace and contentment. It was difficult for us to understand and imagine what he went through to survive." Miss Ann paused briefly and remained silent, and then softly continued as her hands embraced the old white and blue shawl that covered her shoulders, "Children, I need time to rest. Maybe another day we can speak again of life during that time."

Jason was curious and anxious to discover the truth of her knowledge of all of the events that she had spent hours describing. He asked as he arose from the chair and approached Miss Ann, "Before we leave, if I may ask, then how did you learn about his experiences and have the ability to tell us about them."

There was a mischief smile that covered Ann's wrinkled features as she began to speak, "During the war, my uncle kept a diary. One day as I was helping with the washing of laundry, I found it mistakenly in the armoire under his undershirts. From that time on, I would occasionally sneak off when everyone was occupied and read a few pages."

Danny and Jason stood up and said their farewells to Miss Ann. They departed for home, knowing that they would visit another day. The ceremonies had concluded in the park and everyone had departed as evening was fast approaching. Ann sat in her rocking chair with a hot cup of tea that she had just prepared. Once more as she thought of her days at Shenandoah, a glowing, tearful smile appeared. As she lifted her head and gazed at the picture of her Uncle Pete Barker, she whispered, "From Sabers And Roses, A Love Was Born."

Printed in the United States
68889LVS00003B/1-60